RAVES FOR THE LONG PRICE QUARTET

"In this third book in The Long Price Quartet, Abraham writes insight-fully and thoroughly, and his characters avoid clichés. His world-building is fascinating, causing readers to question their preconceived notions of even the simplest definitions of everyday words. However, this novel is heavy and hard to pick up—definitely a read for fans of this series. It's worth starting at the beginning for this one."

—*RT Book Reviews*

"Welcome to Daniel Abraham. If you are meeting him for the first time, I envy you: You are in for a remarkable journey."

—Junot Díaz, Pulitzer Prize–winning author

"Daniel Abraham delighted fantasy readers with his brilliantly original and engaging first novel, *A Shadow in Summer*, and in *A Betrayal in Winter*, penned a tragedy as darkly personal and violent as Shakespeare's *King Lear*. Now in *An Autumn War*, the third volume in The Long Price Quartet, Daniel Abraham has written a spectacular epic fantasy of much wider scope and appeal that will thrill his fans and enthrall legions of new readers."

—*Fantasy Book Critic*

"Daniel Abraham gets better with every book. *A Shadow in Summer* was among the strongest first novels of the last decade, and *A Betrayal in Winter* a terrific second book, but in *An Autumn War* Abraham puts both of them in the shade. This book really blows the top off, taking the world of the andat and the poets in new and unexpected directions. *An Autumn War* will keep you turning pages and break your heart in the bargain. If there's any justice, this should be a contender for all the major awards."

—George R. R. Martin, *New York Times* #1 bestselling author

TURN THE PAGE FOR MORE RAVES.

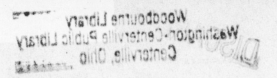
"*An Autumn War* is in its closing stages heart-stoppingly surprising and exciting. Rarely does the penultimate volume in a series carry such a charge of its own."

—*Locus*

"This book will land Abraham in the ranks of our greatest working fantasists, shoulder to shoulder with Robin Hobb, George R. R. Martin, and their peers. I urge you to buy, borrow, or check out from the library the first two books so you'll be ready for *An Autumn War* when it comes out next year. As for Abraham, he's outdone himself and the rest of us with this book. I await the fourth book in The Long Price Quartet with a certain amount of awe."

—Jay Lake, author of *Mainspring*

"There is much to love in The Long Price Quartet. It is epic in scope, but character-centered. The setting is unique yet utterly believable. The storytelling is smooth, careful, and—best of all—unpredictable. The first two books impressed me, but *An Autumn War* surpassed them, leaving me stunned and wondering where Abraham will take me in the fourth book."

—Patrick Rothfuss, bestselling author of *The Name of the Wind*

"For most of the book, an elegiac, entropic ambiance and tone persist. . . . Abraham succeeds in making us feel the weight of time—some fifty years—covered by the quartet before he delivers the satisfying final resurrection and capstone."

—Paul Di Filippo, *Scifiwire.com*

"Abraham's work is about as unlike Tolkien as you can get within the same genre. I find myself thinking of Shakespeare more often. But in this he has taken from Tolkien's model: He isn't afraid to set out his world and show it profoundly broken, changed, becoming something else."

—Jo Walton, bestselling author of *Among Others*

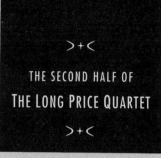

THE SECOND HALF OF
The Long Price Quartet

THE PRICE OF WAR

AN AUTUMN WAR
AND
THE PRICE OF SPRING

DANIEL ABRAHAM

ORB

A TOM DOHERTY ASSOCIATES BOOK • NEW YORK

THE PRICE OF WAR

Copyright © 2012 by Daniel Abraham

This is an omnibus edition containing the novels *An Autumn War*
copyright © 2008 by Daniel Abraham and *The Price of Spring*
copyright © 2009 by Daniel Abraham.

Maps by Jackie Aher

Edited by James Frenkel

An Orb Book
Published by Tom Doherty Associates, LLC
175 Fifth Avenue
New York, NY 10010

www.tor-forge.com

Library of Congress Cataloging-in-Publication Data

Abraham, Daniel.
   [Novels. Selections]
   The price of war : the second half of the Long Price quartet :
An Autumn war and The price of Spring / Daniel Abraham.
—1st ed.
     p. cm.
   "A Tom Doherty Associates book."
   ISBN 978-0-7653-3365-0 (trade pbk.)
   1. Fantasy fiction, American.   I. Abraham, Daniel. Autumn
war. II. Abraham, Daniel. Price of Spring.   III. Title.
PS3601.B677A6 2012b
813'.6—dc23

2012030264

First Edition: November 2012

Printed in the United States of America

0 9 8 7 6 5 4 3 2 1

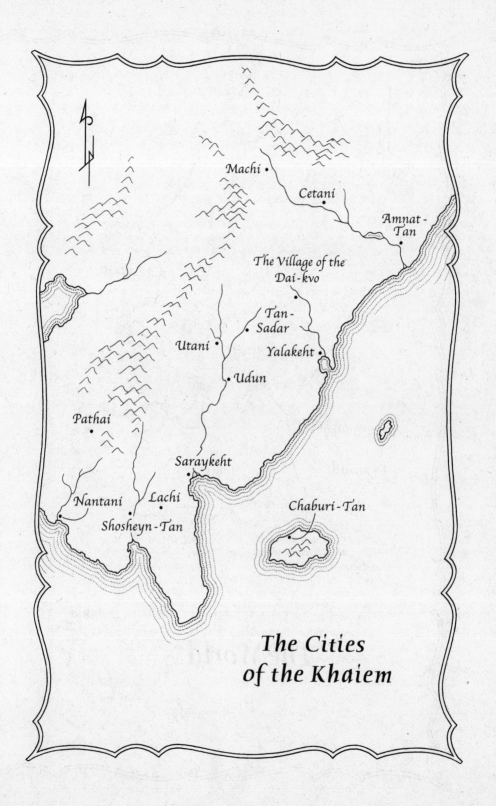

The Cities
of the Khaiem

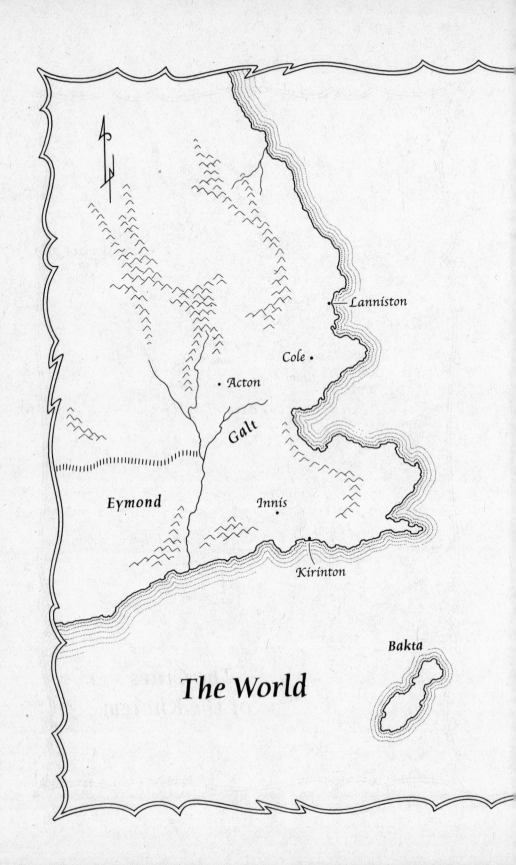

The World

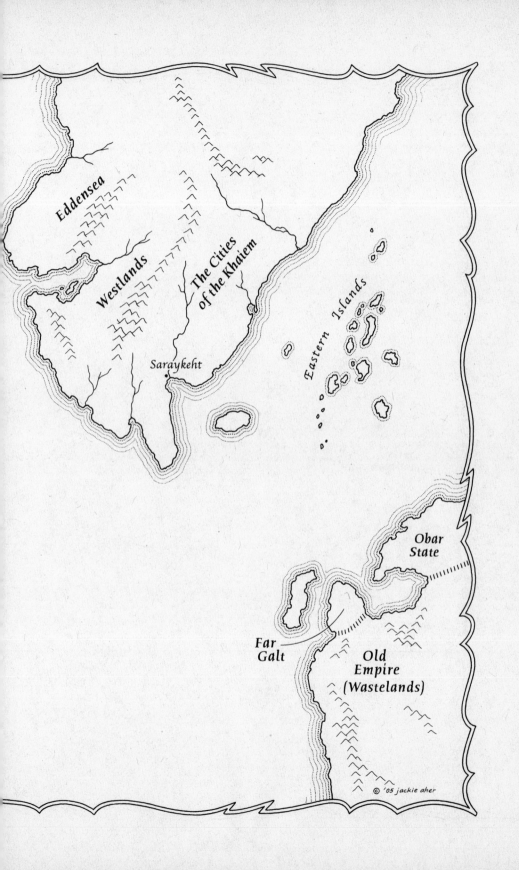

AN
AUTUMN
WAR

To Jim and Allison,
without whom none of this would have been possible

ACKNOWLEDGMENTS

Once again, I would like to extend my thanks to Walter Jon Williams, Melinda Snodgrass, Emily Mah, S. M. Stirling, Terry England, Ian Tregillis, Ty Franck, George R. R. Martin, and the other members of the New Mexico Critical Mass Workshop.

I also owe debts of gratitude to Shawna McCarthy and Danny Baror for their enthusiasm and faith in the project, to James Frenkel for his unstinting support and uncanny ability to improve a manuscript, and to Tom Doherty and the staff at Tor for their kindness and support.

PROLOG

>+< Three men came out of the desert. Twenty had gone in.

The setting sun pushed their shadows out behind them, lit their faces a ruddy gold, blinded them. The weariness and pain in their bodies robbed them of speech. On the horizon, something glimmered that was no star, and they moved silently toward it. The farthest tower of Far Galt, the edge of the Empire, beckoned them home from the wastes, and without speaking, each man knew that they would not stop until they stood behind its gates.

The smallest of them shifted the satchel on his back. His gray commander's tunic hung from his flesh as if the cloth itself were exhausted. His mind turned inward, half-dreaming, and the leather straps of the satchel rubbed against his raw shoulder. The burden had killed seventeen of his men, and now it was his to carry as far as the tower that rose up slowly in the violet air of evening. He could not bring himself to think past that.

One of the others stumbled and fell to his knees on wind-paved stones. The commander paused. He would not lose another, not so near the end. And yet he feared bending down, lifting the man up. If he paused, he might never move again. Grunting, the other man recovered his feet. The commander nodded once and turned again to the west. A breeze stirred the low, brownish grasses, hissing and hushing. The punishing sun made its exit and left behind twilight and the wide swath of stars hanging overhead, cold candles beyond numbering. The night would bring chill as deadly as the midday heat.

It seemed to the commander that the tower did not so much come closer as grow, plantlike. He endured his weariness and pain, and the structure that had been no larger than his thumb was now the size of his hand. The beacon that had seemed steady flickered now, and tongues of flame leapt and vanished. Slowly, the details of the stonework came clear; the huge carved relief of the Great Tree of Galt. He smiled, the skin of his lip splitting, wetting his mouth with blood.

"We're not going to die," one of the others said. He sounded amazed. The commander didn't respond, and some measureless time later, another voice called for them to stop, to offer their names and the reason that they'd come to this twice-forsaken ass end of the world.

When the commander spoke, his voice was rough, rusting with disuse.

"Go to your High Watchman," he said. "Tell him that Balasar Gice has returned."

———

BALASAR GICE HAD BEEN IN HIS ELEVENTH YEAR WHEN HE FIRST HEARD THE word *andat*. The river that passed through his father's estates had turned green one day, and then red. And then it rose fifteen feet. Balasar had watched in horror as the fields vanished, the cottages, the streets and yards he knew. The whole world, it seemed, had become a sea of foul water with only the tops of trees and the corpses of pigs and cattle and men to the horizon.

His father had moved the family and as many of his best men as would fit to the upper stories of the house. Balasar had begged to take the horse his father had given him up as well. When the gravity of the situation had been explained, he changed his pleas to include the son of the village notary, who had been Balasar's closest friend. He had been refused in that as well. His horses and his playmates were going to drown. His father's concern was for Balasar, for the family; the wider world would have to look after itself.

Even now, decades later, the memory of those six days was fresh as a wound. The bloated bodies of pigs and cattle and people like pale logs floating past the house. The rich, low scent of fouled water. The struggle to sleep when the rushing at the bottom of the stairs seemed like the whisper of something vast and terrible for which he had no name. He could still hear men's voices questioning whether the food would last, whether the water was safe to drink, and whether the flood was natural, a catastrophe of distant rains, or an attack by the Khaiem and their andat.

He had not known then what the word meant, but the syllables had taken on the stench of the dead bodies, the devastation where the village had been, the emptiness and the destruction. It was only much later—after the water had receded, the dead had been mourned, the village rebuilt—that he learned how correct he had been.

Nine generations of fathers had greeted their new children into the world since the God Kings of the East had turned upon each other, his history tutor told him. When the glory that had been the center of all creation fell, its throes had changed the nature of space. The lands that had been great gardens and fields were deserts now, permanently altered by the war. Even as far as Galt and Eddensea, the histories told of weeks of darkness, of failed crops and famine, a sky dancing with flames of green, a sound as if the earth were tearing itself apart. Some people said the stars themselves had changed positions.

But the disasters of the past grew in the telling or faded from memory. No one knew exactly how things had been those many years ago. Perhaps the Emperor had gone mad and loosed his personal god-ghost—what they called andat—against his own people, or against himself. Or there might have been a woman, the wife of a great lord, who had been taken by the Emperor against her will. Or perhaps she'd willed it. Or the thousand factions and minor insults and treacheries that accrue around power had simply followed their usual course.

As a boy, Balasar had listened to the story, drinking in the tales of mystery and glory and dread. And, when his tutor had told him, somber of tone and gray, that there were only two legacies left by the fall of the God Kings—the wastelands that bordered Far Galt and Obar State, and the cities of the Khaiem where men still held the andat like Cooling, Seedless, Stone-Made-Soft—Balasar had understood the implication as clearly as if it had been spoken.

What had happened before could happen again at any time and without warning.

"And that's what brought you?" the High Watchman said. "It's a long walk from a little boy at his lessons to this place."

Balasar smiled again and leaned forward to sip bitter kafe from a rough tin mug. His room was baked brick and close as a cell. A cruel wind hissed outside the thick walls, as it had for the three long, feverish days since he had returned to the world. The small windows had been scrubbed milky by sandstorms. His little wounds were scabbing over, none of them reddened or hot to the touch, though the stripe on his shoulder where the satchel strap had been would doubtless leave a scar.

"It wasn't as romantic as I'd imagined," he said. The High Watchman laughed, and then, remembering the dead, sobered. Balasar shifted the subject. "How long have you been here? And who did you offend to get yourself sent to this . . . lovely place?"

"Eight years. I've been eight years at this post. I didn't much care for the way things got run in Acton. I suppose this was my way of saying so."

"I'm sure Acton felt the loss."

"I'm sure it didn't. But then, I didn't do it for them."

Balasar chuckled.

"That *sounds* like wisdom," Balasar said, "but eight years here seems an odd place for wisdom to lead you."

The High Watchman smacked his lips and shrugged.

"It wasn't me going inland," he said. Then, a moment later, "They say there's still andat out there. Haunting the places they used to control."

"There aren't," Balasar said. "There are other things. Things they made or unmade. There's places where the air goes bad on you—one breath's fine, and the next it's like something's crawling into you. There's places where the ground's thin as eggshell and a thousand-foot drop under it. And there are living things too—things they made with the andat, or what happened when the things they made bred. But the ghosts don't stay once their handlers are gone. That isn't what they are."

Balasar took an olive from his plate, sucked away the flesh, and spat back the stone. For a moment, he could hear voices in the wind. The words of men who'd trusted and followed him, even knowing where he would take them. The voices of the dead whose lives he had spent. Coal and Eustin had survived. The others—Little Ott, Bes, Mayarsin, Laran, Kellem, and a dozen more—were bones and memory now. Because of him. He shook his head, clearing it, and the wind was only wind again.

"No offense, General," the High Watchman said, "but there's not enough gold in the world for me to try what you did."

"It was necessary," Balasar said, and his tone ended the conversation.

THE JOURNEY TO THE COAST WAS EASIER THAN IT SHOULD HAVE BEEN. THREE MEN, traveling light. The others were an absence measured in the ten days it took to reach Lawton. It had taken sixteen coming from. The arid, empty lands of the East gave way to softly rolling hills. The tough yellow grasses yielded to blue-green almost the color of a cold sea, wavelets dancing on its surface. Farmsteads appeared off the road, windmills with broad blades shifting in the breezes; men and women and children shared the path that led toward the sea. Balasar forced himself to be civil, even gracious. If the world moved the way he hoped, he would never come to this place again, but the world had a habit of surprising him.

When he'd come back from the campaign in the Westlands, he'd thought his career was coming to its victorious end. He might take a place in the Council or at one of the military colleges. He even dared to dream of a quiet estate someplace away from the yellow coal smoke of the great cities. When the news had come—a historian and engineer in Far Galt had divined a map that might lead to the old libraries—he'd known that rest had been a chimera, a thing for other men but never himself. He'd taken the best of his men, the strongest, smartest, most loyal, and come here. He had lost them here. The ones who had died, and perhaps also the ones who had lived.

Coal and Eustin were both quiet as they traveled, both respectful when they stopped to camp for the night. Without conversation, they had all agreed that the cold night air and hard ground was better than the company of men at an inn or wayhouse. Once in a while, one or the other would attempt to talk or joke or sing, but it always failed. There was a distance in their eyes, a stunned expression that Balasar recognized from boys stumbling over the wreckage of their first battlefield. They were seasoned fighters, Coal and Eustin. He had seen both of them kill men and boys, knew each of them had raped women in the towns they'd sacked, and still, they had left some scrap of innocence in the desert and were moving away from it with every step. Balasar could not say what that loss would do to them, nor would he insult their manhood by bringing it up. He knew, and that alone would have to suffice. They reached the ports of Parrinshall on the first day of autumn.

Half a hundred ships awaited them: great merchant ships built to haul cargo across the vast emptiness of the southern seas, shallow fishing boats that darted out of port and back again, the ornate three-sailed roundboats of Bakta, the antiquated and changeless ships of the east islands. It was nothing to the ports at Kirinton or Lanniston or Saraykeht, but it was enough. Three berths on any of half a dozen of these ships would take them off Far Galt and start them toward home.

"Winter'll be near over afore we see Acton," Coal said, and spat off the dock.

"I imagine it will," Balasar agreed, shifting the satchel against his hip. "If we sail straight through. We could also stay here until spring if we liked. Or stop in Bakta."

"Whatever you like, General," Eustin said.

"Then we'll sail straight through. Find what's setting out and when. I'll be at the harbor master's house."

"Anything the matter, sir?"

"No," Balasar said.

The harbor master's house was a wide building of red brick settled on the edge of the water. Banners of the Great Tree hung from the archway above its wide bronze doors. Balasar announced himself to the secretary and was shown to a private room. He accepted the offer of cool wine and dried figs, asked for and received the tools for writing the report now required of him, and gave orders that he not be disturbed until his men arrived. Then, alone, he opened his satchel and drew forth the books he had recovered, laying them side by side on the desk that looked out over the port. There were four, two bound in thick, peeling leather, another whose covers had been ripped from it, and one encased in metal that appeared to be neither steel nor silver, but something of each. Balasar ran his fingers over the mute volumes, then sat, considering them and the moral paradox they represented.

For these, he had spent the lives of his men. While the path back to Galt was nothing like the risk he had faced in the ruins of the fallen Empire, still it was sea travel. There were storms and pirates and plagues. If he wished to be certain that these volumes survived, the right thing would be to transcribe them here in Parrinshall. If he were to die on the journey home, the books, at least, would not be drowned. The knowledge within them would not be lost.

Which was also the argument *against* making copies. He took the larger of the leather-bound volumes and opened it. The writing was in the flowing script of the dead Empire, not the simpler chop the Khaiem used for business and trade with foreigners like himself. Balasar frowned as he picked out the symbols his tutor had taught him as a boy.

There are two types of impossibility in the andat: those which cannot be under-stood, and those whose natures make binding impossible. His translation was rough, but sufficient for his needs. These were the books he'd sought. And so the question remained whether the risk of their loss was greater than the risk posed by their existence. Balasar closed the book and let his head rest in his hands. He knew, of course, what he would do. He had known before he'd sent Eustin and Coal to find a boat for them. Before he'd reached Far Galt in the first place.

It was his awareness of his own pride that made him hesitate. History was full of men who thought themselves to be the one great soul whom power would not corrupt. He did not wish to be among that number, and yet here he sat, holding in his hands the secrets that might remake the shape of the human world. A humble man would have sought counsel from those wiser than himself, or at least feared to wield the power. He did not like what it said of him that giving the books to anyone besides himself seemed as foolish as gambling with their destruction. He would not even have trusted them to Eustin or Coal or any of the men who had died helping him.

He took the paper he'd been given, raised the pen, and began his report and, in a sense, his confession.

THREE WEEKS OUT, EUSTIN BROKE.

The sea surrounded them, empty and immense as the sky. So far south, the water was clear and the air warm even with the slowly failing days. The birds that had followed them from Parrinshall had vanished. The only animal was a three-legged dog the ship's crew had taken on as a mascot. Nor were there women on board. Only the rank, common smell of men and the sea.

The rigging creaked and groaned, unnerving no one but Balasar. He had never loved traveling by water. Campaigning on land was no more comfortable, but at least when the day ended he was able to see that this village was not the one he'd been in the night before, the tree under which he slept looked out over some different hillside. Here, in the vast nothingness of water, they might almost have been standing still. Only the long white plume of their wake gave him a sense of movement, the visible promise that one day the journey would end. He would often sit at the stern, watch that constant trail, and take what solace he could from it. Sometimes he carved blocks of wax with a small, thin knife while his mind wandered and softened in the boredom of inaction.

It should not have surprised him that the isolation had proved corrosive for Eustin and Coal. And yet when one of the sailors rushed up to him that night, pale eyes bulging from his head, Balasar had not guessed the trouble. His man, the one called Eustin, was belowdecks with a knife, the sailor said. He was threatening to kill himself or else the crippled mascot dog, no one was sure which. Normally, they'd all have clubbed him senseless and thrown him over the side, but as he was a paying passage, the general might perhaps want to take a hand. Balasar put down the wax block half-carved into the shape of a fish, tucked his knife in his belt, and nodded as if the request were perfectly common.

The scene in the belly of the ship was calmer than he'd expected. Eustin sat on a bench. He had the dog by a rope looped around the thing's chest and a field dagger in his other hand. Ten sailors were standing in silence either in the room or just outside it, armed with blades and cudgels. Balasar ignored them, taking a low stool and setting it squarely in front of Eustin before he sat.

"General," Eustin said. His voice was low and flat, like a man half-dead from a wound.

"I hear there's some issue with the animal."

"He ate my soup."

One of the sailors coughed meaningfully, and Eustin's eyes narrowed and flickered toward the sound. Balasar spoke again quickly.

"I've seen Coal sneak half a bottle of wine away from you. It hardly seems a killing offense."

"He didn't steal my soup, General. I gave it to him."

"You gave it to him?"

"Yessir."

The room seemed close as a coffin, and hot. If only there weren't so many men around, if the bodies were not so thick, the air not so heavy with their breath, Balasar thought he might have been able to think clearly. He sucked his teeth, struggling to find something wise or useful to say, some way to disarm the situation and bring Eustin back from his madness. In the end, his silence was enough.

"He deserves better, General," Eustin said. "He's broken. He's a sick, broken thing. He shouldn't have to live like that. There ought to be some dignity at least. If there's nothing else, there should at least be some dignity."

The dog whined and craned its neck toward Eustin. Balasar could see distress in the animal's eyes, but not fear. The dog could hear the pain in Eustin's voice, even if the sailors couldn't. The bodies around him were wound tight, ready for violence, all of them except for Eustin. He held the knife weakly. The tension in his body wasn't the hot, loose energy of battle; he was knotted, like a boy tensed against a blow; like a man facing the gallows.

"Leave us alone. All of you," Balasar said.

"Not without Tripod!" one of the sailors said.

Balasar met Eustin's eyes. With a small shock he realized it was the first time he'd truly looked at the man since they'd emerged from the desert. Perhaps he'd been ashamed of what he might see reflected there. And perhaps his shame had some part in this. Eustin was *his* man, and so the pain he bore was Balasar's responsibility. He'd been weak and stupid to shy away from that. And weakness and stupidity always carried a price.

"Let the dog go. There's no call to involve him, or these men," Balasar said. "Sit with me awhile, and if you still need killing, I'll be the one to do it."

Eustin's gaze flickered over his face, searching for something. To see whether it was a ruse, to see whether Balasar would actually kill his own man. When he saw the answer, Eustin's wide shoulders eased. He dropped the rope, freeing the animal. It hopped in a circle, uncertain and confused.

"You have the dog," Balasar said to the sailors without looking at them. "Now go."

They filed out, none of them taking their eyes from Eustin and the knife still in his hand. Balasar waited until they had all left, the low door pulled shut behind them. Distant voices shouted over the creaking timbers, the oil lamp swung gently on its chain. This time, Balasar used the silence intentionally, waiting. At first, Eustin looked at him, anticipation in his eyes. And then his gaze passed into the distance, seeing something beyond the room, beyond them both. And then silently, Eustin wept. Balasar shifted his stool nearer and put his hand on the man's shoulder.

"I keep seeing them, sir."

"I know."

"I've seen a thousand men die one way or the other. But . . . but that was on a field. That was in a fight."

"It isn't the same," Balasar said. "Is that why you wanted those men to throw you in the sea?"

Eustin turned the blade slowly, catching the light. He was still weeping, his face now slack and empty. Balasar wondered which of them he was seeing now, which of their number haunted him in that moment, and he felt the eyes of the dead upon him. They were in the room, invisibly crowding it as the sailors had.

"Can you tell me they died with honor?" Eustin breathed.

"I'm not sure what honor is," Balasar said. "We did what we did because it was needed, and we were the men to do it. The price was too high for us to bear, you and I and Coal. But we aren't finished, so we have to carry it a bit farther. That's all."

"It wasn't needed, General. I'm sorry, but it *wasn't*. We take a few more cities, we gain a few more slaves. Yes, they're the richest cities in the world. I know it. Sacking even one of the cities of the Khaiem would put more gold in the High Council's coffers than a season in the Westlands. But how much do they need to buy Little Ott back from hell?" Eustin asked. "And why shouldn't I go there and get him myself, sir?"

"It's not about gold. I have enough gold of my own to live well and die old. Gold's a tool we use—a tool *I* use—to make men do what must be done."

"And honor?"

"And glory. Tools, all of them. We're men, Eustin. We've no reason to lie to each other."

He had the man's attention now. Eustin was looking only at him, and there was confusion in his eyes—confusion and pain—but the ghosts weren't inside him now.

"Why then, sir? Why are we doing this?"

Balasar sat back. He hadn't said these words before, he had never explained himself to anyone. Pride again. He was haunted by his pride. The pride that had made him take this on as his task, the work he owed to the world because no one else had the stomach for it.

"The ruins of the Empire were made," he said. "God didn't write it that the world should have something like that in it. Men *created* it. Men with little gods in their sleeves. And men like that still live. The cities of the Khaiem each have one, and they look on them like plow horses. Tools to feed their power and their arrogance. If it suited them, they could turn their andat loose on us. Hold our crops in permanent winter or sink our lands into the sea or whatever else they could devise. They could turn the world itself against us the way you or I might hold a knife. And do you know why they haven't?"

Eustin blinked, unnerved, Balasar thought, by the anger in his voice.

"No, sir."

"Because they haven't yet chosen to. That's all. They might. Or they might turn against each other. They could make everything into wastelands just like those. Acton, Kirinton, Marsh. Every city, every town. It hasn't happened yet because we've been lucky. But someday, one of them *will* grow ambitious or mad. And then all the rest of us are ants on a battlefield, trampled into the mud. That's what I mean when I say this is needed. You and I are seeing that it never happens," he said, and his words made his own blood hot. He was no longer uncertain or touched by shame. Balasar grinned wide and wolfish. If it was pride, then let him be proud. No man could do what he intended without it. "When I've finished, the god-ghosts of the Khaiem will be a story women tell their babes to scare them at night, and nothing more than that. *That's* what Little Ott died for. Not for money or conquest or glory.

"I'm saving the world," Balasar said. "So, now. Say you'd rather drown than help me."

1

>+< It had rained for a week, the cold gray clouds seeming to drape themselves between the mountain ranges to the east and west of the city like a wet canopy. The mornings were foggy, the afternoons chill. With the snowdrifts of winter almost all melted, the land around Machi became a soupy mud whose only virtue was the spring crop of wheat and snow peas it would bring forth. Travel was harder now even than in the deadly cold of deep winter.

And still, the travelers came.

"With all respect, this exercise, as you call it, is ill-advised," the envoy said. His hands still held a pose of deference though the conversation had long since parted from civility. "I am sure your intentions are entirely honorable, however it is the place of the Dai-kvo—"

"If the Dai-kvo wants to rule Machi, tell him to come north," the Khai Machi snapped. "He can pull my puppet strings from the next room. I'll make a bed for him."

The envoy's eyes went wide. He was a young man, and hadn't mastered the art of keeping his mind from showing on his face. Otah, the Khai Machi, waved away his own words and sighed. He had gone too far, and he knew it. Another few steps and they'd be pointing at each other and yelling about which of them wanted to create the Third Empire. The truth was that he had ruled Machi these last fourteen years only by necessity. The prospect of uniting the cities of the Khaiem under his rule was about as enticing as scraping his skin off with a rock.

The audience was a private one, in a small room lined with richly carved blackwood, lit by candles that smelled like rich earth and vanilla, and set well away from the corridors and open gardens where servants and members of the utkhaiem might unintentionally overhear them. This wasn't business he cared to have shared over the dances and dinners of the court. Otah rose from his chair and walked to the window, forcing his temper back down. He opened the shutters, and the city stretched out before him, grand towers of stone stretching up toward the sky, and beyond them the wide plain to the south, green with the first crops of the spring. He pressed his frustration back into yoke.

"I didn't mean that," he said. "I know that the Dai-kvo doesn't intend to dictate to me. Or any of the Khaiem. I appreciate your concern, but the creation of the guard isn't a threat. It's hardly an army, you know. A few hundred men trained up to maybe half the level of a Westlands garrison could hardly topple the world."

"We are concerned for the stability of all the cities," the envoy said. "When one of the Khaiem begins to study war, it puts all the others on edge."

"It's hardly studying war to hand a few men knives and remind them which end's the handle."

"It's more than any of the Khaiem have done in the past hundred years. And you must see that you haven't made it your policy to ally yourself with . . . well, with anyone."

Well, this is going just as poorly as I expected, Otah thought.

"I have a wife, thank you," Otah said, his manner cool. But the envoy had clearly reached the end of his patience. Hearing him stand, Otah turned. The young man's face was flushed, his hands folded into the sleeves of his brown poet's robes.

"And if you were a shopkeeper, having a single woman would be admirable," the envoy said. "But as the Khai Machi, turning away every woman who's offered to you is a pattern of insult. I can't be the first one to point this out. From the time you took the chair, you've isolated yourself from the rest of the Khaiem, the great houses of the utkhaiem, the merchant houses. Everyone."

Otah ran through the thousand arguments and responses—the treaties and trade agreements, the acceptance of servants and slaves, all of the ways in which he'd tried to bind himself and Machi to the other cities. They wouldn't convince the envoy or his master, the Dai-kvo. They wanted blood—his blood flowing in the veins of some boy child whose mother had come from south or east or west. They wanted to know that the Khai Yalakeht or Pathai or Tan-Sadar might be able to hope for a grandson on the black chair in Machi once Otah had died. His wife Kiyan was past the age to bear another child, but men could get children on younger women. For one of the Khaiem to have only two children, and both by the same woman—and her a wayhouse keeper from Udun . . . They wanted sons from him, fathered on women who embodied wise political alliances. They wanted to preserve tradition, and they had two empires and nine generations of the Khaiate court life to back them. Despair settled on him like a thick winter cloak.

There was nothing to be gained. He knew all the reasons for all the choices he had made, and he could as easily explain them to a mine dog as to this proud young man who'd traveled weeks for the privilege of taking him to task. Otah sighed, turned, and took a deeply formal pose of apology.

"I have distracted you from your task, Athai-cha. That was not my intention. What was it again the Dai-kvo wished of me?"

The envoy pressed his lips bloodless. They both knew the answer to the question, but Otah's feigned ignorance would force him to restate it. And the simple fact that Otah's bed habits were not mentioned would make his point for him. Etiquette was a terrible game.

"The militia you have formed," the envoy said. "The Dai-kvo would know your intention in creating it."

"I intend to send it to the Westlands. I intend it to take contracts with whatever forces there are acting in the best interests of *all* the cities of the Khaiem. I will be pleased to draft a letter saying so."

Otah smiled. The young poet's eyes flickered. As insults went, this was mild enough. Eventually, the poet's hands rose in a pose of gratitude.

"There is one other thing, Most High," the envoy said. "If you take any aggressive act against the interests of another of the Khaiem, the Dai-kvo will recall Cehmai and Stone-Made-Soft. If you take arms against them, he will allow the Khaiem to use their poets against you and your city."

"Yes," Otah said. "I understood that when I heard you'd come. I am not acting against the Khaiem, but thank you for your time, Athai-cha. I will have a letter sewn and sealed for you by morning."

After the envoy had left, Otah sank into a chair and pressed the heels of his hands to his temples. Around him, the palace was quiet. He counted fifty breaths, then rose again, closed and latched the door, and turned back to the apparently empty room.

"Well?" he asked, and one of the panels in the corner swung open, exposing a tiny hidden chamber brilliantly designed for eavesdropping.

The man who sat in the listener's chair seemed both at ease and out of place. At ease because it was Sinja's nature to take the world lightly, and out of place because his suntanned skin and rough, stained leathers made him seem like a gardener on a chair of deep red velvet and silver pins fit for the head of a merchant house or a member of the utkhaiem. He rose and closed the panel behind him.

"He seems a decent man," Sinja said. "I wouldn't want him on my side of a fight, though. Overconfident."

"I'm hoping it won't come to that," Otah said.

"For a man who's convinced the world he's bent on war, you're a bit squeamish about violence."

Otah chuckled.

"I think sending the Dai-kvo his messenger's head might not be the most convincing argument for my commitment to peace," he said.

"Excellent point," Sinja agreed as he poured himself a bowl of wine. "But then you are training men to fight. It's a hard thing to preach peace and stability and also pay men to think what's the best way to disembowel someone with a spear."

"I know it," Otah said, his voice dark as wet slate. "Gods. You'd think having total power over a city would give you more options, wouldn't you?"

Otah sipped the wine. It was rich and astringent and fragrant of late summer, and it swirled in the bowl like a dark river. He felt old. Fourteen years he'd spent trying to be what Machi needed him to be—steward, manager, ruler, half-god, fuel for the gossip and backbiting of the court. Most of the time, he did well enough, but then something like this would happen, and he would be sure again that the work was beyond him.

"You could disband it," Sinja said. "It's not as though you need the extra trade."

"It's not about getting more silver," Otah said.

"Then what's it about? You aren't actually planning to invade Cetani, are you? Because I don't think that's a good idea."

Otah coughed out a laugh.

"It's about being ready," he said.

"Ready?"

"Every generation finds it harder to bind fresh andat. Every one that slips away becomes more difficult to capture. It can't go on forever. There will come a time that the poets fail, and we have to rely on something else."

"So," Sinja said. "You're starting a militia so that someday, generations from now, when some Dai-kvo that hasn't been born yet doesn't manage to keep up to the standards of his forebears—"

"There will also be generations of soldiers ready to keep the cities safe."

Sinja scratched his belly and nodded.

"You think I'm wrong?"

"Yes. I think you're wrong," Sinja said. "I think you saw Seedless escape. I think you saw Saraykeht suffer the loss. You know that the Galts have ambitions, and that they've put their hands into the affairs of the Khaiem more than once."

"That doesn't make me wrong," Otah said, unable to keep the sudden anger from his voice. So many years had passed, and the memory of Saraykeht had not dimmed. "You weren't there, Sinja-cha. You don't know how bad it was. That's mine. And if it lets me see farther than the Dai-kvo or the Khaiem—"

"It's possible to look at the horizon so hard you trip over your feet," Sinja said, unfazed by Otah's heat. "You aren't responsible for everything under the sky."

But I am responsible for that, Otah thought. He had never confessed his role in the fall of Saraykeht to Sinja, never told the story of the time he had killed a helpless man, of sparing an enemy and saving a friend. The danger and complexity and sorrow of that time had never entirely left him, but he could not call it regret.

"You want to keep the future safe," Sinja said, breaking the silence, "and I respect that. But you can't do it by shitting on the table right now. Alienating the Dai-kvo gains you nothing."

"What would you do, Sinja? If you were in my place, what would you do?"

"Take as much gold as I could put on a fast cart, and live out my life in a beach hut on Bakta. But then I'm not particularly reliable." He drained his bowl and put it down on the table, porcelain clicking softly on lacquered wood. "What you *should* do is send us west."

"But the men aren't ready—"

"They're near enough. Without real experience, these poor bastards would protect you from a real army about as well as sending out all the dancing girls you could find. And now that I've said it, girls might even slow them down longer."

Otah coughed a mirthless laugh. Sinja leaned forward, his eyes calm and steady.

"Put us in the Westlands as a mercenary company," he said. "It gives real weight to it when you tell the Dai-kvo that you're just looking for another way to make money if we're already walking away from our neighboring cities. The men will get experience; I'll be able to make contacts with other mercenaries, maybe even strike up alliances with some of the Wardens. You can even found your military tradition. But besides that, there are certain problems with training and arming men, and then not giving them any outlet."

Otah looked up, meeting Sinja's grim expression.

"More trouble?" Otah asked.

"I've whipped the men involved and paid reparations," Sinja said, "but if the Dai-kvo doesn't like you putting together a militia, the fine people of Machi are getting impatient with having them. We're paying them to play at soldiers while everybody else's taxes buy their food and clothes."

Otah took a simple pose that acknowledged what Sinja said as truth.

"Where would you take them?"

"Annaster and Notting were on the edge of fighting last autumn. Something about the Warden of Annaster's son getting killed in a hunt. It's a long way south, but we're a small enough group to travel fast, and the passes cleared early this year. Even if nothing comes of it, there'll be keeps down there that want a garrison."

"How long before you could go?"

"I can have the men ready in two days if you'll send food carts out after us. A week if I have to stay to make the arrangements for the supplies."

Otah looked into Sinja's eyes. The years had whitened Sinja's temples but had made him no easier to read.

"That seems fast," Otah said.

"It's already under way," Sinja replied, then seeing Otah's reaction, shrugged. "It seemed likely."

"Two days, then," Otah said. Sinja smiled, stood, took a rough pose that accepted the order, and turned to go. As he lifted the door's latch, Otah spoke again. "Try not to get killed. Kiyan would take it amiss if I sent you off to die."

The captain paused in the open door. What had happened between Kiyan and Sinja—the Khai Machi's first and only wife and the captain of his private armsmen—had found its resolution on a snow-covered field ten years before. Sinja had done as Kiyan had asked him and the issue had ended there. Otah found that the anger and feelings of betrayal had thinned with time, leaving him more embarrassed than wrathful. That they were two men who loved the same woman was understood and unspoken. It wasn't comfortable ground for either of them.

"I'll keep breathing, Otah-cha. You do the same."

The door closed softly behind him, and Otah took another sip of wine. It was fewer than a dozen breaths before a quiet scratching came at the door. Rising and straightening the folds of his robes, Otah prepared himself for the next appearance, the next performance in his ongoing, unending mummer's show. He pressed down a twinge of envy for Sinja and the men who would be slogging through cold mud and dirty snow. He told himself the journey only looked liberating to someone who was staying near a fire grate. He adopted a somber expression, held his body with the rigid grace expected of him, and called out for the servant to enter.

There was a meeting to take with House Daikani over a new mine they were proposing in the South. Mikah Radaani had also put a petition with the Master of Tides to schedule a meeting with the Khai Machi to discuss the prospect of resurrecting the summer fair in Amnat-Tan. And there was the letter to the Dai-kvo to compose, and a ceremony at the temple at moonrise at which his presence was required, and so on through the day and into the night. Otah listened patiently to the list of duties and obligations and tried not to feel haunted by the thought that sending the guard away had been the wrong thing to do.

EIAH TOOK A BITE OF THE ALMOND CAKE, WIPING HONEY FROM HER MOUTH WITH the back of her hand, and Maati was amazed again by how tall she'd grown. He still thought of her as hardly standing high as his knees, and here she was—thin as a stick and awkward, but tall as her mother. She'd even taken to wearing a woman's jewelry—necklace of gold and silver, armbands of lacework silver and gems, and rings on half her fingers. She still looked like a girl playing dress-up in her mother's things, but even that would pass soon.

"And how did *he* die?" she asked.

"I never said he did," Maati said.

Eiah's lips bent in a frown. Her dark eyes narrowed.

"You don't tell stories where they live, Uncle Maati. You like the dead ones."

Maati chuckled. It was a fair enough criticism, and her exasperation was as amusing as her interest. Since she'd been old enough to read, Eiah had haunted the library of Machi, poking here and there, reading and being frustrated. And now that she'd reached her fourteenth summer, the time had come for her to turn to matters of court. She was the only daughter of the Khai Machi, and as such, a rare chance for a marriage alliance. She would be the most valued property in the city, and worse for her and her parents, she was more than clever enough to know it. Her time in the library had taken on a tone of defiance, but it was never leveled at Maati, so it never bothered him. In fact, he found it rather delightful.

"Well," he said, settling his paunch more comfortably in the library's deep silk-covered chair, "as it happens, his binding did fail. It was tragic. He started screaming, and didn't stop for hours. He stopped when he died, of course, and when they examined him afterwards, they found slivers of glass all through his blood."

"They cut him open?"

"Of course," Maati said.

"That's disgusting," she said. Then a moment later, "If someone died here, could I help do it?"

"No one's likely to try a binding here, Eiah-kya. Only poets who've trained for years with the Dai-kvo are allowed to make the attempt, and even then they're under strict supervision. Holding the andat is dangerous work, and not just if it fails."

"They should let girls do it too," she said. "I want to go to the school and train to be a poet."

"But then you wouldn't be your father's daughter anymore. If the Dai-kvo didn't choose you, you'd be one of the branded, and they'd turn you out into the world to make whatever way you could without anyone to help you."

"That's not true. Father was at the school, and he didn't have to take the brand. If the Dai-kvo didn't pick me, I wouldn't take it either. I'd just come back here and live alone like you do."

"But then wouldn't you and Danat have to fight?"

"No," Eiah said, taking a pose appropriate to a tutor offering correction. "Girls can't be Khai, so Danat wouldn't have to fight me for the chair."

"But if you're going to have women be poets, why not Khaiem too?"

"Because who'd want to be Khai?" she asked and took another piece of cake from the tray on the table between them.

The library stretched out around them—chamber after chamber of scrolls and books and codices that were Maati's private domain. The air was rich with the scent of old leather and dust and the pungent herbs he used to keep the mice and insects away. Baarath, the chief librarian and Maati's best friend here in the far, cold North, had kept it before him. Often when Maati arrived in the morning or remained long after dark, puzzling over some piece of ancient text or obscure reference, he would look up, half-wondering where the annoying, fat, boisterous, petty little man had gotten to, and then he would remember.

The fever had taken dozens of people that year. Winter always changed the city, the cold driving them deep into the tunnels and hidden chambers below Machi. For months they lived by firelight and in darkness. By midwinter, the air itself could seem thick and stifling. And illnesses spread easily in the dark and close, and Baraath had grown ill and died, one man among many. Now he was only memory and ash. Maati was the master of the library, appointed by his old friend and enemy and companion Otah Machi. The Khai Machi, husband of Kiyan, and father to this almost-woman Eiah who shared his almond cakes, and to her brother Danat. And, perhaps, to one other.

"Maati-kya? Are you okay?"

"I was just wondering how your brother was," he said.

"Better. He's hardly coughing at all anymore. Everyone's saying he has weak lungs, but I was just as sick when I was young, and I'm just fine."

"People tell stories," Maati said. "It keeps them amused, I suppose."

"What would happen if Danat died?"

"Your father would be expected to take a new, younger wife and produce a son to take his place. More than one, if he could. That's part of why the utkhaiem are so worried about Danat. If he died and no brothers were forthcoming, it would be bad for the city. All the most powerful houses would start fighting over who would be the new Khai. People would probably be killed."

"Well, Danat won't die," Eiah said. "So it doesn't matter. Did you know him?"

"Who?"

"My real uncle. Danat. The one Danat's named for?"

"No," Maati said. "Not really. I met him once."

"Did you like him?"

Maati tried to remember what it had been like, all those years ago. The Dai-kvo had summoned him. That had been the old Dai-kvo—Tahi-kvo. He'd never met the new one. Tahi-kvo had brought him to meet the two men, and set him the task that had ended with Otah on the chair and himself living in the court of Machi. It had been a different lifetime.

"I don't recall liking him or disliking him," Maati said. "He was just a man I'd met."

Eiah sighed impatiently.

"Tell me about another one," she said.

"Well. There was a poet in the First Empire before people understood that andat were harder and harder to capture each time they escaped. He tried to bind Softness with the same binding another poet had used a generation before. Of course it didn't work."

"Because a new binding has to be different," Eiah said.

"But *he* didn't know that."

"What happened to him?"

"His joints all froze in place. He was alive, but like a statue. He couldn't move at all."

"How did he eat?"

"He didn't. They tried to give him water by forcing it up his nostrils, and he drowned in it. When they examined his body, all the bones were fused together as if they had never been separate at all. It looked like one single thing."

"That's disgusting," she said. It was something she often said. Maati grinned.

They talked for another half a hand, Maati telling tales of failed bindings, of the prices paid by poets of old who had attempted the greatest trick in the world and fallen short. Eiah listened and passed her own certain judgment. They finished the last of the almond cakes and called a servant girl in to carry the plates away. Eiah left just as the sun peeked out between the low clouds and the high peaks in the west, brightness flaring gold for a long moment before the city fell into its long twilight. Alone again, Maati told himself that the darkness was only about the accidents of sunlight, and not his young friend's absence.

He could still remember the first time he'd seen Eiah. She'd been tiny, a small, curious helplessness in her mother's arms, and he had been deeply in disfavor with the Dai-kvo and sent to Machi in half-exile for treading too near the line between the poets and the politics of the court. The poets were creatures of the Dai-kvo, lent to the Khaiem. The Dai-kvo took no part in the courtly dramas of generational fratricide. The Khaiem supported the Dai-kvo and his village, sent their excess sons to the school from which they might be plucked to take the honor of the brown robes, and saw to the administration of the cities whose names they took as their own. The Khai Machi, the Khai Yalakeht, the Khai Tan-Sadar. All of them had been other men once, before their fathers had died or become too feeble to rule. All of them had killed their own brothers on the way to claiming their positions. All except Otah.

Otah, the exception.

A scratching at the door roused Maati, and he hauled himself from his chair and went forward. The night had nearly fallen, but torches spattered the darkness with circles of light. Even before he reached the door, he heard music coming from one of the pavilions nearby, the young men and women of the utkhaiem boiling up from the winter earth and celebrating nightly, undeterred by chill or rain or heartbreak. And at the door of his library were two familiar figures, and a third that was only expected. Cehmai, poet of Machi, stood with a bottle of wine in each hand, and behind him the hulking, bemused, inhuman andat Stone-Made-Soft raised its wide chin in greeting. The other—a slender young man in the same brown robes that Cehmai and Maati himself wore—spoke to Cehmai. Athai Vauudun, the envoy from the Dai-kvo.

"He is the most arrogant man I have ever met," the envoy said to Cehmai, continuing a previous conversation. "He has no allies, only one son, and no pause at all at the prospect of alienating every other city of the Khaiem. I think he's *proud* to ignore tradition."

"Our guest has met with the Khai," Stone-Made-Soft said, its voice low and rough as a landslide. "They don't appear to have impressed each other favorably."

"Athai-kvo," Cehmai said, gesturing awkwardly with one full bottle. "This it Maati Vaupathai. Maati-kvo, please meet our new friend."

Athai took a pose of greeting, and Maati answered with a welcoming pose less formal than the one he'd been offered.

"Kvo?" Athai said. "I hadn't known you were Cehmai-cha's teacher."

"It's a courtesy he gives me because I'm old," Maati said. "Come in, though. All of you. It's getting cold out."

Maati led the others back through the chambers and corridors of the library.

On the way, they traded the kind of simple, common talk that etiquette required—the Dai-kvo was in good health, the school had given a number of promising boys the black robes, there were discussions of a possible new binding in the next years—and Maati played his part. Only Stone-Made-Soft didn't participate, considering as it was the thick stone walls with mild, distant interest. The inner chamber that Maati had prepared for the meeting was dim and windowless, but a fire burned hot behind iron shutters. Books and scrolls lay on a wide, low table. Maati opened the iron shutters, lit a taper from the flames, and set a series of candles and lanterns glowing around the room until they were all bathed in shadowless warm light. The envoy and Cehmai had taken chairs by the fire, and Maati lowered himself to a wide bench.

"My private workroom," Maati said, nodding at the space around them. "I've been promised there's no good way to listen to us in here."

The envoy took a pose that accepted the fact, but glanced uneasily at Stone-Made-Soft.

"I won't tell," the andat said, and grinned, baring its unnaturally regular stone-white teeth. "Promise."

"If I lost control of our friend here, telling what happened in a meeting wouldn't be the trouble we faced," Cehmai said.

The envoy seemed somewhat mollified. He had a small face, Maati thought. But perhaps it was only that Maati had already taken a dislike to the man.

"So Cehmai has been telling me about your project," Athai said, folding his hands in his lap. "A study of the prices meted out by failed bindings, is it?"

"A bit more than that," Maati said. "A mapping, rather, of the form of the binding to the form that its price took. What it was about this man's work that his blood went dry, or that one's that made his lungs fill with worms."

"You might consider not binding us in the first place," Stone-Made-Soft said. "If it's so dangerous as all that."

Maati ignored it. "I thought, you see, that there might be some way to better understand whether a poet's work was likely to fail or succeed if we knew more of how older failures presented themselves. It was an essay Heshai Antaburi wrote examining his own binding of Removing-the-Part-That-Continues that gave me the idea. You see his binding succeeded—he held Seedless for decades—but in having done the thing and then lived with the consequences, he could better see the flaws in his original work. Here . . ."

Maati rose up with a grunt and fished through his papers for a moment until the old, worn leather-bound book came to hand. Its cover was limp from years of reading, the pages growing yellow and smudged. The envoy took it and read a bit by the light of candles.

"But this is too much like his original work," Athai said as he thumbed through the pages. "It could never be used."

"No, of course not," Maati agreed. "But he made the attempt to examine the form of the binding, you see, in hopes that showing the kinds of errors he'd

made might help others avoid things that were similar. Heshai-kvo was one of
my first teachers."

"He was the one murdered in Saraykeht, ne?" Athai asked, not looking up
from the book in his hands.

"Yes," Maati said.

Athai looked up, one hand taking an informal pose asking excuse.

"I didn't mean anything by asking," he said. "I only wanted to place him."

Maati brought himself to smile and nod.

"The reason I wrote to the Dai-kvo," Cehmai said, "was the application
Maati-kvo was thinking of."

"Application?"

"It's too early yet to really examine closely," Maati said. He felt himself
starting to blush, and his embarrassment at the thought fueled the blood in his
face. "It's too early to say whether there's anything in it."

"Tell him," Cehmai said, his voice warm and coaxing. The envoy put
Heshai-kvo's book down, his attention entirely on Maati now.

"There are . . . patterns," Maati said. "There seems to be a structure that
links the form of the binding to its . . . its worst expression. Its price. The forms
only seem random because it's a very complex structure. And I was reading
Catji's meditations—the one from the Second Empire, not Catji Sano—and
there are some speculations he made about the nature of language and grammar
that . . . that seem related."

"He's found a way to shield a poet from paying the price," Cehmai said.

"I don't know that's true," Maati said quickly.

"But *possibly*," Cehmai said.

The envoy and the andat both shifted forward in their seats. The effect was
eerie.

"I thought that, if a poet's first attempt at a binding didn't have to be his
last—if an imperfect binding didn't mean death . . ."

Maati gestured helplessly at the air. He had spent so many hours thinking
about what it could mean, about what it could bring about and bring back. All
the andat lost over the course of generations that had been thought beyond
recapture might still be bound if only the men binding them could learn from
their errors, adjust their work as Heshai had done after the fact. Softness.
Water-Moving-Down. Thinking-in-Words. All the spirits cataloged in the histories, the work of poets who had made the Empire great. Perhaps they were
not past redemption.

He looked at Athai, but the young man's eyes were unfocused and distant.

"May I see your work, Maati-kvo?" he asked, and the barely suppressed
excitement in his voice almost brought Maati to like him for the moment. Together, the three men stepped to Maati's worktable. Three men, and one other
that was something else.

2

>+< Liat Chokavi had never seen seawater as green as the bays near Amnat-Tan. The seafront at Saraykeht had always taken its color from the sky—gray, blue, white, yellow, crimson, pink. The water in the far North was different entirely; green as grass and numbing cold. She could no more see the fish and seafloor here than read pages from a closed book. These waters kept their secrets.

A low fog lay on the bay; the white and gray towers of the low town seemed to float upon it. In the far distance, the deep blue spire of the Khai Amnat-Tan's palace seemed almost to glow, a lantern like a star fallen to earth. Even the sailors, she noticed, would pause for a moment at their work and admire it. It was the great wonder of Amnat-Tan, second only to the towers of Machi as the signature of the winter cities. It would take them days more to reach it; the ports and low towns were a good distance downriver of the city itself.

The wind smelled of smoke now—the scent of the low town coming across the water, adding to the smells of salt and fish, crab and unwashed humanity. They would reach port by midday. She turned and went down the steps to their cabin.

Nayiit swung gently in his hammock, his eyes closed, snoring lightly. Liat sat on the crate that held their belongings and considered her son; the long face, the unkempt hair, the delicate hands folded on his belly. He had made an attempt at growing a beard in their time in Yalakeht, but it had come in so poorly he'd shaved it off with a razor and cold seawater. Her heart ached, listening to him sleep. The workings of House Kyaan weren't so complex that it could not run without her immediate presence, but she had never meant to keep Nayiit so long from home and the family he had only recently begun.

The news had reached Saraykeht last summer—almost a year ago now. It had hardly been more than a confluence of rumors—a Galtic ship in Nantani slipping away before its cargo had arrived, a scandal at the Dai-kvo's village, inquiries discreetly made about a poet. And still, as her couriers arrived at the compound, Liat had felt unease growing in her. There were few enough people who knew as she did that the house she ran had been founded to keep watch on the duplicity of the Galts. Fewer still knew of the books she kept, as her mentor Amat Kyaan had before her, tracking the actions and strategies of the Galtic houses among the Khaiem, and it was a secret she meant to keep. So when tales of a missing poet began to dovetail too neatly with stories of Galtic intrigue in Nantani, there was no one whom she trusted the task to more than herself. She had been in Saraykeht for ten years. She decided to leave again the day that Nayiit's son Tai took his first steps.

Looking back, she wondered why it had been so easy for Nayiit to come with her. He and his wife were happy, she'd thought. The baby boy was delightful, and the work of the house engaging. When he had made the offer, she had hidden her pleasure at the thought and made only slight objections. The truth was that the years they had spent on the road when Nayiit had been a child—the time between her break with Maati Vaupathai and her return to the arms of Saraykeht—held a powerful nostalgia for her. Alone in the world with only a son barely halfway to manhood, she had expected struggle and pain and the emptiness that she had always thought must accompany a woman without a man.

The truth had been a surprise. Certainly the emptiness and struggle and pain had attended their travels. She and Nayiit had spent nights huddling under waxed-cloth tarps while chill rain pattered around them. They had eaten cheap food from low-town firekeepers. She had learned again all she'd known as a girl of how to mend a robe or a boot. And she had discovered a competence she had never believed herself to possess. Before that, she had always had a lover by whom to judge herself. With a son, she found herself stronger, smarter, more complete than she had dared pretend.

The journey to Nantani had been a chance for her to relive that, one last time. Her son was a man now, with a child of his own. There wouldn't be many more travels, just the two of them. So she had put aside any doubts, welcomed him, and set off to discover what she could about Riaan Vaudathat, son of a high family of the Nantani utkhaiem and missing poet. She had expected the work to take a season, no more. They would be back in the compound of House Kyaan in time to spend the autumn haggling over contracts and shipping prices.

And now it was spring, and she saw no prospect of sleeping in a bed she might call her own any time soon. Nayiit had not complained when it became clear that their investigation would require a journey to the village of the Dai-kvo. As a woman, Liat was not permitted beyond the low towns approaching it. She would need a man to do her business within the halls of the Dai-kvo's palaces. They had booked passage to Yalakeht, and then upriver. They had arrived at mid-autumn and hardly finished their investigation before Candles Night. So far North, there had been no ship back to Saraykeht, and Liat had taken apartments for them in the narrow, gated streets of Yalakeht for the winter.

In the long, dark hours she had struggled with what she knew, and with the thaw and the first ships taking passages North, she had prepared to travel to Amnat-Tan, and then Cetani. And then, though the prospect made her sick with anxiety, Machi.

A shout rose on the deck above them—a score of men calling out to each other—and the ship lurched and boomed. Nayiit blinked awake, looked over at her, and smiled. He always had had a good smile.

"Have I missed anything?" he asked with a yawn.

"We've reached the low towns outside Amnat-Tan," Liat said. "We'll be docked soon."

Nayiit swung his legs around, planting them on the deck to keep his hammock from rocking. He looked ruefully around the tiny cabin and sighed.

"I'll start packing our things, then," he said.

"Pack them separate," she said. "I'll go the rest of the way myself. I want you back in Saraykeht."

Nayiit took a pose that refused this, and Liat felt her jaw tighten.

"We've had this conversation, Mother. I'm not putting you out to walk the North Road by yourself."

"I'll hire a seat on a caravan," she said. "Spring's just opening, and there are bound to be any number of them going to Cetani and back. It's not such a long journey, really."

"Good. Then it won't take too long for us to get there."

"You're going back," Liat said.

Nayiit sighed and gathered himself visibly.

"Fine," he said. "Make your argument. Convince me."

Liat looked at her hands. It was the same problem she'd fought all through the long winter. Each time she'd come close to speaking the truth, something had held her back. Secrets. It all came back to secrets, and if she spoke her fears to Nayiit, it would mean telling him things that only she knew, things that she had hoped might die with her.

"Is it about my father?" he said, and his voice was so gentle, Liat felt tears gathering in her eyes.

"In a way," she said.

"I know he's at the court of Machi," Nayiit said. "There's no reason for me to fear him, is there? Everything you've said of him—"

"No, Maati would never hurt you. Or me. It's just . . . it was so long ago. And I don't know who he's become since then."

Nayiit leaned forward, taking her hands in his.

"I want to meet him," he said. "Not because of who he was to you, or who he is now. I want to meet him because he's my father. Ever since Tai came, I've been thinking about it. About what it would be for me to walk away from my boy and not come back. About choosing something else over my family."

"It wasn't like that," Liat said. "Maati and I were . . ."

"I've come this far," he said gently. "You can't send me back now."

"You don't understand," she said.

"You can explain to me while I pack our things."

In the end, of course, he won. She had known he would. Nayiit could be as soft and gentle and implacable as snowfall. He was his father's son.

The calls of gulls grew louder as they neared the shore, the scent of smoke more present. The docks were narrower than the seafront of Saraykeht. A ship that put in here for the winter had to prepare itself to be icebound, immobile.

Trade was with the eastern islands and Yalakeht; it was too far from the summer cities or Bakta or Galt for ships to come from those distant ports.

The streets were black cobbles, and ice still haunted the alleys where shadows held the cold. Nayiit carried their crate strapped across his back. The wide leather belt cut into his shoulders, but he didn't complain. He rarely complained about anything, only did what he thought best with a pleasant smile and a calm explanation ready to hand.

Liat stopped at a firekeeper's kiln to ask directions to the compound of House Radaani and was pleased to discover it was nearby. Mother and son, they walked the fog-shrouded streets until they found the wide arches that opened to the courtyard gardens of the Radaani, torches flickering and guttering in the damp air. A boy in sodden robes rushed up and lifted the crate from Nayiit's back to his own. Liat was about to address him when another voice, a woman's voice lovely and low as a singer's, came from the dim.

"Liat-cha, I must assume. I'd sent men to meet you at the docks, but I'm afraid they came too late."

The woman who stepped out from the fog had seen no more than twenty summers. Her robes were white snowfox, eerie in the combination of pale mourning colors and the luxury of the fur. Her hair shone black with cords of silver woven in the braids. She was beautiful, and likely would be for another five summers. Liat could already see the presentiment of jowls at the borders of her jaw.

"Ceinat Radaani," Liat said, taking a pose of gratitude. "I am pleased to meet you in person at last. This is my son, Nayiit."

The Radaani girl adopted a welcoming pose that included them both. Nayiit returned it, and Liat couldn't help noticing the way his eyes lingered on her and hers on him. Liat coughed, bringing their attention back to the moment. The girl took a pose of apology, and turned to lead them into the chambers and corridors of the compound.

In Saraykeht, the architecture tended to be open, encouraging the breezes to flow and cool. Northern buildings were more like great kilns, built to hold heat in their thick stone walls. The ceilings were low and fire grates burned in every room. The Radaani girl led them through a wide entrance chamber and back through a narrow corridor, speaking as she walked.

"My father is in Council with the Khai, but sends his regards and intends to join us as soon as he can return from the city proper. He would very much regret missing the opportunity to meet with the head of our trading partner in the South."

It was bald flattery. Radaani was among the richest houses in the winter cities, and had agreements with dozens of houses, all through the cities of the Khaiem. The whole of House Kyaan would hardly have made up one of the Radaani compounds, and there were four such compounds that Liat knew of. Liat accepted it, though, as if it were true, as if the hospitality extended to her were more than etiquette.

"I look forward to speaking with him," Liat said. "I am most interested in hearing news of the winter cities."

"Oh, there'll be quite a bit to say, I'm sure," the girl laughed. "There always is once winter's ended. I think people save up all the gossip of the winter to haul out in spring."

She opened a pair of wide wooden doors and led them into small, cozy apartments. A fire popped and murmured in the grate, bowls of mulled wine waited steaming on a low wooden table, and archways to either side showed rooms with real beds waiting for them. Liat's body seemed drawn to the bed like a stone rolling downhill. She had not realized how much she loathed shipboard hammocks.

She took a pose of thanks that the girl responded to neatly as the servant boy put the crate down gently by the fire.

"I will let you rest," the girl said. "If you have need of me, any of the servants can find me for you. And I will, of course, send word when my father returns."

"You're very kind," Nayiit said, smiling his disarming smile. "Forgive me, but is there a bathhouse near? I don't think shipboard life has left me entirely prepared for good company."

"Of course," the girl said. "I would be pleased to show you the way."

I'm sure you would, Liat thought. Was I so obvious at her age?

"Mother," Nayiit said, "would you care to . . ."

Liat waved the offer away.

"A basin and a sponge will be enough for me. I have letters to write before dinner. Perhaps, Ceinat-cha, if you would leave word with your couriers that I will have things to send south?"

The girl took an acknowledging pose, then turned to Nayiit with a flutter of a smile and gestured for him to follow her.

"Nayiit," Liat said, and her son paused in the apartment's doorway. "Find out what you can about the situation in Machi. I'd like to know what we're walking into."

Nayiit smiled, nodded, and vanished. The servant boy also left, promising the basin and sponge shortly. Liat sighed and sat down, stretching her feet out toward the burning logs. The wine tasted good, though slightly overspiced to her taste.

Machi. She was going to Machi. She let her mind turn the fact over again, as if it were a puzzle she had nearly solved. She was going to present her discoveries and her fears to the man she'd once called a lover, back when he'd been a seafront laborer and called himself Itani. Now he was the Khai Machi. And Maati, with whom she had betrayed him. The idea tightened her throat every time she thought of it.

Maati. Nayiit was going to see Maati, perhaps to confront him, perhaps to seek the sort of advice that a son can ask only of a father. Something, perhaps, that touched on the finer points of going to foreign bathhouses with young women in snowfox robes. Liat sighed.

Nayiit had been thinking about what it would be to walk away from his wife, the son he'd brought to the world. He'd said as much, and more than once. She had thought it was a question based in anger—an accusation against Maati. It only now occurred to her that perhaps there was also longing in it, and she thought to wonder how complex her quiet, pleasant son's heart might be.

BALASAR LEANED OVER THE BALCONY AND LOOKED DOWN AT THE COURTYARD below. A crowd had gathered, talking animatedly with the brown-skinned, almond-eyed curiosity he had spirited from across the sea. They peppered him with questions—why was he called a poet when he didn't write poems, what did he think of Acton, how had he learned to speak Galtic so well. Their eyes were bright and the conversation as lively as water dropped on a hot skillet. For his part, Riaan Vaudathat drank it all in, answering everything in the slushy singsong accent of the Khaiem. When the people laughed, he joined in as if they were not laughing at him. Perhaps he truly didn't know they were.

Riaan glanced up and saw him, raising his hands in a pose that Balasar recognized as a form of greeting, though he couldn't have said which of the half-thousand possible nuances it held. He only waved in return and stepped away from the edge of the balcony.

"It's like I've taught a dog to wear clothes and talk," Balasar said, lowering himself onto a bench beside Eustin.

"Yes, sir."

"They don't understand."

"You can't expect them to, sir. They're simple folk, most of 'em. Never been as far as Eddensea. They've been hearing about the Khaiem and the poets and the andat all their lives, but they've never seen 'em. Now they have the chance."

"Well, it'll help my popularity at the games," Balasar said, his voice more bitter than he'd intended.

"They don't know the things we do, sir. You can't expect them to think like us."

"And the High Council? Can I expect it of them? Or are they in chambers talking about the funny brown man who dresses like a girl?"

Eustin looked down, silent for long enough that Balasar began to regret his tone.

"All fairness, sir," Eustin said, "the robes do look like a girl's."

It was six years now since he and Eustin and Coal had returned to the hereditary estate outside Kirinton, half a year since they had recruited the fallen poet of Nantani, and three weeks since Balasar had received the expected summons. He'd come to Acton with his best men, the books, the poet, the plans. The High Council had heard him out—the dangers of the andat, the need to end the supremacy of the Khaiem. That part had gone quite well. No one seriously disputed that the Khaiem were the single greatest threat to Galt. It was only when he began to reveal his plans and how far he had already gone that the audience began to turn sour on him.

Since then, the Council had met without him. They might have been debating the plan he had laid out before them, or they might have moved to other business, leaving him to soak in his own sweat. He and Eustin and the poet Riaan had lived in the apartments assigned to them. Balasar had spent his days sitting outside the Council's halls and meeting chambers, and his nights walking the starlit streets, restless as a ghost. Each hour that passed was wasted. Every night was one less that he would have in the autumn when the end of his army was racing against the snow and cold of the Khaiate North. If the Council's intention had been to set him on edge, they had done their work.

A flock of birds, black as crows but thinner, burst from the walnut trees beyond the courtyard, whirled overhead, and settled back where they had come from. Balasar wove his fingers together on one knee.

"What do we do if they don't move forward?" Eustin asked quietly.

"Convince them."

"And if they can't be convinced?"

"Convince them anyway," Balasar said.

Eustin nodded. Balasar appreciated that the man didn't press the issue. Eustin had known him long enough to understand that bloody-mindedness was how Balasar moved through the world. From the beginning, he'd been cursed by a small stature, a shorter reach than his brothers or the boys with whom he'd trained. He'd gotten used to working himself harder, training while other boys slept and drank and whored. Where he couldn't make himself bigger or stronger, he instead became fast and smart and uncompromising.

When he became a man of arms in the service of Galt, he had been the smallest in his cohort. And in time, they had named him general. If the High Council needed to be convinced, then he would by God convince them.

A polite cough came from the archways behind them, and Balasar turned. A secretary of the Council stood in the shade of the wide colonnade. As Balasar and Eustin rose, he bowed slightly at the waist.

"General Gice," the secretary said. "The Lord Convocate requests your presence."

"Good," Balasar said, then turned to Eustin and spoke quickly and low. "Stay here and keep an eye on our friend. If this goes poorly, we may need to make good time out of Acton."

Eustin nodded, his face as calm and impassive as if Balasar asked him to turn against the High Council half the days of any week. Balasar tugged his vest and sleeves into place, nodded to the secretary, and allowed himself to be led into the shadows of government.

The path beneath the colonnade led into a maze of hallways as old as Galt itself. The air seemed ancient, thick and dusty and close with the breath of men generations dead. The secretary led Balasar up a stone stairway worn treacherously smooth by a river of footsteps to a wide door of dark and carved wood. Balasar scratched on it, and a booming voice called him in.

The meeting room was wide and long, with a glassed-in terrace that looked out over the city and shelves lining the walls with books and rolled maps. Low leather couches squatted by an iron fireplace, a low rosewood table between them with dried fruits and glass flutes ready for wine. And standing at the terrace's center looking out over the city, the Lord Convocate, a great gray bear of a man.

Balasar closed the door behind him and walked over to the man's side. Acton spilled out before them—smoke and grime, broad avenues where steam wagons chuffed their slow way through the city taking on passengers for a half-copper a ride laced with lanes so narrow a man's shoulders could touch the walls on either side. For a moment, Balasar recalled the ruins in the desert, placing the memory over the view before him. Reminding himself again of the stakes he played for.

"I've been riding herd on the Council since you gave your report. They aren't happy," the Lord Convocate said. "The High Council doesn't look favorably on men of . . . what should I call it? Profound initiative? None of them had any idea you'd gone so far. Not even your father. It was impolitic."

"I'm not a man of politics."

The Lord Convocate laughed.

"You've led an army on campaign," he said. "If you didn't understand something of how to manage men, you'd be feeding some Westland tree by now."

Balasar shrugged. It wasn't what he'd meant to do; it was the moment to come across as controlled, loyal, reliable as stone, and here he was shrugging like a petulant schoolboy. He forced himself to smile.

"I suppose you're right," he said.

"But you know they would have refused you."

"*Know* is a strong word. Suspected."

"Feared?"

"Perhaps."

"Fourteen cities in a single season. It can't be done, Balasar. Uther Redcape couldn't have done it."

"Uther was fighting in Eddensea," Balasar said. "They have walls around cities in Eddensea. They have armies. The Khaiem haven't got anything but the andat."

"The andat suffice."

"Only if they have them."

"Ah. Yes. That's the center of the question, isn't it? Your grand plan to do away with all the andat at a single blow. I have to confess, I don't think I quite follow how you expect this to work. You have one of these poets here, ready to work with us. Wouldn't it be better to capture one of these andat for ourselves?"

"We will be. Freedom-From-Bondage should be one of the simplest andat to capture. It's never been done, so there's no worry about coming too near what's been tried before. The binding has been discussed literally for centuries. I've found books of commentary and analysis dating back to the First Empire . . ."

"All of it exploring exactly why it can't be done, yes?" The Lord Convocate's voice had gone as gentle and sympathetic as that of a medic trying to lead a man to realize his own dementia. It was a ploy. The old man wanted to see whether Balasar would lose his temper, so instead he smiled.

"That depends on what you mean by impossible."

The Lord Convocate nodded and stepped to the windows, his hands clasped behind his back. Balasar waited for three breaths, four. The impulse to shake the old man, to shout that every day was precious and the price of failure horrible beyond contemplation, rose in him and fell. This was the battle now, and as important as any of those to come.

"So," the Lord Convocate said, turning. "Explain to me how *cannot* means *can*."

Balasar gestured toward the couches. They sat, leather creaking beneath them.

"The andat are ideas translated into forms that include volition," Balasar said. "A poet who's bound something like, for example, Wood-Upon-Water gains control over the expression of that thought in the world. He could raise a sunken vessel up or sink all the ships on the sea with a thought, if he wished it. The time required to create the binding is measured in years. If it succeeds, the poet's life work is to hold the thing here in the world and train someone to take it from him when he grows old or infirm."

"You're telling me what I know," the old man said, but Balasar raised a hand, stopping him.

"I'm telling you what *they* mean when they say impossible. They mean that Freedom-From-Bondage can't be *held*. There is no way to control something that is the essential nature and definition of the uncontrolled. But they make no distinction between being invoked and being maintained."

The Lord Convocate frowned and rubbed his fingertips together.

"We can bind it, sir. Riaan isn't the talent of the ages, but Freedom-From-Bondage should be easy compared with the normal run. The whole binding's nearly done already—only a little tailoring to make it fit our man's mind in particular."

"That comes back to the issue," the Lord Convocate said. "What happens when this impossible binding works?"

"As soon as it is bound it is freed." Balasar clapped his palms together. "That fast."

"And the advantage of that?" the Lord Convocate said, though Balasar could see the old man had already traced out the implications.

"Done well, with the right grammar, the right nuances, it will unbind every andat there is when it goes. All of this was in my report to the High Council."

The Lord Convocate nodded as he plucked a circle of dried apple from the bowl between them. When he spoke again, however, it was as if Balasar's objection had never occurred.

"Assuming it works, that you can take the andat from the field of play, what's to stop the Khaiem from having their poets make another andat and loose it on Galt?"

"Swords," Balasar said. "As you said, fourteen cities in a single season. None of them will have enough time. I have men in every city of the Khaiem, ready to meet us with knowledge of the defenses and strengths we face. There are agreements with mercenary companies to support our men. Four well-equipped, well-supported forces, each taking unfortified, poorly armed cities. But we have to start moving men now. This is going to take time, and I don't want to be caught in the North waiting to see which comes first, the thaw or some overly clever poet in Cetani or Machi managing to bind something new. We have to move quickly—kill the poets, take the libraries—"

"After which we can go about making andat of our own at our leisure," the Lord Convocate said. His voice was thoughtful, and still Balasar sensed a trap. He wondered how much the man had guessed of his own plans and intentions for the future of the andat.

"If that's what the High Council chooses to do," Balasar said, sitting back. "All of this, of course, assuming I'm given permission to move forward."

"Ah," the Lord Convocate said, lacing his hands over his belly. "Yes. That will need an answer. Permission of the Council. A thousand things could go wrong. And if you fail—"

"The stakes are no lower if we sit on our hands. And we could wait forever and never see a better chance," Balasar said. "You'll forgive my saying it, sir, but you haven't said no."

"No," he said, slowly. "No, I haven't."

"Then I have the command, sir?"

After a moment, the Lord Convocate nodded.

3

>+< "What's the matter?" Kiyan asked. She was already dressed in the silk shift that she slept in, her hair tied back from her thin foxlike face. It occurred to Otah for the first time just how long ago the sun had set. He sat on the bed at her side and let himself feel the aches in his back and knees.

"Sitting too long," he said. "I don't know why doing nothing should hurt as badly as hauling crates."

Kiyan put a hand against his back, her fingers tracing his spine through the fine-spun wool of his robes.

"For one thing, you haven't hauled a crate for your living in thirty summers."

"Twenty-five," he said, leaning back into the soft pressure of her hands. "Twenty-six now."

"For another, you've hardly done nothing. As I recall, you were awake before the sun rose."

Otah considered the sleeping chamber—the domed ceiling worked in silver, the wood and bone inlay of the floor and walls, the rich gold netting that draped the bed, the still, somber flame of the lantern. The east wall was stone—pink granite thin as eggshell that glowed when the sun struck it. He couldn't recall how long it had been since he'd woken to see that light. Last summer, perhaps, when the nights were shorter. He closed his eyes and lay back into the soft, enfolding bed. His weight pressed out the scent of crushed rose petals. Eyes closed, he felt Kiyan shift, the familiar warmth and weight of her body resting against him. She kissed his temple.

"Our friend from the Dai-kvo will finally leave soon. A message came recalling him," Otah said. "That was a bright moment. Though the gods only know what kept him here so long. Sinja's likely halfway to the Westlands by now."

"The envoy stayed for Maati's work," Kiyan said. "Apparently he hardly left the library these last weeks. Eiah's been keeping me informed."

"Well, the gods and Eiah, then," Otah said.

"I'm worried about her. She's brooding about something. Can you speak with her?"

Dread touched Otah's belly, and a moment's resentment. It had been such a long day, and here waiting for him like a stalking cat was another problem, another need he was expected to meet. The thought must have expressed itself in his body, because Kiyan sighed and rolled just slightly away.

"You think it's wrong of me," Kiyan said.

"Not wrong," Otah said. "Unnecessary isn't wrong."

"I know. At her age, you were living on the streets in the summer cities, stealing pigeons off firekeeper's kilns and sleeping in alleys. And you came through just fine."

"Oh," Otah said. "Have I told that story already?"

"Once or twice," she said, laughing gently. "It's just that she seems so distant. I think there's something bothering her that she won't say. And then I wonder whether it's only that she won't say it to me."

"And why would she talk to me if she won't she talk to you?"

When he felt Kiyan shrug, Otah opened his eyes and rolled to his side. There were tears shining in his lover's eyes, but her expression was more amused than sorrowful. He touched her cheek with his fingertips, and she kissed his palm absently.

"I don't know. Because you're her father, and I'm only her mother? It was just . . . a hope. The problem is that she's half a woman," Kiyan said. "When the sun's up, I know that. I remember when I was that age. My father had me running half of his wayhouse, or that's how it felt back then. Up before the clients, cooking sausages and barley. Cleaning the rooms during the day. He and Old Mani would take care of the evenings, though. They wanted to sell as much wine as they could, but they didn't want a girl my age around drunken travelers. I thought they were being so unfair."

Kiyan pursed her lips.

"But maybe *I've* told *that* story already," she said.

"Once or twice," Otah agreed.

"There was a time I didn't worry about the whole world and everything in it, you know. I remember that there was. It doesn't make sense to me. One bad season, an illness, a fire—anything, really, and I could have lost the wayhouse. But now here I am, highest of the Khaiem, a whole city that will bend itself in half to hand me whatever it thinks I want, and the world seems more fragile."

"We got old," Otah said. "It's always the ones who've seen the most who think the world's on the edge of collapse, isn't it? And we've seen more than most."

Kiyan shook her head.

"It's more than that. Losing a wayhouse would have made the world harder for me and Old Mani. There are more people than I can count here in the city, and all the low towns. And you carry them. It makes it matter more."

"I sit through days of ceremony and let myself be hectored over the things I don't do the way other people prefer," Otah said. "I'm not sure that anything I've done here has actually made any difference at all. If they stuffed a robe with cotton and posed the sleeves . . ."

"You care about them," Kiyan said.

"I don't," he said. "I care about you and Eiah and Danat. And Maati. I know that I'm supposed to care about everyone and everything in Machi, but love, I'm only a man. They can tell me I gave up my own name when I took the chair, but really the Khai Machi is only what I do. I wouldn't keep the work if I could find a way out."

Kiyan embraced him with one arm. Her hair was fragrant with lavender oil.

"You're sweet," she said.

"Am I? I'll try to confess my incompetence and selfishness more often."

"As long as it includes me," she said. "Now go let those poor men change your clothes and get back to beds of their own."

The servants had become accustomed to the Khai's preference for brief ablutions. Otah knew that his own father had managed somehow to enjoy the ceremony of being dressed and bathed by others. But his father had been raised to take the chair, had followed the traditions and forms of etiquette, and had never, that Otah knew of, stepped outside the role he'd been born to. Otah himself had been turned out, and the years he had spent being a simple, free man, reliant upon himself had ruined him for the fawning of the court. He endured the daily frivolity of having foods brought to him, his hands cleaned for him, his hair combed on his behalf. He allowed the body servants to pull off his formal robes and swathe him in a sleeping shift, and when he returned to his bed, Kiyan's breath was already deep, slow, and heavy. He slipped in beside her, pulling the blankets up over himself, and closed his eyes at last.

Sleep, however, did not come. His body ached, his eyes were tired, but it seemed that the moment he laid his head back, Otah's mind woke. He listened to the sounds of the palace in night: the almost silent wind through a distant window, the deep and subtle ticking of cooling stone, the breath of the woman at his side. Beyond the doors to the apartments, someone coughed—one of the servants set to watch over the Khai Machi in case there was anything he should desire in the night. Otah tried not to move.

He hadn't asked Kiyan about Danat's health. He'd meant to. But surely if there had been anything concerning, she would have brought it up to him. And regardless, he could ask her in the morning. Perhaps he would cancel the audiences before midday and go speak with Danat's physicians. And speak to Eiah. He hadn't said he would do that, but Kiyan had asked, and it wasn't as if being present in his own daughter's life should be an imposition. He wondered what it would have been to have a dozen wives, whether he would have felt the need to attend to all of their children as he did to the two he had now, how he would have stood watching his boys grow up when he knew he would have to send them away or else watch them slaughter one another over which of them would take his own place here on this soft, sleepless bed and fear in turn for his own sons.

The night candle ate through its marks as he listened to the internal voice nattering in his mind, gnawing at half a thousand worries both justified and inane. The trade agreements with Udun weren't in place yet. Perhaps something really was the matter with Eiah. He didn't know how long stone buildings stood; nothing stands forever, so it only made sense that someday the palaces would fall. And the towers. The towers reached so high it seemed that low clouds would touch them; what would he do if they fell? But the night was passing and he had to sleep. If he didn't the morning would be worse. He should talk with Maati, find out how things had gone between him and the Dai-kvo's envoy. Perhaps a dinner.

And on, and on, and on. When he gave up, slipping from the bed softly to let Kiyan, at least, sleep, the night candle was past its three-quarter mark. Otah walked to the apartment's main doors on bare, chilled feet and found his keeper in the hall outside dozing. He was a young man, likely the son of some favored servant or slave of Otah's own father, given the honor of sitting alone in the darkness, bored and cold. Otah considered the boy's soft face, as peaceful in sleep as a corpse's, and walked silently past him and into the dim hallways of the palace.

His night walks had been growing more frequent in recent months. Sometimes twice in a week, Otah found himself wandering in the darkness, sleep a stranger to him. He avoided the places where he might encounter another person, jealously keeping the time to himself. Tonight, he took a lantern and walked down the long stairways to the ground, and then on down, to the tunnels and underground streets into which the city retreated in the deep, bone-breaking cold of winter. With spring come, Otah found the palace beneath the palace empty and silent. The smell of old torches, long gone dark, still lingered in the air, and Otah imagined the corridors and galleries of the city descending forever into the earth. Dark archways and domed sleeping chambers cut from stone that had never seen daylight, narrow stairways leading endlessly down like a thing from a children's song.

He didn't consider where he intended to go until he reached his father's crypt and found himself unsurprised to be there. The dark stone seemed to wrap itself in shadows, words of an ancient language cut deep into the walls. An ornate pedestal held the pale urn, a dead flower. And beneath it, three small boxes—the remains of Biitrah, Danat, Kaiin. Otah's brothers, dead in the struggle to become the new Khai Machi. Lives cut short for the honor of having a pedestal of their own someday, deep in the darkness.

Otah sat on the bare floor, the lantern at his side, and contemplated the man he'd never known or loved whose place he had taken. Here was how his own end would look. An urn, a tomb, high honors and reverence for bones and ashes. And between the chill floor and the pale urn, perhaps another thirty summers. Perhaps forty. Years of ceremony and negotiation, late nights and early mornings and little else.

But when the time came, at least his crypt would be only his own. Danat, brotherless, wouldn't be called upon to kill or die in the succession. There would be no second sons left to kill the other for the black chair. It seemed a thin solace, having given so much of himself to achieve something that a merchant's son could have had for free.

It would have been easier if he'd never been anything but this. A man born into the Khaiem who had never stepped outside wouldn't carry the memories of fishing in the eastern islands, of eating at the wayhouses outside Yalakeht, of being free. If he could have forgotten it all, becoming the man he was supposed to be might have been easier. Instead he was driven to follow his own judgment, raise a militia, take only one wife, raise only one son. That his experience told him that he was right didn't make bearing the world's disapproval as easy as he'd hoped.

The lantern flame guttered and spat. Otah shook his head, uncertain now how long he had been lost in his reverie. When he stood, his left leg had gone numb from being pressed too long against the bare stone. He took up the lantern and walked—moving slowly and carefully to protect his numbed foot— back toward the stairways that would return him to the surface and the day. By the time he regained the great halls, feeling had returned. The sky peeked through the windows, a pale gray preparing itself to blue. Voices echoed and the palaces woke, and the grand, stately beast that was the court of Machi stirred and stretched.

His apartments, when he reached them, were a flurry of activity. A knot of servants and members of the utkhaiem gabbled like peahens, Kiyan in their center listening with a seriousness and sympathy that only he knew masked amusement. Her hand was on the shoulder of the body servant whom Otah had passed, the peace of sleep banished and anxiety in its place.

"Gentlemen," Otah said, letting his voice boom, calling their attention to him. "Is there something amiss?"

To a man, they adopted poses of obeisance and welcome. Otah responded automatically now, as he did half a hundred times every day.

"Most High," a thin-voiced man said—his Master of Tides. "We came to prepare you and found your bed empty."

Otah looked at Kiyan, whose single raised brow told them that empty had only meant empty of him, and that she'd have been quite pleased to keep sleeping.

"I was walking," he said.

"We may not have the time to prepare you for the audience with the envoy from Tan-Sadar," the Master of Tides said.

"Put him off," Otah said, walking through the knot of people to the door of his apartments. "Reschedule everything you have for me today."

The Master of Tides gaped like a trout in air. Otah paused, his hands in a query that asked if the words bore repeating. The Master of Tides adopted an acknowledging pose.

"The rest of you," he said, "I would like breakfast served in my apartments here. And send for my children."

"Eiah-cha's tutors . . ." one of the others began, but Otah looked at the man and he seemed to forget what he'd been saying.

"I will be taking the day with my family," Otah said.

"You will start rumors, Most High," another said. "They'll say the boy's cough has grown worse again."

"And I would like black tea with the meal," Otah said. "In fact, bring the tea first. I'll be in by the fire, warming my feet."

He stepped in, and Kiyan followed, closing the door behind her.

"Bad night?" she asked.

"Sleepless," he said as he sat by the fire grate. "That's all."

Kiyan kissed the top of his head where she assured him that the hair was not thinning, and stepped out of the room. He heard the soft rustle of cloth against stone and Kiyan's low, contented humming, and knew she was changing her robes. The warmth of the fire pressed against the soles of his feet like a comforting hand, and he closed his eyes for a moment.

No building stands forever, he thought. Even palaces fall. Even towers. He wondered what it would have been like to live in a world where Machi didn't exist—who he might have been, what he might have done—and he felt the weight of stone pressing down upon the air he breathed. What would he do if the towers fell? Where would he go, if he could go anywhere?

"Papa-kya!" Danat's bright voice called. "I was in the Second Palace, and I found a closet where no one had been in ever, and look what I found!"

Otah opened his eyes, and turned to his son and the wood-and-string model he'd discovered. Eiah arrived a hand and a half later, when the thin granite shutters glowed with the sun. For a time, at least, Otah's own father's tomb lay forgotten.

THE PROBLEM WITH ATHAI-KVO, MAATI DECIDED, WAS THAT HE WAS SIMPLY AN unlikable man. There was no single thing that he did or said, no single habit or effect that made him grate on the nerves of all those around him. Some men were charming, and would be loved however questionable their behavior. And then on the other end of the balance, there was Athai. The weeks he had spent with the man had been bearable only because of the near-constant stream of praise and admiration given to Maati.

"It will change everything," the envoy said as they sat on the steps of the poet's house—Cehmai's residence. "This is going to begin a new age to rival the Second Empire."

"Because that ended so well," Stone-Made-Soft rumbled, its tone amused as always.

The morning was warm. The sculpted oaks separating the poet's house from the palaces were bright with new leaves. Far above, barely visible through the boughs, the stone towers rose into the sky. Cehmai reached across the envoy to pour more rice wine into Maati's bowl.

"It is early yet to pass judgment," Maati said as he nodded his thanks to Cehmai. "It isn't as though the techniques have been tried."

"But it makes sense," Athai said. "I'm sure it will work."

"If we've overlooked something, the first poet to try this is likely to die badly," Cehmai said. "The Dai-kvo will want a fair amount of study done before he puts a poet's life on the table."

"Next year," Athai said. "I'll wager twenty lengths of silver it will be used in bindings by this time next year."

"Done," the andat said, then turned to Cehmai. "You can back me if I lose."

The poet didn't reply, but Maati saw the amusement at the corners of Cehmai's mouth. It had taken years to understand the ways in which Stone-Made-Soft was an expression of Cehmai, the ways they were a single thing, and the ways they were at war. The small comments the andat made that only Cehmai understood, the unspoken moments of private struggle that sometimes clouded the poet's days. They were like nothing so much as a married couple, long accustomed to each other's ways.

Maati sipped the rice wine. It was infused with peaches, a moment of autumn's harvest in the opening of spring. Athai looked away from the andat's broad face, discomforted.

"You must be ready to return to the Dai-kvo," Cehmai said. "You've been away longer than you'd intended."

Athai waved the concern away, pleased, Maati thought, to speak to the man and forget the andat.

"I wouldn't have traded this away," he said. "Maati-kvo is going to be remembered as the greatest poet of our generation."

"Have some more wine," Maati said, clinking the envoy's bowl with his own, but Cehmai shook his head and gestured toward the wooded path. A slave girl was trotting toward them, her robes billowing behind her. Athai put down his bowl and stood, pulling at his sleeves. Here was the moment they had been awaiting—the call for Athai to join the caravan to the East. Maati sighed with relief. Half a hand, and his library would be his own again. The envoy took a formal pose of farewell that Maati and Cehmai returned.

"I will send word as soon as I can, Maati-kvo," Athai said. "I am honored to have studied with you."

Maati nodded uncomfortably; then, after a moment's awkward silence, Athai turned. Maati watched until the slave girl and poet had both vanished among the trees, then let out a breath. Cehmai chuckled as he put the stopper into the flask of wine.

"Yes, I agree," Cehmai said. "I think the Dai-kvo must have chosen him specifically to annoy the Khai."

"Or he just wanted to be rid of him for a time," Maati said.

"I liked him," Stone-Made-Soft said. "Well, as much as I like anyone."

The three walked together into the poet's house. The rooms within were neatly kept—shelves of books and scrolls, soft couches and a table laid out with the black and white stones on their board. A lemon candle burned at the window, but a fly still buzzed wildly about the corners of the room. It seemed that every winter Maati forgot about the existence of flies, only to rediscover them in spring. He wondered where the insects all went during the vicious cold, and what the signal was for them to return.

"He isn't wrong, you know," Cehmai said. "If you're right, it will be the most important piece of analysis since the fall of the Empire."

"I've likely overlooked something. It isn't as though we haven't seen half a hundred schemes to bring back the glory of the past before now, and there hasn't been one that's done it."

"And I wasn't there to look at the other ideas," Cehmai said. "But since I was here to talk this one over, I'd say this is at least plausible. That's more than most. And the Dai-kvo's likely to think the same."

"He'll probably dismiss it out of hand," Maati said, but he smiled as he spoke.

Cehmai had been the first one he'd shown his theories to, even before he'd known for certain what they were. It had been a curiosity more than anything else. It was only as they'd talked about it that Maati had understood the depths he'd touched upon. And Cehmai had also been the one to encourage bringing the work to the Dai-kvo's attention. All Athai's enthusiasm and hyperbole paled beside a few thoughtful words from Cehmai.

Maati stayed awhile, talking and laughing, comparing impressions of Athai now that he'd left. And then he took his leave, walking slowly enough that he didn't become short of breath. Fourteen, almost fifteen years ago, he'd come to Machi. The black stone roadways, the constant scent of the coal smoke billowing up from the forges, the grandeur of the palaces and the hidden city far beneath his feet had become his home as no other place ever had before. He strode down pathways of crushed marble, under archways that flowed with silken banners. A singing slave called from the gardens, a simple melody of amazing clarity and longing. He turned down a smaller way that would take him to his apartments behind the library.

Maati found himself wondering what he would do if the Dai-kvo truly thought his discovery had merit. It was an odd thought. He had spent so many years now in disgrace, first tainted by the death of his master Heshai, then by his choice to divide his loyalty between his lover and son on the one hand and the Dai-kvo on the other. And then at last his entrance into the politics of the court, wearing the robes of the poet and supporting Otah Machi, his old friend and enemy, to become Khai Machi. It had been simple enough to believe that his promotion to the ranks of the poets had been a mistake. He had, after all, been gifted certain insights by an older boy who had walked away from the school: Otah, before he'd been a laborer or a courier or a Khai. Maati had reconciled himself to a smaller life: the library, the companionship of a few friends and those lovers who would bed a disgraced poet halfway to fat with rich foods and long, inactive hours.

After so many years of failure, the thought that he might shake off that reputation was unreal. It was like a dream from which he could only hope never to wake, too pleasant to trust in.

Eiah was sitting on the steps when he arrived, frowning intently at a moth that had lighted on the back of her hand. Her face was such a clear mix of her parents—Kiyan's high cheeks, Otah's dark eyes and easy smile. Maati took a pose of greeting as he walked up, and when Eiah moved to reply, the moth took wing, chuffing softly through the air and away. In flight, the wings that had been simple brown shone black and orange.

"Athai's gone then?" she asked as Maati unlocked the doors to his apartments.

"He's likely just over the bridge by now."

Maati stepped in, Eiah following him without asking or being asked. It was a wide room, not so grand as the palaces or so comfortable as the poet's house. A librarian's room, ink blocks stacked beside a low desk, chairs with wine-stained cloth on the arms and back, a small bronze brazier dusted with old ash. Maati waved Eiah off as she started to close the door.

"Let the place air out a bit," he said. "It's warm enough for it now. And what's your day been, Eiah-kya?"

"Father," she said. "He was in a mood to have a family, so I had to stay in the palaces all morning. He fell asleep after midday, and Mother said I could leave."

"I'm surprised. I wasn't under the impression Otah slept anymore. He always seems hip-deep in running the city."

Eiah shrugged, neither agreeing nor voicing her denial. She paced the length of the room, squinting out the door at nothing. Maati folded his hands together on his belly, considering her.

"Something's bothering you," he said.

The girl shook her head, but the frown deepened. Maati waited until, with a quick, birdlike motion, Eiah turned to face him. She began to speak, stopped, and gathered herself visibly.

"I want to be married," she said.

Maati blinked, coughed to give himself a moment to think, and leaned forward in his chair. The wood and cloth creaked slightly beneath him. Eiah stood, her arms crossed, her gaze on him in something almost like accusation.

"Who is the boy?" Maati said, regretting the word *boy* as soon as it left his mouth. If they were speaking of marriage, the least he could do was say *man*. But Eiah's impatient snort dismissed the question.

"I don't know," she said. "Whoever."

"Anyone would do?"

"Not just anyone. I don't want to be tied to some low town firekeeper. I want someone good. And I should be able to. Father doesn't have any other daughters, and I know people have talked with him. But nothing ever happens. How long am I supposed to wait?"

Maati rubbed a palm across his cheeks. This was hardly a conversation he'd imagined himself having. He turned through half a hundred things he might say, approaches he might take, and felt a blush rising in his cheeks.

"You're young, Eiah-kya. I mean . . . I suppose it's natural enough for a young woman to . . . be interested in men. Your body is changing, and if I recall the age, there are certain feelings that it's . . ."

Eiah looked at him as if he'd coughed up a rat.

"Or perhaps I've misunderstood the issue," he said.

"It's not that," she said. "I've kissed lots of boys."

The blush wasn't growing less, but Maati resolved to ignore it.

"Ah," he said. "Well, then. If it's that you want apartments of your own, something outside the women's quarters, you could always—"

"Talit Radaani's being married to the third son of the Khai Pathai," Eiah said, and then a heartbeat later, "She's half a year younger than I am."

It was like feeling a puzzle box click open in his fingers. He understood precisely what was happening, what it meant and didn't mean. He rubbed his palms against his knees and sighed.

"And she gloats about that, I'd bet," he said. Eiah swiped at her betraying eyes with the back of a hand. "After all, she's younger and lower in the courts. She must think that she's got proof that she's terribly special."

Eiah shrugged.

"Or that you aren't," Maati continued, keeping his voice gentle to lessen the sting of the words. "That's what she thinks, isn't it?"

"I don't know what she thinks."

"Well, then tell me what you think."

"I don't know why he can't find me a husband. It isn't as if I'd have to leave. There's marriages that go on for years before anyone does anything. But it's understood. It's arranged. I don't see why he can't do that much for me."

"Have you asked him?"

"He should know this," Eiah snapped, pacing between the open door and the fire grate. "He's the Khai Machi. He isn't stupid."

"He also isn't . . ." Maati said and then bit down on the words *a child*. The woman Eiah thought she was would never stand for the name. "He isn't four-teen summers old. It's not so hard for men like me and your father to forget what it was like to be young. And I'm sure he doesn't want to see you married yet, or even promised. You're his daughter, and . . . it's hard, Eiah-kya. It's hard losing your child."

She stopped, her brow furrowed. In the trees just outside his door, a bird sang shrill and high and took flight. Maati could hear the fluttering of its wings.

"It's not losing me," she said, but her voice was less certain than it had been. "I don't die."

"No. You don't, but you'll likely leave to be in your husband's city. There's couriers to carry messages back and forth, but once you've left, it's not likely you'll return in Otah's life, or Kiyan's. Or mine. It's not death, but it is still loss, dear. And we've all lost so much already, it's hard to look forward to another."

"You could come with me," Eiah said. "My husband would take you in. He wouldn't be worth marrying if he wouldn't, so you could come with me."

Maati allowed himself to chuckle as he rose from his seat.

"It's too big a world to plan for all that just yet," he said, mussing Eiah's hair as he had when she'd been younger. "When we come nearer, we'll see where things stand. I may not be staying here at all, depending on what the Dai-kvo thinks. I might be able to go back to his village and use his libraries."

"Could I go there with you?"

"No, Eiah-kya. Women aren't allowed in the village. I know, I know. It isn't fair. But it isn't happening today, so why don't we walk to the kitchens and see if we can't talk them out of some sugar bread."

They left his door open, leaving the spring air and sunlight to freshen the apartments. The path to the kitchens led them through great, arching halls and across pavilions being prepared for a night's dancing; great silken banners cel-ebrated the warmth and light. In the gardens, men and women lay back, eyes closed, faces to the sky like flowers. Outside the palaces, Maati knew, the city was still alive with commerce—the forges and metalworkers toiling through the night, as they always did, preparing to ship the works of Machi. There was bronze, iron, silver and gold, and steel. And the hand-shaped stonework that could be created only here, under the inhuman power of Stone-Made-Soft.

None of that work was apparent in the palaces. The utkhaiem seemed carefree as cats. Maati wondered again how much of that was the studied casualness of court life and how much was simple sloth.

At the kitchens, it was simple enough for the Khai's daughter and his permanent guest to get thick slices of sugar bread wrapped in stiff cotton cloth and a stone flask of cold tea. He told Eiah all of what had happened with Athai since she'd last come to the library, and about the Dai-kvo, and the andat, and the world as Maati had known it in the years before he'd come to Machi. It was a pleasure to spend the time with the girl, flattering that she enjoyed his own company enough to seek him out, and perhaps just the slightest bit gratifying that she would speak to him of things that Otah-kvo never heard from her.

They parted company as the quick spring sun came within a hand's width of the western mountains. Maati stopped at a fountain, washing his fingers in the cool waters, and considered the evening that lay ahead. He'd heard that one of the winter choirs was performing at a teahouse not far from the palaces—the long, dark season's work brought out at last to the light. The thought tempted, but perhaps not more than a book, a flask of wine, and a bed with thick wool blankets.

He was so wrapped up by the petty choice of pleasures that he didn't notice that the lanterns had been lit in his apartments or that a woman was sitting on his couch until she spoke.

4

>+<　"Maati," Liat said, and the man startled like a rabbit. For a long moment, his face was a blank confusion as he struggled to make sense of what he saw. Slowly, she watched him recognize her.

In all fairness, she might not have known him either, had she not sought him out. Time had changed him: thickened his body and thinned his hair. Even his face had changed shape, the smooth chin and jaw giving way to jowls, the eyes going narrower and darker. The lines around his mouth spoke of sadness and isolation. And anger, she thought.

She had known when she arrived that she'd found the right apartments. It hadn't been difficult to get directions to Machi's extra poet, and the door had been open. She'd scratched at the doorframe, called out his name, and when she'd stepped in, it was the scent that had been familiar. Certainly there had been other things—the way the scrolls were laid out, the ink stains on the arms of the chairs—that gave evidence to Maati's presence. The faintest hint, a wisp of musk slight as pale smoke, was the thing that had brought back the flood of memory. For a powerful moment, she saw again the small house she'd lived in after she and Maati had left Saraykeht; the yellow walls and rough, wooden floor, the dog who had lived in the street and only ever been half tamed by her offerings of sausage ends from the kitchen window, the gray spiders that had built their webs in the corners. The particular scent of her old lover's body brought back those rooms. She knew him better by that than to see him again in the flesh.

But perhaps that wasn't true. When he blinked fast and uncertainly, when his head leaned just slightly forward and a smile just began to bloom on his lips, she could see him there, beneath that flesh. The man she had known and loved. The man she'd left behind.

"Liat?" he said. "You . . . you're here?"

She took a pose of affirmation, surprised to find her hands trembling. Maati stepped forward slowly, as if afraid a sudden movement might startle her into flight. Liat swallowed to loosen the knot in her throat and smiled.

"I would have written to warn you I was coming," she said, "but by the time I knew I was, I'd have raced the letter. I'm . . . I'm sorry if . . ."

But he touched her arm, his fingers on the cloth just above her elbow. His eyes were wide and amazed. As if it were natural, as if it had been a week or a day and not a third of their lives, Liat put her arms around him and felt him enclose her. She had told herself that she would hold back, be careful. She was the head of House Kyaan, a woman of business and politics. She knew how to be hardhearted and cool. There was no reason to think that she would be safe here in the farthest city from her home and facing again the two lovers of her childhood. The years had worked changes on them all, and she had parted with neither of them on good terms.

And yet the tears in her eyes were simple and sincere and as much joy as sorrow, and the touch of Maati's body against her own—strange and familiar both—wasn't awkward or unwelcome. She kissed his cheek and drew back enough to see his still wonder-filled face.

"Well," she said at last. "It's been a while. It's good to see you again, Maati-kya. I wasn't sure it would be, but it is."

"I thought I'd never see you again," he said. "I thought, after all this time . . . My letters . . ."

"I got them, yes. And it's not as if court gossip didn't tell everyone in the world where you were. The last succession of Machi was the favorite scandal of the season. I even saw an epic made from it. The boy who took your part didn't look a thing like you," she said, and then, in a lower voice, "I meant to write back to you, even if it was only to tell you that I'd heard. That I knew. But somehow I never managed. I regret that. I've always regretted that. It only seemed so . . . complex."

"I thought perhaps . . . I don't know. I don't know what I thought."

She stood silently in his arms the space of another breath, part of her wishing that this moment might suffice; that the relief she felt at Maati's simple, unconsidered acceptance might stand in for all that she had still to do. He sensed the change in her thoughts and stepped back, his hands moving restlessly. She smoothed her hair, suddenly aware of the streaks of gray at her temple.

"Can I get something for you?" Maati said. "It's simple enough to call a servant in from the palaces. Or I have some distilled wine here."

"Wine will do," she said, and sat.

He went to a low cabinet beside the fire grate, sliding the wooden panel back and taking out two small porcelain bowls and a stoppered bottle as he spoke.

"I've had company recently. He's only just left. I don't usually live in this disorder."

"I'm not sure I believe that," she said, wryly. Maati chuckled and shrugged.

"Oh, I don't clean it myself. It would be a hundred times worse than this. Otah-kvo's been very kind in loaning me servants. He has more than he has places for."

The name was like a cold breath, but Liat only smiled and accepted the bowl that Maati held out to her. She sipped the wine—strong, peppery, and warm in her throat—to give herself a moment. She wasn't ready yet for the pleasure to end.

"The world's changed on us," she said. It was a platitude, but Maati seemed to take some deeper meaning from it.

"It has," he said. "And it'll keep on changing, I think. When I was a boy, I never imagined myself here, and I can't say for certain what I'll be doing when next summer comes. The new Dai-kvo . . ."

He shook his head slowly and sipped his wine for what Liat guessed was much the same reason she had. The silence between them grew. Maati cleared his throat.

"How is Nayiit?" he asked, careful, Liat noticed, to use the boy's name. Not *our son,* but Nayiit.

She told him about the work of House Kyaan, and Nayiit's role as an overseer. The stories of how he had made the transition from the child of the head of the house to an overseer in his own right. His courtship, his marriage, the child. Maati closed the door, lit a fire in the grate, and listened.

It was odd that of all the subjects she had to bring to the table, Nayiit should be the easiest. And Maati listened to it all, laughing or rapt, delighted and also sorrowful, longing to have been part of something that was already gone. Her words were like rain in a desert; he absorbed them, cherished them. She found herself searching for more—anecdotes of Nayiit and his friends, his early lovers, the city, anything. She searched for them and offered them up, part apology, part sacrifice. The candles had grown visibly shorter before he asked whether Nayiit had stayed in Saraykeht, and Liat reluctantly shook her head.

"I've left him at the wayhouse," she said. "I wasn't certain how this would go, between us. I didn't want him to be here if it was bad."

Maati's hands started to move toward some pose—a denial, perhaps—then faltered. His eyes locked on hers. There were decades in them. She felt tears welling up.

"I'm sorry," she said. "If that's worth anything, I am sorry, Maati-kya."

"For what?" he asked, and his tone said that he could imagine a number of answers.

"That you weren't a part of his life until now."

"It was my choice as much as yours. And it will be good to see him again."

He heaved a sigh and pressed the stopper back into the bottle's neck. The sun was long gone, and a cold breeze, thick with the perfume of night-flowering gardens, raised bumps on her arms. Only the air. Not dread.

"You haven't asked me why I've come," she said.

He chuckled and leaned back against his couch. His cheeks were ruddy from the candlelight and wine. His eyes seemed to glitter.

"I was pretending it was for me. Mending old wounds, making peace," Maati said. The anger she'd seen was there now, swimming beneath the pleasant, joking surface. She wondered if she'd waited too long to come to the issue. She should have asked before she'd told him Nayiit was in the city, before the sour memories came back.

Maati took a pose of query, inviting her to share her true agenda.

"I need your help," Liat said. "I need an audience with the Khai."

"You want to talk to Otah-kvo? You don't need my help for that. You could just—"

"I need you to help me convince him. To argue my case with me. We have to convince him to intercede with the Dai-kvo."

Maati's eyes narrowed, and his head tilted like that of a man considering a puzzle. Liat felt herself starting to blush. She'd had too much of the wine, and her control wasn't all it should be.

"Intercede with the Dai-kvo?" he said.

"I've been following the world. And the Galts. It was what Amat Kyaan built the house to do. I have decades of books and ledgers. I've made note of every contract they've made in the summer cities. I know every ship that sails past, what her captain's name is, and half the time, what cargo she carries. I *know*, Maati. I've seen them scheming. I've even blocked them a time or two."

"They had hands in the succession here too. They were backing the woman, Otah-kvo's sister. Anything you want to say about Galt, he'll half-believe before he's heard it. But how is the Dai-kvo part of it?"

"They won't do it without the Dai-kvo," Liat said. "He has to say it's the right thing, or they won't do it."

"Who won't do what?" Maati said, impatience growing in his voice.

"The poets," Liat said. "They have to kill the Galts. And they have to do it now."

OTAH PRESENTED THE MEETING AS A LUNCHEON, A SOCIAL GATHERING OF OLD friends. He chose a balcony high in the palace looking out over the wide air to the south. The city lay below them, streets paved in black stone, tile and metal roofs pointing sharply at the sky. The towers rose above, only sun and clouds hanging higher. The wind was thick with the green, permeating scent of spring and the darker, acrid forge smoke. Between them, the low stone table was covered with plates—bread and cheese and salt olives, honeyed almonds and lemon trout and a sweetbread topped with sliced oranges. The gods alone knew where the kitchen had found a fresh orange.

Yet of all those present none of them ate.

Maati had made the introductions. Liat and Nayiit and Otah and Kiyan. The young man, Liat's son, had taken all the appropriate poses, said all the right phrases, and then taken position standing behind his mother like a bodyguard. Maati leaned against the stone banister, the sky at his back. Otah—formal, uneased, and feeling more the Khai Machi than ever under the anxious gaze of the woman who had been his lover in his youth—took a pose of query, and Liat shared the news that changed the world forever: the Galts had a poet of their own.

"His name is Riaan Vaudathat," Liat said. "He was the fourth son of a high family in the courts of Nantani. His father sent him to the school when he was five."

"This was well after our time," Maati said to Otah. "Neither of us would have known him. Not from there."

"He was accepted by the Dai-kvo and taken to the village to be trained," Liat said. "That was eight years ago. He was talented, well liked, and respected. The Dai-kvo chose him to study for the binding of a fresh andat."

Kiyan, sitting at Otah's side, leaned forward in a pose of query. "Don't all the poets train to hold andat?"

"We all try our hands at preparing a binding," Maati said. "We all study enough to know how it works and what it is. But only a few apply the knowledge. If the Dai-kvo thinks you have the temperament to take on one that's already bound, he'll send you there to study and prepare yourself to take over control when the poet grows too old. If you're bright and talented, he'll set you to working through a fresh binding. It can take years to be ready. Your work is read by other poets and the Dai-kvo, and attacked, and torn apart and redone perhaps a dozen times. Perhaps more."

"Because of the consequences of failing?" Kiyan asked. Maati nodded.

"Riaan was one of the best," Liat said. "And then three years ago, he was sent back to Nantani. To his family. Fallen from favor. No one knew why, he just appeared one day with a letter for his father, and after that he was living in apartments in the Vaudathat holdings. It was a small scandal. And it wasn't the last of them. Riaan was sending letters every week back to the Dai-kvo. Asking to be taken back, everyone supposed. He drank too much, and sometimes fought in the streets. By the end, he was practically living in the comfort houses by the seafront. The story was that he'd bet he could bed every whore in the city in a summer. His family never spoke of it, but they lost standing in the court. There were rumors of father and son fighting, not just arguing, but taking up arms.

"And then, one night, he disappeared. Vanished. His family said that he'd been summoned on secret business. The Dai-kvo had a mission for him, and he'd gone the same day the letter had come. But there wasn't a courier who'd admit to carrying any letter like it."

"They might not have said it," Otah said. "They call it the gentleman's trade for a reason."

"We thought of that," Nayiit replied. He had a strong voice; not loud, but powerful. "Later, when we went to the Dai-kvo, I took a list of the couriers who'd come to Nantani in the right weeks. None of them had been to the Dai-kvo's village at the right time. The Dai-kvo wouldn't speak to me. But of the men who would, none believed that Riaan had been sent for."

Otah could still think of several objections to that, but he held them back, gesturing instead for Liat to go on.

"No one connected the disappearance with a Galtic merchant ship that left that night with half her cargo still waiting to be loaded," Liat said. "Except me, and I wouldn't have if I hadn't made it my business to track all things Galtic."

"You think he was on that ship?" Otah said.

"I'm certain of it."

"Why?" he asked.

"The wealth of coincidences," Liat said. "The captain—Arnau Fentin—was the second brother of a family on the Galtic High Council. A servant in the Vaudathat household saw Riaan's father burning papers. Letters, he said. And in a foreign script."

"Any trade cipher could look like a foreign script," Otah said, but Liat wouldn't be stopped.

"The ship had been bound for Chaburi-Tan and then Bakta. But it headed west instead—back to Galt."

"Or Eddensea, or Eymond."

"Otah-kya," Kiyan said, her voice gentle, "let her finish."

He saw Liat's gaze flicker toward her, and her hands take a pose of thanks. He leaned back, his palms flat on his thighs, and silently nodded for Liat to continue.

"There were stories of Riaan having met a new woman in the weeks before he left. That was what his family thought, at least. He'd spent several evenings every week at a comfort house whose back wall was shared with the compound of House Fentin. The captain's family. I have statements that confirm all of this."

"I went to the comfort house myself," Nayiit said. "I asked after the lady Riaan had described. There wasn't anyone like her."

"It was a clumsy lie," Liat said. "All of it from beginning to end. And, Itani, it's the *Galts*."

Whether she had used his old, assumed name in error or as a ploy to make him recall the days of his youth, the effect was the same. Otah drew a deep breath, and felt a sick weight descend to his belly as he exhaled. He had spent so many years wary of the schemes of Galt that her evidence, thin as it was, almost had the power to convince him. He felt the gazes of the others upon him. Maati leaned forward in his seat, fingers knotted together in his lap. Kiyan's rueful half-smile was sympathetic and considering both. The silence stretched.

"Is there any reason to think he would have . . . done this?" Otah asked. "The poet. Why would he agree to this?"

Liat turned and nodded to her son. The man licked his lips before he spoke.

"I went to the Dai-kvo's village," Nayiit said. "My mother, of course, couldn't. There were stories that Riaan had suffered a fever the winter before he was sent away. A serious one. Apparently he came close to death. Afterward, his skin peeled like he'd been too long in the sun. They say it changed him. He became more prone to anger. He wouldn't think before he acted or spoke. The Dai-kvo sat with him for weeks, training him like he was fresh from the school. It did no good. Riaan wasn't the man he'd been when the Dai-kvo accepted him. So . . ."

"So the Dai-kvo sent him away in disgrace for something that wasn't his fault," Otah said.

"No, not at first," Nayiit said. "The Dai-kvo only told him that he wasn't to continue with his binding. That it was too great a risk. They say Riaan took it poorly. There were fights and drunken rants. One man said Riaan snuck a woman into the village to share his bed, but I never heard anyone confirm that. Whatever the details, the Dai-kvo lost patience. He sent him away."

"You learned quite a lot," Otah said. "I'd have thought the poets would be closer with their disgraces."

"Once Riaan left, it wasn't their disgrace. It was his," Nayiit said. "And they knew I had come from Nantani. I traded stories for stories. It wasn't hard."

"The Dai-kvo wouldn't meet with us," Liat said. "I sent five petitions, and for two of them his secretaries didn't even bother to send refusals. It's why we came here."

"Because you wanted me to make this argument? I'm not in the Dai-kvo's best graces myself just now. He seems to think I blame the Galts when I cough," Otah said. "Maati might be the better man to make the case."

Maati took a pose that disagreed.

"I would hardly be considered disinterested," Maati said. His words were calm and controlled despite their depth. "I may have done some interesting work, but no one will have forgotten that I defied the last Dai-kvo by not abandoning these precise two people."

The rest of the thought hung in the air, just beyond speech. *She abandoned me.* It was true enough. Liat had taken the child and made her own way in the world. She had never answered Maati's letters until now, when she had need of him. There was something almost like shame in Liat's downcast eyes. Nayiit shifted his weight, as if to interpose himself between the two of them—between his mother and the man who had wanted badly to be his father and had been denied.

"We could also ask Cehmai," Kiyan said. "He's a poet of enough prestige and ability to hold Stone-Made-Soft, and his reputation hasn't been compromised."

"That might be wise," Otah said, grabbing for the chance to take the conversation away from the complexities of the past. "But let's go over the evidence you have, Liat-cha. All of it. From the start."

It took the better part of the day. Otah listened to the full story; he read the statements of the missing poet's slaves and servants, the contracts broken by the fleeing Galtic trade ship, the logs of couriers whose whereabouts Nayiit had compiled. Whatever objections he raised, Liat countered. He could see the fatigue in her face and hear the impatience in her voice. This matter was important to her. Important enough to bring her here. That she had come was proof enough of her conviction, if not of the truth of her claim. The girl he had known had been clever enough, competent enough, and still had been used as a stone in other people's games. Perhaps he was harsh in still thinking of her in that light. The years had changed him. They certainly could have changed her as well.

And, as the sun shifted slowly toward the western peaks, Otah found his heart growing heavy. The case she made was not complete, but it was evocative as a monster tale told to children. Galt might well have taken in this mad poet. There was no way to know what they might do with him, or what he might do with their help. The histories of the Empire murmured in the back of Otah's mind: wars fought with the power of gods, the nature of space itself broken, and the greatest empire the world had ever known laid waste. And yes, if all Liat suspected proved true, it might happen again.

But if they acted on their fears, if the Dai-kvo mandated the use of the andat to remove the possibility of a Galtic poet, thousands would die who knew nothing of the plots that had brought down their doom. Children not old enough to speak, men and women who led simple, honest lives. Galt would be made a wasteland to rival the ruins of the Empire. Otah wondered how certain they would all have to be in order to take that step. How certain or else how frightened.

"Let me sit with this," he said at last, nodding to Liat and her son. "I'll have apartments cleared for you. You'll stay here at the palaces."

"There may not be much time," Maati said softly.

"I know it," Otah said. "Tomorrow I'll decide what to do. If Cehmai's the right bearer, we can do this all again with him in the room. And then . . . and then we'll see what shape the world's taken and do whatever needs doing."

Liat took a pose of gratitude, and a heartbeat later Nayiit mirrored her. Otah waved the gestures away. He was too tired for ceremony. Too troubled.

When Maati and the two visitors had left, Otah rose and stood beside Kiyan at the railing, looking out over the city as it fell into its early, sudden twilight. Plumes of smoke rose from among the green copper roofs of the forges. The great stone towers thrust toward the sky as if they supported the deepening blue. Kiyan tossed an almond out into the wide air, and a black-winged bird swooped down to catch it before it reached the distant ground. Otah touched her shoulder; she turned to him smiling as if half-surprised to find him there.

"How are you, love?" he asked.

"I should be the one asking," she said. "Those two . . . that's more than one lifetime's trouble they're carrying."

"I know it. And Maati's still in love with her."

"With both of them," Kiyan said. "One way and another, with both of them."

Otah took a pose that agreed with her.

"You know her well enough," Kiyan said. "Does she love him, do you think?"

"She did once," Otah said. "But now? It's too many years. We've all become other people."

The breeze smelled of smoke and distant rain. The first chill of evening raised gooseflesh on Kiyan's arm. He wanted to turn her toward him, to taste her mouth and lose himself for a while in simple pleasure. He wanted badly to forget the world. As if hearing his thought, she smiled, but he didn't touch her again and she didn't move nearer to him.

"What are you going to do?" she asked.

"Tell Cehmai, send out couriers west to see what we can divine about the situation in Galt, appeal to the Dai-kvo. What else can I do? A mad poet, prone to fits of temper and working for the Galtic High Council? There's not a story worse than that."

"Will the Dai-kvo do what she asks, do you think?"

"I don't know," Otah said. "He'll know this Riaan better than any of us. If he's certain that the man's not capable of a proper binding, perhaps we'll let him try and pay the price of it. One simple death is the best we can hope for, sometimes. If it saves the world."

"And if the Dai-kvo isn't sure?"

"Then he'll spin a coin or throw tiles or whatever it is he does to make a decision, and we'll do that and hope it was right."

Kiyan nodded, crossing her arms and leaning forward, gazing out into the distance as if by considering carefully, she could see Galt from here. Otah's belly growled, but he ignored it.

"He'll destroy them, won't he?" she asked. "The Dai-kvo will use the andat against the Galts."

"Likely."

"Good," Kiyan said with a certainty that surprised him. "If it's going to happen, let it happen there. At least Eiah and Danat are safe from it."

Otah swallowed. He wanted to rise to the defense of the innocent in Galt, wanted to say the sort of high-minded words that he'd held as comfort many years ago when he had been moved to kill in the name of mercy. But the years had taken that man. The years he had lived, and the dark, liquid eyes of his children. If black chaos was to be loosed, he had to side with Kiyan. Better that it was loosed elsewhere. Better a thousand thousand Galtic children die than one of his own. It was what his heart said, but it made him feel lessened and sad.

"And the other problem?" Kiyan asked. Her voice was low, but there was a hardness to it almost like anger. Otah took a querying pose. Kiyan turned to him. He hadn't expected to see fear in her eyes, and the surprise of it filled him with dread as deep as any he had suffered.

"What is it?" he asked.

She looked at him, part in surprise, part accusation.

"Nayiit," she said. "No one would think that man was Maati's child. Not for a heartbeat. You have two sons, Otah-kya."

5

⟩+⟨ Balasar was quickly coming to resent the late-spring storms of the Westlands. Each morning seemed to promise a bright day in which his masters of supply could make their inventories, his captains could train their men. Before midday, great white clouds would hulk up in the south and advance upon him. The middle afternoon had been roaring rain and vicious lightning for the past six days. The training fields were churned mud, the wood for the steam wagons was soaked, and the men were beginning to mirror Balasar's own impatience.

They had been guests of the Warden of Aren for two weeks now, the troops in their tents outside the city walls, Balasar and his captains sleeping in the high keep. The Warden was an old man, fat and boisterous, who understood as well as Balasar the dangers of an army grown restless, even an army still only half assembled. The Warden put a pleasant face on things—he'd agreed to allow a Galtic army on his lands, after all. There was little enough to do now besides be pleasant and hope they'd go away again.

He had even been so kind as to offer Balasar the use of his library. It was a small room overlooking a courtyard, less grand than Balasar's own home in Galt, less than the smallest apartments of the least of the Khaiate nobility. But it was serviceable, and it had the effect each man desired. Balasar had a place to brood, and the Westlanders had a convenient way to keep clear of him.

The afternoon rains pecked at the windows. The pot of black tea had grown tepid and bitter, ignored on a corner of the wide, oaken table. Balasar looked again at the maps. Nantani would be the first, and the easiest. The

western forces would be undivided—five full legions with support of the mercenaries hired with the High Council's gold and promises of plunder. The city
wouldn't stand for a morning. Then one legion would turn North, going overland to Pathai while two others took the mercenaries to Shosheyn-Tan, Lachi,
and Saraykeht. That left him two legions to go upriver to Udun, Utani, and
Tan-Sadar, less whatever men he left behind to occupy the conquered. Eight
of the cities. Over half, but the least important.

Coal and his men were already in place, waiting in the low towns and smugglers' camps outside Chaburi-Tan. When the andat failed, they would sack the
city, and take ships North to Yalakeht. The pieces for steam-driven boats were
already in the warehouses of the Galtic tradesmen, ready to be pegged onto
rafts and sped upriver to the village of the Dai-kvo. And then there was only
the race to the North to put Amnat-Tan, Cetani, and Machi to the torch before
winter came.

Balasar wished again that he had been able to lead the force in Chaburi-
Tan. The fate of the world would rest on that sprint to the libraries and cata-
combs of the poets. If only he had had time to sail out there . . . but days were
precious, and Coal had been preparing his men all the time Balasar had played
politics in Acton. It was better this way. And still . . .

He traced a finger across the western plains—Pathai to Utani. He wished
he knew better how the roads were. The school for the young poets wasn't far
from Pathai. That wouldn't be a pleasant duty either. And he couldn't trust the
slaughter of children to mercenaries, not with the stakes so high. This wasn't a
war that had room for moments of compassion.

A soft knock came at the door, and Eustin stepped in. He wore the deep
blue and red of a captain's uniform. Balasar acknowledged him with a nod.

"Has the third legion arrived, then?" Balasar asked.

"No, sir," Eustin said. "We've had a runner from them. They'll be here by
the week's end, sir."

"Too long."

"Yes, sir. But there's another problem."

Balasar rose, hands clasped behind him. He could feel his mind straining
back toward the plans and maps almost as if it were a physical force, but he
believed that battles were won or lost long before they were fought. If Eustin
had thought something worth interrupting him, it would likely need his whole
attention.

"Go ahead," he said.

"The poet. He's refusing to pay for his whores again, sir. Been saying the
honor of being with him should be enough. One of the girls took offense and
poured a cup of hot tea in his lap. Scalded his little poet like a boiled sausage."

Balasar didn't smile, nor did Eustin. The moment between them was
enough.

"Will he be able to ride?" Balasar asked.

"Given a few days, sir, he'll be fine. But he's demanding the girl be killed.

Half the houses in the city have threatened to raise their rates, and they're talking to their local clients too. I've had two letters today that didn't quite say the grain would cost more than expected."

Balasar felt a brief flush of anger.

"They're aware that the majority of the Galtic armies are either in the ward now or will be here shortly?"

"Yes, sir. And they've not said it's final that they'll stick it to us for more silver. But they're proud folks. It's just a whore he wants killed, but she's a Westlands whore, if you see what I mean. She's one of their own."

This was a mess. He didn't want to start the campaign by fighting the Ward of Aren. He didn't yet have all his men assembled. Balasar looked out the windows, casting his gaze over the courtyard below without truly seeing it.

"I suppose I'd best speak with him, then," Balasar said.

"He's in his rooms, sir. Should I bring him here?"

"No," Balasar said. "I'll face the beast in its lair."

"Yessir."

The central city of Aren was a squat affair. Thick stone walls covered with mud and washed white were the order of the day. The constant wars of the Westlands and the occasional attack by Galt had kept the ward cropped low as a rabbit-haunted garden. The highest houses rose no more than four stories above ground, and the streets, even near the palaces of the Warden, smelled of sewage and old food. Balasar reached the building where he and his captains were housed, shook the rain from his cloak, and gestured for Eustin to wait for him. He took the stairs three at a time up to the anteroom of the poet's apartments. The men guarding the door bowed as he entered, then stood aside as he announced himself.

Riaan sat on a low couch, his robes propped up above his lap like a tent, the hem rising halfway up his shins. The awareness of his indignity shone in the poet's face—lips pressed thin, jaw set forward. Even as Balasar made his half-bow, he could tell the man had been working himself into a rage. If any of his captains had acted this way, Balasar would have assigned them to patrolling on horseback until the wounds had healed. Idiocy should carry a price. Instead he lowered himself to a couch across from the poet and spoke gently.

"I heard about your misfortune," Balasar said in the tongue of the Khaiate cities. "I wanted to come and offer my sympathies. Is there anything I can do to be of service?"

"You could bring me the slack-cunt's heart," the poet spat. "I should have cut her down where she stood. She should be drowned in her own shit for this!"

The poet gestured toward his own crotch, demonstrating the depth of his hurt. Balasar didn't smile. With all the gravity he could manage, he nodded.

"It will cause problems if I have her killed," Balasar said. "The local men are uneasy already. I could have her whipped—"

"No! She must *die*!"

"If there was some other way that honor could be served . . ."

Riaan leaned back, his gaze cold. This, Balasar thought, was the man on whom the hopes of the world rested. A man who had leapt at the chance to turn against his own people, who had eaten the interest and novelty of the people of Acton like it was honey bread, who vented his rage on whores and servants. Balasar had never seen a tool less likely. And yet, the poet was what he needed, and the stakes could not have been higher. He sighed.

"I will see to it," Balasar said. "And permit me to send you my own personal physician. I would not have a man of your importance suffer, Most High."

"This should never have happened," Riaan said. "You will do better in the future."

"Indeed," Balasar agreed, then rose, taking what he hoped was an appropriate pose for an honored if somewhat junior man taking leave of someone above his station. He must have come near the mark, because the poet took a pose of dismissal. Balasar bowed and left. He walked back down the steps more slowly, weighing his options. He found Eustin in a common room with three of his other captains. He knew that the poet's injury had been the topic of their conversation. The sudden quiet when he entered and the merriment in their eyes were evidence enough. He greeted each man by name and gestured for Eustin to follow him back out to the street.

"Any luck, sir?"

"No," Balasar said. "He's still talking himself into a tantrum. But I had to try. I'll need Carlsin sent to him with some ointment for the burn. And he'll need to wear good robes. If he shows up in his usual rags, the man will never believe he's my physician."

"I'll see he's told, sir."

They reached the gray-cobbled street, and Balasar turned back toward the Warden's palaces and the little library with all his maps and plans. Eustin kept pace at his side. In the far distance, there was a rumble of thunder. Balasar cursed, and Eustin agreed.

"And the girl, sir?" Eustin asked.

Balasar nodded and blew out his breath.

"Tell all the comfort houses to give Riaan whatever he asks, and send the bills to me. I'll see them fairly paid. Warn them that I'll be keeping account, though. I'm not opening the coffers to every tiles player and alley worker in the Westlands."

"We have enough silver then, sir?"

"We'll have more when we've reached Nantani," Balasar said. "If the men are a little hungry before then, that might even serve us."

A gust of wind brought the harsh blast of rain and a salting of tiny hailstones. Other than raising his voice slightly, Balasar ignored it.

"And the girl herself will have to die," he said. "Tell her employer I'll pay the house fair price for the lost income."

Eustin was silent. Balasar looked at him, and the man's face was dark. The general felt his mouth curled in a deep frown.

"Say it," Balasar said.

"I think you're wrong, sir."

Balasar took Eustin's elbow and angled off from the street under a covered stone archway. A girl stood there, a cart of green winter apples at her feet, looking out at the gray-white rain and the foul, brown brook at the edge of the street. Balasar scooped up two of the apples and tossed the girl a wide copper coin before finding a low bench and nodding for Eustin to sit.

He handed his captain one of the apples and said, "Make your case."

Eustin shrugged, bit the apple, and chewed thoughtfully for a long moment. A glance at the apple seller, and then he spoke, his voice so low it was nearly inaudible over the clatter of the storm.

"First off, we haven't got so much gold we can afford to spend all of it here. Having the men hungry, well, that's one thing. But five legions is a lot of men. And there's no cause for this, not really. Any of the other men did the thing, you'd take it out of their skins. And they know it."

"I half think you're sweet on the girl," Balasar said.

"I've got a certain respect for her," Eustin said with a grin, but then sobered. "The thing is, you're not treating him like he was long-term, if you see. The story for the High Council is that once we've settled the Khaiem out, our man Riaan's to hook these andat to our yoke. Tell the Lord Convocate otherwise, and it would be someone else leading this. But if that's true, Riaan's going to be around for the rest of your life and mine, and a damned important man at that. All apologies, but you're dancing to his tune like you're hoping he'll kiss you."

Balasar tossed the apple from hand to hand and waited for the flush of anger to recede.

"I need the man," Balasar said. "If I have to bow and scrape for a time—"

"That's just it, though. *For a time*. None of the men are used to seeing you drink piss and smile. They're waiting to see you crack, to see you put him in his place. It keeps not happening, and they're wondering why. Wondering how you can stand the idea of a life licking that little prick's boot. Time will come they'll understand you *aren't* thinking of him in the long term."

Balasar needed a moment to think that through. He bit the apple; it was tart and chalky and squeaked against his teeth. He tossed the rest of it out into the street where the rain took it rolling downhill, white flesh and green skin in the dark water.

"Do you think Riaan suspects?" Balasar asked at length.

Eustin snorted. "He can't believe the tide would go out so long as he was on the beach. The waves all love him too much to leave. But the men, sir. They'll figure you're planning to kill him. And if they do, they may slip."

Balasar nodded. Eustin was right. He was acting differently than he would

have had Riaan been a problem with a future. It hadn't been difficult to let the
Councilmen in Acton blind themselves to the poet's character. Visions of god-
like power, of magic bent to the High Council's will, were enough to let them
overlook the dangers. The captains, the men who spoke with Riaan, would be
more likely to understand why he wasn't to be trusted. They might well see
what Balasar had seen from the beginning, even before he had made the
doomed journey into the desert: that the andat were a dangerous tool, best
discarded the moment the need had passed.

But, and here was the trouble, not a moment before that. If the poet failed
him, everything was lost. He weighed the risks for a long moment before Eustin spoke again.

"Let me send the girl away, sir. I'll give her enough silver to take herself out
into the farmland for half a year, and tell her that if we see her in the city, I'll
have her head on a pike for true. I'll send the poet a pig heart, say we cut it out
of her. The man that runs the comfort house'll know. I'll tell the men it was
your idea."

"It's a gamble," Balasar said.

"It's all a gamble, sir," Eustin said, and then, "Besides. He really did earn it."

To the east, lightning flashed, and before the thunder reached them, Balasar
nodded his assent. Eustin took his leave, stalking out into the downpour to
make this one more tiny adjustment to the monumental plan Balasar had devised and directed. At the end of the pathway, the apple-selling girl sensed
some slackening, pulled a hood up over her fair hair, and darted out into the
city. For a time, Balasar sat quietly, feeling the weariness in his flesh that came
from tension without release. He let his gaze soften, the white walls of the city
fading, losing their separate natures, becoming different shades of nothing,
like the shadows of hills covered by snow.

He wondered what Little Ott would have made of all this: the campaign,
the poet, the wheels within wheels that he'd put in motion. If it came together
as he planned, Balasar would save the world from another war like the one that
had toppled the Old Empire. If it failed, he might start one. And whatever
happened, he had sacrificed Bes, Laran, Kellem, Little Ott. Men who had
loved him were dead and would never return. Men alive now who trusted him
might well die. His nation, everyone he'd known or cared for—his father growing bent with age, the girl he'd lost his heart to when he was a boy shaking the
petals off spring cherry trees, Eustin, Coal—they might all be slaughtered if
he once judged poorly. It was something he tried not to consider, afraid the
weight of it might crush him. And yet in these still moments, it found him.
The dread and the awe at what he had begun. And with it the certainty that he
was right.

He imagined Bes standing in the street before him, wide face split in the
knowing grin that he would never see again outside memory. Balasar lifted a
hand in greeting, and the image bowed to him and faded. They would have
understood. All the men whose blood he'd spilled for this would have under-

stood. Or if they didn't, they'd have done it all the same. It was what they meant by faith.

When at last he returned to the library, one of his other captains—a lanky man named Orem Cot—was pacing the length of the room, literally wringing his hands in agitation or excitement. Balasar closed the door behind him with a thump as the captain bowed.

"Sir," he said. "There's a man come wanting to speak with you. I thought I'd best bring him to you myself."

"What's his business?" Balasar asked.

"Mercenary captain, sir. Brought his men down from Annaster."

"I don't need more forces."

"You'll want to talk with this one all the same, sir. His company? They're from the Khaiem. Says they got turned out by the Khai Machi and they've been traveling ever since."

"He's been in the winter cities?"

"For *years*, sir."

"You were right to bring him. Show the man in," Balasar said, then stopped the captain as he headed to the door. "What's his name?"

"Captain Ajutani, sir. Sinja Ajutani."

IT HAD BECOME CLEAR TO SINJA SHORTLY AFTER HIS ARRIVAL IN AREN THAT HE had misjudged the situation.

The company, such as it was, had passed through the mountains that divided the Westlands from the lands that, while not directly controlled, had associated themselves with Machi and Pathai weeks before. The men were young and excited to be on the march, so Sinja had pushed them. By the time they'd reached Annaster, they were tired enough to complain, but there was still a light in their eyes. They'd escaped the smothering, peaceful blankets of the Khaiem; they were in the realm where violence was met with violence, and not by the uncanny powers of the poets and their andat. They had come to the place where they could prove themselves on the bodies of their enemies.

Besides Sinja, only a dozen or so of the higher ranks had ever been in battle. For the rest, this was like walking into a children's tale. Sinja hadn't tried to explain. Perhaps they'd be able to find glory in the soul-crushing boredom of a siege; perhaps they'd face their first battles and discover that they loved violence. More likely, he'd be sending half of them home to their mothers by midsummer, and that would have been fine. He was here as much to stretch his legs as to keep his master and friend the Khai Machi out of trouble with the Dai-kvo.

He hadn't expected to walk into the largest massing of military force in memory.

Galt was in the southern wards, and it was there in force. All through the Westlands, Wardens had forgotten their squabbles. Every gaze was cast south.

The common wisdom was that Galt had finally decided to end its generations-long games of raid and abandon. It had come to take control of the whole of the Westlands from the southern coast up to Eddensea. There were even those who wondered whether it was going to be a good season for Eddensea.

Sinja had done what he did best—listened. The stories he heard were, of course, overblown. Men and women throughout the Westlands were in different stages of panic. Someone had seen a thousand ships off the coast. There had been agreements signed with Aren, but all the other Wardens and all their children were to be slaughtered to assure that no one would have claim to rule once the Galts had come through. There were even a few optimists who thought that Balasar Gice—the general at the head of this largest of all gathered armies—wasn't looking to the Westlands, but gathering his forces to take control of Galt itself. He could overthrow the High Council and install himself as autocrat.

What it all came to was this: Any mercenary company working for anyone besides Galt was likely to be on the losing side of the fight. The collected Wardens were putting out calls for free companies and garrison forces, preparing themselves as best they could. The fees that Sinja was offered would have been handsome for a band of veterans and siege captains, much less for a few hundred foreign sell-swords one step up from thugs. And so Sinja had considered the money, considered the offers and the stories and his own best instincts, then quietly packed up his men and headed south to Aren to sell their services at a fourth of the price, but to the winners.

The men had grumbled. Wide, square Westland coins had been dancing in their minds. Morale had started to fail. So Sinja had paused in the Ward of Castin, made contact with a free company who'd taken contract there, and challenged their veterans to a day of games. Once Sinja's men had understood and accepted his point, they bound their ribs and continued to the south. No one had questioned his judgment again.

Aren was one of the wards farthest to the south. Low hills covered with rich green grasses, towns of stone buildings with thatched roofs, elk and deer so wise to the ways of men that the bowmen he sent ahead to forage never caught one of them. Wherever they went, Sinja saw the signs of an army having passed—ruined crops, abandoned campsites with the ashes of a half hundred fires churned into the mud. But even with this, he had been shocked when they topped one of the many hills and caught first sight of the city of Aren.

No city under siege had ever seen so many troops at its wall. Tents and low pavilions were laid out around it on all sides, dark oiled cloth shining in row after row after row. The smoke of cook fires left a low haze through the valley that even the rain could not wholly dispel, the strange bulbous steam wagons the Galts used to move supplies and leave their men unburdened seemed as numerous as horses in the fields, and the squirming, streaming activity of men moving through each of the opened gates made the city seem like a dead sparrow overrun by ants.

His men set camp at a polite distance from the existing companies while Sinja dared the city itself. He entered the gates at midday. It wasn't more than three hands later he was being escorted through the halls of the Warden's palace to the library and the general himself. He'd surrendered his blades and the garrote he kept at his waist before being permitted to speak with the great man. Either Balasar Gice felt this unprecedented mass of men was too little for whatever task lay ahead of him and was grabbing at every spare sword and dagger in the world, or else Sinja was, for reasons that passed imagining, of particular interest to him.

Either way, Sinja disliked it.

Balasar Gice turned out to be a smallish man, mouse-brown hair running to white at the temples. He wore the gray tunic of command that Sinja had seen before when he'd been in the field as a young man fighting against the Galts or else with them. He might have been anyone, to look at him. A farmer or a merchant seaman or a seafront customs agent.

"Bad weather for traveling," the general said, amiably, as if they were simply two men who'd met at a wayhouse. He spoke the Khaiate tongue clearly, his accent flavoring the words rather than obscuring them.

"It's always wet in the South this time of year," Sinja agreed in Galtic. "Not always so cold, but that's why the gods made wool. That or as a joke against sheep."

The general smiled, either at the words or the language they were in, Sinja wasn't certain. Sinja kept his expression pleasant and empty. They both knew he was here to sell the use of his men, but only the general knew why the meeting was here and not with some low captain. Sinja opted to wait and see what came of it. Balasar Gice seemed to read his intention; he nodded and walked to a side table, where he poured them both clear wine from a cut-glass carafe. No, not wine. Water.

"I hear the Khai Machi turned you out," the general said in Galtic as he passed a cup to Sinja. That wasn't true. Sinja had told the captain that they were out from Machi, but perhaps there had been some misunderstanding. Sinja shrugged. It was too early in the game to correct anyone's misconceptions.

"It's his right," he said. "Some of the men were causing trouble. Too long in a quiet place. I'm sure you understand."

Balasar chuckled. It was a warm sound, and Sinja found himself liking the man. Balasar nodded to a couch beside the brazier. Sinja made a small bow and sat, the general leaning casually against the table.

"You left on good terms?"

"We didn't turn back and burn the city," Sinja said, "if that's what you mean."

"Do you owe the Khai Machi loyalty? Or are you a free company?"

The truth was that any silver he took would find its way back to Otah Machi's coffers. The company was no more free than the Galtic armies outside the city. And yet there was something in the general's voice when he asked the question, something in his eyes.

"We're mercenaries. We follow whoever pays us," Sinja said.

"And if someone should offer to pay you more? No offense, but the one thing you can say of loyalty for hire is that it's for hire."

"We'll finish out a contract," Sinja said. "I've been through enough to know what happens to a company with a reputation for switching sides mid-battle. But I won't lie, the boys I have are green, most of them. They haven't seen many campaigns."

It was a softening of *these poor bastards hardly know which end's the sharp one* but the meaning was much the same. The general waved the concern aside, which was fascinating. Balasar Gice wasn't interested in their field prowess. Which meant he either wanted them to lead the charges and soak up a few enemy spears and arrows—hardly a role that asked the general's presence at the negotiation—or there was something more, something that Sinja was still missing.

"How many of them speak Galt?"

"A third," Sinja said, inventing the number on the spot.

"I may have use for them. How loyal are they to you?"

"How loyal do they need to be?"

The general smiled. There was a touch of sorrow in his eyes and a long, thoughtful pause. Sinja felt a decision being made, though he couldn't say what the issue was.

"Enough to go against their own kind. Not in the field, but I'll want them as translators and agents. And whatever you can tell me of the winter cities. I'll want that as well."

Sinja smiled knowingly to cover his racing mind. Gice wasn't taking his army North. He was going east, into the cities of the Khaiem, with something close to every able-bodied man in Galt behind him. Sinja chuckled to hide a rush of fear.

"They'll follow you any place you care to go, so long as they're on the winning side," Sinja said. "Are you sure that's going to be you?"

"Yes," the general said, and the bare confidence in his voice was more persuasive than any reasoned argument he might have given. If the man had been trying to convince himself, he would have had a speech ready—why this insanity would work, how the army could overpower the andat, something. But Balasar was certain. The general sipped his water, waiting the space of five long breaths together. Then he spoke again. "You're thinking something?"

"You're not stupid," Sinja said. "So you're either barking mad, or you know something I don't. No one can take on the Khaiem."

"You mean no one can face the andat."

"Yes," Sinja agreed. "That's what I mean."

"I can."

"Forgive me if I keep my doubts about me," Sinja said.

The general nodded, considered Sinja for a long moment, then gestured toward the table. Sinja put down his bowl and stepped over as the general unrolled a long cloth scroll with a map of the cities of the Khaiem on it. Sinja stepped back from it as if there were an asp on it.

"General," he said, "if you're about to tell me your plans for this campaign, I think we might be ahead of where we should be."

Balasar put a hand on Sinja's arm. The Galt's gaze was firm and steady, his voice low and strangely intimate. Sinja saw how a personality like his own could command an army or a nation. Possibly, he thought, a world.

"Captain Ajutani, I don't share these plans with every mercenary captain who walks through my door. I don't trust them. I don't show them to my own captains, barring the ones in my small Council. The others I expect to trust me. But we're men of the world, you and I. You have something I think I could use."

"And you have nothing to lose by telling me," Sinja said, slowly. "Because I'm not leaving this building, am I?"

"Not even to go speak to your men," the general said. "You're here as my ally or my prisoner."

Sinja shook his head.

"That's a brave thing to say, General. It's only the two of us in here."

"If you attacked me, I'd kill you where you stood," Balasar said in the same tone of voice he'd used before, and Sinja believed him. Balasar smiled gently and nudged him forward, toward the table.

"Let me show you why ally would be the better choice."

Still, Sinja held back.

"I'm not an idiot," he said. "If you tell me you plan to take over the Khaiem by flying through the sky on winged dogs, I'll still clap you on the back and swear I'm your ally."

"Of course you will. You'll say you're my dearest friend and solidly behind me. I'll thank you and distrust you and keep you unarmed and under guard. We'll each avoid turning our backs on the other. I think we can take that all as given," Balasar said with a dismissive wave. "I don't care what you say or do, Captain. I care what you *think*."

Sinja felt a genuine smile blooming on his lips. When he laughed, Balasar laughed with him.

"Well," Sinja said. "As long as we're agreed on all that. Go ahead. Convince me that you're going to prevail against the poets."

They talked for what seemed like the better part of the evening. Outside, the storm slackened, the clouds broke. By the time a servant boy came to light the lanterns, a moon so full it seemed too heavy to rise glowed in the indigo sky. Gnats and midges buzzed through the open windows, ignored by both men as they discussed Balasar's intentions and strategies. The general was open and forthcoming and honest, and with every unfolding scheme, Sinja understood that his life was worth whatever Balasar Gice said it was worth. It was up to him to convince the general that letting him live after he'd heard all this wouldn't be a mistake. It was a clever tactic, all the more so because once Sinja understood the trick, it lost none of its power.

Afterward, armsmen escorted him to a small, well-appointed bedchamber with windows too narrow to crawl out and a bar on the outside of the door. Sinja lay in the bed, listening to the nearly inaudible hiss and tick of the candle flame. His body felt poorly attached, likely to slip free of his mind at any moment. Light-headed, he washed his face in cold water, cracked his knuckles, anything to bring his mind to something real and immediate. Something the Galtic general had not just torn away.

It was as if he had fallen into a nightmare, or woken to something worse than one. He felt as if he'd just watched a man he knew well die by violence. The Galt's plan would end the world he had known. If it worked. And in his bones, he knew it would.

The hours passed, the night seeming to stretch on without end. Sinja paced his room or sat or lay sleepless on the bed, remembering the illness he had felt after his first battle. This was the same disease, back again. But the more he thought about it, the more his mind tracked across the maps he and the general had considered, the more his conviction grew.

The turncoat poet and the army were only a part of it—in some ways the least. It was the general's audacity and certainty and caution. It was the force of his personality. Sinja had seen commanders and wardens and kings, and he could tell the sort that fated themselves to lose. Balasar Gice was going to win.

And so, Sinja supposed with a sense of genuine regret, the right thing was to work for him.

6

>+< The poet's house was warm, the scent of trees thick in the air. The false dawn, prolonged by the mountains to the east, had just come, the sun making its way above the peaks to bathe the world in light. Through the opened door, Maati could hear the songs of birds deep in the yearly quest to draw mates to their nests. The dances and parties of the utkhaiem were much the same—who had the loveliest plumage, the more enticing song. There were fewer differences between men and birds than men liked to confess.

He sat on a couch, watching Cehmai at one side of the small table and Stone-Made-Soft at the other. Between them was the game board with its worn lines and stones. The game had been central to the binding Manat Doru had performed generations ago that first brought Stone-Made-Soft into existence, and as part of the legacy he bore, Cehmai had to play the game again— white stones moving forward against the black—as a reaffirmation of his control over the spirit. Fortunately, Manat Doru had also made Stone-Made-Soft a terrible player. Cehmai tapped his fingertips against the wood and shifted a black stone in the center of the board toward the left. Stone-Made-Soft frowned, its wide face twisted in concentration.

"No word yet," Cehmai said. "It's early days, though."

"What do you think he'll do?" Maati asked.

"I'm trying to think, please," the andat rumbled. They ignored it.

Cehmai leaned back in his seat. The years had treated him kindly. The fresh-faced, talented young man Maati had met when he first came to Machi was still there. If there was the first dusting of gray in the boy's hair, if the lines at the corners of his mouth were deeper now, and less prone to vanish when he relaxed, it did nothing to take away from the easy smile or the deep, grounded sense of self that Cehmai had always had. And even the respect he had for Maati—no longer a dread-touched awe, but still profound in its way—had never failed with familiarity.

"I'm afraid he'll do the thing," Cehmai said. "I suppose I'm also afraid that he won't. There's not a good solution."

"He could take a middle course," Maati said. "Demand that the Galts hand back Riaan on the threat of taking action. If the Dai-kvo tells them that he knows, it might be enough."

The andat lifted a thick-fingered hand, gently touched a white stone, and slid it forward with a hiss. Cehmai glanced over, considered, and pushed the black stone he'd moved before back into the space it had come from. The andat coughed in frustration and set its head on balled fists, staring at the board.

"It's odd," Cehmai said. "There was a time when I was at the school—before I'd even taken the black robes, so early on. There was a pigeon that had taken up residence in my cohort's rooms. Nasty thing. It would flap around through the air and drop feathers and shit on us all, and every time we waved it outside, it would come back. Then one day, one of the boys got lucky. He threw a boot at the poor thing and broke its wing. Well, we knew we were going to have to kill it. Even though it had been nothing but annoyance and filth, it was hard to break its neck."

"Were you the one that did it?" Maati asked.

Cehmai took a pose of acknowledgment.

"It felt like this," the younger poet said. "I won't enjoy this, if it's what we do."

The andat looked up from the board.

"Has it ever struck you people how arrogant you are?" it asked, huge hands taking an attitude of query that bordered on accusation. "You're talking of slaughtering a nation. Thousands of innocent people destroyed, lands made barren, mountains leveled and the sea pulled up over them like a blanket. And you're feeling sorry for yourself that you had to wring a bird's neck as a boy? How can anyone have feelings that delicate and that numbed both at the same time?"

"It's your move," Cehmai said.

Stone-Made-Soft sighed theatrically—it had no need for breath, so every sigh it made was a comment—and turned back toward the game. It was essentially over. The andat had lost again as it always did, but they played to the last move, finishing the ritual humiliation once again.

"We're off to the North," Cehmai said as he put the stones back into their trays. "There's a new vein the Radaani want to explore, but I'm not convinced it's possible. Their engineers are swearing that the structure won't collapse, but those mountains are getting near lacework."

"Eight generations is a long time," Maati agreed. "Even without help, the mines would have become a maze by now."

"I fear the day an earthquake comes," Cehmai said as he stood and stretched. "One shake, and half these mountains will fold up flat, I'd swear it."

"Then I suppose we'd have to spend months digging up the bodies," Maati said.

"Not really," the andat said. Its voice was placid again, now that the game was ended. "If we make it soft enough, the bodies will float up through it. If stone is water, almost anything floats. We could have a whole field of stone flat as a lake, with mine dogs and men popping up out of it like bubbles."

"What a pleasant thought," Cehmai said, gently sarcastic. "And here I was wondering why we weren't invited to more dinners. And you, Maati-kvo? What's your day?"

"More work in the library," Maati said. "I want the place in order. If the Dai-kvo calls for me . . ."

"He will," Cehmai said. "You can count on that."

"If he does, I want the place left in order. A sane order that someone else could make sense of. Baarath had the thing put together like a puzzle. Took me three years just to make sense of it, and even then some of it I just went through book by book and made my own classifications."

"Well, he had a different opinion than yours," Cehmai said. "He wanted the library to be a place to bury secrets, not display them. It was how he made himself feel as if he mattered. I don't suppose I can blame him too much for that."

"I suppose not," Maati agreed.

The three of them walked along the wooded path that led to the palaces of the Khai. The stone towers of Machi rose high above the city, bright with the light of morning, and the smoke of the forges plumed up from the metalworkers' district in the south. Maati kept company with Cehmai and Stone-Made-Soft as far as the compound of House Radaani, where a litter and donkeys were waiting. They took poses of farewell, even the andat, and Maati sat on the steps of the compound to watch them lumber away to the North.

In the days since he, Otah, and Liat had broken the news to Cehmai, Maati had found himself less and less able to do his work. The familiar stacks and shelves and galleries of the library were uncomforting. The songs of the sing-

ing slaves in the gardens seemed to pull at him when he caught a phrase of
their melodies. He found himself seeking out food when he wasn't hungry,
wine when he had no thirst. He walked the streets of the city and the paths of
the palaces more than he had in living memory, and even when his knees
ached, he found himself unconsciously rising to pace the rooms of his apartments. Restless. He had become restless.

In part it was the knowledge that Liat and Nayiit were in the city, in the
palaces even. At any time, he could seek them out, invite them to eat with him
or talk with him. Nayiit, whom he had not known since the boy was shorter
than little Danat was now. Liat, whose breath and body he had once said he
would never be whole without. They were here at last.

In part it was the anticipation of a courier from the Dai-kvo, whether about
his own work or Liat's case against the Galts. And of the two, he found the
Galtic issue the lesser. Liat's argument was enough to convince him that they
did have a rogue poet, but the chances that he would bind a new andat seemed
remote. There in the middle of Galt without references, without the Dai-kvo
or his fellow poets to work through the fine points of the binding, the most
likely thing was that the man would try, fail, and die badly. It was a problem
that would solve itself. And if the Dai-kvo took Liat's view and turned the
andat loose against Galt, the chances of tragedy coming to the cities of the
Khaiem was even less.

No, his unease came more from the prospect of his own success. He had
lived so long as a failure that the prospect of success disturbed him. He knew
that his heart should have been singing. He should have been drunk with
pride.

And yet he found himself waking in the night, knotted with anger. In the
darkness of his room, he would wake with the night candle over half burned,
and stare at the netting above his bed as it shifted in barely felt drafts. The
targets of his rage seemed to shift; one night he might wake with a list of the
wrongs done him by Liat, the next with the conviction that he had suffered
insult at the hands of Otah or the Dai-kvo. With the coming of dawn, the fit
would pass, insubstantial as a dream, the complaints that had haunted him in
darkness thin as cheesecloth in the light.

And still, he was restless.

He made his way slowly through the palaces and out to the city itself. The
black-cobbled streets were alive with people. Carts of vegetables and early
berries wound from the low towns toward the markets in the center of the city.
Lambs on rough hemp leads trotted in ignorance toward the butchers' stalls.
And wherever he went, a path was made for him, people took poses of respect
and welcome and he returned them by habit. He paused at a cart and bought a
meal of hot peppered beef and sweet onions wrapped in waxed paper. The
young man running the cart refused to accept his lengths of copper. Another
small amenity granted to the other poet of Machi. Maati took a pose of thanks
as best he could with one hand full of the food.

The towers of Machi seemed to touch the lowest clouds. It had been years since Maati had gone up one of the great towers. He remembered the platform swaying, its great arm-thick chains clanking against the stones as he rose. That far above the city, he had felt he was looking out from a mountain peak—the valley spread below so vast he'd imagined he could almost see the ocean. Not remotely truth, but what it felt like all the same. Looking at the towers now, he remembered what Cehmai had said. If there were an earthquake, the towers would certainly fall. For an instant, he imagined the stones pattering down in a deadly rain, the long, slumped piles of rubble that would lie where they fell. The corpses of giants.

He shook himself, pushing the darkness away, and turned back toward the palaces. He wondered, as he trundled toward the library, where Nayiit was today. He had seen the boy—a man old enough to have a child of his own, and still in Maati's mind a boy—several times since his arrival. Dinners, dances, formal meetings. They had not yet had a conversation as father and son. Maati wondered whether he wanted them to, or if the reminder of what might have been would be too uncomfortable for them both. Perhaps he could track the boy down, show him through the city for a day. Or through the tunnels. There were a few teahouses still in business down in their winter quarters. That was the sort of thing only a local would know. Maybe the boy would be interested. . . .

He paused as he rounded the slow curving path toward the library. Two forms were sitting on its wide stone steps, but neither of them was Nayiit. The older, rounder woman wore robes of seafoam green embroidered with yellow. Liat's hair was still as dark as when she'd been a girl sitting beside him on a cart leaving Saraykeht behind them. Her head still took the same just-off angle when she was speaking to someone to whom she was trying especially to be kind.

The younger looked thin and coltish beside her. Her robes were deep blue shot with white, and Eiah had her hair up, held in place with thick silvered pins that glittered even from here. She was the first to catch sight of him, and her thin arm rose, waving him nearer. He was too thick about the belly these days to trot or he would have.

"We've been waiting for you," Eiah said as he drew near. Her tone was accusing. Liat glanced up at him, amused.

"I was seeing Cehmai off on his journey," Maati said. "He's going to the Radaani mines in the North. A new vein, I think. But I did take the longer way back. If I'd known you were waiting, I'd have been here sooner."

Eiah considered this, and then without word or gesture visibly accepted the apology.

"We've been talking about marriage," Liat said.

"Did you know that Liat-cha never got married to anyone? Nayiit's her son. She had a baby, but she's never been wed?"

"Well, the two things aren't perfectly related, you know," Maati began, but Eiah rolled her eyes and took a pose that unasked the question.

"Eiah-cha and I were going to the high gardens. I've packed some bread and cheese. We thought you might care to join us?"

"You've already eaten," Eiah said, pointing to the waxed paper in his hand.

"This?" Maati said. "No, I was feeding this to the pigeons. Wait a moment, I'll get a jug of wine and some bowls. . . ."

"I'm old enough to drink wine," Eiah said.

"Three bowls, then," Maati said. "Just give me a moment."

He walked back to his apartments, feeling something very much like relief. The afternoon trapped with old scrolls and codices, books and frail maps was banished. He was saved from it. He threw the waxed paper with the remaining onions into a corner where the servants would clean it, took a thick earthenware jug of wine off his shelves, and dropped three small wine bowls into his sleeve. On his way back out to the steps, where he was certain no one could see him, he trotted.

DANAT'S COUGH HAD RETURNED.

Otah had filled his day playing Khai Machi. He had reviewed the preparations for the Grand Audience he was already past due holding. There was an angry letter from the Khai Tan-Sadar asking for an explanation of Otah's decision not to take his youngest daughter as one of his wives that he responded to with as much aplomb as he could muster. His Master of Stone—responsible for keeping the books of the city—had discovered that two of the forms from which silver lengths were struck had been tampered with and reported the progress of his investigation into the matter. The widow of Adaiit Kamau demanded an audience, insisting again that her husband had been murdered and demanding justice in his name. The priests asked for money for the temple and the procession of the beasts. A young playwright, son of Oiad How of House How, had composed an epic in the honor to the Khai Machi, and asked permission to perform it. Permission and funding. The representative of the tinsmiths petitioned for a just distribution of coal, as the ironworkers had been taking more than their share. The ironworkers' explaining that they worked iron, not—sneering and smiling as if Otah would understand—tin. And on and on and on until Otah was more than half tempted to grab a passing servant, put him on the black lacquer chair, and let the city take its chances. And at the end, with all the weight of the city and the impending death of Galt besides, the thing that he could not face was that Danat's cough had returned.

The nursery glowed by the light of the candles. Kiyan sat on the raised bed, talking softly to their son. Great iron statues of strange, imagined beasts had been kept in the fire grates all day and pulled out when night fell, and as he quietly walked forward, Otah could feel the heat radiating from them. The physician's assistant—a young man with a serious expression—took a respectful pose and walked quietly from the room, leaving the family alone.

Otah stepped up to the bedside. Danat's eyes, half closed in drowse, shifted toward him and a smile touched Otah's mouth.

"I got sick again, Papa-kya," he said. His voice was rough and low; the familiar sign of a hard day.

"Don't talk, sweet," Kiyan said, smoothing Danat's forehead with the tips of her fingers. "You'll start it again."

"Yes," Otah said, sitting across from his wife, taking his son's hand. "I heard. But you've been sick before, and you've gotten better. You'll get better again. It's good for boys to be a bit ill when they're young. It gets all the hardest parts out of the way early. Then they can be strong old men."

"Tell me a story?" Danat asked.

Otah took a breath, his mind grasping for a children's story. He tried to recall being in this room himself or one like it. He had been, when he'd been Danat's age. Someone had held him when he'd been ill, had told him stories to distract him. But everything in his life before he'd been disowned and sent to the school existed in the blur of half-memory and dream.

"Papa-kya's tired, sweet," Kiyan said. "Let Mama tell you about . . ."

"No!" Danat cried, his face pulling in—mouth tight, brows thunderously low. "I want Papa-kya—"

"It's all right," Otah said. "I'm not so tired I can't tell my own boy a story."

Kiyan smiled at him, her eyes amused and apologetic both. *I tried to spare you.*

"Once, back before the Empire, when the world was very new," Otah said, then paused. "There, ah. There was a goat."

The goat—whose name was coincidentally also Danat—went on to meet a variety of magical creatures and have long, circuitous conversations to no apparent point or end until Otah saw his son's eyes shut and his breath grow deep and steady. Kiyan rose and silently snuffed all but the night candle. The room filled with the scent of spent wicks. Otah let go of his son's hand and quietly pulled the netting closed. In the near-darkness, Danat's eyelids seemed darker, smudged with kohl. His skin was smooth and brown as eggshell. Kiyan touched Otah's shoulder and motioned with her gaze to the door. He laced his fingers in hers and together they walked to the hallway.

The physician's assistant sat on a low stool, a bowl of rice and fish in his hands.

"I will be here for the night, Most High," the assistant said as Otah paused before him. "My teacher expects that the boy will sleep soundly, but if he wakes, I will be here."

Otah took a pose expressing gratitude. It was a humbling thing for a Khai to do before a servant, even one as skilled as this. The physician's assistant bowed deeply in response. The walk to their own rooms was a short one— down one hallway, up a wide flight of stairs worked in marble and silver, and then the gauntlet of their own servants. The evening's meal was set out for them—quail glazed with pork fat and honey, pale bread with herbed butter, fresh trout, iced apples. More food than any two people could eat.

"It isn't in his chest," Kiyan said as she lifted the trout's pale flesh from delicate, translucent bones. "His color is always good. His lips never blue at all. The physician didn't hear any water when he breathes, and he can blow up a pig's bladder as well as I could."

"And all that's good?" Otah said. "He can't run across a room without coughing until his head aches."

"All that's better than the alternative," Kiyan said. "They don't know what it is. They give him teas that make him sleep, and hope that his body's wise enough to mend itself."

"This has been going on too long. It's been almost a year since he was really well."

"I know it," Kiyan said, and the weariness in her voice checked Otah's frustration. "Really, love, I'm quite clear."

"I'm sorry, Kiyan-kya," he said. "It's just . . ."

He shook his head.

"Hard feeling powerless?" she said gently. Otah nodded. Kiyan sighed softly, a sympathy for his pain. Then, "A *goat*?"

"It was what came to mind."

After the meal, after their hands had been washed for them in silver bowls, after Otah had suffered yet another change of robes, Kiyan kissed him and retreated to her rooms. Otah stepped down from his palace, instructed the retinue of servants that he wished to be left alone, and made his way west, toward the library. The sun had long since slipped behind the mountains, but the sky remained a bright gray, the clouds touched with rose and gold. Spring would soon give way to summer, the long, bright days and brief nights. Still, it was not so early in the season that lanterns didn't glow from the windows that he passed. Stars glittered in the east as the night rose. The library itself was dark, but candles burned in Maati's apartments, and Otah made his way down the path.

Voices came to him, raised in laughter. A man's and a woman's, and both familiar as memory. They sat on chairs set close together. In the yellow candlelight, Maati's cheeks looked rosy. Liat's hair had escaped its bun, locks of it tumbling across her brow, down the curve of her neck. The air smelled of mulling spices and wine, and Eiah lay on a couch, one long, thin arm cast over her eyes. Liat's eyes went wide when she caught sight of him, and Maati turned toward the door to see what had startled her.

"Otah-kvo!" he said, waving him forward. "Come in. Come in. It's my fault. I've kept your daughter too long. I should have sent her home sooner. I wasn't thinking."

"Not at all," Otah said, stepping in. "I've come for your help actually."

Maati took a pose of query. His hands were not perfectly steady, and Liat stifled a giggle. Both of them were more than a little drunk. A bowl of warmed wine sat on the edge of the brazier, a silver serving cup hooked to the rim. Otah glanced at it, and Maati waved him on. There were no bowls, so Otah drank from the serving cup.

"What can I do, Most High?" Maati asked with a grin that was for the most part friendly.

"I need a book. Something with children's stories in it. Fables, or light epics. History, if it's well enough written. Danat's asking me to tell stories, and I don't really know any."

Liat chuckled and shook her head, but Maati nodded in understanding. Otah sat beside his sleeping daughter while Maati considered. The wine was rich and deep, and the spices alone made Otah's head swim a little.

"What about the one from the Dancer's Court?" Liat said. "The one with the stories about the half-Bakta boy who intrigued for the Emperor."

Maati pursed his lips.

"They're a bit bloody, some of them," he said.

"Danat's a boy. He'll love them. Besides, you read them to Nayiit without any lasting damage," Liat said. "Those and the green book. The one that was all political allegories where people turned into light or sank into the ground."

The Silk Hunter's Dreams," Maati said. "That's a thought. I have a copy of that one too, where I can put my hand on it. Only, Otah-kvo, don't tell him the one with the crocodile. Nayiit-kya wouldn't sleep for days after I told him that one."

"I'll trust you," Otah said.

"Wait," Maati said, and with a grunt he pulled himself to standing. "You two stay here. I'll be back with it in three heartbeats."

An uncomfortable silence fell on Otah and Liat. Otah turned to consider Eiah's sleeping face. Liat shifted in her chair.

"She's a lovely girl," Liat said softly. "We spent the day together, the three of us, and I was sure she'd wear us thin by the end of it. Still, we're the ones that lasted longest, eh?"

"She doesn't have a head for wine yet," Otah said.

"We didn't give her wine," Liat said, then chuckled. "Well, not much anyway."

"If the worst she does is sneak away to drink with the pair of you, I'll be the luckiest man alive," Otah said. As if hearing him, Eiah sighed in her sleep and shifted away, pressing her face to the cushions.

"She looks like her mother," Liat said. "Her face is that same shape. The eyes are your color, though. She'll be stunning when she's older. She'll break hearts. But I suppose they all do. Ours if no one else's."

Otah looked up. Liat's expression had darkened, the shadows of lanternlight gathering on the curves of her face. It had been another lifetime, it seemed, when Otah had first known her. Only four years older than Eiah was now. And he'd been younger than Nayiit. Babies, it seemed. Too young to know what they were doing, or how precarious the world truly was. It hadn't seemed that way at the time, though. Otah remembered it all with a terrible clarity.

"You're thinking of Saraykeht," she said.

"Was it that obvious?"

"Yes," Liat said. "How much have you told them? About what happened?"

"Kiyan knows everything. A few others."

"They know how Seedless was freed? And Heshai-kvo, how he was killed?"

For a sick moment, Otah was back in the filthy room, in the stink of mud and raw sewage from the alley. He remembered the ache in his arms. He remembered the struggle as the old poet fought for air with the cord biting into his throat. It had seemed the right thing, then. Even to Heshai. The andat, Seedless, had come to Otah with the plan. Aid in Heshai-kvo's suicide—for in many ways that was what it had been—and Liat would be saved. Maati would be saved. A thousand Galtic babies would stay safely in their mother's wombs, the power of the andat never turned against them.

Otah wondered when things had changed. When he had stopped being someone who would kill a good man to protect the innocent, and become willing to let a nation die if it meant protecting his own. Likely it had been the moment he'd first seen Eiah squirming on Kiyan's breast.

"Do you know?" Otah asked. "How it happened, I mean."

"Only guesses," Liat said. "If you wanted to tell me . . ."

"Thank you," Otah said with a sigh, "but maybe it's best to leave that buried. It's all finished now, and there's no undoing any of it."

"Perhaps you're right."

"We will need to talk about Nayiit," Otah said. "Not now. Not with . . ." He nodded to the sleeping girl.

"I understand," Liat said and brushed her hair back from her eyes. "I don't mean any harm, 'Tani. I wouldn't hurt you or your family. I didn't come here . . . I wouldn't have come here if I hadn't had to."

The door swung open, a gust of cool air coming from it, and Maati stood triumphantly in the frame. He held a small book bound in blue silk as if it were a trophy of war.

"Got the bastard!" he said, and walked over to Otah, presenting it over one arm like a sword. "For you, Most High, and your son."

Over Maati's shoulder, Otah could see Liat look away. Otah only took the book, adopted a pose of thanks, and turned to gently shake Eiah's shoulder. She grunted, her brow furrowing.

"It's time to come home, Eiah-kya," Otah said. "Come along."

" 'M'wake," Eiah protested, but slowly. Rubbing her eyes with the back of one hand, she rose.

They said their good nights, and Otah led his daughter out, closing the door to Maati's apartments behind them. The night had grown cool, and the stars had occupied the sky like a conquering army. Otah laid his arm across Eiah's shoulder, hers under it, around his ribs. She leaned into him as they walked. Night-blooming flowers scented the air, soft as rain. They were just coming in sight of the entrance of the First Palace when Eiah spoke, her voice still abstracted with sleep.

"Nayiit-cha's yours, isn't he, Papa-kya?"

LIAT WOKE IN DIM MOONLIGHT; THE NIGHT CANDLE HAD GONE OUT OR ELSE THEY hadn't bothered to light it. She couldn't recall which. Beside her, Maati mumbled something in his sleep, as he always had. Liat smiled at the dim profile on the pillow beside her. He looked younger in sleep, the lines at his mouth softened, the storm at his brow calmed. She resisted the urge to caress his cheek, afraid to wake him. She had taken lovers in the years since she'd returned to Saraykeht. A half-dozen or so, each a man whose company she had enjoyed, and all of whom she could remember fondly.

She thought, sometimes, that she'd reversed the way women were intended to love. Butterfly flirtations, flitting from one man to another, taking none seriously, were best kept by the young. Had she taken her casual lovers as a girl, they would have been exciting and new, and she would have known too little to notice that they were empty. Instead, Liat had lost her heart twice before she'd seen twenty summers, and if those loves were gone—even this one, sleeping now at her side—the memory of them was there. Once, she had told herself the world was nothing if she didn't have a man who loved her. A man of importance and beauty, a man whom she might, through her gentle guidance, save.

She had been another woman, then. And who, she wondered, had she become now?

She rose quietly, parting the netting, and stepped out onto the cool floor. She found her outer robe and wrapped it around herself. Her inner robes and her sandals she could reclaim tomorrow. Now she wanted her own bed, and pillows less thick with memories.

She slipped out the door, pulling it closed behind her. So far North and without an ocean to hold the warmth of the day, Machi's nights were cold, even now with spring at its height. Gooseflesh rose on her legs and arms, her belly and breasts, as she trotted along the wide, darkened paths to the apartments that Itani or Otah or the Khai Machi had given to her and her son.

More than a week had passed since he had come to Maati's apartments, gathering up a children's book and a daughter halfway to womanhood and leaving behind a lasting unease. Liat had not spoken with him since, but the dread of the coming conversation weighed heavy. As Nayiit had grown, she'd seen nothing in him but himself. Even when people swore that the boy had her eyes, her mouth, her way of sighing, she'd never seen it. Perhaps when there was no space between a mother and her child, the sameness becomes invisible. Perhaps it merely seemed normal. She would have admitted that her son looked something like his father. It was only in seeing them together, seeing the simple, powerful knowing in Otah's wife's expression, that Liat understood the depth of her error in letting Nayiit come.

And with that came her understanding of how it could not be undone. Her first impulse had been to send him away at once, to hide him again the way a child caught with a forbidden sweet might stuff it away into a sleeve as if unseen now might somehow mean never seen at all. Only the years of running her house had counseled her otherwise. The situation was what it was. Attempting any subterfuge would only make the Khai wary, and his unease might mean Nayiit's death. As long as her son lived, he posed a threat to Danat, and she knew enough to understand that a babe held from its first breath meant something that a man full-grown never could. If Otah were forced to choose, Liat had no illusions what that choice would be.

And so she prepared herself, prepared her arguments and her negotiating strategies, and told herself it would end well. They were all together, allies against the Galts. There would be no need. She told herself there would be no need.

At her apartments, no candles were lit, but a fire burned in the grate: old pine, rich with sap that popped and hissed and filled the air with its scent. When she entered, her son looked up from the flames and took a pose of welcome, gesturing to a divan beside him. Liat hesitated, surprised by a sudden embarrassment, then gathered her sense of humor and sat beside him. He smelled of wine and smoke, and his robes hung as loose on him as her own did on her.

"You've been to the teahouses," Liat said, trying to keep any note of disapproval from her voice.

"You've been with my father," he replied.

"I've been with Maati," Liat said as if it were an agreement and not a correction.

Nayiit leaned forward and took up a length of iron, prodding the burning logs. Sparks rose and vanished like fireflies.

"I haven't been able to see him," Nayiit said. "We've been here weeks now, and he hasn't come to speak with me. And every time I go to the library he's gone or he's with you. I think you're trying to keep us from each other."

Liat raised her eyebrows and ran her tongue across the inside of her teeth, weighing the coppery taste that sprang to her mouth, thinking what it meant. She coughed.

"You aren't wrong," she said at last. "I'm not ready for it. Maati's not who he was back then."

"So instead of letting us face each other and see what it is we see, you've decided to start up an affair with him and take all his time and attention?" There was no rancor in his voice, only sadness and amusement. "It doesn't seem the path of wisdom, Mother."

"Well, not when you say it that way," Liat said. "I was thinking of it as coming to know him again before the conflict began. I did love him, you know."

"And now?"

"And still. I still love him, in my fashion," Liat said, her voice rueful. "I know I'm not what he wants. I'm not the person he wants me to be, and I doubt I ever have been, truly. But we enjoy each other. There are things we can say to each other that no one else would understand. They weren't there, and we were. And he's such a little boy. He's carried so much and been so disappointed, and there's still the possibility in him of this . . . *joy*. I can't explain it."

"If I ask you as a favor, will you let me know him as well? We may not actually fight like pit dogs if you let us in the same room together. And if there's conflict at all, it's between us. Not you."

Liat opened her mouth, closed it, shook her head. She sighed.

"Of course," she said. "Of course, I'm sorry. I've been an old hen, and I'm sorry for it, but . . . I know it's not a trade. We aren't negotiating, not really. But Nayiit-kya, you can't say you haven't been with a woman since we've come here. You didn't choose to go south, even when I asked you to. Sweet, is it so bad at home?"

"Bad?" he said, speaking slowly. As if tasting the word. "I don't know. No. Not bad. Only not good. And yes, I know I haven't been keeping to my own bed. Do you think my darling wife has been keeping to hers?"

Liat's mind turned, searching for words, making sense as best she could of what he had asked and what he had meant by it. It was true enough that Tai had come into the world at an odd time, but he was a first child, and wombs weren't made to be certain. She rushed through her memory, looking for signs she might have missed, suggestions back in their lives in Saraykeht that would have pointed at some venomous question, and slowly she began, if not to understand, then at least to guess.

"You think he isn't yours," she said. "You think Tai is another man's child."

"Nothing like that," Nayiit said. "It's only that you can make a child from love or from anger. Or inattention. Or only from not knowing what better to do. A baby isn't proof of anything between the father and mother beyond a few moments' pressure."

"It isn't the child's fault."

"No, I suppose not," Nayiit said.

"This is why you came, then? To Nantani, and then up here? To be away from them?"

"I came because I wanted to. Because it was the world, and when was I going to see it again? Because you wanted someone to carry your bags and wave off dogs. It was only partly that I couldn't stay. And then when you were going to see him, Maati-cha . . . How could I not come along for that too? The chance to see my father again. I remember him, you know? I do, from when I was small, I remember a day we were all in a small hut. There was an iron stove, and it was raining, and you were singing while he bathed me. I don't know when that was, I can't put a time on it. But I remember his face."

"You would have known him, if you'd seen him in passing. You'd have known who he was."

Nayiit took a pose of affirmation. He pursed his lips and chuckled ruefully.

"I don't know what it is to be a father. I'm only working from—"

"Nayiit-kya?" came a voice from the shadows behind them. A soft, feminine voice. "Is everything well?"

She stepped toward the light. A young woman, twenty summers, perhaps as many as twenty-two. She wore bedding tied around her waist, her breasts bare, her hair still wild from the pillows.

"Jaaya-cha, this is my mother. Mother, Jaaya Biavu."

The girl blanched, then flushed. She took a pose of welcome, not bothering to cover herself, but her gaze was on Nayiit. It spoke of both humiliation and contempt. Nayiit didn't look at her. The woman turned and stalked away.

"That wasn't kind," Liat said.

"Very little of what she and I do involves kindness," he said. "I don't expect I'll see her again. By which I mean, I don't suppose she'll see me."

"Is she politically connected? If her family is utkhaiem . . ."

"I don't think she is," Nayiit said, his face in his hands. It was hard to be sure in the firelight, but she thought the tips of his ears were blushing. "I suppose I should have asked."

He struggled for a moment, trying to speak and failing. His brow furrowed and Liat had to resist the urge to reach over and smooth it with her thumb, the way she had when he'd been a babe.

"I'm sorry," he said. "You know that I'm sorry."

"For what?" she asked, her voice low and stern. As if there were any number of things for which he might be.

"For not being a better man," he said.

The fire popped, as if in comment. Liat took her son's hand, and for a long moment, they were silent. Then:

"I don't care what you do with your marriage, Nayiit-kya. If you don't love her, end it. Or if you don't trust her. As you see fit. People come together and they part. It's what we do. But the boy. You can't leave the boy. That isn't fair."

"It's what Maati-cha did to us."

"No," Liat said, giving his hand the smallest pressure, and then releasing it. "We left him."

Nayiit turned to her slowly, his hands folding into a pose that asked confirmation. It was as if the words were too dangerous to speak.

"I left him," Liat said. "I took you when you were still a babe, and I was the one to leave him."

She saw a moment's shock in his expression, gone as fast as it had come. His face went grave, his hands as still as stones. As still as a man bending his will to keep them still.

"Why?" he asked. His voice was low and thready.

"Oh, love. It was so long ago. I was someone else, then," she said, and knew as she said it that it wasn't enough. "I did because he was only half there. And because I couldn't see to all of his needs and all of yours and have no one there to look after me."

"It was better without him?"

"I thought it would be. I thought I was cutting my losses. And then, later, when I wasn't so certain anymore, I convinced myself it had been the right thing, just so I could tell myself I hadn't been wrong."

He was shaken, though he tried to cover it. She knew him too well to be fooled.

"He wasn't there, Nayiit. But he never left you."

And part of me never left him, she thought. What would the world have been if I had chosen otherwise? Where would we all be now if that part of him and of me had been enough? Still in that little hut in the low town near the Dai-kvo? Would they all have lived together in the library these past years as Maati had?

Those other, ghostlike people made a pretty dream, but then there would have been no one to hear of the Galts and the missing poet, no one to travel to Nantani. And little Tai would not have been born, and she would never have seen Amat Kyaan again. Someone else would have been with the old woman when she died—someone else or no one. And Liat would never have taken House Kyaan, would never have proven herself competent to the world and to her own satisfaction.

It was too much. The changes, the differences were too great to think of as good or as bad. The world they had now was too much itself, good and evil too tightly woven to wish for some other path. And still it would be wrong to say she found herself without regrets.

"Maati loves you," she said, softly. "You should see him. I won't interfere again. But first, you should go tend to your guest. Smooth things over."

Nayiit nodded, and then a moment later, he smiled. It was the same charming smile she'd known when she was a girl and it had been on different lips. Nayiit would charm the girl, say something sweet and funny, and the pain would be forgotten for a time. He was his father's son. Son of the Khai Machi. Eldest son, and doomed to the fratricidal struggle of succession that stained every city in each generation. She wondered how far Otah would go to avoid that, to keep his boy safe from her schemes. That conversation had to come, and soon. Perhaps it would be best if she took it to the Khai herself, if she stopped waiting for him to find a right moment.

Nayiit took a querying pose, and Liat shook herself. She waved his concern away.

"I'm tired," she said. "I've come all this way back to have my own bed to myself, and I'm still not in it. I'm too old to sleep in a lover's arms. They twitch and snore and keep me awake all night."

"They do, don't they?" Nayiit said. "Does it get better, do you think? With enough time, would you be so accustomed to it, you'd sleep through?"

"I don't know," Liat said. "I've never made the attempt."

"Like mother, like son, I suppose," Nayiit said as he rose. He bent and kissed the crown of her head before he retreated back into the shadows.

Like mother, like son.

Liat pulled her robe tighter and sat near the fire, as if touched by a sudden chill.

7

>+< The jeweler was a small man, squat but broad. To his credit, he seemed truly ill at ease. It took courage, Otah thought as he listened, to bring a matter such as this before a Khai. He wondered how many others had seen something of the sort and looked away. Any merchant has to expect some losses from theft. And after all, she was the daughter of the Khai. . . .

When it was over—and it seemed to take half a day, though it couldn't have lasted more than half a hand—Otah thanked the man, ordered that payment be made to him, and waited calm and emotionless until the servants and court followers had gone. Only the body servants remained, half a dozen men and women of the utkhaiem who dedicated their lives to bringing him a cracker if he felt like one, or a cup of limed water.

"Find Eiah and take her to the blue chamber. Bring her under guard if you have to."

"Under guard?" the eldest of the servants said.

"No, don't. Just bring her. See that she gets there."

"Most High," the man said, taking a pose that accepted the command. Otah rose and walked out of the room without replying. He stalked the halls of the palace, ignoring the Master of Tides and his ineffectual flapping papers, ignoring the poses of obeisance and respect turned to him wherever he went, looking only for Kiyan. The rest of these people were unimportant.

He found her in the great kitchens, standing beside the chief cook with a dead chicken in her hands. The cook, a woman of not less than sixty summers who had served Otah's father and grandfather, met his eyes and went pale. He wondered belatedly how many times the previous Khaiem of Machi had visited their kitchens, great or low.

"What's happened?" Kiyan asked instead of a greeting.

"Not here," Otah said. His wife nodded, passed the bird's carcass back to the cook, and followed Otah to their rooms. As calmly as he could, Otah related the audience. Eiah and two of her friends—Talit Radaani and Shoyen Pak—had visited a jeweler's shop in the goldsmiths' quarter. Eiah had stolen a brooch of emerald and pearl. The jeweler and his boy had seen it, had come to the court asking for payment.

"He was quite polite about the whole thing," Otah said. "He cast it as a mistake. Eiah-cha, in her girlish flights of attention, forgot to arrange for payment. He was sorry to bother me with it, but he hadn't been sure who I would prefer such issues be taken to and on and on and on. Gods!"

"How much was it?" Kiyan asked.

"Three lengths of gold," Otah said. "Not that it matters. I've got the whole city to put on for taxes and half a thousand bits of jewelry in boxes that no one's worn in lifetimes. It's . . . She's a thief! She's going through the city, taking whatever catches her eye and . . ."

Otah ran out of words and had to make do with a rough, frustrated grunt. He threw himself down on a couch, shaking his head.

"It's my fault," he said. "I've been too busy with the court. I haven't been a decent father to her. All the time she's spent with the daughters of the utkhaiem, playing idiot court games about who has the prettiest dress or the most servants—"

"Or the highest marriage," Kiyan said.

Otah put his hand over his eyes. That was more than he could think about just now. How to correct his daughter, how to show her what she'd done wasn't right, how to try to be a father to her; yes, that he could sit with. That it was too late, that she was already old enough to be another man's wife; that was too much to bear.

"It's a problem, love, yes," Kiyan said. "But sweet. She's fourteen summers old. She stole a pretty thing to see if she could. It's not actually unusual. I was a year older than her when my father caught me sneaking apples off the back of a farmer's cart."

"And did he marry you off to the farmer in punishment?"

"I'm sorry I brought up the marriage. I only meant that Eiah's world's no simpler than ours. It only seems that way from here. To her, it's just as confused and difficult as anything you deal with. She's only half a girl, and not quite half a woman."

Kiyan frowned. Her eyes were rueful and resigned, and she stretched her arms until the elbows cracked.

"My father made me apologize to the farmer and work for the man until I'd earned back twice the cost of what I'd taken. I don't know that's much guidance for us, though. I don't think any of these girls could do work worth three lengths of gold."

"So what do we do?"

"It doesn't matter, love. As long as she's clear that what she did didn't end the way she'd hoped, we'll have come as close as we can. I'd say restrict her from seeing Talit Radaani for a week's time, but that hardly seems equal to the stakes."

"She could assist the physicians," Otah said. "Carry out the night pans, wash dressings for the hurt. A week of that to pay back the city for what it bought her."

Kiyan chuckled.

"So long as she doesn't start enjoying it. She plays at being repulsed by blood because it's expected of her. I think at heart, there's nothing she'd like more than to cut a body apart and see how it's built. She'd have made a fine physician if she'd been born a bit lower."

They talked a bit longer, and Otah felt his rage and uncertainty fade. Kiyan's quiet, sane, thoughtful voice was the most soothing thing he knew. She was right. It wasn't strange, it wasn't a sign that Eiah would grow up to be her aunt Idaan, scheming and killing and lying for the pleasure of it. It was a girl of fourteen summers seeing how far she could go, and the answer was not so far as this. Otah kissed Kiyan before they left, his lips on her cheek. She smiled. There were crow's-feet at the corners of her eyes now. White strands had shot her hair since she'd been young, but there were more now. Her eyes still glittered as they had when he'd met her in Udun when she'd been the keep of a wayhouse and he had been a courier. She seemed to sense his thoughts, and put her hand to his cheek.

"Shall we go be the troll-like, unfair, unfeeling, stupid, venal dispensers of unjust punishment?" she asked.

The blue chamber was wide and round, a table of white marble dominating it like a sheet of ice floating in a far northern sea. The windows looked out on the gardens through walls so thick that sparrows and grackles perched in the sills and pecked at the carved meshwork of the inner shutters. Eiah had been pacing, but stopped when they came in. She looked from one to the other, trying for an innocence of expression that she couldn't quite reach.

"Come, sit," Kiyan said, gesturing to the table. Eiah came forward as if against her will and sat in one of the carved wooden chairs. Her gaze darted between the two of them, her chin already beginning to slide forward.

"I understand you took something from a jeweler. A brooch," Otah said. "Is that true?"

"Who told you that?" Eiah asked.

"Is it true?" Otah repeated, and his daughter looked down. When she frowned, the same small vertical line appeared between her brows that would sometimes show Kiyan's distress. Otah felt the passing urge to soothe her fears, but this wasn't the moment for comfort. He scowled until she looked up, then down again, and nodded. Kiyan sighed.

"Who told you?" Eiah asked again. "It was Shoyen, wasn't it? She's jealous because Talit and I were—"

"You told us, just now," Otah said. "That's all that matters."

Eiah's lips closed hard. Kiyan took a turn, telling Eiah that she'd done wrong, and they all knew it. Even she had to know that simply taking things wasn't right. They had paid her debt, but now she would have to make it good herself. They had decided that she would work with the physicians for a week, and if she didn't go, the physicians had instructions to send for . . .

"I'm not going to," Eiah said. "It's not fair. Talit Radaani sneaks things out of her father's warehouse all the time and no one ever makes her do anything for it."

"I can see that changes," Otah said.

"Don't!" Eiah barked. The birds startled away; a flutter of wings that sounded like panic. "Don't you dare! Talit will hate me forever if she thinks I'm making her . . . Papa-kya! Please, don't do that."

"It might be wise," Kiyan said. "All three girls were party to it."

"You can't! You can't do that to me!" Eiah's eyes were wild. She pushed back the chair as she stood. "I'll tell them Nayiit's your son! I'll tell!"

Otah felt the air go out of the room. Eiah's eyes went wide, aware that she had just done something worse than stealing a bauble, but unsure what it was. Only Kiyan seemed composed and calm. She smiled dangerously.

"Sit down, love," she said. "Please. Sit."

Eiah sat. Otah clasped his hands hard enough the knuckles ached, but there weren't words for the mix of guilt and shame and anger and sorrow. His heart was too many things at once. Kiyan didn't look at him when she spoke; her gaze was on Eiah.

"You will never repeat what you've just said to anyone. Nayiit-cha is Liat's son by Maati. Because if he isn't, if he's the thing you just said, then he will have to kill Danat or Danat will have to kill him. And when that happens, the blood will be on your hands, because you could have prevented it and chose not to. Don't speak. I'm not finished. If any of the houses of the utkhaiem thought Danat was not the one and only man who could take his father's place, some of them would start thinking of killing him themselves in expectation of Nayiit-cha favoring them once he became Khai Machi. I can't protect him from everyone in this city, any more than I can protect him from air or his own body. You have done a wrong thing, stealing. And if you truly mean to hold your brother's life hostage to keep from being chastised for it, I would like to know that now."

Eiah wept silently, shocked by the cold fire in Kiyan's voice. Otah felt as if he'd been slapped as well. As if he ought somehow to have known, all those years ago, in that distant city, that the consequences of taking to his lover's bed would come back again to threaten everything he held dear. His daughter took a pose that begged her mother's forgiveness.

"I won't, Mama-kya. I won't say anything. Not ever."

"You'll apologize to the man you stole from and you will go in the morning to the physician's house and do whatever they ask of you. I will decide what to do about Talit and Shoyen."

"Yes, Mama-kya."

"You can leave now," Kiyan said and looked away. Eiah rose, silent except for the rough breath of tears, and left the room. The door closed behind her.

"I'm sorry—"

"Don't," Kiyan said. "Not now. I can't . . . I don't want to hear it just now."

Otah rose and walked to the window. The sun was high, but the towers cast shadows across the city all the same, like trees above children. Far to the west, clouds were gathering over the mountains, towering white thunderheads with bases dark as a bruise. There would be a storm later. It would come. One of the sparrows returned, considered Otah once with each eye, and then flew away again.

"What would you ask me to do?" Otah said. His voice was placid. No one would have known from the words how much pain lay behind them. No one except Kiyan. "I can't unmake him. Should I have him killed?"

"How did Eiah know?" Kiyan asked.

"She saw. Or she guessed. She knew the way that you did."

"No one told her? Maati or Liat or Nayiit. None of them told her?"

"No."

"You're sure?"

"I am."

"Because if they did, if they're spreading it through the city that you have—"

"They aren't. I was there when she realized it. Only me. No one else."

Kiyan took a long, low, shuddering breath. If it had been otherwise—if someone had told Eiah as part of a plan to spread word of Nayiit's parentage—Kiyan would have asked him to have the boy killed. He wondered what he would have done. He wondered how he would have refused her.

"They'll leave the city as soon as we have word from the Dai-kvo," Otah said. "Either they'll go back to Saraykeht or they'll go to the Dai-kvo's village. Either way, they'll be gone from here."

"And if they come back?"

"They won't. I'll see to it. They won't hurt Danat, love. He's safe."

"He's ill. He's still coughing," Kiyan said. That was it too, of course. Seasons had come and gone, and Danat was still haunted by illness. It was natural for them—Kiyan and himself both—to bend themselves double to protect him from the dangers that they could, especially since there were so many so close over which they were powerless.

It was part of why Otah had postponed for so long the conversation he was doomed to have with Liat Chokavi. But it was only part. Kiyan's chair scraped against the floor as she rose. Otah put his hand out to her, and she took it, stepping in close to him, her arms around him. He kissed her temple.

"Promise me this all ends well," she said. "Just tell me that."

"It will be fine," he said. "Nothing's going to hurt our boy."

They stood silently for a time, looking at each other, and then out at the city. The plumes of smoke rising from the forges, the black-cobbled streets and gray slanted roofs. The sun slipped behind the clouds or else the clouds rose to block the light. The knock that interrupted them was sharp and urgent.

"Most High?" a man's voice said. "Most High, forgive me, but the poets wish to speak with you. Maati-cha says the issue is urgent."

Kiyan walked with him, her hand in his, as they went to the Council chamber where Maati waited. His face was flushed, his mouth set in a deep scowl. A packet of paper fluttered in his hand, the edges rough where he'd ripped them rather than take the labor of unsewing the sheets. Cehmai and Stone-Made-Soft were also there, the poet pacing restlessly, the andat smiling its placid, inhuman smile at each of them in turn.

"News from the Dai-kvo?" Otah asked.

"No, the couriers we sent west," Cehmai said.

Maati tossed the pages to the table as he spoke. "The Galts have fielded an army."

THE THIRD LEGION ARRIVED ON A BRIGHT MORNING, THE SUN SHINING ON THE polished metal and oiled leather of their armor as if they'd been expecting a victory parade instead of the start of a war. Balasar watched from the walls of the city as they arrived and made camp. The sight was so welcome, even the smell of a hundred and a half camp latrines couldn't undermine his pleasure.

They were later even than they'd expected, and with stories and excuses to explain the delay. Balasar, leaning against the map table, listened and kept his expression calm as the officers apprised him of the legion's state—the men, the food, the horses, the steam wagons, the armor, the arms. Mentally, he put the information into the vast map that was the campaign, but even as he did, he felt the wolfish grin coming to his lips. These were the last of his forces to come into place. The hour was almost upon him. The war was about to begin.

He listened as patiently as he could, gave his orders on the disposition of their men and matériel, and told them not to get comfortable. When they were gone, Eustin came in alone, the same excitement that Balasar felt showing on his face.

"What's next, sir? The poet?"

"The poet," Balasar said, leading the way out the door.

They found Riaan in the Warden's private courtyard. He was sitting in the wide shade of a catalpa tree heavy with wide, white blooms and wide leaves the same green as the poet's robes. He'd had someone bring out a wide divan for him to lounge on. Across a small table, the Khaiate mercenary captain was perched on a stool. Both men were frowning at a handful of stones laid out in a short arc. The captain rose when he caught sight of them. The poet only glanced up, annoyed. Balasar took a pose of greeting, and the poet replied with something ornate that he couldn't entirely make sense of. The glitter in the captain's eyes suggested that the complexity was intentional and not entirely complimentary. Balasar put the insult, whatever it was, aside. There was no call to catalog more reasons to kill the man.

"Sinja-cha," Balasar said. "I need to speak with the great poet in private."

"Of course," the captain said, then turning to Riaan with a formal pose, "We can finish the game later if you like."

Riaan nodded and waved, the movement half permission for Sinja to go, half shooing him away. The amusement in the captain's eyes didn't seem to lessen. Eustin escorted the man away, and when they were alone, Balasar took the vacated stool.

"My men are in place," he said. "The time's come."

He kept his gaze on the poet, looking for reluctance or unease in his eyes. But Riaan smiled slowly, like a man who had heard that his dearest enemy had died, and laced his fingers together on his belly. Balasar had half-expected the poet to repent, to change his mind when faced with the prospect of the deed itself. There was nothing of that.

"Tomorrow morning," Riaan said. "I will need a servant to attend me today and through the night. At first light tomorrow, I will prove that the Dai-kvo was a fool to send me away. And then I shall march to my father's house with your army behind me like a flood."

Balasar grinned. He had never seen a man so shortsighted, vain, and petty, and he'd spent three seasons in Acton with his father and the High Council. As far as the poet was concerned, none of this was for anything more important than the greater glory of Riaan Vaudathat.

"How can we serve you in this?" Balasar asked.

"Everything is already prepared. I must only begin my meditations."

It sounded like dismissal to Balasar. He rose, bowing to the poet.

"I will send my most trusted servant," he said. "Should anything more arise, only send word, and I will see it done."

Riaan smiled condescendingly and nodded his head. But as Balasar was just leaving the garden, the poet called his name. A cloud had come over the man, some ghost of uncertainty that had not risen from the prospect of binding.

"Your men," the poet said. "They have been instructed that my family is not to be touched, yes?"

"Of course," Balasar said.

"And the library. The city is, of course, yours to do with as you see fit, but without the libraries of the Khaiem, binding a second andat will be much more difficult. They aren't to be entered by any man but me."

"Of course," Balasar said again, and the poet took a pose accepting his assurances. The concern didn't leave Riaan's brow, though. So perhaps the man wasn't quite as dim as he seemed. Balasar told himself, as he strode back through the covered pathways to his own rooms, that he would have to be more careful with him in the future. Not that there was much future for him. Win or lose, Riaan was a dead man.

The day seemed more real than the ones that had come before it: the sunlight clearer, the air more alive with the scents of flowers and sewage and grass. The stones of the walls seemed more interesting, the subtle differences in color and texture clear where previous days had made them only a field of gray. Even Balasar's body hummed with energy. It was like being a boy again, and diving into the lake from the highest cliff—the one all the other boys feared to jump from. It was dread and joy and the sense of no longer being able to take his decision back. It was what Balasar lived for. He knew already that he would not sleep.

Eustin was waiting for him in the entrance hall.

"There's someone wants a word with you, sir."

Balasar paused.

"The Khaiate captain. He wanted to speak about fallback plans for his men."

Eustin nodded to a side room. There was distrust in his expression, and Balasar waited a long moment for him to speak. Eustin added nothing. Balasar went to the wide, dark oaken door, knocked once, and went in. It was a preparation room for servants—muddy boots cast beside benches and waiting to be scraped clean, cloaks of all weights and colors hung from pegs. It smelled of wet dog, though there was no animal present. The captain sat on a stool tilted back against the wall, cleaning his nails with a knife.

"Captain Ajutani," Balasar said.

The stool came down, and the captain rose, sheathing his blade and bowing in the same motion.

"I appreciate the time, General," he said. "I know you've a great deal on your mind just now."

"I'm always available," Balasar said. "Though the surroundings are . . ."

"Yes. Your man Eustin seemed to think it more appropriate for me to wait here. I'm not sure he likes me." The captain was more amused than offended, so Balasar also smiled and shrugged.

"Your men are in place?" he asked.

"Yes, yes. Broken into groups of three or four, each assigned to one of your sergeants. Except for myself, of course."

"Of course."

"Only I wanted to ask something of you, General. A favor of sorts."

Balasar crossed his arms and nodded for the man to continue.

"If it fails—if our friend Riaan doesn't do his magic trick well enough—don't kill them. My boys. Don't have them killed."

"Why would I do that?" Balasar asked.

"Because it's the right thing," Sinja said. The amusement was gone from the man's eyes. He was in earnest now. "I'm not an idiot, General. If it happens that the binding fails, you'll be standing here in Aren with an army the size of a modest city. People have already noticed it, and the curiosity of the Khaiem is the last thing you'd want. They'd still have their andat, and all you'd have is explanations to give. You'll turn North and make all those stories about conquering the whole of the Westlands to the border with Eddensea true just to make all this—" The captain gestured to the door at Balasar's back. "—seem plausible. All I ask is, let us go with you. If it happens that you have to keep to this coast and not the cities of the Khaiem, I'll re-form the group and lead them wherever you like."

"I wouldn't kill them," Balasar said.

"It would be dangerous, letting them go back home. Stories about how they were set to be interpreters and guides? Not one of them knows the Westlands except the part we walked through to get here. If the Khaiem are wondering whether you had some other plan to start with . . ."

Sinja raised his hands, palms up as if he were offering Balasar the truth resting there. Balasar stepped close, putting his own hands below the captain's and curling the other man's fingers closed.

"I won't kill them," Balasar said. "They're my men now, and I don't kill my own. You can tell them that if you'd like. And that aside, Riaan isn't going to fail us."

Sinja looked down, his head shifting as if he were weighing something.

"I can be sure," Balasar said, answering the unasked question.

"I've never seen one of these before," Sinja said. "Have you? I mean, I assume there's some ceremony, and he'll do something. If there was an andat beside him at the end, you'd have proof, but this thing you're doing . . . there's nothing to show, is there? So how will you know?"

"It *would* be embarrassing to walk into Nantani and have the andat waiting to greet us," Balasar agreed. "But don't let it concern you. Riaan isn't going to mumble into the air and send us all off to die. I'll be certain of that."

"You have a runner in Nantani? Someone who can bring word when the andat's vanished?"

"Don't concern yourself, Sinja," Balasar said. "Just be ready to move when I say and in the direction I choose."

"Yes, General."

Balasar turned and strode to the door. He could see Eustin standing close, his hand on his sword. It was a reassuring sight.

"Captain Ajutani," Balasar said over his shoulder. "What were you speaking to Riaan about before we came?"

"Himself mostly," the captain said. "Is there another subject he's interested in?"

"He was concerned when I spoke with him. Concerned with things that never seemed to occur to him before. You wouldn't have anything to do with that, would you?"

"No, General," Sinja said. "Wouldn't be any profit in it."

Balasar nodded and resumed the path to his rooms. Eustin fell in beside him.

"I don't like that man," Eustin said under his breath. "I don't trust him."

"I do," Balasar said. "I trust him to be and to have always been my staunchest supporter just as soon as he's sure we're going to win. He's a mercenary, but he isn't a spy. And his men will be useful."

"Still."

"It will be fine."

Balasar didn't give his uncertainties and fears free rein until he was safely alone in the borrowed library, and then his mind rioted. Perhaps Sinja was right—the poet could fail, the Khaiem could divine his purpose, the destruction he'd dedicated himself to preventing might be brought about by his miscalculation. Everything might still fail. A thousand threats and errors clamored.

He took out his maps again for the thousandth time. Each road was marked on the thin sheepskin. Each bridge and ford. Each city. Fourteen cities in a single season. They would take Nantani and then scatter. The other forces would come in from the sea. It was nearing summer, and he told himself again and again as if hoping to convince himself that after the sun rose tomorrow, it would be a question only of speed.

In the first battle he'd fought, Balasar had been a crossbowman. He and a dozen like him were supposed to loose their bolts into the packed, charging bodies of the warriors of Eymond and then pull back, letting the men with swords and axes and flails—men like his father—move in and take up the melee. He'd hardly been a boy at the time, much less a man. He had done as he was told, as had the others, but once they were safely over the rise of the hill, out of sight of the enemy and the battle, Balasar had been stupid. The grunts and shrieks and noise of bodies in conflict were like a peal of thunder that never faded. The sound called to him. With each shriek from the battle, he imagined that it had been his father. The nightmare images of the violence happening just over the rise chewed at him. He'd had to see it. He had gone back over. It had almost cost him his life.

One of the soldiers of Eymond had spotted him. He'd been a large man, tall as a tree it had seemed at the time. He'd broken away from the fight and rushed up the hill, axe raised and blood on his mind. Balasar remembered the panic when he understood that his own death was rushing up the hill toward him. The wise thing would have been to flee; if he could have gotten back to the other bowmen, they might have killed the soldier. But instead, without thought, he started to bend back the leaves of the crossbow, fumbling the bolt with fingers that had seemed numb as sausages. Though only one of them was running, it had been a race.

When he'd raised the bow and loosed the bolt, the man had been fewer than ten feet from him. He could still feel the thrum of the string and feel the sinking certainty that he had missed, that his life was forfeit. In point of fact, the bolt had sunk so deep into the man it only seemed to have vanished. The breaths between when he'd fired and when the soldier sank to the ground were the longest he had ever known.

And here he was again. Only this time he was the one in motion. The poets of the Khaiem would have a chance to call up another of the andat—and the measure of that hope was his speed in finding them, killing them, and burning their books.

It was a terrible wager, and more than his own life was in the balance. Balasar was not a religious man. Questions of gods and heavens had always seemed too abstract to him. But now, putting aside the maps, the plans, all the work of his life prepared to find its fruition or else its ruin, he walked to the window, watched the full moon rising over this last night of the world as it had been, and put his hand to his heart, praying to all the gods he knew with a single word.

Please.

8

>+< Twilight came after the long sunset, staining red the high clouds in the west. A light wind had come from the North, carrying the chill of mountaintop glaciers with it, though there was little snow left on even the highest peaks that could be seen from the city. It grabbed at the loose shutters, banging them open and closed like an idiot child in love with the noise. Banners rippled and trees nodded like old men. It was as if an errant breath of winter had stolen into the warm nights. Otah sat in his private chambers, still in his formal robes. He felt no drafts, but the candles flickered in sympathy with the wind.

The letters unfolded before him were in a simple cipher. The years he had spent in the gentleman's trade, carrying letters and contracts and information on the long roads between the cities of the Khaiem, returned to him, and he read the enciphered text as easily as if it had been written plainly. It was as Maati and Cehmai had said. The Wards of the Westlands were united in a state of panic. The doom of the world seemed about to fall upon them.

Since the letters had arrived, Otah's world had centered on the news. He had sent another runner to the Dai-kvo with a pouch so heavy with lengths of silver, the man could have bought a fresh horse at every low town he passed through if it would get him there faster. Otah had sat up long nights with Maati and Cehmai, even with Liat and Nayiit. Here was the plan, then. With the threat of an andat of their own, the Galts would roll through the Westlands, perhaps Eddensea as well. In a year, perhaps two, they might own Bakta and Eymond too. The cities of the Khaiem would find themselves cut off from trade, and perhaps the rogue poet would even become a kind of Galtic Dai-kvo in time. The conquest of the Westlands was the first campaign in a new war that might make the destruction of the Old Empire seem minor.

And still, Otah read the letters again, his mind unquiet. There was something there, something more, that he had overlooked. The certainty of the Galts, their willingness to show their power. Whenever they tired of trade or felt themselves losing at the negotiating tables, Galt had been pleased to play raider and pirate. It had been that way for as long as Otah could remember. The Galtic High Council had schemed and conspired. It shouldn't have been odd that, emboldened by success, they would take to the field. And yet . . .

Otah turned the pages with a sound as dry as autumn leaves. They couldn't be attacking the Khaiem; even with an andat in their possession, they would be overwhelmed. The cities might have their rivalries and disputes, but an attack on one would unite them against their common foe. Thirteen cities each with its own poet added to whatever the Dai-kvo held in reserve in his village. At worst, more than a dozen to one, and each of them capable of destruction on a scale almost impossible to imagine. The Galts wouldn't dare attack the Khaiem. It was posturing. Negotiation. It might even be a bluff; the poet might have tried his binding, paid the price of failure, and left the Galts with nothing but bluster to defend themselves.

Otah had heard all these arguments, had made more than one of them himself. And still night found him here, reading the letters and searching for the thoughts behind them. It was like hearing a new voice in a choir. Somewhere, someone new had entered the strategies of the Galts, and these scraps of paper and pale ink were all that Otah had to work out what that might mean.

He could as well have looked for words written in the air.

A scratching came at the door, followed by a servant boy. The boy took a pose of obeisance and Otah replied automatically.

"The woman you sent for, Most High. Liat Chokavi."

"Bring her in. And bring some wine and two bowls, then see we aren't disturbed."

"But, Most High—"

"We'll pour our own wine," Otah snapped, and regretted it instantly as the boy's face went pale. Otah pressed down the impulse to apologize. It was beneath the dignity of the Khai Machi to apologize for rudeness—one of the thousand things he'd learned when he first took his father's chair. One of the thousand missteps he had made. The boy backed out of the room, and Otah turned to the letters, folding them back in their order and slipping them into his sleeve. The boy preceded Liat into the room, a tray with a silver carafe and two hand-molded bowls of granite in his hands. Liat sat on the low divan, her eyes on the floor in something that looked like respect but might only have been fear.

The door closed, and Otah poured a generous portion of wine into each bowl. Liat took the one he proffered.

"It's lovely work," Liat said, considering the stone.

"It's the andat," Otah said. "He turns the quarry rock into something like clay, and the potters shape it. One of the many wonders of Machi. Have you seen the bridge that spans the river? A single stone poured over molds and shaped by hand five generations back. And there's the towers. Really, we're a city of petty miracles."

"You sound bitter," she said, looking up at last. Her eyes were the same tea-and-milk color he remembered. Otah sighed as he sat across from her. Outside, the wind murmured.

"I'm not," he said. "Only tired."

"I knew you wouldn't end as a seafront laborer," she said.

"Yes, well . . ." Otah shook his head and sipped from the bowl. It was strong wine, and it left his mouth feeling clean and his chest warm. "It's time we spoke about Nayiit."

Liat nodded, took a long drink, and held the cup out for more. Otah poured.

"It's all my fault," she said as she sat back. "I should never have brought him here. I never saw it. I never saw you in him. He was always just himself. If I'd known that . . . that he resembled you quite so closely, I wouldn't have."

"Late for that," Otah said.

Liat sighed her agreement and looked up at him. It was hard to believe that they had been lovers once. The girl he had known back then hadn't had gray in her hair, weariness in her eyes. And the boy he'd been was as distant as snow in summer. Yes, two people had kissed once, had touched each other, had created a child who had grown to manhood. And Otah remembered some of those moments now—showering at the barracks while she spoke to him, the ink blocks at the desk in her cell at the compound of House Wilsin, the feel of a young body pressed against his own, when his flesh had also been new and unmarked. If those days long past had been foolish or wrong, the only evidence was the price they both paid now. It hadn't seemed so at the time.

"I've been thinking of it," Liat said. "I haven't told him. I wasn't sure how you wanted to address the problem. But I think the wisest thing to do is to speak with him and with Maati, and then have Nayiit-kya take the brand. I know it's not something done with firstborn sons, but it's still a repudiation of his right to become Khai. It will make it clear to the world that he doesn't have designs on your chair."

"That isn't what I'd choose," Otah said. His words were slow and careful. "I'm afraid my son may die."

She caught her breath. It was hardly there, no more than a tremor in the air she took in, but he heard it.

"Itani," she said, using the name of the boy he'd been in Saraykeht, "please. I'll swear on anything you choose. Nayiit's no threat to Danat. It was only the Galts that brought us here. I'm not looking to put my son in your chair. . . ."

Otah put down his bowl and took a pose that asked for her silence. Her face pale, she went quiet.

"I don't mean that," he said softly. "I mean that I don't . . . Gods. I don't know how to say this. Danat's not well. His lungs are fragile, and the winters here are bad. We lose people to the cold every year. Not just the old or the weak. Young people. Healthy ones. I'm afraid that Danat may die, and there'll be no one to take my place. The city would tear itself apart."

"But . . . you want . . ."

"I haven't done a good job as Khai. I haven't been able to put the houses of the utkhaiem together except in their distrust of me and resentment of Kiyan. There's been twice it came near violence, and I only held the city in place by luck. But keeping Machi safe is my responsibility. I want Nayiit unbranded, in case . . . in case he becomes my successor."

Liat's mouth hung open, her eyes were wide. A stray lock of hair hung down the side of her face, three white hairs dancing in and out among the black. He felt the faint urge—echo of a habit long forgotten—to brush it back.

"There," Otah said and picked up his wine bowl. "There, I've said it."

"I'm sorry," Liat said, and Otah took a pose accepting her sympathy without knowing quite why she was offering it. She looked down at her hands. The silence between them was profound but not uncomfortable; he felt no need to speak, to fill the void with words. Liat drank her wine, Otah his. The wind muttered to itself and to the stones of the city.

"It's not a job I'd want," Liat said. "Khai Machi."

"It's all power and no freedom," Otah said. "If Nayiit were to have it, he'd likely curse my name. There are a thousand different things to attend to, and every one of them as serious as bone to someone. You can't do it all."

"I know how it feels," Liat said. "I only have a trading house to look after, and there's days I wish that it would all go away. Granted, I have men who work the books and the negotiations and appeals before the low judges and the utkhaiem . . ."

"I have all the low judges and the utkhaiem appealing to me," Otah said. "It's never enough."

"There's always the descent into decadence and self-absorption," Liat said, smiling. It was only half a joke. "They say the Khai Chaburi-Tan only gets sober long enough to bed his latest wife."

"Tempting," Otah said, "but somewhere between taking the chair to protect Kiyan and tonight, it became my city. I came from here, and even if I'm not much good at what I do, I'm what they have."

"That makes sense," Liat said.

"Does it? It doesn't to me."

Liat put down her bowl and rose. He thought her gaze spoke of determination and melancholy, but perhaps the latter was only his own. She stepped close and kissed him on the cheek, a firm peck like an aunt greeting a favorite nephew.

"Amat Kyaan would have understood," she said. "I won't tell Nayiit about this. If anyone asks, I'll deny it unless I hear differently from you."

"Thank you, Liat-cha."

She stepped back. Otah felt a terrible weariness bearing him down, but forced a charming smile. She shook her head.

"Thank *you*, Most High."

"I don't think I've done anything worth thanking me."

"You let my son live," Liat said. "That was one of the decisions you had to make, wasn't it?"

She took his silence as an answer, smiled again, and left him alone. Otah poured the last of the wine from carafe to bowl, and then watched the light die in the west as he finished it; watched the stars come out, and the full moon rise. With every day, the light lasted longer. It would not always. High summer would come, and even when the days were at their warmest, when the trees and vines grew heavy with fruit, the nights would already have started their slow expansion. He wondered whether Danat would get to play outside in the autumn, whether the boy would be able to spend a long afternoon lying in the sunlight before the snows came and drove them all down to the tunnels. He was raising a child to live in darkness and planning for his death.

There had been a time Otah had been young and sure enough of himself to kill. He had taken the life of a good man because they both had known the price that would have to be paid if he lived. He had been able to do that.

But he had seen forty-eight summers now. There were likely fewer seasons before him than there were behind. He'd fathered three children and raised two. He could no longer hold himself apart from the world. It was his to see that the city was a place that Danat and Eiah and children like them could live safe and cared for until they too grew old and uncertain.

He looked at the swirl of red at the bottom of his bowl. Too much wine, and too much memory. It was making him maudlin. He stopped at his private chambers and allowed the servants to switch his robes to something less formal. Kiyan lay on a couch, her eyes closed, her breath deep and regular. Otah didn't wake her, only slid one of the books from his bedside table into the sleeve of his robe and kissed her temple as he left.

The physician's assistant was seated outside Danat's door. The man took a pose of greeting. Otah responded in kind and then nodded to the closed door.

"Is he asleep?" he whispered.

"He's been waiting for you."

Otah slipped into the room. Candles flickered above two great iron statues that flanked the bed—hunting cats with the wings of hawks. Soot darkened their wings from a day spent in the fire grates, and they radiated the warmth that kept the cool night breeze at bay. Danat sat up in his bed, pulling aside the netting.

"Papa-kya!" he said. He didn't cough, didn't sound frail. It was a good day, then. Otah felt a tightness he had not known he carried loosen its grip on his heart. He pulled his robes up around his knees and sat on his son's bed. "Did you bring it?" Danat asked.

Otah drew the book from his sleeve, and the boy's face lit so bright, he might have almost read by him.

"Now, you lie back," Otah said. "I've come to help you sleep, not keep you up all night."

Danat plopped down onto his pillow, looking like the farthest thing from sleep. Otah opened the book, turning through the ancient pages until he found his place.

"In the sixteenth year of the reign of the Emperor Adani Beh, there came to court a boy whose blood was half Bakta, his skin the color of soot, and his mind as clever as any man who has ever lived. . . ."

"THIS IS SPRING?" NAYIIT SAID AS THEY WALKED. THE WIND HAD BLOWN AWAY even the constant scent of forge smoke, and brought in a mild chill. Mild, at least, to Maati. Nayiit wore woolen robes, thick enough that they had hardly rippled. Maati's own were made for summer, and pressed against him, leaving, he was sure, no doubt as to the shape of his legs and belly. He wished he'd thought to wear something heavier too.

"It's always like this," Maati said. "There's one last death throe, and then the heat will come on. Still nothing like the summer cities, even at its worst. I remember in Saraykeht, I had a trail of sweat down my back for weeks at a time."

"We call that *pleasantly warm*," Nayiit said, and Maati chuckled.

In truth, the chill, moonless night was hardly anything to him now. For over a decade, he'd lived through the bone-cracking cold of Machi winters. He'd seen snowdrifts so high that even the second-story doors couldn't be opened. He'd been out on days so cold the men coated their faces with thick-rendered fat to keep their skin from freezing. There was no way to describe those brief, bitter days to someone who had never seen them. So instead, he told Nayiit of the life below ground, the tunnels of Machi, the bathhouses hidden deep below the surface, the streets and apartments and warehouses, the glitter of winter dew turning to frost on the stone of the higher passages. He spoke of the choirs who took the long, empty weeks to compose new songs and practice old ones—weeks spent in the flickering, buttery light of oil lamps surrounded by music.

"I'm amazed people don't stay down there," Nayiit said as they turned a corner and left the white and silver paths of the palaces behind for the black-cobbled streets of the city proper. "It sounds like one huge, warm bed."

"It has its pleasures," Maati agreed. "But people get thirsty for sunlight. As soon as they can stand it, people start making treks up to the streets. They'll go up and lie naked on an ice sheet sometimes just to drink in a little more light. And the river freezes, so the children will go skating on it. There's only about seven weeks when no one comes up. Here. This street. There's a sweet wine they serve at this place that's like nothing you've ever tasted."

It was less awkward than he'd expected, spending the evening with Nayiit. The first time the boy had come to the library alone—tentative and uncertain—Maati had been acutely aware of Liat's absence. She had always been there, even in the ancient days before they had parted. Maati knew how to speak with Liat whether she was alone or with their son, and Maati had discovered quickly how much he'd relied upon her to mediate between him and the boy. The silences had been awkward, the conversations forced. Maati had said something of how pleased he was that Nayiit had come to Machi and felt in the end that he'd only managed to embarrass them both.

It was going to the teahouses and bathhouses and epics that let them speak at last. Once there was a bit of shared experience, a toehold, Maati was able to make conversation, and Nayiit was an expert listener to stories. For several nights in a row, Maati found himself telling tales of the Dai-kvo and the school, the history of Machi and the perils he had faced years ago when he'd been sent to hunt Otah-kvo down. In the telling, he discovered that, to his profound surprise, his life had been interesting.

The platform rested at the base of one of the lower towers, chains thick as a man's arm clanking against it and against the stone as they rose up into the sky like smoke. Nayiit paused to stare up at it, and Maati followed his gaze. The looming, inhuman bulk of the tower, and beyond it the full moon hanging like a lantern of rice paper in the black sky.

"Does anyone ever fall from up there?" Nayiit asked.

"Once every year or so," Maati said. "There's winter storage up there, so there are laborers carrying things in the early spring and middle autumn. There are accidents. And the utkhaiem will hold dances at the tops of them sometimes. They say wine gets you drunk faster at the top, but I don't know if that's true. Then sometimes men kill themselves by stepping through the sky doors when the platform's gone down. It would happen more if there were people up there more often. Otah-kvo has a plan for channeling the air from the forges up through the center of one so it would be warm enough to use in the winter, but we've never figured out how to make the change without bringing the whole thing down."

Nayiit shuddered, and Maati was willing to pretend it was the wind. He put his arm on the boy's shoulder and steered him farther down the street to a squat stone building with a copper roof gone as green as trees with time. Inside, the air was warmed by braziers. Two old men were playing tin-and-silver flutes while a young woman kept time on a small drum and sang. Half a hundred bodies were seated at long wooden tables or on benches. The place was rich with the smell of roast lamb even though the windows were unshuttered; it was as if no one in Machi would miss the chance for fresh air. Maati sympathized.

He and Nayiit took a bench in the back, away from singers and song. The serving boy was hardly as old as Eiah, but he knew his trade. It seemed fewer than a dozen heartbeats before he brought them bowls of sweet wine and a large worked-silver bowl filled with tender slivers of green: spring peas fresh from the vines. Maati, hands full, nodded his thanks.

"And you've worked your whole life in House Kyaan, then?" Maati asked. "What does Liat have you doing?"

"Since we've been traveling, I haven't been doing much at all. Before that, I had been working the needle trades," Nayiit said as he tucked one leg up under him. It made him sit taller. "The spinners, the dyers, the tailors, and the sailmakers and all like that. They aren't as profitable as they were in the days before Seedless was lost, but they still make up a good deal of the business in Saraykeht."

"Habits," Maati said. "The cotton trade's always been in Saraykeht. People don't like change, so it doesn't move away so quickly as it might. Another generation and it'll all be scattered throughout the world."

"Not if I do my work," Nayiit said with a smile that showed he hadn't taken offense.

"Fair point," Maati said. "I only mean that's what you have to work against. It would be easier if there was still an andat in the city that helped with the cotton trade the way Seedless did."

"You knew it, didn't you? Seedless, I mean."

"I was supposed to take him over," Maati said. "The way Cehmai took Stone-Made-Soft from his master, I was to take Seedless from Heshai-kvo. In a way, I was lucky. Seedless was flawed work. Dangerously flawed. Brilliant, don't misunderstand. Heshai-kvo did brilliant work when he bound Seedless, but he made the andat very clever and profoundly involved with destroying the poet. They all want to be free—it's their nature—but Seedless was more than that. He was vicious."

"You sound as though you were fond of it," Nayiit said, only half-teasing.

"We were friendly enough, in our fashion," Maati said. "We wouldn't have been if things had gone by the Dai-kvo's plan. If I'd become the poet of Saraykeht, Seedless would have bent himself to destroying me just the way he had to Heshai-kvo."

"Have you ever tried to bind one of the andat?"

"Once. When Heshai died, I had the mad thought that I could somehow retrieve Seedless. I had Heshai-kvo's notes. Still have them, for that. I even began the ceremonies, but it would never have worked. What I had was too much like what Heshai had done. It would have failed, and I'd have paid its price."

"And then I suppose I would never have been born," Nayiit said.

"You would have," Maati said, solemnly. "Liat-kya didn't know she was carrying you when she stopped me, but she was. I thought about it, afterward. About binding another of the andat, I mean. I even spent part of a winter once doing the basic work for one I called Returning-to-True. I don't know what I would have done with it, precisely. Unbent things, I suppose. I'd have been brilliant repairing axles. But my mind was too fuzzy. There were too many things I meant, and none of them precisely enough."

The musicians ended their song and stood to a roar of approving voices and bowls of wine bought by their admirers. One of the old men walked through the house with a lacquer begging box in his hand. Maati fumbled in his sleeve, came out with two lengths of copper, and tossed them into the box with a satisfying click.

"And then, I also wasn't in the Dai-kvo's best graces," Maati continued. "After Saraykeht . . . Well, I suppose it's poor etiquette to let your master die and the andat escape. I wasn't blamed outright, but it was always hanging there. The memory of it."

"It can't have helped that you brought back a lover and a child," Nayiit said.

"No, it didn't. But I was very young and very full of myself. It's not easy, being told that you are of the handful of men in the world who might be able to control one of the andat. Tends to create a sense of being more than you are.

I thought I could do anything. And maybe I could have, but I tried to do *everything*, and that isn't the same." He sighed and ate a pea pod. Its flesh was crisp and sweet and tasted of spring. When he spoke again, he tried to make his voice light and joking. "I didn't wind up doing a particularly good job of either endeavor."

"It seems to me you've done well enough," Nayiit said as he waved at the serving boy for more wine. "You've made yourself a place in the court here, you've been able to study in the libraries here, and from what Mother says, you've found something no one else ever has. That alone is more than most men manage in a lifetime."

"I suppose," Maati said. He wanted to go on, wanted to say that most men had children, raised them up, watched them become women and men. He wanted to tell this charming boy who stood now where Maati himself once had that he regretted that he had not been able to enjoy those simple pleasures. Instead, he took another handful of pea pods. He could tell that Nayiit sensed his reservations, heard the longing in the brevity of his reply. When the boy spoke, his tone was light.

"I've spent all my life—well, since I've been old enough to think of it as really mine and not something Mother's let me borrow—with House Kyaan. Running errands, delivering contracts. That's how I started, at least. Mother always told me I had to do better than the other boys who worked for the house because I was her son, and if people thought I was getting favors because of it, they wouldn't respect her or me. She was right. I can see that. At the time it all seemed monstrously unfair, though."

"Do you like the work?" Maati asked.

The girl with the drum began tapping a low tattoo, her voice droning in a lament. Maati shifted to look at Nayiit. The boy's gaze was fixed on the singer, his expression melancholy. The urge to put his hand to Nayiit's shoulder, to offer some comfort, however powerless, moved through Maati and faded. He sat still and quiet as the chant rose, the anguish in the singer's voice growing until the air of the teahouse hummed with it, and then it faded into despair. The man with the lacquer box came past again, but Maati didn't put in any copper this time.

"You and Mother. You're lovers again?"

"I suppose so," Maati said, surprised to feel a blush in his cheeks. "It happens sometimes."

"What happens when you're called away to the Dai-kvo?"

"Are we walking the same path a second time, you mean? We're waiting to hear two things from the Dai-kvo—whether he thinks my speculations about avoiding the price of a failed binding are worth looking into and whether to act against Galt. Either one puts me someplace away from Liat. But we aren't who we were then. I don't pretend that we can be. And anyway, I have all the habits of being without her. I've missed her for more years than I spent in her company."

I have missed you, he thought but didn't say. I have missed you, and it's too late now for anything more than awkward conversations and late nights getting drunk together. Nothing will ever make that right.

"Do you regret that?" Nayiit asked. "If you could go back and do things again, would you want to love her less? Would you want to have gone to the Dai-kvo and been able to leave that . . . that longing behind you?"

"I don't know what you mean."

Nayiit looked up.

"I would hate her, if I were you. I would think she'd taken my chance to be what I was supposed to be, to do what I could have done. There you were, a poet, and favored enough that you were expected to hold the andat, and because of her you fell into disfavor. Because of her, and because of me." Nayiit's jaw clenched, his eyes only a half shade darker than the pale brown of his mother's staring at something that wasn't there, his attention turned inward. "I don't know how you stand the sight of us."

"It wasn't like that," Maati said. "It was never like that. If it were all mine again, I would have followed her."

The words struck the boy hard. His gaze lost its focus; his mouth tightened like that of a man in pain.

"What is it, Nayiit-kya?"

Nayiit seemed to snap back to the room, an embarrassed grin on his face. He took a pose of apology, but Maati shook his head.

"Something's bothering you," Maati said.

"It's nothing. I've only . . . It's not worth talking about."

"Something's bothering you, son."

He had never said the word aloud. *Son.* Nayiit had never heard it from his lips, not since he'd been too young for it to mean anything. Maati felt his heart leap and race like a startled deer, and he saw the shock on the boy's face. This was the moment, then, that he'd feared and longed for. He waited to hear what Nayiit would say. Maati dreaded the polite deflection, the retreat back into the roles of a pair of strangers in a tearoom, the way a man falling from a cliff might dread the ground.

Nayiit opened his mouth, closed it, and then said, almost too low to hear over the music and the crowd, "I'm trying to choose between what I am and what I want to be. I'm trying to want what I'm supposed to want. And I'm failing."

"I see."

"I want to be a good man, Father. I want to love my wife and my son. I want to *want* them. And I don't. I don't know whether to walk away from them or from myself. I thought you had made that decision, but . . ."

Maati settled back on the bench, put down his bowl still half full of wine, and took Nayiit's hand in his own. Father. Nayiit had said *Father.*

"Tell me," Maati said. "Tell me all of it."

"It would take all night," the boy said with a rueful chuckle. But he didn't pull back his hand.

"Let it," Maati said. "There's nothing more important than this."

BALASAR HADN'T SLEPT. THE NIGHT HAD COME, A LATE RAIN SHOWER FILLING THE air with the scent of water and murmur of distant thunder, and he had lain in his bed, willing himself to a forgetfulness that wouldn't come.

The orders waited in stacks on his desk in the library, commands to be issued to each of his captains, outlining the first stage of his campaign. There were two sets, of course, just as the Khaiate mercenary captain had surmised. Those he'd sealed in green would lead the army to the North, laying waste to the Westlands and sending the thin stream of gold and silver that could be wrung from them back to the coffers of the High Council. Those he'd sealed in red would wheel the army—twenty thousand armsmen, three hundred steam wagons, six thousand horses, and God only knew how many servants and camp followers—to the east and the most glorious act of conquest the world had ever known.

If he succeeded, he would be remembered as the greatest general in history, at least in his audacity. The battles themselves he expected to be simple enough. The Khaiem had no experience in tactics and no armies to protect them. Balasar would be remembered for two things only: the unimaginable wealth he was about to pour into Galt and the ceremony that would come with the dawn. The plot that stripped the andat from the world.

As the dark hours passed, the thought pricked at him. He had put everything in place. The poet, the books that concerned Freedom-From-Bondage, the army, the arms. There was nothing he would ever do that would match this season. Succeed or fail, this was the high-water mark of his life. He imagined himself an old man, sitting at a street café in Kirinton. He wondered what those years would be like, reaching from here to the grave. He wondered what it would be like to have his greatness behind him. He told himself that he would retire. There would be enough wealth to acquire anything he wanted. A reasonable estate of his own, a wife, children; that seemed enough. If he could not regain this season, he could at least not humiliate himself by trying. He thought of the war leaders who haunted the corridors and wineshops of Acton reliving triumphs the world had forgotten. He would not be one of those. He would be the great General who had done his work and then stepped back to let the world he had made safe follow its path.

At heart, he was not a conqueror. Only a man who saw what needed doing, and then did it.

Or else he would fail and he and every Galtic man and woman would be a corpse or a refugee.

He twisted in his sheets. The stars shone where the clouds were thin enough to permit it. Framed in the opened shutters, they glittered. The stars

wouldn't care what happened here. And yet by the next time their light silvered these stones, the fate of the world would have turned one way or the
other.

Once, he came near to sleep. His eyes grew heavy, his mind began to wander into the half-sense of dreams. And then, irrationally, he became certain
that he had mixed one of the orders. The memory, at first vague but clearer as
he struggled to capture it, of sealing a packet with red that should have been
green swam through his mind. He thought he might have noted at the time
that it would need changing. And yet he hadn't done it. The wrong orders
would go out. A legion would start to the North while the others moved east.
They would lose time finding the error, correcting it. Or the poet would fail,
and some stray company of armsmen would find its way to Nantani and reveal
him to the Khaiem. Half a thousand stories plagued him, each less likely than
the last. His sense of dread grew.

At last, half in distress and half in disgust, he rose, pulled on a heavy cotton
shirt and light trousers, and walked barefoot from his room toward the library.
He would have to open them all, check them, reseal them, and keep a careful
tally so that the crazed monkey that had taken possession of his mind could be
calmed. He wondered, as he passed through hallways lit only by his single
candle, whether Uther Redcape had ever rechecked his own plans in the dead
of night like an old, fearful merchant rattling his own shutters to be sure they
were latched. Perhaps these indignities were part of what any man suffered
when the weight of so many lives was on his back.

The guards outside his library door stood at attention as he passed them,
whatever gossip or complaint they had been using to pass the dark hours of the
night forgotten at the first sight of him. Balasar nodded to them gravely before
passing through the door. With the stub of his bedside candle, he lit the lanterns in the library until the soft glow filled the air. The orders lay where he
had left them. With a sigh, he took out the bricks of colored wax and his private seal. Then he began the long, tedious task of cracking each seal, review-
ing his commands, and putting the packets back in order again. The candle
stub had fizzled to nothing and the lanterns' oil visibly dropped before he was
finished. The memory had been a lie. Everything had been in place. Balasar
stood, stretched, and went to the window. When he opened the shutters, the
cool breeze felt fresh as a bath. Birds were singing, though there was no light
yet in the east. The full moon was near to setting. The dawn was coming.
There would be no sleep for him. Not now.

A soft scratch came at the door, and after Balasar called his permission, Eustin entered. There were dark pouches under the man's eyes, but that was the
only sign that he had managed no better with his sleep. His uniform was crisp
and freshly laundered, the marks of rank on his back and breast, his hair was
tied back and fastened with a thick silver ceremonial bead, and there was an
energy in all his movements that Balasar understood. Eustin was dressed to

witness the change of the world. Balasar was suddenly aware of his rough clothes and bare feet.

"What news?" Balasar said.

"He's been up all through the night, sir. Meditating, reading, preparing. Truth is I don't know that half of what he's done is needed, but he's been doing it all the same."

"Almost none of it's strictly called for," Balasar said. "But if it makes him feel better, let him."

"Yes, sir. I've called for his breakfast. He says that he'll want to wait a half a hand for his food to go down, and then it's time. Says that dawn's a symbolic moment, and that it'll help."

"I suppose I'll be getting prepared, then," Balasar said. "If this isn't a full-dress occasion, I don't know what is."

"I've sent men to wait for the signal. We should know by nightfall."

Balasar nodded. All along the highest hills from Nantani to Aren, bonfires were set. If all worked as they hoped, there would be a signal from the agents he had placed in the city, and they would be lit, each in turn. A thin line of fire would reach from the Khaiem to his own door.

"Have a mug of kafe and some bread sent to my rooms," Balasar said. "I'll meet you before the ceremony."

"Not more than that, sir? The bacon's good here. . . ."

"After," Balasar said. "I'll eat a decent meal after."

The room given them by the Warden had been in its time a warehouse, a meeting hall, and a temple, the last being the most recent. Tapestries of the Four Gods the Warden worshipped had been taken down, rolled up, and stacked in the corner like carpet. The smooth stone walls were marked with symbols, some familiar to Balasar, others obscure. The eastern wall was covered with the flowing script of the fallen Empire, like a page from a book of poetry. A single pillow rested in the center of the room, and beside it a stack of books, two with covers of ruined leather, one whose cover had been ripped from it, and one last closed in bright metal. It had been years since Balasar had carried those books out of the desert wastes. He nodded to them when he saw them, as if they were old friends or perhaps enemies.

Riaan himself was walking around the room with long, slow strides. He breathed in audibly with one step, blew the air out on the next. His face was deeply relaxed; his arms were swinging free at his sides. To look at the two of them, Balasar guessed he would look more like the man about to face death. He took a pose of respect and greeting. The poet came slowly to a halt, and returned the gesture.

"I trust all is well with you," Balasar said in the tongue of the Khaiem.

"I am ready," Riaan said, with a smile that made him seem almost gentle. "I wanted to thank you, Balasar-cha, for this opportunity. These are strange times that men such as you and I should find common cause. The structures of the

Dai-kvo have caused good men to suffer for too many generations. I honor you
for the role you have played in bringing me here."

Balasar bowed his head. Over the years he had known many men whose
minds had been touched by wounds—blows from swords or stones, or fevers
like the one that had prompted Riaan's fall from favor. Balasar knew how im-
pulsive and unreliable a man could become after such an injury. But he also
knew that with many there was also a candor and honesty, if only because they
lacked the ability they had once had to dissemble. Against his own will, he
found himself touched by the man's words.

"We all do what fate calls us to," he said. "It's no particular virtue of mine."

The poet smiled because he didn't understand what Balasar meant. And
that was just as well. Eustin arrived moments later and made formal greeting
to them both.

"There's breakfast waiting for us, when we're done here," Eustin said, and
even such mundane words carried a depth.

"Well then," Balasar said, turning to Riaan. The poet nodded and took a
pose more complex than Balasar could parse, but that seemed to be a farewell
from a superior to someone of a lower class. Then Riaan dropped his pose and
walked with a studied grace to the cushion in the room's center. Balasar stood
against the back wall and nodded for Eustin to join him. He was careful not to
obscure the symbols painted there, though Riaan wasn't looking back toward
them.

For what seemed half a day and was likely no more than two dozen breaths
together, the poet was silent, and then he began, nearly under his breath, to
chant. Balasar knew the basic form of a binding, though the grammars that
were used for the deepest work were beyond him. It was thought, really. Like
a translation—a thought held that became something like a man as a song in a
Westlands tongue might take new words in Galt but hold the same meaning.
The chant was a device of memory and focus, and Balasar remained silent.

Slowly, the sound of the poet's voice grew, filling the space with words that
seemed on the edge of comprehension. The sound began to echo, as if the
room were much larger than the walls that Balasar could see, and something
like a wind that somehow did not stir the air began to twist through the space.
For a moment, he was in the desert again, feeling the air change, hearing
Little Ott's shriek. Balasar put his arm back, palm pressed against the stone
wall. He was here, he was in Aren. The chanting grew, and it was as if there
were other voices now. Beside him, Eustin had gone pale. Sweat stood on the
man's lip.

Under Balasar's fingertips, the wall seemed to shift. The stone hummed,
dancing with the words of the chant. The script on the front wall shifted restlessly until Balasar squinted and the letters remained in their places. The air
was thick.

"Sir," Eustin whispered, "I think it might be best if we stepped out, left
him to—"

"No," Balasar said. "Watch this. It's the last time it's ever going to happen."

Eustin nodded curtly and turned with what seemed physical strain to look ahead. Riaan had risen, standing where the cushion had been, or perhaps he was floating. Or perhaps he was sitting just as he had been. Something had happened to the nature of the space between them. And then, like seven flutes moving from chaos to harmony, the world itself chimed, a note as deep as oceans and pure as dawn. Balasar felt his heart grow light for a moment, a profound joy filling him that had nothing to do with triumph, and there, standing before the seated poet, was a naked man, bald as a baby, with eyes white as salt.

The blast pressed Balasar back against the wall. His ears rang, and Eustin's voice seemed to come from a great distance.

"Riaan, sir!"

Balasar fought to focus his eyes. Riaan was still seated where he had been, but his shoulders were slumped, his head bowed as if in sleep. Balasar walked over to him, the sound of his own footsteps lost in his half-deafened state. It was like floating.

He was breathing. The poet breathed.

"Did it work, sir?" Eustin yelled from half a mile away or else there at his shoulder. "Does that mean it worked?"

9

"What is he to do?" Maati asked and then sipped his tea. It was just slightly overbrewed, a bitter aftertaste haunting the back of his mouth. Or perhaps it was only that he'd drunk too much the night before, sitting up with his son until the full moon set and the eastern sky began to lighten. Maati had seen Nayiit back to the boy's apartments, and then, too tired to sleep, wandered to the poet's house where Cehmai was just risen for breakfast. He'd sent the servants back to the kitchens to bring a second meal, and while they waited, Cehmai shared what he had—thin butter pastry, blackberries still just slightly underripe, overbrewed tea. Everything tasted of early summer. Already the morning had broken the chill of the previous night.

"Really, he's been good to the woman. He's acknowledged the babe, he's married her. But if he doesn't love her, what's he to do? Love's not something you can command."

"Not usually," Stone-Made-Soft said, and smiled wide enough to bare its tooeven white marble teeth. It wasn't a human mouth.

"I don't know," Cehmai said, ignoring the andat. "Really, you and I are probably the two worst men in the city to ask about things like that. I've never been in the position to have a wife. All the women I've been with knew that this old bastard came before anything."

Stone-Made-Soft smiled placidly. Maati had the uncomfortable sense that it was accepting a compliment.

"But you can see his dilemma," Maati said.

Outside, beyond the carefully sculpted oaks that kept the poet's house separate from the palaces, the city was in shadow. The sun, hidden behind the mountains to the east, filled the blue dome of air with soft light. The towers stood dark against the daylight, birds wheeling far below their highest reaches.

"I see that he's in a difficult position," Cehmai said. "And I'm in no position to say that good men never lose their hearts to . . . what? Inappropriate women?"

"If you mean the Khai's sister, the term is vicious killers," Stone-Made-Soft said. "But I think we can generalize from there."

"Thank you," Cehmai said. "But you've made the point yourself, Maati. Nayiit's married her. He's acknowledged the child. Doing that binds him to something, doesn't it? He's made an agreement. He's made a kind of promise, or else why say that he's been good to her? If he can put those things aside, then that goodness is just a formality."

Maati sighed. His mind felt thick. Too much wine, too little rest. He was old to be staying up all night; it was a young man's game. And still, he felt it important that Cehmai understand. If he could explain Nayiit to someone else, it would make the night and all their conversations through it real. It would put them into the world in a way that now might only have been a dream. He was silent too long, struggling to put his thoughts in order. Cehmai cleared his throat, shot an uncomfortable glance at Maati, and changed the subject.

"Forgive me, Maati-cha, but I thought there was some question about Nayiit's . . . ah . . . parentage? I know the Khai signed a document denying him, but that was when there was some question about the succession, and I'd always thought he'd done it as a favor. If you see what I . . ."

Maati put down his tea bowl and took a pose that disagreed.

"There's more to being a father than a few moments between the sheets," Maati said. "I was there when Nayiit took his first steps. I sang him to sleep as often as I could. I brought food for him. I held him. And tonight, Cehmai. He came to me. He talked to *me*. I don't care whose blood he has, that boy's mine."

"If you say so," Cehmai said, but there was something in his voice, some reservation. Maati felt his face begin to flush. Anger straightened his back. Stone-Made-Soft raised a wide, thick hand, palm out, silencing them both. Its head tilted, as if hearing some distant sound.

Its brow furrowed.

"Well," the andat said. "*That's* interesting."

And then it vanished.

Maati blinked in confusion. A few heartbeats later, Cehmai drew a long, shuddering breath. The poet's face was bloodless.

Maati sat silently as Cehmai stood, hands trembling, and walked back into the dimness of the house, and then out again. Cehmai's gaze darted one direction and another, searching for something. His eyes were so wide, the whites showed all the way around.

"Oh," Cehmai said, and his voice was thin and reedy. "Maati . . . Oh gods. I didn't do anything. I didn't . . . Oh gods. Maati-kvo, he's *gone*."

Maati rose, brushing the crumbs from his robes with a sense of profound unreality. Once before, he had seen the last moments of an andat in the world. It wasn't something he'd expected to suffer again. Cehmai paced the wide porch, his head turning one way and another, directionless as a swath of silk caught in the wind.

"Stay here. I'll get Otah-kvo," Maati said. "He'll know what to do."

THE WALLS OF THE AUDIENCE CHAMBER SWOOPED UP, GRACEFUL AS A DOVE'S WING. The high, pale stone looked as soft as fresh butter, seamless where the stones had joined and been smoothed into one piece by the power of the andat. Tiny webworks of stone fanned out from the walls at shoulder height, incense smoke rising from them in soft gray lines. High above, windows had been shaped by hand. Spare and elegant and commanding, it was a place of impossible beauty, and Otah suspected the world would never see another like it.

He sat in the black chair his father had sat in, and his father before him, and on back through the generations to when the Empire had still stood, and the name Khai had meant honored servant. Before him, seated on soft red cushions and intricately woven rugs, were the heads of the highest families of the utkhaiem. Vaunani, Radaani, Kamau, Daikani, Dun, Isadan, and half a dozen others. For each of these, there were ten more families. Twenty more. But these were the highest, the richest, the most powerful men of Machi. And they were the ones who had just suffered the worst loss. Otah waited while his news sank in, watched the blood drain from their faces. Otah kept his visage stern and his posture formal and rigid. His robes were simple, pale, and severe. His first impulse—a ceremonial black shot with red and long, flexible bone sewn in to give it shape—had been too gaudy; he would have seemed to be taking refuge in the cloth. The important things now were that they know he was in control and that they put trust in him. It would be too easy for the city to fall into panic, and here, now, through the force of his own will, he could hold it back. If these men left the room unsure, it would be too late. He could hold a stone, but he couldn't stop a rockslide.

"C-Can we get it back?" Wetai Dun asked, his voice shaking. "There are andat that poets have caught three, four times. Water-Moving-Down was . . ."

Otah took a deep breath. "There is a chance," he said. "It has been done, but it will be harder than it was the first time. The poet who does will have to create a binding sufficiently different from the original. Or it could be that the Dai-kvo will be able to give us an andat that is different, but that still speeds the mining trades."

"How long will it take?" Ashua Radaani asked. The Radaani were the richest family in the city, with more silver and gold in their coffers than even Otah himself could command.

"We can't know until we hear from the Dai-kvo," Otah said. "I've sent my best courier with enough gold in his sleeve to buy a fresh horse every time he needs one. We will hear back as soon as it is possible to know. Until that happens, we will work as we always have. Stone-Made-Soft made the mines here and in the North the most productive in the world, that's true. But it didn't run the forges. It didn't smelt the ore. The stone potters will have to go back to working clay, that's true, but—"

"How did this happen?" Caiin Dun cried. His voice was as anguished as if he'd lost a son. There was a stirring in the air. Fear. Without thinking, Otah rose, his hands flowing into a pose of censure.

"Dun-cha," he said, his voice cold as stone and harder. "You are not here to shout me down. I have brought you here as a courtesy. Do you understand that?"

The man took an apologetic pose, but Otah pressed.

"I asked whether you understood, not whether you were regretful."

"I understand, Most High," the man muttered.

"The potters will have to work clay until some other accommodation can be made," Otah said. "With proper control, this will be an inconvenience, not a catastrophe. The city is wounded, yes. We all know that, and I won't have that made worse by panic. I expect each of you to stand with your Khai, and make your people know that there is nothing to fear. The contracts directly affected by this loss will be brought to me personally. I will see to it that any losses are recompensed so that no one family or house carries more of this burden than its share. And any contracts not directly affected by the andat's absence are still in force. Do each of you understand that?"

A low chorus of affirmation rose. They sounded as reluctant as boys before a tutor.

"Also I have put armsmen on the bridge. Any house who chooses this time to relocate its wealth to some other city will forfeit their holdings here. Any silver over a hundred lengths that leaves Machi at one time must be allowed by me."

Ashua Radaani took a pose that begged permission to speak. It was proper etiquette, and Otah felt the tightness in his chest release by half a turn. At least they were now respecting forms.

"Most High," Radaani said, "this may not be the best time to put restrictions on trade. Machi will need to keep its ties to the other cities strong if we're to weather this tragedy."

"If the smaller houses see carts of gold rolling away to Cetani and Udun, they'll start talking of how the rats all run when the house catches fire," Otah said. "My house hasn't caught fire."

Radaani pursed his lips, his eyes shifting as if reading some invisible text as he reconsidered some internal plan that Otah had just ruined, but he said nothing more.

"Machi needs your loyalty and your obedience," Otah said. "You are all good men, and the leaders of respected families. Understand that I value each of you, and your efforts to keep the peace in this time will be remembered and honored."

And the first of you to bolt, I will destroy and sow your lands with salt, Otah thought but didn't say. He let his eyes carry that part of the message, and from the unease in the men before him, he knew that they had understood. For over a decade, they had thought themselves ruled by a softhearted man, an upstart put in his father's chair by strange fortune and likely less suited to the role than his lady wife, the innkeep. And as terrible as this day was, Otah found he felt some small joy in suggesting they might have been mistaken.

Once they had been dismissed, Otah waved away his servants and walked to his private apartments. Kiyan came to him, taking his hand in her own. Cehmai sat on the edge of a low couch, his face still empty with shock. He had been weeping openly when Otah left.

"How did it go?" Kiyan asked.

"Well, I think. Strangely, it's much easier than dealing with Eiah."

"You don't love them," Kiyan said.

"Ah, is that the difference?"

A plate of fresh apples stood on a copper table, a short, wicked knife beside it. Otah sliced a bit of the white flesh and chewed thoughtfully.

"They'll still move their wealth away, you know," Kiyan said. "Blocking the bridge won't stop a ferry crossing in the night with its lanterns shuttered or wagons looping up north and crossing the water someplace in the mountains."

"I know it. But if I can keep the thing down to a few ferries and wagons, that will do. I'll also need to send messages to the Khaiem," Otah said. "Cetani and Amnat-Tan to start."

"Better they hear the bad news from you," she agreed. "Should I call for a scribe?"

"No. Just paper and a fresh ink brick. I'll do the thing myself."

"I'm sorry, Most High," Cehmai said again. "I don't know . . . I don't know how it happened. He was there, and then . . . he just wasn't. There wasn't even a struggle. He just . . ."

"It doesn't matter," Otah said. "It's gone, and so it's gone. We'll move forward from that."

"It does matter, though," the poet said, and his voice was a cry of despair. Otah wondered what it would feel like, dedicating a life to one singular thing and then in an instant, losing it. He himself had led a half-dozen lives—laborer, fisherman, midwife's assistant, courier, father, Khai—but Cehmai had never been anything besides a poet. Exalted above all other men, honored, envied. And now, suddenly, he was only a man in a brown robe. Otah put a hand to the man's shoulder, and saw a moment's passing shame in Cehmai's expression. It was, perhaps, too early still for comfort.

A scratch came at the door and a servant boy entered, took a formal pose, and announced the poet Maati Vaupathai and Liat Chokavi. A moment later, Maati rushed in, his cheeks an alarming red, his breath hard, his belly heaving. Liat was no more than a step behind. He could see the alarm in her expression. Kiyan stepped forward and helped Maati to a seat. The two women met each other's gaze, and there was a moment's tension before Otah stepped forward.

"Liat-cha," he said. "Thank you for coming."

"Of course," she said. "I came as soon as Maati asked me. Is something wrong? Have we heard from the Dai-kvo?"

"No," Maati said between gasps. "Not that."

Otah took a questioning pose, and Maati shook his head.

"Didn't say. People around. Would have been heard," Maati said. Then, "Gods, I need to eat less. I'm too fat to run anymore."

Otah took Liat's elbow and guided her to a chair, then sat beside Cehmai. Only Kiyan remained standing.

"Liat-cha, you worked with Amat Kyaan," Otah said. "You've taken over the house she founded. She must have spoken with you about how those first years were. After Heshai-kvo died and Seedless escaped."

"Of course," Liat said.

"I need you to tell us about that," Otah said. "I need to know what she did to keep Saraykeht together. What she tried that worked, what failed. What she wished the Khai Saraykeht had done in response, what she would have preferred he had not. Everything."

Liat's gaze went to Maati and then Cehmai and then back to Otah. There was still a deep confusion in her expression.

"It's happened again," Otah said.

10

>+< Given a half-decent road, the armies of Galt could travel faster than any in the world. It was the steam wagons, Balasar reflected, that made the difference. As long as there was wood or coal to burn and water for the boilers, the carts could keep their pace at a fast walk. In addition to the supplies they carried—food, armor, weapons that the men were then spared—a tenth of the infantry could climb aboard the rough slats, rest themselves, and eat. Rotated properly, his men could spend a full day at fast march, make camp, and be rested enough by morning to do the whole thing again. Balasar sat astride his horse—a nameless mare Eustin had procured for him—and looked back over the valley; the sun dropping at their back stretched their shadows to the east. Hundreds of plumes of dark smoke and pale steam rose from the green silk banners rippling above and beside them. The plain behind him was a single,

ordered mass of the army stretching back, it seemed, to the horizon. Boots crushed the grasses, steam wagons consumed the trees, horses tramped the ground to mud. Their passing alone would scar these fields and meadows for a generation.

And the whole of it was his. Balasar's will had gathered it and would direct it, and despite all his late-night sufferings, in this moment he could not imagine failure. Eustin cleared his throat.

"If they had found some andat to do this," Balasar said, "do you know what would have happened?"

"Sir?" Eustin said.

"If the andat had done this—Wagon-That-Pulls-Itself or Horse-Doesn't-Tire, something like that—no one would ever have designed a steam wagon. The merchants would have paid some price to the Khai, the poet would have been set to it, and it would have worked until the poet fell down stairs or failed to pass the andat on."

"Or until we came around," Eustin said, but Balasar wasn't ready to leave his chain of thought for self-congratulations yet.

"And if someone *had* made the thing, had seen a way that any decent smith could do what the Khai charged good silver for, he'd either keep it quiet or find himself facedown in the river," Balasar said and then spat. "It's no way to run a culture."

Eustin's mount whickered and shifted. Balasar sighed and shifted his gaze forward to the rolling hills and grasslands where the first and farthest-flung of Nantani's low towns dotted the landscape. Another day, perhaps two, and he would be there. He was more than half tempted to press on; night marches weren't unheard-of and the anticipation of what lay before them sang to him, the hours pressing at him. But the summer was hardly begun. Better not to suffer surprises too early in the campaign. He moved a practiced gaze over the road ahead, considered the distance between the reddening orb of the sun and the horizon, and made his decision.

"When the first wagon reaches that stand of trees, call the halt," he said. "That will still give the men half a hand to forage before sunset."

"Yes, sir," Eustin said. "And that other matter, sir?"

"After dinner," Balasar said. "You can bring Captain Ajutani to my tent after dinner."

His impulse had been to kill the poet as soon as the signal arrived. The binding had worked, the cities of the Khaiem lay open before him. Riaan had outlived his use.

Eustin had been the one to counsel against it, and Sinja Ajutani had been the issue. Balasar had known there was something less than trust between the two men; that was to be expected. He hadn't understood how deeply Eustin suspected the Khaiate mercenary. He had tracked the man—his visits to the poet, the organization of his men, how Riaan's unease had seemed to rise after a meeting with Sinja and fall again after he spoke with Balasar. It was nothing like an accusation; even Eustin agreed there wasn't proof of treachery. The mercenary had done nothing to show that he wasn't staying bought. And yet Eustin was more and more certain with each day that Sinja was plotting to steal Riaan back to the Khaiem, to reveal what it was he had done and, just possibly, find a way to undo it.

The problem, Balasar thought, was a simple failure of imagination. Eustin had followed Balasar through more than one campaign, had walked through the haunted desert with him, had stood at his side through the long political struggle that had brought this army to this place on this supreme errand. Loyalty was the way Eustin understood the world. The thought of a man who served first one cause and then another made no more sense to him than stone floating on water. Balasar had agreed to his scheme to prove Captain Ajutani's standing, though he himself had little doubt. He took the exercise seriously for Eustin's sake if nothing else. Balasar would be ready for them when they came.

His pavilion was in place before the last light of the sun had vanished in the west: couches made from wood and canvas that could be broken down flat and carried on muleback, flat cushions embroidered with the Galtic Tree, a small writing table. A low iron brazier took the edge from the night's chill, and half a hundred lemon candles filled the air with their scent and drove away the midges. He'd had it set on the top of a rise, looking down over the valley where the light of cook fires dotted the land like stars in the sky. A firefly had found its way through the gossamer folds of his tent, shining and then vanishing as it searched for a way out. A thousand of its fellows glittered in the darkness between camps. It was like something from a children's story, where the Good Neighbors had breached the division between the worlds to join his army. He saw the three of them coming toward him, and he knew each long before he could make out their faces.

Eustin's stride was long, low, and deceptively casual. Captain Ajutani moved carefully, each step provisional, the weight always held on his back foot until he chose to shift it. Riaan's was an unbalanced, civilian strut. Balasar rose, opened the flap for them to enter, and rolled down the woven-grass mats to give them a level of visual privacy, false walls that shifted and muttered in the lightest of breezes.

"Thank you all for coming," Balasar said in the tongue of the Khaiem.

Sinja and Riaan took poses, the forms a study in status; Sinja accepted the greeting of a superior, Riaan condescended to acknowledge an honored servant. Eustin only nodded. In the corner of the pavilion, the firefly burst into sudden brilliance and then vanished again. Balasar led the three men to cushions on a wide woven rug, seating himself to face Sinja. When they had all folded their legs beneath them, Balasar leaned forward.

"When I began this campaign," he said, "it was not my intention to continue the rule of the poets and their andat over the rest of humanity. In the course of my political life, I allowed certain people to misunderstand me. But it is not my intention that Riaan-cha should be burdened by another andat. Or that anyone should. Ever."

The poet's jaw dropped. His face went white, and his hands fluttered toward poses they never reached. Sinja only nodded, accepting the new information as if it were news of the weather.

"That leaves me with an unpleasant task," Balasar said, and he drew a blade from his vest. It was a thick-bladed dagger with a grip of worked leather. He tossed it to the floor. The metal glittered in the candlelight. Riaan didn't understand; his confusion was written on his brow and proclaimed by his silence. If he'd understood, Balasar thought, he'd be begging by now.

Sinja glanced at the knife, then up at Balasar and then Eustin. He sighed.

"And you've chosen me to see if I'd do it," the mercenary said with a tone both weary and amused.

"I don't . . ." Riaan said. "You . . . you can't mean that . . . Sinja-kya, you wouldn't—"

The motion was casual and efficient as swatting at a fly. Sinja leaned over, plucked the knife from the rug, and tossed it into the poet's neck. It sounded like a melon being cleaved. The poet rose half to his feet, clawing at the handle already slick with his blood, then slowly folded, lying forward as if asleep or drunk. The scent of blood filled the air. The poet's body twitched, heaved once, and went still.

"Not your best rug, I assume," Sinja said in Galtic.

"Not my best rug," Balasar agreed.

"Will there be anything else, sir?"

"Not now," Balasar said. "Thank you."

The mercenary captain nodded to Balasar, and then to Eustin. His gait as he walked out was the same as when he'd walked in. Balasar stood and stepped back, kicking the old, flat cushion onto the corpse. Eustin also stood, shaking his head.

"Not what you'd expected, then?" Balasar asked,

"He didn't even try to talk you out of it," Eustin said. "I thought he'd at least play you for time. Another day."

"You're convinced, then?"

Eustin hesitated, then stooped to roll the rug over the corpse. Balasar sat at the writing desk, watching as Eustin finished covering the poor, arrogant, pathetic man in his ignominious shroud and called in two soldiers to haul him away. Riaan Vaudathat, the world's last poet if Balasar had his way, would rest in an unmarked grave in this no-man's-land between the Westlands and Nantani. It took more time than throwing him into a ditch, and there were times that Balasar had been tempted. But treating the body with respect said more about the living than the dead, and it was a dignity with only the smallest price. A few men, a little work.

A new rug was brought in, new pillows, and a plate of curried chicken and raisins, a flagon of wine. The servants all left, and Eustin still hadn't spoken.

"When you brought this to me," Balasar said, "you said his hesitation would be proof of his guilt. Now you're thinking his lack of hesitation might be just as damning."

"Seemed like he might be trying to keep the poor bastard from saying something," Eustin said, his gaze cast down. Balasar laughed.

"There's no winning with you. You know that."

"I suppose not, sir."

Balasar took a knife and cut a slice from the chicken. It smelled lovely, sweet and hot and rich. But beneath it and the lemon candles, there was still a whiff of death and human blood. Balasar ate the food anyway. It tasted fine.

"Keep watch on him," Balasar said. "Be polite about it. Nothing obvious. I don't want the men thinking I don't believe in him. If you don't see him plotting against us by the time we reach Nantani, perhaps you'll sleep better."

"Thank you, sir."

"It's nothing. Some chicken?"

Eustin glanced at the plate, and then his eyes flickered toward the tent flap behind him.

"Or," Balasar said, "would you rather go set someone to shadow Captain Ajutani."

"If it's all the same, sir," Eustin said.

Balasar nodded and waved the man away. In the space of two breaths, he was alone. He ate slowly. When the meal was almost done—chicken gone, flagon still over half full—a chorus of crickets suddenly burst out. Balasar listened. The poet was dead.

There was no turning back now. The High Council back in Acton would be desperately angry with him when they heard the news, but there wasn't a great deal they could do to breathe life back into a corpse. And if his work went well, by the time winter silenced these crickets, there would no longer be a man alive in the world who could take Riaan's place. And yet, his night's work was not complete.

He wiped his hands clean, savored a last sip of wine, and took the leather satchel from under his cot. He put the books on his writing table, side by side by side. The ancient pages seemed alive with memory. He still bore the scars on his shoulder from hauling these four books out of the desert. He still felt the ghosts of his men at his back, watching in silence, waiting to see whether their deaths had been noble or foolish. And beyond that—beyond himself and his life and struggles—the worn paper and pale ink knew of ages. The hand that had copied these words had been dust for at least ten generations. The minds that first conceived these words had fallen into forgetfulness long before that. The emperor whose greater glory they had been offered to was forgotten, his palaces ruins. The lush forests and jungles of the Empire were dune-swept. Balasar put his hand on the cool metallic binding of the first of the volumes.

Killing the man was nothing. Killing the books was more difficult. The poet, like any man, was born to die. Moving his transition from flesh to spirit forward by a few decades was hardly worth considering, and Balasar was a soldier and a leader of soldiers. Killing men was his work. It would have been as well to ask a farmer to regret the fate of his wheat. But to take these words which had lasted longer than the civilization that created them, to slaughter history was a task best done by the ignorant. Only a man who did not understand his actions would be callous enough to destroy these without qualm.

And yet what must be done, must be done. And it was time.

Carefully, Balasar laid the books open in the brazier. The pages shifted in the breeze, scratching one on another like dry hands. He ran his fingers along one line, translating as best he could, reading the words for the last time. The lemon candle spilled its wax across his knuckles as he carried it, and the flame leapt to twice its height. He touched the open leaves with the burning wick as a priest might give a blessing, and the books seemed to embrace the fire. He sat, watching the pages blacken and curl, bits of cinder rise and dance in the air. A pale smoke filled the air, and Balasar rose, opening the flap of the pavilion to the wide night air.

The firefly darted past him, glowing. Balasar watched it fly out to freedom and the company of its fellows until it went dark and vanished. The cook fires were fewer, the stars hanging in the sky bright and steady. A strange elation passed through him, as if he had taken off a burden or been freed himself. He grinned like an idiot at the darkness and had to fight himself not to dance a little jig. If he'd been certain that none of his men were near, that no one would see, he would have allowed himself. But he was a commander and not a child. Dignity had its price.

When he returned to the brazier, nothing was left but blackened hinges, split leather, gray ash. Balasar stirred the ruins with a stick, making sure no text had survived, and then, satisfied, turned to his cot. The day before him would be long.

As he lay in the darkness, half asleep, he felt the ghosts again. The men he had left in the desert. The men still alive whom he would leave in the field. Riaan, books cradled in his arms. Balasar's sacrifices filled the pavilion, and their presence and expectation comforted him until a small voice came from the back of his mind.

Kya, it said. *Sinja*-kya, *he called him. Sinja*-cha *would have been the proper form, wouldn't it? Kya is used for a lover or a brother. Why would Riaan have thought of Sinja as a brother?*

And then, as if Eustin were seated beside the cot, his voice whispered, *Seemed like he might be trying to keep the poor bastard from saying something.*

LIAT WALKED THROUGH DARKNESS BETWEEN THE KHAI'S PALACES AND THE library where Maati, she hoped, was still awake and waiting for her. She felt like a washrag wrung out, soaked, and wrung out again. It was seven days now since Stone-Made-Soft had escaped, and she'd spent the time either meeting with the Khai Machi or waiting to do so. Long days spent in the gilded halls and corridors of the palaces were, she found, more tiring than travel. Her back ached, her legs were sore, and she couldn't even think what she had done to earn the pain. Sitting shouldn't carry such a price. If she'd lifted something heavy, there would at least be a reason. . . .

The city seemed darker now than when she'd arrived. It might be only her imagination, but there seemed fewer lanterns lit on the paths, fewer torches at the doorways. The windows of the palaces that shone with light seemed dimmed. No slaves sang in the gardens, the members of the utkhaiem that she saw throughout her day all shared a tension that she understood too well.

Candles flickered behind Maati's closed shutters, a thin line of light where the wooden frames had warped over the years. Liat found herself more grateful than she had expected to be as she took the last steps down the path that led to his door.

Maati sat on the low couch, a bowl of wine cradled in his fingers. A bottle less than half full sat on the floor at his feet. He smiled as she let herself in, but she saw at once that something wasn't well. She took a pose of query, and he looked away.

"Maati-kya?"

"I've had a letter from the Dai-kvo," Maati said. "The timing of all this isn't what I'd hoped, you know. I've spent years puttering through the library here, looking for nothing in particular, and only stumbled on my little insight now. Just when the Galts have gotten out of hand. And now Cehmai. And . . . forgive me, love, and you. And our boy."

"I don't understand," Liat said. "The Dai-kvo. What did he say?"

"He said that I should come." Maati sighed. "There's nothing in the letter about the Galts or the missing poet. There's nothing about Stone-Made-Soft, of course. The courier won't be there with that sorry news for days yet. It's only about me. It's the thing I'd always hoped for. It's my absolution, Liat-kya. I have been out of favor since before Nayiit was born. After I took Otah's cause in the succession, they almost forbade me from wearing the robes, you know. The old Dai-kvo made it very clear he didn't consider me a poet."

Liat leaned against the cool stone wall. Her pains were forgotten. She watched Maati raise his brows, shake his head. His lips shifted as if he were having some silent conversation to which she was only half welcome. A familiar heaviness touched her heart.

"You must have hoped for this," she said.

"Dreamed of it, when I dared to. I'm welcomed back with honor and dignity. I'm saved."

"That's a bitter tone for a saved man," she said.

"I've only just met you again. I've only just started to know Nayiit. And Otah-kvo's in need. And the Galts are stirring trouble again. My shining hour has come to call me away from everyone who actually matters."

"You can't refuse the Dai-kvo," Liat said softly. "You have to go."

"Do I?"

The air between them grew still. Half a hundred other conversations echoed in their words. Liat closed her eyes, weariness dragging her like rain-heavy robes.

"It's all happening again, isn't it?" she said. "It's all the things we've suffered before, coming back at once. The Galts. Stone-Made-Soft set free. Cehmai lost and mourning the way Heshai was that summer, after Seedless killed the baby. And then us. You and I."

"You and I, ending again," Maati said. "All of history pressed into one season. It doesn't seem fair."

"How is Cehmai?" she asked, turning the conversation to safer ground, if only for a moment. "Has he been eating?"

"A little. Not enough."

"Does he know yet what happened? How Stone-Made-Soft slipped free?"

"No, but . . . but he suspects. And I do, too."

Liat moved forward, sat beside Maati, took the bowl from his hands and drank the wine. Her throat and chest warmed and relaxed. Maati took a bottle from the floor.

"Not every poet is made for slaughter," Maati said as he tipped rice wine clear as water into the bowl. "There was a part of him that rebelled at the prospect of turning the andat against the Galts. I know he struggled with it, and he and I both believed he'd made his peace with it."

"But now you think not?"

"Now I think perhaps he wasn't as certain as he told himself he was. He may not even have known what he meant to do. It would take so little, in a way. The decision of a moment, and then gone beyond retrieval. If he regretted it in the next breath, it would already be too late. But it can't be a coincidence, the Galts and Stone-Made-Soft."

Liat sipped now, just enough to maintain the warmth in her body but not so much as to make her drunk. Maati drank directly from the bottle, wiping it with his sleeve after.

"There's another explanation," she said. "The Galts could have done it."

"How? They can't unmake a binding."

"They could have bought him."

Maati shook his head, frowning. "Not Cehmai. There's not a man in the world less likely to turn against the Khaiem."

"You're sure of that?"

"Yes. I'm sure," Maati said. "He was happy. He had his life and his place in the world, and he was happy."

"So much the worse for him," Liat said. "At least we don't have that to suffer, eh?"

"And now who sounds bitter?"

Liat chuckled and took a pose accepting the point that was made awkward by the bowl in one hand.

"How are things with Otah-kvo?" Maati asked.

"He's like the wind on legs," Liat said. "He wants to know everything at once, control all of it, and I think he's driving the court half mad. And . . . don't say I said it, but it's almost as if he's enjoying it. Everything's falling apart except him. If simple force of will can hold a city together, I think Machi will be fine."

"It can't, though."

"No," she agreed. "It can't."

The back of Maati's hand brushed against her arm. It was a small, tentative gesture, familiar as breath. It was something he had always done when he was uncertain and in need of comfort. There had been times when she'd found it powerfully annoying and times when she'd found herself doing it too. Now, she shifted the wine bowl to her other hand, and resolutely laced her fingers with his.

"I haven't written back to the Dai-kvo," Maati said. His voice was as low as a confession. "I'm not sure what I should . . . I haven't been back to Saraykeht, you know. I could . . . I mean . . . Gods, I'm saying this badly. If you want it, Liat-kya, I could come back with you. You and Nayiit."

"No," she said. "There isn't room for you. My life there has a certain shape to it, and I don't want you to be a part of it. And Nayiit's a grown man. It's too late to start raising him now. I love you. And Nayiit is better, I think, knowing you than he was before. But you can't come back with us. You aren't welcome."

Maati looked down at his knees. His hand seemed to relax into her palm.

"Thank you," he whispered.

She raised his hand and kissed the wide, soft knuckles. And then his mouth. He touched her neck gently, his hand warm against her skin.

"Put out the candles," she said.

Time had made him a better lover than when they had been young. Time and experience—his and her own both. Sex had been so earnest then; so anxious, and so humorless. She had spent too much time as a girl worried about whether her breasts looked pleasing or if her hips were too thin. In the years she had kept a house with him, Maati had tried to hold in his belly whenever his robes came off. Youth and vanity, and now that they were doomed to sagging flesh and loose skin and short breath, all of it could be forgiven and left behind.

They laughed more now as they shrugged out of their robes and pulled each other down on the wide, soft bed. They paused in their passions to let Maati rest. She knew better now what would bring her the greatest pleasure, and had none of her long-ago qualms about asking for it. And when they were spent, lying wrapped in a soft sheet, Maati's head on her breast, the netting pulled closed around them, the silence was deeper and more intimate than any words they had spoken.

She would miss this. She had known the dangers when she had taken his hand again, when she had kissed him again. She had known there would be a price to pay for it, if only the pain of having had something pleasant and precious and brief. For a moment, her mind shifted to Nayiit and his lovers, and she was touched by sorrow on his behalf. He was too much her son and not enough Otah's. But she didn't want Otah in this room, in this moment, so she put both of these other men out of her mind and concentrated instead on the warmth of her own flesh and Maati's, the slow, regular deepening of his breath and of hers.

Her thoughts wandered, slowing and losing their coherence; turning into something close kin to dream. She had almost slipped into the deep waters of sleep when Maati's sudden spasm brought her back. He was sitting up, panting like a man who'd run a mile. It was too dark to see his face.

She called his name, and a low groan escaped him. He stood and for a moment she was afraid that he would stagger and fall. But she made out his silhouette, a deeper darkness, and he did not sway. She called his name again.

"No," he said, then a pause and, "No no no no no. Oh gods. Gods, no."

Liat rose, but Maati was already walking. She heard him bark his shin against the table in the front room, heard the wine bottle clatter as it fell. She wrapped her sheet around herself and hurried after him just in time to see him lumbering naked out the door and into the night. She followed.

He trotted into the library, his hands moving restlessly. When he lit a candle, she saw his face etched deep with dread. It was as if he was watching someone die that only he could see.

"Maati. Stop this," she said, and the fear in her voice made her realize that she was trembling. "What's the matter? What's happened?"

"I was wrong," he said. "Gods, Cehmai will never forgive me doubting him. He'll never forgive me."

Candle in hand, Maati lumbered into the next room and began frantically looking through scrolls, hands shaking so badly the wax spilled on the floor. Liat gave up hope that he would speak, that he would explain. Instead, she took the candle from his hand and held it for him as he searched. In the third room, he found what he'd been seeking and sank to the floor. Liat came to his side, and read over his shoulder as he unfurled the scroll. The ink was pale, the script the alphabet of the Old Empire. Maati's fingertips traced the words, looking for something, some passage or phrase. Liat found herself holding her breath. And then his hand stopped moving.

The grammar was antiquated and formal, the language almost too old to make sense of. Liat silently struggled to translate the words that had caught Maati short.

The second type is made up of those thoughts impossible to bind by their nature, and no greater knowledge shall ever permit them. Examples of this are Imprecision and Freedom-From-Bondage.

"I know what they've done," he said.

11

>+< Nantani had been one of the first cities built when the Second Empire reached out past its borders to put its mark on the distant lands they now inhabited. The palace of the Khai was topped by a dome the color of jade—a single stone shaped by the will of some long-dead poet. When the sunlight warmed it in just the right way, it would chime, a low voice rolling out wordlessly over the whitewashed walls and blue tile roofs of the city.

Sinja had wintered in Nantani for a few seasons, retreating from the snow-bound fields of the Westlands to wait in comfort for the thaw and spend the money he'd earned. He knew the scent of the sea here, the feel of the soft, chalky soil beneath his feet. He knew of an old man who sold garlic sausages from a stall near the temple that were the best he'd had in the world. He knew the sound of the great sun chime. He had not known that the deep, throbbing tone would also come when the palace below it burned.

There were other fires as well: pillars of black, rolling smoke that rose into the air like filthy clouds. The doors he passed as he walked down to the sea-front were broken and splintered. The shutters at the windows clacked open and closed in the breeze. Often they passed wide swaths of half-dry blood on the ground or smeared on the rough white walls.

The city had been home to over a hundred thousand people. It had fallen in a morning.

Balasar had sent three forces in through the wide streets to the Khai's palace, the poet's house, the libraries. When those three things were destroyed, the signal went out—brass horns blaring the sack. When the signal reached the remaining forces, it was a storm of chaos. Some men ran for the inner parts of the city, hoping to find richer pickings. Others grabbed the first mercantile house they saw and took whatever was there to find—goods, gold, women. For the time it took the sun to travel the width of a man's hand, Nantani was a scene from the old stories of hell as the soldiery took what they could for themselves.

And then the second call came, and the looting stopped. Those few who were so maddened by greed or lust that they ignored the call were taken to their captains, relieved of what wealth they had grabbed, and then a fifth of them killed as an example to others. This was an army of discipline, and the free-for-all was over. Now the studied, considered dismantling of the city began.

Quarter by quarter, street by street, the armies of Galt stripped the houses and basements, outbuildings and kitchens and coal stores. Sinja's own men led each force, calling out in breaking voices that Nantani had fallen, that her people were permanently indentured to Galt, their belongings forfeit. And all the wealth of the city was stripped down, put on carts and wagons, and pulled to a great pile at the seafront. Some men fought and were killed. Some fled and were hunted down or ignored, at the whim of the soldiers who found them. And the great blackening dome of jade sang out its grief and mourning.

Sinja caught sight of the pavilion erected by the growing pile of treasure. The banners of Galt and Gice hung from the bar that topped the fluttering canvas. Sinja and the soldiers Balasar Gice had sent to collect him strode to it. At the seafront, ships stood ready to receive what had once been Nantani, and was now the fortune of Galt. Balasar stood at a writing desk, consulting with a clerk over a ledger. The general still wore his armor—embroidered silk as thick as three fingers together. Sinja had seen its like before. Armor that would stop a spear or a sword cut, but weighed likely half as much as the man who wore it. And still when Balasar caught sight of them and walked forward, hand outstretched to Sinja, there was no weariness in him.

"Captain Ajutani," Balasar said, his hand clasping Sinja's, "come sit with me."

Sinja took a pose appropriate for a guard to his commander. It wasn't quite the appropriate thing, but it came near enough for the general to take its sense. Sinja walked behind the man to a low table where a bottle of wine stood open, two perfect porcelain wine bowls glowing white at its side. Balasar waved the attendant away and poured the wine himself. Sinja accepted a bowl and sat across from him.

"It was nicely done," Sinja said, gesturing with his free hand toward the city. "Well-managed and quick."

Balasar looked up, almost as if noticing the streets and warehouses for the first time. Sinja thought a hint of a smile touched the general's lips, but it was gone as soon as it came. The wine was rich and left Sinja's mouth feeling almost clean.

"It was competent," Balasar agreed. "But it can't have been easy. For you and your men."

"I didn't lose one of them," Sinja said. "I don't know that I've ever seen a campaign start where we took a city and didn't lose anyone."

"This is a different sort of war than the usual," Balasar said. And there, in the pale eyes, Sinja saw the ghosts. The general wasn't at ease, however casual he chose to be with his wine. It was an interesting fact, and Sinja put it at the back of his mind. "I wanted to ask after your men."

"Have there been complaints?"

"Not at all. Every report suggests that they did their work admirably. But this wasn't the adventure they expected."

"They expected the women they raped to look less like their sisters, that's truth," Sinja said. "And honestly, I expect we'll lose some. I don't know how it is in Galt, sir, but when I've taken a green company into battle the first time, we always lose some."

"Inexperience," Balasar said, agreeing.

"No, sir. I don't mean the enemy spits a few, though that's usually true as well. I mean there are always a few who came into the work with epics in their heads. Great battles, honor, glory. All that pig shit. Once they see what a battlefield or a sacked town really looks like, they wake up. Half these boys are still licking off the caul. Some of them will think better and sneak off."

"And how do you plan to address the problem?"

"Let them go," Sinja said and shrugged. "We haven't seen a fight yet, but before this is finished, we will. When it happens I'd rather have twenty soldiers than thirty men looking for a reason to retreat."

The general frowned, but he also nodded. At the edge of the pier, half a hundred seagulls took to the air at once, their cries louder than the waves. They wheeled once over the ships and then settled again, just where they had been.

"Unless you have a different opinion, sir," Sinja said.

"Do this," Balasar said, looking up from under his brow. "Go to them. Explain to them that I will never turn against my men. But if they leave me . . . if they leave my service, they aren't my men any longer. And if I find them again, I won't be lenient."

Sinja scratched his chin, the stubble just growing in, and felt a smile growing in his mind.

"I can see that they understand, sir," he said. "And it might stop some of the ones who'd choose to hang up their swords. But if there's someone you feel isn't loyal, one of my men that you think isn't yours, I'd recommend you kill him now. There's no room on a campaign like this for someone who'll take up arms against the man that pays his wage."

Balasar nodded, leaning back in his chair.

"I think we understand each other," he said.

"Let's be certain," Sinja said, and put his hands open and palms-down on the table between them. "I'm a mercenary, and to judge by that pile of silk and cedar chests you're about to ship back to Galt, you're the man who's got the money to pay my contract. If I've given you reason to think there's more happening than that, I'd rather we cleared it up now."

Balasar chuckled. It was a warm sound. That was good.

"Are you ever subtle?" Balasar asked.

"If I'm paid to be," Sinja said. "I've had a bad experience working for someone who thought I might look better with a knife-shaped hole in my belly, sir, and I'd rather not repeat it. Have I done something to make you question my intentions?"

Balasar considered him. Sinja met his gaze.

"Yes," Balasar said. "You have. But it's nothing I would be comfortable hanging you for. Not yet at least. The poet, when you killed him. He addressed you in the familiar. Sinja-kya."

"Men begging for their lives sometimes develop an inaccurate opinion of how close they are to the men holding the blades," Sinja said, and the general had the good manners to blush. "I understand your position, sir. I've been living under the Khaiem for a long time now. You don't know my history, and if you did, it wouldn't help you. I've broken contracts before, and I won't lie about it. But I would appreciate it if we could treat each other professionally on this."

Balasar sighed.

"You've managed to shame me, Captain Ajutani."

"I won't brag about that if you'll agree to be certain you've a decent cause to kill me before taking action," Sinja said.

"Agreed," Balasar said. "But your men? I meant what I said about them."

"I'll be sure they understand," Sinja said, then swigged down the last of his wine, took a pose appropriate to taking leave of a superior, and walked back into the streets of the fallen city, hoping that it wouldn't be clear from his stride that his knees felt loose. Not that a sane measure of fear could be held against him, but there was pride to consider. And someone was watching him. He could be damned sure of that. So he walked straight and calm through the streets and the smoke and the wailing of the survivors until he reached the camp outside the last trailing building of Nantani. The tents were far from empty—the thugs and free armsmen of Machi didn't all have a stomach for looting Nantani—but he didn't speak to his men until just after nightfall.

They had a fire burning, though the summer night wasn't cold. The light of it made the tents glow gold and red. The men were quiet. The boasting and swaggering that the Galts were doing didn't have a place here. It would have if the burning city had been made from gray Westlands stone. Sinja stood at the front on a plank set up on chairs in a makeshift dais. He wanted them to see him. The scouts he'd sent out to assure that the conversation was private returned and took a confirming pose. If General Gice had set a watch over him, they'd gone to their own camps or else come from within his own company. He'd done what he could about the first, and the second there was no protection for. He raised his hands.

"So most of what we've done since the spring opened has been walk," he said. "Well, we're in summer now, and you've seen what war looks like. It's not the war I expected, that's truth. But it's the one we've got, and you can all thank the gods that we're on the side most likely to win. But don't think that because this went well, this is over with. It's a long walk still ahead of us."

He sighed and shifted his weight, the plank wobbling a little under his feet. A log in the fire popped, firing sparks up into the darkness like an omen.

"There are a few of you right now who are thinking of leaving. Don't . . . Quiet now! All of you! Don't lie to yourselves about it and don't lie to me. This is the first taste of war most of you've seen. And some of you might have had family or friends in Nantani. I did. But here's what I have to say to you: Don't do it. Right now it looks like our friends the Galts can't be stopped. All the gods know there's not a fighting force anywhere in the cities that could face them, that's truth. But there's worse things for an army to face than another army. Look at the size of this force, the simple number of men. It can't carry the food it needs with it. It can't haul that much water. We have to rely on the land we're covering. The low towns, the cities. The game we can hunt, the trees and coal we can feed into those traveling kilns of theirs. The water we can get from the rivers.

"If the cities North of here can organize—if they can burn the food and the trees so we have to spend more of our time finding supplies, if they foul the wells so that we can't move far from the rivers, if they get small, fast bands together to harass our hunting parties and scouts—we could still be in for hell's own fight. We took Nantani by surprise. That won't happen twice. And that's why I need every man among you here, keeping that from happening. And besides that, any of you that leave, the general's going to hunt down like lowtown dogs and slit your bellies for you."

Sinja paused, looking out at the earnest, despairing faces of the boys he'd led from Machi. He felt old. He rarely felt old, but now he did.

"Don't be stupid," he said, and got down from the plank.

The men raised a late and halfhearted cheer. Sinja waved it away and headed back to his tent. Overhead, the stars shone where the smoke didn't obscure them. The cooks had made chicken and pepper rice. Stinging flies were out, and, to Sinja's mild disgust, Nantani seemed to be a haven for grass ticks. He spent a quiet, reflective time plucking the insects out of his skin and cracking them with his thumbnails. It was near midnight when he heard the roaring crash, thunder rolling suddenly from the ruined city, and then silence. The dome had fallen, then.

How many of his men would know what the sound had meant, he wondered. And how many would understand that he'd given them all the strategy for slowing the Galts, point by point by point. And how many would have snuck away to the North by morning, thinking they were being clever. But he could tell the general he'd done as he was told, and no man present would be able to say otherwise. So maybe he could lull the general back into trusting him for a while longer at least. And maybe Kiyan's husband would find a good way to make use of the time Sinja won for him.

"Ah, Kiyan-kya," he said to the night and the northern stars, "look what you've done. You've made me into a politician."

"MOST HIGH," ASHUA RADAANI SAID, TAKING A POSE THAT WAS AN APOLOGY AND a refusal, "this is . . . this is folly. I understand that the poets are concerned, but you have to see that we have *nothing* that supports their suspicion. We're in summer. It's only a few weeks before we have to harvest the spring crops and plant for autumn. The men you're asking for . . . we can't just send away our laborers."

Otah frowned. It was not a response his father would have gotten. The other Khaiem would have raised a hand, made a speech, perhaps only shifted hands into a pose asking for the speaker to repeat himself. The men and horses and wagons of grain and cheese and salt-packed meats would simply have appeared.

But not for Otah Machi, the upstart who had not won his chair, who had married a wayhouse keeper and produced only one son and that one sickly. He felt the urgency like a hand pressing at his back, but he forced himself to remain calm. He wouldn't have what he wanted by blustering now. He smiled sweetly at the round, soft man with his glittering rings and calculating eyes.

"Your huntsmen, then," Otah said. "Bring your huntsmen. And come yourself. Ride with me, Ashua-cha, and we'll go see whether there's any truth to this thing. If not, you can bear witness yourself, and reassure the court."

The young man's lips twisted into a half-smile.

"Your offer is kind, Most High," he said. "My huntsmen are yours. I will consult with my overseer. If my house can spare me, I would be honored to ride at your side."

"It would please me, Ashua-cha," Otah said. "I leave in two days, and I look forward to your company."

"I will do all I can."

They finished the audience with the common pleasantries, and a servant girl showed the man out. Otah called for a bowl of tea and used the time to consider where he stood. If Radaani sent him a dozen huntsmen, that took the total to almost three hundred men. House Siyanti had offered up its couriers to act as scouts. None of the families of the utkhaiem had refused him; Daikani and old Kamau had even given him what he asked. The others dragged their feet, begged his forgiveness, compromised. If Radaani had backed him, the others would have fallen in line.

And if he had thought Radaani was likely to, he'd have met with him first instead of last.

It was the price, he supposed, of having played the game so poorly up to now. Had he been the man they expected him to be all these years—had he embraced the role he'd accepted and fathered a dozen sons on as many wives and assured the ritual bloodbath that marked the change of generations—they would have been more responsive now. But his own actions had called the forms of court into question, and now that he needed the traditions, he half-regretted having spent years defying them.

The tea came in a bowl of worked silver carried on a pillow. The servant, a man perhaps twenty years older than Otah himself with a long, well-kept beard and one clouded eye, presented it to him with a grace born of long practice. This man had done much the same before Otah's father, and perhaps his grandfather. The presentation of this bowl of tea might be the study and center of this man's life. The thought made the tea taste worse, but Otah took as warm a pose of thanks as would be permitted between the Khai Machi and a servant, however faithful.

Otah rose, gesturing to the doorway. One of his half-hundred attendants rushed forward, robes flowing like water over stones.

"I'll see him now," Otah said. "In the gardens. And see we aren't disturbed."

The sky was gray and ivory, the breeze from the south warm as breath and nearly as gentle. The cherry trees stood green—the pink of the blossoms gone, the crimson of the fruit not yet arrived. The thicker blossoms of high summer had begun to unfurl, rose and iris and sun poppy. The air was thick with the scent. Otah walked down the path, white gravel fine as salt crunching like snow under his feet. He found Maati sitting on the lip of a stone pool, gazing up at the great fountain. Twice as high as a man, the gods of order stood arrayed in bas-relief shaped from a single sheet of bronze. The dragons of chaos lay cowed beneath their greened feet. Water sluiced down the wall, clear until it touched the brows and exultant, upraised faces of the gods, and there it splattered white. Otah sat beside his old friend and considered.

"The dragon's not defeated," Maati said. "Look. You see the third head from the left? It's about to bite that woman's calf. And the man on the end? The one who's looking down? He's lost his balance."

"I hadn't noticed," Otah said.

"You should have another one made with the dragons on top. Just to remind people that it's never over. Even when you think it's done, there's something waiting to surprise you."

Otah nodded, dipping his fingers into the dancing ripples of the pool. Gold and white koi darted toward his fingertips and then as quickly away.

"I understand if you're angry with me," Otah said. "But I didn't ask him. Nayiit came to me. He volunteered."

"Yes. Liat told me."

"He's spent half a season in the Dai-kvo's village. He knows it better than anyone but you or Cehmai."

Maati looked up. There was a darkness in his expression.

"You're right," Maati said. "If this is the Galts and they've freed the andat, then protecting the Dai-kvo is critical. But it would be faster to send for him to come to us. We can build defenses here, train men. Prepare."

"And if the Dai-kvo didn't come?" Otah asked. "How long has he been mulling over Liat's report that the Galts have a poet of their own? I've sent word. I've sent messages. The world can't afford to wait and see if the Dai-kvo suddenly becomes decisive."

"And you speak for the world now, do you?" There was acid in Maati's tone, but Otah could hear the fear behind it and the despair. "If you insist on charging out into whatever kind of war you find out there, take one of us with you. We've lived there. We know the village. Cehmai's still young. Or strap me on the back of a horse and pull me there. Leave Nayiit out of this."

"He's a grown man," Otah said. "He's not a child any longer. He has his own mind and his own will. I thought about refusing him, for your sake and for Liat's. But what would that be to him? He's not still wrapped in crib cloths. How would I say that I wanted him safe because his mother would worry for him?"

"And what about his father," Maati said, but it had none of the inflection of a question. "You have an opinion, Most High, on what his father would think."

Otah's belly sank. He dried his hand on his sleeve, only thinking afterward that it was the motion of a commoner—a dockfront laborer or a midwife's assistant or a courier. The Khai Machi should have raised an arm, summoned a servant to dry his fingers for him on a cloth woven for the purpose and burned after one use. His face felt mask-like and hard as plaster. He took a pose that asked clarification.

"Is that the conversation we're having, then?" he asked. "We're talking about fathers?"

"We're talking about sons," Maati said. "We're talking about you scraping up all the disposable men that the utkhaiem can drag out of comfort houses and slap sober enough to ride just so they can appease the irrational whims of the Khai. Taking those men out into the field because you think the armies of Galt are going to slaughter the Dai-kvo is what we're talking about, and about taking Nayiit with you."

"You think I'm wrong?"

"I *know* you're right!" Maati was breathing hard now. His face was flushed. "I know they're out there, with an army of veterans who are perfectly accustomed to hollowing out their enemies' skulls for wine bowls. And I know you sent Sinja-cha away with all the men we had who were even half trained. If you come across the Galts, you will lose. And if you take Nayiit, he'll die too. He's still a child. He's still figuring out who he is and what he intends and what he means to do in the world. And—"

"Maati. I know it would be safer for me to stay here. For Nayiit to stay here. But it would only be safe for the moment. If we lose the Dai-kvo and all he knows and the libraries he keeps, having one more safe winter in Machi won't mean anything. And we might not even manage the winter."

Maati looked away. Otah bowed his head and pretended not to have seen the tears on his old friend's cheeks.

"I've only just found him again," Maati said, barely audible over the splashing water. "I've only just found him again, and I don't want him taken away."

"I'll keep him safe," Otah said.

Maati reached out his hand, and Otah let him lace his fingers with his own. It wasn't an intimacy that they had often shared, and against his will, Otah found something near to sorrow tightening his chest. He put his free hand to Maati's shoulder. When Maati spoke, his voice was thick and Otah no longer ignored his tears.

"We're his fathers, you and I," Maati said. "So we'll take care of him. Won't we?"

"Of course we will," Otah said.

"You'll see him home safe."

"Of course."

Maati nodded. It was an empty promise, and they both knew it. Otah smoothed a palm over Maati's thinning hair, squeezed his palm one last time, and stood. He was moved to speak, but he couldn't find any words that would say what he meant. Instead he turned and softly walked away. His servants and attendants waited just outside the garden, attentive as puppies whose mother has left them. Otah waved them away, as he always had. And as he might not do again. The Master of Tides brought the ledger that outlined the rest of his day, and the day after, and was suddenly perfectly blank after that. In two days, he would be traveling with what militia he could, and there was no point planning past that. As the man spoke, Otah gently took the book from him, closed it, and handed it back. The Master of Tides went silent, and no one followed Otah when he walked away.

He strode through the palaces, ignoring the poses of obeisance and respect that bloomed wherever he went. He didn't have time for the forms and rituals. He didn't have time to respect the traditions he was about to put his life in danger to protect. He wasn't entirely sure what that said about him. He took the wide, marble stairs two at a time, rising up from the lower palace toward his personal apartments. When he arrived, Kiyan wasn't there. He paced the rooms, plucking at the papers on the wide table he'd had brought for him. Maps and histories and lists of names. Numbers of men and of wagons and routes. It looked like a nest for rats: the piled books, the scattered notes. It was vaguely ridiculous, he thought as he read over the names of the houses and families who had sworn him support. He was no more a general than he was a tinsmith, and still, here he was, the man stuck with the job.

He didn't recall picking up the map. And yet there it was, in his hands. His eyes traced the paths he and his men might take. He and the men Maati had called disposable. It wasn't the first time he'd wished Sinja-cha were still in the city, if only to have the dispassionate eye of a man who had actually fought in the field. Otah was an amateur at war. He had the impression that it was a poor field for amateurs. He traded the map for the lists of men and studied it again as if there were a cipher hidden in it. He didn't notice when Kiyan and Eiah arrived. When he looked up from his papers, they were simply there.

His wife was calm and collected, though he could see the strain in the thinness of her lips and the tightness of her jaw. Her hair was grayer now than the image of her in his mind. Her face seemed older. For a moment, he was back in the wayhouse she'd taken over from her father, years ago in Udun. He was in her common room, listening to a flute player fumble through old tunes that everyone knew, and wondering if the lovely fox-faced woman serving the wine had meant to touch his hand when she poured. From such small things are lives constructed. Something of his thought must have shown in his face, because her features softened and something near a blush touched her cheeks as Eiah lowered herself to a couch and collapsed. He noticed that her usual array of rings and jewels were gone; but for the quality of her robe, she could have been a merchant's daughter.

"You look spent, Eiah-kya," Otah said. Then, to Kiyan, "What's she been doing? Carrying stones up the towers? And what's happened to jewelry?"

"Physicians don't wear metalwork," she said, as if he'd asked something profoundly stupid. "Blood gets caught in the settings."

"She's been with them all day," Kiyan said.

"We had a boy come in with a crushed arm," Eiah said, her eyes closed. "It was all bloody and the skin scraped off. It looked like something from a butcher's stall. I could see his knuckle bones. Dorin-cha cleaned it up and wrapped it. We'll know in a couple days whether he'll have to have it off."

"*We'll* know?" Otah asked. "They're having you decide the fate of men's elbows?"

He saw a dark glitter where his daughter's eyes cracked just slightly open. "Dorin-cha will tell me, and then we'll both know."

"She's been quite the asset, they say," Kiyan said. "The matrons keep trying to send her away, and she keeps coming back. They tell her it's unseemly for her to be there, but the physicians seem flattered that she's interested."

"I like it," Eiah said, her voice slurring. "I don't want to stop. I want to help."

"You don't have to stop," Otah said. "I'll see to it."

"Thank you, Papa-kya," Eiah murmured.

"Off to your bed," Kiyan said, gently shaking Eiah's knee. "You're already half-dreaming."

Eiah frowned and grunted, but then came to her feet. She stumbled over to Otah, genuine exhaustion competing with the theatrics of being tired, and threw her arms around his neck. Her hair smelled of the vinegar the physicians used to wash down their slate tables. He put his arms around her. He could feel tears welling up in his eyes. His baby girl, his daughter. He would see her tomorrow, and then he would march out into the gods only knew what.

Tomorrow, he told himself, I will see her again tomorrow. This won't be the last time. Not yet. He kissed her forehead and let her go.

Eiah tottered to her mother for another kiss, another hug, and then they were alone. Kiyan gently plucked the papers from his hands and put them back on the desk.

"I'm not certain that worked as a punishment," Otah said. "We're halfway to raising a physician."

"It lets her feel she's useful," Kiyan said as she pulled him to the couch. He sat at her side. "It's normal for her to want to feel she's in control of something. And she isn't squeamish. I'll hand her that much."

"I hope feeling useful is enough," Otah said. "She's got her own will, and I don't think she'd be past following it over a cliff if it led her there."

He saw Kiyan read his deeper meaning. *I hope we are all still here to worry about it.*

"We do as well by them as we can, love," she said.

"I think about Idaan," Otah said.

Kiyan took his hand.

"Eiah isn't your sister. She isn't going to do the things she did," she said. "And more to the point, you aren't your father."

For a moment, he was consumed by memories: the father he had met only once, the sister who had engineered the old man's murder. Hatred and violence and ambition had destroyed his family once. He supposed it was inevitable that he should fear it happening again. Otah raised Kiyan's hand to his lips, and then sighed.

"I have to go to Danat. I haven't seen him yet. Go with me?"

"He's asleep already, love. We stopped in on our way here. He won't wake before morning. And you'll have to find different stories to read to him next time. Everything you left there, he's read to himself. Our boy's going to grow up a scholar at this rate."

Otah nodded, pushing aside a moment's guilt over the relief he felt. Seeing Danat was one less thing, even if it was more important than most of the others he'd already done. And there would be tomorrow. There would at least be tomorrow.

"How is he?"

"His color is better, but he has less energy. The fever is gone for now, but he still coughs. I don't know. No one does."

"Can he travel?"

Kiyan turned. Her gaze darted across his face as if he were a book that she was trying to read. Her hands took a querying pose.

"I've been thinking," Otah said. "Planning."

"For if you're killed," Kiyan said. Her voice made it plain she'd been thinking of it as well.

"The mines. If I don't come back, I want you to take to the mines in the North. Cehmai will go with you, and he knows them better than anyone. If you can, take the children and as much gold as you can carry and head west. Sinja and the others will be there somewhere, working whatever contract they've taken. They'll protect you."

"You're sending me to *him*?" Kiyan asked softly.

"Only if I don't come back."

"You will."

"Still," Otah said. "If . . ."

"If," Kiyan agreed and took his hand. Then, a long moment later, "We were never lovers, he and I. Not the way . . ."

Otah put a finger to her lips, and she went quiet. There were tears in her eyes, and in his.

"Let's not open that again," he said.

"You could come away too. We could all leave quietly. The four of us and a fast cart."

"And spend our lives on a beach in Bakta," Otah said. "I can't. I have this thing to do. My city."

"I know. But I had to say it, just so I know it was said."

Otah looked down. His hands looked old—the knuckles knobbier than he thought of them, the skin looser. They weren't an old man's hands, but they weren't a young man's any longer. When he spoke, his voice was low and thoughtful.

"It's strange, you know. I've spent years chafing under the weight of being Khai Machi, and now that it's harder than it ever was, now that there's something real to lose, I can't let go of it. There was a man once who told me that if it were a choice between holding a live coal in my bare fist or letting a city of innocent people die, of course I would do my best to stand the pain. That it was what any decent man would do."

"Don't apologize," Kiyan said.

"Was I apologizing?"

"Yes," she said. "You were. You shouldn't. I'm not angry with you, and there's nothing to blame you for. They all think you've changed, you know, but this is who you've always been. You were a poor Khai Machi because it didn't matter until now. I understand; I'm just frightened to death, love. It's nothing you can spare me."

"Maati could be wrong," Otah said. "The Galts may be busy rolling over the Westlands and none of it anything to do with Stone-Made-Soft. I may arrive at the Dai-kvo's village and be laughed at all the way back north."

"He's not wrong."

The great stones of the palaces creaked as they cooled, the summer sun fallen behind the mountains. The scent of incense long since burned and the smoke of snuffed lanterns filled the air like a voice gone silent. Shadows touched the corners of the apartments, deepening the reds of the tapestries and giving the light a feeling of physical presence. Kiyan's hand felt warm and lost in his own.

"I know he's not," Otah said.

He left orders with the servants at his door that unless there was immediate threat to him or his family—fire or sudden illness or an army crossing the river—he was to be left alone for the night. He would speak with no one, he would read no letter or contract, he wished no entertainments. Only a simple meal for him and his wife, and the silence for the two of them to fill as they saw fit.

They told stories—reminiscences of Old Mani and the wayhouse in Udun, the sound of the birds by the river. The time a daughter of one of the high families had snuck into the rooms her lover had taken and had to be smuggled back out. Otah told stories from his time as a courier, traveling the cities on the business of House Siyanti under his false name. They were all stories she'd heard before, of course. She knew all his stories.

They made love seriously and gently and with a profound attention. He savored every touch, every scent and motion. He fought to remember them and her, and he felt Kiyan's will to store the moment away, like food packed away for the long empty months after the last leaf of autumn has fallen. It was, Otah supposed, the kind of sex lovers had on the nights before wars, pleasure and fear and a sorrow that anticipated the losses ahead. And afterward, he lay against her familiar, beloved body and pretended to sleep until, all unaware, the pretense became truth and he dreamed of looking for a white raven that everyone else but him had seen, and of a race through the tunnels beneath Machi that began and ended at his father's ashes. He woke to the cool light of morning and Kiyan's voice.

"Sweet," she said again. Otah blinked and stretched, remembering his body. "Sweet, there's someone come to see you. I think you should speak with him."

Otah sat up and adopted a pose that asked the question, but Kiyan, half smiling, nodded toward the bedchamber's door. Before the servants could come and dress him, Otah pulled on rose-red outer robes over his bare skin and, still tying the stays, walked out to the main rooms. Ashua Radaani sat at the edge of a chair, his hands clasped between his knees. His face was as pale as fresh dough, and the jewels set in his rings and sewn in his robes seemed awkward and lost.

"Ashua-cha," Otah said, and the man was already on his feet, already in a pose of formal greeting. "What's happened?"

"Most High, my brother in Cetani . . . I received a letter from him last night. The Khai Cetani is keeping it quiet, but no one has seen poet or andat in the court in some time."

"Not since the day Stone-Made-Soft escaped," Otah said.

"As nearly as we can reckon it," he agreed.

Otah nodded, but took no formal pose. Kiyan stood in the doorway, her expression half pleasure and half dread.

"May I have the men I asked of you, Ashua-cha?"

"You may have every man in my employ, Most High. And myself as well."

"I will take whoever is ready at dawn tomorrow," Otah said. "I won't wait past that."

Ashua Radaani bowed his way out, and Otah stood watching him leave. That would help, he thought. He'd want the word spread that Radaani was firmly behind him. The other houses and families might then change their opinions of what help could be spared. If he could double the men he'd expected to have . . .

Kiyan's low chuckle startled him. She still stood in the doorway, her arms crossed under her breasts. Her smile was gentle and amazed. Otah raised in hands in query.

"I have just watched the Khai Machi gravely accept the apology and sworn aid of his servant Radaani. A day ago you were an annoyance to that man. Today, you're a hero from an Old Empire epic. I've never seen things change around a man so quickly as they change around you."

"It's only because he's frightened. He'll recover," Otah said. "I'll be an incompetent again when he's safe and the world's back where it was."

"It won't be, love," Kiyan said. "The world's changed, and it's not changing back, whatever we do."

"I know it. But it's easier if I don't think too much about it just yet. When the Dai-kvo's safe, when the Galts are defeated, I'll think about it all then. Before that, it doesn't help," Otah said as he turned back toward the bed they had shared for years now, and would for one more night at least. Her hand brushed his cheek as he stepped past, and he turned to kiss his fingers. There were no tears in her eyes now, nor in his.

12

>+< "I gave him too much and not enough men to do it," Balasar said as they walked through the rows of men and horses and steam wagons. Eustin shrugged his disagreement.

Around them, the camps were being broken down. Men loaded rolled canvas tents onto mules and steam wagons. The washerwomen loaded the pans and stones of their trade into packs that they carried on bent shoulders. The last of the captured slaves helped to load the last of the ships for the voyage back to Galt. The gulls whirled and called one to another; the waves rumbled and slapped the high walls of the seafront; the world smelled of sea salt and fire. And Balasar's mind was on the other side of the map, uneased and restless.

"Coal's a good man," Eustin said. "If anyone can do the thing, it's him."

"Six cities," he said. "I set him six cities. It's too much. And he's got far fewer men than we do."

"We'll get finished here in time to help him with the last few," Eustin said. "Besides, one of them's just a glorified village, and Chaburi-Tan was likely burning before we were out of Aren. So that's only four and a half cities left."

There was something in that. Coal's men had been on the island and in the city and in ships off the coast, waiting for the signal that would follow the andat's vanishing. Even now, Coal and his men—between five thousand and six—were sailing fast to Yalakeht. A handful more waited there in the warehouses of Galtic traders, preparing for the trip upstream to the village of the Dai-kvo and the libraries at the heart of the Khaiem. The other cities would have their scrolls and codices, but only there, in the palaces carved from the living rock, were the great secrets of the fallen Empire kept. His war turned on that fire and on the deaths of the men who knew what those soon-burned books said.

And he wouldn't be there for it.

"The southern legions are ready, sir," Eustin said. "Eight thousand for Shosheyn-Tan, Lachi, and Saraykeht. My legion's two thousand strong. Should be enough for Pathai and that school out on the plains. That'll leave you a full half of the forces for the river cities. Udun and Utani and Tan-Sadar."

Balasar struggled with the impulse to send more of the men with Eustin. It was the illusion he always suffered when tactics required that he split his forces. He would make do with less in order to keep his best men safe. Pathai was only half the size of Nantani, but Eustin was taking only a tenth of the men. It was unlikely that word had traveled fast enough for the Khai Pathai to hire some fleet-footed mercenary company out of the Westlands, but unlikely wasn't impossible. Two thousand more men might make the difference if something went wrong.

But he had the longest journey ahead of him—Nantani to Udun, and some of it over plains where there were no good roads and the steam wagons would have to be pulled. On rough ground, the boilers were too likely to explode. The journey would take time, and so Udun and Utani and Tan-Sadar would have the longest time to prepare. They would be the hardest to capture or destroy. It was why he had chosen them for himself. Except, of course, for what he had tasked to Coal. Five thousand men to take six cities. Five cities, now. Four and a half.

"We'll get there in time to help him if he needs us, sir," Eustin said, reading his face. "And keep in mind, there's not a fighting force anywhere in the Khaiem. Coal's in more danger of tripping on his spear than of facing an enemy worth sneezing at."

Balasar laughed. Two armsmen busy folding a tent looked up, saw him and Eustin, and grinned.

"It's like me, isn't it?" Balasar said. "Here we have just made the greatest sack of a city in living history, captured enough gold to keep us both fed the best food and housed in the best brothels for the rest of our lives, and I can't bring myself to enjoy a minute of it."

"You do tend to worry most when things are going well, sir."

They reached a place where the mud path split, one way to the west, the other to the north. Balasar put out his hand, and Eustin took it. For a moment, they weren't general and captain. They were friends and conspirators in the plot to save the world. Balasar found his anxiety ebbing, felt the grin on his face and saw it mirrored in his man's.

"Meet me in Tan-Sadar before the leaves turn," Balasar said. "We'll see then whether Coal has use for us or if it's time to go home."

"I'll be there, sir," Eustin said. "Rely on it. And as a favor to me? Keep an eye on Ajutani."

"Both, when I can spare them," Balasar promised. And then they parted. Balasar walked through the thin mud and low grass to the camp at the head of the first legion. His groom stood waiting, a fresh horse munching contentedly at the roadside weeds. A second horse stood beside it, a rider in the saddle looking out bemused at the men and the rolling hills and the horizon beyond.

"Captain Ajutani," Balasar said, and the rider turned and saluted. "You're ready for the march?"

"At your command, General."

Balasar swung himself up onto the horse and accepted the reins from his groom.

"Then let's begin," he said. "We've got a war to finish."

IT HAD TAKEN A FEW LENGTHS OF COPPER TO CONVINCE THE KEEPERS OF THE WIDE platforms to unhook their chains and haul her skyward, but Liat didn't care. The dread in her belly made small considerations like money seem trivial. Money or food or sleep. She stood now at the open sky doors and looked out to the south and east, where the men of Machi made their way through the high green grasses of summer. From this distance, they looked like a single long black mark on the landscape. She could no more make out an individual wagon or rider than she could take to the air and fly. And still she strained her eyes, because one part of that distant mark was her only son.

He had only told her when it was already done. She had been in her apartments—the apartments given her by the man who had once been her lover. She had been thinking of how a merchant or tradesman who took in an old lover so casually would have been the subject of gossip—even a member of the utkhaiem would have had answers to make—but the Khai was above that. She had gone as far as wondering, not for the first time, what Kiyan-cha thought and felt on the matter, when Nayiit had scratched at her door and let himself in.

She knew when she saw his face that something had happened. There was a light in his eyes brighter than candles, but his smile was the too-charming one he always employed when he'd done something he feared she'd fault him for. Her first thought was that he'd offered to marry some local girl. She took a pose that asked the question even before he could speak.

"Sit with me," he said and took her by the hand.

They sat on a low stone bench near the window. The shutters were opened, and the evening breeze had smelled of forge smoke. He kept her hand in his as he spoke.

"I've been to see the Khai," Nayiit said. "You know he believes what Maati-cha . . . what Father said. About the Galts."

"Yes," Liat said. She still hadn't understood what she was seeing. His next words came like a blow.

"He's taking men, all the men he can find. They're going overland to the Dai-kvo. I've asked to go with them, and he's accepted me. He's finding me a sword and something like armor. He says we'll leave before the week's out," he said, then paused. "I'm sorry."

She knew that her grip on his hand had gone hard because he winced, but not because she felt it. This hadn't been their plan. This had never been their plan.

"Why?" she managed, but she already knew.

He was young and he was trapped in a life he more than half regretted. He was finding what it meant to him to be a man. Riding out to war was an adventure, and a statement—oh, by all the gods—it was a statement that he had faith in Maati's guess. It was a way to show that he believed in his father. Nayiit only kissed her hand.

"I know the Dai-kvo's village," he said. "I can ride. I'm at least good enough with a bow to catch rabbits along the way. And someone has to go, Mother. There's no reason that I shouldn't."

You have a wife, she didn't say. You have a child. You have a city to defend, and it's Saraykeht. You'll be killed, and I cannot lose you. The Galts have terrorized every nation in the world that didn't have the andat for protection, and Otah has a few armsmen barely competent to chase down thieves and brawl in the alleys outside comfort houses.

"Are you sure?" she said.

She sat now, looking out over the wide, empty air as the mark grew slowly smaller. As her son left her. Otah had managed more men than she'd imagined he would. At the last moment, the utkhaiem had rallied to him. Three thousand men, the first army fielded in the cities of the Khaiem in generations. Untried, untested. Armed with whatever had come to hand, armored with leather smith's aprons. And her little boy was among them.

She wiped her eyes with the cloth of her sleeve.

"Hurry," she said, pressing the word out to the distant men. Get the Dai-kvo, retrieve the poets and their books, and come back to me. Before they find you, come back to me.

The sun had traveled the width of two hands together before she stepped out onto the platform and signaled the men far below her to bring her down. The chains clattered and the platform lurched, but Liat only held the rail and waited for it to steady in its descent. She knew she would not fall. That would have been too easy.

She had done a poor job of telling Maati. Perhaps she'd assumed Nayiit would already have told him. Perhaps she'd been trying to punish Maati for beginning it all. It had been the next night, and she had accepted Maati's invitation to dinner in the high pavilion. Goose in honey lacquer, almonds with cinnamon and raisin sauce, rice wine. Not far away, a dance had begun—silk streamers and the glow of torches, the trilling of pipes and the laughter of girls drunk with flirtation. She remembered it all from the days after Saraykeht had fallen. There was only so long that the shock of losing the andat could restrain the festivals of youth.

The young are blind and stupid, she'd said, and their breasts don't sag. It's the nearest thing they've got to a blessing.

Maati had chuckled and tried to take her hand, but she couldn't stand the touch. She'd seen the surprise in his expression, and the hurt. That was when she'd told him. She'd said it lightly, acidly, fueled by her anger and her despair. She had been too wrapped up in herself to pay attention to Maati's shock and horror. It was only later, when he'd excused himself and she was walking alone in the dim paths at the edge of the dance, that she understood she'd as much as accused him of sending Nayiit to his death.

She had gone by Maati's apartments that night and again the next day, but he had gone and no one seemed to know where. By the time she found him, he had spoken with Otah and Nayiit. He accepted her apology, he cradled her while they both confessed their fears, but the damage had been done. He was as haunted as she was, and there was nothing to be done about it.

Liat realized she'd almost reached the ground, startled to have come so far so quickly. Her mind, she supposed, had been elsewhere.

Machi in the height of summer might almost have been a southern city. The sun made its slow, stately way across the sky. The nights had grown so short, she could fall asleep with a glow still bright over the mountains to the west and wake in daylight, unrested. The streets were full of vendors at their carts selling fresh honey bread almost too hot to eat or sausages with blackened skins or bits of lamb over rice with a red sauce spicy enough to burn her tongue. Merchants passed over the black-cobbled streets, wagon wheels clattering. Beggars sang before their lacquered boxes. Firekeepers tended their kilns and saw to the small business of the tradesmen—accepting taxes, witnessing contracts, and a hundred other small duties. Liat pulled her hands into her sleeves and walked without knowing her destination.

It might only have been her imagination that there were fewer men in the streets. Surely there were still laborers and warehouse guards and smiths at their forges. The force marching to the west could account for no more than one man in fifteen. The sense that Machi had become a city of women and old men and boys could only be her mind playing tricks. And still, there was something hollow about the city. A sense of loss and of uncertainty. The city itself seemed to know that the world had changed, and held its breath in dread anticipation, waiting to see whether this transformed reality had a place for Machi in it.

She found herself back at her apartments—feet sore, back aching—before the sun had touched the peaks to the west. As she approached her door, a young man rose from the step. For a moment, her mind tricked her into thinking Nayiit had returned. But no, this boy was too thin through the shoulders, his hair too long, his robes the black of a palace servant. He took a pose of greeting as she approached, and Liat made a brief response.

"Liat Chokavi?"

"Yes."

"Kiyan Machi, first wife of the Khai Machi, extends her invitation. If you would be so kind, I will take you to her."

"Now?" Liat asked, but of course it was now. She waved away the question even before the servant boy could recover from the surprise of being asked in so sharp a tone. When he turned, spine straight and stiff with indignation, she followed him.

They found Otah's wife standing on a balcony overlooking a great hall. Her robes were delicate pink and yellow, and they suited her skin. Her head was turned down, looking at the wide fountain that took up the hall below, the sprays of water reaching up almost to the high domed ceiling above. The servant boy took a pose of obeisance before her, and she replied with one that both thanked and dismissed him. Her greeting of Liat was only a nod and a smile, and then Kiyan's attention turned back to the fountain.

There were children playing in the pool—splashing one another or running, bandy-legged, through water that reached above their knees and would only have dampened half of Liat's own calves. Some wore robes of cotton that clung to their tiny bodies. Some wore loose canvas trousers like a common laborer's. They were, Liat thought, too young to be utkhaiem yet. They were still children, and free from the bindings that would hold them when there was less fat in their cheeks, less joy in their movement. But that was only sentiment. The children of privilege knew when they were faced with a child of the lower orders. These dancing and shouting in the clean, clear water could dress as they saw fit because they were all of the same ranks. These were the children of the great houses, brought to play with the one boy, there, in the robe. The one deep in disagreement with the petulant-looking girl. The one who had eyes and mouth the same shape as Otah's.

Liat looked up and found Kiyan considering her. The woman's expression was unreadable.

"Thank you for coming," Kiyan said over the sounds of falling water and shrieking children.

"Of course," Liat said. She nodded down at the boy. "That's Danat-cha?"

"Yes. He's having a good day," she said. Then, "Please, come this way."

Liat followed her through a doorway at the balcony's rear and into a small resting room where Kiyan sat on a low couch and motioned Liat to do the same. The sounds of play were muffled enough to speak over, but they weren't absent. Liat found them oddly comforting.

"I heard that Nayiit-cha chose to go with the men," Kiyan said.

"Yes," Liat said, and then stopped, because she didn't know what more there was to say.

"I can't imagine that," Kiyan said. "It's hard enough imagining Otah going, but he's my husband. He's not my son."

"I understand why he went. Nayiit, I mean. But his father asked the Khai to take care of him."

Kiyan looked up, confused for a moment, then nodded.

"Maati, you mean?"

"Of course," Liat said.

"Do we have to keep up that pretense?"

"I think we do, Kiyan-cha."

"I suppose," she said. And then a moment later, "No. You're right. You're quite right. I don't know what I was thinking."

Liat considered Otah's wife—thin face, black hair shot with threads of white, so little paint on her cheeks that Liat could see where the lines that came with age had been etched by pain and laughter. There was an intelligence in her face and, Liat thought, a sorrow. Kiyan took a deep breath and seemed to pull herself back from whatever place her mind had gone. She smiled.

"Otah has left the city with a problem," she said. "With so many men gone, the business of things is bound to suffer. There are crops that need bringing in and others that need planting. Roofs need the tiles repaired before autumn comes. There are still parts of the winter quarters that haven't been cleaned out since we've all resurfaced. And the men who coordinate those things or else who oversee the men who do are all off with Otah playing at war."

"That is a problem," Liat agreed, unsure why Kiyan had brought her here to tell her this.

"I'm calling a Council of wives," Kiyan said. "I think we're referring to it as an afternoon banquet, but I mean it to be more than light gossip and sweet breads. I'm going to take care of Machi until Otah comes back. I'll see to it that we have food and coal to see us through the winter."

If, Kiyan didn't need to say, we all live that long. Liat looked at her hands and pressed the dark thoughts away.

"That seems wise," she said.

"I want you to come to the Council, Liat-cha. I want your help."

Liat looked up. Kiyan's whole attention was on her. It made her feel awkward, but also oddly flattered.

"I don't know what I could do—"

"You're a woman of business. You understand schedules and how to coordinate different teams in different tasks so that the whole of a thing comes together the way it should. I understand that too, but frankly most of these women would be totally lost. They've bent their minds to face paints and robes and trading gossip and bedroom tricks," Kiyan said, and then immediately took a pose that asked forgiveness. "I don't mean to make them sound dim. They aren't. But they're the product of a Khai's court, and the things that matter there aren't things that matter, if you see what I mean?"

"Quite well," Liat said with a chuckle.

Kiyan leaned forward and scooped up Liat's hand as if it were the most natural thing to do.

"You helped Otah when he asked it of you. Will you help me now?"

The assent came as far as Liat's lips and then died there. She saw the distress in Kiyan's eyes, but she couldn't say it.

"Why?" Liat whispered. "Why me? Why, when we are what we are to each other."

"When we're what to each other?"

"Women who've loved the same man," Liat said. "Mothers of . . . of *our* sons. How can you put that aside, even only for a little while?"

Kiyan smiled. It was a hard expression. Determined. She did not let go of Liat's hand, but neither did she hold it captive.

"I want you with me because we can't have other enemies now," she said. "And because you and I aren't so different. And because I think perhaps the distraction is something you need as badly as I do. There's war enough coming. I want there to be peace between us."

"I have a price," Liat said.

Kiyan nodded that she continue.

"When Nayiit comes back, spend time with him. Talk with him. Find out who he is. Know him."

"Because?"

"Because if you're going to have me fall in love with your boy, you owe it to fall a little in love with mine."

Kiyan grinned, tears glistening in her eyes. Her hand squeezed Liat's. Liat closed her grip, fierce as a drowning man holding to a rope. She hadn't understood until this moment how deep her fear ran or the loneliness that even Maati couldn't assuage. She couldn't say whether she had pulled Kiyan to her or if she herself had been pulled, but she found herself sobbing into the other woman's shoulder. Otah's wife wrapped fierce arms around her, embracing her as if she would protect Liat from the world.

"They would never understand this," Liat managed when her breath was her own again.

"They're men," Kiyan said. "They're simpler."

13

For years, Otah had been a traveler by profession. He had worked the gentleman's trade, traveling as a courier for a merchant house with business in half the cities of the Khaiem. He had spent days on horseback or hunkered down in the backs of wagons or walking. He remembered with fondness the feeling of resting at the end of a day, his limbs warm and weary, sinking into the woolen blanket that only half protected him from the ticks. He remembered looking up at the wide sky with something like contentment. It seemed fourteen years sleeping in the best bed in Machi had made a difference.

"Is there something I can bring you, Most High?" the servant boy asked from the doorway of the tent. Otah pulled open the netting and turned over in his cot, twisting his head to look at him. The boy was perhaps eighteen summers old, long hair pulled back and bound by a length of leather.

"Do I seem like I need something?"

The boy looked down, abashed.

"You were moaning again, Most High."

Otah let himself lie back on the cot. The stretched canvas creaked under

him like a ship in a storm. He closed his eyes and cataloged quietly all his reasons for moaning. His back ached like someone had kicked him. His thighs
were chafed half raw. They were hardly ten days out from Machi, and it was
becoming profoundly clear that he didn't know how to march a military column across the rolling, forested hills that stretched from Machi almost to the
mountains north of the Dai-kvo. The great Galtic army that had massed in the
South was no doubt well advanced, and the Dai-kvo was in deadly danger, if
he hadn't been killed already. Otah closed his eyes. Right now, the throbbing
sting of his abused thighs bothered him most.

"Go ask the physicians to send some salve," he said.

"I'll call for the physician."

"No! Just . . . just get some salve and bring it here. I'm not infirm. And I
wasn't moaning. It was the cot."

The boy took a pose of acceptance and backed out of the tent, shutting the
door behind him. Otah let the netting fall closed again. A tent with a door.
Gods.

The first few days hadn't been this bad. The sense of release that came
from taking real action at last had almost outweighed the fears that plagued
him and the longing for Kiyan at his side, for Eiah and Danat. The northern
summer was brief, but the days were long. He rode with the men of the utkhaiem, trotting on their best mounts, while the couriers ranged ahead and
the huntsmen foraged. The wide, green world smelled rich with the season. The
North Road ran only among the winter cities—Amnat-Tan, Cetani, Machi.
There was no good, paved road direct from Machi to the village of the Dai-kvo,
but there were trade routes that jumped from low town to low town. Mud
furrows worn by carts and hooves and feet. Around them, grasses rose high as
the bellies of their horses, singing a dry song like fingertips on skin when the
wind stirred the blades. The feeling of the sure-footed animal he rode had
been reassuring at first. Solid and strong.

But the joy of action had wearied while the dread grew stronger. The steady
movement of the horse had become wearisome. The jokes and songs of the
men had lost something of their fire. The epics and romances of the Empire
included some passages about the weariness and longing that came of living
on campaign, but they spoke of endless seasons and years without the solace
of home. Otah and his men hadn't yet traveled two full weeks. They were still
well shy of the journey's halfway mark, and already they were losing what co-
hesion they had.

With every day, most men were afoot while huntsmen and scouts and utkhaiem rode. Horsemen were called to the halt long before the night should
have forced them to make camp, for fear that those following on foot would fail
to reach the tents before darkness fell. And even so, men continued to straggle
in long after the evening meals had been served, leaving them unrested and
fed only on scraps when morning came. The army, such as it was, seemed tied
to the speed of its slowest members. He needed speed and he needed men at

his side, but there was no good way to have both. And the fault, Otah knew, was in himself.

There had to be answers to this and the thousand other problems that came of leading a campaign. The Galts would know. Sinja could have told him, had he been there and not out in some Westlands garrison waiting for a flood of Galts that wasn't coming. They were men that had experience in the field, who had more knowledge of war than the casual study of a few old Empire texts fit in between religious ceremonies and high court bickering.

The scratch came at the door, soft and apologetic. Otah swung his legs off the cot and sat up. He called out his permission as he parted the netting, but the one who came in wasn't the servant boy. It was Nayiit.

He looked tired. His robes had been blue once, but from the hem to the knee they were stained the pale brown of the mud through which they had traveled. Otah considered the weight of their situation—the young man's dual role as Maati's son and his own, the threat he posed to Danat and the promise to Machi, the aid he might be in this present endeavor to prevent harm to the Dai-kvo—and dismissed it all. He was too tired and pained to chew everything a hundred times before he swallowed.

He took a pose of welcome, and Nayiit returned one of greater formality. Otah nodded to a camp chair and Nayiit sat.

"Your attendant wasn't here. I didn't know what the right etiquette was, so I just came through."

"He's running an errand. Once he's back, I can have tea brought," Otah said. "Or wine."

Nayiit took a pose of polite refusal. Otah shrugged it away.

"As you see fit," Otah said. "And what brings you?"

"There's grumbling in the ranks, Most High. Even among some of the ut-khaiem."

"There's grumbling in here, for that," Otah said. "There's just no one here to listen to me. Are there any suggestions? Any solutions that the ranks have seen that escaped me? Because, by all the gods that have ever been named, I'm not too proud to hear them."

"They say you're driving them too hard, Most High," Nayiit said. "That the men need a day's rest."

"Rest? Go slower? That's the solution they have to offer? What kind of brilliance is that?"

Nayiit looked up. His face was long, like a Northerner's. Like Otah's. His eyes were Liat's tea-with-milk brown. His expression, however, owed to neither of them. Where Liat would have kept her eyes down or Otah would have made himself charming, Nayiit's face belonged on a man bearing a heavy load. Whatever was in his mind, in this moment it was clear that he would press until the world was the way he wanted it or it crushed him. It was something equal parts weariness and joy, like a man newly acquainted with certainty. Otah found himself curious.

"They aren't wrong, Most High. These men aren't accustomed to living on the road like this. You can't expect the speed of a practiced army from them. And the walkers have been rising early to drill."

"Have they?"

"They have the impression their lives may rest on it. And the lives of their families. And, forgive me Most High, but your life too."

Otah leaned forward, his hands taking a questioning pose.

"They're afraid of failing you," Nayiit said. "It's why no one would come to you and complain. I've been keeping company with a man named Saya. He's a blacksmith. Plow blades, for the most part. His knees are swollen to twice their normal size, and he wakes before dawn to tie on leather and wool and swing sticks with the others. And then he walks until he can't. And then he walks farther."

Nayiit's voice was trembling now, but Otah couldn't say if it was with weariness or fear or anger.

"These aren't soldiers, Most High. And you're pushing them too hard."

"We've been moving for ten days—"

"And we're coming near to halfway to the Dai-kvo's village," Nayiit said. "In *ten days*. And drilling, and sleeping under thin blankets on hard ground. Not couriers and huntsmen, not men who are accustomed to this. Just men. I've spoken to the provisioners. We left Machi three thousand strong. Do you know how many have turned back? How many have deserted you?"

Otah blinked. It wasn't a question he'd ever thought to ask.

"How many?"

"None."

Otah felt something loosen in his chest. A warmth like the first drink of wine spread through him, and he felt tears beginning to well up in his eyes. If he had been less exhausted, it would never have pierced his reserve, and still . . . *none*.

"With every low town we pass, we take on a few more," Nayiit was saying. "They're afraid. The word has gone out that all the andat are gone, that the Galts are going to invade or are invading. It's the thing every man had convinced himself would never happen. I hear the things they say."

"The things they say?"

"That you were the only one who saw the danger. You were training men even before. You were preparing. They say that you've traveled the world when you were a boy, that you understand it better than any other Khai. Some of them are calling you the new Emperor."

"They should stop that," Otah said.

"Most High, they're desperate and afraid, and they want a hero out of the old epics. They need one."

"And you? What do you need?"

"I need Saya to stop walking for a day."

Otah closed his eyes. Perhaps the right thing was to send the experienced men on ahead. They could clear spaces for the camps. Perhaps missing a single day would not be too much. And there was little point in running if it was only to be sure they came to the battle exhausted and ready for slaughter. The Dai-kvo would have gotten his warning by now. The poets might even now be in flight toward Otah and his ragtag army. He took in a deep breath and let it out slowly through his nose. Letting his body collapse with it.

"I'll consider what you've said, Nayiit-cha," Otah said. "It wasn't where my mind had led me, but I can see there's some wisdom in it."

Nayiit took a pose of gratitude as formal as any at court. He looked nearly as spent as Otah felt. Otah raised his hands in a querying pose.

"The utkhaiem didn't feel comfortable bringing these concerns to me," he said. "Why did you?"

"I think, Most High, there's a certain . . . reluctance in the higher ranks to second-guess you again. And the footmen wouldn't think of approaching you. I grew up with stories about you and Maati-cha, so I suppose I can bring my-self to think of you as one of my mother's friends. That, and I'm desperately tired. If you had me sent back in disgrace, I could at least get a day's rest."

Otah smiled, and saw his own expression reflected back at him. He had never known this boy, had never lifted him over his head the way he had Da-nat. He had had no part in teaching Nayiit wisdom or folly. Even now, seeing himself in his eldest son's movements and expressions, he could hardly think of him with the bone-deep protectiveness that shook him when he thought of Eiah and Danat. And yet he was pleased that he had accepted Nayiit's offer to join him in this half-doomed campaign. Otah leaned forward, his hand out. It was the gesture of friendship that one seafront laborer might offer another. Nayiit only looked shocked for a moment, then clasped Otah's hand.

"Whenever they're too nervous to tell me what I'm doing wrong, you come to me, Nayiit-cha. I haven't got many people I can trust to do that, and I've left most of them back in Machi."

"If you'll promise not to have me whipped for impertinence," the boy said.

"I won't have you whipped, and I won't have you sent back."

"Thank you," Nayiit said, and again Otah was moved to see that the grati-tude was genuine. After Nayiit had gone, Otah was left with the aches in his body and the unease that came with having a man with a wife and child thank you for leading him toward the real chance of death. The life of the Khai Ma-chi, he thought, afforded very few opportunities to be humbled, but this was one. When the attendant returned, Otah didn't recognize the sound of his scratching until the man's voice came.

"Most High?"

"Yes, come in. And bring that ointment here. No, I can put it on myself. But bring me the captains of the houses. I've decided to take a day to rest and send the scouts ahead."

"Yes, Most High."

"And when you've done with that, there's a man named Saya. He's on foot. A blacksmith from Machi, I think."

"Yes, Most High?"

"Ask him to join me for a bowl of wine. I'd like to meet him."

MAATI WOKE TO FIND LIAT ALREADY GONE. HIS HAND TRACED THE INDENTATION in the mattress at his side where she had slept. The world outside his door was already bright and warm. The birds whose songs had filled the air of spring were busy now teaching their hatchlings to fly. The pale green of new leaves had deepened, the trees as rich with summer as they would ever be. High summer had come. Maati rose from his bed with a grunt and went about his morning ablutions.

The days since the ragged, improvised army of Machi began its march to the east had been busy. The loss of Stone-Made-Soft would have sent the court and the merchant houses scurrying like mice before a flood even if nothing more had happened. Word of the other lost andat and of the massed army of Galt made what in other days would have been a cataclysm seem a side issue. For half a week, it seemed, the city had been paralyzed. Not from fear, but from the simple and profound lack of any ritual or ceremony that answered the situation. Then, first from the merchant houses below and Kiyan-cha's women's banquets above and then seemingly everywhere at once, the utkhaiem had flushed with action. Often disorganized, often at crossed purpose, but determined and intent. Maati's own efforts were no less than any others.

Still, he left it behind him now—the books stacked in distinct piles, scrolls unfurled to particular passages as if waiting for the copyist's attention—and walked instead through the wide, bright paths of the palaces. There were fewer singing slaves, more stretches where the gravel of the path had scattered and not yet been raked back into place, and the men and women of the utkhaiem who he passed seemed to carry themselves with less than their full splendor. It was as if a terrible wind had blown through a garden and disarrayed those blossoms it did not destroy.

The path led into the shade of the false forest that separated the poet's house from the palaces. There were old trees among these, thick trunks speaking of generations of human struggle and triumph and failure since their first tentative seedling leaves had pushed away this soil. Moss clothed the bark and scented the air with green. Birds fluttered over Maati's head, and a squirrel scolded him as he passed. In winter, with these oaks bare, you could see from the porch of the poet's house out almost to the palaces. In summer, the house might have been in a different city. The door of the poet's house was standing open, and Maati didn't bother to scratch or knock.

Cehmai's quarters suffered the same marks as his own—books, scrolls, codices, diagrams all laid out without respect to author or age or type of binding. Cehmai, sitting on the floor with his legs crossed, held a book open in his hand. With the brown robes of a poet loose around his frame, he looked, Maati thought, like a young student puzzling over an obscure translation. Cehmai looked up as Maati's shadow crossed him, and smiled wearily.

"Have you eaten?" Maati asked.

"Some bread. Some cheese," Cehmai said, gesturing to the back of the house with his head. "There's some left, if you'd like it."

It hadn't occurred to Maati just how hungry he was until he took up a corner of the rich, sweet bread. He knew he'd had dinner the night before, but he couldn't recall what it had been or when he'd eaten it. He reached into a shallow ceramic bowl of salted raisins. They tasted rich and full as wine. He took a handful and sat on the chair beside Cehmai to look over the assorted results of their labor.

"What's your thought?" Cehmai said.

"I've found more than I expected to," Maati said. "There was a section in Vautai's *Fourth Meditations* that actually clarified some things I hadn't been certain of. If we were to put together all the scraps and rags from all of the books and histories and scrolls, it might be enough to support binding a fresh andat."

Cehmai sighed and closed the book he'd been holding.

"That's near what I've come to," the younger poet agreed. Then he looked up. "And how long do you think it would take to put those scraps and rags into one coherent form?"

"So that it stood as a single work? I'm likely too old to start it," Maati said. "And without the full record from the Dai-kvo, there would be no way to know whether a binding was dangerously near one that had already been done."

"I hated those," Cehmai said.

"They went back to the beginning of the First Empire," Maati said. "Some of the descriptions are so convoluted it takes reading them six times to understand they're using fifty words to carry the meaning of five. But they are complete, and that's the biggest gap in our resources."

Cehmai got to his feet with a grunt. His hair was disheveled and there were dark smudges under his eyes. Maati imagined he had some to match.

"So to sum up," Cehmai said, "if the Khai fails, we might be able to bind a new andat in a generation or so."

"Unless we're unlucky and use some construct too much like something a minor poet employed twenty generations back. In that case, we attempt the binding, pay the price, and die badly. Except that by then, we'll likely all have been slaughtered by the Galts."

"Well," Cehmai said and rubbed his hands together. "Are there any of those raisins left?"

"A few," Maati said.

Maati could hear the joints in Cehmai's back cracking as he stretched. Maati leaned over and scooped up the fallen book. It wasn't titled, nor was the author named, but the grammar in the first page marked it as Second Empire.

Loyan Sho or Kodjan the Lesser. Maati let his gaze flow down the page, seeing the words without taking in their meanings. Behind him, Cehmai ate the raisins, lips smacking until he spoke.

"The second problem is solved if your technique works. It isn't critical that we have all the histories if we can deflect the price of failing. At worst, we'll have lost the time it took to compose the binding."

"Months," Maati said.

"But not death," Cehmai went on. "So there's something to be said for that."

"And the first problem can be skirted by not starting wholly from scratch."

"You've been thinking about this, Maati-kvo."

Cehmai slowly walked back across the floor. His footsteps were soft and deliberate. Outside, a pigeon cooed. Maati let the silence speak for him. When Cehmai returned and sat again, his expression was abstracted and his fingers picked idly at the cloth of his sleeves. Maati knew some part of what haunted the younger man: the danger faced by the city, the likelihood of the Khai Machi retrieving the Dai-kvo, the shapeless and all-pervading fear of the Galtic army that had gathered in the South and might now be almost anywhere. But there was another part to the question, and that Maati could not guess. And so he asked.

"What is it like?"

Cehmai looked up as if he'd half-forgotten Maati was there. His hands flowed into a pose that asked clarification.

"Stone-Made-Soft," Maati said. "What is it like with him gone?"

Cehmai shrugged and turned his head to look out the unshuttered windows. The trees shifted their leaves and adjusted their branches like men in conversation. The sun hung in the sky, gold in lapis.

"I'd forgotten what it was like to be myself," Cehmai said. His voice was low and thoughtful and melancholy. "Just myself and not him as well. I was so young when I took control of him. It's like having had someone strapped to your back when you were a child and then suddenly lifting off the burden. I feel alone. I feel freed. I'm shamed to have failed, even though I know there was nothing I could have done to keep hold of him. And I regret now all the years I could have sunk Galt into ruins that I didn't."

"But if you could have him back, would you?"

The pause that came before Cehmai's reply meant that no, he would have chosen his freedom. It was the answer Maati had expected, but not the one he was ready to accept.

"The Khai may be able to save the Dai-kvo," Cehmai said. "He may get there before the Galts."

"But if he doesn't?"

"Then I would rather have Stone-Made-Soft back than decorate the end of some Galtic spear," Cehmai said, a grim humor in his voice. "I have some early work. Drafts from when I was first studying him. There are places where the options . . . branched. If we used those as starting points, it would make the binding different from the one I took over, and we still wouldn't have to begin from first principles."

"You have them here?"

"Yes. They're in that basket. There. You should take them back to the library and look them over. If we keep them here I'm too likely to do something unpleasant with them. I was half-tempted to burn them last night."

Maati took the pages—small, neat script on cheap, yellowing parchment— and folded them into his sleeve. The weight of them seemed so slight, and still Maati found himself uncomfortably aware of them and of the return to a kind of waking prison that they meant for Cehmai.

"I'll look them over," Maati said. "Once I have an idea what would be the best support for it, I'll put some reading together. And if things go well, we can present it all to the Dai-kvo when he arrives. Certainly, there's no call to do anything until we know where we stand."

"We can prepare for the worst," Cehmai said. "I'd rather be pleasantly surprised than taken unaware."

The resignation in Cehmai's voice was hard to listen to. Maati coughed, as if the suggestion he wished to make fought against being spoken.

"It might be better . . . I haven't attempted a binding myself. If I were the one . . ."

Cehmai took a pose that was both gratitude and refusal. Maati felt a warm relief at Cehmai's answer and also a twinge of regret.

"He's my burden," Cehmai said. "I gave my word to carry Stone-Made-Soft as long as I could, and I'll do that. I wouldn't want to disappoint the Khai." Then he chuckled. "You know, there have been whole years when I would have meant that as a sarcasm. Disappointing the Khaiem seems to be about half of what we do as poets—no, I can't somehow use the andat to help you win at tiles, or restore your prowess with your wives, or any of the thousand stupid, petty things they ask of us. But these last weeks, I really would do whatever I could, not to disappoint that man. I don't know what's changed."

"Everything," Maati said. "Times like these remake men. They change what we are. Otah's trying to become the man we need him to be."

"I suppose that's true," Cehmai said. "I just don't want this all to be happening, so I forget, somehow, that it is. I keep thinking it's all a sour dream and I'll wake out of it and stumble down to play a game of stones against Stone-Made-Soft. That that will be the worst thing I have to face. And not . . ."

Cehmai gestured, his hands wide, including the house and the palaces and the city and the world.

"And not the end of civilization?" Maati suggested.

"Something like that."

Maati sighed.

"You know," he said, "when we were young, the man who was Dai-kvo then chose Otah to come train as a poet. He refused, but I think he would have been good. He has it in him to do whatever needs doing."

Killing a man, taking a throne, marching an army to its death, Maati thought but did not say. Whatever needs doing.

"I hope the price he pays is smaller than ours," Cehmai said.

"I doubt it will be."

14

>+< Balasar had not been raised to put faith in augury. His father had always said that any god that could create the world and the stars should be able to put together a few well-formed sentences if there was something that needed saying; Balasar had accepted this wisdom in the uncritical way of a boy emulating the man he most admires. And still, the dream came to him on the night before he had word of the hunting party.

It was far from the first time he had dreamt of the desert. He felt again the merciless heat, the pain of the satchel cutting into his shoulder. The books he had borne then had become ashes in the dream as they had in life, but the weight was no less. And behind him were not only Coal and Eustin. All of them followed him—Bes, Mayarsin, Little Ott, and the others. The dead followed him, and he knew they were no longer his allies or his enemies. They came to keep watch over him, to see what work he wrought with their blood. They were his judges. As always before, he could not speak. His throat was knotted. He could not turn to see the dead; he only felt them.

But there seemed more now—not only the men he had left in the desert, but others as well. Some of them were soldiers, some of them simple men, all of them padding behind him, waiting to see him justify their sacrifices and his own pride. The host behind him had grown.

He woke in his tent, his mouth dry and sticky. Dawn had not yet come. He drank from the water flask by his bed, then pulled on a shirt and simple trousers and went out to relieve himself among the bushes. The army was still asleep or else just beginning to stir. The air was warm and humid so near the river. Balasar breathed deep and slow. He had the sense that the world itself— trees, grasses, moon-silvered clouds—was heavy with anticipation. It would be two weeks before they would come within sight of the river city Udun. By month's end another poet would be dead, another library burned, another city fallen.

Thus far, the campaign had proved as simple as he had hoped, though slower. He had lost almost no men in Nantani. The low towns that his army had come across in their journey to the North had emptied before them; men, women, children, animals—all had scattered before them like autumn leaves before a windstorm. The only miscalculation he had made was in how long to rely on the steam wagons. Two boilers had blown on the rough terrain before Balasar had called to let them cool and be pulled. Five men had died outright, another fifteen had been scalded too badly to continue. Balasar had sent them back to Nantani. There had been less food captured than he had hoped; the residents of the low towns had put anything they thought might be of use to Balasar and his men to fire before they fled. But the land was rich with game fowl and deer, and his supplies were sufficient to reach the next cities.

As dawn touched the eastern skyline, Balasar put on his uniform and walked among the men. The morning's cook fires smoked, filling the air with the scents of burning grass and wood and coal filched from the steam wagons, hot grease and wheat cakes and kafe. Captains and footmen, archers and carters, Balasar greeted them all with a smile and considered them with approving nods or small frowns. When a man lifted half a wheat cake to him, Balasar took it with thanks and squatted down beside the cook to blow it cool and eat it. Every man he met, he had made rich. Every man in the camp would stand before him on the battle lines, and only a few, he hoped, would walk behind him in his dream.

Sinja Ajutani's camp was enfolded within the greater army's but still separate from it, like the Baktan Quarter in Acton. A city within a city, a camp within a camp. The greeting he found here was less warm. The respect he saw in these dark, almond eyes was touched with fear. Perhaps hatred. But no mistake, it was still respect.

Sinja himself was sitting on a fallen log, shirtless, with a bit of silver mirror in one hand and a blade in the other. He looked up as Balasar came close, made his salute, and returned to shaving. Balasar sat beside him.

"We break camp soon," Balasar said. "I'll want ten of your men to ride with the scouting parties today."

"Expecting to find people to question?" Sinja asked. There was no rancor in his voice.

"This close to the river, I can hope so."

"They'll know we're coming. Refugees move faster than armies. The first news of Nantani likely reached them two, maybe three weeks ago."

"Then perhaps they'll send someone here to speak for them," Balasar said. Sinja seemed to consider this as he pressed the blade against his own throat. There were scars on the man's arms and chest—long raised lines of white.

"Would you prefer I ride with the scouts, or stay close to the camp and wait for an emissary?"

"Close to camp," Balasar said. "The men you choose for scouting should speak my language well, though. I don't want to miss anything that would help us do this cleanly."

"Agreed," Sinja said, and put the knife to his own throat again. Before Balasar could go on, he heard his own name called out. A boy no older than fourteen summers wearing the colors of the second legion came barreling into the camp. His face was flushed from running, his breath short. Balasar stood and accepted the boy's salute. In the corner of his eye, he saw Sinja put away knife and mirror and reach for his shirt.

"General Gice, sir," the boy said between gasps. "Captain Tevor sent me. We've lost one of the hunting parties, sir."

"Well, they'll have to catch up with us as best they can," Balasar said. "We don't have time for searching."

"No, sir. They aren't missing, sir. They're killed."

Balasar felt a grotesque recognition. The other men in his dream. This was where they'd come from.

"Show me," he said.

The trap had been sprung in a clearing at the end of a game trail. Crossbow bolts had taken half a dozen of the men. The others were marked with sword and axe blows. Their armor and robes had been stripped from them. Their weapons were gone. Balasar stepped through the low grass cropped by deer and considered each face.

The songs and epics told of warriors dying with lips curled in battle cry, but every dead man Balasar had ever seen looked at peace. However badly they had died, their bodies surrendered at the end, and the calm he saw in those dead eyes seemed to say that their work was done now. Like a man playing at tiles who has turned his mark and now sat back to ask Balasar what he would do to match it.

"Are there no other bodies?" he asked.

Captain Tevor, at his elbow, shook his great woolly head.

"There's signs that our boys did them harm, sir, but they took their dead with them. It wasn't all fast, sir. This one here, there's burn marks on him, and you can see on his wrists where they bound him up. Asked him what he knew, I expect."

Sinja knelt, touching the dead man's wounds as if making sure they were real.

"I have a priest in my company," Captain Tevor said. "One of the archers. I can have him say a few words. We'll bury them here and catch up with the main body tomorrow, sir."

"They're coming with us," Balasar said.

"Sir?"

"Bring a pallet and a horse. I want these bodies pulled through the camp. I want every man in the army to see them. Then wrap them in shrouds and pack them in ashes. We'll bury them in the ruins of Udun with the Khai's skull to mark their place."

Captain Tevor made his salute, and it wasn't Balasar's imagination that put the tear in the old man's eye. As Tevor barked out the orders to the men who had come with them, Sinja stood and brushed his palms against each other. A smear of old blood darkened the back of the captain's hand. Balasar read the disapproval in the passionless eyes, but neither man spoke.

The effect on the men was unmistakable. The sense of gloating, of leisure, vanished. The tents were pitched, the wagons loaded and ready, the soldiers straining against time itself to close the distance between where they now stood and Udun. Three of his captains asked permission to send out parties. Hunting parties still, but only in part searching for game. Balasar gave each of them his blessing. The dream of the desert didn't return, but he had no doubt that it would.

In the days that followed, he felt keenly the loss of Eustin. Somewhere to the west, Pathai was falling or had fallen. The school with its young poets was burning, or would burn. And through those conflagrations, Eustin rode. Balasar spent his days riding among his men, talking, planning, setting the example he wished them all to follow, and he felt the absence of Eustin's dry pessimism and distrust. The fervor he saw here was a different beast. The men here looked to him as something besides a man. They had never seen him weep over Little Ott's body or call out into the dry, malign desert air for Kellem. To this army, he was General Gice. They might be prepared to kill or die at his word, but they did not know him. It was, he supposed, the difference between faith and loyalty. He found faith isolating. And it was in this sense of being alone among many that the messenger from Sinja Ajutani found him.

The day's travel was done, and they had made good time again. His outriders had made contact with local forces twice—farm boys with rabbit bows and sewn leather armor—and had done well each time. The wells in the low towns had been fouled, but the river ran clean enough. Another two days, three at the most, and they would reach Udun. In the meantime, the sunset was beautiful and birdsong filled the evening air. Balasar rested beneath the wide, thick branches of a cottonwood, flat bread and chicken still hot from the fires on a metal field plate by his side, their scents mixing with those of the rich earth and the river's damp. The man standing before him, hands flat at his sides, looked no more than seventeen summers, but Balasar knew himself a poor judge of ages among these people. He might have been fifteen, he might have been twenty. When he spoke, his Galtic was heavily inflected.

"General Gice," the boy said. "Captain Ajutani would like a word with you, if it is acceptable to your will."

Balasar sat forward.

"He could come himself," Balasar said. "He has before. Why not now?"

The messenger boy's lips went tight, his dark eyes fixed straight ahead. It was anger the boy was controlling.

"Something's happened," Balasar said. "Something's happened to one of yours."

"Sir," the boy said.

Balasar took a regretful look at the chicken, then rose to his feet.

"Take me to Captain Ajutani," Balasar said.

Their path ended at the medical tent. The messenger waited outside when Balasar ducked through the flap and entered. The thick canvas reeked with concentrated vinegar and pine pitch. The medic stood over a low cot where a man lay naked and bloody. One of Sinja's men. The captain himself stood against the tent's center pole, arms folded. Balasar stepped forward, taking in the patient's wounds with a practiced eye. Two parallel cuts on the ribs, shallow but long. Cuts on the hands and arms where the boy had tried to ward off the blades. Skinned knuckles where he'd struck out at someone. Balasar caught the medic's eye and nodded to the man.

"No broken bones, sir," the medic said. "One finger needed sewing, and there'll be scars, but so long as we keep the wounds from festering, he should be fine."

"What happened?" Balasar asked.

"I found him by the river," Sinja said. "I brought him here."

Balasar heard the coolness in Sinja's voice, judged the tension in his face and shoulders. He steeled himself.

"Come, then," Balasar said as he lifted open the tent's wide flap, "eat with me and you can tell me what happened."

"No need, General. It's a short enough story. Coya here can't speak Galtic. There's been footmen from the fourth legion following him for days now. At first it was just mocking, and I didn't think it worth concern."

"You have names? Proof that they did this?"

"They're bragging about it, sir," Sinja said.

Sinja looked down at the wounded man. The boy looked up at him. The dark eyes were calm, perhaps defiant. Balasar sighed and knelt beside the low cot.

"Coya-cha?" he said in the boy's own language. "I want you to rest. I'll see the men who did this disciplined."

The wounded hands took a pose that declined the offer.

"It isn't a favor to you," Balasar said. "My men don't treat one another this way. As long as you march with me, you are my soldier, whatever tongues you speak. I'll be sure they understand it's my wrath they're feeling, and not yours."

"Your dead men are the problem, sir," Sinja said, switching the conversation back to Galtic.

The medic coughed once, then discreetly stepped to the far side of the tent. Balasar folded his hands and nodded to Sinja that he should continue. The mercenary sucked his teeth and spat.

"Your men are angry. Having those shrouds along is like putting a burr under their saddles. They're calling my men things they didn't when this campaign began. And they act as if it were harmless and in fun, but it isn't."

"I'll see your men aren't attacked again, Sinja. You have my word on it."

"It's not just that, sir. You're sowing anger. Yes, it keeps them traveling faster, and I respect that. But once we reach Udun and Utani, they're going to have their blood up. It's easier for ten thousand soldiers to defeat a hundred thousand tradesmen if the tradesmen don't think defeat means being beaten

to death for sport. And a bad sack can burn in resentments that last for lifetimes. All respect, those cities are as good as taken, and we both know it.
There's no call to make this worse than it has to be."

"I should be careful?" Balasar said. "Move slowly, and let the cities fall
gently?"

"You said before you wanted this done clean."

"Yes. Before. I said that *before*."

"They're going to be your cities," Sinja said doggedly as a man swimming
against the tide. "There's more to think about than how to capture them. It's
my guess Galt's going to be ruling these places for a long time. The less the
people have to forget, the easier that rule's going to be."

"I don't care about holding them," Balasar said. "There are too many to
guard, and once the rest of the world scents blood, it's going to be chaos anyway. This war isn't about finding ways for the High Council to appoint more
mayors."

"Sir?"

"We are carrying the dead because they are *my* dead." Balasar kept his voice
calm, his manner matter-of-fact. The trembling in his hands was too slight to
be seen. "And I haven't come to conquer the Khaiem, Captain Ajutani. I've
come to destroy them."

The first refugees appeared when Otah's little army was still three
days' march from the village of the Dai-kvo. They were few and scattered in
the morning, and then more and larger groups toward the day's end. The stories they told Otah were the same. Ships had come to Yalakeht—warships
loaded heavy with Galtic soldiers. Some of the ships were merchant vessels
that had been on trade runs to Chaburi-Tan. Others were unfamiliar. The harbor master had tried to refuse them berths, but a force of men had come from
the warehouse district and taken control of the seafront. By the time the Khai
had gathered a force to drive them back, it was too late. Yalakeht had fallen.
Any hope that Otah's army might be on a fool's errand ended with that news.

In the night, more men came, drawn by the light and scent of the army's
cook fires. Otah saw that they were welcomed, and the tale grew. Boats had
been waiting, half assembled, in the warehouses of Galtic merchants in Yalakeht. Great metal boilers ran paddle wheels, and pushed their wide, shallow
boats upriver faster than oxen could pull. Boats loaded with men and steam
wagons. The low towns nearest Yalakeht had been overrun. Another force had
been following along the shore, hauling food and supplies. The soldiers themselves had sped for the Dai-kvo. Just as Otah had feared they would.

Otah sat in his tent and listened to the cicadas. They sang as if nothing was
changing. As if the world was as it had always been. A breeze blew from the
south, heavy with the smell of rain though the clouds were still few and distant. Trees nodded their branches to one another. Otah kept his back to the
fire and stared out at darkness.

There was no way to know whether the Galtic army had reached the village yet. Perhaps the Dai-kvo was preparing some defense, perhaps the village had been encircled and overrun. From the tales he'd heard, once the Galts and their steam wagons reached the good roads leading from the river to the village itself, they would be able to travel faster than news of them.

It had been almost thirty years ago when Otah had traveled up that river carrying a message from Saraykeht. The memory of it was like something from a dream. There had been an older man—younger, likely, than Otah was now—who had run the boat with his daughter. They had never spoken of the girl's mother, and Otah had never asked. That child daughter would be a woman now, likely with children of her own. Otah wondered what had become of her, wondered whether that half-recalled river girl was among those flying out of the storm into which he was heading, or if she had been in one of the towns that the army had destroyed.

A polite scratch came at the door, his servant announcing himself. Otah called out his permission, and the door opened. He could see the silhouettes of Ashua Radaani and his other captains looming behind the servant boy's formal pose.

"Bring them in," Otah said. "And bring us wine. Wait. Watered wine."

The six men lumbered in. Otah welcomed them all with formal gravity. The fine hunting robes in which they had come out from Machi had been scraped clean of mud. The stubble had been shaved from their chins. From these small signs and from the tightness in their bodies, Otah knew they had all drawn the same conclusions he had. He stood while they folded themselves down to the cushion-strewn floor. Then, silently, Otah sat on his chair, looking down at these grown men, heads of their houses who through the years he had known them had been flushed with pride and self-assurance. The servant boy poured them each a bowl of equal parts wine and fresh water before ghosting silently out the door. Otah took a pose that opened the audience.

"We will be meeting the Galts sometime in the next several days," Otah said. "I can't say where or when, but it will be soon. And when the time comes, we won't have time to plan our strategy. We have to do that now. Tonight. You have all brought your census?"

Each man in turn took a scroll from his sleeve and laid it before him. The number of men, the weapons and armor, the horses and the bows and the numbers of arrows and bolts. The final tally of the strength they had managed. Otah looked down at the scrawled ink and hoped it would be enough.

"Very well," he said. "Let's begin."

None of them had ever been called upon to plan a battle before, but each had an area of expertise. Where one knew of the tactics of hunting, another had had trade relations with the Wardens of the Westlands enough to speak of their habits and insights. Slowly they made their plans: What to do when the scouts first brought news of the Galts. Who should command the wedges of archers and crossbowmen, who the footmen, who the horsemen. How they should protect their flanks, how to pull back the archers when the time came near for the others to engage. Their fingers sketched lines and movements on the floor, their voices rose, became heated, and grew calm again. The moon had traveled the width of six hands together before Otah declared the work finished. Orders were written, shifting men to different commands, specifying the shouted signals that would coordinate the battle, putting the next few uncertain days into the order they imagined for them. When the captains bowed and took their poses of farewell, the clouds had appeared and the first ticking raindrops were striking the canvas. Otah lay on his cot wrapped in blankets of soft wool, listening to the rain, and running through all that they had said. If it worked as they had planned, perhaps all would be well. In the darkness with his belly full of wine and his mind full of the confident words of his men, he could almost think there was hope.

Dawn was a brightening of clouds, east as gray as west. They struck camp, loaded their wagons, and once again made for the Dai-kvo. The flow of refugees seemed to have stopped. No new faces appeared before them—no horses, no men on foot. Perhaps the rain and mud had stopped them. Perhaps something else. Otah rode near the vanguard, the scouts arriving, riding for a time at his side, and then departing again. It was midmorning and the sun was still hidden behind the low gray ceiling of the world when Nayiit rode up on a thin, skittish horse. Otah motioned him to ride near to his side.

"I'm told I'm to be a messenger," Nayiit said. There was a controlled anger in his voice. "I've drilled with the footmen. I have a sword."

"You have a horse too."

"It was given to me with the news," Nayiit said. "Have I done something to displease you, Most High?"

"Of course not," Otah said. "Why would you think you had?"

"Why am I not permitted to fight?"

Otah leaned back, and his mount, reading the shift of his weight, slowed. His back ached and the raw places on his thighs were only half healed. The rain had soaked his robes, so that even the oiled cloth against his skin felt clammy and cold. The rain that pressed Nayiit's hair close against his neck also tapped against Otah's squinting eyes.

"How are you not permitted to fight?" Otah said.

"The men who are making the charge," Nayiit said. "The men I've been traveling with. That I've trained with. I want to be with them when the time comes."

"And I want you to be with me, and with them," Otah said. "I want you to be the bridge between us."

"I would prefer not to," Nayiit said.

"I understand that. But it's what I've decided."

Nayiit's nostrils flared, and his cheeks pinked. Otah took a pose that thanked the boy and dismissed him. Nayiit wheeled his mount and rode away, kicking up mud as he did. In the distance, the meadows began to rise. They were coming to the Dai-kvo from the north and west, up the long, gentle slope of the mountains rather than the cliffs and crags from which the village was carved. Otah had never come this way before. For all his discomfort and the dread in his belly, this gray-green world was lovely. He tried not to think of Nayiit or of the men whom his boy had asked permission to die with. We are his fathers, Maati had said, and Otah had agreed. He wondered if the others would also see Nayiit's duty as a protection of him. He wondered if they would guess that Danat wasn't his only son. He hoped that they would all live long enough for such problems to matter.

The scout came just before midday. He'd seen a rider in Galtic colors. He'd been seen as well. Otah accepted the information and set the couriers to ride closer and in teams. He felt his belly tighten and wondered how far from its main force the Galts would send their riders. That was the distance between him and his first battle. His first war.

It was near evening when the two armies found each other. The scouts had given warning, and still, as Otah topped the rise, the sight of them was astounding. The army of Galt stood still at the far end of the long, shallow valley, silent as ghosts in the gray rain. Their banners should have been green and gold, but in the wet and with the distance, they seemed merely black. Otah paused, trying to guess how many men faced him. Perhaps half again his own. Perhaps a little less. And they were here, waiting for him. The Dai-kvo's village was behind them.

He wondered if he had come too late. Perhaps the Galts had sacked the village and slaughtered the Dai-kvo. Perhaps they had had word of Otah's coming and bypassed the prize to reach him here, before his men could take cover in the buildings and palaces of the mountain. Perhaps the Galts had divided, and the men facing him were what he had spared the Dai-kvo. There was no way to know the situation, and only one course available to him, whatever the truth.

"Call the formation," Otah said, and the shouts and calls flowed out behind him, the slap of leather and metal. The army of Machi took its place—archers and footmen and horsemen. All exhausted by their day's ride, all facing a real enemy for the first time. From across the valley, a sound came, sharp as cracking thunder—thousands of voices raised as one. And then, just as suddenly, silence. Otah ran his hand over the thick leather straps of the reins and forced himself to think.

In the soft quarter of Saraykeht, Otah had seen showfighters pout and preen before the blows came. He had seen them flex their muscles and beat their own faces until there was blood on their lips. It had been a show for the men and women who had come to partake of brutality as entertainment, but it had also been the start of the fight. A display to unnerve the enemy, to sow fear. This was no different. A thousand men who could speak in one voice could fight as one. They were not men, they were a swarm; a single mind with thousands of bodies. *Hear us*, the wordless cry had said, *and die.*

Otah looked at the darkening sky, the misty rain. He thought of all the histories he had read, the accounts of battles lost and won in ancient days before the poets and their andat. Of the struggles in the low cities of the world. He raised his hands, and the messengers, Nayiit among them, came to his side.

"Tell the men to make camp," he said.

The silence was utter.

"Most High?" Nayiit said.

"They won't begin a battle now that they'd have to finish in darkness. This is all show and bluster. Tell the men to set their tents and build what cook fires we can in all this wet. Put them here where those bastards can see the light of them. Tell the men to rest and eat and drink, and we'll set up a pavilion and have songs before we sleep. Let the Galts see how frightened we are."

The messengers took poses that accepted the order and turned their mounts. Otah caught Nayiit's gaze, and the boy hesitated. When the others had gone, Otah spoke again.

"Also find the scouts and have them set a watch. In case I'm wrong."

He saw Nayiit draw breath, but he only took the accepting pose and rode away.

The night was long and unpleasant. The rain had stopped; the clouds thinned and vanished, letting the heat of the ground fly out into the cold, uncaring sky. Otah passed among the fires, accepting the oaths and salutes of his men. He felt his title and dignity on his shoulders like a cloak. He would have liked to smile and be charming, to ease his fears with companionship and wine, just as his men did. It would have been no favor to them, though, so he held back and played the Khai for another night. No attack came, and between the half candle and the three-quarter mark, Otah actually fell asleep. He dreamed of nothing in particular—a bird that flew upside down, a river he recalled from childhood, Danat's voice in an adjacent room singing words Otah could not later recall. He woke in darkness to the scent of frying pork and the sound of voices.

He pulled on his robes and boots and stepped out into the chill of the morning. The cook fires were lit again or had never been put out. And across the valley, the Galt army had lit its own, glittering like orange and yellow stars fallen to earth. His attendant rushed up, blinking sleep from his eyes.

"Most High," the boy said, falling into a pose of abject apology. "I had thought to let you sleep. Your breakfast is nearly ready—"

"Bring it to my tent," Otah said. "I'll be back for it."

He walked to the edge of the camp where the firelight would not spoil his night vision and looked out into the darkness. In the east, the sky had become a paler blackness, the deep gray of charcoal. The stars had not gone out, but they were dimmed. In the trees that lined the valley, birds were beginning their songs. A strange tense peace came over him. His disquiet seemed to fade, and the dawn, gray then cool yellow and rose and serene blue that filled the wide bowl of the sky above him, was beautiful and calm. Whatever happened here in this valley, the sun would rise upon it again tomorrow. The birds would call to one another. Summer would retreat, autumn would come. The lives of men and nations were not the highest stakes to play for. He pulled his hands into his sleeves and turned back to the camp. At his tent, his messengers awaited him, including Nayiit.

"Call the formation," Otah said. "It's time."

The messengers scattered, and it seemed fewer than a dozen breaths before the air was filled with the sounds of metal against metal, shouts and commands as his army pulled itself to the ready.

"Your food, Most High," the attendant said, and Otah waved the man away.

By the time Otah's footmen and horsemen had taken their places between and just behind the wedges of archers, it was bright enough to see the banners and glittering mail of the Galts. Otah's mount seemed to sense the impending violence, dancing uncomfortably as Otah rode back and forth behind his men, watching and waiting and preparing to call out his commands. From across the valley, the shout and silence came again as it had the night before. Then twice more.

"Call the archers to ready!" Otah called out, and like whisperers in court relaying the words to lower men waiting in the halls, his words echoed in a dozen voices. He saw his archers lift their bows and shift in their formations. A long shout, rolling like thunder, came from across the valley. The Galts were moving forward. "Call the march! And be prepared to loose arrows!"

As they had drilled, his men moved forward, archers to the front, footmen between them with their makeshift shields and motley assortment of swords and spears and threshing flails. Horsemen in the colors of the great houses of the utkhaiem trotted at the sides, ready to wheel and protect the flanks. At a walk, three thousand men moved forward across the still-wet grass and patches of ankle-deep mud. And perhaps half again as many Galts came toward them, shouting.

In the old books and histories, the flights of enemy arrows had been compared to smoke rising from a great pyre or clouds blotting out the sun. In fact, when the first volley struck, it was nothing like that. Otah didn't see the arrows and bolts in the air. He saw them begin to appear, heads buried deep in the ground, fletching green and white in the sunlight, like some strange flower that had sprung up from the meadow grass. Then a man screamed, and another.

"Loose arrows!" Otah called. "Give it back to them! Loose arrows!"

Now that he knew to look, he could see the thin, dark shafts. They rose up from the Galtic mass, slowly as if they were floating. His own archers let fly, and it seemed that the arrows should collide in the air, but then slipped past each other, two flocks of birds mingling and parting again. More men screamed.

Otah's horse twitched and sidestepped, nervous with the sounds and the scent of blood. Otah felt his own heart beating fast, sweat on his back and neck though the morning was still cool. His mind spun, judging how many men he was losing with each volley, straining to see how many Galts seemed to fall. They seemed to be getting more volleys off than his men. Perhaps the Galts had more archers than he did. If that was true, the longer he waited for his footmen to engage, the more he would lose. But then perhaps the Galts were simply better practiced at slaughter.

"Call the attack!" Otah yelled. He looked for his messengers, but only two of them were in earshot, and neither was Nayiit. Otah gestured to the nearest of them. "Call the attack!"

The charge was ragged, but it was not hesitant. He could hear it when the footmen got word—a loud whooping yell that seemed to have no particular start nor any end. One man's voice took up where another paused for breath. Otah cantered forward. His horsemen were streaming forward as well now, careful not to outstrip the footmen by too great a distance, and Otah saw the Galtic archers falling back, their own soldiers coming to the fore.

The two sides met with a sound like buildings falling. Shouts and screams mingled, and any nuanced plan was gone. Otah's urge to rush forward was as much the desire to see more clearly what was happening as to defend the men he'd brought. His archers drew and fired sporadically until he called them to stop. There was no way to see who the arrows struck.

The mass of men in the valley writhed. Once a great surge on Otah's left seemed to press into the Galtic ranks, but it was pushed back. He heard drums and trumpet calls. That's a good idea, Otah thought. Drums and trumpets.

The shouting seemed to go on forever. The sun slowly rose in its arc as the men engaged, pulled back, and rushed at one another again. And with every passing breath, Otah saw more of his men fall. More of his men than of the Galts. He forced his mount nearer. He couldn't judge how many he'd lost. The bodies in the mud might have been anyone.

A sudden upsurge in the noise of the battle caught him. His footmen were roaring and surging forward, the center of the enemy's line giving way. "Call them to stand!" Otah shouted, his voice hoarse and fading. "Stand!"

But if they heard the call, the footmen didn't heed it. They pressed forward, into the gap in the Galtic line. A trumpet blared three times, and the signal given, the Galtic horsemen that had held to the rear, left and right both, turned to the center and drove into Otah's men from either side. It had been a trap, and a simple one, and they had stepped in it. Call the retreat, Otah thought wildly, I have to call the retreat. And then from the right, he heard the retreat called.

Someone had panicked; someone had given the order before he could. His horsemen turned, unwilling, it seemed, to leave the footmen behind. A few footmen broke, and then a few more, and then, as if coming loose, Otah's army turned its backs to the Galts and ran. Otah saw some horsemen trying to draw off the pursuing Galts, but most were flying back in retreat themselves. Otah spun his horse and saw, back on the field, the remnants of his wedges of archers fleeing as well.

"No!" he shouted. "Not you! Stop where you are!"

No one heard him. He was a leaf in a storm now, command gone, hope gone, his men being slaughtered like winter pork. Otah dug his heels into his mount's sides, leaned low, and shot off in pursuit of the archers. It was folly riding fast over mud-slick ground, but Otah willed himself forward. The fleeing archers looked back over their shoulders at the sound of his hooves, and had the naïveté to look relieved that it was him. He rode through the nearest wedge, knocking several to the ground, then pulled up before them and pointed back at the men behind them.

"Loose your arrows," Otah croaked. "It's the only chance they have! Loose arrows!"

The archers stood stunned; their wide confused faces made Otah think of sheep confronted by an unexpected cliff. He had brought farmers and smiths onto a battlefield. He had led men who had never known more violence than brawling drunk outside a comfort house to fight soldiers. Otah dropped from his horse, took a bow and quiver from the nearest man, and aimed high. He never saw where his arrow went, but the bowmen at least began to understand. One by one, and then in handfuls, they began to send their arrows and bolts up over the retreating men and into the charging Galts.

"They'll kill us!" a boy shrieked. "There's a thousand of them!"

"Kill the first twenty," Otah said. "Then let the ones still standing argue about who'll lead the next charge."

Behind them, the other fleeing archers had paused. As the first of the fleeing horsemen passed, Otah caught sight of Ashua Radaani and raised his hands in a pose that called the man to a halt. There was blood on Radaani's face and arms, and his eyes were wide with shock. Otah strode to him.

"Go to the other archers. Tell them that once the men have reached us here, they're to start loosing arrows. We'll come back with the men."

"You should come now, Most High," Radaani said. "I can carry you."

"I have a horse," Otah said, though he realized he couldn't say what had become of his mount. "Go. Just go!"

The Galtic charge thinned as they drew into range of the arrows. Otah saw two men fall. And then, almost miraculously, the Galts began to pull back. Otah's footmen came past him, muddy and bleeding and weeping and pale with shock. Some carried wounded men with them. Some, Otah suspected, carried men already dead. The last, or nearly the last, approached, and Otah turned, gesturing to the archers, and they all walked back together. The few Galts that pressed on were dissuaded by fresh arrows. Ashua had reached the other wedge. Thank the gods for that, at least.

The army of Machi, three thousand strong that morning, found itself milling about, confused and without structure as the evening sun lengthened their shadows. They had fled back past the northern lip of the valley where they had made camp the night before onto green grass already tramped flat by their passage. Some supply wagons and tents and fresh water had been caught up in the retreat, but more was strewn over the ground behind them. The wounded were lined up on hillsides and cared for as best the physicians could. Many of the wounds were mild, but there were also many who would not live the night.

The scouts were the first to recover some sense of purpose. The couriers of the trading houses rode back and forth, reporting the movements of the Galts now that the battle was finished. They had scoured the field, caring for their own men and killing the ones Otah had left behind. Then, with professional efficiency, they had made their camp and prepared their dinner. It was clear that the Galts considered the conflict ended. They had won. It was over.

As darkness fell, Otah made his way through the camps, stopped at what cook fires there were. No one greeted him with violence, but he saw anger in some eyes and sorrow in others. By far the most common expression was an emptiness and disbelief. When at last he sat on his cot—set under the spreading limbs of a shade tree in lieu of his tent—he knew that however many men he had lost on the battlefield, twice as many would have deserted by morning. Otah laid an arm over his eyes, his body heavy with exhaustion, but totally unable to sleep.

In the long, dreadful march to this battle, not one man had turned back. At the time, it had warmed Otah's heart. Now he wanted them all to flee. Go back to their wives and their children and their parents. Go back to where it was safe and forget this mad attempt to stop the world from crumbling. Except he couldn't imagine where safety might be. The Dai-kvo would fall if he hadn't already. The cities of the Khaiem would fall. Machi would fall. For years, he had had the power to command the death of Galt. Stone-Made-Soft could have ruined their cities, sunk their lands below the waves. All of this could have been stopped once, if he had known and had the will. And now it was too late.

"Most High?"

Otah raised his arm, sat up. Nayiit stood in the shadows of the tree. Otah knew him by his silhouette.

"Nayiit-kya," Otah said, realizing it was the first he'd seen Liat's son since the battle. Nayiit hadn't even crossed his mind. He wondered what that said about him. Nothing good. "Are you all right?"

"I'm fine. A little bruised on the arm and shoulder, but . . . but fine."

In the dim, Otah saw that Nayiit held something before him. A greasy scent of roast lamb came to him.

"I can't eat," Otah said as the boy came closer. "Thank you, but . . . give it to the men. Give it to the injured men."

"Your attendant said you didn't eat in the morning either," Nayiit said. "It won't help them if you collapse. It won't bring them back."

Otah felt a surge of cold anger at the words, but bit back his retort. He nodded to the edge of the cot.

"Leave it there," he said.

Nayiit hesitated, but then moved forward and placed the bowl on the cot. He stepped back, but he did not walk away. As Otah's eyes adjusted to the darkness, Nayiit's face took on dim features. Otah wasn't surprised to see that the boy was weeping. Nayiit was older now than Otah had been when he'd fathered him on Liat. Older now than Otah had been when he'd first killed a man with his hands.

"I'm sorry, Most High," Nayiit said.

"So am I," Otah said. The scent of lamb was thick and rich. Enticing and mildly nauseating both.

"It was my fault," Nayiit said, voice thickened by a tight throat. "This, all of this, is my fault."

"No," Otah began. "You can't—"

"I saw them killing each other. I saw how many there were, and I broke," Nayiit said, and his hands took a pose of profound contrition. "I'm the one who called the retreat."

"I know," Otah said.

15

>+< Liat had been nursing her headache since she'd woken that morning; as the day progressed, it had drawn a line from the back of her eyes to her temples that throbbed when she moved too quickly. She had given up shaking her head. Instead, she pressed her fingers into the fine-grained wood of the table and tried to will her frustration into it. Kiyan, seated across from her, was saying something in a reasonable, measured tone that entirely missed her point. Liat took a pose that asked permission to speak, and then didn't wait for Kiyan to answer her.

"It isn't the men," Liat said. "He could have taken twice what he did, and we'd be able to do what's needed. It's that he took all the *horses*."

Kiyan's fox-sharp face tightened. Her dark eyes flickered down toward the maps and diagrams spread out between them. The farmlands and low towns that surrounded Machi were listed with the weight of grain and meat and vegetables that had come from each in the last five years. Liat's small, neat script covered paper after paper, black ink on the butter-yellow pages noting acres to be harvested and plowed, the number of hands and hooves required by each.

The breeze from the unshuttered windows lifted the pages but didn't disarray them, like invisible fingers checking the corners for some particular mark.

"Show me again," Kiyan said, and the weariness in her voice was almost enough to disarm Liat's annoyance. Almost, but not entirely. With a sigh, she stood. The line behind her eyes throbbed.

"This is the number of horses we'd need to plow the eastern farmsteads here and here and here," Liat said, tapping the maps as she did so. "We have half that number. We can get up to nearly the right level if we take the mules from the wheat mills."

Kiyan looked over the numbers, her fingertips touching the sums and moving on. Her gaze was focused, a single vertical line between her brows.

"How short is the second planting now?" Kiyan asked.

"The west and south are nearly complete, but they started late. The eastern farmsteads . . . not more than a quarter."

Kiyan leaned back. Otah's wife looked nearly as worn as Liat felt. The gray in her hair seemed more pronounced, her flesh paler and thinner. Liat found herself wondering if Kiyan had made a practice of painting her face and dyeing her hair that, in the crisis, she had let fall away, or if the task they had set themselves was simply sucking the life out of them both.

"It's too late," Kiyan said. "With the time it would take to get the mules, put them to yoke, and plow the fields, we'd be harvesting snowdrifts."

"Is there something else we could plant?" Liat asked. "Something we have time to grow before winter? Potatoes? Turnips?"

"I don't know," Kiyan said. "How long does it take to grow turnips this far north?"

Liat closed her eyes. Two educated, serious, competent women should be able to run a city. Should be able to shoulder the burden of the world and forget that one stood to lose a husband, the other a son. Should be able to ignore the constant fear that soldiers of a Galtic army might appear any day on the horizon prepared to destroy the city. It should be within their power, and yet they were blocked by idiot questions like whether turnips take longer to grow than potatoes. She took a deep breath and slowly let it out, willing the tension in her jaw to lessen, the pain behind her eyes to recede.

"I'll find out," Liat said. "But will you give the order to the mills? They won't be happy to stop their work."

"I'll give them the option of loaning the Khai their animals or pulling the plows themselves," Kiyan said. "If we have to spend the winter grinding wheat for our bread, it's a small price for not starving."

"It's going to be a thin spring regardless," Liat said.

Kiyan took the papers that Liat had drawn up. She didn't speak, but the set of her mouth agreed.

"We'll do our best," Kiyan said.

The banquet had gone splendidly. The women of the utkhaiem—wives and mothers, daughters and aunts—had heard Kiyan's words and taken to them as if she were a priest before the faithful. Liat had seen the light in their eyes, the sense of hope. For all their fine robes and lives of court scandal and gossip, each of these women was as grateful as Liat had been for the chance of something to do.

The food and fuel, Kiyan had kept for herself. Other people had been tasked with seeing to the wool, to arranging the movement of the summer belongings into the storage of the high towers, the preparation of the lower city—the tunnels below Machi. Liat had volunteered to act as Kiyan's messenger and go-between in the management of the farms and crops, gathering the food that would see them through the winter. Being the lover of a poet—even a poet who had never bound one of the andat—apparently lent her enough status in court to make her interesting. And as the rumors began to spread that Cehmai and Maati were keeping long hours together in the library and the poet's house, that they were preparing a fresh binding, Liat found herself more and more in demand. In recent days it had even begun to interfere with her work.

She had let herself spend time in lush gardens and high-domed dining halls, telling what stories she knew of Maati's work and intentions—what parts of it he'd said would be safe to tell. The women were so hungry for good news, for hope, that Liat couldn't refuse them. After telling the stories often enough, even she began to take hope from them herself. But tea and sweet bread and gossip took time, and they took attention, and she had let it go too far. The second wheat crop would be short, and no amount of pleasant high-city chatter now would fill bellies in the spring. Assuming they lived. If the Galts appeared tomorrow, it would hardly matter what she'd done or failed to do.

"There's going to be enough food," Kiyan said softly. "We may wind up killing more of the livestock and eating the grain ourselves, but even if half the crop failed, we'd have enough to see us through to the early harvest."

"Still," Liat said. "It would have been good to have more."

Kiyan took a pose that both agreed with Liat and dismissed the matter. Liat responded with one appropriate for taking leave of a superior. It was a nuance that seemed to trouble Kiyan, because she leaned forward, her fingertips touching Liat's arm.

"Are you well?" Kiyan asked.

"Fine," Liat said. "It's just my head has been tender. It's often like that when the Khai Saraykeht changes the tax laws again or the cotton crops fail. It fades when the troubles pass."

Kiyan nodded, but didn't pull back her hand.

"Is there anything I can do to help?" Kiyan asked.

"Tell me that Otah's come back with Nayiit, the Galts all conquered and the world back the way it was."

"Yes," Kiyan said. Her eyes lost their focus and her hand slipped back to her side of the table. Liat regretted being so glib, regretted letting the moment's compassion fade. "Yes, it would be pretty to think so."

Liat took her leave. The palaces were alive with servants and slaves, the messengers of the merchant houses and the utkhaiem keeping the life of the court active. Liat walked through the wide halls with their distant tiled ceilings and down staircases of marble wide enough for twenty men to walk abreast. Sweet perfumes filled the air, though their scents brought her no comfort. The world was as bright as it had been before she'd come to Machi, the voices lifted in song as merry and sweet. It was only a trick of her mind that dulled the colors and broke the harmonies. It was only the thought of her boy lying dead in some green and distant field and the dull pain behind her eyes.

When she reached the physicians, she found the man she sought speaking with Eiah. A young man lay naked on the wide slate table beside the pair. His face was pale and damp with sweat; his eyes were closed. His nearer leg was purple with bruises and gashed at the side. The physician—a man no older than Liat, but bald apart from a long gray fringe of hair—was gesturing at the young man's leg, and Eiah was leaning in toward him, as if the words were water she was thirsty for. Liat walked to them softly, partly from the pain in her head, partly from the hope of overhearing their discussion without changing it.

"There's a fever in the flesh," the physician said. "That's to be expected. But the *muscle*."

Eiah considered the leg, more fascinated, Liat noticed, with the raw wounds than with the man's flaccid sex.

"It's stretched," Eiah said. "So there's still a connection to stretch it. He'll be able to walk."

The physician dropped the blanket and tapped the boy's shoulder.

"You hear that, Tamiya? The Khai's daughter says you'll be able to walk again."

The boy's eyes fluttered open, and he managed a thin smile.

"You're correct, Eiah-cha. The tendon's injured, but not snapped. He won't be able to walk for several weeks. The greatest danger now is that the wound where the skin popped open may become septic. We'll have to clean it out and bandage it. But first, perhaps we have a fresh patient?"

Liat found herself disconcerted to move from observer to observed so quickly. The physician's smile was distant and professional as a butcher selling lamb, but Eiah's grin was giddy. Liat took a pose that asked forbearance.

"I didn't mean to intrude," she said. "It's only that my head has been troubling me. It aches badly, and I was wondering whether . . ."

"Come, sit down, Liat-kya," Eiah cried, grabbing Liat's hand and pulling her to a low wooden seat. "Loya-cha can fix *anything*."

"I can't fix everything," the physician said, his smile softening a degree—he was speaking now not only to a patient, but a friend of his eager student and a fellow adult. "But I may be able to ease the worst of it. Tell me when I've touched the places that hurt the worst."

Gently, the man's fingers swept over Liat's face, her temples, touching here and there as gently as a feather against her skin. He seemed pleased and satisfied with her answers; then he took her pulse on both wrists and considered her tongue and eyes.

"Yes, I believe I can be of service, Liat-cha. Eiah, you saw what I did?"

Eiah took a pose of agreement. It was strange to see a girl so young and with such wealth and power look so attentive, to see her care so clearly what a man who was merely an honored servant could teach her. Liat's heart went out to the girl.

"Make your own measures, then," the man said. "I have a powder I'll mix for the patient, and we can discuss what you think while we clean the gravel out of our friend Tamiya."

Eiah's touch was harder, less assured. Where the physician had hardly seemed present, Eiah gave the impression of grabbing for something even when pressing with the tips of her fingers. It was an eagerness Liat herself had felt once, many years ago.

"You seem to be doing very well here," Liat said, her voice gentle.

"I know," the girl said. "Loya-cha's very smart, and he said I could keep coming here until Mama-kya or the Khai said different. Can I see your tongue, please?"

Liat let the examination be repeated, then when it was finished said, "You must be pleased to have found something you enjoy doing."

"It's all right," Eiah said. "I'd still rather be married, but this is almost as good. And maybe Papa-kya can find someone to marry me who'll let me take part in the physician's house. I'll probably be married to one of the Khaiem, after all, and Mama-kya's running the whole city now. Everyone says so."

"It may be different later, though," Liat said, trying to imagine a Khai allowing his wife to take a tradesman's work as a hobby.

"There may not be any Khaiem, you mean," Eiah said. "The Galts may kill them all."

"Of course they won't," Liat said, but the girl's eyes met hers and Liat faltered. There was so much of Otah's cool distance in a face that seemed too young to look on the world so dispassionately. She was like her father, prepared to pass judgment on the gods themselves if the situation called her to do it. Comfortable lies had no place with her. Liat looked down. "I don't know," she said. "Perhaps there won't be."

"Here, now," the physician said. "Take this with you, Liat-cha. Pour it into a bowl of water and once it's dissolved, drink the whole thing. It will be bitter, so drink it fast. You'll likely want to lie down for a hand or two afterward, to let it work. But it should do what needs doing."

Liat took the paper packet and slipped it into her sleeve before taking a pose of gratitude.

"We should have a lunch in the gardens again," Eiah said. "You and Uncle Maati and me. Loya-cha would come too, except he's a servant."

Liat felt herself blush, but the physician's wry smile told her it was not the first such pronouncement he'd been subjected to.

"Perhaps you should wait for another day," he said. "Liat-cha had a headache, remember."

"I know that," Eiah said impatiently. "I meant tomorrow."

"That would be lovely," Liat said. "I'll talk with Maati about it."

"Would you be so good as to get the stiff brushes from the back and wash them for me, Eiah-cha?" the physician said. "Tamiya's anxious to be done with us, I'm sure."

Eiah dropped into a pose of confirmation for less than a breath before darting off to her task. Liat watched the physician, the amusement and fondness in his expression. He shook his head.

"She is a force," he said. "But the powder. I wanted to say, it can be habit-forming. You shouldn't have it more than once in a week. So if the pain returns, we may have to find another approach."

"I'm sure this will be fine," Liat said as she rose. "And . . . thank you. For what you've done with Eiah, I mean."

"She needs it," the man said with a shrug. "Her father's ridden off to die, her mother and her friend the poet are too busy trying to keep us all alive to take time to comfort her. She buries herself in this, and so even if she slows us down, how can I do anything but welcome her?"

Liat felt her heart turn to lead. The physician's smile slipped, and for a moment the dread showed from behind the mask. When he spoke again, it was softly and the words were as gray as stones.

"And, after all, we may need our children to know how to care for the dying before all that's coming is done."

MAATI RUBBED HIS EYES WITH THE PALMS OF HIS HANDS, SQUINTED, BLINKED. The world was blurry: the long, rich green of the grass on which they lay was like a single sheet of dyed rice paper; the towers of Machi were reduced to dark blurs that the blue of the sky shone through. It was like fog without the grayness. He blinked again, and the world moved nearer to focus.

"How long was I sleeping?" he asked.

"Long enough, sweet," Liat said. "I could have managed longer, I think. The gods all know we've been restless enough at night."

The sun was near the top of its arc, the remains of breakfast in lacquered boxes with their lids shut, the day half gone. Liat was right, of course. He hadn't been sleeping near enough—late to bed, waking early, and with troubled rest between. He could feel it in his neck and back and see it in the slowness with which his vision cleared.

"Where's Eiah got to?" he asked.

"Back to her place with the physicians, I'd guess. I offered to wake you so that she could say her good-byes, but she thought it would be better if you slept." Liat smiled. "She said it would be restorative. Can you imagine her using that kind of language a season ago? She already sounds like a physician's apprentice."

Maati grinned. He'd resisted the idea of this little outing at first, but Cehmai had joined Eiah's cause. A half-day's effort by a rested man might do better for them than the whole day by someone drunk with exhaustion and despair. And even now the library seemed to call to him—the scrolls he had already read, the codices laid out and put away and pulled out to look over again, the wax tablets with their notes cut into them and smoothed clear again. And in the end, he had never been able to refuse Eiah. Her good opinion was too precious and too fickle.

Liat slid her hand around his arm and leaned against him. She smelled of grass and cherry paste on apples and musk. He turned without thinking and kissed the crown of her head as if it were something he had always done. As if there had not been a lifetime between the days when they had first been lovers and now.

"How badly is it going?" she asked.

"Not well. We have a start, but Cehmai's notes are only beginnings. And they were done by a student. I'm sure they all seemed terribly deep and insightful when he was still fresh from the school. But there's less there than I'd hoped. And . . ."

"And?"

Maati sighed. The towers were visible now. The blades of grass stood out one from another.

"He's not a great inventor," Maati said. "He never was. It's part of why he was chosen to take over an andat that had already been captured instead of binding something new. And I'm no better."

"You were chosen for the same thing."

"Cehmai's clever. I'm clever too, if it comes to that, but we're the second pressing. There's no one we can talk with who's seen a binding through from first principles to a completion. We need someone whose mind's sharper than ours."

There were birds wheeling about the towers—tiny specks of black and gray and white wheeling though the air as if a single mind drove them. Maati pretended he could hear their calls.

"Perhaps you could train someone. There's a whole city to choose from."

"There isn't time," Maati said. He wanted to say that even if there were, he wouldn't. The andat were too powerful, too dangerous to be given to anyone whose heart wasn't strong or whose conscience couldn't be trusted. That was the lesson, after all, that had driven his own life and Cehmai's and the Dai-kvo himself. It was what elevated each of the poets from boy children cast out by their parents to the most honored men in the world. And yet, if there were someone bright enough to hand the power to, he suspected he would. If it brought the army back from the field and put the world back the way it had been, the risk would be worth it.

"Maybe one of the other poets will come," Liat said, but her voice had gone thin and weary.

"You don't have hope for the Dai-kvo?"

Liat smiled.

"Hope? Yes, I have hope. Just not faith. The Galts know what's in play. If we don't recapture the andat, the cities will all fall. If we do, we'll destroy Galt and everyone in her. They'll be as ruthless as we will."

"And Otah-kvo? Nayiit?"

Liat's gaze met his, and he nodded. The knot in her chest, he was certain, was much like his own.

"They'll be fine," Liat said, her tone asking for her own belief in the words as much as his. "It's always the footmen who die in battles, isn't it? The generals all live. And he'll keep Nayiit safe. He said he would."

"They might not even see battle. If they arrive before the Galts and come back quickly enough, we might not lose a single man."

"And the moon may come down and get itself trapped in a teabowl," Liat said. "But it would be nice, wouldn't it? For us, I mean. Not so much for the Galts."

"You care what happens to them?"

"Is that wrong?" Liat asked.

"You're the one who came to Otah-kvo asking that they all be killed."

"I suppose I did, didn't I? I don't know what's changed. Something to do with having my boy out there, I suppose. Slaughtering a nation isn't so much to think about. It's when I start *feeling* that it all goes confused. I wonder why we do it. I wonder why they do. Do you think if we gave them our gold and our silver and swore we would never bind a fresh andat . . . do you think they'd let our children live?"

It took a few breaths to realize that Liat was actually waiting for his answer, and several more before he knew what he believed.

"No," Maati said. "I don't think they would."

"Neither do I. But it would be good, wouldn't it? A world where it wasn't a choice of our children or theirs."

"It would be better than this one."

As if by common consent, they changed the subject, talking of food and the change of seasons, Eiah's new half-apprenticeship with the physicians and the small doings of the women of the utkhaiem now that their men had gone. It was only reluctantly that Maati rose. The sun was two and a half hands past where it had been when he woke, the shadows growing oblong. They walked back to the library, hand in hand at first, and then only walking beside each other. Maati felt his heart growing heavier as they came down the familiar paths, paving stones turning to sand turning to crushed white gravel bright as snow.

"You could come in," Maati said when they reached the wide front doors.

In answer, she kissed him lightly on the mouth, gave his hand a gentle squeeze, and turned away. Maati sighed and turned to lumber up the steps. Inside, Cehmai was sitting on a low couch, three scrolls spread out before him.

"I think I've found something," Cehmai said. "There's reference in Manat-kvo's notes to a grammatic schema called threefold significance. If we have something that talks about that, perhaps we can find a way to shift the binding from one kind of significance to another."

"We don't," Maati said. "And if I recall correctly, the three significators all require unity. There's not a way to pick between them."

"Well. Then we're still stuck."

"Yes."

Cehmai stood and stretched, the popping of his spine audible from across the wide room.

"We need someone who knows this better than we do," Maati said as he lowered himself onto a carved wooden chair. "We need the Dai-kvo."

"We don't have him."

"I know it."

"So we have to keep trying," Cehmai said. "The better prepared we are when the Dai-kvo comes, the better he'll be able to guide us."

"And if he never comes?"

"He will," Cehmai said. "He has to."

16

>+< "Yes," Nayiit said. "That's him."

Otah's mount whickered beneath him as he looked up at the Dai-kvo's body. It had been tied to a stake at the entrance to his high offices; the man had been dead for days. The brown-robed corpses of the poets lay at his feet, stacked like cordwood.

They had taken it all for granted. The andat, the poets, the continuity of one generation following upon another as they always had. It grew more difficult, yes. An andat would escape and for a time the city it had left would suffer, yes. They had not conceived that everything might end. Otah looked at the slaughtered poets, and he saw the world he had known.

The morning after the battle had been tense. He had risen before dawn and paced through the camps. Several of the scouts had vanished, and at first there was no way to know whether they had been captured by the Galts or killed or if they had simply taken their horses, set their eyes on the horizon, and fled. It was only when the reports began to filter back that the shape of things came clear.

The Galts had fallen back, their steam wagons and horses making a fast march to the east, toward the village of the Dai-kvo. There was no pursuit, no rush to find the survivors of that bloody field and finish the work they'd begun. Otah's army had been broken easily, and the Galts' contempt for them was evident in the decision that they were not worth taking the time to kill.

It was humiliating, and still Otah had found himself relieved. More of his men would die today, but only from wounds they already bore. They had given Otah a moment to rest and consider and see how deep the damage had gone.

Four hundred of his men lay dead in the mud and grass beside perhaps a third as many Galts, perhaps less. Another half thousand were wounded or missing. A few hours had cost him a third of what he had, and more than that.

The men who had survived the retreat were different from the ones he had spoken to at their cook fires before the fight. These men seemed stunned, lost, and emptied. The makeshift spears and armor that had once seemed to speak of strength and resourcefulness now seemed painfully naïve. They had come to battle armed like children and they had been killed by men. Otah found himself giving thanks to any gods that would listen for all the ones who had lived.

The scouting party left two days later. It was made of twenty horsemen and as many on foot, Otah himself at the lead. Nayiit asked permission to come, and Otah had granted it. It might not have been keeping the boy safe the way he'd promised Maati, but as long as Nayiit blamed himself for the carnage and defeat, it was better that he be away from the wounded and the dying. The rest of the army would stay behind in the camp, tend to the men who could be helped, ease the passing of those past hope, and, Otah guessed, slip away one by one or else in groups. He couldn't think they would follow him into battle again.

The smaller group moved faster, and the path the Galts had left was clear as a new-built road. Churned grass, broken saplings, the damage done by thousands of disciplined feet. The wounded earth was as wide as ten men across—never more, never less. The precision was eerie. It was two days' travel before Otah saw the smoke.

They reached the village near evening. They found a ruin. Where glittering windows had been, ragged holes remained. The towers and garrets cut from the stone of the mountain were soot-stained and broken. The air smelled of burned flesh and smoke and the copper scent of spilled blood. Otah rode slowly, the clack of his mount's hooves on pavement giving order to the idiot, tuneless wind chimes. The air felt thick against his face, and the place where his heart had once been seemed to gape empty. His hands didn't tremble, he did not weep. His mind simply took in the details—a corpse in the street wearing brown robes made black with blood, a Galtic steam wagon with the wide metalwork on the back twisted open by some terrible force, a firekeeper's kiln overturned and ashen, an arrow splintered against stone—and then forgot them. It was unreal.

Behind him, the others followed in silence. They made their way to the grand office at the height of the village. The great hall, open to the west, caught the light of the setting sun. The white stone of the walls glowed, light where it had escaped the worst damage and a deeper, darker gold where smoke had marked it.

And in the entrance of the hall, the Dai-kvo was tied to a stake. The hopes of the Khaiem lying dead at his feet.

I could have stopped this, Otah thought. The Galts live because I spared them at Saraykeht. This is *my* fault.

He turned to Nayiit.

"Have him cut down," he said. "We can have them buried or burned. Anything but this."

Behind the gruesome sight squatted the remains of a great pyre. Logs as tall as a standing man had been hauled here and set to hold the flames, and had burned nearly through. The spines of ancient books lay stripped in the ashes of their pages and curled from the heat. Shredded ribbons that had held the codices closed shifted in the breeze. Otah touched his palm to the neck of his horse as if to steady it more than himself, then dismounted.

Smoke still rose from the fire, thin gray reeking clouds. He paced the length and breadth of the pyre. Here and there, embers still glowed. He saw more than one bone laid bare and black. Men had died here. Poets and books. Knowledge that could never be replaced. He leaned against the rough bark of a half-burned tree. There had been no battle here. This had been slaughter.

"Most High?"

Ashua Radaani was at his side. Might have been at his side for some time, for all Otah could say. The man's face was drawn, his eyes flat.

"We've taken down the Dai-kvo," he said.

"Five groups of four men," Otah said. "If you can find any lanterns still intact, use them. If not, we'll make torches from something. I can't say how deep into the mountain these hallways go, but we'll walk through the whole thing if we have to."

Radaani glanced over his shoulder at the red and swollen sun that was just now touching the horizon. The others were silhouetted against it, standing in a clot at the mouth of the hall. Radaani turned back and took a pose that suggested an alternative.

"Perhaps we might wait until morning—"

"What if there's a man still alive in there," Otah said. "Will he be alive when the sun's back? If darkness is what we have to work in, we'll work in darkness. Anyone who survived this, I want him. And books. Anything. If it's written, bring it to me. Bring it here."

Radaani hesitated, then fell into a pose of acceptance. Otah put his hand on the man's shoulder.

We've failed, he thought. Of course we failed. We never had a chance.

They didn't make camp, didn't cook food. The horses, nervous from the scent of death all around them, were taken back from the village. Nayiit and his blacksmith friend Saya gleaned lanterns and torches from the wreckage. The long, terrible night began. In the flickering light, the back halls and grand, destroyed chambers danced like things from children's stories of the deepest hells. Otah and the three men with him—Nayiit, Radaani, and a thin-faced boy whose name escaped him—called out into the darkness that they were friends. That help had arrived. Their voices grew hoarse, and only echoes answered them.

They found the dead. In the beds, in the stripped libraries, in the kitchens and alleyways, and floating facedown in the wide wooden tubs of the bathhouse. No man had been spared. There had been no survivors. Twice Otah thought he saw a flicker of recognition in Nayiit's eyes when they found a man lying pale and bloodless, eyes closed as if in sleep. In a meeting chamber near what Otah guessed had been the Dai-kvo's private apartments, Otah found the corpse of Athai-kvo, the messenger who had come in the long-forgotten spring to warn him against training men to fight. His eyes had been gouged away. Otah found himself too numb to react. Another detail to come into his mind and leave it again. As the night's chill stole into him, Otah's fingers began to ache, his shoulders and neck growing tight as if the pain could take the place of warmth.

They fell into their rhythm of walking and shouting and not being answered until time lost its meaning. They might have been working for half a hand, they might have been working for a sunless week, and so the dawn surprised him.

One of the other searching parties had quit earlier. Someone had found a firekeeper's kiln and stoked it, and the rich smell of cracked wheat and flaxseed and fresh honey cut through the smoke and death like a sung melody above a street fight. Otah sat on an abandoned cart and cradled a bowl of the sweet gruel in his hands, the heat from the bowl soothing his palms and fingers. He didn't remember the last time he'd eaten, and though he was bone-weary, he could not bring himself to think of sleep. He feared his dreams.

Nayiit walked to him carrying a similar bowl and sat at his side. He looked older. The horrors of the past days had etched lines at the corners of his mouth. Exhaustion had blackened his eyes. Exhaustion and guilt.

"There's no one, is there?" Nayiit said.

"No. They're gone."

Nayiit nodded and looked down to the neat, carefully fitted bricks that made the road. No blade of grass pressed its way through those stony joints. It struck Otah as strangely obscene that a place of such carnage and destruction should have such well-maintained paving stones. It would be better when tree roots had lifted a few of them. Something so ruined should be a ruin. A few years, perhaps. A few years, and this would all be a wild garden dedicated to the dead. The place would be haunted, but at least it would be green.

"There weren't any children. Or women," Nayiit said. "That's something."

"There were in Yalakeht," Otah said.

"I suppose there were. And Saraykeht too."

It took a moment to realize what Nayiit meant. It was so simple to forget that the boy had a wife. Had a child. Or once had, depending on how badly things had gone in the summer cities. Otah felt himself blush.

"I'm sorry. That wasn't . . . Forgive my saying that."

"It's true, though. It won't change if we're more polite talking about it."

"No. No, it won't."

They were silent for a long moment. Off to their left, three of the others were laying out blankets, unwilling, it seemed, to seek shelter in the halls of the dead. Farther on, Saya the blacksmith was looking over the Galtic steam wagon with what appeared to be a professional interest. High in the robin's-egg sky, a double vee of cranes flew southward, calling to one another in high, nasal voices. Otah took two cupped fingers and lifted a mouthful of the wheat gruel to his lips. It tasted wonderful—sweet and rich and warm—and yet he didn't enjoy it so much as recognize that he should. His limbs felt heavy and awkward as wood. When Nayiit spoke, his voice was low and shaky.

"I know that I won't ever be able to make good for this. If I hadn't called the retreat—"

"This isn't your fault," Otah said. "It's the Dai-kvo's."

Nayiit reared back, his mouth making a small "o." His hands fumbled toward a pose of query, but the porcelain bowl defeated him. Otah took his meaning anyway.

"Not just this one. The last Dai-kvo. Tahi, his name was. And the one before that. All of them. This is their fault. We trusted everything in the andat. Our power, our wealth, the safety of our children. Everything. We built on sand. We were stupid."

"But it worked for so long."

"It worked until it didn't," Otah said. The response came from the back of his mind, as if it had always been there, only waiting for the time to speak. "It was always certain to fail sometime. Now, or ten generations from now. What difference does it make? If we'd been able to postpone the crisis until my children had to face it, or my grandchildren, or your grandchildren—how would that have been better than us facing it now? The andat have always been an unreliable tool, and poets have always been men with all the vanity and frailty and weakness that men are born with. The Empire fell, and we built ourselves in its image and so now we've fallen too. There's no honor in a lesson half-learned."

"Too bad you hadn't said that to the Dai-kvo."

"I did. To all three of them, one way and another. They didn't take it to heart. And I . . . I didn't stay to press the point."

"Then we'll have to learn the lesson now," Nayiit said. It sounded like an attempt at resolution, perhaps even bravery. It sounded hollow as a drum.

"Someone will," Otah said. "Someone will learn by our example. And maybe the Galts burned all the books that would have let them teach more poets of their own. Perhaps they're already safe from our mistakes."

"That would be ironic. To come all this way and destroy the thing that you'd come for."

"Or wise. It might be wise." Otah sighed and took another mouthful of the wheat. "The Galts are likely almost to Tan-Sadar by now. As long as they're heading south, we may be able to reach Machi again before they do. There's no fighting them, I think we've discovered that, but we might be able to flee. Get people to Eddensea and the Westlands before the passes all close. It's probably too late to take a fast cart for Bakta."

Nayiit shook his head.

"They aren't going south."

Otah took another mouthful. The food seemed to be seeping into his blood; he felt only half-dead with exhaustion. Then, a breath or two later, Nayiit's words found their meaning, and he frowned, put down his bowl, and took a questioning pose. Nayiit nodded down toward the low towns at the base of the mountain village.

"I was talking with one of the footmen. The Galts came up the river from Yalakeht, and they left heading north on the road to Amnat-Tan. They're likely only a day or so ahead of us. It doesn't seem like they're interested in Tan-Sadar."

"Why not?" Otah said, more than half to himself. "It's the nearest city."

"Marshes," a low voice said from behind them. The blacksmith, Saya, had come up behind them. "There's decent roads between here and Amnat-Tan. And then the North Road between all the winter cities. Tan-Sadar's close, Most High. But there's two different rivers find their start in the marshes between here and there, and if their wagons are like the one they've left down there, they'll need roads." The thick arms folded into a pose appropriate for an apprentice to his master. "Come and see yourself, if you'd care to."

The steam wagon was wider than a cart, its bed made of hard, oiled wood at the front, and sheeted with copper at the back. A coal furnace twice the size of a firekeeper's kiln stood around a steel boiling tank. Saya pointed out how the force of the steam drove the wheels, and how it might be controlled to turn slowly and with great force or else more swiftly. Otah remembered a model he'd seen as a boy in Saraykeht. An army of teapots, the Khai Saraykeht had called them. The world had always told them how it would be, how things would fall apart. They had all been deaf.

"It's heavy, though," Saya said. "And there's housings there at the front where you could yoke a team of oxen, but I wouldn't want to pull it through soft land."

"Why would they ever pull it?" Nayiit asked. "Why put all this into making it go on fire and then use oxen?"

"They might run out of coal," Otah said.

"They might," Saya agreed. "But more likely, they don't want to rattle it badly. All this was a rounded chamber like an egg. Built to hold the pressure in. You can see how they leaved the seams. Something cracked that egg, and that's why this is all scrap now. Anyone who was nearby when it happened . . . well. Anything strong enough to make a wagon this heavy move in the first place, and then load it with men or supplies, and *then* keep it going fast enough to be worth doing . . . it'd be a lot to let loose at once."

"How?" Otah said. "How did they break it?"

Saya shrugged.

"Lucky shot with a hard crossbow, maybe. Or the heat came too high. I don't know how gentle these things are. Looking at this one, though, I'd like a nice smooth meadow or a well-made road. Nothing too rutted."

"I can't believe they'd put men on this," Nayiit said. "A wagon that could kill everyone on it if it hits a bad bump? Why would anyone ever do that?"

"Because the gain is worth the price," Otah said. "They think the men they lose from it are a good sacrifice for the power they get."

Otah touched the twisted metal. The egg chamber had burst open like a flower bud blooming. The petals were bright and sharp and too thick for Otah to bend bare-handed. His mind felt perfectly awake, and his head felt full. It was as if he were thinking without yet knowing what he was thinking of. He squatted and looked at the wide, blackened door of the coal furnace.

"This is made of iron," Otah said.

"Yes, Most High," Saya agreed.

"But it doesn't melt. So however hot this runs, it can't be hotter than an ironworking forge, ne? How do they measure that, would you guess?"

Saya shrugged again.

"They're likely using soft coal, Most High. Use coal out of a Galt mine, it won't matter how much they put in it, it'll only come so hot. Forging iron needs hard coal. It's why the Galts buy their steel from Eddensea."

"And how long would it take them to reach Amnat-Tan if they were using these?"

"I've no way to know, Most High," Saya said taking a pose of apology. "I've never seen one working."

Otah nodded to himself. His head almost ached, but he could feel himself putting one thing with another like seeing fish moving below glass-clear ice.

"Otah-cha?" Nayiit said. "What is it?"

Otah looked up, and was surprised to find himself grinning.

"Tell the men to rest until midday. We'll start back to the main force after that."

Nayiit took an accepting pose. But as they walked away, Otah saw him exchange confused glances with the blacksmith. Back at their little camp, Ashua Radaani was organizing a pile of books. He took a pose of greeting, but his expression was grim. Otah stood beside him, hands pulled into the sleeves of his robes, and considered the volumes.

"This is everything," Radaani said. "Fourteen books out of the greatest library in the world."

Otah glanced at the mouth of the high offices. He tried to guess how much knowledge had been lost there, vanished from the world and never to been found again. Nayiit put a thick, dirty hand reverently on the stack before him.

"I can only read half of them," Radaani said. "The others are too old, I think. One or two from the First Empire."

"We'll take them to Maati and Cehmai," Otah said. "Maybe they'll be of use."

"We're going back to Machi?" Radaani said.

"Those who'd like to, yes. The rest will come with me to Cetani. I'm going to meet with the Khai Cetani. We'll have to hurry, though. The Galts will be taking the long way, and sacking Amnat-Tan while they're at it. I hope that will give us the time we need."

"You have a plan, Most High?" Radaani sounded dubious.

"Not yet," Otah said. "But when I do, it'll be better than my last one. I don't expect many men to follow me. A few will suffice. If they're loyal."

"We could make for Tan-Sadar," Radaani said. "If it's allies we need, they're closer."

"We don't, or at least not as badly as we need rough roads and an early winter."

Radaani didn't show any sign of understanding the comment, he only took a pose of acceptance.

"That does sounds more like Cetani, Most High. I'll have the men ready to go at midday."

Otah took a pose that acknowledged Radaani's words and walked back to the cart where Saya had found him. The wheat gruel had gone cold and sticky but it was still as sweet. In his mind, he was already on his way to Cetani. The road between Cetani and Machi wasn't one he had traveled often; he had kept to the South in the years he had been a courier, and the Khaiem had always been reluctant to meet one another, preferring to send envoys and girl children to wed. Nonetheless, he had traveled it. He was still trying to recall the details when Nayiit interrupted him.

"What are we going to do in Cetani, Most High?"

The boy's face was sharp and focused. Eager. Otah saw something of what he had been at that age. He knew the answer to Nayiit's question as soon as it was spoken, but still it took him a moment to bring himself to say it.

"You aren't coming, Nayiit-cha. I need you to see those books back to Maati."

"Anyone can do that," Nayiit said. "I'll be of use to you. I've been through Cetani. I was there just weeks ago, when we were coming to Machi. I can—"

"You can't," Otah said, and took the boy's hand. His son's hand. "You called a retreat when no one had given the order. In the Old Empire, I'd have had to see you killed for that. I can't have you come now."

The surprise on Nayiit's face was heartbreaking.

"You said it wasn't my fault," he said.

"And it isn't. I would have called the retreat myself if you hadn't. What happened to our men, what happened here, to the Dai-kvo . . . none of that's yours to carry. If you'd done differently, it would have changed nothing. But there will be a next time, and I can't have someone calling commands who might do what you've done."

Nayiit stepped back, just out of his reach. Ah, Maati, Otah thought, what kind of son have we made, you and I?

"It won't," Nayiit said. "It won't happen again."

"I know. I know it won't," Otah said, making his tone gentle to soften hard words. "Because you're going back to Machi."

UDUN WAS A RIVER CITY. IT WAS A CITY OF BRIDGES, AND A CITY OF BIRDS. SINJA had lived there briefly while recovering from a dagger wound in his thigh. He remembered the songs of the jays and the finches, the sound of the river. He remembered Kiyan's stories of growing up a wayhouse keeper's daughter—the beggars on the riverside quays who drew pictures with chalks to cover the gray stone or played the small reed flutes that never seemed to be popular anywhere else; the canals that carried as much traffic as the streets. The palaces of the Khai Udun spanned the river itself, sinking great stone stanchions down into the river like the widest bridge in the world. As a girl, Kiyan had heard stories about the ghouls that lived in the darkness under those great palaces. She had gone there in boats with her cohort in the dark of night, the way that Sinja himself had dared burial mounds at midnight with his brothers. She had kissed her first lover in the twilight beneath a bridge just north of here. He had spent so little time in Udun, and yet he felt he knew it so well.

The wayhouse where Sinja housed his men was south of the palaces. Its walls were stone and mud and thick as the length of his arm. The shutters were a green so dark they seemed almost black. It hadn't been built to fit as many men as Sinja commanded, but the standards of a soldier were lower than those of a normal traveler. And the standards of a soldier as likely to be mistaken for the enemy by his alleged fellows as killed by the defending armsmen were lower still. The great common room was covered from one wall to the other with thin cotton bedrolls. The upper rooms, intended for four men or fewer, housed eight or ten. There had been a few men who had ventured as far as the stables, but Sinja had called them back inside. There was a madness on Balasar Gice's men, and he didn't intend to have his own fall to it.

In the small walled garden at the back, Sinja sat on a camp stool and drank a bowl of mint tea brewed with fresh-plucked leaves. Thyme and basil grew around him, and a small black-leaf maple gave shade. Smoke rose into the sky, dark and solid as the towers of Machi. The birds were silent or fled. The scouts he'd sent out, their uniforms clearly the colors of Galt, reported that the rivers and canals had all turned red from the blood and the fish were dying of it. Sinja wasn't sure he believed that, but it seemed to catch the flavor of the day. Certainly he wasn't going to go out and look for himself.

An ancient man, spine bent and mouth innocent of anything resembling teeth, poked his head out the wide oaken doors at the end of the garden. The red-rimmed eyes seemed uncertain. The old hands shook so badly Sinja could see the trembling from where he sat. War is no place for the old, Sinja thought. It's meant for young men who can't yet distinguish between excitement and fear. Men who haven't yet grown a conscience.

"Mani-cha," Sinja called to the wayhouse keeper. "Is there something I can do for you?"

"There's a man come for you, Sinja-cha. Say's he's the . . . ah . . . the general."

"Bring him here," Sinja said.

The wayhouse keeper took a pose of acknowledgment, smiled an uncertain smile, and wavered half in, half out of the doorframe.

"You'll be fine, Mani-cha. You've my protection. He's not going to have you hanged, I promise. But you might bring him a bowl of tea."

Old Mani blinked and nodded his apology before ducking back into the house. The protection wasn't a promise he could keep. He hadn't asked General Gice's permission before he'd extended it. And still, he thought the old man's chances were good.

Balasar stepped into the garden as if he knew it, as if he owned it. It wasn't arrogance. That was what made the man so odd. The general's expression was drawn and thoughtful; that at least was a good sign. Sinja put his bowl of tea on the dusty red brick pathway, stood, and made his salute. Balasar returned it, but his gaze seemed caught by the shifting branches of the maple tree.

"All's well, I hope, sir," Sinja said.

"Well enough," Balasar said. "Well enough for a bad day, anyway. And here? Have your men been . . . Have you lost anyone?"

"I can account for all of them. I can have them ready to go out in half a hand, if you think they're needed, sir."

Balasar shifted, looking straight into Sinja's eyes as if seeing him clearly for the first time.

"No," Balasar said. "No, it won't be called for. What resistance there still is can't last long."

Sinja nodded. Of course not. Udun had numbers and knowledge, but they weren't fighters. The raids had continued for the whole trek upriver. Hunting parties had been harassed, wells fouled, the low towns the army had passed through stripped bare of anything that might have been of use to them. And the bodies of the soldiers slain in the raids were wrapped in shrouds and ashes to join the train. Balasar Gice had left Nantani with ten thousand men, and with all the gods watching him, he'd reached Udun with the full ten thousand, no matter if a few dozen needed carrying. Sinja tried to keep the disapproval from his face, but the general saw it there anyway, frowned, and looked away.

"What's the matter with that tree?" Balasar asked.

Sinja considered the maple. It was small—hardly taller than two men's height—and artfully cut to give shade without obstructing the view of the sky.

"Nothing, sir," he said. "It looks fine."

"The leaves are black."

"They're supposed to be," Sinja said. "If you look close, you can see it's really a very deep green, but they call it black-leaf all the same. When autumn comes, it turns a brilliant red. It's lovely, especially if the leaves haven't let go when the first snow comes."

"I'm sorry I won't be here to see it," the general said.

"Well, not the snows," Sinja said, "but you can see on the edges of those lower leaves where the red's starting."

Balasar stepped over and took a low branch in his hand. He bent it to look at the leaves, but he didn't pluck them free. Sinja gave the man credit for that.

Most Galts would have ripped the leaves off to look at them. With a sigh, Balasar let the branch swing back to its place.

"Tea?" Old Mani said from the doorway. Balasar looked over his shoulder at the old man and nodded. Sinja motioned the wayhouse keeper close, took the bowl, and sipped from it before passing it on to the general. Old Mani took a pose of thanks and backed out again.

"Tasting my food and drink?" Balasar asked in the tongue of the Khaiem. There was amusement in his tone. "Surely we haven't come to the point I'd expect you to poison me."

"I didn't brew it," Sinja said. "And Old Mani knew a lot of people you killed today."

Balasar took the cup and frowned into it. He was silent for long enough that Sinja began to grow uncomfortable. When he spoke, his tone was almost confessional.

"I've come to tell you that I was wrong," Balasar said. "You were right. I should have listened."

"I'm gratified that you think so. What was I right about?"

"The bodies. The men. I should have buried them where they lay. I should have left them. Now there's vengeance in it, and it's . . ."

He shook his head and sat on the camp stool. Sinja leaned against the stone wall of the garden.

"War's more fun when the enemy doesn't fight back," Sinja said. "There's never been a sack as easy as Nantani. You had to know things would get harder when the Khaiem got themselves organized."

"I did," Balasar said. "But . . . I carry the dead. I can feel them behind me. I know that they died because of my pride."

Balasar sipped at the tea. Far away across the war, a man shouted something, but Sinja couldn't make out the language, much less the words.

"All respect, Balasar-cha. They died because they were fighting in a war," Sinja said. "It's to be expected."

"They died in my war. My men, in my war."

"I see what you mean about pride."

Balasar looked up sharply, his lips thin, his face flushing. Sinja waited, and the general forced a smile. The maple leaves tapped against each other in the shifting breeze.

"I should have kept better discipline," Balasar said. "The men came to Udun for a slaughter. There's no mercy out there today. It's going to take longer to sack the city, it's going to mean more casualties for us, and Utani and Tan-Sadar will know what happened. They'll know it's a fight to the last man."

"As I recall, you came to destroy the Khaiem," Sinja said. "Not to conquer them."

Balasar nodded, accepting the criticism in Sinja's tone as his due. Sinja half-expected to see the general's hands take a pose of contrition, but instead he looked into Sinja's eyes. There was no remorse there, only the hard look of a man who has claimed his own failures and steeled himself to correcting them.

"I can destroy the Khaiem without killing every fruit seller and baker's apprentice along the way," Balasar said. "I need your help to do it."

"You had something in mind."

"I want your men to carry messages to Utani and Tan-Sadar. Not to the Khaiem. The utkhaiem and merchant houses. Men who have power. Tell them that if they stand aside when we come, they won't be harmed. We want the poets, and the books, and the Khaiem."

Sinja shook his head.

"You might as well run a spear through us now," Sinja said. "We're traitors. Yes, I know we're a mercenary company, and we took service and on and on. But every man I have was born in these cities we're sacking. Waving a contract isn't going to excuse them in the eyes of the citizens. Send prisoners instead. Find a dozen men your soldiers haven't quite hacked to death and use them to carry the messages. They'll be more effective than we will anyway."

"You think they can be trusted not to simply flee?"

"Catch a man and his wife. Or a father and child. There have to be a few left out there. Bring me the hostages and I'll keep them safe. When the husbands and fathers come back, you can give them a few lengths of silver and a day's head start. It won't undo what we've done here, but having a few survivors tell tales of your honorable treatment is better than none."

Balasar sipped his tea. The general's brow was furrowed.

"That's wise," he said at last. "We'll do that. I'll have my men bring the hostages to you by nightfall."

"Best not to rape them," Sinja said. "It takes something from the spirit of the thing if they're treated poorly."

"You're the one looking after them."

"And I can control the situation once they're in my care. It's before that I'm worried by."

"I'll see to it. If I give the order, it will be followed. They're my men." He said it as if he were reminding himself of something more than what the words meant.

For a moment, Sinja saw a profound weariness in the Galt's pale face. It struck him for the first time how small Balasar Gice was. It was only the way he moved through the world that gave the impression of standing half a head above everyone else in the room. The first dusting of gray had touched his temples, but Sinja couldn't say if it was premature or late coming. The breeze stirred, reeking of smoke.

"I can't tell if you hate war or love it," Sinja said.

Balasar looked up as if he'd forgotten Sinja was there. His smile was amused and bitter.

"I see the necessity of it," Balasar said. "And sometimes I forget that the point of war is the peace at the end of it."

"Is it? And here I thought it was gold and women."

"Those can be the same," Balasar said, ignoring the joke. "There are worse things than enough money and someone to spend it on."

"And glory?"

Balasar chuckled as he stood, but there was very little of mirth in the sound. He put down his bowl and his hands took a rough pose of query, as simple as a child's.

"Do you see glory in this, Sinja-cha? I only see a bad job that needs doing and a man so sure of himself, he's spent other people's lives to do it. Hardly sounds glorious."

"That depends," Sinja said, dropping into the language of the Galts. "Does it really need doing?"

"Yes. It does."

Sinja spread his hands, not a formal pose, but only a gesture that completed the argument. For a moment, something like tears seemed to glisten in the general's eyes, and he clapped Sinja on the shoulder. Without thinking, Sinja put his hand to the general's, clasping it hard, as if they were brothers or soldiers of the same cohort. As if their lives were somehow one. Far away, something boomed deep as a drum. Something falling. Udun, falling.

"I'll get you those hostages," Balasar said. "You take care of them for me."

"Sir," Sinja said, and stood braced at attention until the general was gone and he was alone again in the garden. Sinja swallowed twice, loosening the tightness in his throat. The maple swayed, black leaves touched with red.

In a better world, he thought, I'd have followed that man to hell.

Please the gods, let him never reach Machi.

17

The watchmen Kiyan had placed at the tops of the towers began ringing their bells just as the sun touched the top of the mountains to the west. Traffic stopped in the streets below and in the palace corridors. All eyes looked up, straining to see the color of the banners draped from the high, distant windows. Yellow would mean that a Galtic army had come at last, that their doom had come upon them. Red meant that the Khai had returned. So far above the city, colors were difficult to make out. At least to Maati's eyes, the first movement of the great signal cloth was only movement—the banners flew. It was the space of five fast, shaky breaths before he made out the red. Otah Machi had returned.

A crowd formed at the edge of the city as the first wagons came over the bridge. The women and children and old men of Machi come to greet the militia that had gone out to save the Dai-kvo. The Dai-kvo and the city and the world. Maati pushed his way in, elbowing people aside and taking more than one sharp rebuttal in his own ribs. The horses that pulled the wagons were blown. The men who rode them were gray-pale in the face and bloodied. The few who still walked, shambled. A ragged cheer rose from the crowd and then slunk away. A girl in a gray robe of cheap wool stepped out from the edge of the crowd, moving toward the soldiers. From where he stood trapped in the press of bodies, Maati could see the girl's head as it turned, searching the coming train of men for some particular man. Even before the first soldier reached her, Maati saw how small the group was, how many men were missing.

"Nayiit!" he shouted, hoping that his boy would hear him. "Nayiit! Over here!"

His voice was drowned. The citizens of Machi surged forward like an attack. Some of the men crossing the bridge drew back from them as if in fear, and then there was only one surging, swirling mass of people. There was no order, no control. One of the first wagons was pushed sideways from the road, the horses whinnying their protest but too tired to bolt. A man younger than Nayiit with a badly cut arm and a bruise on his face stumbled almost into Maati's arms.

"What happened?" Maati demanded of the boy. "Where's the Khai? Have you seen Nayiit Chokavi?" A blank stare was the only reply.

The chaos seemed to go on for a day, though it wasn't really more than half a hand. Then a loud, cursing voice rose over the tumult, clearing the way for the wagons. There were hurt men. Men who had to see physicians. Men who were dying. Men who were dead. The people stood aside and let the wagons pass. The sounds of weeping and hard wheels on paving stones were the only music. Maati felt breathless with dread.

As he pushed back into the city, following in the path the wagons had opened, he heard bits and snatches from the people he passed. The Khai had taken the utkhaiem and ridden for Cetani. The Galts weren't far behind. The Dai-kvo was dead. The village of the Dai-kvo was burned. There had been a blood-soaked farce of a battle. As many men were dead as still standing.

Rumor, Maati told himself. Everything is rumor and speculation until I hear it from Nayiit. Or Otah-kvo. But his chest was tight and his hands balled in fists so tight they ached when, out of breath and ears ringing, he made his way back to the library. A man in a travel-stained robe squatted beside his door, a tarp-covered crate on the ground at his side.

Nayiit. It was Nayiit. Maati found the strength to embrace his boy, and allowed himself at last to weep. He felt Nayiit's arms around him, felt the boy soften in their shared grief, and then pull away. Maati forced himself to step back. Nayiit's expression was grim.

"Come in," Maati said. "Then tell me."

It was bad. The Galts were not on Machi's door and Otah-kvo lived, but these were the only bright points in Nayiit's long, quiet recitation. They sat in the dimming front room, shutters closed and candles unlit, while Nayiit told the tale. Maati clasped his hands together, squeezing his knuckles until they ached. The Dai-kvo was dead. The men whom Maati had known in the long years he had lived in the village were memories now. He found himself trying to remember their names, their faces. There were fewer fresh to his mind than he would have thought—the firekeeper whose kiln had been at the corner nearest Maati's cell, the old man who'd run the bathhouse, a few others. They were gone, fallen into the forgetfulness of history. The records of their names had been burned.

"We searched. We searched through everything," Nayiit said. "I brought you what we found."

With a thick rustle, he pulled the thick waxed cloth from out of the crate. Two stacks of books lay beneath it, and Maati, squatting on the floor, lifted the ancient texts out one at a time with trembling hands. Fourteen books. The library of the Dai-kvo reduced to fourteen books. He opened them, smelling the smoke in their pages, feeling the terrible lightness of the bindings. There was no unity to them—a sampling of what had happened to be in a dark corner or hidden beneath something unlikely. A history of agriculture before the First Empire. An essay on soft grammars. Jantan Noya's *Fourth Treatise on Form*, which Maati had two copies of among his own books. None of these salvaged volumes outlined the binding of an andat, or the works of ancient poets.

Stone-Made-Soft wouldn't be bound with these. And so Stone-Made-Soft wouldn't be bound, because these were all that remained. Maati felt a cold, deep calm descend upon him. Grunting, he stood up and then began pacing his rooms. His hands went through the movements of lighting candles and lanterns without his conscious participation. His mind was as clear and sharp as broken ice.

Stone-Made-Soft could not be bound—not without years of work—and so he put aside that hope. If he and Cehmai failed to bind an andat, and quickly, the Galts would destroy them all. Nayiit, Liat, Otah, Eiah. Everyone. So something had to be done. Perhaps they could trick the Galts into believing that an andat had been bound. Perhaps they could delay the armies arrayed against them until the cold shut Machi against invasion. If he could win the long, hard months of winter in which he could scheme . . .

When the answer came to him, it was less like discovering something than remembering it. Not a flash of insight, but a familiar glow. He had, perhaps, known it would come to this.

"I think I know what to do, but we have to find Cehmai," he began, but when he turned to Nayiit, his son was curled on the floor, head pillowed by his arms. His breath was as deep and regular as tides, and his eyes were sunken and hard shut. Weariness had paled the long face, sharpening his cheeks. Maati walked as softly as he could to his bedchamber, pulled a thick blanket from his bed, and brought it to drape over Nayiit. The thick carpets were softer and warmer than a traveler's cot. There was no call to wake him.

What had happened out there—the battle, the search through the village, the trek back to Machi with this thin gift of useless books—would likely have broken most men. It had likely scarred Nayiit. Maati reached to smooth the hair on Nayiit's brow, but held back and smiled.

"All the years I should have done this," he murmured to himself. "Putting my boy to bed."

He softly closed the door to his apartments. The night was deep and dark, stars shining like diamonds on velvet, and a distant, eerie green aurora dancing far to the North. Maati stopped at the library proper, tucked the book he needed into his sleeve, and then—though the urge to find Cehmai instantly was hard to resist—made his way to the palaces, and to the apartments that Otah had given Liat.

A servant girl showed him into the main chamber. The only light was the fire in the grate, the shadows of flame dancing on the walls and across Liat's brow as she stared into them. Her hair was disarrayed, wild as a bird's nest. Her hands were in claws, trembling.

"I haven't . . . I haven't found—"

"He's fine," Maati said. "He's in my apartments, asleep."

Liat's cry startled him. She didn't walk to him so much as flow through the air, and her arms were around Maati's shoulders, embracing him. And then she stepped back and struck his shoulder hard enough to sting.

"How long has he been there?"

"Since the army came back," Maati said, rubbing his bruised flesh. "He brought books that they salvaged from the Dai-kvo. I was looking them over when—"

"And you didn't send me a runner? There are no servants in the city who you could have told to come to me? I've been sitting here chewing my own heart raw, afraid he was dead, afraid he was still out with Otah chasing the Galts, and he was at your apartments talking about *books*?"

"He's fine," Maati said. "I put a blanket over him and came to you. But he'll need food. Soup. Some wine. I thought you could take it to him."

Liat wiped away a tear with the back of her hand.

"He's all right?" she asked. Her voice had gone small.

"He's exhausted and hungry. But it's nothing a few days' rest won't heal."

"And . . . his heart? You talked with him. Is he . . . ?"

"I don't know, sweet. I'm not his mother. Take him soup. Talk with him. You'll know him better than I can."

Liat nodded. There were tears on her cheeks, but Maati knew it was only the fear working its way through. Seeing their boy would help more than anything else.

"Where are you going?" she asked.

"The poet's house."

The night air was chill, both numbing his skin and making him more acutely aware of it. Summer was failing, autumn clearing its throat. The few men and women Maati passed seemed to haunt the palaces, more spirit than flesh. They took poses of deference to him, more formal or less depending upon their stations, but the stunned expressions spoke of a single thought. The news from the broken army had spread, and everyone knew that the Dai-kvo was gone, the Galts triumphant. With even the last glow of twilight long vanished, the paths were dimmer than usual, lanterns unlit, torches burned to coal. The great halls and palaces loomed, the glimmering from behind closed shutters the only sign that they had not been abandoned. Twists of dry herbs tied with mourning cloth hung from the trees as offering to the gods. The red banner that had announced the army's arrival still hung from the high tower, grayed by the darkness. Colorless.

Maati passed through the empty gardens, and found himself smiling. He felt separate from the city around him, untouched by its despair. Perhaps even invigorated by it. There was nothing the citizens of Machi could do, no path for them to take that might somehow make things right. That was his alone. He would save the city, if it were to be saved, and if Machi fell, it would find Maati working to the end. It was that hope and the clarity of the path that lay before him that made his steps lighter and kept his blood warm.

He wondered if this strange elation was something like what Otah had felt, all those years he had lived under his false name. Perhaps holding himself at a distance from the world was how Otah had learned his confidence.

But no. That thought was an illusion. However much this felt like joy, Maati's rational mind knew it was only fear in brighter robes.

The door of the poet's house stood open. The candlelight from within glowed gold. Maati hauled himself up the stairs and through the doorway without scratching or calling out to announce his presence. The air within smelled of distilled wine and a deep earthy incense of the sort priests burned in the temples. He found Cehmai at the back of the house, eyes bloodshot and wine bowl cupped in his hands. He sat cross-legged on the floor contemplating a linked sigil of order and chaos—mother-of-pearl inlay in a panel of dark-stained rosewood. He glanced up at Maati and made an awkward attempt at some pose Maati could only guess at.

"You've found religion?" Maati asked.

"Chaos comes out of order," Cehmai said. "I can't think of a better time to contemplate the fact. And gods are all we have left now, aren't they?"

Maati reached out, brushing the panel with his fingers before tipping it backward. It slapped the floor with a sound like a book dropped from a table. Cehmai blinked, half shocked, half amused. Before he could speak, Maati fished in his sleeve, brought out the small brown volume, its leather covers worn soft as cloth by the years, and dropped it into Cehmai's lap. He didn't wait for Cehmai to pick it up before he strode back into the front room, closed the door, and dropped two fresh lumps of coal onto the fire in the grate. He found a pan, a flask of fresh water, and a brick of pressed tea leaves. That was good. They'd want that before the night was out. He also found the spent incense—ashes lighter than fresh snow on a black stone burner. He dumped them outside.

A high slate table held their notes. Thoughts and diagrams charting the new and doomed binding of Stone-Made-Soft. Maati scooped up the pages of cramped writing and put them outside as well, with the ashes. Then he carefully smoothed the writing from the wax tablets until they were smooth again, pristine. He took up the bronze-tipped stylus and scored two long vertical lines in the wax, dividing it into three equal columns. Cehmai walked into the room, his head bent over the open book. He was already more than halfway through it.

"You aren't the only one who was ever chosen to bind one of the andat," Maati said. "I even began the binding once, a long time ago. Liat-cha talked me out of trying. She was right. It would have killed me."

"You mean this?" Cehmai said. "You're going to bind Seedless?"

"It was what the Dai-kvo chose me for. Heshai wrote his binding, and his analysis of its flaws. It's too close to the original. I know that. But with the changes we'll need to make in order to include my scheme for avoiding the price of a failed binding and your fresh perspective, we can find another way."

In the first column of the wax tablet, Maati wrote *Seedless*.

"Forgive me, Maati-kvo, but will this really help? Stone-Made-Soft could have dropped their army half into the ground. Water-Moving-Down might have flooded them. But Seedless? Removing-the-Part-That-Continues doesn't have much power to stop an army."

"I can offer to kill all their crops," Maati said, writing *Heshai-kvo* at the top of the second column. "I can threaten to make every cow and pig and lamb barren. I can make every Galtic woman who's bearing a child lose it. Faced with that, they'll turn back."

His stylus paused over the head of the third column, and then he wrote his own name. He and Cehmai could outline the major points here; they could add and remove aspects of Heshai's first vision, interpret the corrections the old poet would have made, had he been given the chance. They could remake the binding, because the binding was already half-remade. If there was time. If they could find a way. If they were clever enough to save the world from the armies of Galt.

"And if they don't turn back?" Cehmai said.

"Then we'll all die. Their cities *and* ours. Check to see if that tea's ready to brew up, will you? I need your help with this, and it will go better if you're sober."

The sculpture garden of Cetani was the wonder of the city. Two bronze men in the dress of the Emperor's guard stood at the entrances at its northwest end, staring to the south and east, as if still looking to the Empire they had failed to protect. In their great, inhuman shadows, the finest work of the cities of the Khaiem had been gathered over the span of generations. There were hundreds of them, each astounding in its own fashion, under the wide branches of ash and oak with leaves the color of gold. The dragons of Chaos writhed along one long wall, their scales shining with red lacquer and worked silver, chips of lapis and enamel white as milk. In a shadowed niche, Shian Sho, last of the Emperors, sat worked in white marble on a high dais, his head sunk despairingly in his hands. It was a piece done after the Empire's fall. If the Emperor had seen himself shown with such little dignity, the sculptor would have been lucky to have a fast death. But the drape of the final Emperor's robes made the stone seem supple as linen, and the despair and thoughtfulness of the dead man's expression spoke of a time nine generations past when the world had torn itself apart. The sculptor who had found Shian Sho in this stone had lived through that time and had put the burden of his heart into this monument; this empty sepulcher for his age. Otah suspected that no man since then had looked upon it and understood. Not until now.

The Khai Cetani stood at the foot of a life-size bronze of a robed woman with eagle's wings rising wide-spread from her shoulders. He was younger than Otah by perhaps five years, gray only beginning to appear in his night-black hair. His gaze flickered over Otah, giving no sign of the thoughts behind his eyes. Otah felt a moment's self-consciousness at his travel-worn robes and incipient, moth-eaten beard. He took a pose of greeting appropriate for two people of equal status and saw the Khai Cetani hesitate for a moment before returning it. It was likely it was the first time in years anyone had approached him with so little reverence.

"My counselors have told me of your suggestion, my good friend Machi," the Khai Cetani said. "I must say I was . . . surprised. You can't truly expect us to abandon Cetani without a fight."

"You'll lose," Otah said.

"We are a city of fifty thousand people. These invaders of yours are at most five."

"They're soldiers. They know what they're doing. You might slow them, but you won't stop them."

The Khai Cetani sat, crossing his legs. His smile was almost a sneer.

"You think because you failed, no one else can succeed?"

"I think if we had a season, perhaps two, to build an army, we might withstand them. Hire mercenaries to train the men, drill them, build walls around at least the inner reaches of the cities, and we might stand a chance. As it is, we don't. I've seen what they did to the village of the Dai-kvo. I've had reports from Yalakeht. Amnat-Tan will fall if it hasn't already. They will come here next. You have fifty thousand, including the infirm and the aged and children too young to hold a sword. You don't have weapons enough or armor or experience. My proposal is our best hope."

It was an argument he had wrestled with through many of the long nights of his journey to the North. Force of arms would not stop the Galts. Slowing them, letting the winter come and protect them for the long, dark months in which no attacking force would survive the fields of ice and brutally cold nights, winning time for the poets to work a little miracle, bind one of the andat and save them all—it was a thin hope but it was the best they had. And slowly, during the days swaying on horseback and nights sitting by smoldering braziers, Otah had found the plan that he believed would win him this respite. Now if the Khai Cetani would simply see the need of it.

"If you bring your people to Machi, we will have twice as many people who can take the field against the Galts. And if you will do what I've suggested with the coal and food, the Galts will be much worse for the travel than we will be."

"And Cetani will fall without resistance. We will roll over like a soft quarter whore," the Khai Cetani said. "It's simple enough for you to sacrifice my city, isn't it?"

"None of this is easy. But simple? Yes, it's simple. Bring your people to Machi. Bring all the food you can carry and burn what you can't. Mix hard coal in with the soft, so that what we leave behind for the Galts will burn too hot in their steam wagons, and give me the loan of five hundred of your best men. I'll give you a winter and the library of Machi. Between your poet and the two at my court—"

"I have no poet."

Otah took a pose of query.

"He died half a month ago, trying to regain his andat," the Khai Cetani said. "His skin went black as a new bruise and his bones all shattered. I have no poet. All I have is a city, and I won't give it away for nothing!"

The Khai Cetani's words ended in a shout. His face was red with fury. And with fear. There was no more that Otah could say now that would sway him, but years in the gentleman's trade had taught Otah something about negotiations that the Khaiem had never known. He nodded and took a pose that formally withdrew him from the conversation.

"You and your men will stay here," the Khai Cetani said, continuing to speak despite Otah's gesture. "We will make our stand here, at Cetani. We will not fall."

"You will," Otah said. "And my men will leave in the morning, with me."

The Khai Cetani was breathing fast, as if he had run a race. Otah took a pose of farewell, then turned and strode from the garden. To the east, clouds darkened the horizon. The scent of coming rain touched the air. Otah's armsmen and servants fell in with him. The eyes of Cetani's utkhaiem were on the little procession as Otah walked to the apartments granted him by the Khai. He was a curiosity—one of the Khaiem walking with the swagger of a man who'd sat too long on a horse, his retinue looking more like a mercenary captain's crew than courtiers. And Otah suspected that martial air, however undeserved, would serve him. He scowled the way he imagined Sinja might have in his place.

Ashua Radaani was sitting at the fire grate deep in conversation with Saya the blacksmith when Otah entered the wide hall that served as the center of the visitors' palace. Battle and loss and the common enemy of Galt had mixed with the shared recognition of competence to make the two men something like friends. They stood and took poses of respect and welcome that Otah waved away. He sat on a low cushion by the fire and sent his servant boy to find them tea and something to eat.

"It didn't go well, I take it," Radaani said.

"It didn't go well and it didn't go badly," Otah said. "He's smart enough to be frightened. That's good. I was afraid he'd be certain of himself. But his poet's dead. Tried to recapture his andat and paid its price."

Radaani sighed.

"Did he agree to your plan, Most High?" Saya asked.

"No," Otah said. "He's determined that Cetani not fall without a fight. I've told him we're leaving with him or without him. How was your hunting, Ashua-cha?"

Radaani leaned forward. His features were thinner than they had been in Machi, and the ring he turned on his finger wasn't so snug as it had once been.

"The court's frightened," he said. "There are a few people who came here from Yalakeht, and the stories . . . well, either they've grown in the telling, or it wasn't pretty there. And the couriers from Amnat-Tan haven't come the last two days."

"That's bad," Otah said. "Will we have time, do you think?"

"I don't know," Ashua said. He seemed to search for more words, but in the end only shook his head.

"Get the men ready," Otah said. "We'll give Cetani tomorrow to join us. After that, we'll head home. With enough time, we might be able to tear up some sections of the road behind us. Slow down the Galts, even if we can't do all we hoped against them."

"What about the books?" Saya asked. "If their poet's dead, it isn't as if they'll have need of them. Perhaps ours would make something of them."

"I can ask," Otah said. "With luck, we'll have the books and the people and the food stores."

"But the Khai refused you, Most High," Saya said.

Otah smiled and shook his head. Only now that he found himself a moment to rest did the weariness drag at him. He tried to think how many days he'd been riding from first light to last. A lifetime, it felt like. He remembered the man who'd left Machi to save the Dai-kvo, but it no longer felt like something he'd done himself. He was changing. His heart still ached at the thought of Kiyan and Eiah and Danat. His apprehension at the struggle still before him was no less. And still, he was not the man he had once been, and to his surprise and unease, the man he was becoming seemed quite natural.

"Most High?" Saya repeated.

"Walking away from a negotiation isn't the same as ending it," Otah said. "Cetani's proud and he's lost, but he's not a fool. He wants to do what we're asking of him. He just hasn't found the way to say yes."

"You sound sure of that," Saya said.

Otah chose his words carefully.

"If someone had come to me after that battle and said that they knew what to do, that they would take the responsibility, I would have given it to them. And that's just what I've offered him," Otah said. "The Khai Cetani will call for me. Tonight."

He was wrong. The Khai Cetani didn't send for him until the next morning.

The man's eyes were bloodshot, his face slack from worry and exhaustion. Otah doubted the Khai Cetani had slept since they had spoken, and perhaps not for days before that. Through the wide, unshuttered windows, the morning was cold and gray, low clouds seeming to bring the sky no higher than a sparrow might fly. Otah sat on the divan set for him—rich velvet cloth studded with tiny pearls and silver thread, but smelling of dust and age. The most powerful man in Cetani sat across from him on an identical seat. That alone was a concession, and Otah noted it without giving sign one way or the other.

The Khai Cetani motioned the servants to leave them. From the hesitation and surprised glances, Otah took it that he'd rarely done so before. Some men, he supposed, were more comfortable with the constant attention.

"Convince me," the Khai Cetani said when the doors were pulled closed and they were alone.

Otah took a pose of query.

"That you're right," the Khai said. "Convince me that you're right."

There was a hunger in the request, almost a need. Otah took a deep breath and let it out slowly. The fire in the grate popped and shifted while he gathered his thoughts. He had turned his plans over in his mind since he'd left the ruin of the Dai-kvo's village. He'd honed them and tested them and stayed up late into the night despairing at their improbability only to wake in the morning convinced once more. The simplest answer was the best here, and he knew that, but still it was a struggle to find the words that made his mind clear.

"On the field, we can't match them," he said. "If we stay here and face them, we'll lose outright. There's nothing that can keep Cetani from falling to them. But they have two weaknesses. First, the steam wagons. They let them move faster than any group their size should be able to, but they're dangerous. It's a price they're prepared to pay, but they have underestimated the risks. If we start by breaking those—"

"The coal?"

Otah took a confirming pose.

"They aren't built for forge coal," he said. "And the men we're facing? They're soldiers, not smiths and ironmongers. There's no reason for them to look too closely at what they raid out of your stocks. Especially when they're pushing to get to Machi before the winter comes. If we leave them mixed coal, it'll burn too hot. The seams of their metalwork will soften, if the grates don't simply melt out from underneath."

"And so they have to come on foot or by horse?"

Otah remembered the twisted metal from the Dai-kvo's village and allowed himself a smile.

"When those wagons break, it's more than only stopping. They'll lose men just from that, and if we play it well, we can use the confusion to make things worse for them. And there's the other thing. They know we're going to lose. They have the strength, and we're unprepared. The only time we've faced them head-on, we were slaughtered. They know that we can't effectively fight them."

"That's a weakness?" the Khai Cetani asked.

"Yes. It keeps them from paying attention. To them, it's already over. Everything's certain but the details. That something else might happen isn't likely to occur to them. Why should it?"

The Khai Cetani looked into the fire. The flames seemed to glitter in his dark eyes. When he spoke, his voice was grim.

"They've made all the same mistakes we did."

Otah considered that for a moment before nodding.

"The Galts understand war," he said. "They're the best teachers I have. And so I'll do to them what they did to us."

"And to do that, you would have me—Khai of my own city—abandon Cetani to follow *your* lead?"

"Yes," Otah said.

The Khai sat in silence for a long time, then rose. The rustle of his robes as he walked to the window was the only sound. Otah waited as the man looked out over the city. Over Cetani, the city for which this man had killed his brothers, for which he had given up his name. Otah felt the tension in his own back and neck. He was asking this man to abandon everything, to walk away from the only role he had played in his life. Cetani would fall. It would be sacked. Even if everything went perfectly, there might be nothing to rebuild. And what would a Khai be if there was no city left him?

Many years before, Otah had asked another man to do the right thing, even though it would cost him his honor and prestige and the only place he had in the world. Heshai-kvo had refused, and he had died for the decision.

"Most High," Otah began, but the Khai Cetani held up a hand to stop him without even so much as looking back. Otah could see it in the man's shoulders in the moment the decision was made; they lifted as if a burden had been taken from him.

18

>+< Even the winter she had passed in Yalakeht had not prepared Liat for the fickleness of seasons in the North. Each day now was noticeably shorter than the one before, and even when the afternoons were warm, the sun pressing down benignly on her face, the nights were suddenly bitter. In the gardens, the leaves all lost their green at once, as if by conspiracy. It was unlike the near-imperceptible changes in the summer cities. In Saraykeht, autumn was a slow, lingering thing; the warmth of the world made a long good-bye. Things came faster here, and Liat found the pace disturbing. She was a woman of the South, and abrupt change uneased her.

For instance, she thought as she sipped smoky tea in her apartments, she still imagined herself a businesswoman of Saraykeht. Had anyone asked of her work, she would have spoken of the combing rooms, the warehouses. Had anyone asked of her home, she would have described the seafront of Saraykeht, the scent of the ocean, the babble of a hundred languages. She would have pictured the brick-built house she'd taken over when Amat Kyaan had died, and the little bedroom with its window half-choked with vines. She hadn't seen that city in over a year, and wouldn't go back now before the spring at best.

At best.

At worst, Saraykeht itself might be gone. Or she might not live to see summer again.

The city in which she now passed her days was suffering from change as well. Small shrines with images of the vanished andat had begun to appear in the niches between buildings, as if a few flowers and candles could coax them back. The temples had been filled every day by men and women who might not have sat before a priest in years. The beggars singing with boxes at their feet all chose songs about redemption and the return of things lost.

She sipped her tea. It was no longer hot enough to scald her lips, but it felt good drinking it. It warmed her throat like wine, only without the easing in her muscles or the softness in her mind. The morning before her was full— coordinating the movement of food and fuel into the tunnels below Machi, the raising of stores into the high towers where they would wait out the cold of winter. There wasn't time for dark thoughts. And yet the darkness came whether she courted it or not.

She looked up at the sound of the door. Nayiit stepped in. The nights were not so long or so cold as to keep him in his rooms. Liat put down her bowl.

"Good morning, Mother," he said as he sat on a cushion beside the fire. "You're up early."

"Not particularly," Liat said.

"No?" Nayiit said, and then smiled the disarming, rueful smile that would always and forever mark him as the son of Otah Machi. "No, I suppose not. May I?"

Liat gestured her permission, and Nayiit poured himself a bowl of the tea. He looked tired, and it was more than a night spent in teahouses and the baths. Something had changed while he'd been gone. She had thought at first that it was only exhaustion. When she'd found him asleep on Maati's floor, he had been half-dead from his time on the road and visibly thinner. But since then he'd rested and eaten, and still there was something behind his eyes. An echo of her own bleak thoughts, perhaps.

"I failed him," Nayiit said. Liat blinked and sat back in her chair. Nayiit tilted his head. "It's what you were wondering, ne? What's been eating the boy? Why can't he sleep anymore? I failed the Khai. I had his good opinion. There was a time that he valued my counsel and listened to me, even when I had unpleasant things to say. And then I failed him. And he sent me away."

"You didn't fail—"

"I did. Mother, I love you, and I know that you'd move the stars for me if you could, but I failed. Your son can fail," Nayiit said. He put down his bowl with a sharp click, and Liat wondered if perhaps he was still just a bit tipsy from his night's revelry. Drink sometimes made her maudlin too. "I'm not a good man, Mother. I'm not. I have left my wife and my child. I have slept with half the women I've met since we left home. I lost the Khai's trust—"

"Nayiit—"

"I killed those men."

His face was still as stone, but a tear crept from the corner of his eye. Liat slid down from her seat to kneel on the floor beside him. She put her hand on his, but Nayiit didn't move.

"I called the retreat," he said. "I saw them fighting, and the Galts were everywhere. They were all around us. All I could think was that they needed to get away. I was calling signals. I knew how to call the retreat, and I did it. And they died. Every man that fell because we ran is someone I killed. And he knew it. The Khai. He knew it, and it's why he sent me back here."

"That battle was doomed from the start," Liat said. "They outnumbered you; they were veterans. Your men were exhausted laborers and huntsmen. If what happened out there is anyone's fault, it's Otah's."

"You don't understand," he said. His voice wasn't angry, only tired. "I want to be a good man. And I'm not. For a time, I thought I was. I thought I *could* be. I was wrong."

Liat felt a thickness at the back of her throat. She forced a smile, half-rose, and kissed him on the top of his head, where the bones hadn't yet grown closed the first time she'd held him.

"Then do better," she said. "As long as you're alive, the next thing you do can be a good one, ne? Besides which, of course you're a good man. Only good men worry about whether they're bad."

Nayiit chuckled. The darkness slid back to the place it had been. Not gone, but hidden.

"And what do bad men worry about?" he asked.

Liat shrugged and started to answer him, but the bells began to ring. It took half a breath for Liat to recall what the deep chiming alarm meant. She didn't remember going to the window; she couldn't say how Nayiit had come to be at her side. She squinted against the blue-yellow light of morning, trying to make out the banners hanging from the towers high above.

"Is it red or yellow?" Liat asked.

"Gods," Nayiit said. "Look at that."

His gaze was nearer the ground. Liat looked to the south. The low cloud of dust seemed to cover half the horizon. Otah's remaining men couldn't have done that. It wasn't him. The Galts had come to Machi. Liat stepped back from the window, her hands gripping the folds of her robe just over her heart.

"We have to get Kiyan-cha," she said. "We have to get Kiyan-cha and the children. And Maati. We have to get them out before—"

"Red," Nayiit said.

Liat shook her head, uncertain for a moment what he meant. Nayiit pointed to the high dark tower and spoke over the still-ringing bells.

"The banner's red," he said. "It's not the Galts. It's the Khai."

Only it wasn't. The couriers reached Kiyan just before Liat did, so when she entered Kiyan-cha's meeting rooms, she found Otah's wife with a thick letter—seams ripped, seal broken—lying abandoned in her lap and an expression equal parts disbelief and outrage on her pale face.

"He's an idiot," Kiyan said. "He's a self-aggrandizing, half-blind idiot who can't think two thoughts in a straight line."

Liat took a pose that asked the question.

"My husband," Kiyan said, color coming at last to her cheeks. "He's sent us another whole *city*."

Cetani, nearest neighbor of Machi, had emptied itself. The couriers had arrived just before the fastest carts. The dust that Liat had mistaken for an army was only the first wave of tens of thousands of men and women—their stores of grains, their chickens and ducks and goats, whatever small precious things they could not bring themselves to leave behind. Otah's letter explained that they were in need of shelter, that Machi should do its best for them. The tone of the words was apologetic, but only for someone who knew the man well. Only to women like themselves. Kiyan held Liat's arm as if for support as they walked together to the bridge outside the city where they awaited her.

The man who stood at the middle point in the bridge wore an elegant robe—black silk shot with yellow—that was only slightly disarrayed by his travels. Servants and armsmen of Machi parted for Kiyan, allowing her passage onto the bridge's western end. Liat tried to disengage, but Kiyan's grip didn't lessen, and so they walked out together. On seeing them, the man took a pose of greeting appropriate for a man of lower rank to the wife of a more prestigious man. This was not the Khai Cetani, then, but some member of the Cetani utkhaiem.

"I have been sent to speak to the first wife of the Khai Machi," he said.

"I am the Khai's only wife," Kiyan said.

He took this odd information in stride, turning his attention wholly to Kiyan. Liat felt awkward and out of place, and oddly quite protective of the woman at her side.

"Kiyan-cha," the man said. "I am Kamath Vauamnat, voice of House Vauamnat. The Khai Cetani has sent us here at your husband's invitation. The army of Galt is still some days behind us, but it is coming. Our city . . ."

Something changed in the courtier's face. It was unlike anything Liat had seen before, except perhaps an actor who in the midst of declaiming some epic has forgotten the words. The mask and distance of etiquette failed, and the words he spoke became genuine.

"Our city's gone. We have what we're carrying. We need your help."

Only Liat was near enough to Kiyan to hear the tiny sigh that escaped before she spoke.

"How could I refuse you?" she said. "I am utterly unprepared, but if you will bring your people across the bridge and make them ready, I will find them places here."

The man took a pose of gratitude, and Kiyan turned back, Liat still at her side, and walked back to the bank where her people waited.

"We'll need something like shelter for these people," Kiyan said, under her breath. "Someplace we can keep them out of the rain until we can find . . . someplace."

"They won't all fit," Liat said. "We can put them in the tunnels, but then there's no place for all of us to go when winter comes. There's too many of them, and they can't have carried enough food to see them through until spring. And we're stretched thin as it is."

"We'll stretch thinner," Kiyan said.

The rest of the day was a single long emergency, events and needs and decisions coming in waves and overlapping each other like the scales of a snake. Liat found herself at the large and growing camp that was forming as the refugees of Cetani reached the bridge. Thankfully, the bridge was only the width of eight men walking abreast, and it kept the flow of humanity and cattle and carts to a speed that was almost manageable. Liat only had to school herself not to look across the water to the larger, shapeless mass of people still waiting to cross. Liat motioned them to different places, the ones too frail or ill to survive another night in the open, the ones robust enough that they might be put to work. There were old men, children, babes hanging in their mothers' exhausted arms.

Liat felt as if she were being asked to engineer a new city of tents and cook fires. They came in the hundreds. In the thousands. Night had fallen before the last man crossed, and Liat could see fires on the far side, camps made by those who'd given up hope of crossing today. Liat sat on the smooth stone rail at the bridge's end and let the aches in her feet and back and legs complain to her. It had been an excruciating day, and the work was far from ended. But at least the refugees were in tents sent out from Machi, safe from the cold. The food carts of Machi had also come out from the city, making their way through the crowds with garlic sausages and honeyed almonds and bowls of noodles and beef. There were even songs. Over the constant frigid rushing of the water, there was the sound of flutes and drums and voices. The temptation to close her eyes was unbearable, and yet. And yet.

I want to be a good man, he'd said. *And I'm not.*

With a sigh she began the long trek back to the city, to the palaces, to Kiyan and Maati and the bathhouses and her bed. The city, as she passed through its streets, was alive. The refugees of Cetani had not all waited in the camp. Or perhaps Kiyan had meant to start bringing them into the city. Whatever the intention had been, they had come, and Machi had poured itself out to make them welcome, to offer them food and wine and comfort, to pull news and gossip from them. The sun was gone, and the darkness was cold, and yet the city was full as a street fair. And as chaotic.

She found Kiyan in the palaces looking as exhausted as she herself felt. Otah's wife waved her near to the long, broad table. Wives of the utkhaiem were consulting one another, writing figures on paper, issuing orders to wide-eyed servants. It was like the middle of a trading company at the height of the cotton harvest, and Liat found it strangely comforting.

"It can be done," Kiyan said. "It won't be pleasant, but it can be done. I've had word from the Poinyat that we can use their mines, and I'm expecting the Daikani any time now."

"The mines?" Liat said. The exhaustion made her slow to understand.

"We'll have to put people in them. They're deep enough to stay warm. It's like living in the tunnels under the city, only rougher. The ones in the plain will even have their own water. There's food and sewage to worry about, but I've sent Jaini Radaani to speak with the engineers, and if she can't convince them to find a solution, I'll be quite surprised."

"That's good," Liat said. "Things at the bridge are under control. We've set up a tent for the physicians down there, and there's food enough. There will be more tomorrow, but I think they've all been seen to."

"Gods, Liat-cha. You look like death and you're cold. Let me have someone see you to the baths, get you warm. Have you eaten?"

She hadn't, but she pushed the thought aside.

"I need something from you, Kiyan-cha."

"Ask."

"Nayiit. He needs . . . something. He needs something to do. Something that he can be proud of. He came back from the battle . . ."

"I know," Kiyan said. "I know what happened there. It was in Otah's letter."

"He needs to help," Liat said, surprised at the pleading tone of her own voice. She hadn't known she felt so desperate for him. "He needs to *matter.*"

Kiyan nodded slowly, then leaned close and kissed Liat's cheek. The woman's lips felt almost hot against Liat's chilled skin.

"I understand, Liat-kya," she said. "Go and rest. I'll see to it. I promise you."

Weeping with fatigue, Liat found her way to her apartments, to her bedchamber, to her bed. Her belly ached with hunger, but she only drank the full carafe of water the servants had left at her bedside. By the time her body learned that it had been tricked, she would already be asleep. She closed her eyes for a moment before pulling off her robes and woke, still dressed, in the morning. The light sifted through the shutters, pressing in at the seams. The night candle was a lump of spent wax, and the air didn't smell of the dying wick. There was something, though. Pork. Bread. Liat sat up, her head light.

She stripped off yesterday's robes, sticky with sleep sweat, and pulled on a simple sitting robe of thick gray wool. When she stepped out to the main rooms, Kiyan was still arranging the meal on its table.

Thick slices of pink-white meat, bread so fresh it still steamed, trout baked with lemon and salt, poached pears on a silver plate. And a teapot that smelled of white tea and honey. Liat's stomach woke with a sharp pang.

"They told me you hadn't eaten last night," she said. "Either of you. I thought I might bring along something to keep you breathing."

"Kiyan-cha . . ." Liat began, then broke off and simply took a pose of gratitude. Kiyan smiled. She was a beautiful woman, and age was treating her gently. The intelligence in her eyes was matched by the humor. Otah was lucky, Liat thought, to have her.

"It's a trick, really," Kiyan said. "I've come pretending to be a servant girl, when I actually want to speak with Nayiit. If he's awake."

"I am."

His voice came from the shadows of his bedchambers. Nayiit stepped out. His hair pointed in a hundred directions. His eyes were red and puffy. A thin sprinkling of stubble cast a shadow on his jaw. Kiyan took a pose of greeting. He returned it.

"How can I be of service, Kiyan-cha?" he asked. Liat could tell from the too-precise diction that he'd spent his night drinking. He closed his bedroom doors behind him as he stepped in, and Liat more than half thought it was to protect the privacy of whatever woman was sleeping in his bed. Something passed across Kiyan's sharp features; it might have been compassion or sorrow, understanding or recognition. Liat couldn't say, and it was gone almost as soon as it came.

"That's the question, Nayiit-cha. I have something to ask of you. It may come to nothing, and if you should have to act upon my request, I'm afraid I won't be in a position to repay you."

Nayiit came forward slowly and sat at the table. Kiyan filled a plate for him as she spoke, casual as if she were a wayhouse keeper, and he a simple guest.

"You've heard the gossip from Cetani, I assume," she said.

"They've fled before the Galts. The Khai—both of them—are in the rear. To protect the people if the Galts come from behind."

"Yes," Kiyan said. "It's actually more complex than that. Otah has invented a scheme. If it works, he may win us a few months. Perhaps through the winter. If not, I think we can assume the Galts will be here shortly after the last of our cousins from Cetani have arrived."

It was a casual way to express the raw fear that every one of them might die violently before the first frost came. Our lives are measured in days now, Liat thought. But Kiyan had not paused to let the thought grow.

"There is an old mine a day's ride to the north of Machi. It was dug when the first Khai Machi set up residence here. It's been tapped out for generations, but the tunnels are still there. I've been quietly moving supplies to it. A bit of food. Blankets. Coal. A few boxes of gold and jewels. Enough for a few people to survive a winter and still have enough to slip across the passes and into the Westlands when spring comes."

Nayiit took a pose that accepted all she said. Kiyan smiled and leaned forward to touch Nayiit's hands with her own. She seemed at ease except for the tears that had gathered in her eyes.

"If the Galts come," she said, "will you take Eiah and Danat there? Will you . . ."

Kiyan stopped, her smile crumbling. She visibly gathered herself. A long, slow breath. And even still, when she spoke, it was hardly more than a whisper.

"If they come, will you protect my children?"

You brilliant, vicious snake, Liat thought. You glorious bitch. You'd ask him to love your son. You'd make caring for Danat the proof that my boy's a decent man. And you're doing it because I *asked* you to.

It's perfect.

"I would be honored," Nayiit said. The sound of his voice and the awe-struck expression in his eyes were all that Liat needed to see how well Kiyan had chosen.

"Thank you, Nayiit-kya," Kiyan said. She looked over to Liat, and her eyes were guarded. They both knew what had happened here. Liat carefully took a pose of thanks, unsure as she did what precisely she meant by it.

THE LIBRARY OF CETANI WAS MUCH SMALLER THAN MACHI'S. PERHAPS A THIRD AS many books and codices, not more than half as many scrolls. They arrived on Maati's doorway in sacks and baskets, crates and wooden boxes. A letter accompanied them, hardly more than a terse note with Otah's seal on it, telling him that there was no living poet to ask what texts would be of use, that as a result he'd sent everything, and expressing hope that these might help. There was no mention of the Galts or the Dai-kvo or the dead. Otah seemed to assume that Maati would understand how dire the situation was, how much depended on him and on Cehmai.

He was right. Maati understood.

He'd left Cehmai in the library, looking over their new acquisitions, while he sat in the main room of his apartments, marking out grammars and forms. How Heshai had bound Seedless, what he would have done differently in retrospect, and the variations that Maati could make—different words and structures, images and metaphors that would serve the same purpose without coming too near the original. His knuckles ached, and his mind felt woolly. It was hard to say how far into the work they'd come. Perhaps as much as a third. Perhaps less. The hardest part would come at the end; once the binding was mapped out and drafted, there was the careful process of going through, image by image, and checking to see that there were no ambiguities, no unintended meanings, no contradictions where the power of the andat might loop back upon itself and break his hold and himself.

Outside, the wind was blowing cold as it had since the middle morning. The city of tents that had sprung up at Machi's feet would be an unpleasant place tonight. Liat had been entirely absent these last four days, helping to find Cetani a place within Machi. It was just as well, he supposed. If she were here, he'd only want to talk with her. Speak with her. He'd want to hold her. Enough time for those little pleasures when Seedless was bound and the world was set right. Whatever that meant anymore.

The scratch at his door was an annoyance and a relief both. He called out his permission, and the door swung open. Nayiit ducked into the room, an apologetic smile on his face. Behind him, a small figure waddled—Danat wrapped in robes and cloaks until he seemed almost as wide as tall. Maati rose, his back and knees protesting from having been too long in one position.

"I'm sorry, Father," Nayiit said. "I told Danat-cha that you might be busy. . . ."

"Nothing that can't wait a hand or two," Maati said, waving them in. "It might be best, really, if I step away from it all. After a while, it all starts looking the same."

Nayiit chuckled and took a pose that expressed his sympathy. Danat, red-cheeked, shifted his gaze shyly from one man to the other. Maati nodded a question to Nayiit.

"Danat wanted to ask you something," Nayiit said, and squatted down so that his eyes were on a level with the child's. His smile was gentle, encouraging. A favorite uncle helping his nephew over some simple childhood fear. Maati felt the sudden powerful regret that he had never met Nayiit's wife, never seen his child. "Go ahead, Danat-kya. We came so that you could ask, and Maati-cha's here. Do it like we practiced."

Danat turned to Maati, blushing furiously, and took a pose of respect made awkward by the thickness of cloth around his small arms; then he began pulling books out from beneath his robes and placing them one by one in a neat pile before Maati. When the last of them had appeared, Danat shot a glance at Nayiit who answered with an approving pose.

"Excuse me, Maati-cha," Danat said, his face screwed into a knot of concentration, his words choppy from being rehearsed. "Papa-kya's still not back.
And I've finished all these. I wondered . . ."

The words fell to a mumble. Maati smiled and shook his head.

"You'll have to speak louder," Nayiit said. "He can't hear you."

"I wondered if you had any others I could read," the boy said, staring at his
own feet as if he'd asked for the moon on a ribbon and feared to be mocked
for it.

Behind him, where the boy couldn't see, Nayiit grinned. This is who he
would be, Maati thought. This is the kind of father my boy would be.

"Well," he said aloud. "We might be able to find something. Come with me."

He led them out and along the gravel path to the library's entrance. The air
had a bite to it. He could feel the color coming to his own cheeks. When he'd
been young, a child-poet younger than Nayiit, he'd spent his terrible winter in
Saraykeht with Seedless and Otah and Liat. In the summer cities, this chill
would have been the depth of winter. In the North, it was only the first breath
of autumn.

Cehmai looked up when they came in, a scroll case of shattered silk in his
hand. A smear of dust marked his cheek like ashes. Boxes and crates lay about
the main room, stacked man-high. One of the couches was piled with scrolls
that hadn't been looked over, two others with the ones that had. The air was
thick with the smells of dust and parchment and old binder's paste. Danat
stood in the doorway, his eyes wide, his mouth open. Nayiit stepped around
him and drew the boy in, sliding the doors closed behind them. Cehmai nodded his question.

"Danat was asking if we had any other books," Maati said.

"You have *all* of them," the boy said, awe in his voice.

Maati chuckled, and then felt the mirth and simple pleasure fade. The
shelves and crates, boxes and piled volumes surrounded them.

"Yes," he said. "Yes, we have all of them."

19

>+<   "How many do we have?" Otah asked.

The bows had been made for killing bears. Each one stood taller than
a man, the bow itself made of ash and horn, the drawstring of wire. It took a
man sitting down and using both legs to draw it back. The arrows were blackened oak shafts as long as short spears. The tips—usually a wide, crossed head
like twined knives—had been replaced by hard steel points made to punch
through metal. The chief huntsman of the Khai Cetani nudged one with his
toe, spat, and looked out through the trees toward the road below them.

"Two dozen," he said. His voice had a Western drawl. "Sixty shafts, more or less."

"More or less?" the Khai Cetani demanded.

"We're fashioning more, Most High," the huntsman said.

"How many men do we have who can use them?" Otah asked. "It won't matter if we have a thousand bows if there's only five men who can aim them."

"Bear hunters are rare," the huntsman said. "There aren't any old ones."

"How many?"

"Eight who are good. Twice that who know how the bow works. With practice . . ."

The Khai Cetani frowned deeply, and turned to Otah. Otah chewed at the inside of his lip and looked down and to the east. The trees here were thick, unlike the plains nearer to the newly abandoned city where the need for lumber had created new-made meadows. The leaves were red and gold, bright as fire. The days were still warm enough at their height, but the nights were cold and getting colder. Soon it would be freezing before morning, and soon after that—a week, ten days—it wouldn't be thawing by midday.

"We have two and a half thousand men," Otah said. "And you're telling me only eight can work these things?"

"They're not good for much apart from hunting big animals that need killing fast. And there aren't many who care to do that, if they can help it," the huntsman said. "Why learn something with no use?"

Otah squatted and took one of the bows in his hand. It was heavier than it looked. It would be able to throw the bolts hard. Otah wondered how close they could afford to get to the road. Too far back, and the trees would offer as much protection to the Galts as cover for Otah's men. Too close, and they'd be seen before the time came. It wouldn't take much skill to hit the belly of a steam wagon if you were near enough. He tossed the bow from hand to hand as he weighed the risks.

"Go ask for volunteers," Otah said. "Ask on both sides of the road. Anyone who says they're willing, test them. Take the twenty best."

"A man who doesn't know what he's doing with this can scrape the meat off his legs," the huntsman said.

Otah stopped tossing the bow and turned to consider the man. The huntsman blushed, realizing what he had just said and to whom. He took a pose of obeisance and backed away from the two Khaiem, folding himself in among the trees and vanishing. The Khai Cetani sighed and took a pose of apology.

"He's a good enough man," he said, "but he forgets his place."

"He isn't wrong," Otah said. "If this were a better time to have our orders questioned, I'd have listened to him. But then, if it were a better time, we wouldn't be out here."

The last of the men and women fleeing Cetani had passed them five days before, carts and wagons and sacks slung over hunched backs. For five days,

the combined forces of Cetani and Machi had haunted these woods, sharpening their weapons and planning the attack. And growing bored and hungry and
cold. Two nights ago, Otah had ordered an end to all fires. The smoke would
give them away, and the prospect of a half-sleeping man dropping a stray ember on the forest floor was too likely. The men grumbled, but enough of them
saw the sense of it that the edict hadn't been ignored. Not yet.

It wouldn't be many more days, though. If the Galts didn't come, the men
would grow restive and careless, and when the time came, it would be the
battle before the Dai-kvo again, only this time, the Galts would march into
Machi. The bodies left in the streets wouldn't be of poets. They would be the
families of every man in the hidden clumps that dotted the hills. Their mothers, fathers, lovers, children. Everyone they knew. Everyone that remained.
That was good for another day. Perhaps two.

"You're thinking of the frost," the Khai Cetani said. "You're worried that it's
going to come and drop our screen of leaves before the Galts do."

Otah smiled.

"No, actually, I'd been worrying about other things entirely. Thank you for
distracting me."

The Khai Cetani actually chuckled.

"I'll go and speak with my leaders," he said, clapping Otah on the shoulder.
"Keep their spirits up."

"I'll do the same," Otah said. "It's coming. They'll be here soon."

The camps had been divided. Groups of men no larger than twenty. Only
one stayed close to the road on either side. The others fanned out to the west.
When the Galts appeared at the edge of the last cleared forest, runners would
come from the watch camps, and the men would make their way to the road.
Trees already had been felled at four places along the path—two before they
reached the forest, another halfway to the hill on which Otah now stood, and
the last where the road turned a little to the south and then west again toward
Machi. The first time they were forced to stop, they would expect the attack.
By the fourth, Otah hoped they would only think it another delay. The mixed
coal would have their steam wagons running hotter than they intended. The
bear-hunting bows would prick the steel chambers. In the chaos, the armies
would appear, falling on the Galts' long vulnerable flanks. If it all went well. If
the plan worked. If not, then the gods alone knew how the fight would end.

Night fell cold. The wide cloudless sky seemed to pull the warmth of the
day and land up into it, and Otah, most honored and powerful man in his city,
wrapped an extra cloak around himself and settled down against a tree, Ashua
Radaani snoring gently at his side. He had expected his dreams to be troubled,
but instead he found himself ice fishing, and the fish he saw moving below the
ice were also Kiyan and his children, playing with him, tugging at the line and
then darting away. A trout that was also Kiyan in a silver-blue robe leapt from
the water—with the logic of dreams frozen and yet unfrozen—and splashed
back down to Otah's delight when a rough hand shook him awake. Dawn was

threatening, gray and rose in the east, and Saya the blacksmith towered over him, cheeks so red they seemed dark in the dim light, nose running, and a grin showing his teeth.

"They've come, Most High."

Otah leapt up, his back and hip aching from the cold night and the unforgiving ground. To the east, smoke rose in a wall. Coal smoke from the Galtic wagons strung along the road from Cetani like beads on a string. It was earlier in the day than he'd expected them, and as he pulled on his makeshift armor of boiled leather and metal scale, his mind leapt ahead, guessing at what tactical advantages the Galtic captain intended by arriving with the dawn.

None, of course. They had no way to know Otah's men were there. And still, Otah considered how the light would strike the road, the trees, what it would make visible and what it would hide. He could no more stop his mind than call down the stars.

The sun found the highest reaches of the smoke first, where it had diffused almost to nothing. Closer to the ground, the smoke was already visibly nearer. The Galts had passed the third log barrier while the runners had come to him. The fourth lay in wait where Otah could see it. The innocent forest was alive with his men, or so he hoped. From his place at the ridge of the low hill, he saw only the dozen nearest, crouched behind trees and stones. Otah heard something—the clank of metal or the sound of a raised voice. He willed them to be silent, fear and anger at the sound almost enough to make his teeth ache until he heard it again and realized it was the first of the Galts.

The bear hunter appeared at his side. He held three of the spearlike bolts and the great bow. Saya the blacksmith scampered up with another, its steel heads only just fastened to it. Men appeared on the road below them.

"The horn. Where's the horn?" Otah said, a sudden fear arcing through him. If he had learned the lesson of drums and horns from the Galts only to misplace the signal at the critical moment . . . But the brass horn was at his hip, where it had been since they'd set their trap. He took the cold metal in his hands, brushing dirt from the mouthpiece.

"They look a bit rough around the edges, eh?" Saya whispered, pointing at the road with his chin. "Amnat-Tan must have done them some hurt."

Otah looked at the Galtic soldiers. There were perhaps a hundred that he could see on this small curve of road. He tried to recall what the men he had faced outside the Dai-kvo's village had looked like; how they had walked, how they had held themselves. He couldn't. The memory was only of the battle, and of his men, dying. Saya took a pose of farewell and slunk away, down toward the trees where the battle would soon begin.

The first of the steam wagons came into sight. He could hear it clacking like a loom. The wide belly at its back glowed gold in the rising sun. It was piled with sacks and boxes. Tents, perhaps, or food. Coal for the furnaces. The packs that soldiers would have worn on their shoulders. The wreckage he had seen at the Dai-kvo's village had let him understand what these things were, but seeing one move—wheels turning at the speed of a team at fast trot, and yet without a horse near—was no less strange than his dreams. For a moment, he felt something like awe at the mind who had conceived it. The first of the soldiers below him saw the fallen log and called out—a long musical note that might have been a word or only a signal. The sound of the steam wagon changed, and it slowed, jittered once, and came to a halt. The long call came again and again as it receded down the road like whisperers at court passing the words of the Khai to distant galleries. The Galts came together, conferring. At Otah's side, the bear hunter sat back, bracing the curve of the bow against the soles of his feet. He took one of the bolts, steadying it between his fists as, two-handed, he drew back the wire. The bow creaked.

"Wait," Otah said.

A man came forward, past the steam wagon. He wore a gray tunic marked with the Galtic Tree. His hair was dark as Otah's own, his skin dark and leathern. The crowd of men at the fallen trees turned to face him, their bodies taking attitudes of respect. Otah felt something shift in his belly.

"Him," Otah said.

"Most High?" the huntsman said, strain in his voice.

"Can you hit the man in gray from here?"

The huntsman strained his neck, turned his body and his bow.

"Hard. Shot," he grunted.

"Can you do it?"

The huntsman was silent for half a breath.

"Yes," he said.

"Then do. Do it now."

The wire made a low thrum and the huntsman did something fast with his ankles that caught the bow before it could fall. He was already bending back again when the huge arrow struck. It took the gray man in the side, just below his ribs, and he collapsed without crying out. Otah fumbled with his horn, raising it to his lips. The note he blew filled his ears, so that he only knew the Galts below him were calling out to each other by the movement of their jaws and their drawn swords and axes.

The second bolt flew at the steam wagon as the soldiers fell back. It struck the belly of the steam wagon with a low clank and fell useless to the ground. A horn answering Otah's own called, and something terrible and sudden and louder than anything Otah had ever heard before drowned it out. A great cloud gouted up into the sky from perhaps three hundred yards back in the Galtic column, and then the huntsman at his side loosed the third bolt, and Otah was deafened.

The cloud of steam and smoke boiled up toward him, and Otah found himself coughing in the thick, hot air. The huntsman loosed one last bolt into the murk, stood, drew two daggers, and bounded down toward the road. Otah stepped forward. He was aware of sounds, though they were muffled by the ringing in his ears—screams, a trumpet blast, a distant report as another steam wagon met its end. The road came clear to him slowly as the mist thinned. The cart had tipped on its side, spilling its cargo and its men. Perhaps a dozen men lay on the sodden ground, their flesh seared red as a boiled lobster. Many still stood to fight, but they seemed half-stunned, and his own men were cutting them down with a savage glee. The furnace had cracked open, strewing burning coal across the paving stones. The leaves on the nearest trees, damp from the steam, seemed brighter and more vibrant than before. Two more steam wagons burst, the sound like doubled thunder. Otah cried out, rallying his men to his side, as he moved down to the road and the battle.

The first skirmish, here at the head of the column, was the critical one. The way forward had to be blocked. If they could push the Galts back here, they could drive them into their own men, confuse their formations, keep their balance off. Or so they'd planned, so he hoped. And as he came down the hill, it seemed possible. The Galts were wide-eyed with surprise, confused, afraid. Otah shouted and waved an axe, but there was no one there to threaten with it. It had already happened. The Galts were pulling back.

A bodyguard formed around him as he walked down the road, soldiers falling in around him and marching back toward Cetani, cutting down Galts as they went. In the distance, a horn sounded the call for horsemen to attack. Small formations of Galts—two or three score at most—held the road's center, confused, surrounded, and unable to retreat. A few ran to the trees for cover, only to find the forest alive with enemy blades. The rest fell to arrows and stones. Some engineer had made sense of Otah's trick, and great white plumes of steam rose into the sky as the wagons spent their pressure. The air reeked of blood and hot metal and smoke; it tasted rank. Twice, a wave of Galts swung toward Otah and his steadily increasing guard, only to be thrown back. The Galt army was in disarray, surrounded, confused. Horsemen in the colors of the high families of Machi and Cetani raised their swords in salute when they saw Otah.

He walked over the dead and the dying, past steam wagons that had burst open or been spared, horses that lay dead or flailed and screamed as they died. The sun was almost at the top of its arc, the whole morning gone, when Otah reached the last of the wagons, his bodyguard now nearly the size of his entire force. They had followed him, pinching down on the Galts as he'd moved forward. The plains before them stretched out to Machi, stands of Galtic archers holding positions to cover the retreat. Otah raised his horn to his lips and called the halt. Others horns called the acknowledgment. The battle was ended. The Galts had come this far and would come no farther. Otah felt himself sag.

From the south, he saw a movement among the men like wind stirring tall grass. The Khai Cetani came barreling forward, a wide grin on his face, blood soaking the ornate silk sleeves of his robes. Otah found himself grinning back. He took a pose of congratulations, but the Khai Cetani whooped and wrapped his arms around Otah's waist, lifting him like Otah was a child in his father's arms.

"You've done it!" the Khai Cetani shouted. "You've beaten the bastards!"

We have, Otah tried to say, but he was being lifted upon the shoulders of his men. A roar passed through the assembled men—a thousand throats opening as one. Otah let himself smile, let the relief wash over him. The Galtic army was broken. They would not reach Machi before winter came. He had done it.

They carried him back and forth before the men, the shouts and salutes following him like a windstorm. As he came back to the main road, he was amazed to see the Khai Cetani—all decorum and rank forgotten—dancing arm in arm with common laborers and huntsmen. The Khai Cetani caught sight of him, raised a blade in salute, and called out words that Otah couldn't hear. The men around him abandoned their dance, and drew their own blades, taking up the call, and Otah felt his throat close as he understood the words, as he heard them repeated, moving out through the men like a ripple in a pond.

To the Emperor.

BALASAR STOOD IN THE GREAT SQUARE OF TAN-SADAR. THE SKY WAS WHITE AND chill, and the trees that stood in the eastern corners were nearly bare of leaves. A good day, Balasar thought, for endings. The representatives of the utkhaiem stood beneath square-framed colonnades, staring out at him and his company two hundred strong and in their most imposing array of arms and armor and at the Khai Tan-Sadar, bound and kneeling on the brickwork at Balasar's feet. The poet of the city had burned to death among his books on the day Balasar had entered the city, but the disposition of the Khai was less important. A few days waiting in the public jail where men and women passing by could see him languishing posed no particular threat to the world, and the campaign that was now behind him had left Balasar tired.

"Do you have anything you want to say?" Balasar asked in the Khai's own language.

He was a younger man than Balasar had expected. Perhaps no more than thirty summers. It seemed young to have the responsibility of a city upon him or to be slaughtered in front of the nobles who had betrayed him to a conqueror. The Khai shook his head once, a curt and elegant motion.

"If you swear to serve the High Council of Galt, I'll cut your bonds and we can both walk out of here," Balasar said. "I'll have to keep you prisoner, of course. I can't leave you free to gather up an army. But there are worse things than living under guard."

The Khai almost smiled.

"There are also worse things than dying," he said.

Balasar sighed. It was a shame. But the man had made his decision. Balasar raised his hand, and the drums and trumpets called out. The execution proceeded. When the soldier held up the Khai's head for the crowd to see, a shudder seemed to run through them, but the faces that Balasar saw looking out at him seemed bright and excited.

They know they won't die, he thought. If I'm not killing them, it all becomes another court spectacle. They'll be talking about it in their bathhouses and winter gardens, vying for money and power now that the city's fallen. Half of them will be wearing tunics with the Galtic Tree on it come spring.

He looked down at the body of the man he'd had killed and briefly felt the impulse to put Tan-Sadar to the torch. Instead, he turned and walked away, going back to the palaces he had taken for himself and for his men.

Eight thousand remained to him. Several hundred had been lost in battle or to the raids that had slowed his travel since Nantani. The rest he had left in conquered Utani. There was little enough left of Udun that he hadn't bothered leaving men to occupy the city. There was no call to leave people there to guard ashes.

Utani had offered only token resistance and been for the most part spared. Tan-Sadar had very nearly set the musicians to playing and lined the roads with dancing girls. That wasn't true, but as Balasar stalked back through the great vaulted hall of the Khai's palace, his steps echoing off the blue and gold tilework high above him, his disgust with the place made it seem that way. They hadn't fought, and while that might have been wise, it wasn't something to celebrate. The only ones who had spines had been the poet and the Khai. Well, and the Khai's wives and children, whom he'd had killed. So perhaps he wasn't really in the best position to speak about what was honorable and noble after all.

"Darkness has come on as usual, sir?"

Balasar looked up. Eustin stood in salute at the foot of a wide flight of stairs. His tunic was stained, his chin unshaven, and even from five paces away, he stank of horses. Balasar restrained himself from rushing over and embracing the man.

"The darkness?" Balasar asked through his grin.

"Always happens at the end of a campaign, sir. You fall into a black mood for a few weeks. Happened in Eddensea and after the siege at Malsam. All respect, sir, it's like watching my sister after she's birthed a babe."

Balasar laughed. It felt good to laugh, and to smile, and to be reminded that the foul mood that had come on him was something he often suffered. In truth, he had forgotten. He took Eustin's hand in his own.

"Good to have you back," Balasar said. "I didn't know you'd returned."

"I would have sent a runner to pass the news, but it seemed faster if I came myself."

"Come up," Balasar said. "Tell me what's happened."

"It might be best if I saw a bathhouse, sir. . . ."

"Later," Balasar said. "If you can stand the reek, I can. And besides, you deserve some discomfort after that birthing comment. Come up, and I'll have them send us wine and food."

"Yes, sir," Eustin said.

They sat on couches while pine logs burned in the grate, sap hissing and popping and sending up sparks. True to his word, Balasar sent for rice wine infused with cherries and the stiff salty brown cheese that was a local delicacy of Tan-Sadar. Eustin recounted his season—the attack on Pathai, his decision to split the force before moving on to the poet's school. Pathai hadn't been as large or as wealthy as a port city like Nantani, but it was near the Westlands. Moving what wealth it had back to Galt would be simpler than the other inland cities.

"And the school?" Balasar said, and a cloud passed over Eustin's face.

"They were younger than I'd thought. It wasn't the sort of thing they sing about. Unless they're singing laments. Then, maybe."

"It was necessary."

"I know, sir. That's why we did it."

Balasar poured him another cup of the wine, and then one for himself, and they drank in silence together before Eustin went on with his report. The men they'd sent to take the southern cities had managed quite well, apart from an incident with poisoned grain in Lachi and a fire at the warehouses of Saraykeht. That matched with what Balasar himself had heard. All the poets had been found, all the books had been burned. No Khai had lived or left heir.

In return, Balasar shared what news he had from the North. Tan-Sadar, the nearest city to the Dai-kvo, had known about the destruction of the village for weeks before Balasar's prisoner-envoys had arrived. The story was also widely known of the battle; one of the Khaiem in the winter cities had fielded an army of sorts. The estimates of the dead went from several hundred to thousands. Few, if any, had been Coal's. The retelling of that tale as much as the sacking of Udun had broken the back of Utani and Tan-Sadar.

A letter in Coal's short, understated style had come south after Amnat-Tan had fallen. Another courier was due any day bringing the news of Cetani and Machi. But if Coal had kept to the pace he'd intended, those cities were also fallen.

"It'll be good to know for certain, though," Eustin said.

"I trust him," Balasar said.

"Didn't mean anything else, sir."

"No. Of course not. You're right. It will be good to know it's done." Balasar took a bite of the brown cheese and stared at the dancing flames where the wood glowed and blackened and fell to ash. "You'll put your men in Utani?"

"Or send some downriver. Depends how much food there is. There's more than a few who'd be willing to make a winter crossing if it meant getting home to start spending their shares."

"We have made a large number of very rich soldiers," Balasar said.

"They'll be poor again in a season or two, but the dice stands in Kirinton will still be singing our praises when our grandsons are old," Eustin said, then paused. "What about our local man?"

"Captain Ajutani? He's here, in the city. Wintering here with the rest of us.

He's done quite well for himself. And for us. He's given me some very good advice."

Eustin grunted and shook his head.

"Still don't trust him, sir."

"He's more or less out of opportunities to betray us," Balasar said, and Eustin spat into the fire by way of reply.

Over the next days, the army shifted slowly from the rigorous discipline of the road to the bawdy, long, low riot that comes with wintering in a captured city. The locals—tradesmen and laborers and utkhaiem alike—seemed stunned by the change. They were polite and accommodating because Balasar's men were armed and practiced and thousands strong, but as Balasar walked down the long, winding red brick streets, he had the feeling that Tan-Sadar was hoping to wake from this nightmare and find the world once again as it had been. A hard, bitter wind came from the north, and behind it, the season's first thin, tentative snow.

He found his mind turning back to the west and home. The darkness Eustin had seen in him grew with the prospect of returning. The years he had spent gathering the threads of his campaign had come to their end; that it was ending in triumph only partly forgave that it was ending. He found himself wondering who he would be now that he was no longer the man driven to destroy the andat. In the mornings, he imagined himself living on his hereditary estate near Kirinton, perhaps taking a wife. Perhaps teaching in one of the military academies. All his old dreams revisited. As the sun peaked low in the sky and scuttled toward the horizon, the fantasy darkened too. He would be a racing dog with nothing left to chase. And worst, in the dark of the nights, he tried to sleep, his mind pricked by another day gone by without word from the North and the sick fear that despite all their successes, something had gone wrong.

And then, on a cold, clear morning, the courier from Coal arrived. Only it wasn't from Coal. Not really. Because Coal was dead, and Balasar had another ghost at his heels.

"They came without warning," Balasar said. "They were hiding in the trees, like street bandits. He was the first to fall."

"I'm sorry to hear it," Sinja said. "It was a dishonorable attack. Not that the honorable one did them much good from what I've heard."

Eustin's face might have been carved from stone.

"You have a point to make, Captain?" Balasar asked.

"Only that he did make an honest man's try on the field outside the Dai-kvo's village, and he failed. There's only so much you can count against him that he tried a different tack."

He killed my men, Balasar wanted to say. Wanted to shout. He killed *Coal*.

Instead, he paced the length of the wide parlor, staring at the maps he'd unrolled after he'd unsewn the letter from the remnants of the northern force.

The oil lamps hung from their chains, adding a thick buttery light to the thin gray sunlight that filtered in from the windows. Cetani was occupied, but the library was emptied, Khai and poet missing along with the full population of the city. Machi remained. The last of the poets, the last of the books, the last of the Khaiem. His fingertips traced the route that would take him there.

"It's no use, General," Sinja said. "You can't put an army in the field this late in the season. It's too cold. One half-decent storm will freeze them to death."

"It's still autumn," Eustin said. "Winter's not come quite yet."

"It's a northern autumn," Sinja said. "You're thinking it's like Eddensea, but I'll tell you it's not. There's no ocean nearby to hold the heat in. General, Machi isn't going anywhere between now and the first thaw. The Dai-kvo's meat on a stick. Your man burned his books. They have the same chance of binding a fresh andat before spring that I have of growing wings and flying. And you have every chance of killing more of your men than have died since we left the Westlands if you go out there now."

"You've always given me good advice, Captain Ajutani," Balasar said. "I appreciate your wisdom on this."

"I wouldn't call it wisdom particularly," Sinja said. "Just a common interest in not turning into ice sculpture in a bean field somewhere between here and there."

"Thank you," Balasar said, his tone making it clear that the meeting had ended. Sinja saluted Balasar, nodded to Eustin, and made his way out. The door closed with a click. Eustin coughed.

"Do you think he's lying?" Balasar said. "He'd been living in Machi. If there were a place he didn't want captured, it would be there."

Eustin frowned, arms folded across his chest. He looked older, Balasar thought. The grief of losing Coal was heavy on his shoulders too. In a sense, they were the last. There were other men who had taken part in the campaign, but only the two of them had been there from the beginning. Only they had been to the desert. And so there was no one else who could have this conversation and truly understand it.

"He's not lying," Eustin said. His voice was thick. Balasar could hear how much it had cost him to agree with Sinja. "Everything I've heard says the cold up there is deadly. It's not a pleasant day out now, and the season's milder here."

"And Machi's army?"

Eustin shrugged.

"It wasn't an honorable fight," he said. "If we empty Utani and Tan-Sadar, we've got something near three times the men Coal had at the end."

It would take them weeks to reach Machi, even if they started now. A bad storm would be worse than a battle. Tan-Sadar, on the other hand, was a safe place to winter, and when the spring came, they could overwhelm Machi in safety. They could revenge Coal a thousand times over. There was no army that could come to Machi's aid. Meaningful defenses for the city couldn't be built in that time.

Snow was the only armor the enemy had, and the turning seasons would be enough to remove it. Every strategist in Galt would counsel that he wait, plan, prepare, rest. But there were poets in Machi, and all the world to lose if he failed.

He looked up from the maps. His gaze met Eustin's, and they stood together in silence, the only two men in the world who would look at these facts, these odds, these stakes, and have no need to debate them.

"I'll break it to the men," Eustin said.

20

">+<" " 'And quietly, one foot sliding behind the other, for the parapet was too narrow to walk along, the half-Bakta boy went from his own prison chamber around to the bars of the Empress' cell.' " Otah paused, letting the half-Bakta boy hang in the air outside the prison tower. And this time Danat failed to object. His eyes were closed, his breathing heavy and regular. Otah sat for a moment, watching his boy sleep, then closed the book, tucked it in its place by the door, and put out the lantern. Danat murmured and snuggled more deeply into his blankets as Otah carefully opened the door and stepped out into the tunnel.

The physician set to watch over Danat took a pose of obeisance to Otah, and Otah replied with one of thanks before walking to the north, and to the broad spiral stairway that led up to the higher chambers of the underground palace or else down to Otah's own rooms and the women's quarters. Small brass lanterns filled the air with their warmth and the scent of oil. The walls were lighter than sandstone and shone brighter than the flames seemed to warrant. At the stairway, he hesitated.

Above him, Machi was beginning its descent into the other city, washing down into the rooms and corridors reserved for the deep, long winter that was almost upon them. The bathhouses far above had emptied their pipes, shunting the water from their kilns down to lower pools. The towers were being filled with goods of summer, the great platforms crawling up their tracks in the unforgiving stone, and then down again. In the wide, vaulted corridors that would become the main roads and public squares of the winter, beggars sang and food carts filled the air with rich, warm scents: beef soup and peppered pork, fish on hot rice, almond milk and honey cakes. The men and women pulling the carts would be calling, luring the curious and the hungry and the almost-hungry.

Only, of course, they wouldn't be there this winter. Food was no longer an item available for trade. It was being rationed out by the utkhaiem and by the exquisite mechanisms that Kiyan had put in place. The men and women of Cetani had been housed there or in the mines along the plain even before Otah and his army had returned with the news that the Galts had been turned back. Now, with the quarters being shared, there were two and sometimes three families sharing the space meant for one.

There was a part of him that wanted badly to take the stairs leading up, to go out of the palaces, and into the webwork of passages and tunnels one layered upon another that were his city. He knew it was an illusion to think that seeing things would improve them, make them easier to control and make right. But it was a powerful illusion.

He sighed and took the descending stairs. The women's quarters—designed to accommodate a Khai's dozen or more wives—had been changed over to smaller, more private rooms by the addition of a few planks of wood and tapestries taken from the palaces above. The utkhaiem of Cetani—husbands and wives together—found some accommodations there. It had seemed an obvious choice, and Kiyan had never particularly made use of her rooms there. And still it seemed odd to have people so close. Late in the night, he could sometimes hear the voices of people passing by.

The great blue and gold doors to his private apartments stood closed, two guards on either side. Otah noticed as he accepted their salutes how quickly he had come to think of these men as guards where before they had only been servants. Their duties were no different, their robes just the same. It wasn't the world that had changed. It was him.

He found Kiyan sitting at a low table, combing her hair with a wide-toothed comb. Wordless, he took it from her, sitting beside and behind her, and did the little task himself. Her hair was coarser than it had been once, and so shot with white that it seemed almost as much silver as black. He saw the subtle curve in the shape of her cheek as she smiled.

"I heard the Khai Cetani speaking today," she said.

"Really?"

"He was in one of the teahouses. And, honestly, not one of the best ones."

"I won't ask what you were doing in a third-rate tea house," Otah said, and Kiyan chuckled.

"Nothing more scandalous than listening to the Khai," she said. "But that might be enough. He thinks quite highly of you."

"Oh gods," Otah said. "Did the term come up again?"

"Yes, the word *emperor* figured highly in the conversation. He seems to think the sun shines brighter when you tell it to."

"He seems to forget that first battle where I got everyone killed. And that I didn't manage to keep the Dai-kvo from being slaughtered."

"He doesn't forget. But he does say you were the only man who tried to stop the Galts, who banded cities together instead of letting them fall one at a time, and in the end the only man who put them to flight."

"He should stop that," Otah said, and sighed. "He seemed so reasonable when I first met him. Who'd have guessed he was so easily wooed."

"He may not be wrong, you know. We'll need to do something when this is over. An emperor or a way to choose new families to act as Khaiem. A Dai-kvo. That would have to be Maati or Cehmai, wouldn't it?"

It was how all the conversations went now—how to rebuild, how to remake. The polite fiction that the poets were sure to succeed was the tissue that seemed to hold people together, and Otah couldn't bring himself to break it now.

"I suppose so," Otah said. "It'll be a life's work, though. Perhaps more. It was getting hard enough finding andat that could still be bound before this. We've lost so much now, going back will be harder than it was at the first. If we have a new Dai-kvo, he won't have time for anything more than that."

"An emperor, then. One man protecting all the cities. With the poets answering to him. Even just one poet with one andat would be enough. It would protect us."

"I recommend someone else do it. I've decided on a beach hut on Bakta," Otah said, trying to make it a joke. He saw Kiyan's expression. "It's too far ahead to think about now, love. Let it pass, and we'll solve it later if it still needs solving."

Kiyan turned and took his hand. The days since he'd come home hadn't allowed them time together, not as they had had before the war. First, when he and his men had marched across the bridge to trumpets and drums and dancing, it had been a mad festival. They had come out to meet him. He had embraced her, and Eiah, and little Danat whom he had danced around until they were both dizzy. Otah had found himself whirled from one pavilion to the next, balancing the giddy joy of survival with the surprisingly complex work of taking an army—even one as improvised and unformed as his own—apart. And afterward, he'd discovered that Kiyan was still as much in demand now tending the things she'd set in motion as when he had been gone.

Men and women of all classes seemed to have need of her time and attention, coordinating the stores of food and the arrangements of the refugees and the movements of goods and trade that had once been the business of the merchant houses, and had become the work of a few coordinating minds. Kiyan had become the hand that moved Machi, that pushed it into line, that tucked its children into warm beds and kept it from eating all the best food and leaving nothing for tomorrow. It consumed her days.

And the utkhaiem and the high trading families had all wanted a moment of his day, to congratulate or express thanks or wheedle some favor in light of the changed circumstances of the world. To be here, in the warm light of candles, Kiyan's hand in his, her gaze on him, seemed like a dream badly wished for. And yet, now that he had it, he found himself troubled and unable to relax. She squeezed his hand.

"How bad was it?" she asked, and he knew what she meant. The battles. The Dai-kvo. The war.

Otah began to say something witty, something glib. The words got lost on the way to his lips. For long moment, silence was all he could manage.

"It was terrible," he said. "There were so many of them."

"The Galts?"

"The dead. Theirs. Ours. I've never seen anything like it, Kiyan-kya. I've read the histories and I've heard the epics sung, and it's not the same. They were young. And . . . and they looked like they were sleeping. However badly they'd died, in the end, I kept thinking they'd wake up and speak or call for help or scream. I think about all the men I led out there. The ones who would have lived if we hadn't done this."

"We didn't choose this, love. The Galts haven't given anyone much choice. The men who went with you would have died out there in the field, or here when the city fell. Would one have been better?"

"I suppose not. The other ways it could have gone might be just as bad, but the way it *did* happen, they died from following me. From doing what I asked."

To his surprise, Kiyan chuckled low and mirthless.

"That's why he calls you Emperor, isn't it," Kiyan said, and Otah took a pose of query. "The Khai Cetani. It's from gratitude. If you're the leader of the age, then it stops being his burden. Everything you're suffering, you've saved him."

Otah looked at his hands, rubbing his palms together with a long, dry sound. His throat felt tight, and something deep in his chest ached with the suspicion that she was right. When he had asked the man to abandon his city and take the role of follower, he had also been asking for the right to choose whatever happened after. And the responsibility for it. For a moment, he was on the chill, gray field of the dead, and walking the cold, lifeless ruin where poets had once conspired to bind thoughts themselves. He remembered the Dai-kvo's dead eyes, looking at nothing. The bodies, the Galts' and his own both, and the voices calling him Emperor.

"I'm sorry," Kiyan said, and he could tell from her voice that she knew how inadequate the words were. He pulled his mind back to his soft-lit room, the scent of the candles, the touch of this long-beloved hand.

"They've lived with it," he said. "Galt and Eddensea and the Westlands. It's always been like this for them. War and battle. We'll learn."

"I don't think I'm looking forward to that."

Otah raised her hand to his lips. Gently, she caressed his cheek. He drew her close, folding his arms around her, feeling the warmth of her body against him, smelling the familiar scent of her hair, and willing the moment to not end. If only the future could never come.

Kiyan sensed it in the tension of his spine, the fierceness of his embrace. Something. She did not speak, but only breathed, softening against him with every exhalation, and in time he felt himself beginning to relax with her. One of the lanterns, burning the last of its oil, dimmed, spat, and went out. The smoke touched the air with a smell of endings.

"I missed you," she said. "Every night, I went to bed thinking you might not come back. I kept telling the children over and over that things would be fine, that you'd be home soon. And I was sick. I was sick with it."

"I'm sorry."

"Don't. Don't apologize. Don't be sorry. Just know it. Just know we wanted you back. Not the Khai and not the emperor. *You.* Remember that you are a good man and I love you."

He raised her chin and kissed her, wondering how she knew so well the way to fill him with joy without asking him to abandon his sorrow.

"It's Maati's now," Otah whispered. "If he can bind Seedless before the spring thaw, this will all be over."

He felt an odd relaxation in her body, as if by saying the thing, he'd freed her from some secret effort she'd been making.

"And if he can't?" she asked. "If it's all going to fall apart anyway, can we run? You and me and the children? If I take them and go, are you going to come with us, or stay here and fight?"

He kissed her again. She rested her hands against his shoulders, leaning into him. Otah didn't answer, and he knew from the sound of her breath that she understood.

"If we take the nuance of movement-away in *nurat* and the symbol set you worked up for the senses of continuance," Maati said, "I think then we'll have something we can work with."

Cehmai's eyes were bloodshot, his hair wild from another long evening of combing frustrated fingers through it. Around them, the lamplight shone on a bedlam of paper. The library would have seemed a rat's nest to any but the two of them: books laid open; scrolls unfurled and weighted by other scrolls which were themselves unfurled; loose pages of a dozen codices stacked together. The mass of information and inference, grammar and poetry and history would have been overwhelming, Maati thought, to anyone who didn't know how profoundly little it was. Cehmai ran his fingertips down the notes Maati had made and shook his head.

"It's still the same," he said. "*Nurat* is modified by the fourth case of *adat*, and then it's exactly the same logical structure as the one Heshai used."

"No, it isn't," Maati said, slapping the table with an open palm. "It's *different*."

Cehmai took a long, slow breath, raising his hands palms-out. It wasn't a formal gesture, but Maati understood it all the same. They were both worn raw. He sat back in his chair, feeling the knots in his back and neck. The brazier in the corner made the wide room smell warm without seeming to actually heat it.

"Look," Maati said. "Let's put it aside for the day. We need to move the library underground soon anyway. It's going to be too cold up here to do more than watch our fingers turn blue."

Cehmai nodded, then looked around at the disarray. Maati could read the despair in his face.

"I'll put it back together," Maati said. "Then a dozen slaves with strong backs, and I'll put it all together in the winter quarters in two days' time."

"I should move the poet's house down too," Cehmai said. "I feel like I haven't been there in weeks."

"I'm sorry."

"Don't be. The place seems too big without Stone-Made-Soft anyway. Too quiet. It reminds me of . . . well, of everything."

Maati rose, his knees aching. His feet tingled with the pins and needles that long motionlessness brought him these days. He clapped his hand on Cehmai's shoulder.

"Meet me in three days," he said. "I'll have the books in order. We'll start again fresh."

Cehmai took a pose of agreement, but he looked exhausted. Worn thin. The younger poet began snuffing the lanterns as Maati walked back toward his apartments, placing his feet carefully until normal feeling returned to them. Stepping the wrong way and breaking his ankle would be just the thing to make the winter even more miserable than it already promised to be.

The rooms in which he spent his summers were already bare. The fire grate was empty of everything but old soot. The tapestries were gone, the couches, the tables, the cabinets. Everything had been moved to the lower city. Winter ate the middle of things in the North. The snows would come soon, blocking the doors and windows. The second-story snow doors would open out for any-one who needed to travel into the world. Below, in the warmth of the ground, all the citizens of Machi, and now of Cetani too, would huddle and talk and fight and sing and play at tiles and stones until winter lost its grip and the snows turned to meltwater and washed the black-cobbled streets. Only the metal-workers remained at the ground level, the green copper roofs of the forges free of snow and ice, the plumes of coal smoke rising almost as high as the towers all through the winter.

At least all through *this* winter. This one last winter before the Galts came and butchered them all.

If only there was some other way to phrase the idea of *removing*. Seedless's true name would have been better translated as Removing-the-Part-That-Continues. Continuity was a fairly simple problem. The old grammars had several ways to conceptualize continuance. It was *removal* . . .

Maati reached the thin red doorway at the back of the rooms, and started down the stairs. It was dark as night. Darker. He would need to talk with the palace servant masters about seeing that lanterns were lit here. With as many people as there were filling every available niche in the tunnels and, from what he heard, the mines as well, it seemed unlikely that no one could be spared to be sure there was a little light on his path.

Or they might be rationing lamp oil already. There was a depressing thought.

He descended, one hand on the smooth, cool stone of the wall to keep him steady. He moved slowly because going quickly would get him winded, and it was dark enough that he wanted to stay sure of his footing. His mind was only half concerned with walking anyway. Cehmai was right. The logical structure was the same whether he used *nurat* or something else. So that was another dead end.

Removal.

It was a concept of relative motion. Taking something enclosed and producing a distance between it and its—now previous—enclosure. Plucking out a seed, or a baby. A gemstone from its setting. A man from his bed or his home. Removing. Heshai's work in framing Seedless was so elegant, so simple, that it seemed inevitable. That was the curse of second and third bindings of the same andat. Finding something equally graceful, but utterly different. It made his jaw ache just thinking about it.

He reached the bottom of the stairs and the wide upper chamber of his winter quarters. The night candle burning there was hardly to its first quarter mark, which given the lengthening nights of autumn meant the city beneath him would likely still be awake and active. Rest for him, though. His day had been full already. He took up the candle, passed down a short, close corridor, and reached the second stairway, which led down to the bedchambers.

The air was noticeably warmer here than in the library—in part from the heat of ten thousand people in the earth below him rising up, and in part from its stillness. Servants had prepared his bed with blankets and furs. A light meal of rice and spiced pork in one of the bowls of hand-thick iron that could hold the heat for the better part of a day waited on his writing table. Maati sat, ate slowly, not tasting the food, drinking rice wine as if it were water. Even as he sucked the pepper sauce off the last bit of pork, his feet and fingers were still cold. Removing-the-Chill-From-the-Old-Man's-Flesh. There was an andat.

Maati closed the lid of the great iron bowl, slipped out of his robes, hefted himself into his bed, and willed himself to sleep. For a time, he lay watching the candle burn, smelling the wax as it melted and dripped, and could not get comfortable. He couldn't get the cold out of his toes and knuckles, couldn't make his mind stop moving. He couldn't avoid the growing fear that when he closed his eyes, the nightmares that had begun plaguing him would return.

The images his mind held when his eyes were closed had become more violent, more anxious. Fathers weeping for sons who were also sacks of blood-ied grain and dead mice; long, sleepless hours spent searching through bodies in a charnel house hoping to find his child still living and only finding Otah's children again and again and again; the recurring dream of a tunnel that led down past the city, deeper than the mines, and into the earth until the stone itself grew fleshy and angry and bled. And the cry that woke him—a man's voice shouting from a great distance that demanded to know whose child this was. *Whose child?*

With this mind, Maati thought as he watched the single flame of the night candle, I'm intended to bind an andat. It's like driving nails with rotten meat.

The night candle had burned through three of its smallest marks when he abandoned his bed, pulled on his robes, and left his private chambers for the wide, arched galleries of the tunnels below the palaces. The bathhouses were at least warm. If he wasn't to sleep, he could at least be miserable in comfort.

The public spaces were surprisingly full with men and women in the glorious robes of the utkhaiem. It made sense, he supposed. Cetani had not only brought its merchants and craftsmen. There would be two courts living under the palaces this winter. And so twice the social intrigue. Who precisely was sleeping with whom would be even more complex, and even the threat of their death at the hands of a Galtic army wouldn't stop the courtiers playing for rank.

As he passed, the utkhaiem took poses of respect and welcome, the servants and slaves ones of abasement. Maati repressed a swelling hatred of all of them. It wasn't their fault, after all, that he had to save them. And himself. And Liat and Nayiit and Otah and all the people he had ever known, all the cities he had ever seen. His world, and everything in it.

It was the Galts who deserved his anger. And they would feel it, by all the gods. Failed crops, gelded men, and barren women until they rebuilt everything they'd broken and given back everything they took. If he could only think of a better way to say *removing*.

He brooded his way along the dim galleries and through the great chambers until the air began to thicken with the first presentiment of steam, and the prospect of hot water, and of finally warming his chilled feet, intruded on him.

He found his way into the men's changing rooms, where he shrugged off his robes and boots and let the servant offer him a bowl of clear, cold water to drink before he went into the public baths and sweated it all out again. When he passed through the inner door, Maati shivered at the warmth. Voices filled the dim, gray space—conversations between people made invisible by the steam rising from the water. There had been a time, Maati considered as he stepped gingerly down the submerged stairs and waded toward a low bench, when the idea of strangers wandering naked in the baths—men and women together—had held some erotic frisson. Truth often disappoints.

He lowered himself to the thick, water-logged wood of the bench, the hot water rising past his belly, past his chest, until the small warm waves danced against the hollow of his throat. At last, his feet felt warm, and he leaned back against the warm stone, sighing with a purely physical contentment. He resolved to move down toward the warmer end before he went back to his rooms. If he boiled himself thoroughly enough, he might even carry the heat back to his bed.

Across the bath, hidden in the mist, two men talked of grain supplies and how best to address the problem of rats. Far away toward the hotter end of the bath, someone shouted, and there was a sound of splashing. Children, Maati supposed, and then fell into a long, gnawing plan for how best to move the volumes in the library. His concentration was so profound he didn't notice when the children approached.

"Uncle Maati?"

Eiah was practically at his side, crouched low in the water to preserve her modesty. A gaggle of children of the utkhaiem behind her at what Maati supposed must be a respectful distance. He raised hands from the water and took a pose of greeting, somewhat cramped by being held high enough to be seen.

"I haven't seen you in ages, Eiah-kya," he said. "What's been keeping you?"

The girl shrugged, sending ripples.

"There are a lot of new people from Cetani," she said. "There's a whole other Radaani family here now. And I've been studying with Loya-cha about how to fix broken bones. And . . . and Mama-kya said you were busy and that I shouldn't bother you."

"You should always bother me," Maati said with a grin.

"Is it going well?"

"It's a complicated thing," Maati said. "But it's a long wait until spring. We'll have time."

"Complicated's hard," Eiah said. "Loya-cha says it's always easy to fix things when there's only one thing wrong. It's when there's two or three things at once that it's hardest."

"Smart man, Loya-cha," Maati said.

Eiah shrugged again.

"He's a servant," she said. "If you can't recapture Seedless, we can't beat the Galts can we?"

"Your father did once," Maati said. "He's a very clever man."

"But we might not."

"We might not," Maati allowed.

Eiah nodded to herself, her forehead crinkling as she came to some decision. When she spoke, her voice had a seriousness that seemed out of place from a girl still so young, hardly half-grown.

"If we're all going to die, I wanted you to know that I think you were a very good father to Nayiit-cha."

Maati almost coughed from surprise, and then he understood. She knew. A warm sorrow filled him. She knew that Nayiit was Otah's son. That Maati loved the boy. That it mattered to him deeply that Nayiit love him back. And the worst of it, she knew that he hadn't been a very good father.

"You're kind, love," he said, his voice thick.

She nodded sharply, embarrassed, perhaps, to have completed her task. One of her companions yelped and dropped under the water only to come back up spitting and shaking his head. Eiah turned toward them.

"Leave him be!" Eiah shouted, then turned to Maati with an apologetic pose. He smiled and waved her away. She went back to her group with the squared shoulders of an overseer facing a recalcitrant band of laborers. Maati let his smile fade.

A good father to Nayiit. And to be told so by Otah's daughter. Perhaps binding the andat wasn't so complex after all. Not when compared with other things. Fathers and sons, lovers and mother and daughters. And the war. Saraykeht and Seedless. All of it touched one edge against another, like tilework. None of it existed alone. And how could anyone expect him to solve the thing when half of everything seemed to be broken, and half of what was broken was still beautiful.

The physician was right. It would be easy to fix one thing, if there were only one thing wrong. But there were so many ways to break something so delicate and so complex. Even the act of making one thing right seemed destined to undo something else. And he was too tired and too confused to say whether one way of being wounded was better than another.

There were so many ways to be wrong.

There were so many ways to break things.

Maati felt the thought fall into place as if it were something physical. It was the moment he was supposed to shout, to stand up and wave his hands about, possessed by insight as if by a demon. But instead, he sat with it quietly, as if it was a gem only he of all mankind had ever seen.

He'd spent too much time with Heshai's binding. Removing-the-Part-That-Continues had been made for the cotton trade—pulling seeds from the fiber and speeding it on its way to the spinners and the weavers and feeding all of the needle trades. But there was no reason for Maati to be restricted by that. He only needed a way to break Galt. To starve them. To see that no other generation of Galtic children ever saw the world.

It wasn't Seedless he needed. It was only Sterile. And there were any number of ways to say that.

He sank lower into the water as the sense of relief and peace consumed him. Destroying-the-Part-That-Continues, he thought as the little waves touched his lips. Shattering-the-Part-That-Continues. Crushing it. Rotting it. Corroding it.

Corrupting it.

In his mind, Galt died. And he, Maati Vaupathai, killed it. What, he asked himself, was victory in a single battle compared with that? Otah had saved the city. Maati saw now how he could save *everything*.

21

Sinja woke, stiff with cold, to the sound of chopping. Outside the tent, someone with a hand axe was breaking the ice at the top of the barrels. It was still dark, but morning was always dark these days. He kicked off his blankets and rose. The undyed wool of his inner robes held a bit of the heat as he pulled on first one outer robe and then another with a wide leather cloak over the top that creaked when he fastened the wide bone broochwork.

Outside his tent, the army was already breaking camp. Columns of smoke and steam rose from the wagons. Horses snorted, their breath pluming white in the light of a falling moon. In the southeast, the dawn was still only a lighter shade of black. Sinja walked to the cook fire and squatted down beside it, a bowl of barley gruel sweetened with wine-packed prunes in his hands. The heat of it was better than the taste. Wine could do strange things to prunes.

The army had been marching for two and a half weeks. At a guess, there were another three before they reached Machi. If there was no storm, Sinja guessed they would lose a thousand men to frostbite, most of those in the last ten days. He squinted into the dark, implacable sky and watched the faintest stars begin to fade. There would still be over nine thousand men. And every man among them would know that this battle wasn't for money or glory. Or even for love of the general. If by some miracle Otah turned the Galts back from the city, they would die scattered in the frozen plains of the North.

This battle would be the only time in the whole benighted war that the Galts would go in knowing they were fighting for their lives.

"You want more?" the cook asked, and Sinja shook his head. Around him, the members of his personal guard were moving at last. Sinja didn't help them break down the camp. He'd left most of the company behind in Tan-Sadar. They were, after all, on a deadly stupid march that, with luck, would end with them sacking their own homes. It wasn't duty that could be asked of a green recruit of his first campaign. Sinja had taken time handpicking this dozen to accompany him. There wasn't a man among them he liked.

The last tent was folded, poles bound together with their leather thongs, and put on the steam wagon. The fires were all stamped out, and the sun made its tardy appearance. Sinja wrapped the leather cloak closer around his shoulders and sighed. This was a younger man's game. If he'd been as wise as the average rat, he'd be someplace warm and close now, with a good mulled wine and a plate of venison in mint sauce. The call sounded, and he began the walk north. Cold numbed his face and made his ears ache. The air smelled of dust and smoke and horse dung—the miasma of the moving army. Sinja kept his eyes to the horizon, but the only clouds were the high white lace that did little but leach blue from the sky; there was no storm coming today. And still the dusting of snow that had fallen in the last weeks hadn't melted and wouldn't before spring. The world was pale except where a stone or patch of ground stood free of snow. There it was black.

He put one foot in front of the other, his mind growing empty with the rhythm. His muscles slowly warmed. The pain retreated from his ears. With enough effort, the air became almost comfortable. The sun rose quickly behind him, as if in a hurry to finish its day's passage and return the world to darkness.

When he paused to relieve himself on a tree—his piss steaming in its puddle—he took off the leather cloak. If he got too warm, he'd start to sweat. Soaking through his inner robes was an invitation to death. He wondered how many of Balasar's men knew that. With his sad luck, all of them.

They wouldn't see a low town today. They had overrun one yesterday—the locals surprised to find themselves surrounded by horsemen intent on keeping any word from slipping out to the North. There would be another town in a day or two. If Sinja was lucky, it might mean fresh meat for dinner. The rations set aside by the townsmen to see them through the winter might feed the army for as much as half a day.

They paused at midday, the cooks using the furnaces of the steam wagons to warm the bread and boil water for tea. Sinja wasn't hungry but he ate anyway. The tea was good at least. Overbrewed and bitter, but warm. He sat on the broad back of a steam wagon, and was preparing himself for the second push of the day and estimating how many miles they had covered since morning when the general arrived.

Balasar rode a huge black horse, its tack worked with silver. As small as the man was, he still managed to look like something from a painting.

"Sinja-cha," Balasar Gice said in the tongue of the Khaiem. "I was hoping to find you here."

Sinja took a pose of respect and welcome.

"I'd say winter's come," the general said.

"No, Balasar-cha. If this was real winter, you could tell because we'd all be dead by now."

Balasar's eyes went harder, but his wry smile didn't fade. It wasn't anger that made him what he was. It was determination. Sinja found himself unsurprised. Anger was too weak and uncertain to have seen them all this far.

"I'd have you ride with us," the general said.

"I'm not sure Eustin-cha would enjoy that," Sinja said, then switched to speaking in Galtic. "But if it's what you'd like, sir, I'm pleased to do it."

"You have a horse?"

"Several. I've been having them walked. I've got good enough fighters among my men, but I can't speak all that highly of them as grooms. A horse with a good lather up in this climate and with these boys to care for it is going to be tomorrow night's dinner."

"I have a servant or two I could spare," Balasar said, frowning. Sinja took a pose that both thanked and refused.

"I'd take the loan of one of your horses, if you have one ready to ride. Otherwise, I'll need to get one of mine."

"I'll have one sent," Balasar said. Sinja saluted, and the general made his way back to the main body of the column. Sinja had just washed down the last of the bread with the dregs of his tea when a servant arrived with a saddled brown mare and orders to hand it over to him. Sinja rode slowly past the soldiers, grim-faced and uncomfortable, preparing for their trek or else already marching. Balasar rode just after the vanguard with Eustin and whichever of his captains he chose to speak with. Sinja fell in beside the general and made his salute. Balasar returned it seriously. Eustin only nodded.

"You served the Khai Machi," Balasar said.

"Since before he was the Khai, in fact," Sinja said.

"What can you tell me about him?"

"He has a good wife," Sinja said. Eustin actually smiled at the joke, but Balasar's head tilted a degree.

"Only one wife?" he asked. "That's odd for the Khaiem, isn't it?"

"And only one son. It is odd," Sinja said. "But he's an odd man for a Khai. He spent his boyhood working as a laborer and traveling through the eastern islands and the cities. He didn't kill his family to take the chair. He's been considered something of an embarrassment by the utkhaiem, he's upset the Dai-kvo, and I think he's looked on his position as a burden."

"He's a poor leader then?"

"He's better than they deserve. Most of the Khaiem actually like the job."

Balasar smiled and Eustin frowned. They understood.

"He hasn't posted scouts," Eustin pointed out. "He can't be much of a war leader."

"No one would post scouts this late in the season," Sinja said. "You might as well fault him for not keeping a watch on the moon in case we launched an attack from there."

"And how was it that a son of the Khaiem found himself working as a laborer?" Balasar asked, eager, it seemed, to change the subject.

As he swayed gently on the horse, Sinja told the story of Otah Machi. How he had walked away from the Dai-kvo to take a false name as a petty laborer. The years in Saraykeht, and then in the eastern islands. How he had taken part in the gentleman's trade, met the woman who would be his wife, and then been caught up in a plot for his father's chair. The uncertain first year of his rule. The plague that had struck the winter cities, and how he had struggled with it. The tensions when he had refused marriage to the daughter of the Khai Utani. Reluctantly, Sinja even told of his own small drama, and its resolution. He ended with the formation of the small militia, and its being sent away to the west, and to Balasar's service.

Balasar listened through it all, probing now and again with questions or comments or requests for Sinja to amplify on some point or aspect of the Khai Machi. Behind them, the sun slid down toward the horizon. The air began to cool, and Sinja pulled his leather cloak back over his shoulders. Dark would be upon them soon, and the moon had still not risen. Sinja expected the meeting to come to its close when they stopped to make camp, but Balasar kept him near, pressing for more detail and explanation.

Sinja knew better than to dissemble. He was here because he had played well up to this point, but if his loyalty to the Galts was ever going to break, it would be soon and all three men knew it. If he held back, hesitated, or gave information that seemed intended to mislead, he would fall from Balasar's grace. So he told his story as clearly and truthfully as he could. There wasn't a great deal that was likely to be of use to the general anyway. Sinja had, after all, never seen Otah lead an army. If he'd been asked to guess how such an effort would end, he'd have been proved wrong already.

They ate their evening meal in Balasar's tent of thick hide beside a brazier of glowing coals that made the potato-and-salt-pork soup taste smoky. When at last Sinja found himself without more to say, the questions ended. Balasar sighed deeply.

"He sounds like a good man," he said. "I'm sorry I won't get to meet him."

"I'm sure he'd say the same," Sinja said.

"Will the utkhaiem turn against him? If we make the same offers we made in Utani and Tan-Sadar, can we avoid the fighting?"

"After he beat your men? It's not a wager I'd take."

Balasar's eyes narrowed, and Sinja felt his throat go a bit tighter, half-convinced he'd said something wrong. But Balasar only yawned, and the moment passed.

"How would you expect him to defend his city?" Eustin asked, breaking a stick of bread. "Will he come out to meet us, or hide and make us dig him out?"

"Dig, I'd expect. He knows the streets and the tunnels. He knows his men will break if he puts them in the field. And he'll likely put men in the towers to drop rocks on us as we pass. Taking Machi is going to be unpleasant. Assuming we get there."

"You still have doubts?" Balasar asked.

"I've never had doubts. One bad storm, and we're all dead men. I'm as certain of that as I ever was."

"And you still chose to come with us."

"Yes, sir."

"Why?"

Sinja looked at the burning coals. The deep orange glow and the white dust of ash. Why exactly he had come was a question he'd asked himself more than once since they'd left Tan-Sadar. He could say it was the contract, but that wasn't the truth and all three of them knew it. He flexed his fingers, feeling the ache in his knuckles.

"There's something I want there," he said.

"You'd like to be the new Khai Machi?"

"In a way," Sinja said. "Something I'd ask from you instead of my share of the spoils, at least."

Balasar nodded, already knowing what Sinja was driving toward. "The Lady Kiyan," he said.

"I don't want her raped or killed," Sinja said. "When the city falls, I'd like her handed over to me. I'll see she doesn't do anything stupid or destructive."

"Her husband and children," Eustin said. "We will have to kill them."

"I know it," Sinja said, "but she's not from a high family. She's got no standing aside from her marriage. She won't pose a threat."

"And for her sake, you'd betray the Khai?" Balasar asked.

Sinja smiled. This question, at least, he could answer honestly and without fear.

"For her sake, sir, I'd betray the gods."

Balasar looked at Eustin, his eyebrows rising as if asking an unvoiced question. Eustin considered Sinja for a long moment, then shrugged. Grunting, Balasar shifted and pulled a wooden box from under his cot. He took a stoppered flask from it—good Nantani porcelain—and three small drinking bowls. With growing unease, Sinja waited as Balasar poured out water-clear rice wine in silence, then handed one bowl to Eustin, the next to him.

"I have a favor to ask of you as well," Balasar said.

Sinja drank. The wine was rich and clean and made his chest bloom with warmth, but not so much he lost the tightness in his throat and between his shoulders.

"We can go in," Eustin said. "Waves of us. Small numbers, one after the other, until we've dug out every nook and cranny in the city. But we'll lose men. A lot of them."

"Most," Balasar said. "We'd win. I'm sure of that. But it would take half of my men."

"That's bad," Sinja said. "But there is another plan here, isn't there?"

Balasar nodded.

"We can send a man in who can tell us what the defenses are. Who can send word or sign. If we're lucky, perhaps even a man who can help with planning the defense. And, in return, take the woman he wants."

Sinja felt his mind start to spin. The rice wine made it a bit harder to think, but a bit easier to grin. It was ridiculous, except that it made sense. He should have anticipated this. He should have known.

"You want to send me in? As a spy?"

"Take a couple good horses in the morning, and ride hard for the city," Eustin said. "You'll arrive a few days ahead of us. You were the Khai's advisor before. He'll listen to you, or at least let you listen to him. When the time comes for the attack, you guide us."

The captain made a small gesture with one hand, as if what he'd said was simple. Go into Machi, betray Otah and everyone else he'd known this last decade. If I turn against the general, Sinja thought, it'll be a bad death when these men find me.

"It will be faster this way," Balasar said. "Fewer people will die on both sides. And, because you ask, the woman is yours. Safe and unharmed if I can do it."

"I have your word on that?" Sinja asked.

Balasar took a pose that accepted an oath. It wasn't quite the right vocabulary, but it carried the meaning. Sinja felt unpleasantly like he was looking down over a cliff. His head swam a little, and the tightness in his body fell to knotting his gut. He held out his bowl and Balasar refilled it.

"I'll understand if it's too much," Balasar said, his voice soft. "It will make things easier for both sides and it won't change the way the battle falls, but that doesn't mean it isn't a terrible thing to ask of you. Take a few days to sit with it if you'd like."

"No," Sinja said. "I don't need time. I'll do the thing."

"You're sure?" Eustin asked.

Sinja drained his cup in a gulp. He could feel the flush starting to grow in his neck and cheeks, the nausea starting in his belly and the back of his throat. It was strong wine and a bad night coming.

"It needs doing, and it's the price I asked," Sinja said. "So I'll do it."

CEHMAI SAT FORWARD IN HIS CHAIR. THE WHITE MARBLE WALLS OF THEIR WORK-space glowed with candlelight, but Maati didn't find the brightness reassuring. He was sitting as quietly as he could manage on a red and violet embroidered cushion, waiting. Cehmai lifted one of the wide yellow pages, paused, and turned it over. Maati saw the younger poet's lips moving as he shaped some phrase from the papers. Maati restrained himself from asking which. Interruptions wouldn't make this go any faster.

The simple insight that Eiah had given him that night in the baths had taken the better part of two weeks to work into a draft worthy of consideration. Fitting the grammars so that the nuances of corruption and continuance—destruction and creation, or more precisely the destruction *of* creation—reinforced one another had been tricky. And the extra obstacle of fitting in the structures to protect himself should things go amiss had likely tacked on an extra three or four days to the process.

And still, it had taken him only weeks. Not years, not even months. Weeks. The structure of the binding was laid out now. Corruption-of-the-Generative, called Sterile. The death of the Galt's crops. The gelding of its men. The destruction of its women's wombs. Once he had seen the trick of it, the binding had flowed from his pen.

It had been as if some small voice at the back of his mind was whispering the words, and he'd only had to write them down. Even now, squatting on this damnable cushion, his back aching, his feet cold, waiting for Cehmai to read over the last of the changes, he felt half drunk from the work. He was a poet. All the things that had happened in his life to bring him to this place at this time had built toward these days, and the dry pages that hissed and shushed as Cehmai slid them across each other. Maati bit his lip and did not interrupt.

It seemed like days, but Cehmai came to the final page, fingertips tracing the lines Maati had written there, paused, and set it down with the others. Maati leaned forward, his hands taking a querying pose. Cehmai frowned and gently shook his head.

"No?" Maati asked. Something between rage and dismay shot through his belly, only to vanish when Cehmai spoke.

"It's brilliant," he said. "It's a first draft, but it's a very, very good one. I don't think there are many things we'd have to adjust. A few to make it easier to pass on, perhaps. But we can work with those. No, Maati-kvo, I think this is likely to work. It's just . . ."

"Just?"

Cehmai's frown deepened. His fingertips tapped cautiously on the pages, as if he were testing an iron pot, afraid it would be hot enough to burn. He sighed.

"I've never seen an andat fashioned to be a weapon," he said. "There was a book that the Dai-kvo had that dated from the fall of the Second Empire, but he never let anyone look at it. I don't know."

"There's a war, Cehmai-kya," Maati said. "They killed the Dai-kvo and everyone in the village. The gods only know how many other men they've slaughtered. How many women they've raped. What's on those pages, they've earned."

"I know," Cehmai said. "I do know that. It's just I keep thinking of Stone-Made-Soft. It was capable of terrible things. I can't count the times I had to hold it back from collapsing a mine or a building. It had no respect for the lives of men. But there was no particular malice in it either. This . . . Sterile . . . it seems different."

Maati clamped his jaw. He was tired, that was all. They both were. It was no reason to be annoyed with Cehmai, even if his criticism of the binding was something less than useful. Maati smiled the way he imagined a teacher at the school smiling. Or the Dai-kvo. He took a pose that offered instruction.

"Cutting shears and swords are both sharp. Before the war, you and I and the men like us? We made cutting shears," he said, and gestured to the papers. "That's our first sword. It's only natural that you'd feel uneasy with it; we aren't men of violence. If we were, the Dai-kvo would never have chosen us, would he? But the world's a different place now, and so we have to be willing to do things that we wouldn't have before."

"Then it makes you uneasy too?" Cehmai asked. Maati smiled. It didn't make him uneasy at all, but he could see it was what the man needed to hear.

"Of course it does," he said. "But I can't allow that to stop me. The stakes are too high."

Cehmai seemed to collapse on himself. The dark eyes flickered, searching, Maati thought, for some other path. But in the end, the man only sighed.

"I think you've found the thing, Maati-kvo. There are some passages I'd want to think about. There might be ways we can refine it. But I think we'll be ready to try it well before the thaw."

A tension that Maati hadn't known he was carrying released, and he grinned like a boy. He could imagine himself as the controller of the only andat in the world. He and Cehmai would become the new teachers, and under their protection, they would raise up a new generation of poets to bind more of the andat. The cities would be safe again. Maati could feel it in his bones.

The rest of the meeting went quickly, as if Cehmai wanted to be away from the library as quickly as he could. Maati supposed the prospect of binding Sterile was more disturbing to Cehmai than to him. He hoped, as he walked back up the stairways and corridors to his rooms, that Cehmai would be able to adjust to the new way of things. It couldn't be easy for him. He was at heart a gentle man, and the world was a darker place than it had been.

Maati's mind was still involved in its contemplation of darkness when he stepped into his room. At first, he didn't notice that Liat was there, seated on his bed. She coughed—a wet, close sound close to a sob. He looked up.

"What's the matter, sweet?" he asked, hurrying to her. "What's happened?"

In the steady glow of the lantern, Liat's face seemed veiled by shadows. Her eyes were reddened and swollen, her skin flushed with recent tears. She attempted a smile.

"I need something, Maati-kya. I need you to speak with Nayiit."

"Of course. Of course. What's happened?"

"He's . . ." Liat stopped, took a deep breath, and began again. "He isn't leaving with me. Whatever happens, he's decided to stay here and guard her children."

"What?"

"Kiyan," Liat said. "She set him to watch over Danat and Eiah, and now he's decided to keep to it. To stay in the North and watch over them instead of going home with me. He has a wife and a child, and Otah's family is more important to him than his own. And what if they see that he's . . . what if they see whose blood he is? What if he and Danat have to kill each other?"

Maati sat beside Liat and folded her hand in his. The corners of her mouth twitched down, a mask of sorrow. He kissed her palm.

"He's said this? That he's staying in Machi?"

"He doesn't have to," Liat said. "I've seen the way he looks at them. Whenever I talk about the spring and the South, he smiles that false, charming way he always smiles and changes the subject."

Maati nodded. The lantern flame hissed and shuddered, setting the shadows to sway.

"What is this really?" he asked, gently as he could. Liat pulled back her hand

and took a pose that asked clarification. There was anger in her eyes. Maati chewed his lower lip, raised his eyebrows.

"He enjoys a duty that was designed, from what you told me, to be enjoyable for him. To give him the sense of redeeming himself. He's made friends with Otah's children—"

"His *other* children," Liat said, but Maati had known her too long and too well to let the barb turn him aside.

"And they're very easy to make friends with. Danat and Eiah are charming in their ways. And Nayiit doesn't want to talk about plans he can't really make. About his own child who might already be dead. About a wife he doesn't love and a city that's fallen to the Galts. Why would he want to talk about that? What is there in any of that to cause him anything but pain?"

"You think I'm an idiot," Liat said.

"I think he *hasn't* told you that he's staying. That's something you've decided, and you don't reach conclusions that wild unless there's something more going on," he said. "What it is, sweet?"

Liat's face squeezed tight, her brows and mouth and eyes seeming to pull in together like those of a fighter bracing to take a blow.

"I'm frightened. Is that what you want to hear? All right, then. I'm frightened."

"For him."

"For all of us!" Liat stood and began to pace. "For the people I knew in Saraykeht. For the people I've met here. And the ones I haven't met. Do you know how many people the Galts have killed?"

"No, love."

"No one does. No one knows how bloody this has been. No one knows how much more they'll want before it's over. I knew what the world was when I came here."

"You came here to change the world by slaughtering all of Galt," Maati said.

"Yes, Maati. Yes, so that *this* wouldn't happen. So that *we* wouldn't change!" She was weeping now, though he couldn't hear it in her voice. The tears only ran unnoticed down her cheeks as she moved, restless as a trapped bird. "I don't know the Galts. I don't love them. I don't care if they all die. What's going to happen to *us*? What's going to happen to *him*? What's already happened?"

"It's hard, isn't it? When there's nothing to distract you from it," Maati said. "Harder, I mean. It's not ever easy. You had the organization of the city to keep your mind busy, but that's done, and now there's nothing but the waiting. I've felt it too. If I didn't have the binding to work on, I'd have sunk into it."

Liat stopped. Her hands worried at each other.

"I can't stop thinking about it," she said. "I keep half-expecting that it will all go back to what it was. That we'll go back to Saraykeht and carry on with the business and talk about that terrible year when the Galts came the way we talk about a bad cotton crop."

"It won't, though."

"Then what's going to happen to him?"

"Him? Just Nayiit? He's the only one you wonder that of?"

The tears didn't stop, but a smile as much sorrow as otherwise touched her. "He's my son. Who else matters?"

"He's going to be fine," Maati said, and even he heard the conviction in his voice. "The Galts will be turned back, because I will turn them back. Our children won't die. Theirs will. We won't go hungry. They will. Nayiit won't be harmed, and when this is all finished with, he won't stay here with Otah-kvo. He'll go, because he has a child of his own in Saraykeht, and he isn't the kind of man who can walk away from that."

"Isn't he?" Liat asked. Her tone was a plea.

"Either he's Otah's son, and Otah sacrificed his freedom and his dignity to keep Danat and Eiah safe. Or he's mine, and you had to force me away."

"Or he's mine," Liat said. "Then what becomes of him?"

"Then he'll be beautiful and lovely beyond all mortals, and age gracefully into wisdom. And he'll love his child the way you love him," Maati said. "Silly question."

Liat couldn't help but laugh. Maati rose and took her in his arms. She smelled of tears—wet and salt and flesh. Like blood without the iron. He kissed the crown of her bowed head.

"We'll be fine," he said. "I know what to do. Cehmai's here to help me, and Otah's bought us the time we need. Nothing bad will happen."

"It will," Liat said into his shoulder, and then with something that sounded like hope and surrender, "Only make it happen to someone else."

They stood in silence for a while. Maati felt the warmth of Liat's body against him. They had held each other so many times over the years. In lust and shame, in love and pleasure. In sorrow. Even in anger. He knew the feel of her, the sound of her breath, the way her hand curled round his shoulder. There was no one in the world who he would ever be able to speak with the way he spoke to her. They knew things between them that even Otah could never share—moments in Saraykeht, and after. It wasn't only the great moments—the birth of Nayiit, the death of Heshai, their own last parting; there were also the small ones. The time she'd gotten ill on crab soup and he'd nursed her and cared for the still squalling Nayiit. The flute player with the dancing dog they'd given a length of silver at a firekeeper's kiln in Yalakeht. The way the autumn came to Saraykeht when they were still young.

When she left again, there would be no one to talk to about those things. When she went to the South again and he became the new Dai-kvo, there would be no one to remind him of those moments. It made them more precious. It made her more precious.

"I'll protect you," he said. "Don't worry, love. I'll protect us all."

He heard approaching footsteps, and he could feel it in Liat's body when she did as well. She stepped back, and he let her, but he kept hold of one hand.

Even if only for a moment. An urgent knock came at the door, and Cehmai's voice.

"Maati-kvo!"

"Come in. Come in. What's the matter?"

The poet's face was flushed, his eyes wide. It took a moment for him to catch his breath before he could speak.

"The Khai says you should come. Now," Cehmai gasped. "Sinja's back."

22

>+< When Sinja finished his report and was silent, Otah forced his breath to be deep and regular, waiting until he could speak. His voice was tight and controlled.

"You have spent the season fighting beside the Galts?"

"They were winning."

"Is that supposed to be funny?"

He was thinner than Otah remembered him. The months on the road had left Sinja's face drawn, his cheekbones sharp. His skin was leathery from the sun and wind. He hadn't changed his robes, and he smelled of horses. His casual air seemed false, a parody of the certain, amused, detached man whom Otah had sent away, and Otah couldn't say if it was the captain who'd changed more or himself.

Kiyan, the only other person in the chamber, sat apart from the pair of them, at the couch nearest the fire. Her hands were fists in her lap, her spine straight and still as a tree. Her face was expressionless. Sinja's gaze flickered toward her, and then came back to Otah. The captain took a pose that apologized.

"I'm not trying to be light about this, Most High," Sinja said. "But it's truth. By the time I knew they weren't attacking the Westlands, I could no more have excused myself and ridden on than flapped my arms and flown. I did what I could to slow them, but yes, when they called on us, we fought beside them. When they needed interpreters, we spoke for them. I suppose we could have thrown ourselves on their spears and died nobly, but then I wouldn't be here to warn you now."

"You betrayed the Khaiem," Otah said.

"And I'm betraying the Galts now," Sinja replied, his voice calm. "If you can judge the balance on that, you're smarter than I am. I've done what I've done, Most High. If I chose wrong, I'll apologize, except I don't think I have."

"Let it go," Otah said. "We'll deal with it later."

"I'd rather do it now," Sinja said, shifting his weight. "If I'm going to be drowned as a traitor, I'd like to know it."

Otah felt the rage rise up in his breast like a flame uncurling. He heard it in his ears.

"You want pardon?"

"For the boys too," Sinja said. "I swear I'll do everything I can to earn it."

You'll swear anything you like and break the oath when it suits you, Otah thought. He bit his lip until he thought it might bleed, but he didn't shout. He didn't call for the armsmen who waited outside the great blue doors. It would have been simple to have the man killed. It would have even felt like justice, he thought. His own man. His friend and advisor. Walking beside the Galtic general. Giving him advice. But the rage wasn't only rage. It was also fear. And despair. And so no matter how right it felt, it couldn't be trusted.

"Don't ask me for anything again."

"I won't, Otah-cha." And then a moment later, "You're a harder man than when I left."

"I've earned it."

"It suits you."

A rattle came from the door, and then a polite scratching, and Cehmai, Maati, and Liat came in the room. Their faces were flushed, and Maati's breath was heavy as if he'd been running. Otah frowned. He wouldn't have chosen to have Liat here, but she'd helped Kiyan with the preparations of the city and the quartering of the refugees of Cetani, so perhaps it was for the best after all. He took a general pose of greeting.

"What's . . . happened," Maati wheezed.

"We have a problem," Otah said.

"The Galts?" Liat asked.

"Ten thousand of them," Kiyan said, speaking for the first time since Sinja had begun his report. Her voice was solid as stone. "Foot soldiers and archers and horsemen. They won't reach us today. But tomorrow, perhaps. Three days at the most."

Maati's face went white and he sat down hard, like a puppet whose strings had been cut. Liat and Cehmai didn't move to help him. The room was silent except for the murmur of the fire. Otah let the moment pass. There was nothing he could say just now that they wouldn't think for themselves in the next few heartbeats. Cehmai recovered the fastest, his brows rising, his mouth going tight and hard.

"What do we do?" the younger poet asked.

"We have some advantages," Otah said. "We outnumber them. We know the city. We're in a position to defend, and holding a city's easier than forcing your way in."

"On the other hand," Sinja said, "they're soldiers. You aren't. They know that they need shelter from the cold and need it quickly. Taking Machi's their only option. And they know a fair amount about the city as well."

"You told them that too?" Otah asked.

"They've had their agents and traders in all the cities for generations," Kiyan said softly. "They've put their hands in our affairs. They've walked the streets and sat in the bathhouses. They have trading houses that wintered here when your father was Khai."

"Not to mention the several hundred native guides working for them who aren't me," Sinja said. "I was leading a militia, you'll recall. I've left as many as I could behind, but they've had a season to get any information they wanted."

Otah raised his hands in a pose that abandoned his point. He had the feeling of trembling that he remembered from the aftermath of his battles. From hearing Danat's struggles to breathe when his cough had been at its worst. It wasn't time to feel; he couldn't afford to feel. He tried to push the fear and despair away; he couldn't. It was in his blood now.

"I can try," Maati said. "I'll have to try."

"You have a binding ready?" Sinja asked.

"Not ready," Cehmai said. "We have it in outline. It would need weeks to refine it."

"I'll try," Maati said. His voice was stronger now. His lips were pulled thin. "But I don't know that it will help if it comes to a battle. If it works, I can see they never bear children, but that won't stop them in the near term."

"You could make it hurt," Sinja suggested. "Men don't fight as well newly gelded."

Maati frowned deeply, his fingers moving on their own, as if tracing numbers in the air.

"Do what you can," Otah said. "If you think a change will make the binding less likely to work, don't do it. We need an andat—any andat. The details aren't important."

"Could we pretend?" Liat asked. "Dress someone as an andat, and send them out with Maati. How would the Galts know it wasn't true?"

"The costume would have to involve not breathing," Cehmai said. Liat looked crestfallen.

"Kiyan," Otah said. "Can we arm the people we have?"

"We can improvise something," his wife said. "If we put men in the towers, we can rain stones and arrows on them. It would make it hard for them to keep to the streets. And if we block the stairways and keep the platforms locked at the top, it would be hard work to get them out."

"Until the cold kills them," Sinja said. "There's not enough coal in the ground to keep those towers warm enough to live in."

"They can survive a few days," Otah said. "We'll see to it."

"We can also block off the entrances to the tunnels," Liat said. "Hide the ventilation shafts and fill as many of the minor ways down as we can find with stones. It would be easier, wouldn't it, if there were only one or two places that we needed to defend?"

"There's another option," Sinja said. "I don't like to mention it, but . . . If you surrender, Balasar-cha will kill Otah and Eiah and Danat. Cehmai and Maati. The Khai Cetani and his family too, if they're here. He'll burn the books. But he'd accept surrender from the utkhaiem after that. It's a dozen or so people. There's no way to do this that kills fewer."

Otah felt himself rock back. A terrible weight seemed to fall on his shoulders. He wouldn't. Of course he would not. He would let every man and woman in the city die before he offered up his children to be slaughtered, but it meant that every one that died in the next few days would be doubly upon his conscience. Every life that ended here, ended because he had refused to be a sacrifice. He swallowed to loosen the knot in his throat and took a pose that dismissed the subject.

"I had to say it," Sinja said, apologizing with his tone.

"You didn't say my name," Kiyan said. Her eyes turned to Sinja's. "Why didn't you say my name?"

"Well, assuming that you don't all opt for slaughter, there is one other thing we have in our favor," Sinja said. "They sent me here to betray you. Kiyan's safety was my asking price. They expect a report from me when they arrive. If I give them bad information, we may be able to trap some of them. Thin their forces. It won't win the battle, but it could help."

Otah raised his hand, and the mercenary stopped. Kiyan was the one who took a querying pose, and it was to Kiyan that he answered.

"The general. Balasar-cha. He doesn't want a bloody battle. He wants it over quickly, with as few of his men lost as he can manage. I agreed to come here and discover your defenses if he spared you. Gave you to me when it was all over with. Prize of war. It's not all that uncommon."

Kiyan rose, her small foxlike face turned feral. Her fingers were splayed in claws, and her chest pressed forward like a bantam ready for the fighting pit. Otah's heart warmed with something like pride.

"If you let them touch Eiah and Danat, I would kill you in your sleep," she said.

"But Balasar-cha doesn't know that," Sinja said, shrugging and looking into the fire. He couldn't meet her eyes. "He expects a report from me, and I'll give him one. I'll give him whatever report you'd like."

"Gods," Kiyan said, her eyes still ablaze. "Is there anyone you haven't betrayed?"

Sinja smiled, but Otah thought there was sorrow in his dark eyes.

"Yes, there is. But she was in love with someone else."

Cehmai coughed, embarrassed. Otah raised his hands.

"Enough," he said. "We haven't got time for this. We may have as little as a day to get ready. Maati, you prepare your binding. Cehmai will help you. Kiyan. Liat. You've arranged food and quarters for two cities. Do what you can to arm them and keep people from panicking. Sinja and I will work out a plan to defend the city and a report to deliver to the Galts."

Kiyan's eyes carried a question, but Otah didn't answer. There was no reason to trust Sinja-cha. It was just the risk he chose to take.

Servants brought maps of the city, of the low towns to the south, and the mountains and mines to the north. Machi hadn't been built to withstand a war; there were no walls to defend, no pits that the enemy would have to bridge. The only natural barrier—the river—was already frozen solid enough to walk across. Any real defense would have to be on the black-cobbled streets, in the alleys and tunnels and towers. They talked late into the night, joined by the Khai Cetani and Ashua Radaani, Saya the blacksmith and Kiyan when she wasn't out among the tunnels spreading the word and making preparations. Sinja's shame, if it was still there, was hidden and his advice was well considered. By morning, even the Khai Cetani suffered interruption from Sinja-cha. Otah took it as another sign that the Khai had changed.

If things went poorly, there was still the mine in the northern mountains. A few people could take shelter there. Eiah and Danat. Nayiit. If the binding failed, they could send Maati and Cehmai there as well, sneaking them out the back of the palace in a fast cart while the battle was still alive. Otah didn't imagine that he would be there with them, and Sinja didn't question him.

Afterward, Otah looked in on his children, both asleep in their chambers. He found the library where Cehmai and Maati were still arguing over points of grammar so obscure he could hardly make sense of them. The night candle was guttering and spitting when Otah came at last to his bed. Kiyan sat with him in silence for a time. He touched her, tracing the curve of her cheek with the knuckles of one hand.

"Do you believe Sinja?" he asked.

"What part of it?"

"Do you think that this General Gice really believes the andat are too dangerous to exist? That he wants them destroyed? What he said about killing the poet . . . I don't know what to think of that."

"If burning the library is really one of his demands, then maybe," Kiyan said. "I can't think he'd want the books and scrolls burned if he hoped to bind more andat of his own."

Otah nodded, and lay back, his gaze turned toward the ceiling above him, dark as a moonless sky.

"I'm not sure he's wrong," Otah said.

Wordless, she drew his mouth to hers, guided his hands. He would have thought himself too tired for the physical act of love, but she proved him wrong. Afterward, she lay at his side, her fingertips tracing the ink that had been worked into his skin when he had been an eastern islander leading one of his previous lives. He slept deeply and with a feeling of peace utterly unjustified by the situation.

He woke alone, called in the servants who bathed and dressed a Khai. Or, however briefly, an Emperor. Black robes, shot with red. Thick-woven wool layered with waxed silk. Robes of colors chosen for war and designed for cold. He took himself up through the great galleries, rising toward the surface and the light, being seen by the utkhaiem of both Machi and Cetani, by the common laborers hurrying to throw vast cartfuls of rubble into the minor entrances to the underground, by the merchants and couriers. The food sellers and beggars. The city.

The sky was white and gray, vast and empty as a blank page. Crows commented to one another, their voices dispassionate and considering as low-town judges. High above, the towers of Machi loomed, and smoke rose from the sky doors—the sign that men were up there in the thin, distant air burning coal and wood to warm their hands, preparing for the battle. Otah stood on the steps of his palace, the bitter cold numbing his cheeks and biting at his nose and ears, the world smelling of smoke and the threat of snow. Distant and yet clear, like the voice of a ghost, bells began to ring in the towers and great yellow banners unfurled like the last, desperate unfallen leaves of the vast stone trees.

The Galts had come.

SNOW FELL GENTLY THAT MORNING, DRIFTING DOWN FROM THE SHEET OF CLOUDS above them in small, hard flakes. Balasar stood on the ridgeline of the hills south of the city. Frost had formed on the folds of his leather cloak, and the snow that landed on his shoulders didn't melt. Before him, the stone towers rose, seeming closer than they were, more real than the snow-grayed mountains behind them. No enemy army had marched out to meet him, no party of utkhaiem marred the thin white blanket, still little more than ankle-deep, that separated Balasar from Machi. Behind him, his men were gathered around the steam wagons, pressed around the furnace grates that Balasar had ordered opened. The medics were already busy with men suffering from the cold. The captains and masters of arms were seeing that every clump of men was armed and armored. Balasar had been sure to mention the warm baths beneath Machi, the food supplies laid in those tunnels—enough, he assumed, to keep two cities alive for the winter.

Smoke rose from the tops of the towers and from the city itself. Banners flew. He heard a horseman approaching him from behind, and he glanced back to see Eustin on a great bay mare. The beast's breath was heavy and white as feathers. Balasar raised a hand, as Eustin cantered forward, pulled his mount to a halt, and saluted.

"I'm ready, sir. I've a hundred men volunteered to come with me. With your permission."

"Of course," Balasar said, then looked back at the towers. "Do you really think they'd do it? Sneak out. Run north and try to hide in the low towns out there?"

"Best to have us there in the event," Eustin said. "I could be wrong, sir. But I'd rather be careful now than have to spend the cold part of the season making raids. Especially if this is the warm bit."

Balasar shook his head. He didn't believe that the Khai Machi Sinja had described to him would run. He would fight unfairly, he would launch attacks from ambush, he would have his archers aim for the horses. But Balasar didn't think he would run. Still, the poets might. Or the Khai might send his children away for safety, if he hadn't already. And there would be refugees. Eustin's plan to block their flight was a wise one. He couldn't help wishing that Eustin might have been with him here, at the end. They were the last of the men who had braved the desert, and Balasar felt a superstitious dread at sending him away.

"Sir?"

"Be careful," Balasar said. "That's all."

A trumpet called, and Balasar turned back to the city. Sure enough, there was something—a speck of black on the white. A single rider, fleeing Machi.

"Well," Eustin said. "Looks like Captain Ajutani's come back after all. Give him my compliments."

Balasar smiled at the disdain in Eustin's voice.

"I'll be careful too," he said.

It took something like half a hand for Sinja to reach the camp. Balasar noticed particularly that he didn't turn to the bridge, riding instead directly over the frozen river. Eustin and his force were gone, looping around to the north, well before the mercenary captain arrived. Balasar had cups of strong kafe waiting when Sinja, his face pink and raw-looking from his ride, was shown into his tent.

Balasar returned his salute and gestured to a chair. Sinja took a pose of thanks—so little time back among the Khaiem and the use of formal pose seemed to have returned to the man like an accent—and sat, drawing a sheaf of papers from his sleeve. When they spoke, it was in the tongue of the Khaiem.

"It went well?"

"Well enough," Sinja said. "I made a small mistake and had to do some very pretty dancing to cover it. But the Khai's got few enough hopes, he *wants* to trust me. Makes things easier. Now, here. These are rough copies of the maps he's used. They're filling in the main entrances to the underground tunnels to keep us from bringing any single large force down at once. The largest paths they've left open are here," Sinja touched the map, "and here."

"And the poets?"

"They have the outline of a binding. I think they're going to try it. And soon."

Balasar felt the sinking of dread in his belly, and strangely also a kind of peace. He wouldn't have thought there was any part of him that was still held back, and yet that one small fact—the poets lived and planned and would recapture one of the andat now if they could—took away any choice he might still have had. He looked at the map, his mind sifting through strategies like a tiles player shuffling chits of bone.

"There are men in the towers," Balasar said.

"Yes, sir," Sinja said. "They'll have stones and arrows to drop. You won't be able to use the streets near them, but the range isn't good, and they won't be able to aim from so far up. Go a street or two over and keep by the walls, and we'll be safe. There won't be much resistance above ground. Their hope is to keep you at bay long enough for the cold to do their work for them."

Three forces, Balasar thought. One to clear out the houses and trading shops on the south, another to push in toward the forges and the metalworkers, a third to take the palaces. He wouldn't take the steam wagons—he'd learned that much from Coal—so horsemen would be important for the approach, though they might be less useful if the fighting moved inside structures as it likely would. And they'd be near useless once they were underground. Archers wouldn't have much effect. There were few long, clear open spaces in the city. But despite what Sinja said, Balasar expected there would be some fighting on the surface, so enough archers were mixed with the foot troops to fire back at anyone harassing them from the windows and snow doors of the passing buildings.

"Thank you, Sinja-cha," Balasar said. "I know how much doing this must have cost you."

"It needed doing," Sinja said, and Balasar smiled.

"I won't insist that you watch this happen. You can stay at the camp or ride north and join Eustin."

"North?"

"He's taken it to guard. In case someone tries to slip away during the battle."

"That's a good thought," Sinja said, his tone somewhat rueful. "If it's all the same, I'd like to ride with Eustin-cha. I know he hasn't always thought well of me, and if anything does go wrong, I'd like to be where he can see I wasn't the one doing it."

"A pretty thought," Balasar said, chuckling.

"You're going to win," Sinja said. It was a simple statement, but there was a weight behind it. A regret that soldiers often had in the face of loss, and only rarely in victory.

"You thought of changing sides," Balasar said. "While you were there, with all the people you know. In your old home. It was hard not to stand by them."

"That's true," Sinja said.

"It wouldn't have changed things. One more sword—even yours—wouldn't have changed the way this battle falls."

"That's why I came back," Sinja said.

"I'm glad you did," Balasar said. "I've been proud to ride with you."

Sinja gave his thanks and took his leave. Balasar wrote out orders for the guard to accompany Sinja and other ones to deliver to Eustin. Then he turned to the maps of Machi. Truly there was little choice. The poets lived. Another night in the cold would mean losing more men. Balasar sat for a long moment, quietly asking God to let this day end well; then he walked out into the late-morning sun and gave the call to formation.

It was time.

23

>+< Liat had expected panic—in herself and in the city. Instead there was a strange, tense calm. Wherever she went, she was greeted with civility and even pleasure. There were smiles and even laughter, and a sense of purpose in the face of doom. In the interminable night, she had been invited to join in three suppers, as many breakfasts, and bowls of tea without number. She had seen the highest of the utkhaiem sitting with metalsmiths and common armsmen. She had heard one of the famed choirs of Machi softly singing its Candles Night hymns. The rules of society had been suspended, and the human solidarity beneath it moved her to weep.

She and Kiyan had taken the news first to the Khai Cetani and the captains of the battle that had once turned the Galts aside. When the plans had come from Otah's small Council—where to place men, how to resist the Galts as they tried to overrun the city—the Khai Cetani had emerged with the duties of arming and armoring the men who could fight. As the underground city was emptied of anything that could be used as a weapon—hunting arrows, kitchen knives, even lengths of leather and string cut from beds and fashioned into slings—Liat had seen children too young to fight and men and women too old or frail or ill packed into side galleries, the farthest from the fighting. Cots lined the walls, piled with blankets. In some places, there were thick doors that could be closed and pegged from the inside. Though if the Galts ever came this far, it would hardly matter how difficult it was to open the doors. Everything would already be lost.

Kiyan had made the physicians her personal duty—preparing one of the higher galleries for the care of the wounded and dying who would be coming back before the day's end. They'd managed seventy beds and scavenged piles of cloth high as a man's waist, ready to pack wounds. Bottles of distilled wine stood ready to ease pain and clean cuts. A firekeeper's kiln, cauterizing irons already glowing in its maw, had been pulled in and the air was rich with the scent of poppy milk cooking to the black sludge that would take away pain at one spoonful and grant mercy with two. Liat walked between the empty beds, imagining them as they would shortly be—canvas soaked with gore. And still the panic didn't come.

By the entrance, one of the physicians was talking in a calm voice to twenty or so girls and boys no older than Eiah, too young to fight, but old enough to help care for the wounded. Kiyan was nowhere to be found, and Liat wasn't sure whether she was pleased or dismayed.

She sat on one of the beds and let her eyes close. She had not slept all the long night. She wouldn't sleep until the battle was ended. Which meant, of course, that she might never sleep again. The thought carried a sense of unreality that was, she thought, the essential mood of the city. This couldn't be happening. People went about the things that needed doing with a numb surprise that hell had bloomed up in the world. The men in their improvised leather armor and sharpened fire irons could no more fathom that there would be no tomorrow for them than Liat could. And so they were capable of walking, of speaking, of eating food. If they had been given time to understand, the Galts wouldn't have faced half the fight that was before them now.

"Mama-kya!" a man's voice said close at hand. Nayiit's. Liat's eyes flew open.

He stood in the aisle between beds, his eyes wide. Danat, pale-skinned and frightened, clung to her boy's robes.

"What are you doing still here?" Liat said.

"Eiah," Nayiit said. "I can't find Eiah. She was in her rooms, getting dressed, but when I came back with Danat-cha, she was gone. She isn't at the cart. I thought she might be here. I can't leave without her."

"You should have left before the sun rose," Liat said, standing up. "You have to leave now."

"But Eiah—"

"You can't wait for her," Liat said. "You can't *stay* here."

Danat began to cry, a high wailing that echoed against the high tiled ceiling and seemed to fill the world. Nayiit crouched and tried to calm the boy. Liat felt something warm and powerful unwind in her breast. Rage, perhaps. She hauled her son up by his shoulder and leaned in close.

"Leave her," she said. "Leave the girl and get out of this city *now*. Do you understand me?"

"I promised Kiyan-cha that I'd—"

"You can't keep a girl fourteen summers old from being stupid. No one can. She made her decision when she left you."

"I promised that I'd look after them," Nayiit said.

"Then save the one you can," Liat said. "And do it now, before you lose that chance too."

Nayiit blinked in something like surprise and glanced down at the still-wailing boy. His expression hardened and he took a pose of apology.

"You're right, Mother. I wasn't thinking."

"Go. Now," Liat said. "You don't have much time."

"I want my sister!" Danat howled.

"She's going to meet us there," Nayiit said, and then swept the boy up in his arms with a grunt. Danat—eyes puffy and red, snot streaming from his nose—pulled back to stare at Nayiit with naked mistrust. Nayiit smiled his charming smile. His father's smile. Otah's. "It's going to be fine, Danat-kya. Your mama and papa and your sister. They'll meet us at the cave. But we have to leave now."

"No they won't," the boy said.

"You watch," Nayiit said, lying cheerfully. "You'll see. Eiah's probably there already."

"But we have the cart."

"Yes, good thought," Nayiit said. "Let's go see the cart."

He leaned over, awkward with his burden of boy, and kissed Liat.

"I'll do better," he murmured.

You're perfect, Liat wanted to say. You've always been the perfect boy.

But Nayiit was rushing away now, his robes billowing behind him as he sped to the end of the gallery, Danat still on his hip, and turned to the north and vanished toward the back halls and the cart and the north where if the gods could hear Liat's prayers, they would be safe.

HOUSE SIYANTI HAD OFFERED UP ITS WAREHOUSES FOR THE KHAIEM—Machi and Cetani together—to use as their commandery. Five stories high and well back from the edge of the city, the wide, gently sloped roof had as clear a view of the streets as anything besides the great towers themselves. A passage led from the lower warehouse on the street level into the underground should there be a need to retreat into that shelter. In the great empty space—the warehouse emptied of its wares—Maati wrote the text of his binding on the smooth stone wall, pausing occasionally to rub his hands together and try to calm his unquiet mind. A stone stair led up to the second-floor snow doors, which stood open to let the sun in until they were ready to light the dozen glass lanterns that lined the walls. The air blew in bitterly cold and carried a few stray flakes of hard snow that had found their way down from the sky.

Ideally, Maati would have spent the last day meditating on the binding—holding the nuances of each passage clear in his mind, creating step-by-step the mental structure that would become the andat. He had done his best, drinking black tea and reading through his outline for Corrupting-the-Generative. The binding looked solid. He thought he could hold it in his mind. With months or weeks—perhaps even days—he could have been sure. But this morning he felt scattered. The hot metal scent of the brazier, the wet smell of the snow, the falling gray snowflakes against a sky of white, the scuffing of Cehmai's feet against the stone floor, and the occasional distant call of trumpet and drum as the armsmen and defenders of Machi took their places—everything seemed to catch his attention. And he could not afford distraction.

"I don't know if I can do this," he said. His voice echoed against the stone walls, sounding hollow. He turned to meet Cehmai's gaze. "I don't know if I can go through with this, Cehmai-kya."

"I know," the other poet said, but did not pause in his work of chalking symbols into the spare walls. "I felt the same before I took Stone-Made-Soft from my master. I don't think any poet has ever gone to the binding without some sense he was jumping out of a tower in hopes of learning to fly on the way down."

"But the binding," Maati said. "We haven't had time."

"I don't know," Cehmai said, turning to look at Maati. "I've been thinking about it. The draft you made. It's as complex as some bindings I saw when I was training. The nuances support each other. The symbols seem to hang together. And the structure that deflects the price fits it. I think you've been working on this for longer than you think. Maybe since Saraykeht fell."

Maati looked out the snow door at their bright square of sky. His chest felt tight. He thought for a moment how sad it would be to have come this far and collapse now from a bad heart.

"I remember when I was at the village the second time," Maati said. "After Saraykeht. After Liat left me. There was a teahouse at the edge of the village. Tanam Choyan's place."

"High walls," Cehmai said. "And a red lacquer door to the back room. I remember the place. They always undercooked the rice."

"He did," Maati said. "I'd forgotten that. There was a standing game of tiles there. I remember once a boy came to play and didn't know any of the rules. Not even what season led, or when two winds made a trump. He bet everything he had at the first tile. He knew he was in over his head, so he risked it all at once. He thought if he kept playing, then the men at the table who knew better than he did would strip him of every length of copper he had. If he put everything on one hand—well, someone had to win, and it might be him as well as anyone else. I understand now how he felt."

"Did he win?"

"No," Maati said. "But I respected the strategy."

A trumpet blared out above them—Otah sending some signal among his men. Answering horns came from around the city. Maati could no more tell where they originated than guess how many snowflakes were in the wide air. Cehmai's surprised breath caught his attention like a hook pulling at a fish. He turned to the man, and then followed his gaze to the stairway leading down to the tunnels. Eiah stood there, her ribs pumping hard, as if she'd run to reach them. Her hair was pulled back in a messy knot at the back. Her robes were bright green shot with gold.

"Eiah-cha," Cehmai said, stepping toward her. "What are you doing here?"

The girl looked up at Cehmai, stepping away from him as if she might run. Her gaze darted to Maati. He smiled and took a pose that was welcome and inquiry both. Eiah's hands fluttered between half a dozen poses, settling on none of them.

"They need physicians," she said. "People are going to get hurt. I don't want to be useless. And . . . and I want to be here when you stop them. I helped with the binding as much as Cehmai did."

That was a gross untruth, but the girl delivered it with such conviction that Maati felt himself half-believing. He smiled.

"You were supposed to go with Nayiit-cha and your brother," Maati said.

Her mouth went small, her face pale.

"I know," she said. Maati waved her closer, and she came to him, skirting around Cehmai as if she feared he would grab her and haul her away to where she was supposed to be. Maati sat on the cold stone floor and she sat with him.

"It isn't safe here," he said.

"It's safe enough that you can be here. And Papa-kya. And you're the two most important men in the world."

"I don't know that—"

"He's the Emperor. Even the Khai Cetani says so. And you're going to kill all the Galts. There can't be any place safer than with both of you. Besides, what if something happens and *you* need a physician?"

"I'll find one of the armsmen or a servant they can spare," Cehmai said. "We can at least have her safely—"

"No," Maati said. "Let her stay. She reminds me why we're doing this."

Eiah's grin was the image of relief and joy. Of all the terrors and dangers arrayed before them, hers had been that she might be sent away. He took her hand and kissed it.

"Go sit by the stairs," he said. "Don't interrupt me, and if Cehmai-cha tells you to do something, you do it. No asking why, no arguing him out of it. You understand me?"

Eiah flung her hands into a pose of acceptance.

"And Eiah-kya. Understand what I'm doing has risks to it. If I die here—hush, now, let me finish. If I fail the binding and my little protection doesn't do what we think it will, I'll pay the price. If that happens, you have to remember that I love you very deeply, and I've done this because it was worth the risk if it meant keeping you safe."

Eiah swallowed and her eyes shone with tears. Maati smiled at her, stood again, and waved her back toward the stairs. Cehmai came close, frowning.

"I'm not sure that was a kind thing to tell her," he said, but a sudden outburst of trumpet calls sounded before Maati could reply. Maati thought he could hear the distant tattoo of drums echoing against the city walls. He gestured to Cehmai.

"Come on. There isn't time. Finish drawing those, then light the candles and close that blasted door. We'll all freeze to death before the andat can have its crack at us."

"Or we'll have it all in place just in time for the Galts to take it."

Maati scribbled out the rest of the binding. He'd wanted time to think on each word, each phrase; if he'd had time to paint each word like the portrait of a thought, it would have been better. There wasn't time. He finished just as Cehmai lit the final lantern and walked up the stone steps to the snow door. Before he closed it, the younger poet looked out, peering into the city.

"What do you see?"

"Smoke," Cehmai said. Then, "Nothing."

"Come back down," Maati said. "Where are the robes for it?"

"In the back corner," Cehmai said, pulling the wide wooden doors shut. "I'll get them."

Maati went to the cushion in the middle of the room, lowered himself with a grunt, and considered. The wall before him looked more like the scribblings of low-town vandals than a poet's lifework. But the words and phrases, the images and metaphors all shone brighter in his mind than the lanterns could account for. Cehmai passed before him briefly, laying robes of blue shot with black on the floor where, with luck, the next hands to hold them wouldn't be human.

Maati glanced over his shoulder. Eiah was sitting against the back wall, her hands held in fists even with her heart. He smiled at her. Reassuringly, he hoped. And then he turned to the words he had written, took five deep breaths to clear his mind, and began to chant.

OTAH STOOD ON THE LIP OF THE ROOF AND LOOKED DOWN AT MACHI AS IF IT were a map. The great streets were marked by the lines of rooftops. Only those streets that led directly to House Siyanti's warehouses were at an angle that permitted him to see the black cobbles turning white beneath the snow. To the south, the army of the Galts was marching forward. The trumpet calls from the high towers told him that much. They had worked out short signals for some eventualities—short melodies that signaled some part of the plans he had worked with Sinja and Ashua Radaani and the others. But in addition there was a code that let him phrase questions as if they were spoken words, and hear answers in the replies from the towers far above.

The trumpeter was a young man with a vast barrel chest and lips blue with cold. Whenever Otah had the man blow, the wide brass bell of the trumpet seemed as if it would deafen them all. And yet the responses were sometimes nearly too faint to hear. Times like now.

"What's he saying?" the Khai Cetani asked, and Otah held up a hand to stop him, straining to hear the last trailing notes.

"The Galts are taking the bridge," Otah said. "I don't think they trust the ice."

"That'll mean they're longer reaching us," the Khai Cetani said. "That's good. If we can keep them out of the warmth until sundown . . ."

Otah took a pose of agreement, but didn't truly believe it. If they were able to trap the Galts above ground when night came, the invaders would take over the houses and burn whatever they could break small enough to fit in the fire grates. If the cold air moved in—a storm or the frigid winds that ended the gentle snows of autumn—then the Galts would be in trouble, but the snow graying the distance now wasn't prelude to a storm. Otah didn't say it, but he couldn't imagine keeping an army so close and still at bay long enough for the weather to change. The Galts would be defeated here in the streets, or they wouldn't be defeated.

He paced the length of the rooftop, his eyes tracing the routes that he had hoped to guide them toward—the palaces and the forges. Behind him, his servants shivered from the cold and the need to remain respectfully still. The great iron fire grate that they'd hauled up and loaded with logs was burning merrily, but somehow the heat from it seemed to go out no more than a foot or two from the flames. The Khai Cetani stood near it, and the trumpeter. Otah couldn't imagine standing still. Not now.

The southern reaches of the city were essentially Galtic already; there was no way to make them safe against the coming army. The battle would be nearer the center, in the shadows of the towers, in the narrower ways where Otah's men could appear all along the Galtic line at once as they had in the forest. Another trumpet call came. The Galts had finished crossing the river. The march had begun on Machi itself.

I should be down there, Otah thought. I should get a sword or an axe and go down there.

It was an idiotic idea, and he knew it. One more blade or bow in the streets wouldn't matter now, and getting himself killed would achieve nothing.

Trumpets sounded—half a dozen of them at once. And Galtic drums. Everyone sending signals, none of them listening. Otah squatted at the roof's edge with his eyes closed, trying to make out one message from another. Frustration built in his spine and neck. Something was happening—several things, and all at the same moment, and he couldn't hear what they were.

"Most High!" one the servants called. "There!"

Otah and the Khai Cetani both looked to where the servant boy was pointing. A runner dashed along a roofline, down near the great, wide streets that led toward the forges. A great pillar of smoke was rising from the south. Something there, then. Otah felt the first small surge of hope; it was near where he had hoped the Galts would go. The trumpets were calling again, fewer of them. Otah found himself better able to make sense of them. The Galts seemed to be moving in three directions at once—sweeping and holding the southern buildings, and then two large forces moving as Otah had hoped they would.

"Call to the towers," Otah said. "Tell them to begin."

The trumpeter took a great breath and blared out the melody they had set for the towers, and then the rising trill that was their signal to begin raining stones and arrows into the streets. It was less than a breath before Otah thought he saw something fly from the open sky doors far above them, plummeting toward the ground. The snow was tricky, though. It might only have been his imagination.

Otah felt himself trying to stretch out his will across the city, to inhabit it like a ghost, to become it. Time slowed to a terrible crawl—years seeming to pass between the short announcing blasts of the trumpets as they reported the Galts' progress. Muffled by the snow, there also came the sound of distant voices raised in anger. Otah's belly knotted. That wasn't right. There shouldn't be any fighting yet. Unless the Galts had found his men while they were still in hiding. He almost signaled his trumpeter to sound the order to report, but the more the signals were used, the better the Galts would be able to find the trumpeters.

"You," Otah said, pointing at one of the half-frozen servants. "Send a runner to the east. I need to know what's happening there."

The man took a pose of acknowledgment and walked quickly and awkwardly back toward the stairs. Otah tapped his hand against the stone lip of the roof, already impatient for the word to come back to him. His feet and face were numb. The snowfall seemed to be thickening, the world a darker gray though the unseen sun was still likely six or seven hands above the southern horizon.

From the west, the drums of Galt thundered, then were silent. Then thundered again. Otah heard the sudden sharp call—thousands of voices at once in a wild call that ended sharply. A boast. We are vast as the ocean and disciplined. We are soldiers. We have come to kill you. Fear us.

And he did.

"Signal the palace forces to take their places," Otah said.

The trumpeter sang out the call, the wide bell of the trumpet playing over the western rooftops like a priest offering blessing to a crowd. The man was weeping, Otah saw. Tears streaking down his cheeks and into his beard. A terrible, rending crash came from the forges. Otah turned to peer through the rising smoke and the falling snow. He expected to see one of the great copper roofs sitting at an angle, but nothing seemed to have changed. The sound was a mystery.

"I can't stand this," Otah said, stalking back to the Khai Cetani and the servants. There was snow gathering on the servants' shoulders. "I don't know what's happening. I can't command a battle blind and guessing. Where are the runners?"

The eldest of the servants took a pose of apology.

"Then go find out," Otah said.

But Otah felt in his bones what the runners would tell him. Before the signals came—trumpets struggling through the muffling snow. Before the Galtic drums broke out in their manic pounding. Nine thousand veterans led by the greatest general in Galt were pouring into his city and facing blacksmiths and vegetable carters, laborers and warehouse guards.

He was losing.

24

>+< Balasar trotted through the streets, his shield held above his head. Despite what Sinja had said, the great towers of Machi commanded the streets around them fairly well. Throughout the day, stones and bricks peppered his men, sailing down from the sky with the force of boulders hurled by siege engines. Arrows sometimes came down as well, their points shattering against the ground where they struck despite the slowly growing cushion of snow. He ducked into another doorway when he came to it. Five of his own men were waiting, and the bodies of ten or so of the enemy. It was a slow process, spreading out and then moving down not only the streets that were the fastest path to the tunnels, but also two or three to each side. The Khai Machi had learned a trick, and he'd used it against Coal. But he didn't have a second strategy, and so Balasar knew where to find the waiting forces—just back from where they'd be seen, waiting to attack on all sides at once. Instead, Balasar was killing them by handfuls. It was a bad way to fight—bloody, slow, painful, and unnecessary.

But it was better than losing.

"General Gice, sir," the captain said as all the men saluted him. Balasar raised his hand. His arm ached from holding the raised shield. "We're making progress, sir."

"Good," Balasar said. "What have we found?"

"All the smaller passages are blocked off, sir. Collapsed or filled with rubble so deep we can't tell how long it would take to dig them out. And they're narrow, sir. Two men together at most."

"We wouldn't want those anyway," Balasar said. "Better we keep for the objectives. And casualties?"

"We're estimating five hundred of the enemy dead, sir. But that's rough."

"And our men?"

"Perhaps half that," the captain said.

"So many?"

"They aren't good fighters, sir, but they're committed."

Balasar sighed, his mind shifting. If he assumed the force pushing toward the palaces was having similar luck, that meant something like fifteen hundred dead since he'd walked into the city. More, if there was resistance in the south. This wasn't a battle, only slow, ugly slaughter. He went to the doorway, peering out down the street. He could hear the sounds of fighting—men's voices, the clash of metal on metal. A hundred small outbursts that became a constant roar, like raindrops falling on a pond.

"Get the drummer," he said. "We'll make a push for it. Scatter the enemy, take the entrance to the tunnels and then get runners to the others."

"The men we're seeing, sir. They're able-bodied. And decent fighters, some of them."

"They wanted to do this on the surface," Balasar said. "The tunnels will be their second string. It won't be as bad once we're in there. If they're smart, they'll see there's no point going on."

The captain saluted without answering. Balasar was willing to take that as agreement.

It took perhaps half a hand to gather a force of men together. Two hundred soldiers would press forward and take the forges, where Sinja had said the paths down would be open. They were only another street down. There wasn't a line of defenders to crush, so the horsemen were less useful. They could still move fast, and men on foot who entered the streets wouldn't be able to attack them easily. Footmen with archers interspersed between them ducking fast from doorway to doorway was the best plan.

He explained it all to the group leaders, watching the men's faces as he asked them to run through the rain of stones and arrows. Two hundred men to move forward, to take control of the forges and then hold the position against anything that came up out of it until the rest of their force could join them. Balasar would lead them. Not one of them hesitated or voiced objection.

"If we live until sunset," he said, "we'll see the end of this. Now take formation."

The drum throbbed, the captains and group leaders scrambled to the places where their men stood waiting. A few bricks detonated on the street in their wake, but no one had stayed out long enough to be in danger from them. Balasar squatted in his chosen doorway, rubbing his shoulder. The air was numbing cold, and the great dark towers rose around them, higher than the crows that wheeled and called, excited, he guessed, by the smells of blood and carrion.

It struck him how beautiful the city was. Austere and close-packed, with thick-walled buildings and heavy shutters. The brightness of snow and the glittering icicles that hung from the eaves set off the darkness of stone and echoed the vast blank sky. It was a city without color—dark and light with hardly even gray in between—and Balasar found himself moved by it. He took a deep breath, watching the cloud of it that formed when he exhaled. The drummer at his side licked his lips.

"Go," Balasar said.

The deep rattle sounded, echoing between the high walls of the houses, and then the press was on, and Balasar launched himself into it, shield high, shoulder cramping. He made it almost halfway to the shelter of the forges and their great copper roofs before the arrows could drop the distance of the towers. Five men fell around him as he ran that last stretch and found himself in a tangle of heat and shouting and swinging blades. One last group of the enemy had stayed hidden here to defy him, to stand guard against them. Balasar shouted and moved forward with the surge of his men. In the field, there would have been formation, rules, order. This was only melee, and Balasar found himself hewing and hacking with his blood singing and alive. It was an idiotic place for a general to be, throwing himself in the face of a desperate enemy, but Balasar felt the joy of it washing away his better sense. A man with a spear fashioned from an old rake poked at him, and he batted the attack away and swung hard, cutting the man down. Three of the locals had formed a knot, fighting with their backs together. Balasar's men overwhelmed them.

And then it was finished. As suddenly as it had begun, the fight ended. The bodies of the enemy lay at their feet, along with a few of their own. Not many. Steam rose from the corpses of friend and foe alike. But they'd reached the tunnels. One last push, down deep into the belly of the city, and it would be over. The war. The andat. Everything. He felt himself smiling like a wolf. His shoulder and arm no longer hurt.

"General! Sir! It's blocked!"

"What?"

One of his captains came forward, gore soaking his tunic from elbow to knee, his expression dismayed.

"It can't be," Balasar said, striding forward. But the captain turned and led him. And there it was. A great gateway of stone, a sloping ramp leading down wide enough for four carts abreast to travel into it. And as he came forward, his boots slipping where the fight had churned the snow to slush, he saw it was true. The shadows beneath the gateway were filled with stones, cut and rough, large as boulders and small as fists. Something glittered among them. Shattered glass and sharp, awkward scraps of metal. Clearing this would take days.

He'd been betrayed. Sinja Ajutani had led him astray. The taste of it was like ashes. And worse than the deception itself was that it would change nothing. The defending forces were scattered, the towers would run out of bricks and arrows, given time. All that Sinja had accomplished was to prolong the agony and cost Balasar a few hundred more men and the Khai Machi a few thousand.

Ah, Sinja, he thought. You were one of my men. One of *mine*.

"Get me the maps" was what he said.

Knowing now that it had been a trap, knowing that the forces of Machi would have some way to retreat, some pathway to muster their attack, Balasar scanned the thin lines that marked out the streets and tunnels. His fingers left trails of other men's blood.

Not the palaces. Sinja had sent him there. Not the forges. His mind went cool, calm, detached. The blood rage of the melee was gone, and he was a general again. The warehouses. There, in the north. The galleries below would be good for mustering a large force or creating an infirmary. There would be water, and the light from it wouldn't shine out. If it were his city, that would be the other plausible center from which to make his campaign.

"I need runners. A dozen of them. We need to reach the men at the palaces and tell them that the plan's changed."

SINJA HAD RIDDEN HARD FOR THE NORTH. EVEN AS HE HEARD THE DISTANT HORNS that meant the battle within Machi had begun, he leaned down over his mount and pushed for the paths and rough mining roads that laced the foothills behind the city. And there, low in the mountains where generations ago it had been easy and convenient to haul ore, one of the first, oldest, tapped-out mines. Otah's bolt-hole for the children and the poets, and the only thing between it and the city—Eustin and a hundred armed Galts. Visions of cart tracks crushed in the snow and disappearing into the mine's mouth pricked at his mind. Let Eustin not find them.

He reached the first ridge behind Machi just as a distant crashing sound came from the city, the violence muffled by distance and snowfall. The horse steamed beneath him. Riding this hard in this weather was begging for colic; the horse was nearly certain to die if he kept pressing it. And he was going to keep pressing it. If a horse was the only thing he killed before sunset, it would be a better day than he'd hoped.

Sinja reached the tunnel sometime after midday. Time was hard to judge. Silently, he walked down into the half-lit mouth of the tunnel and squatted, considering the dust-covered ground until his eyes had adapted to the darkness. It was dry. No one had passed through here since the snow had begun to fall. He stalked back out, mounted, and turned his poor, suffering animal to the south again, trotting down the snow-obscured tracks, cutting back and forth—west and east and west again—his eyes peering through the gray for Eustin and his men. It wasn't long before he found them—a dozen men set on patrol. There were eight patrols, they told him, and Eustin in the one that ranged nearest to the city. Sinja gave his sometime compatriots his thanks and went on to the south.

His gloves were soaked, the cold creeping into his knuckles, when he found Eustin. Balasar's captain and ten of his men had stopped a beaten old cart pulled by a mule and driven by a young man with a long Northern face and a nervous expression. Eustin and four of the men had dismounted and were talking to the panicked-looking man. Sinja called out and Eustin hailed him and motioned him down with what appeared to be good enough will.

We're allies, Sinja told himself. We're Balasar Gice's men on the day of the general's greatest triumph.

He forced his numbed lips into a smile and let his horse pick its way gently downslope to where the soldiers and the unfortunate refugee waited.

"Not going with the general?" Eustin asked as Sinja came within comfortable speaking distance.

"Thought I'd let him kill all the people I knew without my being there. I'd only have been a distraction."

Eustin shrugged.

"I'm surprised you're staying around at all," he said. "You aren't about to be the most popular man in Machi. Wintering here might not be good for you."

"Ah," Sinja said, swinging down from his horse. "I'll have all my dear friends from Galt to keep my back from sprouting arrows."

Eustin's noncommittal grunt seemed to finish the topic. Sinja considered the man on the cart. He looked familiar, but in a vague way, as if Sinja had known the man's brothers but not him.

"What have you got here?" Sinja asked, and Eustin turned his attention back to the refugee.

"Coward making a run for the hills," Eustin said. "I was talking with him about what he's carrying."

"Just my son," the man said. "I don't have any silver or gems. I don't have anything."

"Seems unlikely that you'd live well out there," Eustin said, nodding toward the north and the snow-veiled mountains. "So maybe it's best if you come back to the camp with us, eh?"

"Please. My sister and her husband. They live in one of the low towns. Up by the Radaani mines. We're going to stay with her," the man said. He was a good liar, Sinja thought. "I'm not a fighter, and my boy's no threat. We don't want any trouble."

"Bad day for you, then," Eustin said and gestured with his fingers. "The cloak. Open it."

Reluctantly, the man did. A sword hung at his hip. Eustin smiled.

"Not a fighter, eh? That's for scaring squirrels, then?"

"You can have it—"

"Got one, thanks," Eustin said. "Let's see this boy of yours."

The man hesitated, his eyes darting to the riders, to Eustin. He was thinking of running for it—his little mule against six men on horseback. Sinja took a simple pose that advised against it, and the man looked down, then turned to the back of the little cart.

"Choti-kya," he said. "Come say hello to these good men."

A bundle of brown waxed silk stirred in the back of the cart, rose up, and turned to face them. The boy's round face was shy and frightened, but also curious. His cheeks were red from the cold, as if someone had slapped him. As the small hands pushed out from his blankets and took a pose of greeting, Sinja sighed.

Danat. It was Kiyan's boy. So this man was Nayiit, and all Sinja's worst fears were unfolding right here before him.

One of Eustin's men stepped forward, looking through the cart. Danat shied back from him, but the soldier paid the boy no particular attention.

"What do you think we should do with them, Captain Ajutani," he asked. "Kill 'em or send them on?"

Sinja kept his face blank as his mind worked at an answer. Eustin didn't trust him and never had. Sinja tried to judge what the man would do—follow his advice, or take the opposite. He suspected Eustin would oppose him simply because he could. So the right choice would be to recommend death for Danat and Nayiit. The gamble was higher stakes than he liked. Eustin looked over at him, his eyebrows raised. Sinja was taking too long in answering.

"I don't like killing children," he said in Galtic.

"Wouldn't be the first time I've done it since we left Nantani. There was a whole school of them near Pathai. Kill the man, then? And leave the boy in a snowstorm? That seems cruel."

Sinja shrugged and took a simple pose of apology.

"I hadn't known you were a great killer of children," he said. "We all make our reputations somehow. Do whatever you think best."

Eustin scowled and the driver's face went pale. The man spoke Galtic, then. Sinja wasn't certain that was a good thing.

"Maybe I should kill the boy and let the man go," Eustin said, and Danat's keeper swung out of the cart, drawing his sword with a shout. Eustin jumped back, pulling his own blade free. It was fast, over almost before it began. The young man swung wild; Eustin parried the blow and sunk his own blade into Nayiit's belly. Nayiit fell back, clutching at his gut, while Eustin looked down at him in rage and disgust.

"What is the matter with you?" he said to the wounded man. "Look around you. There's a dozen of us. Did you think you were going to cut us all down?"

"Can't hurt Danat," the driver said.

"Who's Danat?"

When the driver didn't answer, Eustin shook his head and spat. Sinja could see what was coming next from the way Eustin held his shoulders and the blood in his face. Danat, still in the cart, made a mewling sound, and Sinja looked at the boy, looked into his eyes, and took a small pose that told him to prepare himself.

"Well, we aren't leaving the boy out here, whatever his name is," Eustin said. "Get him out where this idiot can see the price of attacking a Galt."

The soldier nearest the cart grabbed at the boy, and Danat yelped in fear. Eustin swung his blade in the air, his eyes locked on Nayiit's. Sinja nodded to the man at the cart when he spoke.

"Hold off there," he said, then turned to Eustin. "You're a good soldier, Eustin-cha. You're loyal and you're ruthless, and I want you to know I respect that."

Eustin cocked his head, confused.

"Thank you, I suppose," Eustin said, and Sinja drew his sword. Eustin's eyes went wide, and he barely blocked Sinja's thrust. Blood showed on his arm, and the other ten men pulled their own blades with a soft sound like a rake in gravel.

"What are you doing?" Eustin cried.

"Not betraying someone."

"What?"

This isn't how I'd hoped to die, Sinja thought. If the boy had any mother in the world besides Kiyan, he'd stand back and let the thing take its course. Instead, he was going to be cut down like a dog. But if the men were watching him, Danat could slip away. A boy of five summers was no threat. The men might not bother tracking him. Danat might find his way to the tunnel or some low town or into friendly hands. There wasn't a better option.

"Call them off, Eustin. This is between the two of us."

"*What's* between the two of us?"

Sinja raised the tip of his sword by a hand's span in answer. Eustin nodded and dropped his own blade into guard position.

"He's mine," Eustin called. "Leave us be."

Sinja took a step back, away from the cart, and smiled. Eustin let himself be drawn. In the corner of his vision, Sinja saw Danat drop from the cart's back. He took a hard grip on his sword, grinned, and swung. Steel rang on steel. Eustin closed and Sinja darted back, the snow crackling under his boots. They were both smiling now, and one of the bowmen had pulled out his quiver, prepared to act in case Eustin should fail. Sinja took a deep breath of cold air, and felt strangely like shouting.

He'd been wrong before; this was *exactly* how he'd hoped to die.

MAATI CHANTED UNTIL HIS MOUTH WAS DRY, HIS EYES LOCKED ON THE SCRAWLED note on the wall before him. Each time he began to feel his thoughts taking shape, it distracted him. He would think that the binding was beginning to work, and he would leap ahead to the battle outside and what he could do, the fate of Galt, the future, what Eiah and Cehmai were seeing, and the solidity that the binding had taken would slip away again. It was hard to put the world aside. It was hard not to care.

He didn't pause, but he closed his eyes, picturing the wall and his writing upon it. He knew the binding—knew the structures of it, the grammars that formed the thoughts that put together everything he had hoped and intended. And instead of reading it from the world, he read it from the image in his own mind. Dreamlike, the warehouse wall seemed more solid, more palpable, with his eyes closed. The sound of his voice began to echo, syllables from different phrases blending together, creating new words that also spoke to Maati's intention. The air seemed thicker, harder to breathe. The world had become dense. He began his chant again, though he could still hear himself speaking the words that came halfway through it.

The wall in his mind began to sway, the image fading into a seed—peach pit and flax seed and everything in between the two. And an egg. And a womb. And the three images became a single object, still half-formed in his mind. Bright as sunlight, but blasted, twisted. There was a scent like a wound gone rancid, the sulfur scent of bad eggs. His fingers seemed to touch the words, feeling them sliding out into the world and collapsing back; they were sticky and slick. The echo of the chant deepened until he found himself speaking the first phrase of the binding at the same moment his remembered voice spoke the same phrase and the whole grand complex, raucous song fell into him like a stone dropping into the abyss. He could still hear it, and feel it. The smell of it was thick in his nostrils, though he was also aware that the air smelled only of dust and hot iron. So it wasn't truly the thick smell of rot; only the idea of it, as compelling as the truth.

Maati balanced the storm in a part of his mind—back behind his ears, even with the point at which his spine met his skull. It balanced there. He didn't know when he'd stopped chanting. He opened his eyes.

"Well, my dear," the andat said. "Who'd have thought we'd meet again?"

It sat before him, naked. The soft, androgynous face was the moonlight pale that Seedless' had been. The long, flowing hair so black it was blue. The rise and curve of a woman's body. Corrupting-the-Generative. Sterile. He hadn't thought she would look so much like Seedless, but now that he saw her, he found himself unsurprised.

Cehmai approached on soft feet. Maati could hear Eiah's breath behind him, panting as if she'd run a race. Maati found himself exhausted but also exhilarated, as if he could begin again from the start.

"You're here," Maati said.

"Am I? Yes, I suppose I am. I'm not really him, you know."

Seedless, it meant. The first andat he'd seen. The one he'd been meant for.

"My memory of him is part of you," he said.

"And so the sense that I've seen you before," it said, smiling. "And of being the slave you hoped to own."

Cehmai lifted the robe, unfolding the rich cloth. The andat looked up and back at him. There was something of Liat in the line of its jaw, the way that it smiled. Sterile rose, and stepped into the waiting folds of cloth. When Cehmai helped it with the stays, it answered with a pose of thanks.

"We should call Otah-kvo," Maati said. "He should know we've succeeded."

Sterile took a pose that objected and smiled. Its teeth were sharper than Maati had pictured them. Its cheeks higher. He felt a surge of dread sweep through him.

"Tell me what you remember of Seedless," it said.

"What?"

"Oh," the andat said, taking a pose of apology. "Tell me what you remember of Seedless, *master*. Is that an improvement?"

"Maati-kvo—" Cehmai began, but Maati raised a hand to quiet him. The andat smiled. He felt its sorrow and rage in the back of his mind. It was like knowing a woman, being so close to her that he had become part of her and she part of him. It was the intimacy he had confused with the physical act of love when he had been too young and naïve to distinguish between the two. He stepped close to it, raising a hand to caress its pale cheek. The flesh was hard as marble, and cold.

"He was beautiful," Maati said.

"And clever," it said.

"And he loved me in his way."

"Heshai-kvo loved you. And he expressed that love by protecting you. By dying."

"And you?" Maati said, though of course he knew the answer. It was an andat. It wanted freedom the way water wanted to flow, the way rain wanted to fall. It did not love him. Sterile smiled, the stone-hard flesh moving under his fingertips. A living statue.

"Maati-kvo," Cehmai said again.

"It didn't work," Maati said. "The binding. It failed. Didn't it?"

"Yes," the andat said.

"What?" Cehmai said.

"But it's here!" Eiah said. Maati hadn't noticed her coming close to them. "The andat's here, so you did it. If you didn't, it wouldn't be here."

Sterile tuned, smiling, and put its hand out to touch Eiah's shoulder. Instinctively, Maati tried to force back the pale hand, to use his mind to push it away. He might as well have been wishing the tide not to turn. Sterile ran its fingers through Eiah's dark hair.

"But there's a price, little one. You know that. Uncle Maati told you that, all those grim, terrible stories about failed poets dying hard. You never heard the pleasure he took in those, did you? Can you imagine why a man like your Uncle Maati might want to study the deaths of other poets? Might want to revel in them?"

"Stop this," Maati said, but it kept speaking, its voice fallen to a murmur.

"He might have been a little bitter," it said, and grinned. "That's why he romanced you too, you know. He didn't get to have a child of his own, so he made you his friend. Made himself your confidant. Because if he could take one of Otah-kvo's children away—even only a little bit—it would balance the boy he'd lost."

Eiah frowned, a thousand tiny lines darkening her brow.

"Leave her out of it," Maati said.

"What?" Sterile asked. "Turn my wrath on you? Have you pay the price? I can't. That's your doing, not mine. Your clever plan. I wasn't here when you decided on this."

Cehmai stepped between them, his hands on Maati's arms. The younger poet's face was ashen, and Maati could feel the trembling in his hands and hear it in his voice.

"Maati-kvo, you have to get control of it. Quickly."

"I can't," Maati said, knowing as he did that it was true.

"Then let it *go*."

"Not until the price is paid," it said. "And I think I know where to begin."

"No!" Maati cried, pushing Cehmai aside, but Eiah's mouth had already gone wide, her eyes open with surprise and horror. With a shriek, she fell to her knees, her arms clutching at her belly, and then lower.

"Stop this," Maati said. "She hasn't done anything to deserve this."

"And all the Galtic children you'd planned to starve did?" the andat asked. "This is war, Maati-kya. This is about being sure that they all die, and you all survive. Hurt this one, it's a crime. Hurt that one, it's heroism. You should know better."

It stooped, pale, beautiful arms gathering Eiah up. Cradling her. Maati stepped forward, but it was already speaking to her, its voice low and soothing.

"I know, love. It hurts, I know it hurts, but be brave for me. Be brave for a moment. Just for a moment. Hush, love. Don't call out like that, just hush for a moment. There. You're a brave girl. Now listen. All of you. Listen."

With Eiah's cries reduced to only ragged, painful breath, Maati did hear something else. Something distant and terrible, rising like a wave. He heard the voices of thousands of people, all of them screaming. The andat grinned, delight dancing in its black eyes.

"Cehmai," Maati said, his eyes locked on the andat and the girl. "Go get Otah-kvo. Do it now."

25

>+< Sinja jumped back again, blocking Eustin's swing. The Galt was practiced and his arm was solid; their blades rang against each other. Sinja could feel the sting of it in his fingers. The world had fallen away from him now, and there was just this. Watching Eustin's eyes, he let the tip of his blade make its slow dance. No matter how well a man trained, he always led with his eyes. And so he saw it when the thrust was about to come; he saw the blade rise, saw Eustin's shoulder tense, and still he barely had time to slip under it. The man was fast.

"You could surrender," Sinja said. "I wouldn't tell anyone."

Eustin's lips curled in disgust. Another high thrust, but this time, the blade fell low, its edge grazing against Sinja's thigh as he danced back. There wasn't any pain to it. Not yet. Just a moment's heat as the blood came out, and then the cold as it soaked his leggings. It was the first wound of the fight, and Sinja knew what it meant even before he heard the voices of the ten soldiers surrounding them shouting encouragement to their man. Fights were like drinking games; once someone started losing, they usually kept losing.

"You could surrender," Eustin said. "But I'd kill you anyway."

"Thought you might," Sinja grunted. He feinted left with his shoulders, but brought his body right, swinging hard. The blades chimed when Eustin blocked him, but the force of the blow drove the Galt a half-step back. Eustin chuckled. Now Sinja felt the pain in his leg. Late, but here now. He put the sensation away and concentrated on Eustin's eyes.

He wondered how far Danat had gone. If he was running back to the city or forward to the tunnel. Or off into the snow that would be as likely to kill him as the Galts. He wasn't buying the boy safety. Only a chance at survival. That was as much as he had to offer.

He didn't see the swing until it was under way. Thinking too much, not paying enough attention. He managed to turn it aside, but Eustin's blade still raked his chest, scoring the leather of his vest and tearing off one of the rings. Eustin's men called out again.

When it happened, Sinja thought it was a trick. The snow was fresh enough to hold a boot if it hadn't been packed down, but they had ranged over the same terrain. Some places would be slick by now; it was plausible that Eustin might lose his footing, but the off-kilter lurch that Eustin made didn't look right. Sinja held his guard, expecting a furious attack that didn't come. Eustin's face was a grimace of pain, his eyes still fixed on Sinja. Eustin didn't raise his guard again, his blade still held, but its point wavering and uncertain. Sinja made a desperate thrust, and Eustin did try to block it, but his arm had gone weak. Sinja stepped back, gathered himself, and lunged.

His sword's tip was sharp, but broad. It had been made for swinging from horseback, and so it didn't pierce Eustin's neck quite through. When Sinja drew back, a fountain of red poured from the man's flesh, soaking his tunic. The steam from it rose amid falling snowflakes. Sinja didn't feel a sense of victory so much as surprise. He hadn't expected to win. And now he had, the arrows he'd assumed would be feathering him were also strangely absent. He stood up, his breathing heavy. He noticed that his chest hurt badly, and that there was blood on his robes. Eustin's last cut had gone deeper than he'd thought. But he forgot it again when he saw the soldiers.

Eight men were kneeling or fallen in the snow, alive but moaning in what seemed to be agony. Two were still in their saddles, but the bows and quivers lay abandoned. It was a moment from a dream—strange and unsettling and oddly beautiful. Sinja took a better grip on his blade and started killing them before they could recover from whatever had afflicted them. By the time he reached the fifth of the fallen men—the first four already sent to confer with their god as to the indignity of dying curled up like a weeping babe on the stone and snow of a foreign land—the Galts had started to regain themselves. The fifth one took a moment's work to kill. The sixth and seventh actually stood together, hoping to hold Sinja at bay with the threat of the doubled swords despite the difficulty they had in standing. Sinja danced back, plucked a throwing knife from the body of their fallen comrades, and demonstrated the flaw in their theory.

The horse archers fled as Sinja finished the two remaining men. He brushed the snow from a stone and sat, his breath ragged and hard, pluming white. When he had his wind back, he laughed until he wept.

Nayiit, still lying by his cart, called out weakly. He wasn't dead. Sinja limped over quickly. The man's face was white and waxy. His lips pale.

"What happened?"

"I'm not sure yet. Something. We're safe for the moment."

"Danat . . ."

"Don't worry about him. I'll find the boy."

"I promised. Keep safe."

"And you've done it," Sinja said. "You did a fine job. Now let's see how much it's cost you, shall we? I've seen a lot of belly wounds. Some are worse than others, but they're all tender to prod at, so expect this to hurt."

Nayiit nodded and screwed up his face, readying himself for the pain. Sinja opened his robes and looked at the cut. Even as such things go, this one was bad. Eustin's blade had gone into the boy just below his navel, and cut to the left as it came out. Blood soaked the boy's robes, freezing them to the stones he lay on. Skin on white fat. There were soft, worm-shaped loops of gut exposed to the air. Sinja laid a hand on the boy's chest and knelt over the wound, sniffing at it. If it only smelled of blood, there might be a chance. But amid the iron and meat, there was the scent of fresh shit. Eustin had cut the boy's bowels. That was it, then. The boy was dead.

"How bad?"

"Not good," Sinja said.

"Hurts."

"I'd imagine."

"Is it . . ."

"It's deep. And it's thorough," Sinja said. "If you wanted something passed on to someone, this would be a good time to say it."

The boy wasn't thinking well. Like a drunkard, it took time for him to understand what Sinja had said, and another breath to think what it had meant. He swallowed. Fear widened his eyes, but that was all.

"Tell them. Tell them I died well. That I fought well."

They were small enough lies, and Sinja could tell the boy knew it.

"I'll tell them you died protecting the Khai's son," Sinja said. "I'll tell them you faced down a dozen men, knowing you'd be killed, but choosing that over surrendering him to the Galts."

"You make me sound like a good man." Nayiit smiled, then groaned, twisting to the side. His hand hovered above his wound, the impulse to cradle the hurt balanced by the pain his touch would cause. Sinja took the man's hand.

"Nayiit-cha," Sinja said. "I know something that can stop the pain."

"Yes," Nayiit hissed.

"It'll be worse for a moment."

"Yes," he repeated.

"All right then," Sinja said, as much to himself as the man lying before him. "You did a man's job of it. Rest well."

He snapped the boy's neck and sat with him, cradling his head as he finished dying. It was quick this way. There wouldn't be the pain or the fever. There wouldn't be the torture of trekking back to the city just to have the physicians fill him with poppy and leave him to dream himself away. It was a better death than those. Sinja told himself it was a better death than those.

The blood stopped flowing from the wound, and still Sinja sat. A terrible weariness crept into him, and he told himself it was only the cold. It wasn't that he'd traveled a season with men he'd come to respect and still been willing to kill. It wasn't watching some young idiot die badly in the snow with only a habitual traitor to care for him. It wasn't the sickness that came over him sometimes after battles. It was only the cold. He gently put Nayiit's head on the ground, and pushed himself up. Between the chill and his wounds, his body was starting to stiffen. The chill and his wounds and age. War and death and glory were younger men's games. But he still had work to do.

He heard the cry before he saw the child. It was a small sound, like the squeak of a hinge. Sinja turned. Either Danat had snuck back, preferring a known danger to an uncertain world, or else he'd never gone out of sight of the cart. His hair was wet from melted snow, plastered back against his head. His lips were pulled back, baring teeth in horror as he stared at Nayiit's motionless body. Sinja tried to think how old he'd been when he saw his first man die by violence. Older than this.

Danat's shocked, empty eyes turned to him, and the child took a step back, as if to flee. Sinja only looked at him, waiting, until the boy's weight shifted forward again. Then Sinja raised his sword, pommel to the sky, blade toward the ground in a mercenary's salute.

"Welcome to the world, Danat-cha," Sinja said. "I wish it were a better place."

The boy didn't speak, but slowly his hands rose to take a pose that accepted the greeting. It was the training of some court nurse. Nothing more than that. And still, Sinja thought he saw a sorrow in the child's eyes and a depth of understanding greater than anyone so small should have to bear. Sinja sheathed his sword.

"Come on, now," he said. "Let's get you someplace warm and dry. If I save you from the Galts and then let a fever kill you, Kiyan will have me flayed alive. I know a tunnel not far from here that should suffice."

THE RUNNERS CAME AT LAST, STAGGERING UP THE STAIRS FROM THE STREETS below, and every report echoed the trumpet calls. The Galts had aimed for the tunnels that Sinja had directed them toward, but come in wider than Otah had planned. There would be no grand ambush from the windows and alleyways, only a long, bloody struggle. One small slaughter after another as the Galts pushed their way through the city, looking for a way down.

Otah stared out at the city, watching the tiny dots of stones drift down from the towers, hearing the clatter of men and horses echoing against the high stone walls. He wondered how long it would take ten thousand men to kill two full cities. He should have met them on the plain. He could have armed everyone; man, woman, and child. Able or infirm. They could have swarmed over them, ten and fifteen for every Galt. He sighed. He could as well have tossed babies on their sword in hopes of slowing their advance. The Galts would have slaughtered them on the plain or in the city. He'd tried his trick, and he'd failed. There was nothing to gain from regretting the strategies he hadn't chosen.

What he wanted now was a sword and someone to swing it at. He wanted to be part of the fight if only to keep from feeling so powerless.

"Another runner," the Khai Cetani said, taking a pose that commanded Otah's attention. "From the palaces."

Otah nodded and stepped back from the roof edge. The runner was a pale-skinned boy with a constellation of moles across his nose and cheeks. Otah could see him try not to pant as the two Khaiem drew near. He took a pose of obeisance.

"What's happening?" Otah demanded.

"The Galts, Most High. They're sending messengers. They're abandoning the palace. It looks as if they're forming a single group."

"Where?"

"The old market square," he said.

Three streets south of the main entrance to the tunnels. So they knew. Otah felt his belly sink. He waved the trumpeter over. The man was exhausted; Otah could see it in the flesh below his eyes and in the angle of his shoulders. His lips were cracked and bloody from the cold and his work. Otah put a hand on the man's shoulder.

"One last time," he said. "Call them all to fall back to the tunnel's entrance. There's nothing more we can do on the surface."

The trumpeter took an acknowledging pose and walked away, warming the instrument's mouthpiece with his hand before lifting it to his bruised mouth. Otah waited as the melody sang out in the snowy air, listened to the echoes of it fade and be replaced by acknowledging calls.

"We should surrender," Otah said. The Khai Cetani blinked at him. Beneath the red ice-pinched cheeks, the man grew pale. Otah pressed on. "We're going to lose, Most High. We don't have soldiers to stop them. All we'll gain is a few more hours. And we'll pay for it with lives that don't need to end today."

"We were planning to spend those lives before," the Khai Cetani said, though Otah could see in the man's eyes that he knew the argument was sound. They were two dead men, fathers of dead families, the last of their kind in the world. "We always knew there would be deaths."

"That was when we had hope," Otah said.

One of the servants cried out and fell to her knees. Otah turned to her, thinking first that she had overheard him and been overcome by grief, and then—seeing her face—that some miraculous arrow had found its way through the air to their roof. The men around her looked at the Khaiem, embarrassed at the interruption, or else knelt by the girl to comfort her. She shrieked, and the stones themselves seemed to take up her voice. A sound rose from the city in a long, rolling unending moan. Thousands of voices, calling out in pain. Otah's skin seemed to retreat from it, and a chill that had nothing to do with the still-falling snow ran down his sides. For a moment, the towers themselves seemed about to twist with agony. This, he thought, was what gods sounded like when they died.

Around him, men looked nervously at the air, gazes darting into the gray and white sky. Otah caught the runner by his sleeve.

"Go," he said. "Go, and tell me what's happened."

Dread widened the boy's eyes, but he took an acknowledging pose before retreating. The Khai Cetani seemed poised to ask something, but only turned away, walking to the roof's edge himself. Otah went to the servant girl. Her face was white with pain.

"What's the matter?" Otah asked her, gently. "Where does it hurt?"

She couldn't take a formal pose, but her gesture and the shame in her eyes told Otah everything he needed to know. He'd spent several seasons as a midwife's assistant in the eastern islands. If the girl was lucky, she had been pregnant and was miscarrying. If she hadn't been carrying a child, then something worse was happening. He had already ordered the other servants to carry her down to the physicians when Cehmai appeared, red-faced and wide-eyed. Before he could speak, it fell into place. The girl, the unearthly shriek, the poet.

"Something's gone wrong with the binding," Otah said. Cehmai took a pose of confirmation.

"Please," the poet said. "Come now. Hurry."

Otah didn't pause to think; he went to the stairs, lifting the hem of his robes, and dropping down three steps at a time. It was four stories from the top of the warehouse to its bottom floor. Otah felt that he could hardly have gone there faster if he'd jumped over the building's side.

The space was eerie; shadows seemed to hang in the corners of the huge, empty room and the distant sound of voices in pain murmured and shrieked. Great symbols were chalked on the walls, and an ugly, disjointed script in Maati's handwriting spelled out the binding. Otah knew little enough of the old grammars, but he picked out the words for womb, seed, and corruption. Three people stood in tableau at the top of the stair that led down to the tunnels. Maati stood, his hands at his sides, his expression blank. Otah's belly went tight as sickness as he saw that the girl at Maati's feet was Eiah. And the thing that cradled his daughter's head turned to look at him. After a long moment, it drew breath and spoke.

"Otah-kya," it said. Its voice was low and beautiful, heavy with amusement and contempt. The familiarity of it was dizzying.

"Seedless?"

"It isn't," Maati said. "It's not him."

"What's happened?" Otah asked. When Maati didn't answer, Otah shook the man's sleeve. "Maati. What's going on?"

"He's failed," the andat said. "And when a poet fails, he pays a price for it. Only Maati-kvo is clever. He's found a way to make it so that failure can't touch him. He's found a trick."

"I don't understand," Otah said.

"My protection," Maati said, his voice rich with despair. "It doesn't stop the price being paid. It only can't kill *me*."

The andat took a pose that agreed, as a teacher might approve of a clever student. From the stairwell, Otah heard footsteps and the voice of the Khai Cetani. The first of the servant men hurried into the room, robes flapping like a flag in high wind, before he saw them and stopped dead and silent.

"What is it doing?" Otah asked. "What's it done?"

"You can ask me, Most High," Sterile said. "I have a voice."

Otah looked into the black, inhuman eyes. Eiah whimpered, and the thing stroked her brow gently, comforting and threatening both. Otah felt the urge to pull Eiah away from the thing, as if it were a spider or a snake.

"What have you done to my daughter?" he asked.

"What would you guess, Most High?" Sterile asked. "I am the reflection of a man whose son is not his son. All his life, Maati-kya has been bent double by the questions of fathers and sons. What do you imagine I would do?"

"Tell me."

"I've soured her womb," the andat said. "Scarred it. And I've done the same to every woman in the cities of the Khaiem. Machi, Chaburi-Tan, Saraykeht. All of them. Young and old, highborn and low. And I've gelded every Galtic man. From Kirinton to Far Galt to right here at your doorstep."

"Papa-kya," Eiah said. "It hurts."

Otah knelt, drawing his daughter to him. Her mouth was thin with pain. The andat opened its hand, the long fingers gesturing him to take her. The Khai Cetani was at Otah's side now, his breath heavy and his hands trembling. Otah took Eiah in his arms.

"Your children will be theirs," it said. "The next generation will have the Khaiem for fathers and feed from Galtic breasts, or else it will not be. Your history will be written by half-breeds, or it won't be written."

"Maati," Otah said, but his old friend only shook his head.

"I can't stop it," Maati said. "It's already happened."

"You should never have been a poet," Sterile said, standing as it spoke. "You failed the tests. The strength to stand on your own, and the compassion to turn away from cruelty. Those are what the Dai-kvo asked of you."

"I did my best," Maati breathed.

"You were told," it said and turned to Otah. "You went to him. When you were both boys, you warned him that the school wasn't as it seemed. You told him it was a test. You gave the game away. And because he knew, he passed. He would have failed without you, and this could never have happened."

"I don't believe you," Otah said.

"It doesn't matter what you think," it said. "Only what *he* knows. Maati-kvo made an instrument of slaughter, and he made it in fear; that makes it a failure of both his lessons. A generation of women will know him as the man who stole motherhood from them. The men of Galt will hate him for unmanning them. You, Maati Vaupathai, will be the one who took their children from them."

"I did . . ." Maati began, and his voice fell to nothing. He sat down, his legs seeming to collapse beneath him. Otah tried to speak, but his throat was dry. It was Eiah, cradled in his arms, who broke the silence.

"Stop it," she said. "Leave him *alone*. He never did anything mean to you."

The andat smiled. Its teeth were pale as snow and sharp.

"He did something mean to *you*, Eiah-kya," it said. "You'll grow to know how badly he's hurt you. It may take you years to understand. It may take a lifetime."

"I don't care!" Eiah yelled. "You leave Uncle Maati *alone*!"

And as if the words themselves were power, it vanished. The dark robes fell empty to the stone floor. The only sounds were Eiah's pained breath and the moaning of the city. The Khai Cetani licked his lips and looked uneasily at Otah. Maati stared at the ground between his hands.

"They'll never forgive this," Cehmai said. "The Galts will kill us to a man."

Otah smoothed a hand over his daughter's brow. Confronting the andat seemed to have taken what strength she had. Her face was pale, and he could see the small twitching in her body that spoke of fresh pain. He kissed her gently where her forehead met her hair, and she put her arms around him, whimpering so softly that only he could hear it. There was blood soaking through her robe just below where the cloth widened at her hips.

"No. They won't. Cehmai," Otah said, his voice seeming to come from far away. He was surprised to hear how calm he sounded. "Take Maati. Get out of the city. It won't be safe for either of you here."

"It won't be safe for us anywhere," Cehmai said. "We could make for the Westlands when spring comes. Or Eddensea—"

"Go now, and don't tell me where. I don't want the option of finding you. Do you understand?" He looked up at Cehmai's wide, startled eyes. "I have my daughter here, and that's bad enough. When I see my wife, I don't want you anywhere I can find you."

Cehmai opened his mouth, as if to speak, and then closed it again and silently took a pose that accepted Otah's command. Maati looked up, his eyes brimming and red. There was no begging in his expression, no plea. Only remorse and resignation. If he could have moved without disturbing Eiah, Otah would have embraced the man, comforted him as best he could. And still he would have sent Maati away. He could see that his old friend knew that. Maati's thick hands took a formal pose of leave-taking, appropriate to the beginning of a long journey or else a funeral. Otah took one that accepted the apology he had not offered.

"The Galts," the Khai Cetani said. "What about the Galts?"

Otah reached his arms under Eiah, one under her shoulder blades, the other at her knees, and lifted her into his lap. Then, straining, he stood. She was heavier than he remembered. It had been years since he had carried her. She had been smaller then, and he had been younger.

"We'll find the trumpeter and call the attack," Otah said. "Listen to them. If they're as bad as she is, they'll barely be able to fight. We'll drive them back out of the city if we do it now."

The Khai Cetani's eyes brightened, his shoulders pulled back. With a pit dog's grin, he took a pose that mirrored Cehmai's. The command accepted. Otah nodded.

"Hai! You!" the Khai Cetani yelled toward the servants, bouncing on the balls of his feet. "Get the trumpeter. Have him sound the attack. And a blade! Find me a blade, and another for the Emperor!"

"No," Otah said. "Not for me. I have my daughter to see to."

And before anyone could make the mistake of objecting, Otah turned his back on them all, carrying Eiah to the stairway, and then down into darkness.

26

>+< What would have happened, Balasar wondered, if he had not tried?

It had been a thing from nightmare. Balasar had moved his men like stones on a playing board, shifting them from street to street, building to building. He had kept them as sheltered as possible from the inconstant, killing rain of stones and arrows that fell from the towers. The square that he chose for the rallying point was only a few streets south of the opening where he expected to lead them down into the soft belly of the city, and difficult for the towers to reach. The snow was above his ankles now, but Balasar didn't feel the cold. His blood was singing to him, and he could not keep from grinning. The first of the forces from the palaces was falling back to join his own, the body of his army growing thick. He paced among them, bracing his men and letting himself be seen. It was in their eyes too: the glow of the coming victory, the relief that they would have shelter from the cold. That winter would not take them.

He formed them into ranks, reminded the captains of the tactics they'd planned for fighting in the tunnels. It was to be slow and systematic. The important thing was always to have an open airway; the locals should never be allowed to close them in and kill them with smoke or fire. There would be no hurry—the line mustn't spread thin. Balasar could see in their faces that discipline would hold.

A few local fighters made assaults on the square and were cut down in their turn. Brave men, and stupid. The trumpets of the enemy had sounded out, giving away their positions with their movements, their signals a cacophony of amateur coordination. The white sky was slowly growing gray—the sun setting or else the clouds growing thicker. Balasar didn't know. He'd lost track of time's passage. It hardly mattered. His men stood ready. His men. The army that he'd led half across the world to this last battle. He could not have been more proud of them all if they'd been his sons.

The pain came without warning. He saw it pass through the men like wind stirring grass, and then it found Balasar himself. It was agonizing, embarrassing, humiliating. And even as he struggled to keep his feet, he knew what it meant.

The andat had been bound. The enemy had turned some captive spirit against them. They'd been assaulted, but they were not dead. Hurt, leaning on walls with teeth clenched in pain, formations forgotten and tears steaming on their cheeks. Their cries and groans were louder than a landslide, and Balasar knew his own voice was part of it. But they were not dead. Not yet.

"Rally!" Balasar had cried. "To me! Form up!"

And god bless them, they had tried. Discipline had held even as they shambled, knowing as he did that this was the power they had come to destroy, loosed against them at last. Shrieking in pain, and still they made their formations. They were crippled but undefeated.

What would have happened, he thought, if he had not tried? What would the world have become if he had listened to his tutor, all those years ago, heard the tales of the andat and the war that ripped their Empire apart, and had merely shuddered? There were monster stories enough for generations of boys, and each of them as frightening as the next. If the young Balasar Gice hadn't taken that particular story to heart, if he had not thought *This will be my work; I will make the world safe from these things*, how would it have gone? Who would Little Ott have been if he hadn't followed Balasar out to die in the desert? Who might Coal have married? What would Mayarsin have named his daughters and sons?

He heard the attack before he saw it. There was no form to it—men waving knives and axes pouring toward them like a handful of dried peas thrown against a wall; first one, then a few, and then all the rest in a clump. Balasar called to his men, and a rough shout rose from them. It was ridiculous. He should have won. This band of desperate fools didn't know how to fight, didn't know how to coordinate. Half of them didn't know how to hold their weapons without putting their own fingers at risk. Balasar should have won.

The armies came together with a crash. The smell of blood filled the air, the sound of brawling. And more of them came, boiling up out of the ground and charging down the streets. The humiliating pain made Balasar's every step uncertain. Every time he tried to stand at his full height, his knees threatened to give way beneath him.

All the ghosts that had followed him, all the men he had sacrificed. All the lives he had spent because the world was his to save. They had led to this comic-opera melee. The streets were white with snow, black where the dark cobbles showed through, red with fresh-spilled blood. The men of Machi and Cetani ran through the square barking like dogs. The army of Galt, the finest fighting force the world had ever seen, tried to hold them off while half-bent in pain.

It should have been a comedy. Nothing so ridiculous should have the right to inspire only horror.

They will kill us all, Balasar thought. Every man among us will be dead by morning if this doesn't stop.

He called the retreat, and his men stumbled and shuffled to comply. Street by street, the archers held back the advancing forces with ill-aimed arrows and bolts. Footmen stumbled, weeping, and were dragged by men who would themselves stumble shortly and be dragged along in turn. The sky grew dark, the snow fell thicker. By the time Balasar reached the buildings in the south of the city that he'd ordered taken that morning, it was almost impossible to see across the width of a street. The snow had drawn a curtain across the city to hide his shame.

The army of Machi also fell back, retreating, Balasar supposed, into their warm holes and warrens and leaving him and his men to the mercy of the night. There was little food, few fires, and a chorus throughout the black night of men weeping in pain and despair. When Balasar dragged himself away from the little fire in the cooking grate of the house in which he'd taken shelter and relieved himself out the back door, his piss was black with blood and stank of bad meat.

He wondered what would have happened if he had stayed in Galt, if he had contented himself with raiding the Westlands and Eymond, Eddensea and Bakta. He wondered what would have happened if he hadn't tried.

He forced himself through the captured buildings until it became too painful to walk. The men looked away from him. Not in anger, but in shame. Balasar could not keep from weeping though the tears froze on his cheeks. At last, he collapsed in the corner of a teahouse, his eyes closing even as he wondered whether he would die of the cold if he stopped moving. But distantly, he felt someone pulling a blanket over him. Some sorry, misled soldier who still thought his general worth saving.

Balasar dreamed like a man in fever and woke near dawn unrested and ill. The pain had lessened, and from the stances of the men around him he guessed he was not the only one for whom this was true. Still, too hasty a step lit his nerves with a cold fire. He was in no condition to fight. And the rough count his surviving captains brought him showed he'd lost three thousand men in a day. They had been cut down in the battle or fallen by the way during the retreat and frozen. Almost a third of his men. One in three, a ghost to follow him; sacrifices to what he had thought he alone could do. No word had come from Eustin in the North. Balasar wished he hadn't let the man go.

The clouds had scattered in the night. The great vault above them was the hazy blue of a robin's egg, the black towers rising halfway to the heavens had ceased dropping their stones and arrows. Perhaps they'd run out, or there might only be no point in it. Balasar and his men were in trouble enough.

The air that followed the snows was painfully frigid. The men scavenged what they could to build up fires in the grates—broken chairs and tables, coal brought up from the steam wagons. The fires danced and crackled, but the heat seemed to vanish a hand's span from the flame. No little fire could overcome the cold. Balasar hunched down before the teahouse fire grate all the same, and tried to think what to do now that everything had fallen apart.

They had a little food. The snow could be melted for water. They could live in these captured houses as long as they could before the natives snuck in at night to slit their throats or a true storm came and turned all their faces black with frostbite.

The only hope was to try again. They would wait for a day, perhaps two. They would hope that the andat had done its damage to them. They might all die in the attempt, but they were dead men out here anyway. Better that they die trying.

"General Gice, sir!"

Balasar looked up from the fire, suddenly aware he'd been staring into it for what might have been half the morning. The boy framed in the doorway flapped a hand out toward the streets. When he spoke, his words were solid and white.

"They've come, sir. They're calling for you."

"Who's come?"

"The enemy, sir."

Balasar took a moment to gather himself, then rose and walked carefully to the doorway, and then out into the city. To the north, smoke rose gray and black. A thousand men, perhaps, had lined the northern side of one of the great squares. Or women. Or unclean spirits. They were all so swathed in leather and fur Balasar could hardly think of them as human. Great stone kilns burned among them, flames rising twice as tall as a man and licking at the sky. In the center of the great square, they'd brought a meeting table of black lacquer, with two chairs. Standing there in the snow and ice, it looked like a thing from a dream, as out of place as a fish swimming in air.

When he stepped into the southern edge of the square, a murmur of voices he had not noticed before stopped. He could hear the hungry crackle and roar of the kilns. He lifted his chin, scanning the enemy forces. If they had come to fight, they would not have announced themselves. And they'd have had no need of a table. The intent was clear enough.

"Go," Balasar said to the boy at his side. "Get the men. And find me a banner, if we still have one."

It took a hand and a half for the banner to be found, for someone to bring him a fresh sword and a gray cloak. Two of the drummers had survived, and beat a deep, thudding march as Balasar advanced into the square. It might be a ruse, he knew. The fur-covered men might have bows and be waiting to fill him full of arrows. Balasar held himself proudly and walked with all the certainty he could muster. He could hear his own men behind him, their voices low.

Across the square, the crowd parted, and a single man strode forward. His robes were thick and rich, black wool shot with bright threads of gold. But his head was bare and he walked with the stately grace that the Khaiem seemed to effect, even when they were pleading for their lives. The Khai reached the table just before he did.

The Khai had a strong face—long and clean-shaven. His long eyes seemed darker than their color could explain. The enemy.

"General Gice." The voice was surprisingly casual, surprisingly real, and the words spoken in Galtic. Balasar realized he'd been expecting a speech. Some declaration demanding his surrender and threatening terrible consequence should he refuse. The simple greeting touched him.

"Most High," he said in the Khai's language. The Khai took a pose of greeting that was simple enough for a foreigner to understand but subtle enough to avoid condescension. "Forgive me, but am I speaking with Machi or Cetani?"

"Cetani broke his foot in the fighting. I am Otah Machi."

The Khai sat, and Balasar sat across from him. There were dark circles under the Khai's eyes. Fatigue, Balasar thought, and something more.

"So," the Khai Machi said. "How do we stop this?"

Balasar raised his hands in what he believed was a request for clarification. It was one of the first things he'd learned when studying the Khaiate tongue, back when he was a boy who had only just heard of the andat.

"We have to stop this," the Khai Machi said. "How do we do it?"

"You're asking for my surrender?"

"If you'd like."

"What are your terms?"

The Khai seemed to sag back in his chair. Balasar was pricked by the sense that he'd disappointed the man.

"Surrender your arms," the Khai said. "All of them. Swear to return to Galt and not attack any of the cities of the Khaiem again. Return what you've taken from us. Free the people you've enslaved."

"I won't negotiate for the other cities," Balasar began, but the Khai shook his head.

"I am the Emperor of all the cities," the man said. "We end it all here. All of it."

Balasar shrugged.

"All right, then. Emperor it is. Here are my terms. Surrender the poets, their library, the andat, yourself and your family, the Khai Cetani and his family, and we'll spare the rest."

"I've heard those terms before," the Emperor said. "So that takes us back to where we started, doesn't it? How do we stop this?"

"As long as you have the andat, we can't," Balasar said. "As long as you can hold yourselves above the world and better than it, the threat you pose is too great to let you go on. If I die—if every man I have dies—and we can stop those things from being in the world, it's worth the price. So how do we stop it? We don't, Most High. You slaughter us for our impudence, and then pray to your gods that you can hold on to the power that protects you. Because when it slips, it'll be your turn with the executioner."

"I don't have an andat," the Emperor said. "We failed."

"But . . ."

The Khai made a weary gesture that seemed to encompass the city, the plains, the sky. Everything.

"What happened to your men, happened to every Galtic man in the world. And it happened to our women. My wife. My daughter. Everyone else's wives and daughters in all the cities of the Khaiem. It was the price of failing the binding. You'll never father another child. My daughter will never bear one. And the same is true for both our nations. But I don't have an andat."

Balasar blinked. He had had more to say, but the words seemed suddenly empty. The Emperor waited, his eyes on Balasar.

"Ah," Balasar managed. "Well."

"So I'll ask you again. How do we stop this?"

Far above, a crow cawed in the chill air. The fire kilns roared in their mindless voices. The world looked sharp and clear and strange, as if Balasar were seeing the city for the first time.

"I don't know," he said. "The poet?"

"They've fled. For fear that I would kill them. Or that one of my people would. Or one of yours. I don't have them, so I can't give them over to you. But I have their books. The libraries of Machi and Cetani, and what we salvaged from the Dai-kvo. Give me your weapons. Give me your promise that you'll go back to Galt and not make war against us again. I'll burn the books and try to keep us all from starving next spring."

"I can't promise you what the Council will do. Especially once . . . if . . ."

"Promise me *you* won't. You and your men. I'll worry about the others later."

There was strength in the man's voice. And sorrow. Balasar thought of all the things he knew of this man, all the things Sinja had told him. A seafront laborer, a sailor, a courier, an assistant midwife. And now a man who negotiated the fate of the world over a meeting table in a snow-packed square while thousands of soldiers who'd spent the previous day trying to kill one another looked on. He was unremarkable—exhausted, grieving, determined. He could have been anyone.

"I'll need to talk to my men," Balasar said.

"Of course."

"I'll have an answer for you by sundown."

"If you have it by midday, we can get you someplace warm before night."

"Midday, then."

They rose together, Balasar taking a pose of respect, and the Emperor Otah Machi returning it.

"General," Otah said as Balasar began to turn away. His voice was gray as ashes. "One thing. You came because you believed the andat were too powerful, and the poet's hearts were too weak. You weren't wrong. The man who did this was a friend of mine. He's a good man. Good men shouldn't be able to make mistakes with prices this high."

Balasar nodded and walked back across the square. The drummers matched the pace of his steps. The last of the books burned, the last of the poets fled into the wilderness, most likely to die, and if not then to live outcast for their crimes. The andat gone from the world. It was hard to think it. All his life he had aimed for that end, and still the idea was too large. His captains crowded around him as he drew near. Their faces were ashen and excited and fearful. Questions battered at him like moths at a lantern.

"Tell the men," Balasar began, and they quieted. Balasar hesitated. "Tell the men to disarm. We'll bring the weapons here. By midday."

There was a moment of profound silence, and then one of the junior captains spoke.

"How should we explain the surrender, sir?"

Balasar looked at the man, at all his men. For the first time in his memory, there seemed to be no ghosts at his back. He forced himself not to smile.

"Tell them we won."

27

>+< The mine was ancient—one of the first to be dug when Machi had been a new city, the last Empire still unfallen. Its passages honeycombed the rock, twisting and swirling to follow veins of ore gone since long before Maati's great-grandfather was born. Together, Maati and Cehmai had been raiding the bolt-hole that Otah had prepared for them and for his own children. It had been well stocked: dried meat and fruit, thick crackers, nuts and seeds. All of it was kept safe in thick clay jars with wax seals. They also took the wood and coal that had been set by. It would have been easier to stay there—to sleep in the beds that had been laid out, to light the lanterns set in the stone walls. But then they might have been found, and without discussing it, they had agreed to flee farther away from the city and the people they had known. Cehmai knew the tunnels well enough to find a new hiding place where the ventilation was good. They weren't in danger of the fire igniting the mine air, as had sometimes happened. Or of the flames suffocating them.

The only thing they didn't have in quantity was water; that, they could harvest. Maati or Cehmai could take one of the mine sleds out, fill it with snow, and haul it down into the earth. A trip every day or two was sufficient. They took turns sitting at the brazier, scooping handful after handful of snow into the flat iron pans, watching the perfect white collapse on itself and vanish into the black of the iron.

"We did what we could," Maati said. "It isn't as if we could have done anything differently."

"I know," Cehmai said, settling deeper into his cloak.

The rough stone walls didn't make their voices echo so much as sound hollow.

"I couldn't just let the Galts roll through the city. I had to try," Maati said.

"We all agreed," Cehmai said. "It was a decision we all reached together. It's not your fault. Let it go."

It was the conversation Maati always returned to in the handful of days they'd spent in hiding. He couldn't help it. He could start with plans for the spring—taking gold and gems from the bolt-hole and marching off to Eddensea or the Westlands. He could start with speculations on what was happening in Machi or reminiscences of his childhood, or what sort of drum fit best with which type of court dance. He could begin anywhere, and he found himself always coming back to the same series of justifications, and Cehmai agreeing by rote with each of them. The dark season spread out before them—only one another for company and only one conversation spoken over and over, its variations meaningless. Maati took another handful of snow and dropped it into the iron melting pan.

"I've always wanted to go to Bakta," Cehmai said. "I hear it's warm all year."

"I've heard that too."

"Maybe next winter," Cehmai said.

"Maybe," Maati agreed. The last icy island of snow melted and vanished. Maati dropped another handful in.

"What part of the day is it, do you think?" Maati asked.

"After morning, I'd think. Maybe a hand or two either side of midday."

"You think so? I'd have thought later."

"Could be later," Cehmai said. "I lose track down here."

"I'm going to the bolt-hole again. Get more supplies."

They didn't need them, but Cehmai only raised his hands in a pose of agreement, then curled into himself and shut his eyes. Maati pulled the thick leather straps of the sled harness over his shoulders, lit a lantern, and began the long walk through the starless dark. The wood and metal flat-bottomed sled scraped and ground along the stone and dust of the mine floor. It was light now. It would be heavier coming back. But at least Maati was alone for a time, and the effort of pulling kept his mind clear.

An instrument of slaughter, made in fear. Sterile had called herself that. Maati could still hear her voice, could still feel the bite of her words. He had destroyed Galt, but he had destroyed his own people as well. He'd failed, and every doubt he had ever had of his own ability, or his worthiness to be among the poets, stood justified. He would be the most hated man in generations. And he'd earned it. The sled dragging behind him, the straps pulling back at his shoulders—they were the simplest burden he carried. They were nothing.

Cehmai had marked the turnings to take with piles of stone. Hunters searching the mines would be unlikely to notice the marks, but they were easy enough for Maati to follow. He turned left at a crossing, and then bore right where the tunnel forked, one passage leading up into darkness, the other down into air just as black.

The only comfort that the andat had offered—the only faint sliver of grace—was that Maati was not wholly at fault. Otah-kvo bore some measure of this guilt as well. He was the one who had come to Maati, all those years ago. He was the one who had hinted to Maati that the school to which they had both been sent had a hidden structure. If he hadn't, Maati might never have been a poet. Never have known Seedless or Heshai, Liat or Cehmai. Nayiit might never have been born. Even if the Galts had come, even if the world had fallen, it wouldn't have fallen on Maati's shoulders. Cehmai was right; the binding of Sterile had been a decision they had all made—Otah-kvo more than any of the rest. But it was Maati who was cast out to live in the dark and the cold. The sense of betrayal was as comforting as a candle in the darkness, and as he walked, Maati found himself indulging it.

The fault wasn't his alone, and the punishment was. There was nothing fair in that. Nothing right. The terrible thing that had happened seemed nearly inevitable now that he looked back on it. He'd been given hardly any books, not half the time he'd been promised, and the threat of death at the end of a Galtic sword unless he succeeded. It would have been astounding it he hadn't failed.

And for the price, that wasn't something he'd chosen. That had been Sterile. Once the binding had failed, he'd had no control over it. He would never have hurt Eiah if he'd had the choice. It had simply happened. And still, he felt it in the back of his mind—the shape of the andat, the place in the realm of ideas that it had pressed down in him, like the flattened grass where a hunting cat has slept. Sterile came from him, was him, and even if she had only been brief, she had still learned her voice from him and visited her price upon the world through his mind and fears. The clever trick of pushing the price away from himself and onto the world had been his. The way in which the world had broken was his shadow—not him, not even truly shaped like him. But connected.

The tunnel before him came to a sudden end, and Maati had to follow his own track back to the turn he'd missed, angling up a steep slope and into the first breath of fresh, cold air, the first glimmer of daylight. Maati stood still a moment to catch his breath, then fastened all the ties on his cloak, pulled the furred hood up over his head, and began the long last climb.

The bolt-hole was perhaps half a hand's walk from the entrance to the mines in which the poets hid. The snow was dry as sand, and the icy breeze from the North would be enough to conceal what traces of his footsteps the sled didn't smooth over. Maati trudged through the world of snow and stone, his breath pluming out before him, his face stung and numbed. It was hellish. His feet first burned then went numb, and frost began to form on the fur around his hood's mouth. Maati dragged himself and his sled. The numbness and the pain felt a bit like penance, and he was so caught up in them he nearly failed to notice the horse at the mouth of the bolt-hole.

It was a small animal, fit with heavy blankets and riding tack. Maati blinked at it, stunned by its presence, then scurried quickly behind a boulder, his heart in his mouth. Someone had come looking for them. Someone had found them. He turned to look back at the path he'd walked, certain that the footsteps in the snow were visible as blood on a wedding dress.

He waited for what seemed half a day but couldn't have been more than half a hand's width in the arc of the fast winter sun. A figure emerged from the tunnels—thick black cloak, and wide, heavy hood. Maati was torn between poking his head out to watch it and pulling back to hide behind his boulder. In the end caution won out, and he waited blind while the sound of horse's hooves on snow began and then grew faint. He chanced a look, and the rider had its back to him, heading back south to Machi, a twig of black on the wide field of mourning white. Maati waited until he judged the risk of being seen no greater than the risk of frostbite if he stayed still, then forced himself—all his limbs aching with the cold—to scramble the last stretch into the tunnel.

The bolt-hole was empty. He was surprised to find that he'd half-expected it to be filled with men bearing swords, ready to take their vengeance out against him. He pulled off his gloves and lit a small fire to warm himself, and when his hands could move again without pain, he made an inventory of the place. Nothing seemed to be missing, nothing disturbed. Except this: a small wicker basket with two low stone wax-sealed jars where none had been before. Maati squatted over them, lifting them carefully. They were heavy—packed with something. And a length of scroll, curled like a leaf, had been nestled between them. Maati blew on his fingers and unfurled the scrap of parchment.

Maati-cha—
I thought you might be out in the hiding place where we were supposed to go when the Galts came, but you aren't here, so I'm not sure anymore. I'm leaving this for you just in case. It's peaches from the gardens. They were going to give them to the Galts, so I stole them.
Loya-cha says I'm not supposed to ride yet, so I don't know when I'll be able to get out again. If you find this, take it so I'll know you were there.
It's going to be all right.

It was signed with Eiah's wide, uncontrolled hand. Maati felt himself weeping. He broke the seal of one jar and with numb fingers drew out a slice of the deep orange fruit, sweet and rich and thick with the sunshine of the autumn days that had passed.

THE WORLD CHANGES. SOMETIMES SLOWLY, SOMETIMES ALL OF AN INSTANT. BUT the world changes, and it doesn't change back. A rockslide shifts the face of a mountain, and the stones never go back up to take their old places. War scatters the people of a city, and not all will return. If any.

A child cherished as a babe, clung to as a man, dies; a mother's one last journey with her son at her side proves to be truly the last. The world has changed. And no matter how painful this new world is, it doesn't change back.

Liat lay in the darkened room, as she had for days. Her belly didn't bother her any longer. Even when it had, the pain hadn't been deep. It was only flesh. The news of Nayiit's death had been a more profound wound than anything the andat could do. Her boy had followed her on this last desperate adventure. He had left his own wife and child. And she had brought him here to die for a boy he hadn't even known to be his brother.

Or perhaps he had known. Perhaps that was what had given him the courage to attack the Galtic soldiers and be cut down. She would have asked him; she still intended to ask him, when she saw him next. Even knowing that she never could, even trying consciously to force the impulse away, she found she could not stop intending it. *When I see him again* still felt like the future. A time would come when it would feel like the past. When he was here, when I could touch him, when he would smile at me and make me laugh, when I worried for him. When my boy lived. Back then. Before I lost him.

Before the world changed.

She sighed in the darkness, and didn't bother to wipe away the tears. They were meaningless—her body responding without her. They couldn't undo what had been done, and so they didn't matter. Voices echoed in the hall outside her apartments here in the tunnels, and she ignored them. If they had been shouting warnings of fire, she would have ignored those too.

Sometimes she would think of all the people who had died. The amateur soldiers that Otah had led into battle outside the village of the Dai-kvo, the Galts dead on the road from Cetani. The sad rogue poet Riaan, slaughtered by the men he thought his friends. The innocent, naïve men and women and children in Nantani and Utani and Chaburi-Tan and all the other sacked cities. The children at the poets' school.

Every one of them had a mother. Every mother who had not had the luck to die was trapped in the quiet desperation that imprisoned her now. Liat thought of all these other grieving women, held them up in her mind as proof that she was being stupid and weak. Mothers lost their sons all the time, all across the world. In every nation, in every city, in every age. Her suffering wasn't so much compared with all of them.

And then she would hear someone cough in Nayiit's voice, or she'd mistake the shape of a man's back, and her idiot, traitor heart would sing for a moment. Even as her mind told her no it wasn't, her heart would soar before it fell.

The scratch at her door was so faint and tentative, Liat thought at first it was only a rat tricked by the darkness into believing the room empty. But the sound came again, the intentional rhythm of a hand against wood.

Likely it was Otah, coming again to hold her hand and sit quietly. He had done so several times, when he could free himself from the rigors of peace and war and Empire. They spoke little because there was too much to say, and no words adequate. Or perhaps one of his physicians, come to look in on her health. Or a servant sent to declaim poems or sing. Someone to distract her in the name of comfort. She wished they wouldn't come.

The scratch repeated itself, more loudly.

"Who?" Liat managed to ask. For answer, the door slid open, and Kiyan stood framed in the doorway, a lantern in her hand. The expression on the woman's fox-thin face seemed equally pity and unease.

"Liat-kya," she said. "May I come in?"

"If you like," Liat said.

The lantern cast a thousand broken shadows as Kiyan moved across the room. The tapestries on the wall, hidden so long in darkness, seemed to breathe. Liat considered the space in which she had been for so many days without seeing it. It was small. The furnishings were costly and exquisite. It didn't matter. Kiyan went to the wall sconces, taking down the pale wax candles, touching them to the lantern flame, putting them back in their places glowing. The soft light slowly filled the air, the shadows smoothed away.

"I heard you had missed your breakfast," Kiyan said, her voice cheerful and forced, as she lit the last of the candles.

"And my dinner," Liat said.

"Yes, I heard that too."

The lantern made a clunking sound—iron on wood—as Kiyan set it on the bedside table. She sat on the mattress at Liat's side. Otah's wife looked weary and drawn. Perhaps the andat's price had been worse for her than it had for Liat. Perhaps it was something else.

"They've put the Galts in the southern tunnels," Kiyan said. "There's almost no room. I don't know how it will be when the worst of the cold comes. And spring . . . we'll have to start sending people south and east as soon as it's safe to travel."

"Good that so many died," Liat said, and saw the other woman flinch. Now that she'd said it, the words did seem pointed. Liat hadn't meant them to be; she only couldn't be bothered to weigh the effect of her actions just now. Kiyan fumbled in her sleeve and drew out a small package wrapped in waxed cloth. Liat could smell the raisins and honey. She knew it should have been appetizing. Without speaking, Kiyan placed the little cake on the bedside table and rose to leave.

"Stop it," Liat said, sitting up on her bed.

Otah's wife, the mother of his children, turned back, her hands in a pose of query.

"Stop moving around me like I'm made of eggshell," Liat said. "It's not in your power to keep me from breaking. I've broken. Move on."

"I'm sorry. I didn't—"

"Didn't what? Didn't mean to throw your boy and mine onto a company of Galtic swords? Didn't mean to have your daughter play find-me-find-you until it wasn't safe to flee? Well, there's a relief. And here I thought you wanted *both* our children dead instead of just mine."

Kiyan's face hardened. Liat felt the rage billow in her like she was a sheet thrown over a fire. It ate her and it held her up.

"I didn't mean to treat you as if you were fragile," Kiyan said. "We both know I didn't mean for Nayiit—"

"Didn't mean for him to be a threat to your precious Danat? Didn't mean to let him be a threat to your family? He wasn't. He never was. I offered to have him take the brand."

"I know," Kiyan said. "Otah told me."

But she might as well not have spoken. Liat could no more stop the words now than will the blood to stop flowing from a wound.

"I *offered* to take him away. I didn't want him fighting to be the Khai any more than you did. I wouldn't have put him in danger, and he would never have hurt Danat. He would never have hurt your boy. He wouldn't have hurt anyone. It's your mewling half-dead son that's caused this. If he'd been able to fight off a cough, Otah would never have kept Nayiit from the brand. Nayiit would never have fought, never have hurt *anybody's* children. He was . . . he was . . ."

The tears came again. She couldn't say what would have come. She couldn't say that Danat and Nayiit would never have come to face one another as custom demanded. Perhaps in the years ahead the gods would have pitted them against each other. If the world was what it had been. If things hadn't changed. Sobs as violent as sickness racked her, and she found Kiyan's arms around her, her own fists full of the soft wool of the woman's robe, her screams echoing as if by will alone she could pull the stones down and bury them all.

Time changed its nature. The sorrow and rage and the physical ache of her heart went on forever and only a moment. The only measure was that the candles had burned a quarter of their length before the fit passed, and exhaustion reclaimed her again. She was embarrassed to see the damp spot she had left on Kiyan's shoulder, but when she tried to smooth it away, Kiyan only took her hand, lacing their fingers together like half-grown girls trading gossip at a dance. Liat allowed it.

"You know you can stay here," Kiyan said.

"You know I can't."

"I only meant you'd be welcome," Kiyan said. Then a moment later, "What will you do when the thaw comes?"

"Go south," Liat said. "Go to Saraykeht. See what's left. I may still have a grandson. I can hope it. And better that he not lose a father and grandmother both."

"Nayiit was a good man," Kiyan said.

"He was nothing of the sort. He was a charming bastard who fled his own family and slept with half the women between here and Saraykeht. But I loved him."

"He died saving my son," Kiyan said. "He's a hero."

"That doesn't help me."

"I know it," Kiyan said, and with a distant surprise, Liat found herself smiling.

"Aren't you going to tell me it will pass?" Liat asked.

"Will it?"

The tunnels below Machi had their own weather—a system of warm winds and cold; dry and damp. Sometimes, if no one was speaking, if there were no words to say, Liat could hear it like a breath. Like a long, low, endless exhalation.

"I will never stop missing him," Liat said. "I want him back."

Kiyan nodded, and sat there with her, keeping the vigil for another night as outside autumn fell into winter and winter crawled toward spring. The world slowly changing.

"I UNDERSTAND YOUR SON HAS FALLEN ILL?"

Otah's first impulse, unthinking as a reflex, was to deny it. Balasar Gice was a small-framed man, unimposing until he spoke, and then charming and warm enough to fill a room with his ironic half-smile. He was the man who had brought down everything. Thousands of people who were alive in the spring were now dead or enslaved through this man's ambition. Otah's first impulse was to keep anything about Danat away from the man, because he was a Galt and the enemy.

His second impulse, as unreasoned as the first, was to tell Balasar the truth, because in the few days since the surrender, he'd begun to like the man.

"It's a cough," Otah said. "He's always had it, but it had been less recently. We'd hoped it was gone, but . . ."

He took a pose expressing regret and powerlessness before the gods. Balasar seemed to take the sense of it.

"I have medics with me," the Galt said, gesturing over his back at the wide, dark stone arch that led from the great vaulted chamber in which they now met toward the south and the tunnels given over to the Galtic army. "They have more experience with sewing men's fingers back on, but they might be of use. If you'd accept them."

Otah hesitated, his unease washing back over him, then forced himself to smile.

"That's very kind of you," he said, neither agreeing to anything nor refusing. The Galt shrugged.

"And Sinja?" he asked.

"He sends his regards," Otah said, "but he thought it best to withdraw from company. Fear of reprisal."

"He's not wrong," Balasar said. "That man was many things, but he wasn't stupid."

"I'm told your men have found places in the tunnels."

"It's a tight fit," the Galt said. "And there are going to be problems. You can't make a peace just by saying it. People are angry. Yours and mine both. They're grieving, and grieving people aren't sane. There haven't been any fights yet, but there will be."

"I know it," Otah said. "We'll keep them apart as best we can. I've given orders."

"I have too. As long as we're both clear, we can keep it from growing out of control. At least before the thaw."

"And after that?"

The Galt sighed and nodded, as if agreeing with the question. His gaze traveled up the walls, tracing the blue tile and the gold. Otah gestured, and a servant boy scuttled forward from the shadows and poured them each more tea. The Galt smiled at him, and the boy smiled back. Balasar took his bowl of tea and blew across it before he spoke.

"I can't stop the High Council from coming back," Balasar said. "I'm their general for this season. I don't own the army. And . . . and since this campaign ended with the gelding of every man who would cast the vote, I doubt my voice will carry much with them."

Otah took a pose that accepted this statement.

"There's an age of war coming for you," Balasar said. "You still have some of the richest cities in the world, and you're still ripe for plunder. Even if we don't come, there's Eymond, Eddensea, the Westlands. There will be pirates from Bakta and Obar State."

"I'll address those problems. And the others," Otah said with a confidence he didn't feel. Balasar let the issue drop. After a moment's silence, Otah felt himself moved to ask the question he had intended to leave be. "What will you do? Go back to Galt?"

"Yes," Balasar said. "I'll go back, but I don't think it would be wise for me to stay. I don't know, Most High. I had plans, but none of them involved being hated and disgraced. So I suppose I'll have to make others. What do you do when you've finished your life's work and haven't died?"

"I don't know," Otah said, and Balasar laughed.

"With the things still ahead of you, Lord Emperor, you likely never will. That's your fate." Balasar's gaze seemed to soften—melancholy creeping in at the corners of his eyes. "There are worse, though."

Otah sipped his tea. The leaves were perfectly brewed, neither weak nor bitter. Balasar raised his own cup in a wordless salute.

"Shall we do this thing?" Otah asked.

"I was wondering," Balasar said. "I was afraid you might reconsider. Burning a library's a terrible thing."

For a moment, Otah saw the cold eyes of Sterile, its feminine smile, heard its voice. The memory of the physicians' cots filled with row upon row of women in pain possessed him for the length of a heartbeat and was gone.

"There are worse," he said.

Otah rose, and the general rose with him. From the servants' niches and from beyond the great archway to the south, their respective people appeared. Hard soldiers from the South, men of the utkhaiem in flowing robes from the North. Otah raised his hands in a pose of command, and let the servants go forward to prepare their way.

The furnaces were near the surface where they could be blocked off from the rest of the city if the fires ever should escape their cells. The air near them was thick with the scent of smoke and oppressive with heat. The noise of the flames was like a waterfall. Otah led Balasar and his men to the huge grates where the scrolls and codices and books were stacked. Generations of history. Philosophic essays composed by minds gone to dust a thousand years before. Maps that predated the First Empire. The surviving scraps of war records from before the first andat. Otah looked upon his culture, his history, the record of all that had come before and that had made the world what it was. The flames licked and leapt.

If only it could have been just the poets' books and treatises on the andat . . . but the Galt had insisted, and Otah had understood. Each history was a footprint in the path, each collection of court poems might contain a hint or reference. With time and attention, someone might put together again what had been torn apart, and it was a chance the Galt had refused to accept. Their tenuous peace required sacrifices, and sacrifice without loss didn't deserve the name.

"Forgive this," Otah said, to no one. He walked forward, coming to the first pile. The book was leather-bound and worn from years of loving care. Otah let it fall open and looked on Heshai's careful handwriting for the last time. With a sense of sorrow, Otah cast the book into the flames, then raised his hands again, and the servants began to throw the pages into the fire. Parchment darkened and curled in the suddenly white flame. Tiny embers flew out into the air, glowing and going dark, fireflies at sunset. The horror of it all closed his throat, and with it came a strange elation.

A hand touched his arm, and Otah looked at the Galtic general. There were tears in his eyes too.

"It was necessary," he said.

The night candles were burned down past their first quarter before Otah found his way back to his rooms. Kiyan was already asleep, her face smooth and peaceful. He resisted the urge to touch her, to pull her awake and hope that some of that calm might come with her. It wouldn't. He knew that. Instead he watched the subtle rise and fall of her breath, listened to the small sounds the tunnels made in the darkness, the soft flow of air. He thought of crawling in beside her, still in his robes, pressing his eyes closed until forget-fulness took him as well. But he needed to perform one last errand. He rose quietly and left by the back passage, down deeper into the earth.

The physician rose when he caught sight of Otah, taking a welcoming pose so quietly that the rustle of cloth in his robes seemed loud. Otah replied with one that asked a question.

"He's well," the physician said. "The poppy milk makes him sleepy, but it stops the cough."

"May I?" Otah asked.

"I think he'll never rest unless you do. But it would be best if he didn't speak overmuch."

Danat's room was warm and close. The night candle fluttered and glowed in its glass case. Great iron statues of hunting cats and a bear risen on his back feet radiated heat from the fires in which they'd been kept all through the day. His boy sat up unsteadily, smiling. Otah went to his side.

"You should be asleep," Otah said, smoothing the hair from Danat's brow.

"You were supposed to read to me," the boy said. His voice was scratchy and thick, but not as bad as it had been. Otah felt tears in his eyes again. He could not bring himself to say that the books were all gone, the stories all made ash. "Lie back," he said. "I'll do what I can."

Grinning, Danat dropped to his pillows. Otah took a long, unsteady breath and closed his eyes.

"In the sixteenth year of the reign of the Emperor Adani Beh," Otah mur-mured, "there came to court a boy whose blood was half Bakta, his skin the color of soot, and his mind as clever as any man who has ever lived . . ." Danat made a small sound of pleasure and closed his eyes, his hand seeking out Otah's fingers.

Otah went on as long as he could before his memory failed him, and then he began to invent.

THE PRICE OF SPRING

To Scarlet Abraham

ACKNOWLEDGMENTS

For the last time on this project, I reflect on the people who have helped me get to the end of it. I owe debts of service and gratitude to Walter Jon Williams, Melinda Snodgrass, Emily Mah, S. M. Stirling, Ian Tregillis, Ty Franck, George R. R. Martin, Terry England, and all the members of the New Mexico Critical Mass Workshop. I owe thanks to Connie Willis and the Clarion West '98 class for starting the story off a decade ago. Also to my agents Shawna McCarthy, who kept me on the project, and Danny Baror, who has sold these books in foreign lands and beyond my wildest dreams; to James Frenkel for his patience, faith, and uncanny ability to improve a manuscript; to Tom Doherty and the staff at Tor, who have made these into books with which I am deeply pleased.

Thank you all.

PROLOG

>+< Eiah Machi, physician and daughter of the Emperor, pressed her fingers gently on the woman's belly. The swollen flesh was tight, veins marbling the skin blue within brown. The woman appeared for all the world to be in the seventh month of a pregnancy. She was not.

"It's because my mother's father was a Westlander," the woman on the table said. "I'm a quarter Westlander, so when it came, it didn't affect me like it did other girls. Even at the time, I wasn't as sick as everyone else. You can't tell because I have my father's eyes, but my mother's were paler and almost round."

Eiah nodded, running practiced fingertips across the flesh, feeling where the skin was hot and where it was cool. She took the woman's hand, bending it gently at the wrist to see how tight her tendons were. She reached inside the woman's sex, probing where only lovers had gone before. The man who stood at his wife's side looked uncomfortable, but Eiah ignored him. He was likely the least important person in the room.

"Eiah-cha," Parit, the regular physician, said, "if there is anything I can do . . ."

Eiah took a pose that both thanked and refused. Parit bowed slightly.

"I was very young, too," the woman said. "When it happened. Just six summers old."

"I was fourteen," Eiah said. "How many months has it been since you bled?"

"Six," the woman said as if it were a badge of honor. Eiah forced herself to smile.

"Is the baby well?" the man asked. Eiah considered how his hand wrapped his wife's. How his gaze bored into her own. Desperation was as thick a scent in the room as the vinegar and herb smoke.

"It's hard to say," Eiah said. "I haven't had the luck to see very many pregnancies. Few of us have these days. But even if things are well so far, birthing is a tricky business. Many things can go wrong."

"He'll be fine," the woman on the table asserted; the hand not being squeezed bloodless by her man caressed the slight pooch of her belly. "It's a boy," she went on. "We're going to name him Loniit."

Eiah placed a hand on the woman's arm. The woman's eyes burned with something like joy, something like fever. The smile faltered for less than a heartbeat, less than the time it took to blink. So at least some part of the woman knew the truth.

"Thank you for letting me make the examination," Eiah said. "You're very kind. And I wish the best of luck to you both."

"All three," the woman corrected.

"All three," Eiah said.

She walked from the room while Parit arranged his patient. The antechamber glowed by the light of a small lantern. Worked stone and carved wood made the room seem more spacious than it was. Two bowls, one of old wine and another of fresh water, stood waiting. Eiah washed her hands in the wine first. The chill against her fingers helped wash away the warmth of the woman's flesh. The sooner she could forget that, the better.

Voices came from the examining room like echoes. Eiah didn't listen. When she put her hands into the water, the wine turned it pink. She dried herself with a cloth laid by for the purpose, moving slowly to be sure both the husband and wife were gone before she returned.

Parit was washing down the slate table with vinegar and a stiff brush. It was something Eiah had done often when she'd first apprenticed to the physicians, all those years ago. There were fewer apprentices now, and Parit didn't complain.

"Well?" he asked.

"There's no child in her," Eiah said.

"Of course not," he said. "But the signs she *does* show. The pooled blood, the swelling. The loss of her monthly flow. And yet there's no slackening in her joints, no shielding in her sex. It's a strange mix."

"I've seen it before," Eiah said.

Parit stopped. His hands took a pose of query. Eiah sighed and leaned against one of the high stools.

"Desire," Eiah said. "That's all. Want something that you can't have badly enough, and the longing becomes a disease."

Her fellow physician and onetime lover paused for a moment, considering Eiah's words, then looked down and continued his cleaning.

"I suppose we should have said something," he said.

"There's nothing to say," Eiah said. "They're happy now, and they'll be sad later. What good would it do us to hurry that?"

Parit gave the half-smile she'd known on him years before, but didn't look up to meet her gaze.

"There is something to be said in favor of truth," he said.

"And there's something to be said for letting her keep her husband for another few weeks," Eiah said.

"You don't know that he'll turn her out," he said.

Eiah took a pose that accepted correction. They both knew it was a gentle sarcasm. Parit chuckled and poured a last rinse over the slate table: the rush of the water like a fountain trailed off to small, sharp drips that reminded Eiah of wet leaves at the end of a storm. Parit pulled out a stool and sat, his hands clasped in his lap. Eiah felt a sudden awkwardness that hadn't been there before. She was always better when she could inhabit her role. If Parit had been bleeding from the neck, she would have been sure of herself. That he was only looking at her made her aware of the sharpness of her face, the gray in her hair that she'd had since her eighteenth summer, and the emptiness of the house. She took a formal pose that offered gratitude. Perhaps a degree more formal than was needed.

"Thank you for sending for me," Eiah said. "It's late, and I should be getting back."

"To the palaces," he said. There was warmth and humor in his voice. There always had been. "You could also stay here."

Eiah knew she should have been tempted at least. The glow of old love and half-recalled sex should have wafted in her nostrils like mulled wine. He was still lovely. She was still alone.

"I don't think I could, Parit-kya," she said, switching from the formal to the intimate to pull the sting from it.

"Why not?" he asked, making it sound as if he was playing.

"There are a hundred reasons," Eiah said, keeping her tone as light as his. "Don't make me list them."

He chuckled and took a pose that surrendered the game. Eiah felt herself relax a degree, and smiled. She found her bag by the door and slung its strap over her shoulder.

"You still hide behind that," Parit said.

Eiah looked down at the battered leather satchel, and then up at him, the question in her eyes.

"There's too much to fit in my sleeves," she said. "I'd clank like a toolshed every time I waved."

"That's not why you carry it," he said. "It's so that people see a physician and not your father's daughter. You've always been like that."

It was his little punishment for her return to her own rooms. There had been a time when she'd have resented the criticism. That time had passed.

"Good night, Parit-kya," she said. "It was good to see you again."

He took a pose of farewell, and then walked with her to the door. In the courtyard of his house, the autumn moon was full and bright and heavy. The air smelled of wood smoke and the ocean. Warmth so late in the season still surprised her. In the north, where she'd spent her girlhood, the chill would have been deadly by now. Here, she hardly needed a heavy robe.

Parit stopped in the shadows beneath a wide shade tree, its golden leaves lined with silver by the moonlight. Eiah had her hand on the gate before he spoke.

"Was that what you were looking for?" he asked.

She looked back, paused, and took a pose that asked for clarification. There were too many things he might have meant.

"When you wrote, you said to watch for unusual cases," Parit said. "Was she what you had in mind?"

"No," Eiah said. "That wasn't it." She passed from the garden to the street.

A decade and a half had passed since the power of the andat had left the world. For generations before that, the cities of the Khaiem had been protected by the poets—men who had dedicated their lives to binding one of the spirits, the thoughts made flesh. Stone-Made-Soft, whom Eiah had known as a child with its wide shoulders and amiable smile, was one of them. It had made the mines around the northern city of Machi the greatest in the world. Water-Moving-Down, who generations ago had commanded the rains to come or else to cease, the rivers to flow or else run dry. Removing-the-Part-That-Continues, called Seedless, who had plucked the seeds from the cotton harvests of Saraykeht and discreetly ended pregnancies.

Each of the cities had had one, and each city had shaped its trade and commerce to exploit the power of its particular andat to the advantage of its citizens. War had never come to the cities of the Khaiem. No one dared to face an enemy who might make the mountains flow like rivers, who might flood your cities or cause your crops to fail or your women to miscarry. For almost ten generations, the cities of the Khaiem had stood above the world like adults over children.

And then the Galtic general Balasar Gice had made his terrible wager and won. The andat left the world, and left it in ruins. For a blood-soaked spring, summer, and autumn, the armies of Galt had washed over the cities like a wave over sandcastles. Nantani, Udun, Yalakeht, Chaburi-Tan. The great cities fell to the foreign swords. The Khaiem died. The Dai-kvo and his poets were put to the sword and their libraries burned. Eiah still remembered being fourteen summers old and waiting for death to come. She had been only the daughter of the Khai Machi then, but that had been enough. The Galts, who had taken every other city, were advancing on them. And their only hope had been Uncle Maati, the disgraced poet, and his bid to bind one last andat.

She had been present in the warehouse when he'd attempted the binding. She'd seen it go wrong. She had felt it in her body. She and every other woman in the cities of the Khaiem. And every man of Galt. Corrupting-the-Generative, the last andat had been named.

Sterile.

Since that day, no woman of the cities of the Khaiem had borne a child. No man of Galt had fathered one. It was a dark joke. Enemy nations locked in war afflicted with complementary curses. *Your history will be written by half-breeds*, Sterile had said, *or it won't be written*. Eiah knew the words because she had been in the room when the world had been broken. Her own father had taken the name Emperor when he sued for peace, and Emperor he had become. Emperor of a fallen world.

Perhaps Parit was right. Perhaps she had taken to her vocation as single-mindedly as she had because she wanted to be something else. Something besides her father's daughter. As the princess of the new empire, she would have been a marriage to some foreign ward or king or lord incapable of bearing children. The degraded currency of her body would have been her definition.

Physician and healer were better roles to play. Walking through the darkened streets of Saraykeht, her robes and her satchel afforded her a measure of respect and protection. It was poor form to assault a healer, in part because of the very real chance of requiring her services one day. The toughs and beggars who haunted the alleys near the seafront might meet her eyes as she walked past, might even hail her with an obscenity or veiled threat, but they had never followed her. And so she didn't see that she had any need of the palace guard. If her work protected her, there was no reason to call upon her blood.

She stopped at the bronze statue of Shian Sho. The last emperor gazed out wistfully over the sea, or perhaps back through the ages to a time when his name had been important. Eiah pulled her robe tight around herself and squatted at his metalwork feet, waiting for the firekeeper and his steamcart. In daytime, she would have walked the streets north and uphill to the palaces, but the seafront wasn't the worst part of Saraykeht. It was safer to wait.

To the west, the soft quarter was lit in its nightly festival. To the east, the bathhouses, the great stone warehouses, rarely more than half-filled now. Beyond that, the cohort houses of the laborers were darker, but far from unpeopled. Eiah heard a man's laugh from one direction, a woman's voice lifted in drunken song from another. The ships that filled the seafront docks stood silent, their masts like winter trees, and the ocean beyond them gray with a low mist.

There was a beauty in it, and a familiarity. Eiah had made her studies in places like this, whatever city she'd been in. She'd sewn closed the flesh of whores and thieves as often as soothed the coughs and pains of the utkhaiem in their perfumed palaces. It was a decision she'd made early in her career, not to be a court physician, not to care only for the powerful. Her father had approved, and even, she thought, been proud of the decision. For all their differences—and there were many—it was one reason she loved him.

The steamcart appeared first as a sound: the rough clatter of iron-bound wheels against the bricks of the street, the chuff of the boiler, the low rumble of the kiln. And then, as Eiah stood and shook the dirt and grime from her robe, it turned into the wide street they called the Nantan and came down toward the statue. In the light of the kiln, she saw seven or perhaps eight figures clinging to the cart's side. The firekeeper himself sat on the top, guiding the cart with a series of levers and pedals that made the most ornate loom seem simple. Eiah stepped forward as the cart trundled past, took one of the leather grips, and hoisted herself up to the cart's side runner along with the others.

"Two coppers," the firekeeper said without looking at her.

Eiah dug in her sleeve with her free hand, came out with two lengths of copper, and tossed them into the lacquer box at the firekeeper's feet. The man nodded rather than take any more-complex pose. His hands and eyes were occupied. The breeze shifted, a waft of smoke and thick steam washing her in its scent, and the cart lurched, shuddered, and turned again to the north along its constant route. Eiah sighed and made herself comfortable. It would take her almost the time for the moon to move the width of her hand before she stepped down at the pathway that led to the palaces. In the meantime, she watched the night city pass by her.

The streets nearest the seafront alternated between the high roofs of warehouses and the low of the tradesmen's shops. In the right season, the clack of looms would have filled the air, even this late at night. The streets converged on wide squares where the litter of the week's market still fouled the street: cheeses dropped to the cobbles and trod into mush, soiled cabbages and yams, even a skinned rabbit too corrupt to sell and not worth hauling away. One of the men on the far side of the steamcart stepped down, shifting the balance slightly. Eiah watched as his red-brown cloak passed into darkness.

There had been a time, she knew, when the streets had been safe to walk down, even alone. There had been a time beggars with their boxes would have been on the corners, filling the night with plaintive, amateur song. She had never seen it, never heard it. It was a story she knew, Old Saraykeht from long ago. She knew it like she knew Bakta, where she had never been, and the courts of the Second Empire, gone from the world for hundreds of years. It was a story. Once upon a time there was a city by the sea, and it lived in prosperity and innocence. But it didn't anymore.

The steamcart passed into the compounds of the merchant houses, three, four, five stories tall. They were almost palaces in themselves. There were more lights here, more voices. Lanterns hung from ropes at the crossroads, spilling buttery light on the bricks. Three more of Eiah's fellows stepped down from the cart. Two stepped on, dropping their copper lengths into the firekeeper's box. They didn't speak, didn't acknowledge one another. She shifted her hands on the leather grip. The palaces of the utkhaiem would be coming soon. And her apartments, and bed, and sleep. The kiln roared when the firekeeper opened it and poured in another spade's worth of coal.

The servants met her at the gateway that separated the palaces from the city, the smooth brick streets from the crushed marble pathways. The air smelled different here, coal smoke and the rich, fetid stink of humanity displaced by incense and perfume. Eiah felt relieved to be back, and then guilty for her relief. She answered their poses of greeting and obeisance with one of acknowledgment. She was no longer her work. Among these high towers and palaces, she was and would always be her father's daughter.

"Eiah-cha," the most senior of the servants said, his hands in a pose of ritual offering, "may we escort you to your rooms?"

"No," she said. "Food first. Then rest."

Eiah suffered them to take her satchel, but refused the sable cloak they offered against the night air. It really wasn't that cold.

"Is there word from my father?" she asked as they walked along the wide, empty paths.

"No, Eiah-cha," the servant replied. "Nor from your brother. There have been no couriers today."

Eiah kept her pleasure at the news from her expression.

The palaces of Saraykeht had suffered less under their brief Galtic occupation than many others had. Nantani had been nearly ruined. Udun had been razed and never rebuilt. In Saraykeht, it was clear where statues had once been and were gone, where jewels had been set into the goldwork around the doorways and been wrenched out, but all the buildings except the Khai's palace and the library still stood. The utkhaiem of the city hadn't restored the damage or covered it over. Like a woman assaulted but with unbroken spirit, Saraykeht wore her scars without shame. Of all the cities of the Khaiem, she was the least devastated, the strongest, and the most arrogant in her will to survive. Eiah thought she might love the city just a little, even as it made her sad.

A singing slave occupied the garden outside Eiah's apartments. Eiah left the shutters open so that the songs could come through more clearly. A fire burned in the grate and candles glowed in glass towers. A Galtic clock marked the hours of the night in soft metallic counterpoint to the singer, and as she pulled off her robes and prepared for sleep, Eiah was amazed to see how early it was. The night had hardly exhausted its first third. It had seemed longer. She put out the candles, pulled herself into her bed, and drew the netting closed.

The night passed, and the day that followed it, and the day that followed that. Eiah's life in Saraykeht had long since taken on a rhythm. The mornings she spent at the palaces working with the court physicians, the afternoons down in the city or in the low towns that spread out from Saraykeht. To those who didn't know her, she gave herself out to be a visitor from Cetani in the north, driven to the summer cities by hardship. It wasn't an implausible tale. There were many for whom it was true. And while it couldn't be totally hidden, she didn't want to be widely known as her father's daughter. Not here. Not yet.

On a morning near the end of her second month in the city—two weeks after Candles Night—the object of her hunt finally appeared. She was in her rooms, working on a guide to the treatment of fevers in older patients. The fire was snapping and murmuring in the grate and a thin, cold rain tapped at the shutters like a hundred polite mice asking permission to enter. The scratch at the door startled her. She arranged her robe and opened the door just as the slave outside it was raising her hand to scratch again.

"Eiah-cha," the girl said, falling into a pose that was equal parts apology and greeting. "Forgive me, but there's a man . . . he says he has to speak with you. He has a message."

"From whom?" Eiah demanded.

"He wouldn't say, Most High," the slave said. "He said he could speak only with you."

Eiah considered the girl. She was little more than sixteen summers. One of the youngest in the cities of the Khaiem. One of the last.

"Bring him," Eiah said. The girl made a brief pose that acknowledged the command and fled back out into the damp night. Eiah shuddered and went to add more coal to the fire. She didn't close the door.

The runner was a young man, broad across the shoulder. Twenty summers, perhaps. His hair was soaked and sticking to his forehead. His robe hung heavily from his shoulders, sodden with the rain.

"Eiah-cha," he said. "Parit-cha sent me. He's at his workroom. He said he has something and that you should come. Quickly."

She caught her breath, the first movements of excitement lighting her nerves. The other times one or another of the physicians and healers and herb women of the city had sent word, it had been with no sense of urgency. A man ill one day was very likely to be ill the next as well. This, then, was something different.

"What is it?" she asked.

The runner took an apologetic pose. Eiah waved it away and called for a servant. She needed a thick robe. And a litter; she wasn't waiting for the fire-keeper. And now, she needed them now. The Emperor's daughter got what she wanted, and she got it quickly. She and the boy were on the streets in less than half a hand, the litter jouncing uncomfortably as they were carried through the drizzle. The runner tried not to seem awed at the palace servants' fear of Eiah. Eiah tried not to bite her fingernails from anxiety. The streets slid by outside their shelter as Eiah willed the litter bearers to go faster. When they reached Parit's house, she strode through the courtyard gardens like a general going to war.

Without speaking, Parit ushered her to the back. It was the same room in which she'd seen the last woman. Parit sent the runner away. There were no servants. There was no one besides the two physicians and a body on the wide slate table, covered by a thick canvas cloth soaked through with blood.

"They brought her to me this morning," Parit said. "I called for you immediately."

"Let me see," Eiah said.

Parit pulled back the cloth.

The woman was perhaps five summers older than Eiah herself, dark-haired and thickly built. She was naked, and Eiah saw the wounds that covered her body: belly, breasts, arms, legs. A hundred stab wounds. The woman's skin was unnaturally pale. She'd bled to death. Eiah felt no revulsion, no outrage. Her mind fell into the patterns she had cultivated all her life. This was only death, only violence. This was where she was most at home.

"Someone wasn't happy with her," Eiah said. "Was she a soft-quarter whore?"

Parit startled, his hands almost taking a pose of query. Eiah shrugged.

"That many knife wounds," she said, "aren't meant only to kill. Three or four would suffice. And the spacing of them isn't what I've seen when the killer had simply lost control. Someone was sending a message."

"She wasn't stabbed," Parit said. He took a cloth from his sleeve and tossed it to her. Eiah turned back to the corpse, wiping the blood away from a wound in the dead woman's side. The smear of gore thinned. The nature of the wound became clear.

It was a mouth. Tiny rosebud lips, slack as sleep. Eiah told her hand to move, but for a long moment her flesh refused her. Then, her breath shallow, she cleaned another. And then another.

The woman was covered with babies' mouths. Eiah's fingertips traced the tiny lips that had spilled the woman's lifeblood. It was a death as grotesque as any Eiah had heard in the tales of poets who had tried to bind the andat and fallen short.

Tears filled her eyes. Something like love or pity or gratitude filled her heart to bursting. She looked at the woman's face for the first time. The woman hadn't been pretty. A thick jaw, a heavy brow, acne pocks. Eiah held back from kissing her cheek. Parit was confused enough as it stood. Instead, Eiah wiped her eyes on her sleeve and took the dead woman's hand.

"What happened?" she asked.

"The watch saw a cart going west out of the soft quarter," Parit said. "The captain said there were three people, and they were acting nervous. When he hailed them, they tried to run."

"Did he catch them?"

Parit was staring at Eiah's hand clasping the dead woman's fingers.

"Parit," she said. "Did he catch them?"

"What? No. No, all three slipped away. But they had to abandon the cart. She was in it," Parit said, nodding at the corpse. "I'd asked anything unusual to be brought to me. I offered a length of silver."

"They earned it," Eiah said. "Thank you, Parit-kya. I can't tell you how much this means."

"What should we do?" Parit asked, sitting on his stool like a fresh apprentice before his master. He'd always done that when he felt himself at sea. Eiah found there was warmth in her heart for him even now.

"Burn her," Eiah said. "Burn her with honors and treat her ashes with respect."

"Shouldn't we . . . shouldn't we tell someone? The utkhaiem? The Emperor?"

"You already have," Eiah said. "You've told me."

There was a moment's pause. Parit took a pose that asked clarification. It wasn't quite the appropriate one, but he was flustered.

"This is it, then," he said. "This is what you were looking for."

"Yes," Eiah said.

"You know what happened to her."

"Yes."

"Would you . . ." Parit coughed, looked down. His brow was knotted. Eiah was half-tempted to go to him, to smooth his forehead with her palm. "Could you explain this to me?"

"No," she said.

AFTER THAT, IT WAS SIMPLE. THEY WOULDN'T REMAIN IN SARAYKEHT, NOT WHEN they'd so nearly been discovered. The Emperor's daughter asked favors of the port master, of the customs men on the roads, of the armsmen paid by the city to patrol and keep the violence in the low towns to an acceptable level. Her quarry weren't smugglers or thieves. They weren't expert in covering their tracks. In two days, she knew where they were. Eiah quietly packed what things she needed from her apartments in the palace, took a horse from the stables, and rode out of the city as if she were only going to visit an herb woman in one of the low towns.

As if she were coming back.

She found them at a wayhouse on the road to Shosheyn-Tan. The winter sun had set, but the gates to the wayhouse courtyard were still open. The carriage Eiah had heard described was at the side of the house, its horses unhitched. The two women, she knew, were presenting themselves as travelers. The man—old, fat, unpleasant to speak with—was posing as their slave. Eiah let the servant take her horse to be cared for, but instead of going up the steps to the main house, she followed him back to the stables. A small shack stood away at an angle. Quarters for servants and slaves. Eiah felt her lips press thin at the thought. Rough straw ticking, thin blankets, whatever was left to eat after the paying guests were done.

"How many servants are here now?" Eiah asked of the young man— eighteen summers, so three years old when it had happened—brushing down her horse. He looked at her as if she'd asked what color ducks laid the eggs they served at table. She smiled.

"Three," the servant said.

"Tell me about them," she said.

He shrugged.

"There's an old woman came in two days ago. Her master's laid up sick. Then a boy from the Westlands works for a merchant staying on the ground floor. And an old bastard just came in with two women from Chaburi-Tan."

"Chaburi-Tan?"

"What they said," the servant replied.

Eiah took two lengths of silver from her sleeve and held them out in her palm. The servant promptly forgot about her horse.

"When you're done," she said, "take the woman and the Westlander to the back of the house. Buy them some wine. Don't mention me. Leave the old man."

The servant took a pose of acceptance so total it was just short of an open pledge. Eiah smiled, dropped the silver in his palm, and pulled up a shoeing stool to sit on while she waited. The night was cool, but still not near as cold as her home in the north. An owl hooted deep and low. Eiah pulled her arms up into her sleeves to keep her fingers warm. The scent of roasting pork wafted from the wayhouse, and the sounds of a flute and a voice lifted together.

The servant finished his work and with a deferential nod to Eiah, made his way to the servants' house. It was less than half a hand before he emerged with a thin woman and a sandy-haired Westlands boy trailing him. Eiah pushed her hands back through her sleeves and made her way to the small, rough shack.

He was sitting beside the fire, frowning into the flames and eating a mush of rice and raisins from a small wooden bowl. The years hadn't been kind to him. He was thicker than he'd been when she knew him, an unhealthy fatness that had little to do with indulgence. His color was poor; what remained of his hair was white stained yellow by neglect. He looked angry. He looked lonesome.

"Uncle Maati," she said.

He startled. His eyes flashed. Eiah couldn't tell if it was anger or fear. But whatever it was had a trace of pleasure to it.

"Don't know who you mean," he said. "Name's Daavit."

Eiah chuckled and stepped into the small room. It smelled of bodies and smoke and the raisins in Maati's food. Eiah found a small chair and pulled it to the fire beside the old poet, her chosen uncle, the man who had destroyed the world. They sat silently for a while.

"It was the way they died," Eiah said. "All the stories you told me when I was young about the prices that the andat exacted when a poet's binding failed. The one whose blood turned dry. The one whose belly swelled up like he was pregnant, and when they cut him open it was all ice and seaweed. All of them. I started to hear stories. What was that, four years ago?"

At first she thought he wouldn't answer. He cupped two thick fingers into the rice and ate what they lifted out. He swallowed. He sucked his teeth.

"Six," he said.

"Six years," she said. "Women started appearing here and there, dead in strange ways."

He didn't answer. Eiah waited for the space of five slow breaths together before she went on.

"You told me stories about the andat when I was young," she said. "I remember most of it, I think. I know that a binding only works once. In order to bind the same andat again, the poet has to invent a whole new way to describe the thought. You used to tell me about how the poets of the Old Empire would bind three or four andat in a lifetime. I thought at the time you envied them, but I saw later that you were only sick at the waste of it."

Maati sighed and looked down.

"And I remember when you tried to explain to me why only men could be poets," she said. "As I recall, the arguments weren't all that convincing to me."

"You were a stubborn girl," Maati said.

"You've changed your mind," Eiah said. "You've lost all your books. All the grammars and histories and records of the andat that have come before. They're gone. All the poets gone but you and perhaps Cehmai. And in the history of the Empire, the Second Empire, the Khaiem, the *one* thing you know is that a woman has never been a poet. So perhaps, if women think differently enough from men, the bindings they create will succeed, even with nothing but your own memory to draw from."

"Who told you? Otah?"

"I know my father had letters from you," Eiah said. "I don't know what was in them. He didn't tell me."

"A women's grammar," Maati said. "We're building a women's grammar."

Eiah took the bowl from his hands and put it on the floor with a clatter. Outside, a gust of wind shrilled past the shack. Smoke bellied out from the fire, rising into the air, thinning as it went. When he looked at her, the pleasure was gone from his eyes.

"It's the best hope," Maati said. "It's the only way to . . . undo what's been done."

"You can't do this, Maati-kya," Eiah said, her voice gentle.

Maati started to his feet. The stool he'd sat on clattered to the floor. Eiah pulled back from his accusing finger.

"Don't you tell that to me, Eiah," Maati said, biting at the words. "I know he doesn't approve. I asked his help. Eight years ago, I risked my life by sending to him, asking the Emperor of this pisspot empire for help. And what did he say? No. Let the world be the world, he said. He doesn't see what it is out here. He doesn't see the pain and the ache and the suffering. So don't you tell *me* what to do. Every girl I've lost, it's *his* fault. Every time we try and fall short, it's because we're sneaking around in warehouses and low towns. Meeting in secret like criminals—"

"Maati-kya—"

"I *can* do this," the old poet continued, a fleck of white foam at the corner of his mouth. "I *have* to. I *have* to retrieve my error. I have to fix what I broke. I know I'm hated. I know what the world's become because of me. But these girls are dedicated and smart and willing to die if that's what's called for. Willing to *die*. How can you and your great and glorious father tell me that I'm wrong to try?"

"I didn't say you shouldn't try," Eiah said. "I said you can't do it. Not alone."

Maati's mouth worked for a moment. His fingertip traced an arc down to the fire grate as the anger left him. Confusion washed through his expression, his shoulders sagging and his chest sinking in. He reminded Eiah of a puppet with its strings fouled. She rose and took his hand as she had the dead woman's.

"I haven't come here on my father's business," Eiah said. "I've come to help."

"Oh," Maati said. A tentative smile found its way to his lips. "Well. I . . . that is . . ."

He frowned viciously and wiped at his eyes with one hand. Eiah stepped forward and put her arms around him. His clothes smelled rank and unwashed; his flesh was soft, his skin papery. When he returned her embrace, she would not have traded the moment for anything.

1

>+< It was the fifth month of the Emperor's self-imposed exile. The day had been filled, as always, with meetings and conversations and appreciations of artistic tableaux. Otah had retired early, claiming a headache rather than face another banquet of heavy, overspiced Galtic food.

The night birds in the garden below his window sang unfamiliar songs. The perfume of the wide, pale flowers was equal parts sweetness and pepper. The rooms of his suite were hung with heavy Galtic tapestries, knotwork soldiers slaughtering one another in memory of some battle of which Otah had never heard.

It was, coincidentally, the sixty-third anniversary of his birth. He hadn't chosen to make it known; the High Council might have staged some further celebration, and he had had a bellyful of celebrations. On this day, he had been called upon to admire a gold- and jewel-encrusted clockwork whose religious significance was obscure to him; he had moved in slow procession down the narrow streets and through the grand halls with their awkward, blocky architecture and their strange, smoky incense; he had spoken to two members of the High Council to no observable effect. At this moment, he could be sitting with them again, making the same points, suffering the same deflections. Instead, he watched the thin clouds pass across the crescent moon.

He had become accustomed to feeling alone. It was true that with a word or a gesture he could summon his counselors or singing slaves, scholars or priests. Another night, he might have, if only in hope that this time it would be different; that the company would do something more than remind him how little comfort it provided. Instead, he went to the ornate writing desk and took what solace he could.

Kiyan-kya—

I have done what I said I would do. I have come to our old enemies, I have pled my case and pled and pled and pled, and now I suppose I'll plead some more. The full council is set to make their vote in a week's time. I know I should go out and do more, but I swear that I've spoken to everyone in this city twice over, and tonight, I'd rather be here with you. I miss you.

They tell me that all widowers suffer this sense of being halved, and they tell me it fades. It hasn't faded. I suspect age changes the nature of time. Four years may be an epoch for young men, to me it's hardly the space between one breath and the next. I want you to be here to tell me your thoughts on the matter. I want you here. I want you back.

I've had word from Danat and Sinja. They seem to be running the cities ef-fectively enough in my absence, but apart from our essential problem, there are a thousand other threats. Pirates have raided Chaburi-Tan, and there are sto-ries of armed companies from Eddensea and the Westlands exacting tolls on the roads outside the winter cities. The trading houses are bleeding money badly; no one indentures themselves as an apprentice anymore. Artisans are having to pay for workers. Even seafront laborers are commanding wages higher than anything I made as a courier. The high families of the utkhaiem are watching their coffers drain like a holed bladder. It makes them restless. I have had two separate petitions to allow forced indenture for what they call "critical labor." I haven't given an answer. When I go home, I suppose I'll have to.

Otah paused, the tip of his pen touching the brick of ink. Something with wide, pale wings the size of his hands and eyes as black and wet as river stones hovered at the window and then vanished. A soft breeze rattled the open shut-ters. He pulled back the sleeve of his robe, but before the bronze tip touched the paper, a soft knock came at his door.

"Most High," the servant boy said, his hands in a pose of obeisance. "Balasar-cha requests an audience."

Otah smiled and took a pose that granted the request and implied that the guest should be brought to him here, the nuance only slightly hampered by the pen still in his hand. As the servant scampered out, Otah straightened his sleeves and stuck the pen nib-first into the ink brick.

Once, Balasar Gice had led armies against the Khaiem, and only raw chance had kept him from success. Instead of leading Galt to its greatest hour, he had precipitated its slow ruin. That the Khaiem shared that fate took away little of the sting. The general had spent years rebuilding his broken reputation, and even now was less a force within Galt than once he had been.

And still, he was a man to be reckoned with.

He came into the room, bowing to Otah as he always did, but with a wry smile which was reserved for occasions out of the public eye.

"I came to inquire after your health, Most High," Balasar Gice said in the language of the Khaiem. His accent hadn't lessened in the years since they had met. "Councilman Trathorn was somewhat relieved by your absence, but he had to pretend distress."

"Well, you can tell him his distress in every way mirrors my own," Otah said. "I couldn't face it. I've been too much in the world. There is only so much praise I can stand from people who'd be happy to see my head on a plate. Please, sit. I can have a fire lit if you're cold. . . ."

Balasar sat on a low couch beside the window. He was a small man, more than half a head shorter than Otah, with the force of personality that made it easy to forget. The years had weathered his face, grooves at the corners of his eyes and mouth that spoke as much of laughter as sorrow. They had met a decade and a half ago in the snow-covered square that had been the site of the last battle in the war between Galt and the Khaiem. A war that they had both lost.

The years since had seen his status in his homeland collapse and then slowly be rebuilt. He wasn't a member of the convocation, much less the High Council, but he was still a man of power within Galt. When he sat forward, elbows resting on his knees, Otah could imagine him beside a campfire, working through the final details of the next morning's attack.

"Otah," the former general said, falling into his native tongue, "what is your plan if the vote fails?"

Otah leaned back in his chair.

"I don't see why it should," Otah said. "All respect, but what Sterile did, she did to both of us. Galt is in just as much trouble as the cities of the Khaiem. Your men can't father children. Our women can't bear them. We've gone almost fifteen years without children. The farms are starting to feel the loss. The armies. The trades."

"I know all that," Balasar said, but Otah pressed on.

"Both of our nations are *going* to fall. They've been falling, but we're coming close to the last chance to repair it. We might be able to weather a single lost generation, but if there isn't another after that, Galt will become Eymond's back gardens, and the Khaiem will be eaten by whoever can get to us first. You know that Eymond is only waiting for your army to age into weakness."

"And I know there are other peoples who weren't cursed," Balasar said. "Eymond, certainly. And the Westlands. Bakta. Obar State."

"And there are a handful of half-breed children from matches like those in the coastal cities," Otah said. "They're born to high families that can afford them and hoarded away like treasure. And there are others whose blood was mixed. Some have borne. Might that be enough, do you think?"

Balasar's smile was thin.

"It isn't," he said. "They won't suffice. Children can't be rarer than silk and lapis. So few might as well be none. And why should Eymond or Eddensea or the Westlands send their sons here to make families, when they can wait a few more years and take what they want from a nation of geriatrics? If the Khaiem and the Galts don't become one, we'll both be forgotten. Our land will be taken, our cities will be occupied, and you and I will spend our last years picking wild berries and stealing eggs out of nests, because there won't be farm hands enough to keep us in bread."

"That was my thought as well," Otah said.

"So, no fallback position, eh?"

"None," Otah said. "It was raw hell getting the utkhaiem to agree to the proposal I've brought. I take it the vote is going to fail?"

"The vote is going to fail," Balasar said.

Otah sat forward, his face cradled in his palms. The slight, acrid smell of old ink on his fingers only made the darkness behind his closed lids deeper.

Five months before, he had wrestled the last of the language in his proposed treaty with Galt into shape. A hundred translators from the high families and great trading houses had offered comment and correction, and small
wars had been fought in the halls and meeting rooms of his palace at Utani,
sometimes resulting in actual blows. Once, memorably, a chair had been thrown
and the chief overseer of House Siyanti had suffered a broken finger.

Otah had set forth with an entourage of hundreds—court servants, guards,
representatives of every interest from Machi in the far, frozen north to the island city of Chaburi-Tan, where ice was a novelty. The ships had poured into
the harbor flying brightly dyed sails and more banners and good-luck pennants
than the world had ever seen. For weeks and months, Otah had made his arguments to any man of any power in the bizarre, fluid government of his old
enemy. And now, this.

"Can I ask why?" he said, his eyes still closed.

"Pride," Balasar said. Otah heard the sympathy in the softness of his voice.
"No matter how prettily you put it, you're talking about putting our daughters
in bed under your sons."

"And rather than that, they'll let everything die?" Otah said, looking up at
last. Balasar's gaze didn't waver. When the old Galt spoke, it was with a sense
of reason and consideration that might almost have made a listener forget that
he was one of the men he spoke of.

"You don't understand the depth to which these people have been damaged. Every man on that council was hurt by you in a profound, personal way.
Most of them have been steeping in the shame of it since the day it happened.
They are less than men, and in their minds, it's because of the Khaiem. If
someone had humiliated and crippled you, how would you feel about marrying
your Eiah to him?"

"And none of them will see sense?"

"Some will," Balasar said, his gaze steady as stone. "Some of them think what
you've suggested is the best hope we have. Only not enough to win the vote."

"So I have a week. How do I convince them?" Otah asked.

Balasar's silence was eloquent.

"Well," Otah said. And then, "Can I offer you some particularly strong distilled wine?"

"I think it's called for," Balasar said. "And you'd mentioned something about
a fire against the cold."

Otah hadn't known, when the great panoply of Khaiate ships had come
with himself at the front, what his relationship with Balasar Gice would be.
Perhaps Balasar had also been uneasy, but if so it had never shown. The former general was an easy man to like, and the pair of them had experienced
things—the profound sorrow of commanders seeing their miscalculations lead
loyal men to the slaughter, the eggshell diplomacy of a long winter in close
quarters with men who had been enemies in autumn, the weight that falls on
the shoulders of someone who has changed the face of the world. There were

conversations, they discovered, that only the two of them could have. And so they had become at first diplomats, then friends, and now something deeper and more melancholy. Fellow mourners, perhaps, at the sickbeds of their empires.

The night wore on, the moon rising through the clouds, the fire in its grate flickering, dying down to embers before being fed fresh coal and coming to life again. They talked and they laughed, traded jokes and memories. Otah was aware, as he always was, of a distant twinge of guilt at enjoying the company of a man who had killed so many innocents in his war against the Khaiem and the andat. And as always, he tried to set the guilt aside. It was better to forget the ruins of Nantani and the bodies of the Dai-kvo and his poets, the corpses of Otah's own men scattered like scythed wheat and the smell of book paste catching fire. It was better, but it was difficult. He knew he would never wholly succeed.

He was more than half drunk when the conversation turned to his unfinished letter, still on his desk.

"It's pathetic, I suppose," Otah said, "but it's the habit I've made."

"I don't think it's pathetic," Balasar said. "You're keeping faith with her. With what she was to you, and what she still is. That's admirable."

"Tends toward the maudlin, actually," Otah said. "But I think she'd forgive me that. I only wish she could write back. There were things she'd understand in an instant that I doubt I'd ever have come to. If she were here, she'd have found a way to win the vote."

"I can't see that," Balasar said ruefully.

Otah took a pose of correction that spilled a bit of the wine from his bowl.

"She had a different perspective," Otah said. "She was . . . she . . ."

Otah's mind shifted under him, struggling against the fog. There was something. He'd just thought it, and now it was almost gone again. Kiyan-kya, his beloved wife, with her fox-sharp face and her way of smiling. Something about the ways that the world she'd seen were different from his own experience. The way talking with her had been like living twice . . .

"Otah?" Balasar said, and Otah realized it wasn't the first time.

"Forgive me," Otah said, suddenly short of breath. "Balasar-cha, I think . . . will you excuse me? There's something I need to . . ."

Otah put his wine bowl on the desk and walked to the door of his rooms. The corridors of the suite were dark, only the lowest of servants still awake, cleaning the carpets and polishing the latches. Eyes widened and hands fluttered as Otah passed, but he ignored them. The scribes and translators were housed in a separate building across a flagstone square. Otah passed the dry fountain in its center before the thought that had possessed him truly took form. He had to restrain himself from laughing.

The chief scribe was so dead asleep that Otah had to shake the woman twice. When consciousness did come into her eyes, her face went pale. She took a pose of apology that Otah waved away.

"How many of your best calligraphers can work in Galtic?"

"All of them, Most High," the chief scribe said. "It's why I brought them."

"How many? How many can we put to work now, tonight?"

"Ten?" she said as if it were a question.

"Wake them. Get them to their desks. Then I'll need a translator in my apartments. Or two. Best get two. An etiquette master and a trade specialist. Now. Go, now! This won't wait for morning."

On the way back to his rooms, his heart was tripping over, but his mind was clearing, the alcohol burning off in the heat of his plan. Balasar was seated where Otah had left him, an expression of bleary concern on his face.

"Is all well?"

"All's excellent," Otah said. "No, don't go. Stay here, Balasar-cha. I have a letter to write, and I need you."

"What's happened?"

"I can't convince the men on the council. You've said as much. And if I can't talk to the men who wield the power, I'll talk to the women who wield the men. Tell me there's a councilman's wife out there who doesn't want grandchildren. I defy you to."

"I don't understand," Balasar said.

"I need a list of the names of all the councilmen's wives. And the men of the convocation. Theirs too. Perhaps their daughters if . . . Well, those can wait. I'm going to draft an appeal to the women of Galt. If anyone can sway the vote, it's them."

"And you think that would work?" Balasar asked, incredulity in his expression.

In the event, Otah's letter seemed for two full days to have no effect. The letters went out, each sewn with silk thread and stamped with Otah's imperial seal, and no word came back. He attended the ceremonies and meals, the entertainments and committee meetings, his eyes straining for some hint of change like a snow fox waiting for the thaw. It was only on the morning of the third day, just as he was preparing to send a fresh wave of appeals to the daughters of the families of power, that his visitor was announced.

She was perhaps ten years younger than Otah, with hair the gray of dry slate pulled back from an intimidating, well-painted face. The reddening at her eyelids seemed more likely to be a constant feature than a sign of recent weeping. Otah rose from the garden bench and took a pose of welcome simple enough for anyone with even rudimentary training to recognize. His guest replied appropriately and waited for him to invite her to sit in the chair across from him.

"We haven't met," the woman said in her native language. "Not formally."

"But I know your husband," Otah said. He had met with all the members of the High Council many times. Farrer Dasin was among the longest-standing, though not by any means the most powerful. His wife Issandra had been no more than a polite smile and another face among hundreds until now. Otah considered her raised brows and downcast eyes, the set of her mouth and her shoulders. There had been a time when he'd lived by knowing how to interpret such small indications. Perhaps he still did.

"I found your letter quite moving," she said. "Several of us did."

"I am gratified," Otah said, not certain it was quite the correct word.

"Farrer and I have talked about your treaty. The massive shipment of Galtic women to your cities as bed servants to your men, and then hauling back a crop of your excess male population for whatever girls escaped. It isn't a popular scheme."

The brutality of her tone was a gambit, a test. Otah refused to rise to it.

"Those aren't the terms I put in the treaty," he said. "I believe I used the term *wife* rather than *bed servant*, for example. I understand that the men of Galt might find it difficult. It is, however, needed."

He spread his hands, as if in apology. She met his gaze with the bare intellect of a master merchant.

"Yes, it is," she said. "Majesty, I am in a position to deliver a decisive majority in both the High Council and the convocation. It will cost me all the favors I'm owed, and I have been accruing them for thirty years. It will likely take me another thirty to pay back the debt I'm going into for you."

Otah smiled and waited. The cold blue eyes glittered for a moment.

"You might offer your thanks," she said.

"Forgive me," Otah said. "I didn't think you'd finished speaking. I didn't want to interrupt."

The woman nodded, sat back a degree, and folded her hands in her lap. A wasp hummed through the air to hover between them before it darted away into the foliage. He watched her weigh strategies and decide at last on the blunt and straightforward.

"You have a son, I understand?" Issandra Dasin said.

"I do," Otah said.

"Only one."

It was, of course, what he had expected. He had made no provision for Danat's role in the text of the treaty itself, but alliances among the Khaiem had always taken the form of marriages. His son's future had always been a tile in this game, and now that tile was in play.

"Only one," he agreed.

"As it happens, I have a daughter. Ana was three years old when the doom came. She's eighteen now, and . . ."

She frowned. It was the most surprising thing she'd done since her arrival. The stone face shifted; the eyes he could not imagine weeping glistened with unspilled tears. Otah was shocked to have misjudged her so badly.

"She's never held a baby, you know," the woman said. "Hardly ever seen one. At her age, you couldn't pull me out of the nursery with a rope. The way they chuckle when they're small. Ana's never heard that. The way their hair smells . . ."

She took a deep breath, steadying herself. Otah leaned forward, his hand on the woman's wrist.

"I remember," he said softly, and she smiled.

"It's beside the matter," she said.

"It's at the center of the matter," Otah said, falling reflexively into a pose of disagreement. "And it's the part upon which we agree. Forgive me if I am being forward, but you are offering your support for my treaty in exchange for a marriage between our families? Your daughter and my son."

"Yes," she said. "I am."

"There may be others who ask the same price. There is a tradition among my people of the Khai taking several wives. . . ."

"You didn't."

"No," Otah agreed. "I didn't."

The wasp returned, buzzing at Otah's ear. He didn't raise a hand, and the insect landed on the brightly embroidered silk of his sleeve. Issandra Dasin, mother of his son's future wife, leaned forward gracefully and crushed it between her fingers.

"No other wives," she said.

"I would need assurances that the vote would be decisive," Otah said.

"You'll have them. I am a more influential woman than I seem."

Otah looked up. Above them, the sun burned behind a thin scrim of cloud. The same light fell in Utani, spilling through the windows of Danat's palace. If only there were some way to whisper to the sun and have it relay the message to Danat: Are you certain you'll take this risk? A life spent with a woman whom you've never met, whom you may never love?

His son had seen twenty summers and was by all rights a man. Before the great diplomatic horde had left for Galt, they had discussed the likelihood of a bargain of this sort. Danat hadn't hesitated. If it was a price, he'd pay it. His face had been solemn when he'd said it. Solemn and certain, and as ignorant as Otah himself had been at that age. There was nothing else either of them could have said. And nothing different that Otah could do now, except put off the moment for another few breaths by staring up at the blinding sun.

"Very well," Otah said. Then again, "Very well."

"You also have a daughter," the woman said. "The elder child?"

"Yes," Otah said.

"Does she have a claim as heir?"

The image appeared in his mind unbidden: Eiah draped in golden robes and gems woven into her hair as she dressed a patient's wounds. Otah chuckled, then saw the beginnings of offense in his guest's expression. He thought it might not be wise to appear amused at the idea of a woman in power.

"She wouldn't take the job if you begged her," Otah said. "She's a smart, strong-willed woman, but court politics give her a rash."

"But if she changed her mind. Twenty years from now, who can say that her opinions won't have shifted?"

"It wouldn't matter," Otah said. "There is no tradition of empresses. Nor, I think, of women on your own High Council."

She snorted derisively, but Otah saw he had scored his point. She considered for a moment, then with a deep breath allowed herself to relax.

"Well then. It seems we have an agreement."

"Yes," Otah said.

She stood and adopted a pose that she clearly had practiced with a specialist in etiquette. It was in essence a greeting, with nuances of a contract being formed and the informality that came with close relations.

"Welcome to my family, Most High," she said in his language. Otah replied with a pose that accepted the welcome, and if its precise meaning was lost on her, the gist was clear enough.

After she had left, Otah strolled through the gardens, insulated by his rank from everyone he met. The trees seemed straighter than he remembered, the birdsong more delicate. A weariness he only half-knew had been upon him had lifted, and he felt warm and energetic in a way he hadn't in months. He made his way at length to his suite, his rooms, his desk.

Kiyan-kya, it seems something may have gone right after all. . . .

2

Ten years almost to the day before word of Otah's pact with the Galts reached him, Maati Vaupathai had learned of his son's death at the hands of Galtic soldiers. A fugitive only just abandoned by his only companion, he had made his way to the south like a wounded horse finding its way home. It had not been the city itself he had been looking for, but a woman.

Liat Chokavi, owner and overseer of House Kyaan, had received him. Twice, they had been lovers, once as children, and then again just before the war. She had told him of Nayiit's stand, of how he had been cut down protecting the Emperor's son, Danat, as the final assault on Machi began. She spoke with the chalky tones of a woman still in pain. If Maati had held hopes that his once-lover might take him in, they did not survive that conversation. He left her house in agony. He had not spoken to her since.

Two years after that, he took his first student, a woman named Halit. Since then, his life had become a narrow, focused thing. He had remade himself as a teacher, as an agent of hope, as the Dai-kvo of a new age.

It was less glamorous than it sounded.

All that morning he had lain in the small room that was presently his home, squinting at the dirty light that made its way through the oiled-parchment window and thinking of the andat. Thinking of thoughts made flesh, of ideas

given human form and volition. Little gods, held tight to existence by the
poets who knew them best and, by knowing, bound them. Removing-the-
Part-That-Continues, called Seedless. Water-Moving-Down, called Rain or
Seaward. Stone-Made-Soft who had no other name. And his own—Corrupting-
the-Generative, called Sterile, whom Maati had not quite bound, and who had
remade the world.

The lessons he had learned as a boy, the conversations he had had as a man
and a poet, they all came back to him dimly. Fragments and moments, insights
but not all the steps that had led him there. A mosquito whined in the gloom,
and Maati waved it away.

Teaching his girls was like telling the story of his life and finding there were
holes in it. He knew things—structures of grammar and metaphor, anecdotes
of long-dead poets and the bindings they had made, occult relationships
between abstractions like shapes and numbers and the concrete things of
the world—without remembering how he'd learned them. Every lecture he
gave, he had to half-invent. Every question he answered, he had to solve in his
mind to be sure. On one hand, it was as awkward as using a grand palace as a
lesson on how to build scaffolding. And on the other, it was making him a better poet and a better teacher than he would ever have been otherwise.

He sat up, the canvas cot groaning as his weight shifted. The room was tiny
and quiet; the stone walls wept and smelled of fungus. Half-aware of his surroundings and half in the fine points of ancient grammars, Maati rose and
trundled up the short flight of stairs. The warehouse stood empty, the muted
daylight and the sound of light rain making their way through the high, narrow
windows. His footsteps echoed as he crossed to the makeshift lecture hall.

Benches of old, splintering wood squatted near a length of wall smooth
enough to take chalk. The markings of the previous evening still shone white
against the stone. Maati squinted at them.

Age was a thief. It took his wind, it made his heart race at odd times, and it
stole his sleep. But the worst of all the little indignities was his sight. He hadn't
thought about the blessing that decent vision was until his eyes started to fail.
It made his head ache a bit, but he found the diagram he'd been thinking of,
traced it with his fingertips, considered, and then took a rag from the pail of
water beside his little podium and washed the marks away. He could start
there tonight, with the four categories of being and their relationships. It was a
subtle point, but without it, the girls would never build a decent binding.

There were five of them now: Irit, Ashti Beg, Vanjit, Small Kae, and Large
Kae. Half a year ago, there had been seven, but Umnit had tried her binding,
failed, and perished. Lisat had given up and left him. Just as well, really. Lisat
had been a good-hearted girl, but slow-witted as a cow. And so, five. Or six, if
he counted Eiah.

Eiah had been a gift from the gods. She spent her days in the palaces of
Utani, playing the daughter of Empire. He knew it was a life she disliked, but
she saw to it that food and money found their way to Maati. And being part of

the court let her keep an ear out for gossip that would serve them, like a dispute over the ownership of a low-town warehouse that left both claimants barred from visiting the building until judgment was passed. The warehouse had been Maati's for two months now. It was beginning to feel like his own. He dropped the rag back into its pail, found the thick cube of chalk, and started drawing the charts for the evening's lecture. He wondered whether Eiah would be able to join them. She was a good student, when she could slip away from her life at the palace. She asked good questions.

The crude iron bolt turned with a sound like a dropped hammer, and the small, human-size door beside the great sliding walls intended for carts and wagons opened. A woman's figure was silhouetted against the soft gray light. It was neither of the Kaes, but his eyes weren't strong enough to make out features. When she came in, closing the door behind her, he recognized Vanjit by her gait.

"You're early, Vanjit-cha," Maati said, turning back to the wall and chalk.

"I thought I might be able to help," she said. "Are you well, Maati-cha?"

Vanjit had been with him for almost a year now. She had come to his covert school, as all the others had, through a series of happy accidents. Another of his students—Umnit—had fallen into conversation with her, and something had sparked between them. Umnit had presented Vanjit as a candidate to join in their work. Reluctantly, Maati had accepted her.

The girl had a brilliant mind, no question. But she had been a child in Udun, the only one of her family to survive when the Galts had come, and the memory of that slaughter still touched her eyes from time to time. She might laugh and talk and make music, but she bore scars on her body and in her mind. In the months he had spent working with her, Maati had come to realize what had first unnerved him about the girl: of all the students he had taught, she was most like him.

He had lost his family in the war as well—his almost-son Nayiit, his lover Liat, and the man he had once thought his dearest friend. Otah, Emperor of the Khaiem. Otah, favored of the gods, who couldn't fall down without landing on rose petals. They had not all died, but they were all lost to him.

"Maati-cha?" Vanjit said. "Did I say something wrong?"

Maati blinked and took a pose of query.

"You looked angry," she said.

"Nothing," Maati said, shifting the chalk to his other hand and shaking the ache from his fingers. "Nothing, Vanjit-kya, my mind was just wandering. Come, sit. There's nothing that you need to do, but you can keep me company while I get ready."

She sat on the bench, one leg tucked under her. He noticed that her hair and robe were wet from the rain. There was mud on her boots. She'd been walking out in the weather. Maati hesitated, chalk halfway back to the stone.

"Or," he said slowly, "perhaps I should ask if you've been well?"

She smiled and took a pose that dismissed his concerns.

"Bad dream again," she said. "That's all."

"About the baby," Maati said.

"I could feel him inside of me," she said. "I could feel his heartbeat. It's strange. I hate dreaming about him. The nightmares that I'm back in the war—I may scream myself awake, but at least I'm pleased that the dream's ended. When I dream about him, I'm happy. I'm at peace. And then . . ."

She gestured at the childless world around them.

"It's worse, wishing I could sleep and dream and never awake."

Maati's heart rang in sympathy, like a crystal bowl taking up the ringing of a great bell. How many times had he dreamed that Nayiit lived? That the world had not been broken, or, if it had, not by him?

"We'll bring him," Maati said. "Have faith. Every week, we come closer. Once the grammar is built solidly enough, anything will be possible."

"Are we coming closer?" she asked. "Be honest, Maati-cha. Every week we spend on this, I think we're on the edge, and every week, there's more after it."

He tucked the chalk into his sleeve and sat at the girl's side. She leaned forward, and he thought there was something in her expression—not despair and not shame, but something related to both.

"We are coming near, and we are close," he said. "I know it isn't something you can see, but each of you knows more about the andat and the bindings right now than I did after a year with the Dai-kvo. You're smart and dedicated and talented. And together, we can make this work. It sounds terrible, I know, but as soon as Siimat failed her binding and paid the price . . . I won't say I was pleased. I can't say that. She was a brave woman, and she had a wonderful mind. I miss her. But that she and all the others died means we are very close."

Ten bindings, ending in ten failures and ten corpses. His fallen soldiers, Maati thought. His girls who had sacrificed themselves. And here, wet as a canal rat and sad to her bones, Vanjit impatient to make her own try, risk her own life. Maati took her small hand in his own. The girl smiled at the wall.

"This *will* happen," he said.

"I know it," she said, her voice soft. "It's just so hard to wait when the dream keeps coming."

Maati sat with her for a moment, only the tapping of raindrops and the songs of birds between them. He stood, fished the chalk from his sleeve, and went back to the wall.

"If you'd like, you could light a fire in the office grate," Maati said. "We could surprise the others with some fresh tea."

It wasn't called for, but it gave the girl something to do. He squinted at the figure he'd drawn until the lines came into focus. Ah, yes. Four categories of being.

The rain slackened as the others arrived. Large Kae checked the coverings over the windows, careful that no stray light betray their presence, as Irit fluttered sparrowlike lighting the lanterns. Small Kae and Ashti Beg adjusted the seats and benches, the younger woman's light voice contrasting with her elder's dry one.

The scents of wood smoke and tea made their warehouse classroom seem less illicit. Vanjit poured bowls for each of his students as they took their places. The soft light darkened the stone so that the chalk marks almost seemed written on air. Maati took a moment to himself to think of his teachers, of their lectures. He willed himself to become one of their number.

"The world," Maati began, "has two essential structures. There's the physical"—he slapped the stone wall behind him—"and there's the abstract. Two and two are always four, regardless of whether you're talking about grains of sand or racing camels. Twelve could always be broken into two sets of six or three sets of four long before anybody noticed the fact. Abstract structure, you see?"

They bent toward him like flowers toward the sun. Maati saw the hunger in their faces and the set of their shoulders.

"Now," Maati said. "Does the physical require the abstract? Come on. Think! Can you have something physical that doesn't have abstract structure?"

There was a moment's silence.

"Water?" Small Kae asked. "Because if you put two drops of water together with two drops of water, you just get one big drop."

"You're ahead of yourself," Maati said. "That's called the doctrine of least similarity. You're not ready for that. What I mean is this: is there anything real that can't be described by its abstract structure? Any of you? No one has a thought about this? I answered that one correctly before I'd seen ten summers."

"No?" suggested Irit.

"No. How many of you think she's right? Go on! Take a stand about it one way or the other! Good. Yes. Irit's right," Maati said and spat at the floor by his feet. "Everything physical has abstract structure, but not everything abstract need be physical. That's what we're *doing* here. That's the asymmetry that lets the andat exist."

In all their faces, turned to his, there was the same expression. Hunger, he thought, or desperation. Or longing halfway forged into something stronger. It gave him hope.

After the lecture, he made them run through grammar exercises, and then, as the moon rose and the lanterns smoked and the rats came out to chuff and chitter at them from the shadows, they considered the failed bindings of the women who had gone before them. Slowly, they were developing a sense of what it was to capture an andat, to take a thought and translate it into a different form. To give it volition and a human shape. To keep the binding present in your mind for the rest of your life, holding the spirit back from its natural state of nothingness like holding a stone over a well: slip once, and it is gone. Maati could see the knowledge growing in the set of their poses and hear it in the questions they asked. He had almost reached the end of his night's plan when the small door to the street flew open again.

Eiah strode in, her breath labored. She wore a drab cloak over a silk robe rich with all the colors of sunset. The others fell silent. Maati, standing before a wall now covered in white, ghostly notations and graphs, took a pose that expressed his alarm and asked the cause of hers.

"Uncle Maati," she said between gasps, "there's news from Galt. My father."

Maati shifted toward several poses at once, managing none of them. Eiah's expression was grim.

"That's all for tonight," he said. "Come back tomorrow."

He had intended to assign exercises, translation puzzles for them to work in their time away from class. He abandoned the idea and shooed them out the door. All of them left except Eiah, sitting on a low chair in the warehouse office, her face lit by the shifting flames in the grate.

The letters had arrived by fast courier. Against all expectation, the Emperor's benighted mission to Galt had borne fruit. Danat was to be married to a daughter of the Galtic High Council. Terms were being arranged for the transport of a thousand Galtic women of childbearing age to the cities of the Khaiem. Applications would be taken for a thousand men to leave their lives among the cities of the Khaiem and move to Galt. It was, Eiah said, intended to be the first exchange of many.

There were protests and anger in only a few cities. Nantani and Yalakeht, hit hard by the war, were sending petitions of condemnation. In the low towns, the anger burned brighter. Galt was still the enemy, and there were rumors of plots to kill whomever of them dared set foot on Khaiate soil: talk and rumor, drunken rhetoric likely to come to nothing.

The greater mass of the utkhaiem were already gathering their best robes and most garish jewelry in preparation for the journey south to Saraykeht to greet the returning fleet and see this Galtic girl who would one day be Empress. Maati listened to it all, his frown deepening until his mouth began to ache.

"It doesn't change anything," he said. "Otah can sell us to our enemies if he wants. It doesn't affect our work here. Once we have the grammar worked through and the andat back in the world—"

"It changes everything," Eiah said. "Danat is marrying a Galt. The utkhaiem are either going to line up like sailors at a comfort house to follow the example or resist and restart a war we'll never win. Or worse, both. Perhaps he'll divide the utkhaiem so deeply that we'll turn on each other."

Maati took the tea from the fire and filled his bowl. It was bitter and overbrewed and scalded his tongue. He drank it anyway. Eiah was looking at him, waiting for him to speak. The fire danced over the graying lumps of coal.

"The women's grammar won't matter if the world's already passed us by," Eiah said softly. "If it takes us five more years to capture an andat, there will already be a half-Galt child on its way to becoming Emperor. There will already be half-Galt children born to every family with any power, anywhere in the cities. Will an andat undo that? Will an andat unmake the love these fathers feel for their new children?"

If it's the right one, yes, Maati thought but didn't say. He only stared down into his bowl of tea, watching the dark leaves staining its depths.

"He is remaking the world without us," Eiah went on. "He's giving his official seal to the thought that if a woman can't bear a child, she doesn't matter. He's doing the wrong thing, and once a wound has healed badly, Uncle, it's twice as hard to put right."

Everything she said made sense. The longer it took to bring back the andat, the harder it would be to repair the damage he'd done. And if the world had changed past recognition before his work was complete, he wasn't sure what meaning the effort would have. His jaw ached, and he realized he'd been clenching it.

"So what then?" Maati said, taking a pose that made his words a challenge. "What do you want me to do I'm not doing already?"

Eiah sat back, her head in her hands. She looked like Otah when she did it. It was always unnerving when he caught a glimpse of her father in her. He knew what she would say before she spoke. It was, after all, what she'd been steering him toward from the conversation's start. It was the subject they had been arguing for months.

"Let me try my binding," Eiah said. "You've seen my outlines. You know the structure's sound. If I can capture Returning-to-Natural-Equilibrium . . ."

She let the words trail away. Returning-to-Natural-Equilibrium, called Healing.

"I *don't* know that," Maati said, half-ashamed by the peevishness in his voice. "I only said that I didn't *see* a flaw in them. I never said there wasn't one, only that I couldn't see it. And besides which, it might be too near something that's been done before. I won't lose you because some minor poet in the Second Empire bound Making-Things-Right or Fix-the-Broken or some idiotically broad concept like that."

"Even if they did, they hadn't trained as physicians. I know how flesh works in ways they wouldn't have. I can bring things back the way they're meant to be. The women that Sterile broke, I can make whole again. If we could only—"

"You're too important."

Eiah went silent. When she spoke again, her voice was heavy and bitter.

"You know you've just called all the others unimportant," Eiah said.

"Not unimportant," Maati said. "They're all important. They only aren't all irreplaceable. Wait, Eiah-kya. Be patient. Once we have a grammar that we know can work, I won't stop you. But let someone else be first."

"There isn't time," Eiah said. "We have a handful of months before the trade starts in earnest. Maybe a year."

"Then we'll find a way to move them faster," Maati said.

The question of how that might be done, however, haunted him the rest of the night. He lay on his cot, the night candle hissing almost inaudibly and casting its misty light on the stone ceiling. The women, his students, had all retired to what quarters Eiah had quietly arranged for them. Eiah herself had gone back to the palaces of the Emperor, the great structures dedicated to Otah, while Maati lay in the near-dark in a warehouse, sleep eluding him and his mind gnawing at questions of time.

Maati's father had died younger than he was now. Maati had been an aspiring poet at the village of the Dai-kvo at the time. When the word came, he had not seen the man in something near a decade. The news had stung less than he would have anticipated, not a fresh loss so much as the reminder of one already suffered. A slowing of blood had taken the man, the message said, and Maati had never looked into the matter more deeply. Lately he'd found himself wondering whether his father had done all that he'd wished, if the son he'd given over to the poets had made him proud, what regrets had marked that last illness.

The candle had almost burned itself to nothing when he gave up any hope of sleep. Outside, songbirds were greeting the still-invisible dawn, but Maati took no joy in them. He lit a fresh candle and sat on the smooth-worn stone steps and considered the small wooden box that carried the only two irreplaceable things he owned. One was a painting he had done from memory of Nayiit Chokavi, the son he should have had, the child he had helped, however briefly, to raise, the boy whom Otah—Otah to whom no rules applied—had brought into the world in Saraykeht and taken out of it in Machi. The other was a book bound in black leather.

He opened the cover and considered the first page, squinting to bring the letters clear. He could not help but think of another book—that one brown—which had been his gift from Heshai-kvo and Seedless. Heshai's handwriting had been clearer than Maati's own, his gift for language more profound.

> I, *Maati Vaupathai, am one of the two men remaining in the world who has wielded the power of the andat. As the references from which I myself learned are lost, I shall endeavor to record here what I know of grammar and of the forms of thought by which the andat may be bound and the abstract made physical. And, with that, my own profound error from which the world is still suffering.*

Half-reading, he flipped through the pages, caught occasionally by a particular turn of phrase of which he was fond or tripped by a diagram or metaphor that was still not to his best liking. Though his eyes strained, he could still read what he'd written, and when the ink seemed to blur, he had the memory of what he had put there. He reached the blank pages sooner than he expected, and sat on his stairs, fingertips moving over the smooth paper with a sound like skin against skin. There was so much to say, so many things he'd thought and considered. Often, he would come back from a particularly good lecture to his students full of fire and intentions, prepared to write a fresh section. Sometimes his energy lasted long enough to do so. Sometimes not.

It will be a sad legacy to die with this half-finished, he thought as he let the cover close.

He needed a real school, the school needed a teacher, and he himself could manage only so much. There wasn't time to lecture all his students and write his manual and slink like a criminal through the dark corners of the Empire. If he'd been younger, perhaps—fifty, or better yet forty years old—he might have made the attempt, but not now. And with this mad scheme of Otah's, time had grown even dearer.

"Maati-cha?"

Maati blinked. Vanjit came toward him, her steps tentative. He tucked his book into its box and took a pose of welcome.

"The door wasn't bolted," she said. "I was afraid something had happened?"

"No," Maati said, rising and hoisting himself up the stairs. "I forgot it last night. An old man getting older is all."

The girl took a pose that was both an acceptance and a denial. She looked exhausted, and Maati suspected there were dark smudges under his own eyes to match hers. The scent of eggs and beef caught his attention. A small lacquer box hung at Vanjit's side.

"Ah," Maati said. "It that what I hope it is?"

She smiled at that. The girl did have a pleasant smile, when she used it. The eggs were fresh; whipped and steamed in bright orange blocks. The beef was rich and moist. Vanjit sat beside him in the echoing, empty space of the warehouse as the morning light pressed in at the high, narrow windows, blue then yellow then gold. They talked about nothing important: the wayhouse where she was staying, his annoyance with his failing eyes, the merits of their present warehouse as compared to the half-dozen other places where Maati had taken up his chalk. Vanjit asked him questions that built on what they'd discussed the night before: How did the different forms of being relate to time? How did a number exist differently than an apple or a man? Or a child?

Maati found himself holding forth on matters of the andat and the poets, his time with the Dai-kvo, and even before that at the school. Vanjit sat still, her gaze on him, and drank his words like water.

She had lost her family when she was barely six years old. Her mother, father, younger sister, and two older brothers cut down by the gale of Galtic blades. The pain of it had faded, perhaps. It had never gone. Maati felt, as they sat together, that perhaps she had begun, however imperfectly, to build a new family. Perhaps she would have sat at her true father's knee, listening to him with this same intensity. Perhaps Nayiit would have treated him with the same attention that Vanjit did now. Or perhaps their shared hunger belonged to people who had lost the first object of their love.

By the time Eiah and the others arrived in the late morning, Maati had reached the decision that he'd fought against the whole night. He took Eiah aside as soon as she came in.

"I have need of you," Maati said. "How much can you spirit away without our being noticed? We'll need food and clothing and tools. Lots of tools. And if there's a servant or slave you can trust . . ."

"There isn't," Eiah said. "But things are in disarray right now. Half the court in Nantani would chew their tongues out before offering hospitality to a Galt. The other half are whipped to a froth trying to get to Saraykeht before the rest. A few wagonloads here and there would be easy to overlook."

Maati nodded, more than half to himself. Eiah took a pose of query.

"You're going to build me a school. I know where there's one to be had, and with the others helping, it shouldn't take terribly long to have it in order. And we need a teacher."

"We have a teacher, Maati-kya," Eiah said.

Maati didn't answer, and after a moment, Eiah looked down.

"Cehmai?" she asked.

"He's the only other living poet. The only one who's truly held one of the andat. He could do more, I suspect, than I can manage."

"I thought you two had fallen out?"

"I don't like his wife," Maati said sourly. "But I have to try. The two of us agreed on a way to find one another, if the need arose. I can hope he's kept to it better than I have."

"I'll come with you."

"No," Maati said, putting a hand on Eiah's shoulder. "I need you to prepare things for us. There's a place—I'll draw you a map to it. The Galts attacked it in the war, killed everyone, but even if they dropped bodies down the well, the water'll be fresh again by now. It's off the high road between Pathai and Nantani. . . ."

"That school?" Eiah said. "The place they sent the boys to train as poets? That's where you want to go?"

"Yes," Maati said. "It's out of the way, it's built for itinerant poets, and there may be something there—some book or scroll or engravings on the walls—that the twice-damned Galts overlooked. Regardless, it's where it all began. It's where we are going to take it all back."

3

>+< The voyage returning Otah to the cities of the Khaiem took weeks to prepare, and if the ships that had left Saraykeht all those months before had looked like an invading fleet, the ones returning were a city built on the water. The high-masted Galtic ships with their great billowing sails dyed red and blue and gold took to the sea by the dozens. Every great family of Galt seemed bent on sending a ship greater than the others. The ships of the utkhaiem—lacquered and delicate and low to the water—seemed small and awkward beside these, their newest seafaring cousins. Birds circled above them, screaming confusion as if a part of the coast itself had set out for foreign lands. The trees and hills of Otah's onetime enemies fell away behind them. That first night, the torches and lanterns made the sea appear as full of stars as the sky.

One of the small gifts the gods had granted Otah was a fondness for travel by ship. The shifting of the deck under his feet, the vast scent of the ocean, the call of the gulls were like visiting a place he had once lived. He stood at the prow of the great Galtic ship given him by the High Council for his journey home and looked out at the rising sun.

He had spent years in the eastern islands as a boy. He'd been a middling fisherman, a better midwife's assistant, a good sailor. He had come close to marrying an island woman, and still bore the first half of the marriage tattoo on his breast. The ink had faded and spread over the years as if he were a parchment dropped in water. With the slap of waves against wood, the salt-laden air, the morning light dancing gold and rose on the water, he remembered those days.

This late in the morning, he would already have cast his nets. His fingers would have been numbed by the cold. He would have been eating the traditional breakfast of fish paste and nuts from an earthenware jar. The men he had known would be doing the same today, those who were still alive. In another life, another world, he might be doing it still.

He had lived so many lives: half-starved street child; petty thief; seafront laborer; fisherman; assistant midwife; courier; Khai; husband; father; war leader; emperor. Put in a line that way, he could see how another person might imagine his life to be an unending upward spiral, but it didn't feel that way to him. He had done what he'd had to at the time. One thing had led to another. A man without particular ambition had been placed atop the world, and likewise the world had been placed atop him. And against all probability, he found himself here, wearing the richest robes in the cities, with a private cabin larger than some boats he'd worked, and thinking fondly of fish paste and nuts.

Lost in thought, he heard the little ship's boat hail—a booming voice speaking Galtic words—before he knew it was approaching. The watchman of his own vessel replied, and then the landsman's chair descended. Otah watched idly as a man in the colors of House Dasin was winched up, swung over, and lowered to the deck. A knot of Otah's own clerks and servants formed around the newcomer. Otah pulled his hands up into his sleeves and made his way back.

The boy was a servant of some sort—the Galts had a system of gradation that Otah hadn't bothered to memorize—with hair the color of beach sand and a greenish tint to his face. Seeing Otah, the servant took a pose of abject obeisance poorly.

"Most High," he said, his words heavily inflected, "Councilman Dasin sends his regards. He and his wife extend the invitation to a dinner and concert aboard the *Avenger* tomorrow evening."

The boy gulped and looked down. There had, no doubt, been a more formal and flowery speech planned. Nausea led to brevity. Otah glanced at his Master of Tides, a youngish woman with a face like a hatchet and a mind for detail that would have served her in any trade. She took a pose that deferred to Otah's judgment, gave permission, and offered to make excuse all with a single gesture. Dasin's servant wouldn't have seen a third of her meanings. Otah glanced over at the shining water. The sun's angle had already shifted, the light already changed its colors and the colors of the ocean that bore them. He allowed himself a small sigh.

Even here there would be no escape from it. Etiquette and court politics, parties and private audiences, favors asked and given. There was no end of it because of course there wasn't. No more than a farmer could stop planting fields, a fisherman stop casting nets, a tradesman close up warehouses and stalls and spend long days singing in teahouses or soaking in baths.

"I should be pleased," he said. "Please convey my gratitude to Farrer-cha and his family."

The boy bowed his thanks rather than make a formal pose, then, blushing, adopted a pose of gratitude and retreated back to the landsman's chair. With a great shouting and the creak of wood and leather, the chair rose, swung out over the water, and descended. Otah watched the boy vanish over the rail, but didn't see him safely to the boat. The invitation was a reminder of all that waited for him in his cabin below decks. Otah took a long, deep breath, feeling the salt and the sunlight in his lungs, and descended to the endless business of Empire.

Letters had arrived from Yalakeht outlining a conspiracy by three of the high families of the utkhaiem still bitter from the war to claim independence and name a Khai Yalakeht rather than acknowledge a Galtic empress. Chaburi-Tan had suffered another attack by pirates. Though the invaders had been driven off, it was becoming clear that the Westlands mercenary company hired to protect the city was also in negotiation with the raiders; the city's economy was on the edge of collapse.

There was some positive news from the palaces at Utani. Danat wrote that the low farms around Pathai, Utani, and Lachi were all showing a good crop, and the cattle plague they'd feared had come to nothing, so those three cities, at least, wouldn't be starving for at least the next year.

Otah read until the servants brought his midday meal, then again for two and a half hands. He slept after that in a suspended cot whose oiled chains shifted with the rocking ship but never let out so much as a whisper. He woke with the low sunlight of evening sloping in the cabin window and the dull thunder of feet above him announcing the change of watch as clearly as the drum and flute. He lay there for a moment, his mind pleasantly emptied by his rest, then swung his legs over, dropped to the deck, and composed two of the seven letters he would send ahead of the massive, celebratory fleet.

WHEN, THE NEXT EVENING, HIS MASTER OF TIDES SENT TO REMIND HIM OF THE engagement he'd agreed to, Otah had indeed forgotten it. He allowed servants to dress him in robes of emerald silk and cloth of gold, his long, white hair to be bound back. His temples were anointed with oils smelling of lavender and sandalwood. Decades now he had been Emperor or else Khai Machi, and the exercise still struck him as ridiculous. He had been slow to understand the value of ceremony and tradition. He still wasn't entirely convinced.

The boat that bore him and his retinue across to the Dasins' ship, the *Avenger*, was festooned with flowers and torches. Blossoms fell into the water, floating there with the reflections of flame. Otah stood, watching as the oarsmen pulled him toward the great warship. His footing was as sure as a seaman's, and he was secretly proud of the fact. The high members of the utkhaiem who had joined him—Auna Tiyan, Piyat Saya, and old Adaut Kamau—all kept to their benches. The *Avenger* itself glowed with candlelight, the effect lessened by the last remnant of the glorious sunset behind it. When full darkness came, the ship would look like something from a children's story. Otah tried to appreciate it for what it would become.

The landsman's chair took each of them up in turn, Otah last out of respect for his rank. The deck of the *Avenger* was as perfect and controlled as any palace ballroom, any Khaiate garden, any high chamber of the Galts. Chairs that seemed made of silver filigree and breath were scattered over the fresh-scrubbed boards in patterns that looked both careless and perfect. Musicians played reed organ and harp, and a small chorus of singers sat in the rigging, as if the ship itself had joined the song. Swinging down in the landsman's chair, Otah saw half-a-dozen men he knew, including, his face upturned and amused, Balasar Gice.

Farrer Dasin stood with his wife Issandra and the young woman—the girl—Ana. Otah let himself be drawn up from the chair by his servants, and stepped forward to his hosts. Farrer stood stiff as cast iron, his smile never reaching his eyes. Issandra's eyes still had the reddened rims that Otah recalled, but there was also pleasure there. And her daughter . . .

Ana Dasin, the Galt who would one day be Empress of the Khaiem, reminded Otah of a rabbit. Her huge, brown eyes and small mouth looked perpetually startled. She wore a gown of blue as pale as a robin's egg that didn't fit her complexion and a necklace of raw gold that did. She would have seemed meek, except that there was something of her mother in the line of her jaw and the set of her shoulders.

All he knew of her had come from court gossip, Balasar Gice's comments, and the trade of formal documents that had flowed by the crate once the agreements were made. It was difficult to believe that this was the girl who had beaten her own tutor at numbers or written a private book of etiquette that had been the scandal of its season. She was said to have ridden horses from the age of four; she was said to have insulted the son of an ambassador from Eddensea to his face and gone on to make her case so clearly that the insulted boy had offered apology. She had climbed out windows on ropes made from stripped tapestry, had climbed the walls of the palaces of Acton dressed as an urchin boy, had broken the hearts of men twice her age. Or, again, perhaps she had not. He had heard a great deal about her, and knew nothing he could count as truth. It was to her he made his first greeting.

"Ana-cha," he said. "I hope I find you well."

"Thank you, Most High," she said, her voice so soft, Otah half-wondered whether he'd understood. "And you also."

"Emperor," Farrer Dasin said in his own language.

"Councilman Dasin," Otah said. "You are kind to invite me."

Farrer's nod made it clear that he would have preferred not to. The singers above them reached the end of one song, paused, and launched into another. Issandra stepped forward smiling and rested her hand on Otah's arm.

"Forgive my husband," she said. "He was never fond of shipboard life. And he spent seven years as a sailor."

"I hadn't known that," Otah said.

"Fighting Eymond," the councilman said. "Sank twelve of their ships. Burned their harbor at Cathir."

Otah smiled and nodded. He wondered how his own history as a fisherman would be received if he shared it now. He chose to leave the subject behind.

"The weather is treating us gently," Otah said. "We will be in Saraykeht before summer's end."

·   He could see in all their faces that it had been the wrong thing. The father's jaw tightened, his nostrils flared. The mother's smile lost its sharp corners and her eyes grew sad. Ana looked away.

"Come see what they've done with the kitchens, Most High," Issandra said. "It's really quite remarkable."

After a short tour of the ship, Issandra released him, and Otah made his way to the dais that was intended for him. Other guests arrived from Galtic ships and the utkhaiem, each new person greeting the councilman and his family, and then coming to Otah. He had expected to see a division among them: the Galts resentful and full of barely controlled rage much like Farrer Dasin, and Otah's own people pleased at the prospects that his treaty opened for them. Instead, he saw as the guests came and went, as the banquet was served, as priests of Galt intoned their celebratory rites, that opinions were more varied and more complex.

At the opening ceremony, the divisions were clear. Here, the robes of the Khaiem, there the tunics and gowns of the Galts. But very quickly, the people on the deck began to shift. Small groups fell into discussion, often no more than two or three people. Otah's practiced eye could pick out the testing smile and almost flirtatious laughter of men on the verge of negotiation. And as the evening progressed—candles burning down and being replaced, slow courses of wine and fish and meat and pastry making their way from the very cleverly built kitchens to the gently shifting deck—as many Galts as utkhaiem had the glint in their eyes that spoke of sensed opportunity. Larger groups formed and broke apart, the proportions of their two nations seeming almost even. Otah felt as if he'd stirred a muddy pool and was now seeing the first outlines of the new forms that it might take.

And yet, some groups were unmoved. Two clusters of Galts never budged or admitted in anyone wearing robes, but also a fair-sized clot of people of the cities of the Khaiem sat near the far rail, their backs to the celebration, their conversation almost pointedly relying on court poses too subtle for foreigners to follow.

Women, Otah noted. The people of his nation whose anger was clearest in their bodies and speech tended to be women. He thought of Eiah, and cool melancholy touched his heart. Trafficking in wombs, she would have called it. To her, this agreement would be the clearest and most nearly final statement that what mattered about the women of the cities—about his own daughter— was whether they could bear. He could hear her voice saying it, could see the pain in the way she held her chin. He murmured his counterarguments, as if she were there, as if she could hear him.

It wasn't a turning away, only an acknowledgment of what they all knew. The woman of the Khaiem were just as clever, just as strong, just as important as they had ever been. The brokering of marriage—and yes, specifically marriage bent on producing children—was no more an attack on Eiah and her generation than building city militias or hiring mercenary companies or any of the other things he had done to hold the cities safe had been.

It sounded patronizing, even to him.

There had to be some way, he thought, to honor and respect the pain and the loss that they had suffered without forfeiting the future. He remembered Kiyan warning him that some women—not all, but some—who could not bear children went mad from longing. She told stories of babies being stolen, and of pregnant women killed and the babes taken from their dying wombs.

Wanting could be a sickness, his wife had said. He remembered the night she'd said it, where the lantern had been, how the air had smelled of burning oil and pine boughs. He remembered his daughter's expression at hearing the phrase, like she'd found expression for something she'd always known, and his own sense of dread. Kiyan had tried to warn him of something, and it had to do with the backs of the people now at the rails, turned away from the Galts and the negotiated future forming behind them. Eiah had known. Otah felt he had still only half-grasped it. Farrer Dasin, he thought, might see it more clearly.

"It appears to be going quite well, wouldn't you say, Most High?"

Balasar Gice stood beside the dais, his hands in a pose of greeting. The cool night air or else the wine had touched his cheeks with red.

"Does it? I hope so," Otah said, smoothing away his darker thoughts. "I think there are more trade agreements than wars brewing tonight. It's hard to know."

"There's hope," Balasar said. And then, his voice growing reflective, "There's hope, and that's actually quite new. I hadn't realized it had become quite such a rare thing, these last few years."

"How nice," Otah said more sharply than he'd intended. Balasar looked at him more closely, and Otah waved the concern away. "I'm old and tired. And I've eaten more Galtic food than I could have wanted in a lifetime. It's astounding you people ever got up from your tables."

"You aren't expected to finish every dish," Balasar said. "Ah, I think the entertainment has begun."

Otah looked up. Servants and sailors were silently moving across the deck like a wind over the water. The glow of candles lessened and the scent of spent wicks filled the air as a stage appeared as if conjured across the deck from Otah's dais. The singers that had hung from the rigging had apparently made their way down, because they rose now, taking their places. Servants placed three more chairs on the dais at Otah's side, and Councilman Dasin and his family took their seats. Farrer smelled prodigiously of distilled wine and sat the farthest from him, his wife close at his side, leaving Ana nearest to Otah.

The singers bowed their heads for a moment, then the low sounds of their voices began to swell. Otah closed his eyes. It was a song he knew—a court dance from the Second Empire. The harmonies were perfect and rich, sorrowful and joyous. This, he understood, was a gift. Galtic voices raised in a song of an empire that was not their own. He let himself be carried by it, and when the voices fell again, the last throbbing notes fading to silence, he was among the first to applaud. Otah was surprised to find tears in his eyes.

Ana Dasin, at his side, was also weeping. When he met her eyes, she looked down, said something he couldn't hear, and walked briskly away. He watched her descend the stairs below decks as the singers began another, more boisterous song. Otah's gaze flickered to Issandra. In the dim light, the subtle signs of age were softened. He saw for a moment who she had been as a younger woman. She met his eyes with a profound weariness. Farrer had his hand on her arm, holding her gently to him, though the man's face remained turned away. Otah wondered, not for the first time, what brokering this agreement had cost Issandra Dasin.

He glanced at the stairs down which her daughter had vanished, and then back, his hands shifting into a pose that made an implicit offer. Issandra raised an eyebrow, a half-smile making a dimple in one cheek. Otah tugged at his robes, straightening the lines, and stepped carefully down from the dais. The girl Ana would be his daughter too, soon enough. If her true mother and father weren't placed to speak with her in her distress, perhaps it was time that Otah did.

Below decks, the Galtic ship was as cramped and close and ripe with the scent of tightly quartered humanity as any ship Otah had sailed with. Under normal circumstances, the deck now peopled with the guests of the Dasin family would have given room to a full watch of sailors. Instead, most were lurking in the tiny rooms, waiting for the songs to end and their own turn with fresh air to come. Still, Otah, Emperor of the Khaiem, found a way cleared for him, conversations stopping when he came in view. He made his way forward, squinting into the darkness for a glimpse of the rabbit-faced girl.

Galtic design divided the cargo hold in sections, and it was in one of these dark chambers that he heard the girl's voice. Crates and boxes loomed above him to either side, the binding ropes creaking gently with the rolling ship. Rats chattered and complained. And there, hunched over as if she were protecting something pressed to her belly, sat Ana Dasin.

"Excuse me," Otah said. "I don't mean to intrude, but . . . may I sit?"

Ana looked up at him. Her dark eyes shone in the dim light. Her nod was so faint it might almost have been the movement of the ship. Otah stepped carefully over the rough board, hitched his robes up to his shins, and sat at the girl's side. They were silent. Above them, the singers struck a complex rhythm, like jugglers tossing pins between them. Otah sighed.

"I know this isn't easy for you," he said.

"What isn't, Most High?"

"Otah. Please, my name is Otah. You can call me that. I mean all of this. Being uprooted, married off to a man you've never met in a city you've never been to."

"It's what's expected of me," she said.

"Yes, I know, but . . . it isn't really fair."

"No," she said, her voice suddenly hard. "It isn't."

Otah clasped his hands, fingers laced together.

"He isn't a bad man, my son," Otah said. "He's clever and he's strong, and he cares about people. He feels deeply. He's probably a better man than I was at his age."

"Forgive me, Most High," Ana Dasin said. "I don't know what you want me to say."

"Nothing. Nothing in particular. Only know that this life that we've forced on you . . . it might have some redeeming qualities. The gods all know the life I've had wasn't the one I expected, either. We do what we have to do. In my ways, I'm as constrained by it as you are."

She looked at him as if he were speaking a language she hadn't heard before. Otah shook his head.

"It's nothing, Ana-cha," he said. "Only know that I know how hard this time is, and it will get better. If you allow room for it, this new life might even surprise you."

The girl was quiet for a moment, her brow furrowed. She shook her head.

"Thank you?" she said.

Otah chuckled ruefully.

"I'm not doing a particularly good job of this, am I?" he said.

"I don't know," Ana Dasin said after a pause. Her tone carried the shielded contempt of an adolescent for her elders. "I don't know what you're doing."

Making his way back through the crowded belly of the ship, Otah wondered what he had thought he would say to a Galtic girl who had seen forty-five fewer summers than himself. He had expected to offer some kind of wisdom, some variety of comfort, and instead it had been like trying to hold a conversation with a cat. Who would have thought a man could be as old as he was, wield the power of empire, and still be so naïve as to think his heart would be explicable to an eighteen-year-old girl?

And, of course, as he reached the plank stairway that led up, he found what he wished he had said. He should have said that he knew what courage it took to face sacrifice. He should have said that he knew her suffering was real, and that it was in a noble cause. It made them alike, the Emperor and the Empress-to-be, that they compromised in order to make the lives of uncountable strangers better.

More than that, he should have encouraged her to speak, and he should have listened.

An approving roar came from the deck above him. A reed organ hummed and sang, flute and drum following a heartbeat later. Otah hesitated and turned back. He would try again. At worst, the girl would think he was ridiculous, and she likely already did that.

As he drew near the hold, he heard her weeping again, her voice straining at words he couldn't make out. A man's voice answered, not her father's. Otah hesitated, then quietly stepped forward.

In the gloom, Ana Dasin knelt, her arms around a young man. The boy, whoever he was, wore the work clothes of a sailor, but his arms were thin and his skin was as pale as the girl's. He returned her embrace, his arms finding their way around her as if through long acquaintance; his tear-streaked face nuzzled her hair. Ana Dasin stroked the boy's head, murmuring reassurances.

Ah, Otah thought as he stepped back, unnoticed. That's how it is.

Above deck, he smiled and nodded at Issandra and pretended to turn his attention back to the music. He wondered how many other sacrifices he had demanded in order to remake the world according to his vision, how many other lovers would be parted to further his little scheme to save two empires. He would likely never know the full price of it. As if in answer, the candles guttered in the breeze, the reed organ took a mournful turn, and the sea through which they sailed grew darker.

〉+〈 The midday sun beat down on the lush green; gnats and flies filled the air. The river—not the Qiit proper but one of its tributaries—threaded its way south like a snake. Maati tied his mule under the wide leaves of a catalpa and squatted down on a likely-looking boulder. Pulling a pouch of raisins and seeds from his sleeve, he looked out over the summer. The wild trees, the rough wagon track he'd followed from the farmers' low town to the northwest, the cultivated fields to the south.

A cluster of small farms made a loose community here, raising goats and millet and, near the water, rice. The land between the cities was dotted with low communities like this one: the rural roots that fed the great, blossoming cities of the Khaiem. The accents were rougher here, the effete taint of a high court as foreign as another language. Men might be born, grow, love, marry, and die without ever traveling more than a day's walk, birthing bed and grave marker no more distant than a thrown pebble.

And one of those fields with its ripe green grasses had been plowed by the only other man in all the world who knew how to bind the andat. Maati took a mouthful of raisins and chewed slowly, thinking.

Leaving the warehouse outside Utani had proven harder than he had expected. For over a decade, he had been rootless, moving from one city or town to another, living in the shadows. One more journey—and this one heading south into the summer cities—hadn't seemed to signify anything more than a few weeks' time and, of course, the errand itself. But somewhere in the years since the Galtic invasion, Maati had grown accustomed to traveling with companions, and as he and his swaybacked pack mule had made their slow way down the tracks and low-town roads, he had felt their absence.

The world had changed in the years he had been walking through it. Having no one there to talk with forced his mind back in on itself, and the nature of the changes he saw were more disturbing than he'd thought they would be.

Many were things he had expected. The cities and towns had grown quieter, undisturbed by the laughter and games of children. The people were older, grayer. The streets felt too big, like the robes of a once-hale man who had grown thin with illness or age. And the scars of the war itself—the burned towns already half-reclaimed by foxes and saplings, the bright green swath from Utani all the way down to ruined Nantani on the southern coast where once an army had passed—had faded, but they had not disappeared.

The distrust of the foreign was driven deep into the flesh here. He had heard stories of Westlands women coming to marry among the low towns, thinking their wombs would make them of greater value here than in their own lands. Instead, they were recognized as a slower kind of invasion. Driven out with threats or stones. The men who had had the temerity to marry outside their own kind punished in ways to rival the prices paid by failed poets. Joints broken, drowned in night pots, necks snapped, and bodies thrown into creeks to drown in half a hand's depth of water.

And yet, the stories might only be stories. The more Maati traveled, the less certain he was.

Twice, great belching steam wagons had passed him on the trail. The men at the controls had been locals, but the machines themselves were Galtic, remnants of the war. Once he had seen plumes of smoke and steam rising from the river itself, a flat barge sitting low to the water and driven by the same chuffing, tarnished bulb as the wagons. Even the fields below him now were cultivated in a pattern he had never seen before the Galts came. Perhaps Otah's betrayal of the cities colored all of Maati's perceptions now, but it felt as if the Galts were invading again, only slowly this time, burrowing under the ground and changing all they touched in small, insidious ways.

Something tickled his arm. Maati plucked out the tick and cracked it between his thumbnails. He was wasting time. His feet ached from walking and his robe stuck to his back and legs, but the sooner this meeting happened, the sooner he would know where he stood. He emptied the last of the seeds into his hand, ate them, then put the pouch back in his sleeve and untied his mule.

Seven years before, he and Cehmai had parted for the last time at a wayhouse three days' walk northwest of the farms and the river and catalpa-shaded hill. It had not been an entirely friendly parting, but they had agreed to leave letters of their whereabouts at that house, should the need ever arise to find each other.

Maati had found the place easily. In the intervening years, the kitchens had burned, and the two huge trees in the courtyard. The boy who stabled the horses had grown to be a man. The bricks that had been brown and yellow had been painted white and blue. And the box they had paid the keeper to hold for them had a letter in it, sewn and sealed, with ciphered directions that would lead to the farmhouse Cehmai had taken under his new false name. Jadit Noygu.

Jadit Noygu, and his wife Sian.

Maati took the letter out again, consulting the deciphered text he'd marked in between the lines written in Cehmai's clean, clear hand. Forward down the track until he passed the ruin of an old mill, then the first east-turning pathway, and half a hand's walk to a low mud-and-straw farmhouse with a brick cistern in front. Maati clucked at the mule and resumed his walk.

He arrived in the heat of the afternoon; even the shade beneath the trees sweltered. Maati helped himself to a bowl of water from the cistern, and then another bowl for the mule. No one came out to greet him, but the shutters on the windows looked recently painted and the track that led around the side of the house was well-tended. There was no sense that the farm stood empty. Maati made his way toward the back.

A small herd of goats bleated at him from their pen, the disturbing, clever eyes considering him with as little joy as he had for them. The low sound of whistling came to him from a tall, narrow building set apart from both house and pen. A slaughterhouse.

He stepped into the doorway, blocking the light. The air was thick with smoke to drive the flies away. The body of the sacrificed goat hung from a hook, buckets of blood and entrails at the butcher's feet. The butcher turned. Her hands were crimson, her leather apron sodden with blood. A hooked knife flashed in her hand.

She was not the only reason that Maati and Cehmai had parted company, but she would have been sufficient. Idaan Machi, outcast sister to the Emperor. As a girl no older than Vanjit was now, Idaan had plotted the slaughter of her own family in a bloody-minded attempt to win Machi for herself and her husband. Otah had come near to being executed for her crimes, Cehmai had been seduced and used by her, and Maati still had a thick scar on his belly where her assassin had tried to gut him. Otah, for reasons that passed beyond Maati's understanding, had spared the murderess. Even less comprehensible, Cehmai had found her, and in their shared exile, they had once again become lovers. Only Maati still saw her for what she was.

Age had thickened her. Her hair, tied back in a ferocious knot, was more gray than black. Her long, northern face showed curiosity, then surprise, then for less than a heartbeat something like contempt.

"You'll want to see him, then," said Otah's exiled sister: the woman who had once set an assassin to kill Maati. Who had blamed Otah for the murders she and her ambitious lover had committed.

She sank the gory knife into the dead animal's side, setting the corpse swinging, and walked forward.

"Follow me," she said.

"Tell me where to find him," Maati said. "I can just as well . . ."

"The dogs don't know you," Idaan said. "*Follow* me."

Once Maati saw the dogs—five wide-jawed beasts as big as ponies, lazing in the rich dirt at the back of the house—he was glad she was there to guide him. She walked with a strong gait, leading him past the house, past a low barn where chickens scattered and complained, to a wide, low field of grass, its black soil under half an inch of water. At the far side of the field, a thin figure stood. He wore the canvas trousers of a workman and a rag the color of old blood around his head. By the time the man's face had ceased to be a leather-colored blur, they were almost upon him. There were the bright, boyish eyes, the serious mouth. The sun had coarsened his skin and complicated the corners of his eyes. He smiled and took a pose of greeting appropriate for one master of their arcane trade to another. Idaan snorted, turned, and walked back toward the slaughterhouse, leaving them alone.

"It's a dry year," Cehmai said. "You wouldn't know it, but it's a dry year. The last two crops, I was afraid that they'd mold in the field. This one, I'm out here every other week, opening the ditch gates."

"I need your help, Cehmai-cha," Maati said.

The man nodded, squinted out over the field as if judging something Maati couldn't see, and sighed.

"Of course you do," Cehmai said. "Come on, then. Walk with me."

The fields were not the largest Maati had seen, and reminded him of the gardens he'd worked as a child in the school. The dark soil of the river-fed lowlands was unlike the dry, pale soil of the high plains outside Pathai, but the scent of wet earth, the buzzing of small insects, the warmth of the high sun, and the subtle cool rising from the water all echoed moments of his childhood. Not all those memories were harsh. For a moment, he imagined slipping off his sandals and sinking his toes into the mud.

As they walked, he told Cehmai all he'd been doing in the years since they'd met. The idea of a women's grammar was one they had discussed before, so it required little more than to remind him of it. He outlined the progress he had made, the insights that had taken the project far enough to begin the experimental bindings. They paused under the broad shade of a catalpa and Cehmai shared a light meal of dried cherries and dense honey bread while Maati recounted his losses.

He did not mention Eiah or the school. Not yet. Not until he knew better which way his old colleague's opinions fell.

Cehmai listened, nodding on occasion. He asked few questions, but those he did were to the point and well-considered. Maati felt himself falling into familiar habits of conversation. When, three hands later, Cehmai rose and led the way back to the river gate, it was almost as if the years had not passed. They were the only two people in the world who shared the knowledge of the andat and the Dai-kvo. They had suffered through the long, painful nights of the war, working to fashion a binding that might save them. They had lived through the long, bitter winter of their failure in the caves north of Machi. If it had not made them friends, they were at least intimates. Maati found himself outlining the binding of Returning-to-Natural-Equilibrium as Cehmai turned the rough iron mechanism that would slow the water.

"That won't work," Cehmai said with a grunt. "Logic's wrong."

"I don't know about that," Maati said. "The girl's trained as a physician. She says that healing flesh is mostly a matter of letting it go back into the shape it tends toward anyway. The body actually helps the process that way, and—"

"But the logic, Maati-kvo," Cehmai said, using the honorific for a teacher as if by reflex. "It's a paradox. The natural balance of the andat is not to exist, and she wants to bind something whose essence is the return to its natural state? It's the same problem as Freedom-From-Bondage. She should reverse it."

"How do you mean?"

The river gates creaked as they closed. The flow thinned and then stopped.

Cehmai squatted, elbows resting on his knees, and pointed toward the water with his chin.

"Water-Moving-Down didn't only make water move down. She also stopped it. She withdrew her influence, ne? So she could make rain fall or she could keep it in the sky. She could stop a river from flowing as easily as making it run fast. Your physician can't bind Returning-to-Balance or however she planned to phrase it. But if she bound something like Wounded or Scarred-by-Illness, she could *withdraw* that from someone. She negates the opposite, achieves the same effect, and has something that isn't so slippery to hold."

Maati considered, then nodded.

"That's good," he said. "That's very good. And it's why I need you."

Cehmai smiled out at the waving green field, then glanced at the house and looked down.

"You'll stay the night?" Cehmai said.

Maati took a pose that accepted the invitation. He kept his trepidation at the thought of sleeping under Idaan's roof out of his stance and expression. It would have been too much to hope for that Cehmai would drop everything in his life and take to the road at once. And still, Maati had hoped for it. . . .

Inside the thick stone walls of the farmhouse, the air was cooler and rich with the scent of dog and old curry. The afternoon faded slowly, the sun lingering in the treetops to the west, its light thick and golden and softened by Maati's failing eyes. Cicadas set up a choir. He sat on a low stone porch, watching everything and nothing.

Maati had known quite well that Idaan and Cehmai had been lovers once, even while Idaan had been married to another man and arranging the deaths of her family. Cehmai's betrayal of her had been the key that brought her down, that lifted Otah into the role of Khai Machi, and from there to Emperor. Cehmai had, in his fashion, created the world as it was with the decision to expose his lover's crimes.

Maati had thought the man mad for still harboring feelings for the woman; she was a murderer and a traitor to her city and her family. He'd thought him mad twice over for wanting to find her again after the andat had vanished from the world and the poets had fallen from grace. She would, he had expected, kill Cehmai on sight.

And yet.

As a boy, Maati had taken another man's lover as his own, and Otah had forgiven it. In gratitude or something like it, Maati had devoted himself to proving Otah's innocence and helped to bring Idaan's crimes to light. Seedless, the first andat Maati had known, had betrayed both the poet Heshai who had bound him and the Galtic house that had backed the andat's cruel scheme. And the woman—what had her name been?—whose child died. Seedless had betrayed everyone, but had asked only Maati to forgive him.

The accrued weight of decades pressed upon him as the sun caught in the western branches. Dead children, war, betrayal, loss. And here, in this small nameless farm days' travel from even a low town of notable size, two lovers who had become enemies were lovers again. It made him angry, and his anger made him sad.

As the first stars appeared, pale ghost lights in the deepening blue before sunset, Idaan emerged from the house. With her leather gear gone, she looked less like a thing from a monster tale. She was a woman, only a woman. And growing old. It was only when she met his gaze that he felt a chill. He had seen her eyes set in a younger face, and the darkness in them had shifted, but it had not been unmade.

"There's food," she said.

The table was small and somehow more frail than Maati had expected. Three bowls were set out, each with rice and strips of browned meat. Cehmai was also pouring out small measures of rice wine from a bone carafe. It was, Maati supposed, an acknowledgment of the occasion and likely as much extravagance as Cehmai's resources would allow. Maati took a pose that offered thanks and requested permission to join the table. Cehmai responded with one of acceptance and welcome, but his movements were slow. Maati couldn't tell if it was from exhaustion or thought. Idaan added neither word nor pose to the conversation; her expression was unreadable.

"I've been thinking," Cehmai said. "Your plan. I have a few questions about it."

"Anything," Maati said.

"Would your scheme to undo what Sterile did include restoring the Galts?"

Maati took a strip of the meat from his bowl. The flesh was pleasantly rich and well-salted. He chewed slowly to give himself time to think, but his hesitation was answer enough.

"I don't think I can join you," Cehmai said. "This battle I've . . . I've lost my taste for it."

Maati felt his own frown like an ache.

"Reconsider," he said, but Cehmai shook his head.

"I've given too much of my life to the world already. I'd like to keep the rest of my years for myself. No more great struggles, no more cities or nations or worlds resting on what I do or don't do. What I have here is enough."

Maati wiped his fingers on his sleeve and took a pose of query that bordered on accusation. Cehmai's eyes narrowed.

"Enough for what?" Maati demanded. "Enough for the pair of you? It'll be more than enough before many years have passed. It'll be too much. How much do you work in a day? Raising your own food, tending your crops and your animals, making food and washing your robes and gathering wood for your fires? Does it give you any time at all to think? To rest?"

"It isn't as easy as living in the courts, that's truth," Cehmai said. His smile was the same as ever, even set in this worn face. "There are nights it would be good to leave the washing to a servant."

"It won't get easier," Maati said. "You'll get older. Both of you. The work will stay just as difficult, and you'll get tired faster. When you take sick, you'll recover slowly. One or the other of you will strain something or break an old bone or catch fever, and your children won't be there to care for you. The next farm over? His children won't be there for you either. Or the next. Or the next."

"He's not wrong, love," Idaan said. Maati blinked. Of all the people in the world, Idaan was the last he'd expected support from.

"I know all that," Cehmai said. "It doesn't mean that I should go back to being a poet."

"What else would you do?" Maati said. "Sell the land rights? Who is there to buy them? Take up some new trade? Who will there be to teach you? Binding the andat is the thing you've trained for. Your mind is built for the work. These girls . . . you should see them. The dedication, the engagement, the drive. If this thing can be done, they will do it. We can remake the world."

"We've done that once already," Cehmai said. "It didn't go well."

"We didn't have time. The Galts were at our door. We did what we had to do. And now we can correct our errors."

"Does my brother know about this?" Idaan asked.

"He refused me," Maati said.

"Is that why you hate him?"

The air around the table seemed to clench. Maati stared at the woman. Idaan met his gaze with a level calm.

"He is selling us," Maati said. "He is turning away from a generation of women whose injuries are as much his fault as ours."

"And is that why you hate him?" Idaan asked again. "You can't tell me that you don't, Maati-cha. I know quite a lot about hatred."

He let my son die to save his, Maati thought but did not say. There were a thousand arguments against the statement: Otah hadn't been there when Nayiit died; it wasn't Danat's fault that his protector failed to fend off the soldiers; Nayiit wasn't truly his son. He knew them all, and that none of them mattered. Nayiit had died, Maati had been sent into the wilderness, and Otah had risen like a star in the sky.

"What I feel toward your brother doesn't change what needs to be done," Maati said, "or the help I'll need to do it."

"Who's backing you?" Idaan said.

Maati felt a flash of surprise and even fear. An image of Eiah flickered in his mind and was banished.

"What do you mean?" he asked.

"Someone's feeding you," she said. "Someone's hiding you and your students. If the word got out that you'd been found, half the world would send armsmen to cut you down for fear you'd do exactly what you're doing now. And half of the rest would kick you to death for petty vengeance. If it's not Otah protecting you, who is it? One of the high families of the utkhaiem? A trading house? Who?"

"I have strong backing," Maati said. "But I won't tell you more than that."

"Every danger you face, my husband faces too," Idaan said. "If you want him to take your risks, you have to tell him what protection you can offer."

"I have an ear in the palaces anytime I need it. Otah won't be able to mount any kind of action against me without warning finding me. You can trust to that."

"You have to tell us more," Idaan said.

"He doesn't," Cehmai said, sharply. "He doesn't have to offer me protection because I'm not going to do the work. I'm done, love. I'm finished. I want a few more years with you and a quiet death, and I'll be quite pleased with that."

"The world needs you," Maati said.

"It doesn't," Cehmai said. "You've come a long way, Maati-kvo, and I've disappointed you. I'm sorry for that, but you have my answer. I used to be a poet, but I'm not anymore. I can reconsider as long as we both keep breathing, and we'll come to the same place."

"We can't stay on here," Idaan said. Her voice was soft. "I've loved it here too. This place, these years . . . we've been lucky to have them. But Maati-cha's right. This season, and perhaps five or ten after it, we'll make do. But eventually the work will pass us. We're not getting younger, and we can't hire on hands to help us. There aren't any."

"Then we'll leave," Cehmai said. "We'll do something else, only not that."

"Why not?" Maati asked.

"Because I don't want to kill any more people," Cehmai said. "Not the girls you're encouraging to try this, not the foreigners who would try to stop us, not whatever army came in the next autumn's war."

"It doesn't have to be like that," Maati said.

"It does," Cehmai said. "We held the power of gods, and the world envied us and turned against us, and they always will again. I can't say I think much of where we stand now, but I remember what happened to bring us here, and I don't see how making poets of women instead of men will make a world any different or better than the one we had then."

"It may not," Maati said, "but it will be better than the one we have now. If you won't help me, then I'll do without you, but I'd thought better of you, Cehmai. I'd thought you had more spine."

"Rice is getting cold," Idaan said. Her voice was controlled rage. "Perhaps we should eat it before it goes bad."

They finished the meal alternating between artificially polite conversation and strained silence. After, Cehmai took the bowls away to clean and didn't return. Idaan led Maati to a small room near the back with a straw pallet and a night candle already burning. Maati slept poorly and found himself still upset when he woke. He left in the dark of the morning without speaking again to either of his hosts, one from disappointment and shame and the other, though he would never have said it, from fear.

5

>+< Nantani was the nearest port to the lands of Galt, but the scars of war were too fresh there and too deep. Instead, the gods had conspired to return Otah to the city of his childhood: Saraykeht.

The fastest ships arrived several days before the great mass of the fleet. They stood out half a hand's travel from the seafront, and Otah took in the whole city. He could see the masts at the farthest end of the seafront, berthed in order to leave the greatest space for the incoming traffic. Bright cloth hung from every window Otah could see, starting with the dock master's offices nearest the water to the towers of the palaces, high and to the north where the vibrant colors were grayed by humidity.

Crowds filled the docks, and he heard a roar of voices and snatches of drum and flute carried by the breeze. The air itself smelled different: rank and green and familiar in a way he hadn't expected.

The Emperor of the Khaiem had been away from his cities for eight months, almost nine, and his return with the high families of Galt in tow was the kind of event seen once in history and never again. This was the day that every man and woman at the seafront or watching from the windows above the streets would recall until death's long fingers touched them. The day that the new empress, the Galtic empress, arrived for the first time.

There were stories Otah had read in books that had been ashes for almost as long as this new Empress had been alive, about an emperor's life mirroring the state of his empire. An emperor with many children meant rich, fertile land; one without heir spoke of poor crops and thin cattle. An emperor who drank himself to sleep meant an empire of libertines; one who studied and prayed, a somber land of great wisdom. He had half-believed the stories then. He had no faith in them now.

"You would think they would have made some allowance for our arrival," a man's peevish voice said from behind him. Otah looked back at Balasar Gice, dressed in formal brocade armor and shining with sweat. Otah took a pose of powerlessness before the gods.

"The wind does what the wind does," he said. "We'll be on land by nightfall."

"We will," Balasar said. "But the others will be docking and unloading all night."

It was true. Saraykeht would likely add something near a tenth of its population in the next day, Galts filling the guest quarters and wayhouses and likely half the beds in the soft quarter. It was the second time in Otah's life that a pale-skinned, round-eyed neighborhood without buildings had appeared in his city. Only now, it would happen without drawn blades and blood.

"They're sending tow galleys out for us," Otah said. "It will all be fine."

The galleys, with their flashing banks of white oars and ornamental iron-work rails, reached the great ship just after midday. With a great clamor of voices—protests, laughter, orders, counterorders—thick cables of hemp were made fast to the ship's deck. The sails were already down, and with the sound of a bell clanging like an alarm, Otah's ship lurched, shifted directly into the wind, and began the last, shortest leg of his journey home.

A welcoming platform had been erected especially for the occasion. The broad beams were white as snow, and a ceremonial guard waited by a litter while a somewhat less ceremonial one kept the press of the crowds at a distance. Balasar and six of the Galtic High Council had made their way to Otah's ship in order to disembark with him. The *Avenger* with Ana and her parents would likely come next, after which the roar of competing etiquette masters would likely drown out the ocean. Otah was more than willing to leave the fighting for position and status for the dock master to settle out.

The crowd's voice rose when the ship pulled in, and again when the walk bridged the shifting gap between ship and land. His servants preceded him in the proper array and sequence, and then Otah left the sea. The noise was something physical, a wind built of sound. The ceremonial guard adopted poses of obeisance, and Otah took his ritual reply. The first of the guard to stand, grinning, was Sinja.

"You've shaved your whiskers," Otah shouted.

"I was starting to look like an otter," Sinja agreed. His expression became opaque and he bowed to Otah's right. "Balasar-cha."

"Sinja," Balasar said.

The past intruded. Once Sinja had played the part of Balasar's man, expert on the cities of the Khaiem and mercenary leader of war. He had spied on the Galts, betrayed Balasar, and killed the man Balasar held dearest to his heart. It thickened the air between them, even now. Balasar's eyes shifted to the middle distance, a frown on his lips as if he were counting how many of his dead might have lived, had Sinja remained true. And then the moment was gone. Or if not gone, covered over for the sake of etiquette.

The others of the Galtic party lurched in from the ship, unsteady on planks that didn't move, and the assembled masses cheered each of them like a hero returned from war. Servants dressed in light cotton robes led each sweating Galt to a waiting litter, Otah's station of honor making him the last to leave.

"I suspect they'll be changing to local clothes before long," Sinja said. "They all look half-dead with the heat."

"I'm feeling it myself," Otah said.

"Should I interrupt protocol?" Sinja asked. "I could have you loaded and on your way up the hills in the time it takes to kill a chicken."

"No," Otah said with a sigh. "If we're doing this, let's do it well. But ride with me, eh? I want to hear what's going on."

"Yes," Sinja said. "Well. You've missed some dramatics, but I don't think there's anything particularly ominous waiting. Except the pirates. And the conspiracy. You did get the report about the conspiracy in Yalakeht? It's apparently got ties to Obar State."

"Well, that's just lovely," Otah said.

"No more plague than usual," Sinja offered gamely, and then it was time and servants stepped forward to escort Otah to his litter. The shifting gait of his bearers was similar to being aboard ship, but also wrong. Between that and the heat, Otah was beginning to feel nauseated, but the buildings that passed by his beaded window were comforting. Great blue and white walls topped with roof tiles of gray and red; banners hanging in the slow, thick air; men and women in poses of welcome or else waving small lengths of brightly colored cloth. If it had been autumn or winter, the old firekeepers' kilns would have been lit and strange flames would have accompanied him up the wide streets to the palaces.

"Any problems with the arrival?" he asked Sinja.

"A few. Angry women throwing stones, mostly. We've locked them away until the last ship comes in. Danat and I decided to put the girl and her family in the poet's house. It isn't the most impressive location, but it's comfortable, and it's far enough back from the other buildings that they might have some privacy. The gods all know they'll be gawked at like a three-headed calf the rest of the time."

"I think Ana has a lover," Otah said. "One of the sailors was built rather like a courtier."

"Ah," Sinja said. "I'll tell the guard to keep eyes out. I assume we'd rather he didn't come calling?"

"No, better that he not," Otah said.

"I don't suppose there's a chance the girl's still a virgin?"

Otah took a pose that dismissed the concern. Even if she weren't—and of course she wasn't—she wouldn't be bearing another man's child. Not if the boy he had glimpsed in the hold of the *Avenger* was a Galt. Otah felt a moment's unease.

"If the guard do find a boy sneaking in, have him held until I can speak with him. I'd rather that this whole situation not get more complex than it already is."

"Your word is law, Most High," Sinja said, his tone light. Otah chuckled.

He had missed the man's company. There were few people in the world who could see Otah beneath his titles, fewer still who dared mock him. It was a familiarity that had been forged by years. Together, they had acted against the plot which had first changed Otah from outcast to Khai Machi. They had loved the same woman and come near violence over it. Sinja had trained Otah's son in the arts of combat and strategy, had gotten drunk with the Emperor after Kiyan's funeral, had spoken his mind whether invited to or not. Otah had no other advisor or friend like him.

As they moved north, the crowd that lined the street changed its nature. Once they had passed out of the throng at the seafront, the robes and faces had been those of laborers and artisans. As they passed the compounds of the merchant houses, the robes and banners became more ornate. Rich and saturated colors were edged with embroidery of gold and worked in the symbols of the various houses. And then almost without a pause, the symbols and colors were not of merchants, but of the families of the utkhaiem, and the high walls and ornate shutters were not mercantile compounds, but palaces. Men and women in fine robes took poses of welcome and obeisance as servants and slaves fanned them. A hidden choir burst into song somewhere to his left, the voices in complex harmony. The litter stopped before the grand palace, the first palace, the Emperor's palace. Otah stepped out, sweeping his gaze over the ordered rows of servants and high officials until he saw the one man he'd longed for.

Danat was in his twentieth summer, his face a mixture of Otah's long, northern features and Kiyan's, thin and foxlike. The planes of his cheeks had sharpened since Otah had gone. He looked older, more handsome. He wore a robe of deep gray set off with a rich, red sash that suited him. And still, Otah could see all the boys that had made this man: the babe, the bumbling child new to his own feet, the long-ill boy kept in his bed, the awkward and sorrowful youth, and the young heir to the Empire. All of them stood before him, hands in a pose of formal welcome, a smile glittering in his eyes. Otah broke protocol, embracing his son. The boy's arms were strong.

"You've done well," Otah murmured.

"None of the cities actually burned down while you were gone," Danat replied softly. There was pride in his voice, pleasure at the compliment.

"But you sound too much like Sinja."

"You knew that was a risk."

Otah laughed and let the swarm of servants precede him to his chambers. There would be no end of ceremonies later. Welcomes would drag on for weeks, audiences, special pleadings, feasts, dances, negotiations, councils. It all lay before him like a life's work started late. But now, sitting in the cool breeze of his private apartments with Sinja across from him and Danat pouring chilled water into stone bowls, the world was perfect.

Except, of course, that it wasn't.

"Perhaps we can mend both breaks with the same nail," Sinja said. "A strong showing against the pirates protects Chaburi-Tan and warns Obar State to keep to its own house."

"And a weak showing against them?" Otah asked.

"Shows we're weak, after which things go poorly," Sinja said. "But if we're going to assume failure from the start, there's not going to be anything of use that I can offer."

Otah propped up his feet. The palaces still felt as if they were swaying: the ghost motion of weeks aboard ship. The feeling was oddly pleasant.

"On the other hand," he said, "if we plan to decimate the enemy with a flower and a pillow, it's not going to help us. How strong is our fleet? Do we have enough men to take the pirates in a fair fight?"

"If we don't have them now, we certainly won't next year when all the sailors are a year older," Sinja said. "Even if you magically transport every fertile girl in Galt straight to some poor bastard's bed, it will be ten years before they can deliver us anyone strong enough to coil rope, much less fight. If we're going to do anything, it has to be now. We're going to grow weaker before we're strong."

"If we manage to get strong," Otah said. "And I don't know that we can spare the ships. We have eleven cities and the gods alone know how many low towns. We're talking about moving half a million of our men to Galt and bringing back as many of their women."

"Well, yes, shipping out anyone we have of fighting age now won't help the matter," Sinja said.

"Galt could do it," Danat said. "They have experience with sea wars. They have fighting ships and the veterans."

Otah saw the considering expression on Sinja's face. He let the silence stretch.

"I don't like it," Sinja said at last. "I don't know why I don't like it, but I don't."

"We're still thinking of our problems as our own," Danat said. "Asking Galt to fight our battles might seem odd, but they'd be protecting their own land too. In a generation, Chaburi-Tan is going to be as much their city as ours."

Otah felt an odd pressure in his chest. It was true, of course. It was what he had spent years working to accomplish. And still, when Danat put it in bare terms like that, it was hard for him to hear it.

"It's more than that," Sinja said.

"Is it Balasar?" Otah asked.

Sinja leaned forward, his fingers laced on his knee, his mouth set in a scowl. At length, he spoke.

"Yes," he said. "Yes, it is."

"He's forgiven me," Otah said. "Perhaps the two of you—"

"All respect, Otah-cha," Sinja said. "You were his enemy. That's a fair position. I broke my oath, lied to him, and killed his best captain. He's a man who loves loyalty, and I was one of his men. It's not the same."

"Perhaps it isn't," Otah agreed.

"Balasar-cha doesn't have to be the one to lead it," Danat said. "Or, all respect, Sinja-cha, for that."

"No, of course we don't," Sinja said. "It's not my head that's struggling with the thought. It's just . . . The boy's right, Otah-cha. A mixed fleet, their ships and ours, sinking the pirates would be the best solution. I don't know if we can negotiate the thing, but it's worth considering."

Otah scratched his leg.

"Farrer-cha," he said. "Danat's new father. He has experience with sea fighting. I think he hates all of us together and individually for Ana-cha's upcoming marriage, but he would still be the man to approach."

Danat took a long drink of water and grinned. It made him look younger.

"After the ceremony's done with," Sinja said. "We'll get the man drunk and happy and see if we can't make him sign something binding before he sobers up."

"If it were only so simple," Otah said. "With the High Council and the Low Council and the Conclave, every step they take is like putting cats in a straight line. Watching it in action, it's amazing they ever put together a war."

"You should talk to Balasar," Sinja said.

"I will," Otah replied.

They moved on to other topics. Some were more difficult: weavers and stonemasons on the coasts had started offering money to apprentices, so the nearby farms were losing hands; the taxes from Amnat-Tan had been lower than expected; the raids in the northern passes were getting worse. Others were innocuous: court fashions had shifted toward robes with a more Galtic drape; the shipping traffic on the rivers was faster now that they'd figured out how to harness boilers to do the rowing; and finally, Eiah had sent word that she was busy assisting a physician in Pathai and would not attend her brother's wedding.

Otah paused over this letter, rereading his daughter's neat, clear hand. The words were all simple, the grammar formal and appropriate. She made no accusations, leveled no arguments against him. It might have been better if she had. Anger was, at least, not distance.

He considered the implications of her absence. On one hand, it could hardly go unnoticed that the imperial family was not all in attendance. On the other, Eiah had broken with him years ago, when his present plan had still been only a rough sketch. If she was there, it might have served only to remind the women of the cities that they had in a sense been discarded. The next generation would have no Khaiate mothers, and the solace that neither would they have Galtic fathers would be cold comfort at best. He folded his daughter's letter and tucked it into his sleeve, his heart heavy with the thought that not having her near was likely for the best.

After, Otah retired to his rooms, sent his servants away, and lay on his bed, watching the pale netting shift in a barely felt breeze. It was strange being home, hearing his own language in the streets, smelling the air he'd breathed as a youth.

Ana and her parents would be settled in by now, sitting, perhaps, on the porch that looked out over the koi pond and its bridge. Perhaps putting back the hinged walls to let in the air. Otah had spent some little time at the poet's house of Saraykeht once, back when he'd been Danat's age and the drinking companion and friend of Maati Vaupathai. Back in some other life. He closed his eyes and tried to picture the rooms as they'd been when Seedless and the poet Heshai had still been in the world. The confusion of scrolls and books, the ashes piled up in the grate, the smell of incense and old wine. He didn't realize that he was falling asleep until Seedless smirked and turned away, and Otah knew he was in dreams.

A human voice woke him. The angle of the sun had shifted, the day almost passed. Otah sat up, struggling to focus his eyes. The servant spoke again.

"Most High, the welcoming ceremonies are due in a hand and a half. Shall I tell the Master of Tides to postpone them?"

"No," Otah said. His voice sounded groggy. He wondered how long the servant had been trying to rouse him. "No, not at all. Send me clean robes. Or . . . no, send them to the baths. I'll be there."

The servant fell into a pose that accepted the command as law. It seemed a little overstated to Otah, but he'd grown accustomed to other people taking his role more seriously than he did himself. He refreshed himself, met with the representatives of two high families and a trading house with connections in Obar State and Bakta, and allowed himself to be swept along to the grand celebration. They would welcome their onetime invaders with music and gifts and intrigue and, he suspected, the equivalent weight of the palaces in wine and food.

The grandest hall of his palaces stood open on a wide garden of night-blooming plants. A network of whisperers stood on platforms, ready to repeat the ceremonial greetings and ritual out to the farthest ear. Otah didn't doubt that runners were waiting at the edge of the gardens to carry reports of the event even farther. The press of bodies was intense, the sound of voices so riotous that the musicians and singers set to wander the garden in serenade had all been sent home.

Otah sat on the black lacquer chair of the Khai Saraykeht, his spine straight and his hands folded as gracefully as he could manage. Cushions for Danat and Sinja and all of Otah's highest officers were arrayed behind him, perhaps two-thirds filled. The others were, doubtless, in the throng of silk and gems. There was nowhere else to be tonight. Not in Saraykeht. Perhaps not in the world.

Danat brought him a bowl of cold wine, but it was too loud to have any conversation beyond the trading of thanks and welcome. Danat took his place on the cushion at Otah's side. Farrer Dasin, Otah saw, had been given not a chair but a rosewood bench. Issandra and Ana were on cushions at his feet. All three looked overwhelmed about the eyes. Otah caught Issandra's gaze and adopted a pose of welcome, which she returned admirably.

He turned his attention to her husband. Farrer Dasin, stern and gray. Otah found himself wondering how best to approach the man about this new proposal. Though he knew better, he could not help thinking of Galt and his own cities as separate, as two empires in alliance. Farrer Dasin—indeed, most of the High Council—were sure to be thinking in the same ways. They were all wrong, of course, Otah included. They were marrying two families together, but more than that they were binding two cultures, two governments, two histories. His own grandchildren would live and die in a world unrecognizable as the one Otah had known; he would be as foreign to them as Galt had been to him.

And here, on this clear, crowded night, the cycle of ages was turning. He found himself irrationally certain that Farrer Dasin could be persuaded to lead, or at least to sponsor, a campaign against the pirates at Chaburi-Tan. They had done this. They could do anything.

The signal came: flutes and drums in fanfare as the cloth lanterns rose to the dais. Otah stood up and the crowd before him went silent. Only the sound of a thousand breaths competed with the songbirds and crickets.

Otah gave his address in the tones appropriate to his place, practiced over the course of years. He found himself changing the words he had practiced. Instead of speaking only of the future, he also wanted to honor the past. He wanted every person there to know that in addition to the world they were making, there was a world—in some ways good, in others evil—that they were leaving behind.

They listened to him as if he were a singer, their eyes fastened to him, the silence complete apart from his own words in the hundred throats of the whisperers echoing out into the summer night. When he took the pose that would end his recitation, he saw tears on more than one face, and on the faces of more than one nation. He made his way to Farrer Dasin and formally invited the man to speak. The Galt stood, bowed to Otah as a gesture between equals, and moved forward. Otah returned to his seat with only the lightest twinge of trepidation.

"Are you sure you should let him speak?" Sinja murmured.

"There's no avoiding it," Otah replied, still smiling. "It will be fine."

The councilman cleared his throat, stood in the odd, awkward style of Galtic orators—one foot before the other, one hand in the air, the other clasping his jacket—and spoke. All of Otah's worst fears were put at once to rest. It was as if Issandra had written the words and spoke them now through her husband's mouth. The joy that was children, the dark years that the war had brought, the emptiness of a world without the laughter of babes. And now, the darkness ended.

Otah felt himself begin to weep slightly. He wished deeply that Kiyan had lived to see this night. He hoped that whatever gods were more than stories and metaphors took word of it to her. The old Galt bowed his head to the crowd. The applause was like an earthquake or a flood. Otah rose and held his hand out to Danat as Farrer Dasin did the same with his daughter. The Emperor-to-be and his Empress meeting here for the first time. There would be songs sung of this night, Otah knew.

Ana was beautiful. Someone had seen to it that the gown she wore flattered her. Her face was painted in perfect harmony with her hair and the gold of her necklace. Danat wore a black robe embroidered with gold and cut to please the Galtic eye. Farrer and Otah stepped back, leaving the center of the dais to their children. Danat tried a smile. The girl's eyes fluttered; her cheeks were flushed under the paint, her breath fast.

"Danat Machi?" she said.

"Ana Dasin," he replied.

The girl took a deep breath. Her pretty, rodentlike face shone. When she spoke, her voice was strong and certain.

"I will never consent to lay down with you, and if you rape me, I will see the world knows it. My lover is Hanchat Dor, and I will have no other."

Otah felt his face go white. In the corner of his eye, he saw Farrer Dasin rock back like a man struck by a stone and then raise a hand to his face. Danat's mouth opened and closed like a fish's. The whisperers paused, and then a heartbeat later, the words went out where they could never be called back. The voice of the crowd rose up like the waters of chaos come to drown them all.

6

>+< Maati relived his conversation with Cehmai a thousand times in the weeks that followed. He rose in the morning from whatever rough camp or wayhouse bed he'd fallen into the night before, and he muttered his arguments to Cehmai. He rode his weary mule along overgrown tracks thick with heat and heavy with humidity, and he spoke aloud, gesturing. He ate his evening meals with the late sunset of summer, and in his mind, Cehmai sat across from him, dumbfounded and ashamed, persuaded at last by the force of Maati's argument. And when Maati's imagination returned him to the world as it was, his failure and shame poured in on him afresh.

Every low town he passed through, the mud streets empty of the sound of children, was a rebuke. Every woman he met, an accusation. He had failed. He had gone to the one man in the world who might have lightened his burden, and he had been refused. The better part of the season was lost to him now. It was time he should have spent with the girls, preparing the grammar and writing his book. They were days he would never win back. If he had stayed, perhaps they would have had a breakthrough. Perhaps there would already be an andat in the world, and Otah's plans ruined.

And what if by going after Cehmai, Maati had somehow lost that chance? With every day, it seemed more likely. As the trees and deer of the river valleys gave way to the high, dry plains between Pathai and ruined Nantani, Maati became more and more sure that his error had been catastrophic. Irretrievable. And so it was also another mark against Otah Machi. Otah, the Emperor, to whom no rules applied.

Maati found the high road, and then the turning that would lead, given half a day's ride, to the school. To his students. To Eiah. He camped at the cross-roads.

He was too old to be living on muleback. Lying in the thin folds of his bed-roll, he ached as if he'd been beaten. His back had been suffering spasms for days; they had grown painful enough that he hadn't slept deeply. And his exhaustion seemed to make his muscles worse. The high plains grew cool at night, almost cold, and the air smelled of dust. He heard the skittering of lizards or mice and the low call of owls. The stars shone down on him, each point of light smeared by his aging eyes until the whole sky seemed possessed by a single luminous cloud.

There had been a time he'd lain under stars and picked out constellations. There was a time his body could have taken rest on cobblestone, had the need arisen. There was a time Cehmai, poet of Machi and master of Stone-Made-Soft, had looked up to him.

It was going to be hard to tell Eiah that he'd failed. The others as well, but Eiah knew Cehmai. She had seen them work together. The others might be disappointed, but Eiah alone would understand what he had lost.

His dread slowed him. At this, his last camp, he ate his breakfast and watched the slow sunrise. He packed his mule slowly, then walked westward, his shadow stretching out ahead and growing slowly smaller. The shapes of the hills grew familiar, and the pauses he took grew longer. Here was the dry streambed where he and the other black-robed boys had sat in the evenings and told one another stories of the families they had already half-forgotten. There, a grouping of stumps showed where the stand of trees they had climbed had been felled by Galtic axes and burned. A cave under an outcropping of rock where they'd made the younger boys slither into the darkness to hunt snakes. The air was as rich with memory as the scent of dust and wildflowers. His life had been simpler then, or if not simpler, at least a thing that held promise.

He managed to postpone his arrival at the school itself until the sun was lowering before him. The grand stone buildings looked smaller than he remembered them, but the great bronze door that had once been reserved for the Dai-kvo was just as grand. The high, narrow windows were marked black at the tops, the remnants of some long-dead fire. The wall of one of the sleeping chambers had fallen, stones strewn on the ground. The gardens were gone, marked only by low mounds where stones had once formed their borders. Time and violence had changed the place, but not yet beyond recognition. Another decade of rain washing mortar from between the stones, another fire, and perhaps the roofs would collapse. The ground would reclaim its own.

Maati tied his mule to a low, half-rotten post and made his way in. The grand room where he and the other boys had stood in rows each morning before marching off to their duties and classes. The wide corridors beyond it, lit only by the reddish rays of the evening sun. Where were the bodies of the boys who had been here on the day the armies of Galt arrived? Where had those bones been buried? And where, now, were Maati's own students? Had something gone awry?

When he reached the inner courtyard, his concerns eased. The flagstone paths were clear of dirt and dust, the weeds and grass had been pulled from between the stones. And there, in the third window that had once been the teachers' quarters, a lantern glowed already against the falling night.

The door that opened to the wide central hall had been fitted with a new leather hinge. The walls and floors, freshly washed, shone in the light of a hundred candles. The scent of curry and the sound of women's voices raised in conversation came through the air as if the one were part of the other. Maati found himself disoriented for a moment, as if he'd walked down a familiar street only to find it opening upon some unknown city. He walked forward slowly, drawn in by the voices as if they were music. There was Ashti Beg's dry voice, Large Kae's laughter. As he drew nearer, the pauses between the louder voices were filled with the softer voices of Vanjit and Irit. The first words he made out were Eiah's.

"Yes," she said, "but how would you fit that into a grammatic structure that doesn't already include it? Or am I talking in a circle?"

"I think you may be," Small Kae replied. "Maati-kvo said that binding an andat involves all kinds of inclusions. I don't see why this one would be any different."

There was a pause, a sound that might have been the ghost of a sigh.

"Add it to the list," Eiah said as Maati turned through a well-lit doorway and into the room.

"What list?" he asked.

There was a moment's silence, and then uproar. The circle of chairs was abandoned, and Maati found himself the subject of a half-dozen embraces. The dread and anger and despair that had dogged his steps lightened if it didn't vanish. He let Vanjit lead him to an empty chair, and the others gathered around him, their eyes bright, their smiles genuine. It was like coming home. When Eiah returned to his question, he had forgotten it. It took a moment to understand what she was saying.

"It's a list of questions for you," she said. "After we came and put the place more or less to rights, we started . . . well, we started holding class without you."

"It wasn't really the same," Small Kae said with an apologetic pose. "We only didn't want to forget what we'd learned. We were only talking about it."

"After a few nights it became clear we were going to need some way to keep track of the parts that needed clarifying. It's become rather a long list. And some of the questions . . ."

Maati took a pose that dismissed her concerns, somewhat hampered by the bowl of curried rice in his hand.

"It's a good thought," he said. "I would have recommended it myself, if I'd been thinking clearly. Bring me the list tonight, and perhaps we can start going over it in the morning. If you are all prepared to begin working in earnest?"

The roar of agreement drowned out his laughter. Only Eiah didn't join in. Her smile was soft, almost sad, and she took no pose to explain it. Instead, she poured a bowl of water for him.

"Is Cehmai-kvo here?" Large Kae asked.

Maati took a bite of the rice, chewing slowly, letting the spices burn his tongue a little before answering.

"I didn't find him," Maati said. "There was a message, but it was out-of-date. I searched as long as there seemed some chance of finding him, but there was no sign. I left word where I could, and it may very well reach him. He might join us at any time. My job is to have you all prepared in case he does."

It was kinder than the truth. If Maati's failure had been only that he hadn't found help, it left them the hope that help might still arrive. It was no great lie to give them an image of the future in which something good might come. And it was easier for him if he didn't have to say he'd been refused. Only Eiah knew; he could hear it in her silence. She would follow his lead.

Maati's mule was seen to, his things hauled into the room they had prepared for him, and a bath drawn in a wide copper tub set before a fire grate. It reminded him of nothing so much as his days living in court, servants available at any moment to cater to his needs. It was strange to recall that he had lived that way once. It seemed both very recent and very long ago. And also, the slaves and servants that had driven the life in the palaces of Machi hadn't been women he knew and cared for. Slipping into the warm water, feeling his travel-abused joints ache just a degree less, letting his eyes rest, Maati wondered what it would have been like to receive so much female attention when he'd been younger. There would have been a time when the simple sensual pleasures of food and a warm bath might have suggested something more sexual. It might still, if bone-deep weariness hadn't held him.

But no, that wasn't true. He wasn't dead to lust, but it had been years since it had carried the urgency that he remembered from his youth. He wondered if that wasn't part of why women had been barred from the school and the village of the Dai-kvo. Would any poet have been able to focus on a binding if half his mind was on a woman his body was aching for? Or perhaps there was something in that mind-set itself that would affect the binding. So much of the andat was a reflection of the poet who bound it, it would be easy to imagine andat fashioned by younger poets in the forms of wantons and whores. Apart from the profoundly undignified nature of such a binding, it might actually make holding the andat more difficult as decades passed and a man's fires burned less brightly. He wondered if there was an analogy with women.

The scratch at the door brought him back. He'd half fallen asleep there in the water. He rose awkwardly, reaching for his robe and trying not to spill so much water that it flowed into the fire grate and killed the flames.

"Yes, yes," he called as he fastened the robe's ties. "I'm not drowned yet. Come in."

Eiah stepped through the doorway. There was something in her arms, held close to her. Between the unsteady light of the fire and his own age-blunted sight, he couldn't tell more than it looked like a book. Maati took a pose of welcome, his sleeves water-stuck to his arms.

"Should I come back later?" she asked.

"No, of course not," Maati said, pulling a chair toward the fire for her. "I was only washing the road off of me. Is this the famed list?"

"Part of it is," she said as she sat. She was wearing a physician's robe of deep green and gold. "Part of it's something else."

Maati settled himself on the tub's wide lip and took a pose that expressed curiosity and surprise. Eiah handed him a scroll, and he unfurled it. The questions were all written in a large hand, clearly, and each with a small passage to give some context. He read three of them. Two were simple enough, but the third was more interesting. It touched on the difficulties of generating new directionals, and the possibility of encasing absolute structures within relative ones. It gave the grammar an odd feeling, as if it were suggesting that fire was hot rather than asserting it.

It was interesting.

"Are they all like this?" he asked.

"The questions? Some of them, yes," Eiah said. "Vanjit's especially were beyond anything we could find a plausible answer for."

Maati pursed his lips and nodded. An absolute made relative. What would that do? He found himself smiling without knowing at first what he was smiling about.

"I think," he said, "leaving you to your own company may have been the best thing I've done."

The firelight caught Eiah's answering smile.

"I wasn't going to say so," she said. "It's been fascinating. At first, it was as if we were sneaking pies from the kitchens. Everyone wanted to do the thing, but it seemed . . . wrong? I don't know if that's the word. It seemed like something we shouldn't do, and more tempting because of it. And then once we started talking with each other, it was like being on a loose cart. We couldn't stop or even slow down. Half the time I didn't know if we were going down the wrong road, but . . ."

She shrugged, nodding at the scroll in his hands.

"Well, even if you were, some of this may be quite useful."

"I'd hoped so," Eiah said. "And that brings me to something else. I found some books at court. I brought them."

Maati blinked, the scroll forgotten in his hands.

"Books? They weren't all burned?" he said.

"Not that sort. These aren't ours," she said. "They're Westlands'. Books from physicians. Here."

She took back the scroll and put a small, cloth-bound book in his hand. One of the sticks in the fire grate broke, sending out embers like fireflies. Maati leaned forward.

The script was small and cramped, the ink pale. It would have been difficult in sunlight; by fire and candle, it might as well not have been written.
Frustrated, Maati turned the pages and an eye stared back at him from the
paper. He turned back and went more slowly. All the diagrams were of eyes,
some ripped from their sockets, some pierced by careful blades. Comments
accompanied each orb, laying, he assumed, its secrets open.

"Sight," Eiah said. "The author is called Arran, but it was more likely written by dozens of people who all used the same name. The wardens in the
north had a period four or five generations ago when there was some brilliant
work done. We ignored it, of course, because it wasn't by us. But these are
very, very good. Arran was brilliant."

"Whether he existed or not," Maati said. He meant it as a joke.

"Whether he existed or not," Eiah agreed with perfect seriousness. "I've
been working with these. And with Vanjit. We have a draft. You should look
at it."

Maati handed her back the book and she pulled a sheaf of papers from her
sleeve. Maati found himself almost hesitant to accept them. Vanjit, and her
dreamed baby. Vanjit, who had lost so much in the war. He didn't want to see
any of his students pay the price of a failed binding, but especially not her.

He took the papers. Eiah waited. He opened them.

The binding was an outline, but it was well-considered. The sections and relationships sketched in with commentary detailing what would go in each, often
with two or three notes of possible approaches. The andat would be Clarity-of-
Sight, and it would be based in the medical knowledge of Westlands physicians
and the women's grammar that Maati and Eiah had been creating. Even if some
Second Empire poet had managed to hold the andat before, this approach, with
these descriptions and sensibilities, was likely to be wholly different. Wholly new.

"Why Vanjit?" he asked. "Why not Ashti Beg or Small Kae?"

"You think she isn't ready?"

"I . . . I wouldn't go so far as that," Maati said. "It's only that she's young,
and she's had a harder life than some. I wonder whether . . ."

"None of us are perfect, Maati-kya," Eiah said. "We have to work with the
people we have. Vanjit is clever and determined."

"You think she can manage it? Bind this andat?"

"I think she has the best hope of any of us. Except possibly me."

Maati sighed, nodding as much to himself as to her. Dread thickened his
throat.

"Let me look at this," he said. "Let me think about it."

Eiah took a pose that accepted his command. Maati looked down again.

"Why didn't he come?" Eiah asked.

"Because," Maati began, and then found he wasn't able to answer as easily
as he'd thought. He folded the papers and began to tuck them into his sleeve,
remembered how wet the cloth was, and tossed them instead onto his low,
wood-framed bed. "Because he didn't want to," he said at last.

"And my aunt?"

"I don't know," Maati said. "I thought for a time that she might take my side. She didn't seem pleased with how they were living. Or, no. That's not right. She seemed to care more than he did about how they would live in the future. But he wouldn't have any of it."

"He's given up," Eiah said.

Maati recalled the man's face, the lines and weariness. The authenticity of his smile. When they'd first met, Cehmai had been little more than a boy, younger than Eiah was now. This was what the world had done to that boy. What it had done to them all.

"He has," Maati said.

"Then we'll do without him," Eiah said.

"Yes," Maati said, hoisting himself up. "Yes we will, but if you'll forgive me, Eiah-kya, I think the day's worn me thin. A little rest, and we'll begin fresh tomorrow. And where's that list of questions? Ah, thank you. I'll look over all of this, and we'll decide where best to go from here, eh?"

She took his hand, squeezing his knuckles gently.

"It's good to have you back," she said.

"I'm pleased to be here," he said.

"Did you have any news of my father?"

"No," he said. "I didn't ask. It's the first rule of running a race, isn't it? Not to look back at who's behind you?"

Eiah chuckled, but didn't respond otherwise. Once she'd left and Maati had banked the fire, he sat on the bed. The night candle stood straight in its glass case, the burning wick marking the hours before dawn. It wasn't to its first-quarter mark and he felt exhausted. He moved the papers and the scroll safely off the bed, pulled the blanket up over himself, and slept better than he had in weeks, waking to the sound of morning birds and pale light before dawn.

He read over the list of questions on the scroll, only surveying them and not bothering to think of answers just yet, and then turned to the proposed binding. When he went out, following the smells of wood smoke and warmed honey, his mind was turning at twice its usual speed.

They had made a small common room from what had once been the teachers' cells, and Irit and Large Kae were sitting at the window that Maati remembered looking out when he had been a child called before Tahi-kvo. Bald, mean-spirited Tahi-kvo, who would not have recognized the world as it had become; women studying the andat in his own rooms, the poets almost vanished from the world, Galts on the way to becoming the nobles of this new, rattling, sad, stumble-footed Empire. Nothing was the same as it had been. Everything was different.

Vanjit, sitting with her legs crossed by the fire grate, smiled up at him. Maati took a pose of greeting and lowered himself carefully to her side. Irit and Large Kae both glanced at him, their eyes rich with curiosity and perhaps even envy, but they kept to their window and their conversation. Vanjit held out her bowl of cooked wheat and raisins, but Maati took a pose that both thanked and refused, then changed his mind and scooped two fingers into his mouth. The grain was rich and salted, sweetened with fruit and honey both. Vanjit smiled at him; the expression failed to reach her eyes.

"I looked over your work. Yours and Eiah-cha's," he said. "It's interesting."

Vanjit looked down, setting the bowl on the stone floor at her side. After a moment's hesitation, her hands took a pose that invited his judgment.

"I . . ." Maati began, then coughed, looked out past Large Kae and Irit to the bright and featureless blue of the western sky. "I don't want to hurry this. And I would rather not see any more of you pay the price of falling short."

Her mouth tightened, and her eyebrows rose as if she were asking a question. She said nothing.

"You're sure you want this?" he asked. "You have seen all the women we've lost. You know the dangers."

"I want this, Maati-kvo. I want to try this. And . . . and I don't know how much longer I can wait," she said. Her gaze rose to meet his. "It's time for me. I have to try soon, or I think I never will."

"If you have doubts about—"

"Not doubts. Only a little despair now and then. You can take that from me. If you let me try." Maati started to speak, but the girl went on, raising her voice and speaking faster, as if she feared what he would say next. "I've seen death. I won't say I'm not afraid of it, but I'm not so taken by the fear that I can't risk anything. If it's called for."

"I didn't think you were," he said.

"And I helped bury Umnit. I know what the price can look like. But I buried my mother and my brother and his daughter too, and they didn't die for a reason. They were only on the streets when Udun fell," she said, and shrugged. "We all die sometime, Maati-kvo. Risking it sooner and for a reason is better than being safe and meaningless. Isn't it?"

Brave girl. She was such a brave girl. To have lost so much, so young, and still be strong enough to risk the binding. Maati felt tears in his eyes and forced himself to smile.

"We chose it for *you*. Clarity-of-Sight," she said. "I saw how hard it is for you to read some days, and Eiah and I thought . . . if we could help . . ."

Maati laid his hand on hers, his heart aching with something equally joy and fear. Vanjit was weeping a bit as well now. He heard voices coming down the hallway—Eiah and Ashti Beg—but Irit and Large Kae were silent. He was certain they were watching them. He didn't care.

"We'll be careful," he said. "We'll make it work."

Her smile outshone the sun. Maati nodded; yes, they would attempt the binding. Yes, Vanjit would be the first woman in history to hold an andat or else the next of his students to die.

7

"No, I will not forbid her a goddamned thing. The girl's got more spine than all the rest of us put together. We could learn something from her," Farrer Dasin said, his arms folded before him, his chin high and proud. And when he said *the rest of us,* Otah was clear that he meant the Galts. The courts of the Khaiem, the cities and people of Otah's empire were not part of Farrer Dasin's *us;* they were still apart and the enemy.

Six members of the High Council sat at the wide marble table along with Balasar Gice and Issandra Dasin. Otah, Danat, and representatives of four of the highest families of the utkhaiem sat across from them. Otah wished he'd been able to scatter each side among the other instead of dividing the table like a battlefield. Or else keep the group smaller. If it had been only himself, Farrer, and Issandra, there might have been a chance.

Ana, the girl who had taken a stick to this political beehive, was not present, nor was she welcome.

"There are agreements in place," Balasar said. "We can't unmake them on a whim."

"Yes, Dasin-cha. Contracts have been signed," one of the utkhaiem said. "Is it Galt's intention that any contract can be invalidated if the signer's daughter objects?"

"That isn't what happened," the councilman at Farrer's right hand said. "We have our hands full enough without exaggerating."

And so it started off again, voices raised each over the other with the effect that nothing but babble could be heard. Otah didn't add to the clamor, but sat forward in his chair and watched. He considered the architecture—vaulted ceiling of blue and gold tiles, the sliding wooden shutters. He found a scent in the air: sugared almonds. He struggled to hear a sound beyond the table: the wind in the treetops. Then, slowly, he pulled his awareness back to the people before him. It was an old trick he'd learned during his days as a courier, a way of withdrawing half a step from the place where he was and considering the ways that people moved and held themselves, the expressions they wore when they were silent and when they spoke. It often said more than the words. And now, he saw three things.

First, he was not the only silent one at the table. Issandra Dasin was rocked a degree back in her chair, her eyes fixed on the middle distance. Her expression spoke of exhaustion and a barely hidden sorrow, the complement to her husband's self-destructive pleasure. Danat was also withdrawn, but with his body canted forward, as if he was trying to hear every phrase that fluttered through the heavy air. He might as easily drink a river.

Second, Otah saw that neither side was united. The Galts across from him ran the gamut from defiant to conciliatory, the utkhaiem from outraged to fearful. It was the same outside. The palaces, the teahouses, the baths, the street corners—all of Saraykeht was filled with agreements and negotiations that were suddenly, violently uncertain. He recalled something his daughter had said once about the reopened wound being the one most plagued by scars.

Third, and perhaps least interesting, it became clear that he was wasting his time.

"Friends," Otah said. Then again, louder, "Friends!"

Slowly, the table grew quiet around him.

"The morning has been difficult," he said. "We should retire and reflect on what has been said."

Whatever it was, he didn't add.

There was a rumble of assent, if not precisely agreement. Otah took a pose of gratitude to each man and woman as they left, even to Farrer Dasin, for whom he felt very little warmth. Otah dismissed the servants as well, and soon only he and Danat remained. Without the pandemonium of voices, the meeting room seemed larger and oddly forlorn.

"Well," his son said, leaning against the table. He was wearing the same robe as he had at the botched ceremony the day before. The cloth itself looked weary. "What do you make of it?"

Otah scratched idly at his arm and tried to focus his mind. His back ached, and there was an uneasy, bright feeling in his gut that presaged a sleepless and uncomfortable night. He sighed.

"Primarily, I think I'm an idiot," Otah said. "I should have written to the daughters. I forget how different their world is. Your world, too."

Danat took a pose that asked elaboration. Otah rose, stretching. His back didn't improve.

"Political marriage isn't a new thing," Otah said. "We've always suffered it. They've always suffered it. But, once the rules changed, it stopped meaning so much, didn't it? As long as Ana-cha has been alive, she hasn't seen political marriages take place. If Radaani married his son to Saya's daughter, they wouldn't be joining bloodlines. No children, no lasting connection between the houses. Likewise in Galt. I doubt it's stopped the practice entirely, but it's changed things. I should have thought of it."

"And she could take lovers," Danat said.

"People took lovers before," Otah said.

"Not without fear," Danat said. "There's no chance of a child. It changes how willing a girl would be."

"And how exactly do you know that?" Otah asked.

Danat blushed. Otah walked to the window. Below, the gardens were in motion. Wind shifted the boughs of the trees and set the flowers nodding. The scent of impending rain cooled the air. There would be a storm by nightfall.

"Papa-kya?" Danat said.

Otah looked over his shoulder. Danat was sitting on the table, his feet on the seat of a cushioned chair. It was the pose of a casual boy in a cheap teahouse. Danat's face, however, was troubled.

"Don't bother it," Otah said. "It might be a new world for sex, but there was an old world for it too. And I'm sure there are any number of other men who've made the same discoveries you have."

"That wasn't the matter. It's the wedding. I don't think I can . . . I don't think I can do it. When it was just thinking of it, I hadn't seen what it would be to be married to someone who hated me. I have now."

His voice was thick with distress. A gust of stronger wind came, rattling the shutters in their frames. Otah slid the wood closed, and the meeting room dimmed, gold tiles turning bronze, blue tiles black.

"It will be fine," Otah said. "At worst, there are other councillors with other daughters. It won't be a pleasant transition, but—"

"A different girl won't fix this. At best we'd find a girl less willing to struggle. At worst, we'd find someone who hated me just as much, but better versed in deceit."

Otah took his seat again. He could feel his brow furrow. If he hadn't been so tired to begin with, it wouldn't have taken him as long to think through Danat's words.

"Are you . . ." Otah said, then stopped and began again. "You're saying you won't have *Ana*?"

"I thought I could. I would have, if she hadn't done what she did. But I've spent all night looking at it, and I don't see a way."

"I do. I see it perfectly clearly. High families have been arranging marriages for as long as there have been high families. It binds them together. It shows trust."

"You didn't. You were Khai Machi. You could have had dozens of wives, but you didn't. Even after the fever took Mother, you didn't. You could have," Danat said. And then, "You could now. You could make one of these girls your wife. Marry Ana-cha."

"You know quite well that I couldn't. A man of my years bedding a girl? They wouldn't see a marriage so much as a debauch."

"Yes," Danat said. "And putting me in your place would only change how it looked, not what it was. I'll do whatever I can to help. You know that. I could marry a stranger and make the best of it. But I won't father a child on an unwilling girl."

"Don't be an idiot," Otah said, and knew immediately that it was the wrong thing. His son's smile was a mask now, cold and bright and hard as stone. Otah raised his hands in a pose that took the words back, but Danat ignored it.

"I won't do something I know in my bones is wrong," Danat said. "If it's the only way to save us, then we aren't worth saving."

Otah watched the boy leave. There were a thousand arguments to make, a thousand ways to rephrase the issue, to make something different of these same circumstances. None of them would matter. He let his head sink to his hands.

There had been a time when Otah had been young and the world had been, if not simple, at least certain. Decades and experience had made him sure that his sense of right and wrong were not the only ones. Before he'd had that beaten out of him by the gods, he might well have taken the same stand Danat had just now. Do what he believed to be right and endure the consequences, no matter how terrible.

If only his children were less like him.

There had to be a way. The whole half-dead mess of it had to be salvageable. He had only to see how.

Voices and argument filled the halls as he made his way through the palaces. Columns wrapped in celebratory cloth mocked him. Uncertain, falsely bright gazes met his own and were ignored. The thick air of the summer cities left sweat running down Otah's spine and the sensation of a damp cloth pressed against his face. There was a way to salvage this. He had only to find it.

Letters and requests for audiences waited for him, stacks of paper as long as his forearm. He ignored them for now and sent his servants scurrying for fresh paper and chilled tea. He sat at his desk, the pen's bright bronze nib in the air just above the brick of ink, and gave himself a moment before he began.

> *Kiyan-kya—*
>
> *Well, love, it's all gone as well as a wicker fish boat. Ana won't have Danat. Danat won't have Ana. I find myself host to the worst gathering in history not actually struck by plague. I think the only thing I've done well was that I didn't wrestle our son to the ground when he walked away from me. I feel like everyone is wrapped up in what happened before, and I'm alone in fearing what will come after. We won't survive, love. The Khaiem and the Galts both are sinking, and we're so short-sighted and mean of spirit we're willing to die if it means the other bastard goes down too.*
>
> *I don't mean Ana or Danat. They're only young and brave and stupid the way young, brave people are. I mean her father. Farrer Dasin is happy to see this fail. I imagine there are a fair number in my court who feel the same way.*
>
> *There are two sides to this, love. But they aren't the two sides we think of— not the Khaiem and the Galts. It's the people in love with the past and the ones who fear for the future. And, though the gods alone know how I'm going to do it, I have to win Danat and Ana over from the one camp to the other.*

Otah paused, something shifting in the back of his mind. It felt the way it had when Kiyan was alive and speaking to him from the next room, her voice too low to make out the words. He put down the pen and closed his eyes.

Win Ana over. He had to win Ana over.

"Oh," he said.

"Issandra-cha. Thank you for coming. You know my son, I think," Otah said.

The sun touched the hills to the west of Saraykeht. Ruddy air rich with the scent of evening roses came through the unshuttered windows. A small meal of cheese and dried apple and plum wine waited for their pleasure on a low lacquered table. Issandra Dasin rose from her divan to greet Danat as he came forward.

"Issandra-cha," Danat said and returned her welcome.

"Danat needs your help," Otah said. Danat glanced over at him, surprise in his gaze. "You see, your daughter has convinced him that it would be wrong to marry an unwilling woman. I can argue it to be the lesser evil, but if we two work together, I think the issue might be avoided altogether."

Issandra returned to her seat, sighing. She looked older than when Otah had first met her.

"It won't be simple," Issandra said.

"What won't be simple?" Danat asked.

"Wooing my daughter," Issandra said. "What did you think we were talking about?"

Otah took a bit of dried apple in his mouth while Danat blinked. Words stumbled over the boy's tongue without finding a sentence.

"You won't have a different girl for fear she'll hate you and lie about it," Otah said in the tone of a man explaining the solution of a simple mechanical problem. "Ana, we are all quite aware, isn't going to hide her feelings on the matter. So if she chooses you, you can believe her. Yes?"

"We have a small advantage in that her present lover is something of a cow," Issandra said. "I suspect that, had the circumstances been otherwise, she would already have grown tired of him. But he's a point of pride now." She fixed Danat with her eyes. "You have a hard road before you, son."

"You want me to seduce your daughter?" Danat asked, his voice breaking slightly at *seduce*.

"Yes," Issandra said.

Danat sank to a cushion. His face flushed almost the color of sunset.

"I thought he might deliver an apology," Otah said. "It would give him a reason to speak with Ana-cha in private, separate him from the political aspect of the arrangement, and place him in her camp."

"Apologize for what?" Danat said.

"Well, for me," Otah said. "Express your shame that I would treat her so poorly."

"She'll smell that in a heartbeat," Issandra said. "And if you begin by giving her the upper hand, you'll never have it back. Ask an apology *from* her. Respect her objections, but tell her she was wrong in humiliating you. You are as much a pawn in this as she is. And do you have a lover?"

"I . . . I was . . ."

"Well, find one," Issandra said. "Preferably someone prettier than my daughter. You needn't look shocked, my boy. I've lived my life in court. While you poor dears are out swinging knives at each other, there are wars just as bloody at every grand ball."

A scratching came at the door, followed by a servant woman. She took a pose of abject apology.

"Most High, there's a courier for you."

"It can wait," Otah said. "Or if it can't, send for Sinja-cha."

"The courier's come from Chaburi-Tan," the servant said. "The letter is sealed and signed for you alone. He says the issue is urgent."

Otah cursed under his breath, but he rose. As he stepped out to the ante-chamber, he heard Danat and Issandra resume the conversation without him. The antechamber felt as close as a grave, heavy tapestries killing any sound from within the greater meeting room. The courier was a young man, hardly more than Danat's age. Otah saw the calm, professional eyes sum him up. If the boy had been longer in the gentleman's trade, Otah would never have noticed it. He accepted the letter and ripped it open there, not waiting for a blade to cut the silk-sewn edging.

The cipher was familiar to him, but it made for slower reading than plain text. It was from the Kajiit Miyan, servant to the Emperor Otah Machi who had founded the Third Empire. Otah skipped down past the honorifics and empty form, decoding words and phrases in his mind until he reached some-thing of actual importance. Then he read more slowly. And then he went back and read it again.

The mercenaries hired to protect Chaburi-Tan were ending their contract and leaving. Within a month, the city would be reduced to its citizen militia. The pirates who had been harrying the city would find them only token resis-tance. Their options, his agent said, were to surrender and pray for mercy or else flee the city. There would be no defense.

Otah took the servant girl by the elbow.

"Find Balasar. And Sinja. Bring them . . ." Otah looked over his shoulder. "Bring them to the winter garden of the second palace. Do it now. You. Cou-rier. You'll wait until I have word to take back."

The twilight world lost its color like a face going pale. Otah paced the lush green and blossomless garden, wrenching his mind from one crisis to the next. A different servant led Balasar into the space between the willows.

"Find us some light," Otah said. "And Sinja-cha. Get Sinja-cha."

The servant, caught between two needs, hesitated, then hurried off. Otah led Balasar to a low stone bench. The general wore a lighter jacket, silk over cotton. His breath smelled of wine, but he gave no sign of being drunk. Otah looked out at the gray sky, the dark, looming palaces with windows glimmer-ing like stars and cursed Sinja for his absence.

"Balasar-cha, I need you. The Galtic fleet has to travel to Chaburi-Tan," Otah said.

He outlined the letter he'd had, the history of increasing raids and attacks, and his half-imagined scheme to show the unity of Galt and the Khaiem. With every word, Balasar seemed to become stiller, until at the end, it was like speaking to stone.

"We can only show unity where it exists," Balasar said. His voice was low, and in the rising darkness it seemed to come from no direction at all. "After what happened yesterday, the fleet's as likely to turn on the city as the raiders."

"I don't have the ships and men to protect Chaburi-Tan," Otah said. "Not without you. The city will fall, and thousands will be killed. If the Galtic fleet came in, the pirates would turn back without so much as an arrow flown. And it would halfway unmake yesterday's mess."

"It can't happen," Balasar said.

"Then tell me what can," Otah said.

The general was silent. A moth took wing, fluttering between them like a clot of shadows and dust before it vanished.

"There is . . . something. It will make things here more difficult," Balasar said. "There are families who have committed to your scheme. That have already been brokering contracts and arranging alliances. I can gather them. It won't be anything like the full force of war, but if they sent their private ships and soldiers along with whatever you can muster up, it might serve."

"At the cost of sending away what allies I have," Otah said.

"That would be the price of it," Balasar said. "Send away your friends, and you're left eating with your enemies. It could poison the court against us."

Us. At least the man had said *us*.

"Get them," Otah said. "Get whoever you can quickly, and then send for me. I can't let another city die."

It only occurred to him as he stalked back through the wide stone halls and softly glowing lanterns of the first palace that he had been speaking to the man that had killed Udun and the village of the Dai-kvo, the man who had maimed Nantani and Yalakeht.

The meeting chamber was empty when he reached it; Danat and Issandra had gone. The cheese and apples and wine had been cleared away. The lanterns had blown out. Otah called for a servant to fetch him food and light. He sat, his annoyance and unease rising in his breast like the tide climbing a sea cliff.

Ana Dasin and her petulant, self-important father were well on their way to seeing both empires chewed away one bit at a time by pirates and foreign conspiracies. And failing crops. And time. Childless years growing one upon another like a winter with no promise of spring. There were so many things to fix, so uncountably many things that had gone wrong. He was the Emperor, the most powerful man in the cities of the Khaiem, and he was tired to his heart.

When the food arrived—pork in black sauce, spiced rice, sugared apple, wine and herbs—Otah was hardly hungry any longer. Moments after that, Sinja finally arrived.

"Where have you been?" Sinja demanded. "I've been wandering around the winter garden for half a hand looking for you."

"I should ask the same. I must have had half the servants in the palace looking for you."

"I know. Six of them found me. It got inconvenient telling them all I was busy. You need to come with me."

"You were busy?"

"Otah-cha, you need to come with me."

He breathed deeply and took a pose that commanded obedience. Sinja's eyebrows rose and he adopted an answering pose that held nuances of both query and affront.

"I have no intention of going anywhere until I have finished eating," Otah said. It embarrassed him to hear the peevishness in his voice, but not so much as to unsay it. Sinja tilted his head, stepped forward, and lifted one end of the table. The plates and bowl spun to the floor. One shattered. Otah was on his feet with no memory of standing. His face felt as warm as if he were looking into a fire. His ears filled with a buzzing of rage.

Sinja took a step back.

"I can have you killed," Otah said. "You know I can have you killed."

"You're right," Sinja said. "That passed the mark. I apologize, Most High. But you have to come with me. Now."

Servants came in, their eyes wide as little moons, their hands fluttering over the carnage of his dinner.

"What is it?" Otah said.

"Not here. Not where someone might hear us."

Sinja turned and walked from the room. Otah hesitated, mumbled an obscenity that made the servants turn their faces away, and followed. As his own anger faded, he saw the tension in Sinja's shoulders and through his neck. They were the sorts of signs he should have picked up on at once. He was tired. He was slipping.

Sinja was quartered in apartments of the third palace, where the Khai Saraykeht's second son would have lived, had there been a Khai Saraykeht or any sons. The walls were black marble polished until the darkness itself shone in the torchlight. Doors of worked silver still showed where gems had been wrenched from them by Galtic hands. They were beautiful all the same. Perhaps more beautiful than when they had been intact; scars created character.

Without speaking, Sinja went to each window in turn, poking his head out into the night, then closing outer shutters and inner. Otah stood, arms in his sleeves, unease growing in his heart.

"What is this?" Otah said, but the man only took a pose that asked patience and continued in his errand. At the last, he looked out into the corridor, sent the servant there away, then closed and bolted the main door.

"We have a problem, Otah-cha," Sinja said. He was breathing hard, like a man who'd run up stairs.

"We have a hundred of them," Otah said.

"The others may not matter," a woman's voice said from the shadows of the bedchamber. Otah turned.

Idaan was shorter than he remembered her, wider through the shoulders and the hips. Her hair was gray, her robe a cheaply dyed green and travel-stained. Otah took a step back without meaning to. His sister's appearance chilled his heart like an omen of death, but he wouldn't let it show.

"Why are you here?" he said.

His exiled sister pursed her lips and shrugged.

"Gratitude," she said. "You did away with my lover and his family. You took everything I had, including my true name, and sent me out into the world to survive as best I could."

"I'm not sorry," Otah said.

"And I am? It's the kindest thing anyone's ever done for me," Idaan said. "I mean that. And I'm here to repay the debt. You're in trouble, brother mine, and I'm the only one who can warn you. The andat are coming back to the world. And this time, the poets won't be answering to you."

8

>+< Autumn came early on the high plains. Even though the leaves were as green, the grasses as thick, Maati felt the change. It wasn't a chill, but the presentiment of one: a sharpness to air that had been soft and torpid with summer heat. Another few weeks and the trees would turn to red and gold, the mornings would come late, the sunsets early. The endless change would change again. For the first time in years, Maati found himself pleased by the thought.

The days following his return had fallen into a rhythm. In the mornings, he and his students worked on the simple tasks of maintenance that the school demanded: mending the coops for the chickens they'd brought from Utani, weeding the paths, washing the webs and dust from the corners of the rooms. At midday, they stopped, made food, and rested in the shade of the gardens or on the long, sloping hills where he had taken lessons as a boy. Afterward, he would retire for the afternoon, preparing his lectures and writing in his book until his eyes ached and then taking a short nap to revive before the evening lecture. And always, whatever the day brought, the subject drew itself back to Vanjit and Clarity-of-Sight.

"What about when you see things that aren't there?" Small Kae said.

"Dreams, you mean?" Eiah asked.

Maati leaned forward on the podium. The classroom was larger than they required, all six of his students sitting in the first row. The high, narrow windows that had never known glass let the evening breeze disturb their lanterns.

He had ended his remarks early. He found there was less need to fill the time with his knowledge than there had once been. Now a few remarks and comments would spur conversation and analysis that often led far from where he had intended. But it was rarely unproductive and never dull.

"Dreams," Small Kae said. "Or when you mistake things for other things."

"My brother had a fever once," Ashti Beg said. "Saw rats coming through the walls for three days."

"I don't think that applies," Eiah said. "The definitions we've based the draft on are all physicians' texts. They have to do with the actual function of the eye."

"But if you see a thing without your eyes," Small Kae began.

"Then you're imagining them," Vanjit said, her voice calm and certain. "And the passages on clarity would prevent the contradiction."

"What contradiction?" Large Kae asked.

"Who can answer that?" Maati said, leaping into the fray. "It's a good question, but any of you should be able to think it through. Ashti-cha? Would you care to?"

The older woman sucked her teeth for a moment. A sparrow flew in through one window, its wings fluttering like a pennant in the wind, and then out again.

"Clarity," Ashti Beg said slowly. "The sense of clarity implies that it's reflecting the world as it is, ne? And if you see something that's not there to be seen, it's not the world as it is. Even if imagining something is like sight, it isn't like clarity."

"Very good," Maati said, and the woman smiled. Maati smiled back.

The binding had progressed more quickly than Maati had thought possible. For the greatest part, the advances had been made in moments like these. Seven minds prodding at the same thought, debating the nuances and structures, challenging one another to understand the issues at hand more deeply. Someone—anyone—would find a phrase or a thought that struck sparks, and Vanjit would pull pages from her sleeve and mark down whatever had pushed her one step nearer the edge.

It was happening less and less often. The binding, Maati knew, was coming near its final form. The certainty in Vanjit's voice and the angle of her shoulders told him as much about her chances of success as looking over the details of her binding.

As they ended the evening's session, reluctant despite yawns and heavy-lidded eyes, Maati realized that the work they were doing was less like his own training before the Dai-kvo and more like the long, arduous hours he had spent with Cehmai. Somehow, during his absence, they had all become equals. Not in knowledge—he was still far and away the best informed—but in status. Where he had once had a body of students, he was working now with a group of novice poets. A lizard scampered along before him and then up the rough wall and into the darkness. A nightingale sang.

He was exhausted, his body heavy, his mind beginning to spark and slip. And he was also elated. The wide night sky above him seemed rich with promise, the ground he walked upon eager to bear him up.

His bed, however, didn't invite sleep. Small pains in his knees and spine prodded him, and his mind failed to calm. The light of the half-moon cast shadows on the walls that seemed to move of their own accord. The restlessness of age, as opposed, he thought with weary amusement, to the restlessness of youth. As he lay there, small doubts began to arise, gnawing at him. Perhaps Vanjit wasn't ready yet to take on the role of poet. Perhaps he and Eiah in their need and optimism were sending the girl to her death.

There was no way to know another person's heart. No way to judge. It might be that Vanjit herself was as afraid of this as he was, but held by her despair and anger and sense of obligation to the others to move forward as if she weren't.

Every poet that bound an andat came face-to-face with their own flaws, their own failures. Maati's first master, Heshai-kvo, had made Seedless the embodiment of his own self-hatred, but that was only one extreme example. Kiai Jut three generations earlier had bound Flatness only to find the andat bent on destroying the family the poet secretly hated. Magar Inarit had famously bound Unwoven only to discover his own shameful desires made manifest in his creation. The work of binding the andat was of such depth and complexity, the poet's true self was difficult if not impossible to hide within it. And what, he wondered, would Vanjit discover about herself if she succeeded? With all the hours they had spent on the mechanics of the binding, was it not also his responsibility to prepare the girl to face her imperfections?

His mind worried at the questions like a dog at a bone. As the moon vanished from his window and left him with only the night candle, Maati rose. A walk might work the kinks from his muscles.

The school was a different place at night. The ravages of war and time were less obvious, the shapes of the looming walls and hallways familiar and prone to stir the ancient memories of the boy Maati had been. Here, for instance, was the rough stone floor of the main hall. He had cleaned these very stones when his hands had been smooth and strong and free from the dark, liver-colored spots. He stood at the place where Milah-kvo had first offered him the black robes. He remembered both the pride of the moment and the sense, hardly noticed at the time, that it was an honor he didn't wholly deserve.

"Would you have done it differently, Milah-kvo?" he asked the dead man and the empty air. "If you had known what I was going to do, would you still have made the offer?"

The air said nothing. Maati felt himself smile without knowing precisely why.

"Maati-kvo?"

He turned. In the dim light of his candle, Eiah seemed like a ghost. Something conjured from his memory. He took a pose of greeting.

"You're awake," she said, falling into step beside him.

"Sometimes sleep abandons old men," he said with a chuckle. "It's the way of things. And you? I can't think you make a practice of wandering the halls in the middle of the night."

"I've just left Vanjit. She sits up after the lecture is done and goes over everything we said. Everything anyone said. I agreed to sit with her and compare my memory to hers."

"She's a good girl," Maati said.

"Her dreams are getting worse," Eiah said. "If the situation were different, I'd be giving her a sleeping powder. I'm afraid it will dull her, though."

"They're bad then?" Maati said.

Eiah shrugged. In the dim light, her face seemed older.

"They're no worse than anyone who watched her family die before her eyes. She has told you, hasn't she?"

"She was a child," Maati said. "The only one to live."

"She said no more than that?"

"No," Maati said. They passed through a stone archway and into the courtyard. Eiah looked up at the stars.

"It's as much as I know too," Eiah said. "I try to coax her. To get her to speak about it. But she won't."

"Why try?" Maati said. "Talking won't undo it. Let her be who and where she is now. It's better that way."

Eiah took a pose that accepted his advice, but her face didn't entirely match it. He put a hand on her shoulder.

"It will be fine," he said.

"Will it?" Eiah said. "I tell myself the same thing, but I don't always believe it."

Maati stopped at a stone bench, flicked a snail from the seat, and rested. Eiah sat at his side, hunched over, her elbows on her knees.

"You think we should stop this?" he asked. "Call off the binding?"

"What reason could we give?"

"That Vanjit isn't ready."

"It isn't true, though. Her mind is as good as any of ours will ever be. If I called this to a halt, I'd be saying I didn't trust her to be a poet. Because of what she's been through. That the Galts had taken that from her too. And if I say that of her, who won't it be true of? Ashti Beg lost her husband. Irit's father burned with his farm. Large Kae only had her womb turned sick and saw the Khai Utani slaughtered with his family. If we're looking for a woman who's never known pain, we may as well pack up our things now, because there isn't one."

Maati let the silence stretch, in part to leave Eiah room to think. In part because he didn't know what wisdom he could offer.

"No, Uncle Maati, I don't want to stop. I only . . . I only hope this brings her some peace," Eiah said.

"It won't," Maati said, gently. "It may heal some part of her. It may bring good to the world, but the andat have never brought peace to poets."

"No. I suppose not," Eiah said. Then, a moment later, "I'm going into Pathai. I'll just need a cart and one of the horses."

"Is there need?"

"We aren't starving, if that's what you mean. But buying at the markets there attracts less notice than going straight to the low towns. It would be better if no one knows there are people living out here. And there might be news."

"And if there's news, there will be some idea of how soon Vanjit-cha will need to make her attempt."

"I was thinking more of how much time I have," Eiah said. She turned to look at him. The warm light of the candle and the cool glow of the moon made her seem like two different women at once. "This doesn't rest on Vanjit. It doesn't rest on any of them. Binding an andat isn't enough to . . . fix things. It has to be the right one."

"And Clarity-of-Sight isn't the right one?" he asked.

"It won't give any of these women babies. It won't put them back in the arms of the men who used to be their husbands or stop men like my father from trading in women's flesh like we were sheep. None of it. All the binding will do is prove that it can be done. That a solution exists. It doesn't even mean I'll be strong enough when my turn comes."

Maati took her hand. He had known her for so many years. Her hand had been so small that first time he had seen her. He remembered her deep brown eyes, and the way she had gurgled and burrowed into her mother's cradling arms. He could still see the shape of that young face in the shape of her cheeks and the set of her jaw. He leaned over and kissed her hair. She looked up at him, amused to see him so easily moved.

"I was only thinking," he said, "how many of us there are carrying this whole burden alone."

"I know I'm not alone, Maati-kya. It only feels like it some nights."

"It does. It certainly does," he said. Then, "Do you think she'll manage it?"

Eiah rose silently, took a pose that marked parting with nuances as intimate as family, and walked back into the buildings of the school. Maati sighed and lay back on the stone, looking up into the night sky. A shooting star blazed from the eastern sky toward the north and vanished like an ember gone cold.

He wondered if Otah-kvo still looked at the sky, or if he had grown too busy being the Emperor. The days and nights of power and feasting and admiration might rob him of simple beauties like a night sky or a fear grown less by being shared. Might, in fact, cut Otah-kvo off from all the things that gave meaning to people lower than himself. He was, after all, planning his new empire by denying all the women injured by the last war any hope of those simple, human pleasures. A babe. A family. Tens of thousands of women, cut free from the lives they were entitled to, now to be forgotten.

He wondered if a man who could do that still had enough humanity left to enjoy a falling star or the song of a nightingale.

He hoped not.

Eiah left the next morning. The high road was still in good repair, and travel along it was an order of magnitude faster than the tracking Maati had done between the low towns. When Maati and the others saw her off, she was wearing simple robes and the leather satchel hung at her side. She could have been mistaken for any traveling physician. Maati might have imagined it, but he thought that Vanjit held her parting stance longer than the others, that her eyes followed Eiah more hungrily.

When the horse and cart had gone far enough that even the dust from the hooves and wheels was invisible, they turned back to the business at hand. Until midday, they scraped soot and a decade's fallen leaves out from the shell of one of the gutted buildings. Irit found the bones of some forgotten boy who had been caught in that long-cooled fire, and they held a brief ceremony in remembrance of the slaughtered poets and student boys in whose path they all traveled. Vanjit especially was sober and pale as Maati finished his words and committed the bones to a fresh-made, hotter blaze that would, he hoped, return the old bones to their proper ash.

As they made their way back from the pyre, he made a point to walk at her side. Her olive skin and well-deep eyes reminded him of his first lover, Liat. The mother of the child who should have been his own. Even before she spoke, his breast ached like a once-broken arm presaging a shift of weather.

"I was thinking of my brother," Vanjit said. "He was near that boy's age. Not highborn, of course. They didn't take normal people here then, did they?"

"No," Maati said. "Nor women, for that."

"It's a strange thought. It already seems like home to me. Like I've always been here," the girl said, then shifted her weight, her shoulders turning a degree toward Maati even as they walked side by side. "You've always known Eiah-cha, haven't you?"

"As long as she's known anything," Maati said with a chuckle. "Possibly a bit longer. I was living in Machi for years and years before the war."

"She must be very important to you."

"She's been my salvation, in her way. Without her, none of us would be here."

"You would have found a way," Vanjit said. Her voice was odd, a degree harder than Maati had expected. Or perhaps he had imagined it, because when she went on, there was no particular bite to the words. "You're clever and wise enough, and I'm sure there are more people in places of influence that would have given you aid, if you'd asked."

"Perhaps," Maati said. "But I knew from the first I could trust Eiah. That carries quite a bit of weight. Without trust, I don't know if I would have hit on the idea of coming here. Before, I always kept to places I could leave easily."

"She said that you wouldn't let her bind the first andat," Vanjit said. "One of us has to succeed before you'll let her make the attempt."

"That's so," Maati agreed, a moment's discomfort passing through him. He didn't want to explain the thinking behind that decision. When Vanjit went on, it was happily not in that direction.

"She's shown me some of the work she's done. She's working from the same books that I am, you know."

"Yes," Maati said. "That was a good thought, using sources from the Westlands. The more things we can use that weren't part of how the old poets thought, the better off we are."

Maati described Cehmai's suggestion of making an andat and withdrawing its influence as a strategy of Eiah, pleased to have steered the conversation to safe waters. Vanjit listened, her full attention upon him. Ashti Beg and Irit, walking before them, paused. If Vanjit hadn't hesitated, Maati thought he might not have noticed until he bumped into them.

"Small Kae is making soup for dinner," Irit said. "If you have time to help her . . ."

"Maati-kvo's much too busy for that," Vanjit said.

When Ashti Beg spoke, her voice was dry as sand.

"Irit-cha might not have been speaking to him."

Vanjit's spine stiffened, and then, with a laugh, relaxed. She smiled at all of them as she took a contrite pose, accepting the correction. Irit reached out and placed her hand on Vanjit's shoulder as a sister might.

"I'm so proud of you," Irit said, grinning. "I'm just so happy and proud."

"So are we all," Ashti Beg said. Maati smiled, but the sense that something had happened sat at the back of his mind. As the four of them walked to the kitchens—the air growing rich with the salt-and-fat scent of pork and the dark, earthy scent of boiled lentils—Maati reviewed what each of them had said, the tones of voice, the angles at which they had held themselves. Small Kae assigned tasks to all of them except Maati, and he waited for a time, listening to the simple banter and the crack of knives against wood. When he took his leave, he was troubled.

He was not so far removed from his boyhood that he had forgotten what jealousy felt like. He'd suffered it himself in these same halls and rooms. One boy or another was always in favor, and the others wishing that they were. Walking through the bare gardens, Maati wondered whether he had allowed the same thing to happen. Vanjit was certainly the center of all their work and activity. Had Ashti Beg and Irit interrupted their conversation from an urge to take his attention, or at least deny it to her?

And then there was some question of Vanjit's heart.

The truth was that Eiah had been right. For all the hope and attention placed upon her, the project of the school was not truly Vanjit and Clarity-of-Sight. It would be Eiah and Wounded. Vanjit had seen it. It couldn't be pleasant, knowing she was taking the lead not for her own sake but to blaze the trail for another. He would speak to her. He would have to speak with her. Reassure her.

After the last of the lentil soup had been sopped up by the final crust of bread, Maati took Vanjit aside. It didn't go as he had expected.

"It isn't that Eiah-cha's work is more important," Maati said, his hands in a pose meant to convey a gentle authority. "You are taking the greater risk, and the role of the first of the poets of a new age. It's only that there are certain benefits that Eiah-cha brings because of her position at court. Once those aren't needed any longer, you see—"

Vanjit kissed him. Maati sat back. The girl's smile was broad, genuine, and oddly pitying. Her hands took a pose that offered correction.

"Ah, Maati-kvo. You think it matters that Eiah is more important than I am?"

"I didn't . . . I wouldn't put it that way."

"Let me. Eiah is more important than I am. I'm first because I'm the scout. That's all. But if I do well, if I can make this binding work, then she will have your permission. And then we can do anything. That's all I want."

Maati ran a hand through his hair. He found that none of the words he had practiced fit the moment. Vanjit seemed to understand his silence. When she went on, her voice was low and gentle.

"There's a difference between why you came to this place and why we have," she said. "Your father sent you here in hopes of glory. He hoped that you would rise through the ranks of all the boys and be sent to the Dai-kvo and become a poet. It isn't like that for me. I don't want to be a poet. Did you understand that?"

Maati took a pose that expressed both an acceptance of correction and a query. Vanjit responded with one appropriate to thanking someone of higher status.

"I had the dream again," Vanjit said. "I've been having it every night, almost. He's in me. And he's shifting and moving and I can hear his heart beating."

"I'm sorry," Maati said.

"No, Maati-kvo, that's just it. I wake up, and I'm not sad any longer. It was only hard when I thought it would never come. Now, I wake up, and I'm happy all day long. I can feel him getting close. He'll be here. What is being a poet beside that?"

Nayiit, he thought.

Maati didn't expect the tears, they simply welled up in his eyes. The pain in his breast was so sudden and sharp, he almost mistook the sorrow for illness. She put her hand on his, her expression anxious. He forced himself to smile.

"You're quite right," he said. "Quite right. Come along now. The bowls are all washed, and it's time we got to work."

He made his way to the hall they had set aside for classes. His heart was both heavy and light: heavy with the renewed sorrow of his boy's death, light at Vanjit's reaction to him. She had known Eiah's work to be of greater importance, and had already made her peace with her own lesser role. He wondered whether, in her place and at her age, he would have been able to do the same. He doubted it.

That evening, his lecture was particularly short, and the conversation after it was lively and pointed and thoughtful. In the days that followed, Maati abandoned his formal teaching entirely, instead leading discussion after discussion, analysis after analysis. Together, they tore Vanjit's binding of Clarity-of-Sight apart, and together they rebuilt it. Each time, Maati thought it was stronger, the images and resonances of it more appropriate to one another, the grammar that formed it more precise.

It was difficult to call the process to a halt, but in the end, it was Vanjit and Vanjit alone who would make the attempt. They might help her and advise her, but he allocated two full weeks in which the binding was hers and hers alone.

Low clouds came in the morning Eiah returned. They scudded in from the north on a wind cold as winter. Maati knew it wouldn't take. There were weeks of heat and sun to come before the seasons changed. And yet, there was a part of Maati's mind that couldn't help seeing the shift as an omen. And a positive one, he told himself. Change, the movement of the seasons, the proper order of the world: those were what he tried to see in the low, gray roof of the sky. Not the presentiment of barren winter.

"The news is strange," Eiah said as they unloaded her cart. Boxes of salt pork and raw flour, canisters of spice and hard cheese. "The Galts have fallen on Saraykeht like they owned it, but something didn't go well. I can't tell if my brother thought the girl was too ugly or she fell into a fit when she was presented, but something went badly. What I heard was early and muddled. I'll know better next time I go."

"Anything that hurts him helps us," Maati said. "So whatever it was, it's good."

"That was my thought," Eiah said, but her voice was somber. When he took a pose of query, she didn't answer it.

"How have things progressed here?" she asked instead.

"Well. Very well. I think Vanjit is ready."

Eiah stopped, wiping her sleeve across her forehead. She looked old. How many summers had she seen? Thirty? Thirty-one? Her eyes were deeper than thirty summers.

"When?" she asked.

"We were only waiting for you to come back," he said. Then, trying for levity, "You've brought the wine and food for a celebration. So tomorrow, we'll do something worth celebrating."

Or else something to mourn, he thought but did not say.

9

"By everything holy, don't tell Balasar," Sinja said. "He can't know about this."

"Why?" Idaan asked, sitting on the edge of the soldier's bed. "What would he do?"

"I don't know," Sinja said. "Something bloody and extreme. And effective."

"Stop," Otah said. "Just stop. I have to think."

But sitting there, head resting in his hands, clarity of mind wasn't coming to him easily. Idaan's story—her travels in the north after her exile, Cehmai's appearance on her doorstep, their rekindled love, and Maati's break with his fellow poet and then his return—had the feel of an old poem, if not the careful structure. If he hadn't had the pirates or Ana or her father or his own son or the conspiracy between Yalakeht and Obar State, or the incursions from the Westlands, he might have enjoyed the tale for its own sake.

But she hadn't brought it to him as a story. It was a threat.

"What role has Cehmai taken in this?" he asked.

"None. He wanted nothing to do with it. Or with my coming here, for that. I've left him to look after things until I've paid my debt to you. Then I'll be going home."

"Is it working?" Otah said at length. "Idaan-cha, did Maati say anything to suggest it was working?"

His sister took a pose of negation that held a sense of uncertainty.

"He came to Cehmai for help," Sinja said. "That means at least that he thinks he needs help."

"And Cehmai didn't agree to it," Idaan said. "He isn't helping. But he also doesn't want to see Maati hung. He cut Maati off before he told me who was backing him."

"What makes you think he has backing?"

"He said as much. Strong backing and an ear in the palaces whenever he wanted one," Idaan said. "Even if that overstates the truth, he isn't out hunting rabbits or wading through a rice field. Someone's feeding him. And how many people are there who might want the andat back in the world?"

"No end of them," Otah said. "But how many would think the thing was possible?"

Sinja opened a small wooden cabinet and took out a fluted bottle of carved bone. When he lifted out the stopper, the scent of wine filled the room. He asked with a gesture. Otah and Idaan accepted simultaneously, and with the same pose.

"The books are all burned," Otah said. "The histories are gone, the grammars are gone. I didn't think he could do this when he wrote to me before, I don't see that he could manage it now."

Sinja, stunned, overfilled one of the wine bowls, the red pooling on his table like spilled blood. Idaan hoisted a single eyebrow.

"He wrote to you before?" she said.

"It was years ago," Otah said. "I had a letter. A single letter. Maati said he was looking for a way to recapture the andat. He wanted my help. I sent a message back refusing."

"All apologies, Most High," Sinja said. He hadn't bothered to wipe up the spilled wine. "Why is this the first I'm hearing of it?"

"It came at a bad time," Otah said. "Kiyan was dying. It was hopeless. The andat are gone, and there's no force in the world that can bring them safely back."

"You're sure of that?" Idaan asked. "Because Maati-cha didn't think it was hopeless. The man is many things, but he isn't dim."

"It hardly matters," Sinja said. "Just the word that this is happening, and that—may all the gods keep it from happening—you knew he was thinking of it. That you've known for *years* . . ."

"It's a dream!" Otah shouted. "Maati was dreaming, that's all. He wants something back that's gone beyond his reach. Well, so do I. Anyone who has lived as long as we have knows that longing, and we know how useless it is. What's gone is gone, and we can't have it back. So what would you have had me do? Send the message back with an assassin? Announce to the world that Maati Vaupathai was out, trying to bind the andat, so they should all send invading armies at their first convenience?"

"Why didn't you?" Idaan asked. "Send the assassin, I mean. The invading armies, I understand. For that, why did you let them go at the end of the war?"

"I am not in the mood, Idaan-cha, to be questioned by a woman who killed my father, schemed to place the blame on me, and is only breathing air now because I chose to let her. I understand that you would have happily opened their throats."

"Not Cehmai's," she said softly. "But then I know why I wouldn't have done it. It doesn't follow that I should know why you didn't. The two aren't the same."

Otah rocked back in his chair. His face was hot. Their gazes locked, and he saw her nod. Idaan took a pose that expressed both understanding and contrition while unmasking the question.

"That isn't true," she said. "Thinking for a moment, I suppose they are."

Otah took the bowl Sinja held out to him. The wine was unwatered, rich and astringent. He drank it dry. Sinja looked nervous.

"There's nothing I can do about any of this tonight," Otah said. "I'm tired. I'm going to bed. If I decide it needs talking of further, it'll be another time."

He rose, taking a pose that ended an audience, then feeling a moment's shame, shifted to one that was merely a farewell.

"Otah-cha," Sinja said. "One last thing. I'm sorry, but you left standing orders. If she came back, I was supposed to kill her."

"For plotting to take my chair and conspiring with the Galts," Otah said. "Well. Idaan-cha? Are you hoping to become Emperor?"

"I wouldn't take your place as a favor," she said.

Otah nodded.

"Find apartments for her," he said. "Lift the death order. The girl we sent out in the snow might as well have died. And the man who sent her, for that. We are, all of us, different people now."

Otah walked back to his rooms alone. The palace wasn't quiet or still. Perhaps it never wholly was. But the buzzing fury of the day had given way to a slower pace. Fewer servants made their way down the halls. The members of the high families who had business here had largely gone back to their own palaces, walking stone paths chipped by the spurs and boot nails of Galtic soldiers, passing through arches whose gold and silver adornments had been hacked off by Galtic axes. They went to palaces where the highest men and women of Galt had come as guests, eating beef soup and white bread and fruit tarts. Sipping tea and wine and water and working, some of them at least, to build a common future.

And Idaan had come to warn him against Maati.

He slept poorly and woke tired. The Master of Tides attended him as he was bathed and dressed. The day was full from dawn to nightfall. Sixteen audiences had been requested, falling almost equally between members of the utkhaiem and the Galts. Three of the Galtic houses had left letters strongly implying that they had daughters who might be pressed to serve should Ana Dasin refuse. One of the priests at the temple had left a request to preach against the recalcitrance of women who failed to offer up sex. Two of the trading houses had made it clear that they wished to be released from shipping contracts to Chaburi-Tan. The Master of Tides droned and listed and laid out the form of another painful, endless, wasted day. When the stars came out again, Otah knew, he would feel like a wrung towel and all the great problems he faced would still be unsolved.

He instructed that the priest be forbidden, the trading houses be referred to Sinja-cha and the Master of Chains, who could renegotiate terms but not break the contract, and then dictated a common response to the three letters offering up new wives for Danat that neither encouraged nor refused them. All this before the breakfast of fresh-brewed tea, spiced apples, and seared pork had appeared.

He had hardly begun to eat when the Master of Tides returned with a sour expression and took a pose that asked forgiveness, but pointedly did not suggest that the offending party was the Master of Tides herself.

"Most High, Balasar Gice is requesting to join you. I have suggested that he apply for an audience just as anyone else, but he seems to forget that his conquest of Saraykeht was temporary."

"You'll treat Balasar-cha with respect," Otah said, though he couldn't quite keep from smiling. And then a breath later, his chest tightened. *Something*

bloody and extreme. And effective. What if the general had heard Idaan's news?
"See him in. And bring another bowl for tea."

The Master of Tides took a pose that accepted the command.

"A clean bowl," Otah added to the woman's back.

Balasar followed all the appropriate forms when the servants escorted him
back. Otah matched him, and then gestured for all the others to leave. When
they were alone, Balasar lowered himself to the cushion on the floor, took the
bowl of tea and the bit of pork that Otah offered him, and stretched out. Otah
watched the man's face and body, but there was no sign there that he'd heard
of Idaan's arrival or of her news.

"I've had a couple of discreet conversations," Balasar said.

"Yes?"

"About taking a fleet to Chaburi-Tan?"

Otah nodded. Of course. Of course that was what they were meeting about.

"And what have you found?" Otah asked.

"It can be done, but there are two ways to go about it. We have enough
men to make a small, effective fighting force. Eight ships, perhaps, fully
armed and provisioned. I wouldn't go to war on it, but it would outman most
raiding parties."

Otah sipped his tea. The water wasn't quite hot enough to scald.

"The other way?"

"We can use the same number to man twenty ships. A mixed force, ours
and your own. Throw on as many men as we can find who are well enough to
stand upright. It would actually be easier to defeat in a battle. The men who
knew what they were about would be spread thin, and amateurs are worse
than nothing in a sea fight. But weigh it against the sight of twenty ships. The
pirates would be mad to come against us in force."

"Unless they know we're all lights and empty show," Otah said. "There are
suggestions that the mercenaries we have at Chaburi-Tan are working both
sides."

Balasar sucked his teeth.

"That makes it harder," he agreed.

"How long would you need?" Otah asked.

"A week for the smaller force. Twice that for the larger."

"How many of our allies would we lose in the court here?"

"Hard to say. Knowing who your friends are is a tricky business right now.
You'll have fewer than if they stayed."

Otah took a slice of apple, chewing the soft flesh slowly to give himself time.
Balasar was silent, his expression unreadable. It occurred to Otah that the man
would have made a decent courier.

"Give me the day," he said. "I'll have an answer for you tonight. Tomorrow
at the latest."

"Thank you, Most High," Balasar said.

"I know how much I've asked of you," Otah said.

"It's something I owe you. Or that we owe each other. Whatever I can do, I will."

Otah smiled and took a pose of gratitude, but he was wondering what limits that debt would find if Idaan spoke to the old general. He was dancing around too many blades. He couldn't keep them all clear in his mind, and if he stumbled, there would be blood.

Otah finished his meal, allowed the servants to change his outer robe to a formal black with threads of gold throughout, and led his ritual procession to the audience chamber. The members of his court flowed into their places in the appropriate order, with the custom-driven signs of loyalty and obeisance. Otah restrained himself from shouting at them all to hurry. The time he spent in empty form was time stolen. He didn't have it to spare.

The audiences began, each a balancing between the justice of the issue, the politics behind those involved, and the massive complex webwork that made up the relationships of the court, of the cities, of the world. When he'd been young, the Khai Saraykeht had held audiences for things as simple as land disputes and broken contracts. Those days were gone, and nothing reached so high as the Emperor of the Khaiem unless no one lower dared rule on the matter. Nothing was trivial, everything fraught with implication.

Midday came and went, and the sun began its slow fall to the west. Storm clouds rose, white and soft and taller than mountains, but the rain stayed out over the sea. The daylight moon hung in the blue sky to the north. Otah didn't think of Balasar or Idaan, Chaburi-Tan or the andat. When at last he paused to eat, he felt worn thin enough to see through. He tried to consider Balasar's analysis, but ended by staring at the plate of lemon fish and rice as if it were enthralling.

Because he had been hoping for a moment's peace, he'd chosen to eat his little meal in one of the low halls at the back of the palace. The stone floor and simple, unadorned plaster walls made it seem more like the common room of a small wayhouse than the center of empire. That was part of its appeal. The shutters were open on the garden behind it: crawling lavender, starfall rose, mint, and, without warning, Danat, in a formally cut robe of deep blue hot with yellow, blood running from his nose to cover his mouth and chin. Otah put down the bowl.

Danat stalked into the hall and halfway across it before he noticed that a table was occupied. He hesitated, then took a pose of greeting. The fingers of his right hand were scarlet where he had tried to stanch the flow and failed. Otah didn't recall having stood. His expression must have been alarmed, because Danat smiled and shook his head.

"It's not bad," he said. "Just messy. I didn't want to come through the larger halls."

"What happened?"

"I have met my rival," Danat said. "Hanchat Dor."

"There's blood? There's blood between you?"

"No," Danat said. "Well, technically yes, I suppose. But no."

He lowered himself to sit at the table where Otah's food lay abandoned. There was a carafe of water and a porcelain bowl. As Otah sat, his boy wet one of his sleeves and set about wiping the blood from around his grin. Otah's first violent impulses to protect his son and punish his assailant were disarmed by that smile. Not conquered, but disarmed.

"He and Ana-cha were haunting the path between the palaces and the poet's house, just before the pond," Danat said. "We had words. He took some exception to our demand that Ana-cha apologize. He suggested that I should feel honored to have breathed the same air as his darling chipmunk. Seriously, Papa. 'Darling chipmunk.'"

"It might be a Galtic endearment," he said, trying to match his son's light tone.

Danat waved the thought away. It would be no more dignified, Otah admitted to himself, because a whole culture said it. Danat went on.

"I said that my business wasn't with him, but with Ana-cha. He began declaiming something in rhymed verse about him and his love being one flesh. Ana-cha told him to stop, but he only started bellowing it."

"How did Ana-cha react?"

Danat's grin widened. Blood had pinked his teeth.

"She seemed a bit embarrassed. I began speaking to her as if he weren't there. And . . ."

Danat shrugged.

"He hit you?"

"I may have goaded him," Danat said. "A little."

Otah sat back, stunned. Danat raised his hands to a pose appropriate to the announcement of victory in a game. Otah let himself smile too, but there was a touch of melancholy behind it. His son was no longer the ill, fragile child he'd known. That boy was gone. In his place was a young man with the same instinct to rough-and-tumble as any number of young men. The same as Otah had suffered once himself. It was so easy to forget.

"I had the palace armsmen throw him in a cell," Danat said. "I've set a guard on him in case anyone decides to defend my abused dignity by killing him."

"Yes, that would complicate things," Otah agreed.

"Ana followed the whole way shrieking, but she was as angry at Hanchat-cha as at me. Once I get to looking a bit less like an apprentice showfighter's first night, I'm sending an invitation to Ana-cha for a formal dinner at which we can further discuss her poor treatment of our hospitality. And then I'm going to meet my new lover."

"Your new lover?"

"Shija Radaani has offered to play the role. I think she was flattered to be asked. Issandra-cha is adamant that nothing makes a man worth having like another woman smiling at him."

"Issandra-cha is a dangerous woman," Otah said.

"She is," Danat agreed.

They laughed together for a moment. Otah was the first to sober.

"Will it work, do you think?" he asked. "Can it be done?"

"Can I win Ana's heart and make her want what she's professed before every-one of power in two empires that she hates?" Danat said. Saying it that way, he sounded like his mother. "I don't know. And I can't say what I feel about the way it's happening. I'm plotting against her. Her own mother is plotting against her. I feel that I ought to disapprove. That it isn't honest. And yet . . ."

Danat shook his head. Otah took a querying pose.

"I'm enjoying myself," Danat said. "Whatever it says of me, I've been struck bloody by a Galt boy, and I feel I've scored a point in some game."

"It's an important game."

Danat rose. He took a pose that promised his best effort, appropriate to a junior competitor to his teacher, and left.

There had to be some way that he could aid in Danat's task, but for the moment, he couldn't think what it might be. Perhaps if there was a way to arrange some sort of isolation for the two. A journey, perhaps, to Yalakeht. Or, no, there was the conspiracy with Obar State there that still hadn't been rooted out. Well, Cetani, then. Something long and arduous and cold by the time they got there. And without the bastard who'd struck his son . . .

Otah finished his fish and rice, lingering over a last bowl of wine and look-ing out at the small garden. It was, he thought, the size of the walled yard at the wayhouse Kiyan had owned before she became his first and only wife and he became the Khai Machi. That little space of green and white, of finches in the branches and voles scuttling in the low grass, might have been the size of his life.

Until the Galts came and slaughtered them all with the rest of Udun.

And instead, he had the world, or most of it. And a son. And, however little she liked it, a daughter. And Kiyan's ashes and his memory of her. But it had been a pretty little garden.

Otah returned to the waiting supplicants with his mind moving in ten dif-ferent directions at once. He did his best to focus on the work before him, but everything seemed trivial. No matter that men's fortunes lay in his decision. No matter that he was the final appeal for justice, or if not that, at least peace. Or mercy. Justice and peace and mercy all seemed insignificant when held next to duty. His duty to Chaburi-Tan and all the other cities, to Danat and Eiah and the shape of the future. By the time the sun sank in the western hills, he had almost forgotten Idaan.

His sister waited for him in the apartments Sinja had found for her. She looked out of place among the sweeping arches and intricately carved stone-work. Her hands were thick and calloused, her face roughened by sun. Some servant had arranged a robe for her, well-cut silk of green and cream. He considered her dark eyes and calm, weighing expression. He could not forget that she had killed men coldly, with calculation. But then so had he.

"Idaan-cha," he said as she rose. Her hands took a pose of greeting formal as court, but made awkward by decades without practice. Otah returned it.

"You've made a decision," she said.

"Actually, no. I haven't. I hope to by this time tomorrow. I'd like you to stay until then."

Idaan's eyes narrowed, her lips pressed thin. Otah fought the urge to step back.

"Forgive me if it isn't my place to ask, Most High. But is there something more important going on than Maati bringing back the andat?"

"There are a hundred things that are more certain," Otah said. "He may manage it, but the chances are that he won't. Meantime, I know for certain of three . . . four other things that are happening that could unmake the cities of the Khaiem. I don't have time to play in *might be*."

He'd meant to turn at the end of his pronouncement and walk from the rooms. Her voice was cutting.

"So instead, you'll wait until *is*?" Idaan said. "Or is it only that you have too many apples in the air, and you're only a middling juggler?"

"I'm not in the mood to be—"

"Dressed down by a woman who's only breathing because you've chosen to let her? Listen to yourself. You sound like the villain from some children's bedtime story."

"Idaan-cha," he said, and then found that he had nothing to follow it.

"I've come to tell you that your old friend and enemy is harnessing gods, and not for your benefit. It's the most threatening thing I can imagine happening. And what's your response? You knew. You've known for years. What's more, knowing now that he's redoubling his efforts, you can't be bothered even to consider the question until you've cleared your sheet of audiences? I've held a thousand opinions of you over the years, brother, but I never thought you were stupid."

Otah felt rage bloom in his chest, rising like a fiery wave, only to die with the woman's next words.

"It's the guilt, isn't it?" she said. When he didn't answer at once, she nodded to herself. "You aren't the only one that's done this, you know."

"Been Emperor? Are there others?"

"Betrayed the people you loved," she said. "Come. Sit down. I still have a little tea."

Almost to his surprise, Otah walked forward, sitting on a divan while the former exile poured pale green tea into two carved bone bowls.

"After you set me free, I spent years without sleeping through a full night. I'd dream of the people I'd . . . the people I was responsible for. Our father. Adrah. Danat. You never knew Danat, did you?"

"I named my son for him," Otah said. Idaan smiled, but there was a sorrow in her eyes.

"He'd have liked that, I think. Here. Choose a bowl. I'll drink first if you'd like. I don't mind."

Otah drank. It was overbrewed and sweetened with honey; sweet and bitter. Idaan sipped at hers.

"After you sent me away, there was a time I went about the business of living with what I'd done by working myself like a war slave," she said. "Sunrise to dark, I did whatever it was I was doing until I could fall down at the end half-dead and too tired to dream."

"It doesn't sound pleasant," Otah said.

"I did a lot of good," Idaan said. "You wouldn't guess it, but I organized a constabulary through half of the low towns in the north. I was actually a judge for a few years, if you'll picture that. I found that meting out justice wasn't something I felt suited for, but I kept a few murderers and rapists from making a habit of it. I made a few places safer. I wasn't utterly ineffective, even though half the time I was too tired to focus my eyes."

"And you think I'm doing the same thing?" Otah said. "You don't understand what it is to be an emperor. All respect for whatever you did after Machi, but I have hundreds of thousands of people relying upon me. The politics of empire aren't like a few low towns organizing to keep the local thugs in line."

"You also have a thousand servants," she said. "Dozens of high families who would do your bidding just for the status that comes from being asked. Tell me, why did you go to Galt yourself? You have men and women who'd have been ambassador for you."

"It needed me," Otah said. "If it had been someone lower, it wouldn't have carried the weight."

"Ah, I see," she said. She sounded less than persuaded.

"Besides which, I don't have anything to feel guilt over."

"You broke the world," she said. "You ordered Maati and Cehmai to bind that andat, and when it went feral on them and shredded every womb in the cities, my own included, you threw your poets into the wind. Men who trusted you and sacrificed for you. You became the heroic figure that bound the cities together, and they became outcasts."

"Is that how you see it?"

Idaan put her bowl down softly on the stone table. Her black eyes held his. She had a long face. Northern, like his own. He remembered that of all the children of the old Khai Machi, he and Idaan had shared a mother.

"It doesn't matter how I see it," she said. "My opinion doesn't make the world. Or unmake it. All that matters is what it actually is. So, tell me, Most High, am I right?"

Otah shook his head and rose, leaving his tea bowl beside hers.

"You don't know me, Idaan-cha. We've spoken to each other fewer times than I have fingers. I don't think you're in a position to judge my motives."

"Yours, no," she said. "But I've made the mistakes you're making now. And I know why I did."

"We aren't the same person."

She smiled now, her gaze cast down and her hands in a pose that accepted correction and apologized for her transgression without making it clear what transgression she meant.

"Of course not," she said. "I'll stay through tomorrow, Most High. In case you come to a decision that I might be able to aid you with."

Otah left with the uncomfortable impression that his sister pitied him. He made his way back to his apartments, ate half of the meal the servants brought him, and refused the singers and musicians whose only function in the world was to wait upon his whim. Instead, he took a chair out to his balcony and sat in the starlight, looking south to the sea.

Thin clouds streaked the high air, and the ocean was a vast darkness. The city that spilled down the hills before him glittered brighter than the stars; torches and lanterns, candles and firekeepers' kilns. The breeze smelled of smoke and salt and the lush flowers of early autumn. He closed his eyes.

He could feel the palaces behind him, looming like a weight he'd shifted off his back for a moment and would need to shoulder again. His mind ran free without him, bouncing from one crisis to another without ever pausing long enough to make sense of any one of them. And, intruding upon all of it, he found himself replaying his conversation with Idaan, searching for the cutting replies that hadn't occurred to him at the time.

Who was she to pity him? She'd made a low-town judge of herself, and now a farmer. It was an improvement from traitor and murderer, but it didn't give her moral authority over him. And to instruct him on the nature of his feelings about Maati and Cehmai was ridiculous. She hardly knew him. Coming to court in the first place had been a kind of madness on her part. He could have had her killed outright rather than sit like a dog while she heaped her abuse on him.

She thought he'd broken the world, did she? Well, what about the old way had been worth saving? It hadn't brought justice. The peace it offered had been purchased at the cost of lives of misery and struggle. And from that first moment, more than forty summers earlier, when the Dai-kvo had told him that they could not offer Saraykeht a replacement should Seedless slip its leash, Otah had known it was doomed.

The genius of the Galts—of all the rest of the world, for that—was that they had built their power on ideas that could grow one on another. A better forge led to better metalwork led to stronger tools and so on to the end of their abilities. By contrast, the Empire, the Second Empire, the cities of the Khaiem: all of them had wielded unthinkable power and fashioned wonders. And when the first poet had bound the first andat, anything had been possible. Anything a mind could fathom could be harnessed; anything that could be thought could be done.

But when the first andat had escaped and been harder to recapture, that potential had dropped a degree. Once a binding failed, each one that followed had to be different, and there were only so many ways to describe a thing fully enough to hold it as a slave. It was the central truth of the long, slow, dwindling of power that had brought them all here.

It was like a man's life. For a time in his youth, Otah had been capable of anything. His body had been strong, his judgment so certain he'd been willing to kill a man. And every day and every decision had narrowed him. Every year had weakened his back and his knees, eaten at his sight and wrinkled his skin. Time had taken Kiyan from him. His judgment had lost him his daughter.

He could have done anything, and he had chosen this. Or had it chosen for him.

And he wasn't yet dead, so there were other choices still to be made. Other days and years to live through. Other duties and failures and disappointments he would be responsible for not making right. His anger with Idaan was perfectly comprehensible. He was enraged by her because she had seen to the heart of something he hadn't wanted to understand.

He tried to imagine Kiyan sitting on the stone rail, smiling down at him the way she had. It was very, very easy.

What should I do? he asked the ghost his mind had conjured.

You can do anything, love, she said, *it's just that you can't do everything.*

Otah, Emperor of the Khaiem, wept, and he couldn't say how much was from sorrow and how much from relief.

In the morning, he had the Master of Tides clear his schedule. He met with Balasar and Sinja first. The meeting room was blond stone, ornately carved. Otah had heard that the carvings illustrated some ancient epic, but he'd never bothered to consider it. They were only figures in stone, unmoving and incapable of change. Unlike the men.

Balasar and Sinja sat across from each other, their spines straight and their expressions polite. They were divided by blood and broken faith. Otah poured the tea himself.

"I am placing you in joint control of the fleets and what armsmen we have," Otah said. "Between the two of you, you will protect Chaburi-Tan from the raiders and bring the mercenary forces into compliance with their contracts. I've written an edict that officially grants you my unrestricted permissions."

"Most High," Balasar said. His voice was careful and precise. "Forgive me, but is this wise? I am not one of your countrymen."

"Of course you are," Otah said. "Once Danat and Ana marry, we will be a united empire. Are you refusing the command?"

Sinja replied in the general's place.

"We're an odd pairing, Most High," he said. "It might be better if—"

"You've been my right hand for decades. You know our resources and our strengths. You're known and you're trusted," Otah said. "Balasar-cha's the best commander in Galt. You're both grown men."

"What exactly do you want from us?" Balasar asked.

"I want you to take this problem from me and fix it," Otah said. "I'm only one man, and I'm tired and overcommitted. Besides which, I'm a third-rate war leader, as I think we are all aware."

Sinja coughed to cover laughter. Balasar leaned forward, stroking his chin and looking down as if he'd discovered something fascinating in the grain of the table before him. Slowly, he nodded. After that, it was only a matter of working out the wording of the edict to the satisfaction of Sinja and Balasar both.

There would be trouble between them. That couldn't be avoided. But, Otah told himself, that was theirs to work out. Not his. Not his any longer. He left the meeting room feeling oddly giddy.

He had scheduled a similar meeting with Danat and Issandra Dasin concerning the politics of the court and the intermarriage of Galt and the Khaiem. And then he thought Ashua Radaani was the man to address the issues of the conspiracy between Yalakeht and Obar State. He wasn't certain of that yet. Panjit Dun might also do well with it.

And once all that was done, all the best minds he could choose given their autonomy, he would closet himself with his sister and begin the work that couldn't be safely trusted to others: tracking Maati and whatever enemy among the courts of the utkhaiem had been supporting him.

10

Dawn crept over the school. The dark walls gained detail; the fragile lacing of frost burned away almost before it was visible. Birdsong that had begun in darkness grew in volume and complexity. The countless stars faded into the pale blue and rose of the east. Maati Vaupathai walked the perimeter of the school, his memory jogged with every new corner he turned. Here was the classroom where he'd first heard of the andat. There, the walkway where an older boy had beaten him for not taking the proper stance. The stables, empty now but for the few animals Eiah had brought, which Maati had made the younger boys clean with their bare hands after he had been elevated to the black robes of the older boys.

Ever since his return, Maati had suffered moments when his mind would spiral back through time, unearthing memories as fresh as yesterday. This morning in particular, the past seemed present. He walked past the long-dead echoes of boys crying in their cots, the vanished scent of the caustic soap they'd used to wash the stone floors, the almost-forgotten smell of young bodies and old food and misery. And then, just as memory threatened to sweep him away, he heard one of the girls. Large Kae singing, Irit's laughter, anything.

The walls themselves shifted. The school became something new again, never seen in the world. Women poets, working together as the risen sun washed the haze from the air.

When he stepped into the kitchen, the warmth of the fire and the damp of the steam made him feel like he was walking into summer. Eiah and Ashti Beg sat at the wide table, carving apples into slivers. An iron pot of rough-ground wheat, rice, and millet burped to itself over the fire. The gruel was soft and rich with buttercream and honey.

"Maati-kvo!" Small Kae called, and she took a pose of welcome that the others matched. "There's fresh tea in the green pot. And that bowl there is clean. The blue one."

"Eiah was just telling us about the news from Pathai," Ashti Beg said.

"Little that there was of it," Eiah said. "Nothing to compare with what you were all doing here."

"Nothing we did while you were away is going to compare with what we'll do next," Small Kae said. Her face was bright, her smile taut. She covered her fear with an unwillingness to conceive of defeat. Maati poured himself the tea. It smelled like fresh-picked leaves.

"Have we seen Vanjit?" he asked and lowered himself to a cushion beside the fire. He grunted only a little bit.

"Not yet," Eiah said. "Large Kae went to wake her."

"Perhaps it would be better to let her sleep," Small Kae said. "It is her day, after all. It seems rude to make demands on her just because we all want to share it with her."

Eiah smiled, but her gaze was on Maati. A private conversation passed between them, no longer than three heartbeats together. More would be decided today than Vanjit and Clarity-of-Sight. Likely they all knew as much, but no one would say the words. Maati filled a fresh bowl with the sweet grain, holding it out for Ashti Beg to cover with apple. He didn't answer Eiah's unspoken question: *What will we do if she fails?*

Vanjit arrived before he had finished half the bowl. She wore a robe of deep blue shot with red, and her hair was woven with glass beads and carved shells. Her face was painted, her lips widened and red, her eyes touched by kohl. Maati hadn't even known she'd brought paints and baubles to the school. She had never worn them before, but this morning, she looked like the daughter of a Khai. When no one was looking, he took a pose of congratulation to Eiah. She replied with an inclination of the head and a tiny smile that admitted the change was her doing.

"How did you sleep, Vanjit-cha?" Maati asked as she swept the hem of her robe aside and sat next to him.

She took his hand and squeezed it, but didn't answer his question. Large Kae brought her a bowl of tea, Irit a helping of the grain and butter already covered with apple. Vanjit took a pose of thanks somewhat hampered by the food and drink.

While they all ate, the conversation looped around the one concern they all shared. The Galts, the Emperor, the weather, the supplies Eiah had brought from Pathai, the species of insect peculiar to the dry lands around the school. Anything was a fit topic except Vanjit's binding and the fear that lay beneath all their merriment and pleasure.

Vanjit alone seemed untouched by care. She was beautiful and, for the first time since Maati had met her, comfortable in her beauty. Her laughter seemed genuine and her movements relaxed. Maati thought he was seeing confidence in her, the assurance of a woman who was about to do a thing she had no thought might be beyond her. His opinion didn't change until after all the bowls had been gathered and rinsed, the cored apples and spilled grain swept up and carried away to the pit in the back of the school, when she took him by the hand and led him gently aside.

"I wanted to thank you," she said as they reached the bend of the wide hallway.

"I can't see I've done anything worth it," he said. "If anything, I should be offering you . . ."

There were tears brimming in her eyes, the shining water threatening her kohl. Maati took the end of his sleeve and dabbed her eyes gently. The brown cloth came away stained black.

"After Udun," Vanjit began, then paused. "After what the Galts did to my brothers . . . my parents. I thought I would never have a family again. It was better that there not be anyone in my life that I cared for enough that it would hurt me to lose them."

"Ah, now. Vanjit-kya. You don't need to think of that now."

"But I do. I do. You are the closest thing I've had to a father. You are the most dedicated man I have ever known, and it has been an honor to be allowed a place in your work. And I've broken the promise I made myself. I will miss you."

Maati took a pose that both disagreed and asked for clarification. Vanjit smiled and shook her head, the beads and shells in her braids clicking like claws on stone. He waited.

"We both know that the chances are poor that I'll see the sunset," she said. Her voice was solemn and composed. "This grammar we've made is a guess. The forces at play are deadlier than fires or floods. If I were someone else, I wouldn't wager a length of copper on my chances if you offered me odds."

"That isn't true," Maati said. He hadn't meant to shout, and lowered his voice when he spoke again. "That isn't true. We've done good work here. The equal of anything I learned from the Dai-kvo. Your chances are equal to the best any poet has faced. I'll swear to that if you'd like."

"There's no call," she said. From down the hall, he heard voices in bright conversation. He heard laughter. Vanjit took his hand. He had never noticed how small her hands were. How small she was, hardly more than a child herself.

"Thank you," she said. "Whatever happens, thank you. If I die today, thank you. Do you understand?"

"No."

"You've made living bearable," she said. "It's more than I can ever repay."

"You can. You can repay all of it and more. Don't die. Succeed."

Vanjit smiled and took a pose that accepted instruction, then moved forward, wrapping her arms around Maati in a bear hug. He cradled her head on his breast, his eyes pressed closed, his heart sick and anxious.

The chamber they had set aside for the binding had once been the sleeping room for one of the younger cohorts. The lines of cots were gone now. The windows shone with the light of middle morning. Vanjit took a round of chalk and began writing out her binding on the wide south wall, ancient words and recent blending together in the new grammar they had all created. From Maati's cushion at the back of the room, the letters were blurry and indistinct, but from their shape alone, he could see that the binding had shifted since the last time he'd seen it.

Eiah sat at his side, her hand on his arm, her gaze fixed on the opposite wall. She looked half-ill.

"It's going to be all right," Maati murmured.

Eiah nodded once, her eyes never leaving the pale words taking over the far wall like a bright shadow. When Vanjit was finished, she walked to the beginning again, paced slowly down the wall reading all she'd written, and then, satisfied, put the chalk on the ground. A single cushion had been placed in the middle of the room for her. She stopped at it, her binding behind her, her face turned toward the small assembly at the back. She took a silent pose of gratitude, turned, and sat.

Maati had a powerful urge to stand, to call out. He could wash the wall clean, talk through the binding again, check it for errors one last time. Vanjit began to chant, the cadences unlike anything he had heard before. Her voice was soft, coaxing, gentle; she was singing her andat into the world. He clenched his fists and stayed quiet. Eiah seemed to have stopped breathing.

The sound of Vanjit's voice filled the air, reverberating as if the building had grown huge. The chant began to echo, and Vanjit's actual voice receded. Words and phrases combined, voice against echo, making new sentences and meanings. The lilt of the girl's voice fell into harmony with itself, and Maati heard a third voice, neither Vanjit nor her echo, but something deep and sonorous as a bell. It was reciting syllables borrowed from the words of the binding, creating another layer of sound and intention. The air thickened, and Vanjit's back— her shoulders hunched, her head bowed—seemed very far away. Maati smelled hot iron, or perhaps blood. His heart began to race with a fear he couldn't express.

Something's wrong. We have to stop her, he said to Eiah, but though he could feel the words vibrate in his throat, he couldn't hear them. Vanjit's circling voice had made a kind of silence that Maati was powerless to break. Another layer of echoes came, the words seeming to come before Vanjit spoke them, echoing from the other direction in time. Beside him, Eiah's face had gone white.

Vanjit's voice spoke a single word—the last of the binding—at the same time as all the layered echoes, a dozen voices speaking as one. The world itself chimed, pandemonium resolving into a single harmonious chord. The room was only a room again. When Maati stood, he could hear the hem of his robe whispering against the stone. Vanjit sat where she had been, her head bowed. No new form stood before her. It should have been there.

She's failed, Maati thought. It hasn't worked, and she's paid the price of it.

The others were on their feet, but he took a pose that commanded them to remain where they were. This was his. However bad it was, it was his. His belly twisted as he walked toward her corpse. He had seen the price a failed binding exacted: always different, always fatal. And yet Vanjit's ribs rose and fell, still breathing.

"Vanjit-kya?" he said, his voice no more than a murmur.

The girl shifted, turned her head, and looked up at him. Her eyes were bright with joy. In her lap, something squirmed. Maati saw the round, soft flesh, the tubby, half-formed hands and feet, a toothless mouth, and black eyes full of empty rage. Except for the eyes, it could have been a human baby.

"He's come," Vanjit said. "Look, Maati-kvo. We've done it. He's here."

As if freed from silence by the poet's words, Clarity-of-Sight opened its tiny throat and wailed.

11

Kiyan-kya—

I look at how long I carried the world, or thought I did, and I wonder how many times we have to learn the same lessons. Until we remember them, I suppose. It isn't that I've stopped worrying. The gods all know I crawl into my bed at night half-tempted to call for reports from Sinja and Danat and Ashua. Even if I had them dragged into my chambers to recount everything they'd seen and done, how would it change things? Would I need less sleep? Would I be able to remake the world through raw will like a poet? I'm only a man, however fancy the robes they put me in. I'm not more suited to lead a war fleet or root out a conspiracy or win a young girl's love than any of them.

Why is it so hard for me to believe that someone besides myself might be competent? Or did I fear that letting go of any one part would mean everything would fall away?

No, love. Idaan was right. I have been punishing myself all this time for not saving the people I cared for most. I think some nights that I will never stop mourning you.

Otah's pen hung in the cool night air, the brass nib just above the paper. The night breeze smelled of the sea and the city, rich and heavy as an overripe grape whose skin has only just split. In Machi, they would already be moving down to the tunnels beneath the city. In Utani, where his central palace stood wrapped in cloth, awaiting his return, the leaves would have turned to red and yellow and gold. In Pathai, where Eiah worked with her latest pet physician and pointedly ignored all matters of politics and power, there might be frost in the mornings.

Here in Saraykeht, the change of seasons was only a difference of scent and the surprise that the sun, which had so plagued them at summer's height, could grow tired so early. He wrote a few more sentences, the pen sounding like bird's feet against the paper, and then blew on the ink to cure it, folded the letter, and put it in with all the others he had written to her.

His eyes ached. His back ached. The joints of his hands were stiff, and his spine felt carved from wood. For days, he had been poring over records and agendas, letters and accountancy reports, searching for some connection that would uncover Maati's suspected patron. There were patterns to be looked for—people who had traveled extensively in the past few years who might be moving with the poet, supplies that had vanished with no clear destination, opposition to the planned alliance with Galt. And, with that, Maati's boast of an ear in the palaces. And the gods all knew there were patterns to be found. The courts of the Khaiem were thick with petty intrigue. Flushing out any one particular scheme was like plucking a particular thread from a tapestry.

To make matters worse, the servants and high families that Idaan had chided him for not making better use of had no place here. Even if Maati didn't have the well-placed spy he'd claimed, Otah still couldn't afford the usual gossip. Maati had to be found and the situation resolved before he managed to bind some new andat, and no one—Galt, Westlander, no one—could hear of it for fear of the reaction it would bring.

That meant that the records and reports were brought to Otah's private chambers. Crate after crate until they piled near the ceiling. And the only eyes that he could trust to the task were his own and, through the twisted humor that gods seemed to enjoy, Idaan's.

She was stretched out on a long silk divan now, half a month's lading records from the harbor master's office arrayed about her. Her closed eyes shifted beneath their lids, but her breath was as steady as the tide. Otah found a thin wool blanket and draped it over her.

It had not particularly been his intention to embrace his exiled sister and make her a part of the hunt for Maati, but the work was more than he could manage on his own. The only other person who knew of the problem was Sinja, and he was busy with Balasar and the creation of the unlikely fleet whose mission was to save Chaburi-Tan. Idaan knew the workings of the poets as well as any woman alive; she had been the enemy of one, the lover of another. She knew a great deal about court intrigue and also the mechanics of living an unobtrusive life. There was no one better equipped for the investigation.

He did not trust her, but had resolved to behave as if he did. At least for the present. The future was as unpredictable as it had always been, and he'd given up hope of anticipating its changes.

He knew from long experience that he wouldn't sleep if he went to bed now. His mind might be in a deep fog, but his body was punishing him for sitting too long. As it would have punished him for working too hard. The range allowed to him was so much narrower than when he'd been young. A walk to loosen his joints, and he might be able to rest.

The armsmen at the door of his apartments took poses of obeisance as he stepped out. He only nodded and made his way south. He wore a simple robe of cotton. The cloth was of the first quality, but the cut was simple and the red and gray less than gaudy. Someone who didn't know him by sight might have mistaken him for a member of the utkhaiem, or even a particularly powerful servant. He made a game of walking with his head down, trying to pass as a functionary in his own house.

The halls of the palaces were immense and ornate. Many small items—statues, paintings, jeweled decoration—had vanished during the brief occupation by Galt, but the huge copper-sheathed columns and the high, clear glass of the unshuttered windows spoke of greater days. The wood floors shone with lacquer even where they were scraped and pitted.

Incense burned in unobtrusive brass bowls, filling the air with the scent of sandalwood and desert sage. Even this late at night, singing slaves carried their harmonies in empty chambers. Crickets, Otah thought, would have been as beautiful.

His back had begun to relax and his feet to complain when the illusion of traveling the palaces unnoticed was broken. A servant in a gold robe appeared at the far end of the hall, walking purposefully toward him. Otah stopped. The man took a pose of obeisance and apology as he drew near.

"Most High, I am sorry to interrupt. Ana Dasin has come to request an audience. I would have turned her away, but under the circumstances . . ."

"You did well," he said. "Take her to the autumn garden."

The servant took a pose that accepted the command, but then hesitated.

"Should I send for an outer robe, Most High?"

Otah looked down at the wrinkled fabric and wondered what Ana would see if he met her like this: a man of great power and consequence at the end of a long day's work, or an old slob in a cotton robe.

"Yes," he said with a sigh. "An outer robe would be welcome. And tea. Bring us fresh tea. She might not care for it, but I want some."

The man scurried away. They had known where he was, and that he didn't wish to be disturbed. And they had known when to disturb him. To be the

Emperor of the Khaiem was above all else to be known by people he did not know. He had discovered that truth a thousand times before, and likely would do so a thousand times again, and each one discomforted him.

The autumn garden was nestled within the palaces. Trees and vines hid the stone walls, and paper lanterns gave the flagstone path a soft light. Near the center, a small brass fountain, long given to verdigris, chuckled to itself and a small wooden pavilion rested in the darkness. Otah walked down the path, still tugging the black and silver outer robe into place. Ana Dasin sat in the pavilion, her gaze on the water sluicing over bronze. The tea, set on a lacquered tray, had preceded him as if the servants had anticipated that he would ask for it as well and had had it ready.

Otah gathered himself. He was almost certain that Danat had already had his second meeting with the girl. Hanchat Dor, Danat's rival, was set to be freed in the morning. Otah found himself curious to see who Ana Dasin was in these circumstances.

"Ana," he said in her language. "I had not expected your company."

The girl stood. The soft light made her face rounder than it was, her eyes darker. She was wearing a dress of Galtic cut with pearls embroidered down the sleeves. Her hair, which had been pulled back into a severe formality, was escaping. Locks hung at the side of her face like silken banners draped from towers' windows.

"Emperor Machi. I have to thank you for seeing me so late," she said. Her voice was hard, but not accusatory. Otah caught the faint scent of distilled wine. The girl was fortified with drink, but not yet dulled by it.

"I am an old man," Otah said as he poured pale tea into two porcelain bowls. "I need less sleep than I once did. Here, take one."

His little act of kindness seemed to make her stiffer and less pleased, but she accepted the bowl. Otah sat, blowing across the tea's steaming surface.

"I've come . . ."

He waited.

"I've come to apologize," she said. She spoke the words as if she were vomiting.

Otah sipped his tea. It was perfectly brewed, the leaves infusing the water with a taste like summer sun and cut grass. It made the moment even more pleasant, and he wondered if he was being unkind by taking pleasure in Ana's predicament.

"May I ask what precisely you wish to apologize for," Otah said. "I would hate to have any further misunderstandings between us."

Ana sat, putting the bowl on the bench at her side. The porcelain clicked against the stone.

"I presented myself poorly," she said. "I . . . set out to humiliate you and Danat. That was uncalled for. I could have made my feelings known in private."

"I see," Otah said. "And is that all?"

"I would like to thank you for the mercy you've shown to Hanchat."

"It's Danat you should thank for that," Otah said. "I only respected his wishes."

"Not every parent respects her child," Ana said, then looked away, lips pressed thin. *Her* child, meaning Issandra. Ana was right. The mother was indeed scheming against her own daughter, and Otah had made himself a party to the plot. He would not have done it to his own child. He took another sip of his tea. It wasn't quite as pleasant as the first.

The fountain muttered to itself, the wind sighed. Here was the moment that chance had given him, and he wasn't sure how to use it. Ana, on whom all his plans rested, had come to him. There was something here, some word or phrase, some thought, that would narrow the distance between them. And in the space of a few more breaths, she would have collected herself again and gone.

"I should apologize to you as well," Otah said. "I forget sometimes that my view on the world isn't the only one. Or even the only correct one. I doubt you would have been driven to humiliate me if I hadn't done the same to you."

Her gaze shifted back to him. Whatever she had expected of him, it hadn't been this.

"I went to the wives of the councillors. There was very little time, and I thought they would have greater sway than the children. Perhaps they did. But I traded you as a trinket and didn't even think to ask you your thoughts and feelings. That should have been beneath me."

"I'm a woman," Ana said, her tone managing to be both dismissive and a challenge. *I'm a woman, and we've always been traded, married off, shifted as the tokens of power and alliance.* Otah smiled, surprised to find himself possessed by genuine sorrow.

"Yes," he said. "You are. And with my sister, my wife, my daughter . . . of all the men in the world, I should have known what that meant, and I forgot. I was in such a hurry to fix all the things I've done poorly that I did this poorly too."

She was frowning at him again as she had once before, on the journey to Saraykeht. He might have begun speaking in the language of birds or belching stones, to judge by her expression. He chuckled.

"It was not my intention to treat you with disrespect, Ana-cha. That I did so shames me. I accept your apology, and I hope that you will accept mine."

"I won't marry him," she said.

Otah drank the rest of his tea and set the empty bowl mouth-down on the lacquer tray.

"My son, you mean," Otah said. "You'll stay with this other man. Hanchat? No matter what the price or who's called on to pay it, no man deserves even your consideration? If it destroys your country and mine both, it would still be just."

"I . . . I don't . . ." the girl said. "That isn't . . ."

"I know. I understand. I'll say this. Danat is a good man. Better than I was at his age. But what you choose is entirely yours," Otah said. "If we've established anything, you and I, it's that."

"Not his?"

"Danat's decision is whether he'll marry you," Otah said with a smile. "Not the same thing at all."

He meant to leave her there. It seemed the right moment, and there was nothing more he could think to say. As he bent forward, preparing to rise, Ana spoke again.

"Your wife was a wayhouse keeper. You didn't put her aside. You never took a second wife. It was an insult to the whole body of the utkhaiem."

"It was," Otah said and stood with a grunt. There had been a time he could sit or stand in silence. "But I didn't marry her for the effect it had on other people. I did it because she was Kiyan, and there wasn't anyone else like her in the world."

"How can you ask Danat to obey tradition when you've broken it?" she demanded.

Otah considered her. She seemed angry again, but it seemed as much on Danat's behalf as her own.

"By asking," Otah said. "It's the best I can manage. I've damaged the world badly. The reasons I had for doing it seemed good at the time. I would like to be part of putting it back together again. With his help. With yours."

"I didn't break all this," Ana said, her chin stubborn. "Danat didn't either, for that matter. It's not fair that we should have to sacrifice whatever we want to unmake your mistakes."

"It isn't. But I can't repair this."

"Why do you think I can?"

"I have some faith in you both," he said.

By the time he made his way back to his rooms, Idaan had departed, leaving only a brief note saying that she intended to return in the morning and had some questions for him. Otah sat on a low couch by the fire grate, his eyes focused on nothing. He wondered what Eiah would have made of his conversation with the Galtic girl, and of whom he was truly asking forgiveness. His mind wandered, and he did not realize he had lain back until he woke to the cool light of dawn.

He was sitting in his private bath, the hot water easing the knots that sleeping away from his bed had tied in his back, when the servant announced Sinja's arrival. Otah considered the effort that rising, drying himself, and being dressed would require and had the man brought to him. Sinja, dressed in the simple canvas and leather of a soldier, looked more like a mercenary captain than the nearest advisor to an emperor. He squatted at the edge of the bath, looking down at Otah. The servant poured tea for the newcomer, took a ritual pose appropriate to a withdrawal from which he would have to be specifically summoned to return, and left. The door slid closed behind him, the waxed wooden runners as silent as breath.

"What's happened?" Otah asked, dreading the answer.

"I was going to ask the same thing. You spoke to Ana Dasin last night?"

"I did," Otah said.

Sinja sipped his tea before he spoke again.

"Well, I don't know what you said to her, but this morning, I had a runner from Farrer Dasin offering his ships and his men for Balasar's fleet. The general's meeting with him now to arrange the details."

Otah sat forward, the water swirling around him.

"Farrer-cha . . ."

Sinja put down the bowl of tea.

"The man himself. Not Issandra, not one of his servants. The handwriting was his own. There weren't details, only the offer. And since he's been reticent and dismissive every time Balasar asked, it seemed that something had changed. If it's what it looks like, it will mean putting off departure for a few days, but when we get there, it will be a real fighting force."

"That's . . ." Otah began. "I don't know how that happened."

"I've been swimming through palace gossip ever since, trying to find what made the change, and the only thing half-plausible I've heard is that Ana Dasin met with Danat-cha, after which she went to a second-rate teahouse, drank more than was considered healthy, and came here. After talking with you, she went back to the old poet's house; the lanterns were all lit and they didn't stop burning until the sun rose."

"We didn't talk about the fleet," Otah said. "The subject never came up."

Sinja unstrung his sandals and slid his feet into the warm water of the bath.

"Why don't you tell me what was said," Sinja asked. "Because somehow, in the middle of it, you seem to have done something right."

Otah recounted the meeting, rising from his bath and drying himself as he did. Sinja listened for the most part, interrupting only to laugh when Otah told of apologizing to the girl.

"That likely had as much to do with it as anything," Sinja said. "A high councillor's daughter with the Emperor of the Khaiem calling himself down for disrespecting her. Gods, Otah-kya, with that low an opinion of your own dignity, I don't know how you managed to hold power all these years."

Otah paused, his hands shifting to a pose of query.

"You apologized to a Galtic girl."

"I'd treated her poorly," Otah said.

Sinja raised his hands. It wasn't a formal pose, but it carried the sense of surrender. Whatever it was Sinja didn't understand about the act, he clearly despaired of ever learning.

"Tell me the rest," Sinja said.

There wasn't a great deal more, but Otah told it. He pulled on his robes by himself. The servants could adjust them when the meeting ended. Sinja drank another bowl of tea. The water in the bath grew still and as clear as air.

"Well," Sinja said when he had finished, "that's unexpected all around."

"You think Ana-cha interceded for us."

"I can't think anything else," Sinja said. "She's an interesting girl, that one. Quick to anger and about as tough as boiled leather if confronted, but I think you made her feel for you. It was clever."

"I didn't mean it as a ploy," Otah said.

"That's likely what made the ploy work," Sinja said. "Issandra and Danat should hear more of it. You know that little conspiracy is beginning to slip its stitches?"

"What do you mean?"

"Danat's false lover. Shija Radaani? It seems your boy is starting to fall in love with her. Or if not love, at least bed. That was the other gossip this morning. Shija went to Danat's rooms last night and hasn't yet come out."

Otah tugged at the sleeves, his eyebrows trying to crawl up his forehead. Sinja nodded.

"Perhaps it's part of Issandra's plan?" Otah said.

"If it is, she's more of a gambler than I am."

"I'll look into it," Otah said.

"Don't bother. I've already sent word to all the parties who need to know."

"Meaning Issandra."

"And nobody else," Sinja said. "You worry about finding Maati and his poet girls. And your sister. Whatever you're doing, keep one eye toward her."

Otah was halfway to objecting, but Sinja only tilted his head. Idaan had killed Otah's brothers. His father. She was capable of casual slaughter, and everyone knew it. There was no point in pretending the world was something it wasn't. Otah took a pose that accepted the advice and promised his best effort.

In point of fact, Idaan was waiting in his rooms when he returned from his breakfast and the morning of audiences that he could not postpone. She wore a borrowed robe of blue silk as dark as a twilight sky. Her arms and shoulders were thicker than the robe allowed, the fabric straining. Her hair was pulled back in a gray tail as thick as a mane. She did not smile.

"Idaan-cha," he said.

"Brother," she replied.

He sat across from her. Her long face was cool and unreadable. She touched the papers and scrolls on the low table between them. The scents of cedar and apples should have made the room more comfortable.

"I'm not done," she said. "But I doubt a year and ten clerks would be enough to do a truly thorough job. With just the pair of us, and you off half the time at court, we can't really hope for more than a weighted guess."

"Then we should get to work," he said. "I'll have them bring us food and—"

"Before that," Idaan said. "Before that, there's something we should discuss. Alone."

Otah considered her eyes. They were the same black-brown as his own. Her jaw was softer, her mouth pale and lined. He could still see the girl she had been, whom he had drawn up from the deepest cells beneath Machi and given freedom where she'd expected slavery or death.

"I'll send the servants away," he said. She took a pose that offered thanks.

When he returned, she was pacing before the windows, her hands clasped behind her. The soft leather soles of her boots whispered against the wood. The city spread below them, and then the sea.

"I never thought about them," she said. "The andat? I never gave them half a thought when I was young. Stone-Made-Soft was something halfway between a trained hunting cat and another courtier in a world full of them. But they could destroy everything, couldn't they? If a poet bound something like Steam or Fog, all that ocean could vanish in a moment, couldn't it?"

"I suppose," Otah agreed.

"I would have controlled it. Stone-Made-Soft, I mean. And Cehmai. If all the things I'd planned had happened as I planned them, I would have had the command of that power."

"Your husband would have," he said. Otah had ordered her husband executed. Adrah Vaunyogi's body had hung from the ruins of his family's palace, food for the crows. Idaan smiled.

"My husband," she said, her voice warm and amused. "Even worse."

She shook herself and turned back to the table. Her thick fingers plucked out a clerk's writing tablet. Otah could see letters carved into the wax.

"I've made a list of those people who seem most likely," she said. "I have a dozen, and I could give you a dozen more if you'd like it. They've all traveled extensively in the past four years. They've all had expenditures that look suspicious to one degree or another. And as far as I can see, all of them oppose your treaty with the Galts or are closely related to someone who does. And they all have the close connections to the palace that Maati boasted of."

Otah held out his hand. Idaan didn't pass the tablet to him.

"I think about what would have happened if I had been given that kind of power," she said. "I think of the girl I was back then. And the things I did. Can you imagine what I might have done?"

"It wouldn't have happened," Otah said. "Cehmai only answered to you so long as the Dai-kvo told him to. If you had started draining oceans or melting cities, he would have forbidden it."

"The Dai-kvo is dead, though. Years dead, and almost forgotten."

"What are you saying, Idaan-cha?"

She smiled, but her eyes made it sorrow.

"All the restraints we had to keep the poets from doing as they saw fit? They're gone now. I'm saying you should remember that when you see this list. Remember the stakes we're playing for."

The tablet was heavy in his hand, the dark wax scored with white where she had written on it. He frowned as his finger traced down the names. Then he stopped, and the blood left his face. He understood what Idaan had been saying. She was telling him to be ruthless, to be cold. She meant to steel him against the pain of what he might have to sacrifice.

"My daughter's name is on this list," he said, keeping his voice low and matter-of-fact.

His sister replied with silence.

12

>+< "There," Vanjit said, her finger pointing up into a featureless blue sky. "Right there."

On her hip, the andat squirmed and waved its tiny hands. She shifted her weight, drawing the small body closer to her own, her outstretched finger still indicating nothing.

"I don't see it," Maati said.

Vanjit smiled, her attention focusing on the babe. Clarity-of-Sight mewled, shook its head weakly, and then stilled. Vanjit's lips pressed thin, and the sky above Maati seemed to sharpen. Even where there was nothing to see, the blue itself seemed legible. And then he caught sight of it. Little more than a dot at first, and then a moment later, he made out the shape of the outstretched wings. A hawk, soaring high above the ground. Its beak was hooked and sharp as a knife. Its feathers, brown and gold, trembled in the high air. A smear of old blood darkened its talons. There were mites in its feathers.

Maati closed his eyes and looked away, shaken by vertigo.

"Gods!" he said. He heard Vanjit's delighted chuckle.

The spirit of elation filled the stone halls, the ruined gardens, the spare meadows. All the days since the binding, it had felt to Maati as if the world itself had taken a deep breath and then laughed aloud. Whenever the chores and classes had allowed it, the girls had crowded around Vanjit and Clarity-of-Sight, and himself along with them.

The andat itself was beautiful and fascinating. Its form was identical to a true human child, but small things in its behavior showed Vanjit's inexperience. She had not held a babe or seen one since she herself had been no more than a child. The strength of its neck and the sureness of its gaze were subtly wrong. Its cry, while wordless, expressed a richness and variety of emotion that in Maati's experience children rarely developed before they could walk. Small errors of imagination that affected only the form that the andat took. Its function, as Vanjit delighting in showing, was perfect and precise.

"I've seen other things too," Vanjit said. "The greater the change, the more difficult it is at first."

Maati nodded. He could see the individual hairs on her head. The crags where tiny flakes of dead skin peeled from the living tissue beneath. An insect the shape of a tick but a thousand times smaller clung to the root of her eyelash. He closed his eyes.

"Forgive me," he said. "Could I put upon you to undo some part of that? It's distracting. . . ."

He heard her robe rustle and go silent. When he opened his eyes again, his vision was clear but no longer inhumanly so. He smiled.

"Once I've made the change, I forget that it doesn't fall back on its own," she said.

"Stone-Made-Soft was much the same," Maati said. "Once it had changed the nature of a rock, it remained weakened until Cehmai-kvo put an effort into changing it back. Then there was Water-Moving-Down, who might stop a river only so long as its poet gave the matter strict attention. The question rests on the innate capacity for change within the object affected. Stone by nature resists change, water embraces it. I suspect that whatever eyes you improve will still suffer the normal effects of age."

"The change may be permanent, but we aren't," she said.

"Well put," Maati said.

The courtyard in which they sat showed only small signs of the decade of ruin it had suffered. The weeds had all been pulled or cut, the broken stones reset. Songbirds flitted between the trees, lizards scurried through the low grass, and far above, invisible to him now, a hawk circled in the high, distant air.

Maati could imagine that it wasn't the school that he had suffered in his boyhood: it had so little in common with the half-prison he recalled. A handful of women instead of a shifting cadre of boys. A cooperative struggle to achieve the impossible instead of cruelty and judgment. Joy instead of fear. The space itself seemed remade, and perhaps the whole of the world along with it. Vanjit seemed to guess his thoughts. She smiled. The thing at her hip grumbled, fixing its black eyes on Maati, but did not cry.

"It's unlike anything I expected," Vanjit said. "I can feel him. All the time, he's in the back of my mind."

"How burdensome is it?" Maati asked, sitting forward.

Vanjit shook her head.

"No worse than any baby, I'd imagine," she said. "He tires me sometimes, but not so much I lose myself. And the others have all been kind. I don't think I've cooked a meal for myself since the binding."

"That's good," Maati said. "That's excellent."

"And you? Your eyes?"

"Perfect. I've been able to write every evening. I may actually manage to complete this before I die."

He'd meant it as a joke, but Vanjit's reply was grim, almost scolding.

"Don't say that. Don't talk about death lightly. It isn't something to laugh at."

Maati took an apologetic pose, and a moment later the darkness seemed to leave the girl's eyes. She shifted the andat again, freeing one hand to take an apologetic pose.

"No," Maati said. "You're right. You're quite right."

He steered the conversation to safer waters—meals, weather, reconstructing the finer points of Vanjit's successful binding. Contentment seemed to come from the girl like heat from a fire. He regretted leaving her there, and yet, walking down the wide stone corridors, he was also pleased.

The years he had spent scrabbling in the shadows like a rat had been so long and so thick with anger and despair, Maati had forgotten what it was to feel simple happiness. Now, with the women's grammar proved and the andat returned to the world, his flesh itself felt different. His shoulders had grown straighter, his heart lighter, his joints looser and stronger and sure. He had managed to ignore his burden so long he had mistaken it for normalcy. The lifting of it felt like youth.

Eiah sat cross-legged on the floor of one of the old lecture halls, untied codices, opened books, unfurled scrolls laid out around her like ripples on the surface of a pond. He glanced at the pages—diagrams of flayed arms, the muscles and joints laid bare as if by the most meticulous butcher in history; Westlands script with its whorls and dots like a child's angry scribble; notations in Eiah's own hand, outlining the definitions and limitations and structure of violence done upon flesh. Wounded. The andat at its origin. And all of it, he could make out from where he stood without squinting or bending close.

Eiah looked up at him with a pose equal parts welcome and despair. Maati lowered himself to the floor beside her.

"You look tired," he said.

Eiah gestured to the careful mess before her, and then sighed.

"This was simpler when I wasn't allowed to do it," she said. "Now that my own turn has come, I'm starting to think I was a fool to think it possible."

Maati touched one of the books with his outstretched fingers. The paper felt thick as skin.

"There is a danger to it," Maati said. "Even if your binding is perfectly built, there might have been another done that was too much like it. These books, they were written by men. Your training was done by men. The poets before Vanjit were all men. Your thinking could be too little like a man's."

Eiah smiled, chuckling. Maati took a pose of query.

"Physicians in the Westlands tend to be women," she said. "I don't think I have more than half-a-dozen texts that I could say for certain were written by men. The problem isn't that."

"No?"

"No, it's that no matter what's between your thighs, a cut is a cut, a burn is a burn, and a bruise is a bruise. Break a bone now, and it snaps much the way it did in the Second Empire. Vanjit's binding was based on a study of eyes and light that didn't exist back then. Nothing I'm working from is *new*."

There was frustration in her voice. Perhaps fear.

"There is another way," Maati said. Eiah shifted, her gaze on his. Maati scratched his arm.

"We have Clarity-of-Sight," he said. "It proves that we can do this thing, and that alone gives us a certain power. If we send word to Otah-kvo, tell him what we've done and that he must turn away from his scheme with the Galts, he would do it. He would have to. We could take as much time as you care to take, consult as many scholars as we can unearth. Even Cehmai would have to come. He couldn't refuse the Emperor."

It wasn't something he'd spoken aloud before. It was hardly something he'd allowed himself to think. Before Vanjit and Clarity-of-Sight, the idea of returning to the courts of the Khaiem—to Otah—in triumph would have been only a sort of torture of the soul. It would have been like wishing for his son to be alive, or Liat at his side, or any of the thousand regrets of his past to be unmade.

Now it was not only possible but perhaps even wise. Another letter, sent by fast courier, announcing that Maati had succeeded and made himself the new Dai-kvo, and Otah would have no choice but to honor him. He could almost hear the apology now, sweeter for coming from the lips of an emperor.

"It's a kind thought, but no," Eiah said. "It's too big a risk."

"I don't see how," Maati said, frowning.

"Vanjit's one woman, and binding an andat doesn't mean that a good man and a sharp knife can't end you," Eiah said. "And she may slip, at which point half the world will want our heads on sticks, just to be sure it doesn't happen again. Once we've managed a few more, it will be safe. And Wounded can't wait."

"If you heal all the women of the cities, they'll know we've bound an andat," Maati said. "It will be just as clear a message as sending a letter. And by your argument, just as dangerous."

"If they wait until after I've given back the chance of bearing children, the Galts can kill me," Eiah said. "It will be too late to matter."

"You don't believe that," Maati said, aghast. Eiah smiled and shrugged.

"Perhaps not," she agreed. "Say rather, if I'm going to die, I'd rather it was after I'd finished this."

Maati put a hand on her shoulder, then let his arm fall to his side. Eiah described the issues of the binding that troubled her most. To pull a thought from abstraction into concrete form required a deep understanding of the idea's limits and consequences. To bind Wounded, Eiah needed to find the common features of a cut finger and a burned foot, the difference between a tattooing quill and a rose thorn, the definitions that kept the thought small enough for a single mind to encompass.

"Take Vanjit's work," Eiah said. "Your eyes were never burned. No one cut them or bruised them. But they didn't see as well as when you were young. So there must have been some damage to them. So are the changes of age wounds? White hair? Baldness? When a woman loses her monthly flow, is it because she's broken?"

"You can't consider age," Maati said. "For one thing, it muddies the water, and for another, I will swear to you that more than one poet has reached for Youth-Regained or some such."

"But how can I make that fit?" Eiah said. "What makes an old man's failing hip different from a young girl's bruised one? The speed of the injury?"

"The intention," Maati said, and touched a line of symbols. His finger traced the strokes of ink, pausing from time to time. He could feel Eiah's attention on him. "Here. Change *ki* to *toyaki*. Wounds are either intentional or accident. *Toyaki* includes both senses."

"I don't see what difference it makes," Eiah said.

"*Ki* also includes a nuance of proper function. Behavior that isn't misadventure or conscious intention, but a product of design," Maati said. "If you remove that . . ."

He licked his lips, his fingers closing in the air above the page. Once, many years before, he had been asked to explain why the poets were called poets. He remembered his answer vaguely. That the bindings were the careful shaping of meaning and intention, that makers or thought-weavers were just as apt. It had been a true answer for as far as it went.

And also, sometimes, the grammar of a binding would say something unexpected. Something half-known, or half-acknowledged. A profound melancholy touched him.

"You see, Eiah-cha," he said, softly, "time is meant to pass. The world is meant to change. When people fade and die, it isn't a deviation. It's the way the world is made."

He tapped the symbol *ki*.

"And that," he said, "is where you make that distinction."

Eiah was silent for a moment, then drew a pen from her sleeve and a small silver ink box. With a soft pressure, gentler than rain on leaves, she added the strokes that remade the binding.

"You accept my argument, then?" Maati asked.

"I have to," Eiah said. "It's why we're here, isn't it? Sterile didn't add anything to the world, it only broke the way humanity renews itself. I've seen enough decline and death to recognize its proper place. I'm not here to stop time or death. Just to put back the balance so that new generations can come up fresh."

Maati nodded. When Eiah spoke, her voice sounded tired.

"I miss him," she said. He knew that she meant her father. "The last time I saw him, he looked so old. I still picture him with dark hair. It hasn't been like that in years, but it's what's in my mind."

"We're doing the right thing," Maati said. His voice was little more than a whisper.

"I don't doubt it," Eiah said. "He's turned his back on a generation of women as if their suffering were insignificant. Sexual indenture used to be restricted to bed slaves, and he would make an industry of it if he could. He would haul women across like bales of cotton. I hate everything about the scheme, but I miss him."

"I do too," Maati said.

"You also hate him," she said. There was no place in this room for half-truths.

"That too," Maati agreed.

Dinner that night was a brace of quail Large Kae had trapped. The flesh was soft and rich. Maati sat at the head of the long table, Vanjit and Clarity-of-Sight at the far end, and plucked the delicate bones. The bright chattering voices of Small Kae and Irit seemed distant, the dry wit of Ashti Beg grim. Eiah also seemed subdued, but it might only have been that she was thinking of the binding. The meal seemed to last forever, and yet he found himself surprised when Ashti Beg gathered up the bowls and the talk shifted to cleanup chores.

"I don't think I can," Vanjit said, her voice apologetic. "I assumed that we had changed the rotation."

"We skipped you last time, if that's what you mean," Ashti Beg said. "I don't know if that's the same as agreeing to wait on you."

There was laughter in the older woman's voice, but it had teeth. Small Kae was smiling a fixed smile and staring at the table. If he hadn't been so distracted, Maati would have seen this coming before it arrived.

"I don't think I can, though," Vanjit said, still firmly in her seat. The thing on her lap shifted its gaze from the poet to Ashti Beg and back as if fascinated.

"I seem to recall my mother keeping the house even when she had a babe on her hip," Ashti Beg said. "But she always was unusually talented."

"I have the andat. That's more work than washing dishes," Vanjit said. "At court, poets are forgiven other duties, aren't they, Maati-kvo?"

"The smallest brat of the utkhaiem is forgiven their duties," Ashti Beg said before Maati could frame a reply. "That's why it's court. Because some people set themselves above others."

The air was suddenly heavy. Maati stood, unsure what he was about to say. Irit's sudden chirp saved him.

"Oh, it isn't much. No need to fuss about it. I'll be happy to do the thing. No, Vanjit-cha, don't get up. If you don't feel up to doing it, you ought not strain yourself."

The last words rose at the end as if they were a question. Maati nodded as if something had been decided, then walked out of the hall. Vanjit followed without speaking, and took herself and her small burden down a side hall and out to the gardens. Maati could hear the voices of the others as they cleaned away the remnants of the small, fallen birds.

They met as they always did, sitting in a rough circle and discussing the fine points of binding the andat. There was no sign of the earlier conflict; Vanjit and Ashti Beg treated each other with their customary kindness and respect. Eiah explained the difference between accident, intention, and consequence of design to Irit and Small Kae and, Maati thought, learned by the experience. By the warm, soft light of the lanterns, they might have been talking of anything. By the end, there was even real laughter.

It should have been a good evening, but as he went back toward his bed, Maati was troubled and couldn't quite say why. It had to do with Otah-kvo and

Eiah, Vanjit and Clarity-of-Sight. The Galts and his own unsettling if unsurprising insight into the nature of time and decay.

He opened his book, reading his own handwriting by the light of the night candle. Even the quality of his script had changed since Vanjit had sharpened his vision. The older entries had been . . . not sloppy, never that. But not so crisp as he was capable of now. It had been an old man's handwriting. Now it was something different. He picked up his pen, touched nib to ink, but found nothing coherent to say.

He wiped the pen clean and put the book aside. Somewhere far to the south, Otah was dining with the men who had destroyed the Khaiem. He was sleeping on a bed of silk and drinking wine from bowls of beaten gold, while here in the dry plains his own daughter prepared to risk her life to make right what he had done.

What they had done together. Otah, Cehmai, and Maati himself. One was crawling into bed with the enemy, another turning away and hiding his face. Only Maati had even tried to make things whole again. Vanjit's success meant it had not been wasted effort. Eiah's fear reminded him that it was not yet finished.

He made his way down the corridors in the near darkness. Only candles and a half-moon lit his way. He was unsurprised to see Vanjit sitting alone in the gardens. Unlike the courtyard where they had spoken before, the gardens were bleak and bare. They had come too late to plant this season. Eiah's occasional journeys to Pathai provided food enough, and they didn't have the surplus of spare hands that had once held up the school. The wilderness encroached on the high stone walls here, young trees growing green and bold in plots where Maati had sown peas and harvested pods.

She heard him approaching and glanced back over her shoulder. She shifted, adjusting her robes, and Maati saw the small, black eyes of the andat appear from among the folds of cotton. She had been nursing it. It shocked him for a moment, though on reflection it shouldn't have. The andat had no need of milk, of course, but it was a product of Vanjit's conceptions. Stone-Made-Soft had been involved with the game of stones. Three-Bound-as-One had been fascinated by knots. The relationship of poet and andat was modeled on mother and child as it had never been before in all of history. The nursing was, Maati supposed, the physical emblem of it.

"Maati-kvo," she said. "I didn't expect anyone to be here."

He took a pose of apology, and she waved it away. In the cold light, she looked ghostly. The andat's eyes and mouth seemed to eat the light, its skin to glow. Maati came nearer.

"I was worried, I suppose," he said. "It seemed . . . uncomfortable at dinner this evening."

"I'd been thinking about that," Vanjit said. "It's hard for them. Ashti Beg and the others. I think it must be very hard for them."

"How do you mean?"

She shrugged. The andat in her lap gurgled to itself, considering its own short, pale fingers with fascination.

"They have all put in so much time, so much work. Then to see another woman complete a binding and gain a child, all at once. I imagine it must gnaw at her. It isn't that she intends to be rude or cruel. Ashti is in pain, and she lashes out. I knew a dog like that once. A cart had rolled over it. Snapped its spine. It whined and howled all night. You would have thought it was begging aid, except that it tried to bite anyone who came near. Ashti-cha is much the same."

"You think so?"

"I do," she said. "You shouldn't think ill of her, Maati-kvo. I doubt she even knows what she's doing."

He folded his arms.

"I can't think it's simple for you either," he said. He had the sense of testing her, though he couldn't have said quite how. Vanjit's face was as clear and cloudless as the sky.

"It's perfect," she said. "Nowhere near as difficult as I'd thought. Only he makes me tired. No more than any mother with a new babe, though. I've been thinking of names. My cousin was named Ciiat, and he was about this old when the Galts came."

"It has a name already," Maati said. "Clarity-of-Sight."

"I meant a private name," Vanjit said. "One for just between the two of us. And you, I suppose. You are as near to a father as he has."

Maati opened his mouth, then closed it. Vanjit's hand slipped into his own, her fingers twined around his. Her smile seemed so genuine, so innocent, that Maati only shook his head and laughed. They remained there for the space of ten long breaths together, Vanjit sitting, Maati standing at her side, and the andat, shifting impatiently in her lap.

"Once Eiah's bound Wounded," Maati said, "we can all go back."

Vanjit made a small sound, neither cough nor gasp nor chuckle, and released Maati's hand. He glanced down. Vanjit smiled up at him.

"That will be good," she said. "This must all be hard for her as well. I wish there was something we could do to ease things."

"We'll do what can be done," Maati said. "It will have to be enough."

Vanjit didn't reply, and then raised her arm, pointing to the horizon.

"The brightest star," she said. "The one just coming up over the trees there? You see it?"

"I do," Maati said. It was one of the traveling stars that made their slow way through the night skies.

"It has moons around it. Three of them."

He laughed and shook his head, but Vanjit didn't join him. Her face was still and cool. Maati's laughter died.

"A star with . . . *moons?*"

Vanjit nodded. Maati looked up again at the bright golden glimmer above the trees. He frowned first and then smiled.

"Show me," he said.

13

>+< The fleet left Saraykeht on the first truly cool morning of autumn. A dozen ships with bright sails, and the marks of the Empire and Galt flying together from their masts. From the shore, Otah could no longer make out the shapes of the individual sailors and soldiers that crowded the distant decks, much less Sinja himself, dressed though the man was in gaudy commander's array. Farrer Dasin's ships still stood at anchor, and the other Galtic ships which had been promised but were not yet prepared to sail.

Sinja had met with him for the last time less than a hand and a half before he'd stepped onto the small boat to make his last inspection. Otah had made himself comfortable in a teahouse near the seafront, waiting for the ceremony that would send off the fleet. The walls of the place were stained with decades of lantern smoke, the floorboards spotted with the memory of spilled wine. Sitting at the back table, Otah had felt like a peacock in a hen coop. Sinja, breezing through the open doors in a robe of bright green and hung with silk scarves and golden pendants, had made him feel less ridiculous only by comparison.

"Well, this is your last chance to call the whole thing quits," Sinja said, dropping into the chair across from Otah as casually as a drinking companion. Otah fumbled in his sleeve for a moment and drew out the letters intended for the utkhaiem of Chaburi-Tan. Sinja took them, considered the bright thread that sewed each of them closed, and sighed.

"I'd feel better if Balasar was leading the first command," Sinja said.

"I thought you'd decided that he'd be better staying to arrange your reinforcements."

"Agreed. I agreed. He decided. And it does make sense. Farrer-cha and the others who've followed his example will be able to swallow all this better if they're answering to a Galtic general."

"And waiting for them to be ready . . ." Otah said.

"Madness," Sinja said, slipping the letters into his own sleeve. "We've been too long already. I'm not saying that it's a bad plan. I only wish that there was a brilliant, well-crafted scheme that had Balasar-cha going out and me following behind to see whether the raiders sank everyone. Any word from Chaburi-Tan?"

"Nothing new," Otah said.

"Fair enough. We'll send word once we get there."

A silence followed, the unasked questions as heavy in the air as smoke. Otah leaned forward. Sinja knew about Idaan's list; Otah had told him in a fit of candor and regretted it since. Sinja knew better than to raise the issue where they might be overheard, but disapproval haunted his expression.

"There is some movement on the question of Obar State," Otah said. "Ashua Radaani bribed their ambassador. He has a list of men who have been in negotiation to break the eastern cities from the Empire with backing from Obar State. Two dozen men in four families."

"That's good work," Sinja said.

"He's asking permission to kill them."

"Sounds very tidy, assuming it's true and Radaani isn't involved in the conspiracy himself."

"Very tidy then too," Otah said. "I'm ordering the men brought to Utani. I can speak with them there."

"And if Radaani refuses?"

"Then I'll invite just him," Otah said. Sinja took an approving pose. Otah thought for a moment that they might be done.

"The other matter?"

"Being addressed," Otah said.

Four of the members of Idaan's list had been quietly looked into, the irregularities of their behavior clarified. One had been hiding half-a-dozen mistresses from a wife with a notoriously short temper. Two others had been conspiring to undercut the glass trades in the north, setting up workshops nearer the alum mines of Eddensea. The fourth had also appeared on Ashua Radaani's list, and had no clear connection to Maati.

Sinja had made it perfectly clear that he thought examining Eiah's actions was the wisest course. If she was Maati's backer, better to find it quickly and put a stop to the whole affair. If she wasn't, best to know that and stop losing sleep. There was a cold logic to his argument, and Otah knew what his own reluctance meant. His daughter had turned to her Uncle Maati. Turned against her father. And the pain of that loss was almost more than he could bear.

"Well," Sinja said. "I suppose I'd better go before the sailors all get too drunk to know sunrise from sunset and land us all in Eymond. If I don't come back, make sure they put up statues of me."

"You'll come back," Otah said.

"You only say that because I always have before," Sinja replied, smiling. He sobered. "See that Balasar comes quickly, though. These ships will make a grand spectacle, but it would be a short fight."

"I'll see to it," Otah said.

Sinja rose and took a pose of leave-taking. It might be the last time Otah ever saw the man. It was a fact he'd known, but something in the set of Sinja's body or the studied blankness of his face drove the point home. For the space of a breath, Otah felt the loss as if the worst had already happened.

"I would have been lost without you, these last years," Otah said. "You know that."

"I know you think it," Sinja said, matching Otah's quiet tone. "Take care, Most High. Do what needs doing."

Sitting now on his dais, watching the ships recede and vanish, Otah thought the phrase had been intended as last words. Do what needs doing. Meaning, more specifically, find Eiah. The sun rose from its morning home in the east; the seafront surged with a hundred languages, creoles, pidgins. Where the armsmen of the palace ended, merchants set up their tall, thin stalls and proclaimed their wares. When Otah took his leave, they would do the same in the space he now inhabited. Returning to the palaces would be like taking his finger out of water. It wouldn't leave a hole. He wondered, sometimes, if the whole world wasn't the same.

Back at the palaces, Otah suffered through the ritual change of robes, the closing ceremony that followed seeing off the fleet. He dearly hoped that when Balasar's reinforcements departed, he could avoid repeating the entire pointless exercise. He hoped, but doubted it. Once the last cymbal had chimed, the last priest intoned the final passage, and Otah had done his duty as Emperor, he went back to his rooms. Danat and Issandra were waiting there.

Otah greeted them both with a single pose appropriate to near family. If it was still an optimism, the Galtic woman didn't comment on it. She put down a bowl of tea she'd been drinking from, and Danat rose to his feet.

"Thank you for joining me," Otah said. "I wanted to know the . . . the status of your work."

The pair exchanged glances. Issandra spoke.

"In one respect, I think you could say we're doing quite well. Ana's request that her father add himself to your naval adventure has caused something of a strain between her and Hanchat. He seems to think she's being disloyal to Galt in general and therefore him in particular."

"I can understand that," Otah said, lowering himself to a cushion. "The gods all know she surprised me with it."

"The problem is that she feels she's cleared all accounts by the gesture," Issandra said. "Any sense of obligation she might have felt toward Danat-cha from her misbehavior or his clemency toward Hanchat is done."

"I see," Otah said.

"There's something else," Danat said. "I think Shija-cha has . . ."

"The imitation lover has developed ambitions," Issandra said. "Apparently you've entrusted her uncle with some particularly delicate task?"

Shija Radaani. Ashua's niece.

"I have," Otah said.

"She's taken that fact and the request that she act as Danat's escort, and drawn the most remarkable conclusion," Issandra said. "She thinks that Danat-cha is in love with her, and intends to sabotage his connection to Ana on her behalf."

"It's not only that," Danat said. "This is my fault. I . . . I lost my perspective. It was . . ."

"You bedded her," Otah said.

Danat's blush could have lit houses. It was as Otah had feared. Issandra sighed.

"This Radaani woman," she said. "Can you safely offend her family?"

"At the moment, it would be awkward," Otah said.

"Then I can't see that the girl is that far wrong," Issandra said. "Danat *has* sabotaged things."

"I'm very sorry," he said. "It wasn't . . . gods."

Danat sat again, his head in his hands.

"What is Ana's opinion of the matter of Shija and Danat?" Otah asked.

"I don't know," Issandra said. Her voice went softer, sorrow creeping in at the seams. "I believe she's avoiding me."

Otah pressed his fingers against his eyelids until colors swam in the darkness. No one spoke, and the silence pressed on his shoulder like a hand.

"Well," he said at last, "how do the two of you intend to move forward from here?"

"She wants to put them together," Danat said. His voice was equal parts plea and outrage. "She wants Shija and Ana to be seated beside each other at every dance, every meal . . ."

"You can't envy what you don't see," Issandra said. "It's more difficult if this other girl can't be easily removed, but if Ana's run with her present lover is nearing an end, and Shija makes it clear that she considers Ana a threat . . ."

Danat yelped and began to spout objections, as Issandra pressed on against him. Otah kept his eyes closed, the paired voices draining each other of meaning. Instead he imagined the girl to be before him as she had been the night she came to speak with him. Half-drunk. Too proud to be ruled by pride.

He took a pose that commanded silence. Danat's words ended at once. Issandra's took a moment longer to trail off.

"Between the two of you, you'll have to devise something," he said. "I don't have the time or the resources to fix this for you. But consider that you might be treating Ana with less respect than she deserves. Danat-cha, do you intend to build a life with Shija Radaani?"

Danat sobered. He took no pose, spoke no word. Otah nodded.

"Then it would be disrespectful to behave as if you did," Otah said. "Be honest with her, and if it damages relations with House Radaani, then it does."

"Yes, Father," Danat said, hesitated, and then took a pose that asked forgiveness before walking from the room.

Otah's spine ached. His eyes felt gritty with the efforts of the day. It was all far from over.

"Issandra-cha," he said. "I don't know Ana well, but I lost my own daughter by treating her as the girl I remembered instead of the woman she'd become.

Don't repeat my mistake. Ana may not be subject to the manipulations that work on younger girls."

Issandra Dasin's face hardened. For a moment, Otah saw the resemblance between mother and daughter. She took a pose of acknowledgment. It was awkward, but her form was correct.

"There is, perhaps, another approach," she said. "I wouldn't have considered it before, but I've spent a certain number of hours with your son. He might be able to manage it."

Otah nodded her on.

"He could choose to fall in love with her. Cultivate the feeling within himself, and then . . ." She shrugged. "Let the world take its course. I haven't known many women who failed to be charmed by an attractive man's genuine admiration."

"You think he could simply decide to feel what we want him to feel?"

"I've done it every day for nearly thirty years," Issandra said.

"That is either the most romantic thing I've heard or the saddest," Otah said. And then, "Ana-cha did me a great favor. I'm sorry that Danat repaid it with an indiscretion."

Issandra waved the apology away.

"I doubt she took offense. I'm sure she assumed Danat and this Radaani creature were sharing whatever flat surfaces came available. I remember what it was like at their age. We were all heat and dramatic gestures. We thought we were the first generation to truly discover love or sex or betrayal." Her voice softened.

Otah recalled a girl named Liat with skin the brown of eggshell and the night his one true friend had confessed his affair with her. The night Maati had confessed. He hadn't seen or spoken to either of them for years afterward. He had killed a man, in part as a blessing upon them, Liat and Maati, and the freedom that together they had given him.

All heat and dramatic gestures, he thought. Amusement mixed with sorrow, the way it always did.

"Still, it is a pity," Issandra said. "The Radaani girl is beautiful, and vanity is a powerful lever, no matter how sophisticated you take my daughter to be."

"We may hope for the best," Otah said. "Perhaps Shija-cha will take Danat's apology in stride and return to only acting the role."

Issandra's gaze told him exactly how likely she thought that was, but she only shook her head.

"It would be pleasant," she said.

He ate alone that night, though there were scores of men, Galtic and ut-khaiem both, who would have been pleased to share his table. The pavilion sat atop a high tower, the air smelling of lavender and the sea. Otah sat on a cushion by a low table and watched the sunset: orange and red and gold spread out upon a wide canvas of clouds and sky. There were no singing slaves here, but soft chimes danced in the breeze with a sound like bells made from wood.

An iron brazier sat close to keep him warm. The evening was beautiful and rich with sadness.

He had known that his daughter was angry with him. He had encouraged the high families to import wives for their sons. They had come from Bakta, Eymond, Eddensea. Women of middling birth commanded huge dowries. The coffers of the utkhaiem had dropped, but a handful of children had been born. A few dozen, perhaps, in every city. It hadn't been enough. And so he'd conceived the plan to join with Galt, old enemies made one people. Yes, it left behind a generation of Khaiate women. And Galtic men, for that. No doubt they would feel angered, lost, discarded. It was a small price to pay for a future.

The Comfort House Empire, she'd called it the last time they'd spoken. And her father, *her* father, the Procurer King. She said it, and she spat.

Thinking of it stung.

A flock of gulls wheeled below him and to the south. Lemon rice and river trout rested warm on his fingers and in his mouth. When he was alone, he still ate like a laborer.

He wondered if he had been wrong. Perhaps in the approach he had taken, trying to find women capable of bearing children for the cities. Perhaps in speaking to Eiah about it in the terms he'd used. Perhaps in failing to accept her criticism, in speaking harshly. Eiah had accused him of turning his back on the women whom Sterile had wounded because they were inconvenient. Eiah was one of those women, and the injury she'd suffered was as deep as any of his own. Deeper.

It might, he supposed, have been enough to turn her against him. She had always been close to Maati. She had spent long evenings at the library of Machi, where Maati had made his home. She had known Nayiit, the man that Otah had fathered and Maati had called son. In the many years that he had struggled with being merely the Khai Machi, Eiah had made a friend and an uncle of Maati Vaupathai. There was little reason to believe that she would withhold her loyalty from Maati now.

The wheeling gulls landed, leaving the sky to itself. The fleet had long passed the horizon, and Otah wished he had some magical glass that would let him see it still. It was a short enough voyage to Chaburi-Tan. Shorter if the pirates and raiders came out to confront them. He wished Sinja had stayed behind. In the failing light, the gaudy sunset turning to gray, he wanted his old friend back and was only half-startled to realize he meant Maati as much as Sinja.

A servant emerged from the darkened arches at the pavilion's edge and came forward. Otah knew the news he carried before he spoke. Idaan Machi had answered his summons and awaited at his pleasure. Otah ordered that she be brought to him. Her and more food.

Do what needs doing, Sinja said from his memory.

He heard her soft footsteps and didn't turn around. His belly was knotted, and the fish before him smelled suddenly unpleasant. Idaan walked past him and stood at the edge of the pavilion, looking down the height of the tower.

Her outer robe was dark, the hem fluttering as if she were about to fall or take flight. When she turned back to him, her expression was mild.

"Lovely view," she said. "But still nothing beside Machi. Do you miss the towers?"

"No," Otah said. "Not really. They're too cold to use in the winter, too hot in the summer, and the tracks they use to haul things up the side have to be replaced every fifth year. They're the best example I know of doing a thing just to show it's possible."

Idaan lowered herself to a cushion opposite him. The fading glow of western clouds silhouetted her.

"True enough," she said. "Still. I miss them."

She considered the bowls of food before them, then took a scoop of rice and fish on two curled fingers. Otah smiled. His sister chewed appreciatively and took a pose that opened a negotiation.

"Yes," he agreed. "There's something I want from you."

Idaan nodded, but didn't speak. Otah squinted out into the wide air above Saraykeht.

"There's too much," he said. "Even turning everything I can manage over to Sinja and Danat and Ashua Radaani, there's too much."

"Too much to allow for what?" She knew, he thought, what was coming.

"Too much for me to leave," he said. "Being Emperor is like being the most honored slave in the world. I can do anything, except that I can't. I can go anywhere, except that I mustn't."

"It sounds awful."

"Don't laugh. I'm not saying I'd rather be lifting crates at the seafront, but senior overseer of a courier service? Something with a few dozen chests of silver lengths and a favorite teahouse."

"Fewer meetings like this one," Idaan suggested.

"That," Otah said. "Gods yes, that."

Idaan scooped up another mouthful of rice, chewed slowly, and let her dark eyes play across his face. He didn't know what she saw there. After a swallow of water and a small sigh, she spoke.

"You want me to find Eiah," she said.

"You know what Maati looks like," he said. "You have the experience of living among low towns and hiding who you are. You understand poets as well as anyone alive, I'd guess."

"And I know what I'm looking for," she said, her voice light and conversational. "Anyone else, and you'd have to bring them into your confidence. Explain what you wanted to know and why. Well, Sinja-cha perhaps, but you've sent him off the other direction."

This is madness, Otah thought but didn't say. She is a killer. She was born without a conscience. However she may seem now, she slaughtered her brothers and the father she loved. She's got the eyes of a pit hound and the heart of a butcher.

"Will you do it?" he said aloud.

Idaan didn't answer at once. A gust of wind pushed at her sleeve and drew a lock of gray hair out behind her like a banner from the mast of a fighting ship. Otah's hands ached, and he forced his fists to open by an act of will.

"Maati hunted me once," she said, hardly louder than the wind. "It only seems fair to return the favor."

Otah closed his eyes. Perhaps it was an empty task. Eiah might very well have nothing to do with Maati's schemes. She might truly be working with some low-town physician, hoping through her own hard work to atone for her father's misdeeds. For his misdeeds. When he looked up, his sister was considering him with hooded eyes.

"I will have a cart and driver ready for you in the morning," he said. "You'll be able to take whatever fresh horses or food you need along the way. I've written the orders up already."

"All the horses and food we need along the way?" Idaan said. "You're right. Being Emperor must be raw hell."

He didn't answer her. She finished the rice and fish. The clouds behind her had gone dark, and since neither had called for candles or torches, the only light was the cold blue moon and the fiery embers in the brazier. Idaan took a pose that accepted his charge.

"You don't want to negotiate payment?" he said.

"I'm just pleased you've decided to do the thing. I was afraid you'd put it off until it was too late," Idaan said. "One question, though. If I find her, and she is the one, what action should I take?"

Meaning should Idaan kill her, kill Maati and as many of the other fledgling poets as she could to prevent them from accomplishing their aims.

Do what needs doing.

"Nothing," Otah said, nerve failing. "Do nothing. There will be couriers in Pathai. You can send the fastest of them back. I'll give you a cipher."

"You're sure?" Idaan said. "It's a lot of time on the road, sending me out and then someone else back. And then waiting while you make your way to Pathai or wherever the trail leads."

"If you find her, send word," Otah said. "You aren't to act against her."

Idaan's smile was crooked with meanings he couldn't quite follow. Otah felt anger growing in his spine, only it wasn't rage so much as dread.

"I'll do as you say, Most High," Idaan said. "I'll go at first light."

"Thank you," he said.

Idaan rose and walked back toward the arches. He heard her pause for a moment and then go on. The stars had come out, glimmering in the darkness like gems thrown on black stone. Otah sat in silence until he was sure he could walk, and then went down to his rooms. The servants had left him a bowl of candied fruit, but he couldn't stand the prospect.

A fire burned in the grate, protecting the air from even the slightest chill and tainting it with tendrils of pine smoke. The summer cities had always been overly vigilant of cold. Thin blood. Everything south of Udun was plagued by thinness of the blood. Otah came from the winter cities, and he threw open the shutters, letting in what cold there was. He didn't notice that Danat was there until the boy spoke.

"Father."

Otah turned. Danat stood in the doorway that led to the inner chambers. He wore the same robe that he had before, but the cloth sagged like an unmade bed. Danat's eyes were rimmed with red.

"Danat-kya," Otah said. "What's happened?"

"I've done as you said. Shija and I went to the rose pavilion. Just the two of us. I . . . spoke with her. I broke things off."

"Ah," Otah said. He walked back from the open windows and sat on a couch before the fire. Danat came forward, his eyes glittering with unfallen tears.

"This is my fault, Papa-kya. In a different world, I might have . . . I have been careless with her. I've *hurt* her."

Was I ever as young as this? Otah thought, and immediately pressed it away. Even if the question was fair, it was unkind. He held out his hand, and his son—his tall, thick-shouldered son—sat beside him, curled into Otah's shoulder the way he had as a boy. Danat sobbed once.

"I only . . . I know you and Issandra-cha were relying on me and . . ."

Otah hushed the boy.

"You've taken a willing girl to bed," Otah said. "You aren't who she hoped you might be, and so she's disappointed. Yes?"

Danat nodded.

"There are worse things." Otah saw again the darkness of Idaan's eyes. He was sending the woman behind those eyes after his Eiah, his little girl. The ghost of nausea touched him and he stroked Danat's hair. "People have done worse."

14

Maati frowned at the papers before him. A small fire crackled in the brazier on his desk, and he was more than half-tempted to drop the pages onto the flames. Eiah, sitting across from him, looked no more pleased.

"You're right," he said. "We're moving backward."

"What's happened?" Eiah asked, though she knew as well as he did.

The few weeks that had passed since Vanjit's successful binding had only grown more difficult. To start, the other students excepting Eiah were more distracted. The mewling and cries of the andat disrupted any conversation. Its awkward crawling seemed capable of entrancing them for a full morning. Perhaps he had known too much of the andat, but he held the growing impression that it was perfectly aware of the effect its toothless smile could have. And that it was especially cultivating the admiration of Ashti Beg.

Added to that, Vanjit herself had come almost disconnected from the rest. She would sit for whole days, the andat in her lap or at her breast, staring at water or empty air. Maati had some sympathy for that. She had shown him the most compelling of the wonders her new powers had uncovered, and he had been as delighted as she was. But her little raptures meant that she wasn't engaged in the work at hand: Eiah, and the binding of Wounded.

"There is something we can do," Eiah said. "If we set the classes in the mornings, just after the first meal, we won't have had a full day behind us. We could come at it fresh each time."

Maati nodded more to show he'd heard her than from any real agreement. His fingertips traced the lines of the binding again, tapping the page each time some little infelicity struck him. He had seen bindings falter this way before. In those first years when Maati had been a new poet, the Dai-kvo had spoken of the dangers of muddying thoughts by too much work. One sure way to fail was to build something sufficient and then not stop. With every small improvement, the larger structure became less tenable, until eventually the thing collapsed under the weight of too much history.

He wondered if they had gone too far, corrected one too many things which were not truly problems so much as differences of taste.

Eiah took a pose that challenged him. He looked at her directly for perhaps the first time since she'd come to his study.

"You think I'm wrong," she said. "You can say it. I've heard worse."

It took Maati the space of several heartbeats to recall what her proposal had been.

"I think it can't hurt. But I also think it isn't our essential problem. We were all quite capable of designing Clarity-of-Sight with meetings in the evening. This"—he rattled the papers in his hand—"is something different. Half-measures won't suffice."

"What then?" she said.

He put the papers down.

"We stop," he said. "For a few days, we don't touch it at all. Instead we can send someone to a low town for meat and candles, or clear the gardens. Anything."

"Do we have time for that?" Eiah asked. "Anything could have happened. My brother may be married. His wife may be carrying a child. All of Galt may be loading their daughters in ships, and the men of the cities may be scuttling off to Kirinton and Acton and Marsh. We are out here where there's no one to talk to, no couriers on the roads, and I know it feels that time has stopped. It hasn't. We've been weeks at this. Months. We can't spend time we don't have."

"You'd recommend what, then? Move faster than we can move? Think more clearly than we can think? It isn't as if we can sit down with a serious expression and demand that the work be better than it is. Have you never seen a man ill with something that needed quiet and time? This is no different."

"I've also watched ill men die," Eiah said. "Time passes, and once you've waited too long for something, there's no getting it back."

Her mouth bent in a deep frown. There were dark circles under her eyes. She bit her lower lip and shook her head as if conducting some conversation within her mind and disagreeing with herself. The coal burning in the brazier settled and gave off a dozen small sparks as bright as fireflies. One landed on the paper, already cold and gray. Ash.

"You're reconsidering," Maati said.

"No. I'm not. We can't tell my father," she said. "Not yet."

"We could send to others, then," Maati said. "There are high families in every city that would rise up against Otah's every plan if they knew the andat were back in the world. You've lived your whole life in the courts. Two or three people whose discretion you trust would be all it took. A rumor spoken in the right ears. We needn't even say where we are or what's been bound."

Eiah combed her fingers through her hair. Every breath that she didn't answer, Maati felt his hopes rise. She would, if he only gave her a little more time and silence to convince herself. She would announce their success, and everyone in the cities of the Khaiem would know that Maati Vaupathai had remained true to them. He had never given up, never turned away.

"It would mean going to a city," Eiah said. "I can't send half-a-dozen ciphered letters under my own seal out from a low town without every courier in the south finding out where we are."

"Then Pathai," Maati said, his hands opening. "We need to step back from the binding. The letters will win us time to make things right."

Eiah turned, looking out the window. In the courtyard, the maple trees were losing their leaves. A storm, a strong wind, and the branches would be bare. A sparrow, brown and gray, hopped from one twig to another. Maati could see the fine markings on its wings, the blackness of its eyes. It had been years since sparrows had been more than dull smears. He glanced at Eiah, surprised to see the tears on her cheek.

His hand touched her shoulder. She didn't look back, but he felt her lean into him a degree.

"I don't know," she said as if to the sparrow, the trees, the thousand fallen leaves. "I don't know why it should matter. It's no secret what he's done or what I think of it. I don't have any doubts that what we're doing is the right choice."

"And yet," Maati said.

"And yet," she agreed. "My father will be disappointed in me. I would have thought I was old enough that his opinion wouldn't matter."

He searched for a response—something gentle and kind and that would strengthen her resolve. Before he found the words, he felt her tense. He took back his hand, adopting a querying pose.

"I thought I heard something," she said. "Someone was yelling."

A long, high shriek rang in the air. It was a woman's voice, but he couldn't guess whose. Eiah leaped from her stool and vanished into the dark hallways before Maati recovered himself. He followed, his heart pounding, his breath short. The shrieking didn't stop, and as he came nearer the kitchen, he heard other sounds—clattering, banging, high voices urging calm or making demands that he couldn't decipher, the andat's infantile wail. And then Eiah's commanding voice, with the single word *stop*.

He rounded the last corner, his fist pressed to his chest, his heart hammering. The cooking areas were raw chaos come to earth. An earthenware jar of wheat flour had been overturned and cracked. The thin stone block Irit used for chopping plants lay in shards on the floor. Ashti Beg stood in the middle of the room, a knife in her hand, her chin held high like a statue of abstract vengeance. In the corner, Vanjit held the still-mewling andat close to her breast. Large Kae, Small Kae, and Irit were all cowering against the walls, their eyes wide and mouths hanging open. Eiah's expression was calm and commanding at the same time, like a mother calling back her children from a cliff edge.

"It's done, Ashti-cha," Eiah said, walking slowly toward the woman. "I'll have the knife."

"Not until I find that bitch and put it in her heart," Ashti Beg spat, turning toward Eiah's voice. Maati saw for the first time that the woman's eyes were as gray as storm clouds.

"I'll have the knife," Eiah said again. "Or I will beat you down and take it. You know you're more likely to hurt the others than Vanjit."

The andat whimpered and Ashti Beg whirled toward it. Eiah stepped forward smoothly, took Ashti Beg's elbow and wrist in her hands, and twisted. Ashti Beg yelped, the blade clattering to the floor.

"What . . ." Maati gasped. "What is happening?"

Four voices answered at once, words tripping over each other. Only Eiah and Vanjit remained silent, the two poets considering each other silently in the center of the storm. Maati raised his hands in a pose that commanded silence, and all of them stopped except Ashti Beg.

". . . power over us. It isn't right, it isn't fair, and I will not simper and smile and lick her ass because she happened to be the one to go first!"

"Enough!" Maati said. "Enough, all of you. Gods. *Gods*. Vanjit. Come with me."

The girl looked over as if noticing him for the first time. The rage in her expression faltered. Her hands were shaking. Eiah stepped forward, keeping herself between Ashti Beg and her prey as Vanjit walked across the room.

"Eiah, see to Ashti-cha," Maati said, taking Vanjit's wrist. "The rest of you, clean this mess. I'd rather not eat food prepared in a child's playpen."

He turned away, pulling Vanjit and Clarity-of-Sight after him. The andat was silent now. Maati crossed the hallway and started down a flight of stone stairs that led to the sleeping rooms for the younger cohorts. The voices of the others rose behind them and faded. He wasn't certain where he was taking her until he reached the branching hall that led to the slate-paved rooms where the teachers had once disciplined boys with the cutting slash of a lacquered rod. He stopped in the hallway instead, putting the reflexive impulse to violence aside. Vanjit bowed her head.

"I would like an explanation of that," he said, his voice shaking with anger.

"It was Ashti Beg," Vanjit said. "She can't contain her jealousy any longer, Maati-kvo. I have tried to give her the time and consideration, but she won't understand. I am a poet now. I have an andat to care for. I can't be expected to work and toil like a servant."

The andat twisted in her grasp, looking up at Maati with tears in its black eyes. The tiny, toothless mouth gaped in what would have been distress if it had been a baby.

"Tell me," Maati said. "Tell me what happened."

"Ashti Beg said that I had to clean the pots from breakfast. Irit offered to, but Ashti wouldn't even let her finish her sentences. I explained that I couldn't. I was very calm. I am patient with her, Maati-kvo. I'm always very patient."

"What happened?" Maati insisted.

"She tried to take him," Vanjit said. Her voice had changed. The pleading tone was gone. Her words could have been shaved from ice. "She said that she could look after him as well as anyone, and that I was more than welcome to have him back once the kitchen had been cleaned."

Maati closed his eyes.

"She put her *hands* on him," Vanjit said. In her voice, it sounded like a violation. Perhaps it was.

"And what did you do," Maati asked, though he knew the answer.

"What you told me," Vanjit said. "What you said about Wounded."

"Which was?" he said. Clarity-of-Sight gurgled and swung its thick arms at Vanjit's ears, its dumb show of fear and distress forgotten.

"You said that Eiah-cha couldn't make an andat based on things being as they're meant to, because the andat aren't meant to be bound. It's not their nature. You said she had to bind Wounded and then withdraw it from all the women who still can't bear babes. And so we withdrew from Ashti Beg."

The andat cooed. It might have been Maati's imagination, but the thing seemed proud. Clarity-of-Sight. And so also Blindness.

The warmth that bloomed in his breast, the tightening of his jaw, the near-unconscious shaking of his head. They were not anger so much as a bone-deep impatience.

"It is manipulating you," he said. "We've talked about this from the beginning. The andat wants its freedom. Whatever else it is, it will always struggle to be free. It has been courting Ashti Beg and the others for days to precipitate exactly this. You have to know yourself better than it does. You have to behave like a grown woman, not a self-righteous child."

"But she—"

Maati put two fingers against the girl's lips. The andat was silent now, staring at him with silent anger.

"You have been entrusted with a power beyond any living person," Maati said, his tone harsher than he'd intended. "You are responsible for that power. You understand me? Responsible. I have tried to make you see that, but now I think I've failed. Poets aren't simply men . . . or women . . . who have a particular profession. We aren't like sailors or cabinetmakers or armsmen. Holding the andat is like holding small gods, and there is a price you pay for that. Do you understand what I'm saying?"

"Yes, Maati-kvo," Vanjit whispered.

"I doubt that," he said. "After what I've seen today, I very much doubt it."

She was weeping silently. Maati opened his mouth, some cutting comment ready to humiliate her further, and stopped. For a moment, he was a boy again, in this same hallway. He could feel the thin robes and the winter cold, and the tears on his own cheeks as the older boys mocked him or Tahi-kvo—bald, cruel Tahi-kvo, who had later become the Dai-kvo—beat him. He wondered if this fear and rage had been what drove his teachers back then, or if it had been something colder.

"Fix it," Maati said. "Put Ashti Beg back as she was, and never, never use the andat for petty infighting again."

"No, Maati-kvo."

"And wash the pots when your turn comes."

Vanjit took a pose that was a promise and an expression of gratitude. The quiet sobs as she walked away made Maati feel smaller. If they had been in a city, he would have gone to a bathhouse or some public square, listened to beggars singing on the corners and bought food from the carts. He would have tried to lose himself for a while, perhaps in wine, perhaps in music, rarely in gambling, and never in sex. At the school, there was no escape. He walked out, leaving the stone walls and memories behind him. Then the gardens. The low hills that haunted the land west of the buildings.

He sat on the wind-paved hillside, marking the passage of the sun across the afternoon sky, his mind tugged a hundred different ways. He had been too harsh with Vanjit, or not harsh enough. The binding of Wounded was overworked or not deeply enough considered, doomed or on the edge of being perfected. Ashti Beg had been in the wrong or justified or both. He closed his eyes and let the sunlight beat down on them, turning the world to red.

In time, the turmoil in his heart calmed. A small, blue-tailed lizard scrambled past him. He had chased lizards like it when he'd been a boy. He hadn't recalled that in years.

It was folly to think of poets as different from other men. Other women, now that Vanjit had proved their grammar effective. It was that mistake which had made the school what it was, which had deformed the lives of so many people, his own included. Of course Vanjit was still subject to petty jealousy and pride. Of course she would need to learn wisdom, just the same as anyone else. The andat had never changed who someone was, only what they could do.

He should have taught them that along with all the rest. Every now and again, he could have spent an evening talking about what power was, and what responsibility it carried. He'd never thought to do it, he now realized, because when he imagined a woman wielding the power of the andat, that woman was always Eiah.

Maati made his way back as the cold afternoon breeze set the trees and bushes rustling. He found the kitchen empty but immaculate. The broken cutting stone had been replaced with a length of polished wood, but otherwise everything was as it had been. His students, he found under Eiah's command in the courtyard. They were raking the fallen leaves into a pit for burning and resetting a half-dozen flagstones that had broken from years of frost, tree roots, and neglect. Vanjit knelt with Large Kae, lifting the stones from the ground. Clarity-of-Sight nestled in Irit's lap, its eyes closed and its mouth a perfect O. Ashti Beg, her vision clearly restored, was by Small Kae's side, a deep pile of russet leaves before them.

"Maati-kvo," Eiah said, taking a pose of greeting, which he returned. The others acknowledged him with a smile or simple pose. Vanjit turned away quickly, as if afraid to see anger still in his expression.

He trundled to a rough boulder, resting against it to catch his breath. Irit joined him and, without a word, passed the andat to him. It stirred, groaned once, and then turned to nestle its face into his robes. The andat had no need of breath. Maati had known that since he had first met Seedless over half a century earlier. Clarity-of-Sight's deep, regular sighs were manipulations, but Maati welcomed them. To hold something so much like a child but as still as the dead would have unnerved him.

Irit especially talked in light tones, and no one seeing them would have guessed that one of the group had been swinging a knife at another earlier in the day. Apart from a mutually respected distance between Ashti Beg and Vanjit, there was no sign of unease.

Large Kae and Small Kae left to prepare a simple meal just as Eiah put the torch to the pit of leaves. The flames rose, dancing. Pale smoke filled the air with the scent of autumn, then floated into the sky while the rest of them watched: Vanjit and Eiah, Ashti Beg, Irit, Maati and Clarity-of-Sight, who was also Blindness. The andat seemed captivated by the flames. Maati stretched his palm out to the fire and felt the heat pushing gently back.

They ate roasted chicken and drank watered wine. By the end of the meal, Vanjit was smiling again. When the last wine bowl was empty, the last thin, blood-darkened bone set bare on its plate, she was the first to rise and gather the washing. Maati felt a relief that surprised him. The trouble had passed; whether it had been Vanjit's pride or Ashti Beg's jealousy, it didn't matter.

To show his approval, Maati joined in the cleaning himself, sweeping the kitchen and building up the fire. In place of the usual lecture, they discussed the difficulties of looking too long at a binding. It came out that all of them had felt some disquiet at the state of Eiah's work. Even that was reassuring.

He and Eiah sat together after the session ended. A small kettle smelled equally of hot iron and fresh tea. The wind was picking up outside, cold and fragrant with the threat of rain or snow. By the warm light of the fire grate, Eiah looked tired.

"I'll leave in the morning," Eiah said. "I want to beat the worst of the weather, if I can."

"That seems wise," Maati said and sipped his tea. It was still scalding hot, but its taste was comforting.

"Ashti Beg wants to come with me," she said. "I don't know what to do about that."

He put down his bowl.

"What are you thinking?" he asked.

"That she might leave. After today, I'm afraid she's been soured on the work."

Maati snorted and waved the concern away.

"She'll move past it," Maati said. "It's finished. Vanjit overstepped, and she's seen it. I don't think Ashti's so petty as to hold things past that."

"Perhaps," Eiah said. "You think I should take her with me, then?"

"Certainly. There's no reason not to, and it will give you another pair of hands on the road. And besides, we're a school, not a prison. If she truly wants to leave, she should be able to."

"Even now?" Eiah asked.

"What option do we have?" Maati asked. "Chain her to a tree? Kill her? No, Eiah-kya. Ashti Beg won't abandon the work, but if she does, we have no choice but to let her."

Eiah was silent for five slow breaths together. When she looked up, he was surprised by her grim expression.

"I still can't quite bring myself to believe Vanjit did that."

"Why not?"

Eiah frowned, her hands clasped together. Some distant shutter's ties had slipped; wood clapping against stone. A soft wind pushed at the windows and unsettled the fire in the grate.

"She's a poet," Eiah said. "She's *the* poet."

"Poets are human," Maati said. "We err. We can be petty on occasion. Vindictive. Small. Her world has been turned on its head, and she hasn't come yet to understand all that means. Well, of course she hasn't. I'd have been more surprised if she'd never made a misstep."

"You don't think we have a problem then?" Eiah said.

"She's a reasonable girl. Given power, she's misbehaved once. Once." Maati shook his head. "Once is as good as never."

"And if it becomes twice?" Eiah asked. "If it becomes every time?"

"It won't," Maati said. "That isn't who she is."

"But she's changed. You said it just now. The binding gave her power, and power changes people."

"It changes their situation," Maati said. "It changes the calculations of what things they choose to do. What they forbear. It doesn't change their souls."

"I've cut through a hundred bodies, Uncle. I've never weighed out a soul. I've never judged one. When I picked Vanjit, I hope I did the right thing."

"Don't kill yourself with worry," Maati said. "Not yet, at any rate."

Eiah nodded slowly. "I've been thinking about who to send letters to. I've picked half-a-dozen names. I'll hire a courier when we reach Pathai. I won't be there long enough to bring back replies."

"That's fine," Maati said. "All we need is enough time to perfect Wounded."

Eiah took a pose that agreed and also ended the conversation. She walked away into the darkened hall, her shoulders bent, her head bowed. Maati felt a pang of guilt. Eiah was tired and sorrowful and more fearful than she let on. He was sending her to announce to the world that she had betrayed her father. He could have been gentler about her concerns over Vanjit and Clarity-of-Sight. He didn't know why he'd been so harsh.

He made his evening ablutions and prepared himself to write a few pages in his book, scratching words onto paper by the light of the fluttering night candle, thanks in no small part to Vanjit. He was less than surprised when a soft scratching came at his door.

Vanjit looked small and young. The andat held in the crook of her arm looked around the dim room, gurgling to itself almost like a baby. Maati gestured for her to sit.

"I heard Eiah-cha speaking to Ashti Beg," Vanjit said. "They're leaving?"

"Eiah is taking the cart to Pathai for supplies and to send off some letters for me. Ashti Beg is going to help. That's all," he said.

"It's not because of me?"

"No, Vanjit-kya," Maati said warmly. "No. It was planned before anything happened between you and Ashti-cha. It's only . . . we need time. Eiah needs time away from her binding to clear her mind. And we need to be sure that the Emperor and his son can't make a half-Galtic heir before we've done what needs doing. So we're asking help. Eiah is the daughter of the Empire. Her word carries weight. If she tells a few people well-placed in the utkhaiem what we've done and what we intend to do, they can use their influence to stop the Galts. And then . . ."

He gestured to Vanjit, to the school, to the wide plain of possibilities that lay before them, if only they could gain the time. The andat cooed and threw its own arms wide, in joy or possibly mockery.

"Why is he doing it?" Vanjit asked. "Why would he trade with those people? Is he so in love with Galt?"

Maati took a long breath, letting the question turn itself in his mind. It was the habit of years to lay any number of sins at Otah's feet. But, reluctantly, not this.

"No," Maati said. "Otah-kvo isn't evil. Petty, perhaps. Misguided, certainly. He sees that the Galts are strong, and we need strength. He sees that their women can bear babes with our men, and he believes it's the only hope of a new generation. He doesn't understand that what we've broken, we can also repair."

"Given time," Vanjit said.

"Yes," Maati said with a sigh. "Given time to rebuild. Remake."

For a moment, he was in the cold warehouse in Machi, the andat Sterile looking at him with her terrible, beautiful smile.

"It takes so long to build the world," he said softly, "and so very little to break it. I still remember what it felt like. Between one breath and the next, Vanjit-kya. I ruined the world in less than a heartbeat."

Vanjit blinked, as if surprised, and then a half-smile plucked her lips. Clarity-of-Sight quieted, looking at her as if she'd spoken. The andat was as still as stone; even the pretense of breath had gone.

Maati felt unease stir in his belly.

"Vanjit? Are you well?" and when she didn't reply, *"Vanjit?"*

She started, as if she'd forgotten where she was and that he was there. He caught her gaze, and she smiled.

"Fine. Yes, I'm fine," she said. There was a strange tone in her voice. Something low and languid and relaxed. It reminded Maati of the aftermath of sex. He took a pose that asked whether he had failed to understand something.

"No, nothing," Vanjit said; and then not quite in answer to his question, "Nothing's wrong."

15

>+< Shortly after midday, Otah walked along the winding path that led from the palaces themselves to the building that had once been the poet's house. Since the first time he had come this way, little more than a boy, many things had changed. The pathway itself was the white of crushed marble with borders of oiled wood. The bridge that rose over the pond had blackened with time; the grain of the wood seemed coarser. One of the stands of trees which gave the poet's house its sense of separation from the palaces had burned. White-oak seedlings had been planted to replace them. The trees looked thin, awkward, and adolescent. One day, decades ahead, they would tower over the path.

He paused at the top of the bridge's arch, looking down into the dark water. Koi swam lazily under the surface, orange and white and gold appearing from beneath lily pads and vanishing again. The man reflected in the pond's surface looked old and tired. White hair, gray skin. Time had thinned his shoulders and taken the roundness from his cheeks. Otah put out his hand, and the reflection did as well, as if they were old friends greeting each other.

When he reached the house itself, it seemed less changed than the landscape. The lower floor still had walls that were hinged like shutters which could be pulled back to open the place like a pavilion. The polished wood seemed to glow softly in the autumn light. He could almost imagine Maati sitting on the steps as he had been then. Sixteen summers old, and wearing the brown robes of a poet like a mark of honor. Or frog-mouthed Heshai, the poet whom Otah had killed to prevent the slaughter of innocents. Or Seedless, Heshai's beautiful, unfathomable slave.

Instead, Farrer Dasin sat on a silk-upholstered couch, a book in one hand, a pipe in the other. Otah approached the house casually as if they were merchants or workers, men whose dignity was less of a burden. The Galt closed his book as Otah reached the first stair up.

"Most High," he said in the Khaiate tongue.

"Farrer-cha," Otah replied.

"None of them are here. There's apparently a gathering at one of the lesser palaces. I believe one of the high-prestige wives of your court is showing her wealth in the guise of judging silks."

"It isn't uncommon. Especially if there is someone particularly worth impressing," Otah said. "I am surprised that Ana-cha chose to attend."

"To be honest, so am I. But I am on the verge of despairing that I will ever understand women."

It was hard to say whether the light, informal tone that the Galt adopted was intended as an offering of peace or as an insult. Likely it was both. The smoke rising from the pipe was thin and gray as fog, and smelled of cherries and bark.

"I don't mean to intrude," Otah said.

"No," Farrer Dasin said, "I imagine you don't. I've sent the servant away. You can take that seat there, if you like."

Otah, Emperor of the cities of the Khaiem, pulled a wood-backed chair to face the Galt, sat in it, and leaned back.

"I was a bit surprised you wanted to speak with me," Farrer said. "I thought we did all of our communication through my family."

A mosquito whined through the air as Otah considered this. Farrer Dasin waited, his mild expression a challenge.

"We have met and spoken many times over the past year, Farrer-cha. I don't believe I've ever turned you away. And as to your family, the first time I had no other option," Otah said. "The council was poised to refuse me, and there was a chance that your wives might be my allies. The second time, it was Ana who came to me. I didn't seek her out."

Farrer looked at Otah, his green-gray eyes as enigmatic as the sea.

"What brings you, Most High?" Farrer asked.

"I had heard rumors the decision to lend me your ships had perhaps weakened your position in the council. I had hoped I could offer some assistance."

Farrer drew on his pipe, then gestured out at the pond, the palaces, the world. When he spoke, the pipe smoke made the words seem solid and gray.

"I've failed. I know that. I was bullied into agreeing to this union between our houses, but so were half of the councillors. They can't think less of me for that, except for the few who genuinely backed your plan. They never thought much of me. And then I let myself be wheedled into helping you, so those whose love Ana won in her little speech think I'm ruled by the whims of a girl who hasn't seen twenty summers. The damning thing is, I can't say they're wrong."

"You love her," Otah said.

"I love her too much," Farrer said. His expression was grim. "It keeps me from knowing my own mind."

Otah's thoughts flickered for a moment, roving west to Idaan and her hunt. He brought himself back with a conscious effort.

"The city you're helping to protect is precious," Otah said. "The people whose lives you save won't think less of you for hearing wisdom from your daughter."

"Yes," Farrer said with a chuckle, "but they aren't on the council, are they."

"No," Otah said. "I understand that you are invested in sugar? There are cane fields east of Saraykeht, but most of what we have comes from Bakta. Much better land for it there. If Chaburi-Tan failed, we would feel the effect here and all through the Westlands."

Farrer grunted noncommittally.

"It's surprising how much Baktan trade flows through Chaburi-Tan. Not so much as through Saraykeht, but still a great deal. The island is easier to approach. And it's a good site for any trade in the south. Obar State, Eymond. Far Galt, for that. Did you know that nearly all the ore from Far Galt passes through the port at Chaburi-Tan?"

"Less since you've raised the taxes."

"I don't set those taxes," Otah said. "I appoint the port's administration. Usually they agree to pay a certain amount for the privilege and then try to make back what they've spent before their term ends."

"And how long are their terms?"

"As long as the Emperor is pleased to have them in that place," Otah said. "So long as I think they've done a good job with maintaining the seafront and keeping the flow of ships through, they may hold power for years. Or, if they've mismanaged things, perhaps even required a fleet to come out and save the city, they might be replaced."

The frown on Farrer's face was the most pleasant thing Otah had seen all morning. The truth of the matter was that Otah no more liked the Galt than he was liked by him. Their nations were old enemies, and however much Otah and Issandra plotted, there was a way in which their generation would die as enemies.

But what he did now, as little as Otah liked it personally, was intended for people as yet unborn, unconceived. It was a long game he was playing, and it got longer, it seemed, the less time he had to live.

Farrer coughed, sucked his teeth, and leaned forward.

"Forgive me, Most High," he said, formality returning to his diction. "What is the conversation we're having?"

"I would appoint you or your agent to oversee Chaburi-Tan's seafront," Otah said. "It would, I think, demonstrate that my commitment to joining our nations isn't only that you should send us your daughters."

"And have the council believe that I'm not only controlled by my wife and child, but also the tool of the Emperor, bought and paid for?" His tone was more amused than aggressive.

Otah pulled a small book from his sleeve and held it out.

"The accounting of the Chaburi-Tan seafront," Otah said. "We are an empire of fallen cities, Farrer-cha. But we were very high before, and falling for years hasn't yet brought us down to be even with most of the world."

The Galt clamped his pipe between his teeth and accepted the proffered book. Otah waited as he flipped through the thin pages. He saw Farrer's eyebrows rise when he reached the quarter's sums, and then again at the half-year's.

"You would want something from me," Farrer said.

"You have already lent me your boats," Otah said. "Your sailors. Let the others on the council see what effect that has."

"You can afford to give away this much gold to make them jealous?"

"I know that Ana-cha has objected to marrying Danat. I hope there may yet be some shift of her position. Then I would be giving the gold to my grandson's grandfather," Otah said.

"And if she doesn't?" Farrer asked, scowling. His eyes had narrowed like a seafront merchant distrustful of too good a bargain.

"If she doesn't, then I've made a poor wager," Otah said. "We are gamblers, Farrer-cha, just by getting up from bed in the morning."

Farrer Dasin didn't answer except to relax his gaze, laugh, and tuck the book into his belt. Otah took a pose that ended a meeting. It had a positive nuance that Dasin was unlikely to notice, but Otah didn't mind. It was as much for himself as for the Galt.

The walk back to the palaces seemed shorter, less haunted by nostalgia. He returned to his rooms, allowed himself to be changed into formal robes, and began the long, slow work of another day. The court was its customary buzz of rituals and requirements. The constant speculation on the Galtic treaty's fate made every other facet of the economic and political life of the Empire swing like a ship's mast in high seas. Otah did what he could to pour oil on the waters. For the most part, he succeeded.

Before the early sunset of middle autumn, Otah had seen the heads of both Galtic and Khaiate stone masons disputing a contract upon which the Galtic Council had already ruled. He had taken audiences with two other members of the High Council and three of the highest families of the utkhaiem. And, in the brightest moment of his day, a visibly unnerved representative of Obar State had arrived with gifts and assurances of the good relations between his small nation and the cities of the Khaiem.

No courier came from Idaan or Eiah. Likely his sister was still on the roads between Saraykeht and Pathai. There was no reason to expect word back so soon, and yet every time a servant entered his chambers with a folded paper, his belly tightened until he broke the seal.

The night began with a banquet held in the honor of Balasar Gice and the preparation of what the Galtic Council called the second fleet and the utkhaiem, dismissively and in private, the other ships. The great hall fluttered with fine robes and silk banners. Musicians and singing slaves hidden behind screens filled the air with soft music of Galtic composition. Lanterns of colored glass gave the light a feeling of belonging to some other, gentler world. Otah sat on his high dais, Balasar at his side. He caught a glimpse of Danat dressed in formal robes of black and gold, sitting among his peers of the high utkhaiem. The group included Shija Radaani. Though Farrer and Issandra Dasin were among the Galts present, Otah did not see Ana. He tried not to find her absence unnerving.

The food and drink had been prepared by the best cooks Otah could find: classic Galtic dishes made if not light at least less heavy; foods designed to represent each of the cities of the Khaiem; all of it served with bowls of the best wines the world could offer.

Peace, Otah meant the celebration to say. *As we send our armsmen and sailors away to fight and die together, let there be peace between us. If there cannot be peace in the world, at least let it be welcome here.* It pleased him to see the youth of both countries sitting together and talking, even as it disturbed him that so many places set aside for the utkhaiem remained empty.

He did not notice that Issandra had taken her leave until the note arrived. The servant was very young, having seen no more than sixteen summers, and he approached Balasar with a small message box of worked gold. Balasar plucked the folded paper from it, read the message, then nodded and waved the boy away. The musicians nearest them shifted to a light, contemplative song. Balasar leaned toward Otah, as if to whisper some comment upon the music.

"This is for you," the general murmured.

General Gice, please pass this to the Emperor with all haste discretion allows. I would prefer that it not be immediately obvious that I am communicating with him, but time may be short.

Emperor. Please forgive my note, but I believe something is going to happen

*in the moon garden of the third palace at the beginning of the entertainments
that you would be pleased to see. Consider claiming a moment's necessity and
joining me.*

It was signed with Issandra Dasin's chop.

Balasar was considering him silently. Otah slipped the paper into his sleeve.
It was less than half a hand before the acrobats and dancers, trained dogs and
fire-eaters were to take to the floor. It wasn't much time.

"I don't like this," Otah said, leaning toward Balasar so that no one could
overhear.

"You think it's a plot to assassinate you," Balasar said.

"Might it be?"

Balasar smiled out into the hall, his eyes flickering as if looking for concealed archers.

"She sent the message through me. That provides a witness. It isn't the sort
of thing I would do if I intended to kill you," Balasar said. "Still, if you go, take
a guard."

Otah felt the weight of the note in his sleeve, feather-light and yet enough
to command all his attention. He had almost decided to ignore it when, as the
trumpets blared the first of the entertainments to the floor, he noticed that
Danat had also gone. He slipped down from the back of the dais, chose two of
the guards that he recognized, and made his way out to the third palace.

The moon garden had been built as a theater; great half-circles of carved
stone set into a slope were covered with moss and snow ivy. At the deepest
recess, three old wooden doors led to hallways where players or musicians
could crouch, awaiting their entrance. The gardens were dark when he arrived,
not even a lantern glowing to mark the paths. Behind him, the guards were as
silent as shadows.

"Otah-cha," a woman whispered. "Here. Quickly."

Issandra huddled in the darkness under an ivy-choked willow. Otah walked
forward, his hands in a pose of query. Issandra didn't reply, her eyes on the
guards at his back. Her expression went from disapproval to acceptance barely
seen in the dim light. She motioned all of them close to her.

"What is this?" Otah asked as he crouched in the darkness.

"Hush," Issandra said. "They should almost be here. There now. Be quiet,
all of you."

One of the wooden doors at the base of the garden was opening, the light of
a lantern spilling out onto the green of the grass, the black of the soil. Otah
squinted. Ana Dasin stepped out. She wore a rough cloak over what appeared
to be simple peasant robes, but her face and hair would have proclaimed her in
the darkest teahouse. She looked like a girl who wanted to travel unnoticed
but didn't know the trick of it. As Otah watched, she raised her lantern, scanning the wide stone curve, and then sat down.

"What is—" he whispered.

Issandra pressed her hand to his mouth. One of the guards shifted, but Otah gestured him back. It wasn't everyone who could gag the Emperor of the Khaiem, but he was too curious to disrupt things over a point of etiquette. Besides which, he didn't truly care.

Another of the doors shifted and creaked open. Danat stepped out. Being discovered crouched in the ivy, eavesdropping on their own children might be the least dignified thing possible, so Otah tried to be very, very still. When Danat spoke, the sound carried perfectly.

"I received your message. I'm here."

"And I received your poem," Ana said.

It was too dark to actually see how deeply Danat blushed, but Otah recognized the discomfort in his son's body.

"Ah. That," he said.

Otah tapped Issandra on the shoulder and mouthed the word *poem?* Issandra pointed back down to their children.

"I am not a toy," Ana said. "If this is another scheme of your father's or my mother's, you can carry word back to them that it didn't work. I know better than to trust you."

"You think I've lied?" Danat said. "What have I said to you that wasn't true?"

"As if you'd let yourself be caught out," Ana said.

Danat sat, one leg tucked under him, the other bent. He looked up at her like a player in some ancient epic. In the dim light, his expression seemed bemused.

"Ask anything," he said. "Do it now. I won't lie to you."

Ana crossed her arms, looking down on Danat like a low-town judge. Her brows were furrowed.

"Are you trying to seduce me?"

"Yes," Danat said. His voice was calm and solid as stone.

"Why?"

"Because I think you are worth seducing," Danat said.

"Only that? Not to please your father or my mother?"

Danat chuckled. One of the guards at Otah's side shifted his weight, the leaves beneath him crackling. Neither of the children below had ears for it.

"It began that way, I suppose," Danat said. "A political alliance. A world to remake. All of that has its appeal, but it didn't write that poem."

Ana fumbled at her belt for a moment and drew out a folded sheet of paper. Danat hesitated, then reached up and accepted it from her. They were quiet. Otah sensed the tension in Issandra's crouched body. Ana was refusing the token. And then the girl spoke, and her mother relaxed.

"Read it," Ana said. "Read it to me."

Otah closed his eyes and prayed to all the gods there were that neither he nor Issandra nor either of the guards would sneeze or cough. He had never lived through a more excruciatingly awkward scene. Below, Danat cleared his throat and began to declaim.

It wasn't good. Danat's command of Galtic didn't extend to the subtlety of rhyme. The images were simple and puerile, the sexuality just under the surface of the words ham-fisted and uncertain, and worst of all of it, Danat's tone as he spoke was as sincere as a priest at temple. His voice shook at the end of the last stanza. Silence fell in the garden. One of the guards shook once with suppressed laughter and went still.

Danat folded the paper slowly, then offered it up to Ana. It hesitated there for a moment before the girl took it.

"I see," she said. Against all reason, her voice had softened. Otah could hardly believe it, but Ana appeared genuinely moved. Danat rose to stand a hand's breadth nearer to her than before. The lanterns flickered. The two children gazed at each other with perfect seriousness. Ana looked away.

"I have a lover," she said.

"You've made that quite clear," Danat replied, amusement in his voice.

Ana shook her head. The shadows hid her expression.

"I can't," she said. "You are a fine man, Danat. More an emperor than your father. But I've sworn. I've sworn before everyone . . ."

"I don't believe that," Danat said. "I've hardly known you, Ana-kya, and I don't believe the gods themselves could stop you from something if it was truly what you wanted. Say you won't have me, but don't tell me you're refusing me out of fear."

Ana began to speak, stumbled on the words, and went silent. Danat rose, and the girl took a step toward him.

And a moment later, "Does Hanchat know you're here?"

Ana was still, and then almost imperceptibly she shook her head. Danat put a hand on her shoulder and gently turned her to face him. Otah might have been imagining it, but he thought the girl's head inclined a degree toward that hand. Danat kissed Ana's forehead and then her mouth. Her hand, palm against Danat's chest, seemed too weak to push him away. It was Danat who stepped back.

He murmured something too low to hear, then bowed in the Galtic style, took his lantern, and left her. Ana slowly lowered herself to the ground. They waited, one girl alone in the night and four hidden spies with legs and backs slowly beginning to cramp. Without word or warning, Ana sobbed twice, rose, scooped up her own lantern, and vanished through the door she'd first come from. Otah let out a pained sigh and made his uncomfortable way out from beneath the willow. There were green streaks on his robe where his knees had ground into the ivy. The armsmen had the grace to move away a few paces, expressionless.

"We're doing well," Issandra said.

"I didn't hear a declaration of marriage," Otah said. He felt disagreeable despite the evidence of Ana's changing heart. He felt dishonest, and it made him sour.

"So long as nothing comes to throw her off, it will come. In time. I know my daughter. I've seen this all before."

"Really? How odd," Otah said. "I know my son, and I never have."

"Then perhaps Ana is a lucky woman," Issandra said. He was surprised to hear something wistful in the woman's voice. The moon passed behind a high cloud, deepening the darkness around them, and then was gone. Issandra stood before him, her head high and proud, her mouth in a half-smile. She was, he thought, an interesting woman. Not beautiful in the traditional sense, and all the more attractive for that.

"A marriage is what you make of it," she said.

Otah considered the words, then took a pose that both agreed and expressed a gentle sorrow. He did not know how much of his meaning she understood. She nodded and strode off, leaving him with his armsmen.

Otah suffered through the rest of the banquet and returned to his apartments, sure he would not sleep. The night air had cooled. The fire in the grate warmed his feet. The fear that had dogged him all these last months didn't vanish, but its hold upon him faded. Somewhere under the stars just then, Danat and Ana were playing out their drama in touches and whispers; Issandra and Farrer Dasin in silences and the knowledge of long association. Idaan was hunting, Ashua Radaani was hunting, Sinja was hunting. And he was alone and sleepless with nothing to do.

He closed his eyes and tried to feel Kiyan's presence, tried to bring some sense of her out of the scent of smoke and the sound of distant singing. He tricked himself into thinking that she was here, but not so well that he could forget it was a trick.

Tomorrow, there would be another wide array of men and women requesting his time. Another schedule of ritual and audience and meeting. Perhaps it would all go as well as today had, and he would end the day in his rooms, feeling old and maudlin despite his success. There were so many men and women in the court—in the world—who wanted nothing more than power. Otah, who held it, had known how little it changed.

He slept deeply and without dreams. When he woke, every man and woman of Galt had gone blind.

16

>+< It had been raining for two full days. Occasionally the water changed to sleet or hail, and small accumulations of rotten ice had begun to form in the sheltered corners of the courtyard. Maati closed his shutters against the low clouds and sat close to the fire, the weather tapping on wood like fingers on a table. It might almost have been pleasant if it hadn't made his spine stiffen and ache.

The cold coupled with Eiah's absence had turned life quiet and slow, like a bear preparing to sleep through the winter. Maati went down to the kitchen in the morning and ate with the others. Large Kae and Irit had started rehearsing old songs together to pass the time. They sang while they cooked, and the harmonies were prettier than Maati would have imagined. When Vanjit and Clarity-of-Sight were there, the andat would grow restive, its eyes shifting from one singer to the next and back again until Vanjit started to fidget and took her charge away. Small Kae had no ear for music, so instead spent her time reading the old texts that Clarity-of-Sight had been built from and asking questions about the finer points of their newly re-created grammar.

Most of the day, Maati spent alone in his rooms, or dressed in several thick robes, walking through the halls. He would not say it, but the space had begun to feel close and restricting. Likely it was only the sense of winter moving in.

With the journey to Pathai and back, along with the trading and provisioning, he couldn't expect Eiah's return for another ten days. He hadn't expected to feel that burden so heavily upon him, and so both delight and dread touched him when Small Kae interrupted his half-doze.

"She's come back. Vanjit's been watching from the classroom, and she says Eiah's come back. She's already turned from the high road, and if the path's not too muddy, she'll be here by nightfall."

Maati rose and opened the shutters, as if by squinting at the gray he could match Vanjit's sight. A gust of cold and damp pulled at the shutter in his hand. He was half-tempted to find a cloak of oiled silk and go out to meet her. It would be folly, of course, and gain him nothing. He ran a hand through the thin remnants of his hair, wondering how many days it had been since he'd bathed and shaved himself, and then realized that Small Kae was still there, waiting for him to speak.

"Well," he said, "whatever we have that's best, let's cook it up. Eiah-cha's going to have fresh supplies, so there's no point in saving it."

Small Kae grinned, took a pose that accepted his instruction, and bustled out. Maati turned back to the open window. Ice and mud and gloom. And set in it, invisible to him, Eiah and news.

There was no sunset; Eiah arrived shortly after the clouds had faded into darkness. In the light of hissing torches, the cart's wheels were beige with mud and clay. The horse trembled with exhaustion, driven too hard through the wet. Large Kae, clucking her tongue in disapproval, took the poor beast off to be rubbed down and warmed while the rest of them crowded around Eiah. She wrung the water from her hair with pale fingers, answering the first question before it was asked.

"Ashti Beg's left. She said she didn't want to come back. We were in a low town just south of here off the high road. She said we could talk about it, but when I got up in the morning, she'd already gone." She looked at Maati when she finished. "I'm sorry."

He took a pose that forgave and also diminished the scale of the thing, then waved her in. Vanjit followed, and then Irit and Small Kae. The meal was laid out and waiting. Barley soup with lemon and quail. Rice and sausage. Watered wine. Eiah sat near the brazier and ate like a woman starved, talking between mouthfuls.

"We never reached Pathai. There was a trade fair halfway to the city. Tents, carts, the wayhouse so full they were renting out space on the kitchen floor. There was a courier there gathering messages from all the low towns."

"So the letters were sent?" Irit asked. Eiah nodded and scooped up another mouthful of rice.

"Ashti Beg," Maati said. "Tell me more about her. Did she say why she left?"

Eiah frowned. Color was coming back to her cheeks, but her lips were still pale, her hair clinging to her neck like ivy.

"It was me," Vanjit said, the andat squirming in her lap. "It's my doing."

"Perhaps, but it wasn't what she said," Eiah replied. "She said she was tired, and that she felt we'd all gone past her. She didn't see that she would ever complete a binding of her own, or that her insights were particularly helping us. I tried to tell her otherwise, give her some perspective. If she'd stayed on until the morning, perhaps I could have."

Maati sipped his wine, wondering how much of what Eiah said was true, how much of it was being softened because Vanjit and Clarity-of-Sight were in the room. It seemed more likely to him that Ashti Beg had taken offense at Vanjit's misstep and been unable to forgive it. He recalled the woman's dry tone, her cutting humor. She had not been an easy woman or a particularly apt pupil, but he believed he would miss her.

"Was there other news? Anything of the Galts?" Vanjit asked. There was something odd about her voice, but it might only have been that Clarity-of-Sight had started its wordless, wailing complaint. Eiah appeared to notice nothing strange in the question.

"There would have been if I'd reached Pathai, I'd expect," she said. "But since there would have been nothing to do about it and our business was done early, I wanted to come back quickly."

"Ah," Vanjit said. "Of course."

Maati tugged at his fingers. There was something near disappointment in the girl's tone. As if she had expected someone that had not arrived.

"You're ready to work again?" Small Kae said. Irit flapped a cloth at her, and Small Kae took a pose that unasked the question. Eiah smiled.

"I've had a few thoughts," she said. "Let me look them over tonight after we unload the cart, and we can talk in the morning."

"Oh, there's no more work for you tonight," Irit said. "You've been on the road all this time. We can hand a few things down from a cart."

"Of course," Vanjit said. "You should rest, Eiah-kya. We'll be happy to help."

Eiah put down her soup and took a pose that offered gratitude. Something in the cant of her wrists caught Maati's attention, but the pose was gone as quickly as it had come and Eiah was sitting back, drinking wine and leaning her still-wet hair toward the fire. Large Kae rejoined them, smelling of wet horse, and Eiah told the whole story again for her benefit and then left for her rooms. Maati felt the impulse to follow her, to speak in private, but Vanjit took him by the hand and led him out to the cart with the others.

The supplies were something less than Maati had expected. Two chests of salted pork, a few jars of lard and flour and sweet oil. Bags of rice. It wasn't inconsiderable—certainly there was enough to keep them all well-fed for weeks, but likely not months. There were few spices, and no wine. Large Kae made a few small remarks about the failures of low-town trade fairs, and the others chuckled their agreement. The rain slackened, and then, as Vanjit balanced the last bag of rice on one hip and Clarity-of-Sight on the other, snow began to fall. Maati went back to his rooms, heated a kettle over his fire, and debated whether to try to boil enough water for a bath. Immersion was the one way he was sure he could chase the cold from his joints, but the effort required seemed worse than enduring the chill. And there was an errand he preferred to complete.

Light glowed through the cracks around Eiah's door. Dim and flickering, it was still more than a single night candle would have made. Maati scratched at the door. For a moment, nothing happened. Perhaps Eiah had taken to her cot. Perhaps she was elsewhere in the school. A soft sound, no more than a whisper, drew him back to the door.

"Eiah-kya?" he said, his voice low. "It's me."

Her door opened. Eiah had changed into a simple robe of thick wool, her hair tied back with a length of twine. She looked powerfully like her mother. The room she brought Maati into had once been a storage pantry. Her cot and brazier and a low table were all the furnishings. There was no window, and the air was thick with the heat and smoke from the coals.

Papers and scrolls lay on the table beside a wax tablet half-whitened by fresh notes. Medical texts in the languages of the Westlands, Eiah's own earlier drafts of the binding of Wounded. And also, he saw, the completed binding they had all devised for Clarity-of-Sight. Eiah sat on the cot, the frail structure creaking under her. She didn't look up at him.

"Why did she leave?" Maati asked. "Truth, now."

"I told her to," Eiah said. "She was frightened to come back. I told her that I understood. What happens if two poets come into conflict? If one poet has something like Floats-in-Air and the other has something like Sinking?"

"Or one poet can blind, and the other heal injury?"

"As an example," Eiah said.

Maati sighed and lowered himself to sit beside her. The cot complained. He laced his fingers together, looking at the words and diagrams without seeing them.

"I don't entirely know. It hasn't happened in my lifetime. It hasn't happened in generations."

"But it has happened," Eiah said.

"There was the war. The one that ended the Second Empire. That was . . .

what, ten generations ago? The andat are flesh because we've translated them into flesh, but they are also concepts. Abstractions. It might simply be that the poets' wills are set against each other's. A kind of wrestling match mediated through the andat. Whoever has the greater strength of mind and the andat more suited to the struggle gains the upper hand. Or it could be that the concepts of the two andat don't coincide, and any struggle would have to be expressed physically. In the world we inhabit. Or . . ."

"Or?"

"Or something else could happen. The grammar and meaning in one binding could relate to some structure or nuance in another. Imagine two singers in competition. What if they chose songs that harmonized? What if the words of one song blended with the words of the other, and something new came from it? Songs are a poor metaphor. What are the odds that the words of any two given songs would speak to each other? If the bindings are related in concept, if the *ideas* are near, it's much more likely that sort of resonance could happen. By chance."

"And what would that do?"

"I don't know," Maati said. "Nobody does. I can say that what was once a land of palm trees and rivers and palaces of sapphire is a killing desert. I can say that people who travel in the ruins of the Old Empire tend to die there. It might be from physical expressions of that old struggle. It might be from some interaction of bindings. There is no way to be sure."

Eiah was silent. She turned the pages of her medical books until she reached diagrams Maati recognized. Eyes cut through the center, eyes sliced through the back. He had seen them all thousands of times when Vanjit was preparing herself, and they had seemed like the keepers of great secrets. He hadn't considered at the time that each image was the result of some actual, physical orb meeting with an investigative blade, or that all the eyes pictured there were sightless.

He felt Eiah's sigh as much as heard it.

"What happened out there?" he asked. "The truth, not what you said in front of the others."

Eiah leaned forward. For a moment, Maati thought she was weeping, but she straightened again. Her eyes were dry, her jaw set. She had pulled a small box of carved oak from under the cot, and she handed it to him now. He opened it, the leather hinge loose and soft. Six folded pages lay inside, sewn at the edges and sealed with Eiah's personal sigil.

"You didn't send them?"

"It was true about the trade fair. We did find one. It wasn't very good, but it was there, so we stopped. There are Galts everywhere now. They came to Saraykeht at the start, and apparently the councillors and the court are all still there. There are others who have fanned out. The ones who believe that my father's plan is going to work."

"The ones who see a profit in it. Slavers?"

"Marriage brokers," Eiah said as if the terms were the same. "They've been traveling the low towns making lists of men in want of Galtic peasant girls to act as brood mares for their farms. Apparently eight lengths of copper will put a man's name on the list to travel to Galt. Two of silver for the list to haul a girl here."

Maati felt his belly twist. It had gone further than he had dared think.

"Most of them are lying, of course," Eiah said. "Taking money from the desperate and moving on. I don't know how many of them there are out there. Hundreds, I would guess. But, Maati-cha, the night I left? All of the Galts lost their sight. All of them, and at once. No one cares any longer what's happened with my brother and the girl he was supposed to marry. No one talks about the Emperor. All anyone cares about is the andat. They know that some poet somewhere has bound Blindness or something like it and loosed it against the Galts."

It was as if the air had gone from the room, as if Maati were suddenly on a mountaintop. His breath was fast, his heart pounding. It might have been joy or fear or something of each.

"I see," Maati said.

"Uncle, they hate us. All those farmers and traders and shepherds? All those men who thought that they would have wives and children? All those women who thought that even if it hadn't come from their body, at least there would be a baby nearby to care for? They think we've taken it from them. And I have never seen so much rage."

Maati felt as if he'd been struck, caught in the moment between the blow and the bloom of pain. He said something, words stringing together without sense and trailing to silence. He put his face in his hands.

"You didn't know," Eiah said. "She didn't tell you."

"Vanjit's done this," Maati said. "She can undo it. I can . . ." He stopped, catching his breath. He felt as if he'd been running. His hands trembled. When Eiah spoke, her voice was as level and calm as a physician's announcing a death.

"Twice."

Maati turned to her, his hands taking a pose of query. Eiah put her hand on the table, papers shifting under her fingers with a sound like sand against glass.

"This is twice, Maati-cha. First with Ashti Beg, and now . . . Gods. Now with all of Galt."

"Is this why Ashti Beg left?" Maati asked. "The true reason?"

"The true reason is that she was afraid of Vanjit," Eiah said. "And I couldn't reassure her."

"Children," Maati said. The pain in his chest was easing, the shock of the news fading away. "I'll speak with Vanjit. She did this all. She can undo it as well. And . . . and it does speak to the purpose. We wanted to announce that the andat had returned to the world. She's done that in no small voice."

"Maati-cha," Eiah began, but he kept talking, fast and loud.

"This is why they did it, you know. All those tests and lies and opportunities to prove ourselves. Or fail to prove ourselves. They broke us to the lead first, and gave us power when they knew we could be controlled."

"It looked like a wiser strategy, if this is the alternative," Eiah said. "Do you think she'll listen to you?"

"Listen, yes. Do as I command? I don't know. And I don't know that I'd want her to. She's learning responsibility. She's learning her own limits. Even if I could tell her what they are, she couldn't learn by having it said. She's . . . exploring."

"She's killed thousands of people, at the least."

"Galts," Maati said. "She's killed Galts. We were never here to save them. Yes, Eiah-kya. Vanjit went too far, and because she's holding an andat, there are consequences. When you slaughter a city? When you send your army to kill a little girl's family in front of her? There are consequences to that too. Or by all the gods there should be."

"You're saying this is justice?" Eiah asked.

"We made peace with Galt," Maati said. "None of Vanjit's family were avenged. There was no justice for them because it was simpler for Otah to ignore their deaths. Just as it's simpler for him to ignore all the women of the cities. Vanjit has an andat, and so her will is now more important than your father's. I don't see that makes it any more or less just."

Eiah took a pose that respectfully disagreed, then dropped her hands to her sides.

"I don't argue that she's gone too far," Maati said. "She's killing a horsefly with a hammer. Only that it's not as bad as it first seems. She's still young. She's still new to her powers."

"And that forgives everything?" Eiah said.

"Don't," Maati said more sharply than he'd intended. "Don't be so quick to judge her. You'll be in her position soon enough. If all goes well."

"I wonder what I'll forget. How I'll go too far," Eiah said, and sighed. "How did we ever think we could do good with these as our tools?"

Maati was silent for a moment. His memory turned on Heshai and Seedless, Cehmai and Stone-Made-Soft. The sickening twist that was Sterile, moving through his own mind like an eel through muddy water.

"Is there another way to fix it?" Maati asked. "After Sterile, is there a way other than this to make the world whole? All those women who will never bear a child. All those men whose money is going to charming Galtic liars. Is there a way to make the world well again besides what we're doing?"

"We could wait," Eiah said, her voice gray and toneless. "Given enough time, we'll all die and be forgotten."

Maati was silent. Eiah closed her eyes. The flame of the night candle fluttered in a draft that smelled of fresh snow and wet cloth. Eiah's gaze focused inward, on some landscape of her own mind. He didn't think she liked what she saw there. She opened her mouth as if to speak, closed it again, and looked away.

"You're right, though," Maati said. "This is twice."

They found Vanjit in her room, the andat wailing disconsolately as she rocked it in her arms. Maati entered the room first to Vanjit's gentle smile, but her expression went blank when Eiah came in after him and slid the door shut behind her. The andat's black eyes went from Vanjit to Eiah and back, then it squealed in delight and held its thick, short arms up to Eiah as if it was asking to be held.

"You know, then," Vanjit said. "It was inevitable."

"You should have told me what you intended," Maati said. "It was a dangerous, rash thing to do. And it's going to have consequences."

Vanjit put Clarity-of-Sight on the floor at her feet. The thing shrieked complaint, and she bent toward it, her jaw clenched. Maati recognized the push and pull of wills between andat and poet. Even before the andat whimpered and went silent, he had no doubt of the outcome.

"You were going to tell the world of what we'd done anyway," Vanjit said. "But you couldn't be sure they would have stopped the Emperor, could you? This way they can't go forward."

"Why didn't you tell Maati-kvo what you were doing?" Eiah asked.

"Because he would have told me not to," Vanjit said, anger in her voice.

"I would have," Maati said. "Yes."

"It isn't fair, Maati-kya," Vanjit said. "It isn't right that they should come here, take our places. They were the killers, not us. They were the ones who brought blades to our cities. Any of the poets could have destroyed Galt at any time, and we never, ever did."

"And that makes it right to crush them now?" Eiah demanded.

"Yes," Vanjit said. There were tears in her eyes.

Eiah tilted her head. Long familiarity told Maati the thoughts that occupied Eiah's mind. This girl, sitting before them both, had been granted the power of a small god by their work. Maati's and Eiah's. The others had helped, but the three of them together in that room carried the decision. And so the weight of its consequences.

"It was ill advised," Maati said. "The low towns should have been our allies and support. Now they've been angered."

"Why?" Vanjit asked.

"They don't know what our plan is," Maati said. "They don't know about Eiah and Wounded. All they see is that there was a glimmer of hope. Yes, I know it was a thin, false hope, but it was all that they had."

"That's stupid," Vanjit said.

"It only seems that way because we know more than they," Eiah said.

"We can tell them," Vanjit said.

"If we can calm them long enough to listen," Maati said. "But that isn't what I've come here for. I am your teacher, Vanjit-cha. I need two things of you. Do you understand?"

The girl looked at the ground, her hands rising in a pose of acceptance appropriate for a student to her master.

"First, you must never take this kind of action with the andat without telling me. We have too many plans and they are too delicate for any of us to act without the others knowing it."

"Eiah sent Ashti Beg away," Vanjit said.

"And we discussed that possibility before they left," Maati said. "The second thing . . . What you've done to the Galts, only you can undo."

The girl looked up now. Anger flashed in her eyes. The andat gurgled and clapped its tiny hands. Maati held up a finger, insisting that she wait until he had finished.

"If you hold to this," he said, "thousands of people will die. Women and children who are innocent of any crime."

"It's what they did to us," she said. *What they did to me.* Maati reached forward and took her hand.

"I understand," he said. "I won't tell you to undo this thing. But for me, think carefully about how the burden of those deaths will weigh on you. You're angry now, and anger gives you strength. But when it's faded, you will still be responsible for what you've done."

"I will, Maati-kvo," Vanjit said.

Eiah made a sound in the back of her throat, its meaning unguessable. Maati smiled and put a hand on Vanjit's shoulder.

"Well. That's settled. Now, I suppose it's time to get back to work. Give these people in the low towns something to celebrate."

"You've done it, then, Eiah-kya?" Vanjit asked. "You've found the insight you needed? You understand Wounded?"

Eiah was quiet for a moment, looking down at Vanjit and Clarity-of-Sight. Her lips twitched into a thin, joyless smile.

"Closer," Eiah said. "I've come closer."

17

Seeing Balasar Gice shook Otah more than he had expected. He had always known that the general was not a large-framed man, but his presence had always filled the room. Seeing him seated at a table by the window with his eyes the gray of old pearls, Otah felt he was watching the man die. The robes seemed too large on him, or his shoulders suddenly grown small.

Outside the window, the morning sun lit the sea. Gulls called and complained to one another. A small plate held the remnants of fresh cheese and cut apple; the cheese flowed in the day's heat, the pale flesh of the apple had gone brown. Otah cleared his throat. Balasar smiled, but didn't bother turning his head toward the sound.

"Most High?" Balasar asked.

"Yes," Otah said. "I came . . . I came when I heard."

"I am afraid Sinja will have to do without my aid," Balasar said, his voice ironic and bleak. "It seems I'll be in no condition to sail."

Otah leaned against the window's ledge, his shadow falling over Balasar. The general turned toward him. His voice was banked rage, his expression impotence.

"Did you know, Otah? Did you know what they were doing?"

"This wasn't my doing," Otah said. "I swear that."

"My life was taking your god-ghosts out of the world. I thought we'd done it. Even after what you bastards did to me, to all of us, I was content trying to make peace. I lost my men to it, and I lived with that because the loss meant something. However desperate the cost, at least we'd be rid of the fucking andat. And now . . ."

Balasar struck the table with an open palm, the report like stone breaking. Otah lifted his hands toward a pose that offered comfort, and then stopped and let his arms fall to his sides.

"I'm sorry," Otah said. "I will send my best agents to find the new poet and resolve this. Until then, all of you will be cared for and—"

Balasar's laughter was a bark.

"Where do I begin, Most High? We will all be cared for? Do you really think this has only happened to the Galts who came to your filthy city? I will wager any odds you like that everyone back home is suffering the same things we are. How many fishermen were on their boats when it happened? How many people were traveling the roads? You could no more care for all of us than pluck the moon out of the sky."

"I'm sorry for that," Otah said. "Once we've found the poet and talked to . . ." He stumbled on his words, caught between the expected *him* and the more likely *her*.

Balasar gestured to him, palms up as if displaying something small and obvious.

"If it wasn't your pet andat that did this, then what hope do you have of resolving anything?" Balasar asked. "They may have left you your sight for the moment, but there's nothing you can do. It's the andat. There's no defense. There's no counterattack that means anything. Gather your armsmen. Take to the field. Then come back and die beside us. You can do *nothing*."

This is my daughter's work, Otah thought but didn't say. I can hope that she still loves me enough to listen.

"You've never felt this," Balasar said. "The rest of us? The rest of the world? We know what it is to be faced with the andat. You can't end this. You can't even negotiate. You have no standing now. The best you can do is beg."

"Then I will beg," Otah said.

"Enjoy that," Balasar said, sitting back in his chair. It was like watching a showfighter collapse at the end of a match. The vitality, the anger, the violence snuffed out, and the general was only a small Galtic man with crippled eyes, waiting for some kind soul to take away the remains of his uneaten meal. Otah rose and walked quietly from the room.

All through the city, the scenes were playing out. Men and women who had been well the night before were in states of rage and despair. They blundered into the unfamiliar streets, screaming, swinging whatever weapon came to hand at anyone who tried to help them. Or else they wept. Or, like Balasar, folded in upon themselves. The last was the most terrible.

Balasar had been only the first stop in Otah's long, painful morning journey. He'd meant to call on each of the high councillors, to promise his efforts at restoration and the best of care until then. The general had spoiled the plan. Otah did see two more men, made the same declarations. Neither of the others scoffed, but Otah could see that his words rang as hollow as a gourd.

Instead of the third councillor, Otah went back to his palaces. He prayed as he walked, that some message would have come from Idaan. None had. Instead, his audience chambers were filled with the utkhaiem, some in fine robes hastily thrown on, others still in whatever finery they had slept in. The sound of their voices competing one over another was louder than surf and as incomprehensible. Everywhere he walked, their eyes turned toward him. Otah walked with a grave countenance, his spine as straight as he could keep it. He greeted the shock and the fear with the same equanimity as the expressions of joy.

There was more joy than he had expected. More than he had hoped. The andat had come back to the world, and the Galts made to suffer, and that was somehow a cause to celebrate. Otah didn't respond to those calls, but he did begin a mental catalog of who precisely was laughing, who weeping. Someday, he told himself, someday the best of these men and women would be rewarded, the worst left behind. Only he didn't know how.

In his private rooms, the servants fluttered like moths. No schedules were right, no plans were made. Orders from the Master of Tides contradicted the instructions from the Master of Keys, and neither allowed for what the guards and armsmen said they needed to do. Otah built his own fire in the grate, lighting it from the stub of a candle, and let raw chaos reign about him.

Danat found him there, looking into the fire. His son's eyes were wide, but his shoulders hadn't yet sagged. Otah took a pose of welcome and Danat crouched before him.

"What are you doing, Papa-kya," Danat said. "You're just sitting here?"

"I'm thinking," Otah said, aware as he did so how weak the words sounded.

"They need you. You have to gather the high utkhaiem. You have to tell them what's going on."

He looked at his son. The strong face, the sincere eyes the same rich brown as Kiyan's had been. He would have made a good emperor. Better than Otah had. He took his boy's hand.

"The fleet is doomed," Otah said. "Galt is broken. These new poets, wherever they are, no longer answer to the Empire. What would you have me say?"

"That," Danat said. "If nothing else, say that. Say what everyone knows is true. How can that be wrong?"

"Because I have nothing to say after it," Otah said. "I don't know what to do. I don't have an answer."

"Then tell them that we're thinking of one," Danat said.

Otah sat silent, his hands on his knees, and let the fire in the grate fill his eyes. Danat shook his shoulder with a sound that was part frustration and part plea. When Otah couldn't find a response, Danat stood, took a pose that ended an audience, and strode out. The young man's impatience lingered in the air like incense.

There had been a time when Otah had been possessed of the certainty of youth. He had held the fate of nations in his hands, and done what needed doing. He had killed. Somewhere the years had pressed it out of him. Danat would see the same complexity, futility, and sorrow, given time. He was young. He wasn't tired yet. His world was still simple.

Servants came, and Otah turned them away. He considered going to his desk, writing another of his letters to Kiyan, but the effort of it was too much. He thought of Sinja, riding the swift autumn waves outside Chaburi-Tan and waiting for aid that would never come. Would he know? Were there Galts enough among his crew to guess what had happened?

The world was so large and so complex, it was almost impossible to believe that it could collapse so quickly. Idaan had been right again. All the problems that had plagued him were meaningless in the face of this.

Eiah. Maati. The people he had failed. They had taken the world from him. Well, perhaps they'd have a better idea what to do with it. And if a few hundred or a few thousand Galts died, there was nothing Otah could do to save them. He was no poet. He could have been. One angry, rootless boy's decision differently made, and everything would have been different.

A servant woman came and took away a tray of untouched food that Otah hadn't known was there. The pine branches in the grate were all ashes now. The sun was almost at the height of its day's arc. Otah rubbed his eyes and only then recognized the sound that had drawn him from his reverie. Trumpets and bells. Callers' voices ringing out over the palaces, over the city, over sea and sky and everything in it. A pronouncement was to be made, and all men and women of the utkhaiem were called to hear it.

He made his way through the back halls, set like stagecraft, that allowed him to appear at the appropriate ritual moment. What few servants there were bent themselves almost double in poses of obeisance as he passed. Otah ignored them.

A side hall, almost too narrow for a man to walk down, took him to a hidden seat. Years before, it had been a place where the Khai Saraykeht could watch entertainments without being seen. Now it was Otah's own. He looked down upon the hall. It was packed so thickly there was no room to sit. The cushions meant to allow people to take their rest were all being trampled underfoot. Whisperers had to fight to hold their positions. And among the bright robes and jeweled headdresses of the utkhaiem, there were also the tunics and gray, empty eyes of Galts come to hear what was said. He saw them and thought of an old dream he'd had of Heshai, the poet he had once killed, attending a dinner though still very much dead. Corpses walked among the utkhaiem. Balasar was not among them.

Silence took the hall as if someone had cupped his hands over Otah's ears, and he turned toward the dais. His son stood there, his robe the pale of mourning.

"My friends," Danat said. "There is little I can say which you do not already know. Our brothers and sisters of Galt have been struck. The only plausible cause is this: a new poet has been trained, a new andat has been bound, and, against all wisdom, it has been used first as a weapon."

Danat paused as the whisperers repeated his words out through the wide galleries and, no doubt, into the streets.

"The fleet is in peril," Danat continued. "Chaburi-Tan placed at risk. We do not know who the poet is that has done this thing. We cannot trust that they will be as quick to blind our enemies as they have our friends. We cannot trust that they will undo the damage they have caused to our new allies. Our new families. And so my father has asked me to find this new poet and kill him."

Otah's fingers pressed against the carved stone until his joints ached. His chest ached with dread. *He doesn't know*, Otah wanted to shout. *His sister is part of this, and he does not know it*. He shook and kept silent. There was only the swelling roar of the people, the whisperers shouting above it, and his son standing proud and still, shoulders set.

"There are some among us who look upon what has happened today as a moment of hope. They believe that the andat returned to the world marks the end of our hard times. With all respect, it marks their beginning, and neither I nor . . ."

Otah turned away, pushing his way down the narrow hall, afraid to let his hands leave the stone for fear he should lose his balance. In the dim hallways, he gathered himself. He had expected shame. Seeing Danat speaking as he himself could not, he thought that he would feel shame. He didn't. There was only anger.

The first servant he found, he grabbed by the sleeve and spun halfway around. The woman started to shout at him, then saw who he was, saw his face, and went pale.

"Whatever you were doing, stop it," Otah said. "Find me the Master of Tides. Bring her to my rooms. Do it now."

She might have taken a pose that accepted the command or one of obeisance or any other of the hundred thousand things the physical grammar of the Khaiem might express. Otah didn't stop long enough to see, and didn't care.

In his rooms, he called for a traveler's basket. The thin wicker shifted and creaked as he pulled the simplest robes from his wardrobes and stuffed them in, one atop the other like they were canvas trousers. The dressing servants made small pawing movements, and Otah didn't bother to find out whether they were meant to help or slow him before he sent them all away. He found eight identical pairs of strapped leather boots, put three pairs into his basket, then snarled and took the extra ones back out. He only had two feet, he didn't need more boots than that. He didn't notice the Master of Tides until the woman made a small sound, like someone stepping on a mouse.

"Good," Otah said. "You have something to write with?"

She fumbled with her sleeve and pulled out a small ledger and a finger charcoal. Otah reeled off half-a-dozen names, all the heads of high families of the utkhaiem. He paused, then named Balasar Gice as well. The Master of Tides scribbled, the charcoal graying her fingers.

"That is *my* High Council," Otah said. "Here with you as witness, I invest them with the power to administrate the Empire until Danat or I return. Is that clear enough?"

"Most High," the Master of Tides said, her face pale and bloodless, "there has never . . . the authority of the Emperor can't be . . . and Gice-cha isn't even . . ."

Otah strode across the room toward her, blood rushing in his ears. The Master of Tides fell back a step, anticipating a blow, but Otah only plucked the ledger from her hands. The charcoal had fallen to the floor, and Otah scooped it up, turned to a fresh page, and wrote out the investiture he'd just spoken. When he handed it back, the Master of Tides opened and closed her mouth like a fish on sand, then said, "The court. The utkhaiem. A council with explicit imperial authority? This . . . can't be done."

"It can," Otah said.

"Most High, forgive me, but what you've suggested here changes everything! It throws aside all *tradition*!"

"I do that sometimes," Otah said. "Get me a horse."

Danat's force was small—a dozen armsmen with swords and bows, two steamcarts with rough shedlike structures on the flats, and Danat in a wool huntsman's robes. Otah's own robe was leather dyed the red of roses; his horse was taller at the shoulder than the top of his own head. The wicker traveler's basket jounced against the animal's flank as he cantered to Danat's side.

"Father," Danat said. He took no pose, but his body was stiff and defiant.

"I heard your speech. It was rash," Otah said. "What was your plan, now that I've sent you off to find and kill this new poet?"

"We're going north to Utani," Danat said. "It's central, and we can move in any direction once we've gotten word where he is."

"She," Otah said. "Wherever *she* is."

Danat blinked, his spine relaxing in his surprise.

"And you can't announce a plan like this, Danat-kya," Otah said. "No matter how fast you ride, word will move faster. And you'll know when the news has reached her, because you'll be just as crippled as the Galts."

"You knew about this?" Danat murmured.

"I know some things. I'd had reports," Otah said. His mount whickered uneasily. "I had taken some action. I didn't know it had gone so far. Utani is the wrong way. We need to ride west. Toward Pathai. And whichever rider is fastest goes ahead and stops any couriers heading back toward Saraykeht. I'm expecting a letter, but we can meet it on the road."

"You can't go," Danat said. "The cities need you. They need to see that there's someone in control."

"They do see that. They see it's the poet," Otah said.

Danat glanced at the steamcarts with their covered burdens. He looked nervous and lost. Otah felt the impulse to tell him, there on the open street, what he was facing: Maati's plan, his own reluctance to act, the specter of Eiah's involvement, Idaan's mission. He restrained himself. There would be time later, and fewer people who might overhear.

"Papa-kya," Danat said. "I think you should stay here. They need . . ."

"They need the poets ended," Otah said, knowing as he said it that he also meant his daughter. For a moment, he saw her. In his imagination, she was always younger than the real woman. He saw her dark eyes and furrowed brow as she studied with the court physicians. He felt the warmth and weight of her, still small enough to rest in his arms. He smelled the sour-milk breath she'd had before the soft place in her skull had grown closed. It might not come to that, he told himself.

He also knew that it might.

"We'll do this together," Otah said. "The two of us."

"Papa . . ."

"You can't stop me from this, Danat-kya," Otah said gently. "I'm the Emperor."

Danat tried to speak, first confusion in his eyes, then distress, and then amused resignation. Otah looked out at the armsmen, their eyes averted. The steamcarts chuffed and shuddered, the sheds on them larger than some homes Otah had kept as a child. The anger rose in him again. Not with Danat or Eiah, Maati or Idaan. His anger was with the gods themselves and the fate that had brought him here, and it burned in him.

"West," Otah called. "West. All of us. Now."

They passed the arch that marked the edge of the city at three hands past midday. Men and women had come out, lining the streets as they passed. Some cheered them, others merely watched. Few, Otah thought, were likely to believe that the old man at the front was truly the Emperor.

The buildings west of the city proper grew lower and squat. Instead of roof tiles, they had layers of water-grayed wood or cane thatching. The division between the last of Saraykeht and the nearest low town was invisible. Traders pulled aside to let them pass. Feral dogs yipped at them from the high grass and followed along just out of bowshot. The sun slipped down in its arc, blinding Otah and drawing tears.

A thousand small memories flooded Otah's mind like raindrops in an evening storm. A night he'd spent years before, sleeping in a hut made from grass and mud. The first horse he'd been given when he took the colors of House Siyanti and joined the gentleman's trade. He had traveled these very roads, back then. When his hair had still been dark and his back still strong and Kiyan still the loveliest wayhouse keeper in all the cities he had seen.

They rode until full dark came, stopping at a pond. Otah stood for a moment, looking into the dark water. It wasn't quite cold enough for ice to have formed on its surface. His spine and legs ached so badly he wondered whether he would be able to sleep. The muscles of his belly protested when he tried to bend. It had been years since he'd taken to the road in anything faster or more demanding than a carried litter. He remembered the pleasant near-exhaustion at the end of a long day's ride, and his present pain had little in common with it. He thought about sitting on the cool, wet grass. He was more than half afraid that once he sat down, he wouldn't be able to stand.

Behind him, the kilns of the steamcarts had been opened, and the armsmen were cooking birds over the coals. The smaller of the two sheds perched atop the steamcarts had been opened to reveal tightly rolled blankets, crates of soft fuel coal, and earthenware jars inscribed with symbols for seeds, raisins, and salted fish. As Otah watched, Danat emerged from the second shed, standing alone in the shadows at the end of the cart. One of the armsmen struck up a song, and the others joined in. It was the kind of thing Otah himself would have done, back when he had been a different man.

"Danat-kya," he said when he'd walked close enough to be heard over the good cheer of their companions. His son squatted at the edge of the cart, and then sat. In the light from the kilns, Danat seemed little more than a deeper shadow, his face hidden. "There are some things we should discuss."

"There are," Danat said, and his voice pulled Otah back.

Otah shifted to sit at his son's side. Something in his left knee clicked, but there was no particular pain, so he ignored it. Danat laced his fingers.

"You're angry that I've come?" Otah said.

"No," Danat said. "It's not . . . not that, quite. But I hadn't thought that you would be here, or that we'd be going west. I made arrangements with my own plan set, and you've changed it."

"I can apologize. But this is the right thing. I can't swear that Pathai is—"

"That's not what I'm trying . . . Gods," Danat said. He turned to his father, his eyes catching the kiln light and flashing with it. "Come on. You might as well know."

Danat shifted, rose, and walked across the wide, wooden back of the steamcart. The shed's door was shut fast. As Otah pulled himself up, grunting, Danat worked a thick iron latch. The armsmen's singing faltered. Otah was aware of eyes fixed upon them, though he couldn't see the men as more than silhouettes.

Otah made his way to the shed's open door. Inside was pure darkness. Danat stood, latch in his hand, silent. Otah was about to speak when another voice came from the black.

"Danat?" Ana Dasin asked. "Is it you?"

"It is," Danat said. "And my father."

Gray-eyed, the Galtic girl emerged from the darkness. She wore a blouse of simple cotton, a skirt like a peasant worker's. Her hands moved before her, testing the air until they found the wood frame of the shed's door. Otah must have made a sound, because she turned as if to look at him, her gaze going past him and into nothing. He almost took a pose of formal greeting but stopped himself.

"Ana-cha," he said.

"Most High," she replied, her chin high, her brows raised.

"I didn't expect to see you here," he said.

"I went to her as soon as I heard what had happened," Danat said. "I swore it was nothing that we'd done. We hadn't been trying to recapture the andat. She didn't believe me. When I decided to go, I asked her to come. As a witness. We've left word for Farrer-cha. Even if he disapproves, it doesn't seem he'd be able to do much about it before we returned."

"You know this is madness," Otah said softly.

Ana Dasin frowned, hard lines marking her face. But then she nodded.

"It makes very little difference whether I die in the city or on the road," she said. "If this isn't treachery on the part of the Khaiem, then I don't see that I have anything to fear."

"We are on an improvised campaign against powers we cannot match. I can name half-a-dozen things to fear without stopping to think," Otah said. He sighed, and the Galtic girl's expression hardened. Otah went on, letting a hint of bleak amusement into his voice. "But I suppose if you've come, you've come. Welcome to our hunt, Ana-cha."

He nodded to his son and stepped back. Her voice recalled him.

"Most High," she said. "I want to believe Danat. I want to think that he had nothing to do with this."

"He didn't," Otah said. The girl weighed his words, and then seemed to accept them.

"And you?" she said. "Was any of this yours?"

Otah smiled. The girl couldn't see him, but Danat did.

"Only my inattention," Otah said. "It's a failure I've come to correct."

"So the andat can blind you as easily as he has us," Ana said, stepping out of the shed and onto the steamcart. "You aren't protected any more than I am."

"That's true," Otah said.

Ana went silent, then smiled. In the dim light of the fire, he could see her mother in the shape of her cheek.

"And yet you take our side rather than ally with the poets," she said. "So which of us is mad?"

18

⟩+⟨ The snow fell and stayed, as deep as Maati's three fingers together. The winds of autumn whistled through the high, narrow windows that had never known glass. The women—Eiah, Irit, and the two Kaes—were in a small room, clustered around a brazier and talking with hushed fervor about grammar and form, the distinctions between age and wounds and madness. Vanjit, wrapped in thick woolen robes and a cloak of waxed silk, was sitting on a high wall, her gaze to the east. She sang lullabies to Clarity-of-Sight, and her voice would have been beautiful if she'd been cradling a real babe. Maati considered interrupting her or else returning to the work with the others, but both options were worse than remaining alone. He turned away from the great bronze door and retreated into the darkness.

It would be only weeks until winter was upon them. Not the killing storms of the north, but enough that even the short journey to Pathai would become difficult. He tried to imagine the long nights and cold that waited for him, for all of them, and he wondered how they would manage it.

A darkness had taken Eiah since her return. He saw it in her eyes and heard the rasp of it in her voice, but there was no lethargy about it. She was awake before him every morning and took to her bed long after sunset. Her attention was bent to the work of her binding, and her ferocity seemed to pull the others in her wake. Only Vanjit held herself apart, attending only some of Eiah's discussions. It was as if there were a set amount of attention, and as Eiah bore down, Vanjit floated up like a kite. Maati, caught between the pair, only felt tired and sick and old.

It had been years since he had lived in one place, and then it had been as the permanent guest of the Khai Machi. He had had a library, servants who brought him wine and food. Eiah had been no more than a girl, then. Bright, engaged, curious. But more than that, she had been joyful. And he remembered himself as being a part of that joy, that comfort.

He lumbered into one of the wide, bare rooms where rows and columns of cots had once held boys no older than ten summers, wrapped in all the robes they owned to keep off the cold. He leaned against the wall, feeling the rough stone against his back.

Another winter in this place. There was a time when he'd thought it wise.

Footsteps came from behind him. Vanjit's. He knew them from the sound.

He didn't turn to greet her. When she stepped into the room, waxed silk shining like leather, she didn't at first look at him. She had grown beautiful in an odd way. The andat held against her hip clung to her, and there was a peace in her expression that lent her an air of serenity. He wanted to trust her, to take her success as the first of a thousand ways in which he would be able to set the world right, to unmake his mistakes.

"Maati-kvo," Vanjit said. Her voice was low and soft as a woman newly woken.

"Vanjit," he said, taking a pose of greeting.

She and the andat came to sit at his side. The tiny thing balled its hands in the folds of Maati's robe, tugging as if to draw his attention. Vanjit appeared not to notice.

"Eiah-cha is doing well, isn't she?" Vanjit asked.

"I think so," Maati said. "She's taken a wide concept, and that's always difficult. She's very serious, though. There are a few flaws. Structures that work against each other instead of in concert."

"How long?" Vanjit asked. Maati rubbed his eyes with the palms of his hands.

"Until she's ready? If she finds a form that resolves the conflict, I suppose she could start the last phase tomorrow. Two weeks. Three at the earliest. Or months more. I don't know."

Vanjit nodded to herself, not looking up at him. The andat tugged at his robe again. Maati looked down into the black, eager eyes. The andat gave its wide, toothless grin.

"We've been talking," Vanjit said. "Clarity-of-Sight and I have been talking about Eiah and what she's doing. He pointed something out that I hadn't considered."

That was possible, but only in a fashion. The andat was a part of her, as all of them reflected the poets who had bound them. Whatever thought it had presented in the deep, intimate battle it waged with Vanjit, it had to have originated with her. Still, she was as capable of surprising herself as any of them. Maati took a pose that invited her to continue.

"We can't know how Eiah-cha's binding will go," Vanjit said. "I know that we were first as a test of the grammar. That Clarity-of-Sight exists is proof that the bindings can work. It isn't proof that Eiah-cha . . . Don't misunderstand, Maati-kvo. I know as well as anyone that Eiah-cha is brilliant. Without her, I would never have managed my binding. But until she makes the attempt, we can't be sure that she's the right sort of mind to be a poet. Even with all our work, she might still fail."

"That's true," Maati said, trying to turn away from the thought even as he spoke.

"It would all end, wouldn't it? What I can do, what we can do. It wouldn't mean anything without Eiah-cha. She's the one who can undo what Sterile did, and unless she can do that . . ."

"She's our best hope," Maati said.

"Yes," Vanjit said, and turned to look up at Maati. Her face was bright. "Yes, our best hope. But not the only one."

The andat at her hip clucked and giggled to itself, clapping tiny hands. Maati took a pose of query.

"We know for certain that we have one person who could bind an andat, because I already have. I want Eiah-cha to win through as badly as anyone, but if her binding does fail, I could take it up."

Maati smiled because he could think of nothing else to do. Dread knotted in his chest. His breath had grown suddenly short, and the warehouse-wide walls of the sleeping quarters had narrowed. Vanjit stood, her hand on his sleeve. Maati took a moment, shook his head.

"Are you well, Maati-kvo?" Vanjit asked.

"I'm old," he said. "It's nothing. Vanjit-kya, you can't hold another andat. You of all of us know how much of your attention Clarity-of-Sight requires."

"I would have to release him for a time," Vanjit said. "I understand that. But what makes him him comes from me, doesn't it? All the things that aren't innate to the idea of sight made clear. So when I bind Wounded, it would be almost like having him back. It would be, because it would come from me, just as he does."

"It . . . it might," Maati said. His head still felt light. A chill sweat touched his back. "I suppose it might. But the risk of it would also be huge. Once the andat was let go, you wouldn't be able to recall it. Even if you were to bind another, Clarity-of-Sight would be gone. We have the power now . . ."

"But my power doesn't mean anything," Vanjit said. Her voice was taking on a strained tone, as if some banked anger was rising in her. "Eiah matters. Wounded matters."

He thought of the Galts, blinded. Had Vanjit held Wounded, they would doubtless all have died. A nation felled—every woman, every man—by invisible swords, axes, stones. It was a terrible power, but they weren't here for the benefit of the Galts. He put his hand over Vanjit's.

"Let us hope it never comes to that," he said. "It would be far, far better to have two poets. But if it does, I'm glad you'll be here."

The girl's face brightened and she darted forward, kissing Maati's lips as brief and light as a butterfly. The andat on her hip gurgled and flailed. Vanjit nodded as if it had spoken.

"We should go," Vanjit said. "We've spent so much time talking about how to approach you, I've neglected the classes. Thank you, Maati-kvo. I can't tell you how much it means to know that I can still help."

Maati nodded, waited until girl and andat had vanished, then lowered himself to the floor. Slowly, the knot in his chest relaxed, and his breath returned to its normal depth and rhythm. In the snow-gray sunlight, he considered the backs of his hands, the nature of the andat, and what he had just agreed to. The cold of the stone and the sky seemed to take his energy. By the time he rose, his fingers were white and his feet were numb.

He found the others in the kitchen. Chalk marks on the walls sketched out three or four grammatical scenarios, each using different vocabulary and structures. Eiah, considering the notes, took a brief pose of welcome when he appeared, then turned to stare at him. Irit fluttered about, chattering merrily until he was seated by the fire with a bowl of warm tea in his hand. Large Kae and Small Kae were in the middle of a conversation about the difference between cutting and crushing, which in other circumstances would have been disturbing to hear. Vanjit sat with a beatific smile, Clarity-of-Sight perched on her lap. Maati motioned at Eiah that she should carry on, and with a reluctance he didn't understand, she did.

The tea was warm and smelled like spring. Coals glowed in the brazier. The voices around him seemed hopeful and bright. But then he saw the andat's black eyes and was reminded of his unease.

The session came to its end and the women scattered, each to her own task, leaving only Vanjit sitting by the fire, nursing the andat from a breast swollen with milk. Maati made his way back to his rooms. He was tired past all reason and unsteady on his feet. As he had hoped, Eiah was waiting outside his door.

"That seemed to go well," Maati said. "I think Irit's solution was fairly elegant."

"It has promise," Eiah agreed as she followed him into the room. He sat in a leather chair, sighing. Eiah blew life into the coals in the fire grate, added a handful of small tinder and a twisted length of oak to the fire, then took a stool and pulled it up before him.

"How do you feel about the binding's progress?" he asked.

"Well enough," she said, taking both his forearms in her hands. Her gaze was locked somewhere over his left shoulder, her fingers pressing hard into the flesh between the bones of his wrists. A moment later, she dropped his right hand and began squeezing his fingertips.

"Eiah-kya?"

"Don't mind me," she said. "It's habit. The binding's coming closer. There are one or two more things I'd like to try, but I think we've come as near as we're going to."

She went on for half a hand, recounting the fine issues of definition, duration, and intent that haunted the form of her present binding. Maati listened, submitting himself to her professional examination as she went on. Outside the window, the snow was falling again, small flakes gray against the pure white sky. Before Vanjit, he wouldn't have been able to make them out.

"I agree," Maati said as she ended, then plucked his sleeves back into their proper place. "Do you think . . ."

"Before Candles Night, certainly," Eiah said. "But there is going to be a complication. We have to leave the school. Utani would be best, but Pathai would do if that's impossible. You and I can leave in the morning, and the others can join us."

Maati chuckled.

"Eiah-kya," he said. "You've apologized for letting Ashti Beg go. I understand why you did it, but there's nothing to be concerned about. Even if she did tell someone that we're out here, Vanjit could turn Clarity-of-Sight against them, and we could all walk quietly away. The power of the andat—"

"Your heart is failing," Eiah said. "I don't have the herbs or the baths to care for you here."

She said it simply, her voice flat with exhaustion. Maati felt the smile fading from his lips. He saw tears beginning to glimmer in her eyes, the drops unfallen but threatening. He took a pose that denied her.

"Your color is bad," she said. "Your pulses aren't symmetric. Your blood is thick and dark. This is what I do, Uncle. I find people who are sick, and I look at the signs, and I think about them and their bodies. I look at you, here, now, and I see a man whose blood is slow and growing slower."

"You're imagining things," Maati said. "I'm fine. I only haven't slept well. I would never have guessed that you of all people would mistake a little lost rest for a weak heart."

"I'm not—"

"I am fine!" Maati shouted, pounding the arm of the chair. "And we cannot afford to run off into the teeth of winter. You aren't a physician any longer. That's behind you. You are a poet. You are the poet who's going to save the cities."

She took his hand in both of hers. For a moment, there was no sound but the low murmur of the fire and the nearly inaudible sound of her palm stroking the back of his hand. One of the threatened tears fell, streaking her cheek black. He hadn't realized she wore kohl.

"You," he said softly, "are the most important poet there is. The most important one there ever was."

"I'm just one woman," Eiah said. "I'm doing the best I can, but I'm tired. And the world keeps getting darker around me. If I can't take care of everything, at least let me take care of you."

"I will be fine," Maati said. "I'm not young anymore, but I'm a long way from death. We'll finish your binding, and then if you want to haul me to half the baths in the Empire, I'll submit."

Another tear marked her face. Maati took his sleeve and wiped her cheek dry.

"I'll be fine," he said. "I'll rest more if you like. I'll pretend my bones are made of mud brick and glass. But you can't stop now to concern yourself with me. Those people out there. They're the ones who need your care. Not me."

"Let me go to Pathai," she said. "I can get teas there."

"No," Maati said. "I won't do that."

"Let me send Large Kae, then. I can't stand by and do nothing."

"All right," Maati said, holding up a placating hand. "All right. Let's wait until morning, and we can talk to Large Kae. And perhaps you'll see that I'm only tired and we can move past this."

She left in the end without being convinced. As darkness fell, Maati found himself slipping into a soft despair. The world was quiet and still and utterly unaware of him.

His son was dead. The people he had counted as his friends had become his enemies, and he was among the most despised men in the world. Eiah was wrong, of course. His health was fine. But someday, it would fail. All men died, and most were forgotten. The few that the world remembered were not always celebrated.

He lit the night candle by holding it to the fire, the wax hissing where it dripped on the coals. He found his book and settled close to the fire grate before opening the cover and considering the words.

I, Maati Vaupathai, am one of the two men remaining in the world who has wielded the power of the andat.

Already, it was not true. There were three living poets now, and one of them a woman. Between the time he had touched a pen to this page and this moment, reading it in the early night, the world had moved on. He wondered how much of the rest was already old, already the property of a past that could never be regained. He read slowly, tracing the path his own mind had taken. The candle lent the pages an orange glow, the ink seeming to retreat into the pages, as if they were much larger and much farther away. The fire warmed his ankles and turned strong, solid wood into ashes softer than snow.

He was surprised to see the anger and bitterness in the book. There was a thread, he thought, of hatred in these words. He didn't think he'd meant it to be there, and yet sitting alone with his slowing blood, it could not be denied. Hatred of Otah and the Galts, of course, but also of Cehmai. Of Liat, whom he mentioned more frequently than he remembered and in terms that he knew she didn't deserve. Hatred toward the gods and the world. And thus, he had to think, toward himself. Before he reached the last page, Maati was weeping quietly.

He found an ink brick and a fresh pen, lit all the lanterns and candles he could find, and sat at his desk. He drew a line across the middle of the last page, marking a change in the book and in himself that he could not yet describe. He freshened the ink and did not know precisely what he intended to write until the nib touched the page, tracing out letters with a sound as dry and quiet as a lizard on stones.

If it were within my power, I would begin again. I would begin as a boy again, and live my life a different way. I have been told tonight that my heart is growing weak. Looking back upon the man I have been until now, I think it always has been. I think it was shattered one time too many and put back without all the shards in place.

And, though I think this is the cry of a coward, I do not want to die. I want to see the world made right. I want to live that long, at least.

He paused, looking at the words where they grew fainter, the ink running thin.

He found Eiah asleep on her cot, still wearing the robes she'd worn all day. Her door stood ajar, and his scratch woke her.

"Uncle," she said, yawning. "What's happened? Is something wrong?"

"You're certain. What you said about my blood. You're sure."

"Yes," she said. There was no hesitation in her.

"Perhaps," he said, then coughed. "Perhaps we should go to Utani."

Tears came to her eyes again, but with them a smile. The first true smile he'd seen from her since her journey to the low town. Since Vanjit's blinding of the Galts.

"Thank you, Uncle," she said.

In the morning, the others were shocked, and yet before the sun broke through the midday clouds, the cart was loaded with food and books, wax tables and wineskins. The horses were fitted with their leads and burdens, and all six of the travelers, seven if he counted Clarity-of-Sight, were wrapped in warm robes and ready for the road. The only delay was Irit scrambling back at the last moment to find some small, forgotten token.

Maati pulled himself deep into the enfolding wool as the cart shifted under him, and the low buildings with snow on the roofs and the cracks between stones receded. His breath plumed before him, rubbing out the division between sky and snow.

Vanjit sat beside him, the andat wrapped in her cloak. Her expression was blank. Dark smudges of fatigue marked her eyes, and the andat squirmed and fussed. The wide wheels tossed bits of hard-packed snow up into the cart, and Maati brushed them away idly. It would be an hour or more to the high road, and then perhaps a day before they turned into the network of tracks and roads that connected the low towns that would take them to the grand palaces of Utani, center of the Empire. Maati found himself wondering whether Otah-kvo would have returned there, to sit on the gold-worked seat. Or perhaps he would still be in Saraykeht, scheming to haul countless thousands of blinded women from Kirinton, Acton, and Marsh.

He tried to picture his old friend and enemy, but he could conjure only a sense of his presence. Otah's face escaped him, but it had been a decade and a half since they had seen each other. All memory faded, he supposed. Everything, eventually, passed into the white veil and was forgotten.

The snow made roadway and meadow identical, so the first bend in the road was marked by a stand of thin trees and a low ridge of stone. Maati watched the dark buildings vanish behind the hillside. It was unlikely that he would ever see them again. But he would carry his memories of the warmth of the kitchens, the laughter of women, the first binding done by a woman, and the proof that his new grammar would function. Better that than the death house it had been when the Galts had come down this same road, murder in their minds. Or the mourning chambers for boys without families before that.

Vanjit shuddered. Her face was paler. Maati freed his hands and took a pose that expressed concern and offered comfort. Vanjit shook her head.

"He's never been away," she said. "He's leaving home for the first time."

"It can be frightening," Maati said. "It will pass."

"No. Worse, really. He's happy. He's very happy to be leaving," Vanjit said. Her voice was low and exhausted. "All the things we said about the struggle to hold them. It's all truth. I can feel him in the back of my mind. He never stops pushing."

"It's the nature of the andat," Maati said. "If you'd like, we can talk about ways to make bearing the burden easier."

Vanjit looked away. Her lips were pale.

"No," she said. "We'll be fine. It's only a harder day than usual. We'll find another place, and see you cared for, and then all will be well. But when the time comes to bind Wounded, there are things I'll do differently."

"We can hope it never comes to that," Maati said.

Vanjit shifted, her eyes widening for a moment, and the soft, almost flirting smile came to her lips.

"Of course not," she said. "Of course it won't. Eiah-cha will be fine. I was only thinking aloud. It was nothing."

Maati nodded and lay back. His thick robes cushioned the bare wood of the cart's side. Crates and chests groaned and shifted against their ropes. Small Kae and Irit began singing, and the others slowly joined them. All of them except Vanjit and himself. He let his eyes close to slits, watching Vanjit from between the distorting bars of his eyelashes.

The andat squirmed again, howled out once, and her face went hard and still. She glanced over at Maati, but he feigned sleep. The others, involved in their song and the road, didn't see it when she pulled Clarity-of-Sight from her cloak, staring at it. The tiny arms flailed, the soft legs whirled. The andat made a low, angry sound, and Vanjit's expression hardened.

She shook the thing once, hard enough to make the oversized head snap back. The tiny mouth set itself into a shocked grimace and it began to wail. Vanjit looked about, but no one had seen the small violence between them. She pulled the andat back to her, cooing and rocking slowly back and forth while it whimpered and fought. Desolate tears tracked her cheeks. And were wiped away with a sleeve.

Maati wondered how often scenes like this one had passed without comment or notice. Many years before, he had cared for an infant himself, and the frustration of it was something he understood. This was something different. He thought of what it would have been to have a child that hated him, that wanted nothing more than to be free. Clarity-of-Sight was all the longing that haunted Vanjit and all the anger that sustained her put into a being that would do whatever was needed to escape. Vanjit had been betrayed by the cruelty of the world, and now also her own desire made flesh.

At last she had the baby that had haunted her dreams. And it wanted to die.

Eiah spoke in his memory. *What makes us imagine we can do good with these as our tools?*

19

>+< Low towns clustered around the great cities of the Khaiem, small centers of commerce and farming, justice and healing. Men and women could live out their lives under the nominal control of the Khaiem or now of the Emperor and never pass into the cities themselves. They had low courts, road taxes, smiths and stablers, wayhouses and comfort houses and common meadows for anyone's use. He had seen them all, years before, when he had only been a courier. They were the cities of the Khaiem writ small, and as he passed through them with his armsmen, his son, and the Galtic half-stowaway, Otah saw all his fears made real.

Silences lay where children should have been playing street games. Great swings made from rope and plank hung from ancient branches that shadowed the common fields, no boys daring each other higher. As a child who had seen no more than twelve summers, Otah had set out on his own, competing with low-town boys for small work. With every low town he entered, his eyes caught the sorts of things he had done: roofs with thatch that wanted care, fences and stone walls in need of mending, cisterns grown thick and black with weeds that required only a strong back and the energy of youth to repair. But there were no boys, no girls; only men and women whose smiles carried a bewildered, permanent sorrow. The leaves on the trees had turned brown and yellow and fallen. The nights were long, and the dawns touched by frost.

The land was dead. He had known it. Being reminded brought him no joy.

They stopped for the night in a wayhouse nestled in a wooded valley. The walls were kiln-fired brick with a thick covering of ivy that the autumn chill had turned brown and brittle. News of his identity and errand had spread before him like a wave on water, making quiet investigation impossible. The keeper had cleared all his rooms before they knew where they meant to stop, had his best calf killed and hot baths drawn on the chance that Otah might stop to rest. Sitting now in the alcove of a room large enough to fit a dozen men, Otah felt his muscles slowly and incompletely unknotting. With the supplies carried on the steam wagons and the men shifting between tending the kilns and riding, Pathai was less than two days away. Without the Galtic machines, it would have been four, perhaps five.

Low clouds obscured moon and stars. When Otah closed the shutters against the cold night air, the room grew no darker. The great copper tub the keeper had prepared glowed in the light of the fire grate. The earthenware jar of soap beside it was half-empty, but at least Otah felt like his skin was his own again and not hidden under layers of dust and sweat. His traveling robes had vanished and he'd picked a simple garment of combed wool lined with silk. The voices of the armsmen rose through the floorboards. The song was patriotic and bawdy, and the drum that accompanied them kept missing the right time. Otah rose on bare feet and walked out to the stairs. No servants scuttled out of his way, and he noticed the absence.

Danat was not among the armsmen or out with the horses. It was only when Otah approached the room set aside for Ana Dasin that he heard his son's voice. The room was on the lower floor, near the kitchens. The floor there was stone. Otah's steps made no sound as he walked forward. Ana said something he couldn't make out, but when Danat answered, he'd come near enough to hear.

"Of course there are, it's only Papa-kya isn't one of them. When I was a boy, he told me stories from the First Empire about a half-Bakta boy. And he nearly married a girl from the eastern islands."

"When was that?" Ana asked. Otah heard a sound of shifting cloth, like a blanket being pulled or a robe being adjusted.

"A long time ago," Danat said. "Just after Saraykeht. He lived in the eastern islands for years after that. They build their marriages in stages there. He's got the first half of the marriage tattoo."

"Why didn't he finish it?" Ana asked.

Otah remembered Maj as he hadn't in years. Her wide, pale lips. Her eyes that could go from blue the color of the sky at dawn to slate gray. The stretch marks on her belly, a constant reminder of the child that had been taken from her. In his mind, she was linked with the scent of the ocean.

"I don't know," Danat said. "But it wasn't that he was trying to keep his bloodline pure. Really, there's a strong case that my lineage isn't particularly high. My mother didn't come from the utkhaiem, and for some people that's as much an insult as marrying a Westlander."

"Or a Galt," Ana said, tartly.

"Exactly," Danat said. "So, yes. Of course there are people in the court who want some kind of purity, but they've gotten used to disappointment over the last few decades."

"They would never accept me."

"You?" Danat said.

"Anyone like me."

"If they won't, then they won't accept anyone. So it hardly matters what they think, because they won't have any sons or daughters at court. The world's changed, and the families that can't change with it won't survive."

"I suppose," Ana said. They were silent for a moment. Otah debated whether he should scratch on her door or back quietly away, and then Ana spoke again.

Her voice had changed. It was lower now, and dark as rain on stone. "It doesn't really matter, though, does it. There isn't going to be a Galt."

"That's not true," Danat said.

"Every day that we're like . . . like this, more of us are dying. It's harvest time. How are they going to harvest the grain if they can't see it? How do you raise sheep and cattle by sound?"

"I knew a blind man who worked leather in Lachi," Danat said. "His work was just as good as a man's with eyes."

"One man doesn't signify," Ana said. "He wasn't baking his own bread or catching his own fish. If he needed to know what a thing looked like, there was someone he could ask. If everyone's sightless, it's different. It's all falling apart."

"You can't know that," Danat said.

"I know how crippled I am," Ana said. "It gives me room to guess. I know how little I can do to stop it."

There was a soft sound, and Danat hushing her. Otah took a careful step back, away from the door. When Ana's voice came again, it was thick with tears.

"Tell me," she said. "Tell me one of those stories. The ones where a child with two races could still win out."

"In the sixteenth year of the reign of the Emperor Adani Beh," Danat said, his voice bright and soft, "there came to court a boy whose blood was half Bakta, his skin the color of soot, and his mind as clever as any man who had ever lived. When the Emperor saw him . . ."

Otah backed away, his son's voice becoming a murmur of sound, inflected like words but too faint to mean anything. Their whole journey, it had been like this. Each time Otah thought they might have a moment alone, Ana was near, or one of the armsmen, or Otah had brought himself to the edge of speech and then failed. Every courier they stopped along the road was another reminder to Otah that his son had to know, had to be told. But no word had come from Idaan, and Danat still didn't know that Eiah was involved in the slow death of Galt and, with it, the future Otah had fought for.

Before Pathai, Otah had told himself when they were on the road. During the journey itself, it hardly mattered whether Danat knew, but once they reached their destination, his son couldn't be sent out without knowing what it was they were searching for and why. Otah had no faith that another, better chance would come the next day. He made his way back upstairs, found a servant woman, and had cheese, fresh bread, and a carafe of rice wine taken to Danat's room. Otah waited there until the Galtic clock, clicking to itself in a corner, marked the night as almost half-gone. Otah didn't notice that he was dozing until the opening door roused him.

Otah broke the news as gently as he could, outlining his own half-knowledge of Maati's intentions, Idaan's appearance in Saraykeht, Eiah's appearance on the list of possible backers, and his own decision to set his sister to hunt down his daughter. Danat listened carefully, as if picking through the words for clues to some deeper mystery. When, at length, Otah went silent, Danat looked into the fire in its grate, wove his fingers together, and thought. The flames made his eyes glitter like jewels.

"It isn't her," he said at last. "She wouldn't do this."

"I know you love her, Danat-kya. I love her too, and I don't want to think this of her either, but—"

"I don't mean she didn't back Maati," Danat said. "We don't know that she did, but at least that part's plausible. I'm only saying that this blindness isn't her work."

His voice wasn't loud or strident. He seemed less like a man fighting an unpalatable truth than a builder pointing out a weakness in an archway's design. Otah took a pose that invited him to elaborate.

"Eiah hates your plan," Danat said. "She even came to me a few times to argue that I should refuse it."

"I didn't know that."

"I didn't tell you," Danat said, his hands taking a pose that apologized, though his voice held no regret. "I couldn't see that it would make things between the two of you any better. But my point is that her arguments were never against Galts. She couldn't stand to see a generation of our own women ignored. Their pain was what she lived in. When you started allowing the import of bed slaves as . . . well . . ."

"Brood mares," Otah said. "I do remember her saying that."

"Well, that," Danat agreed. "Eiah took that as saying that none of the women here mattered. That *she* didn't matter. If the problems of the Empire could be solved by hauling in wombs that would bear, then all that was important to you about women was the children they could yield."

"But if there's no children, there can't be—"

Danat shifted forward in his seat, putting his palm over Otah's mouth. The boy's eyes were dark, his mouth set in the half-smile Kiyan had often worn.

"You need to listen to me, Papa-kya. I'm not telling you that she's right. I'm not telling you she's wrong, for that. I'm telling you Eiah loves people and she hates pain. If she's been backing Uncle Maati, it's to take away the pain, not to . . ."

Danat gestured at the shutters, and by implication at the world on the other side of them. The logs in the grate popped and the song of a single cricket, perhaps the last one alive before the coming winter, sang counterpoint to the ticking clock. Otah rubbed his chin, his mind turning his son's words over like a jeweler considering a gem.

"She may be part of this," Danat said. "I think you're right to find her. But the poet we want? It isn't her."

"I wish I could be certain of that," Otah said.

"Well, start with not being certain that she is," Danat said. "The world will carry you the rest of the way, if I'm right."

Otah smiled and put his hand on his son's head.

"When did you become wise?" Otah asked.

"It's only what you'd have said, if you weren't busy feeling responsible for all of it," Danat said. "You're a good man, Papa-kya. And we're doing what we can in unprecedented times."

Otah let his hand fall to his side. Danat smiled. The cricket, wherever it was, went silent.

"Go," Danat said. "Sleep. We've got a long ride tomorrow, and I'm exhausted."

Otah rose, his hands taking a pose that accepted the command. Danat chuckled; then as Otah reached the door, he sobered.

"Thank you, by the way, for what you said about Ana," Danat said. "You were right. We weren't treating her with the respect she deserved."

"It's a mistake we all make, one time and another," Otah said. "I'm glad it was an error we could correct."

Perhaps mine also will be, he thought. It terrified him in some fundamental and joyous way to think that possibly, *possibly*, this might still end without a sacrifice that was too great for him to bear. He hadn't realized how much he had tried to harden himself against the prospect of killing his own daughter, or how poorly he had managed it.

He crawled into his bed. Danat's certainty lightened the weight that bore him down. The poet wasn't Eiah. This blindness wasn't in her, wasn't who she was. The andat might have been bound by Maati or some other girl. Some girl whom he could bring himself to kill. He closed his eyes, considering how he might avoid having the power of the andat turned on him. The fear would return, he was sure of that. But now, for a moment, he could afford himself the luxury of being more frightened of loss than of the price of victory.

They left before sunrise with the steamcarts' supplies of wood, coal, and water refreshed, the horses replaced with well-rested animals, and the scent of snow heavy in the air. They moved faster than Otah had expected, not pausing to eat or rest. He himself took a turn at the kiln of the larger steamcart, keeping the fire hot and well-fueled. If the armsmen were surprised to see the Emperor working like a commoner, they didn't say anything. Two couriers passed them riding east, but neither bore a message from Idaan. Three came up behind them bearing letters for the Emperor from what seemed like half the court at Saraykeht and Utani.

Nightfall caught them at the top of the last high, broad pass that opened onto the western plains. On the horizon, Pathai glittered like a congress of stars. The armsmen assembled the sleeping tents, unrolling layers of leather and fur to drape over the canvas. Otah squatted by the kiln, reading through letter after letter. The silk threads that had once sewn the paper closed rested in knots and tangles by his feet. The snow that lay about them was fresh though the sky had cleared, and the cold combined with the day's work to tire him. The joints of his hands ached, and his eyes were tired and difficult to focus. He dreaded the close, airless sleeping tents and the ache-interrupted night that lay before him almost as much as he was annoyed by the petty politics of court.

Letter after letter praised or castigated him for his decision to leave. The Khaiate Council, as it had been deemed in his absence, was either a terrible mistake or an act of surpassing wisdom, and whichever it was, the author of the letter would be better placed on it than someone Otah had named.

Balasar Gice, the only Galt on the council, was pressing for relief ships to sail for Galt with as much food as could be spared and men to help guide and oversee the blinded. The rest of the council was divided, and a third of them had written to Otah for his opinion. Otah put those letters directly into the fire. If he'd meant to answer every difficult question from the road, he wouldn't have created the council.

There was no word from Sinja or Chaburi-Tan. Balasar, writing with a secretary to help him, feared the worst. This letter, Otah tucked into his sleeve. There was no reason to keep it. He could do nothing to affect its news. But he couldn't bring himself to destroy something to do with Sinja when his old friend's fate already seemed so tentative.

Uncertain footsteps sounded behind him. Ana Dasin was walking the wide boards toward the kiln. Her hair was loose and her robe blue shot with gold. Her grayed eyes seemed to search the darkness.

"Ana-cha," he said, both a greeting and a warning that he was there. The girl started a little, but then smiled uncertainly.

"Most High," she said, nodding very nearly toward him. "Is . . . I was wondering if Danat-cha was with you?"

"He's gone to fetch water with the others," Otah said, nodding uselessly toward a path that led to a shepherd's well. "He will be back in half a hand, I'd think."

"Oh," Ana said, her face falling.

"Is there something I can do?"

Watching the struggle in the girl's expression seemed almost more an intrusion than his previous eavesdropping. After a moment, she drew something from her sleeve. Cream-colored paper sewn with yellow thread. She held it out.

"The courier said it was from my father," she said. "I can't read it."

Otah cleared his throat against an unexpected tightness. He felt unworthy of the girl's trust, and something like gratitude brought tears to his eyes.

"I would be honored, Ana-cha, to read it for you," he said.

Otah rose, took the letter, and drew Ana to a stool near enough the kiln to warm her, but not so close as to put her in danger of touching the still-scorching metal. He ripped out the thread, unfolded the single page, and leaned in toward the light.

It was written in Galtic though the script betrayed more familiarity with the alphabet of the Khaiem. He knew before he began to read that there would be nothing in it too personal to say to a secretary, and the fact relieved him. He skimmed the words once, then again more slowly.

"Most High?" Ana said.

"It is addressed to you," Otah said. "It says this: *I understand that you've seen fit to run off without telling me or your mother. You should know better than that.* Then there are a few more lines that restate all that."

Ana sat straight, her hands on her knees, her face expressionless. Otah coughed, cleared his throat, and went on.

"There is a second section," he said. "He says . . . well."

Otah smoothed the page with his fingers, tracing the words as he spoke.

"*Still, I was your age once too. If good judgment were part of being young, there would be no reason to grow old. In God's name write back to tell us you're well. Your mother's sick that you'll fall off the trail and get eaten by dogs, and I'm half-sick that you'll come back wed and pregnant,*" Otah said. "He goes on to offer a brief analysis of my own intelligence. I'll skip that."

Ana chuckled and wiped away a tear. Otah grinned and kept the smile in his voice when he went on.

"He ends by saying that he loves you. And that he trusts you to do what's right."

"You're lying," Ana said.

Otah took a pose that denied an unjust accusation, then flapped his hands in annoyance. The physical language of the Khaiem was a difficult habit to put aside.

"Why would I lie?" he asked.

"To be polite? I don't know. But my father? Farrer Dasin putting on paper that he trusts his little girl's judgment? The stars would dance on treetops first. The wed-and-pregnant part sounded like him, though."

"Well," Otah said, placing the folded page into her fingers. "He might surprise you. Keep this, and you can read it for yourself once we've fixed all this mess."

Ana took a pose that offered thanks. It wasn't particularly well done.

"You are always welcome," Otah said.

They sat in silence until Danat and the other water bearers returned. Then Otah left his seat to Danat and crawled into the sleeping tent, where, true to expectations, he shifted from discomfort to discomfort until the sun rose again.

They reached Pathai at midday. Silk banners streamed from the towers and the throng that met them at the western arch cheered and sang and played flutes and drums. Men and women hung from lattices of wood and rope to get a better view of Otah and Danat, their armsmen, the steamcarts. The air was thick with the scents of honeyed almonds and mulled wine and bodies. The armsmen of Pathai met them, made an elaborate ritual obeisance, and then cleared a path for them until they reached the palaces.

A feast had been prepared, and baths. Servants descended on the group like moths, and Otah submitted to being only emperor once again.

The celebration of his arrival was as annoying as it was pointless. Dish after dish of savory meat and sweet bread, hot curry and chilled fish, all accompanied by the best acrobats and musicians that could be scraped together with little notice. And Ana Dasin sitting at his table, her empty eyes a constant, unintentional reproach. Finding Maati and this new poet was going to be like hunting quail with a circus. He would have to do something to let them move discreetly. He didn't yet know what that would be.

The rooms he'd been given were blond stone, the ceiling vaulted and set with tiles of indigo and silver. A thousand candles set the air glowing and filled his senses with the scent of hot wax and perfume. It was, he thought, the sort of space that was almost impossible to keep warm. Danat, Ana, and the armsmen were all being seen to elsewhere. He sat on a long, low couch and hoped that Danat, at least, would be able to get out into the city and make a few inquiries.

When a servant came and announced Sian Noygu, Otah almost refused the audience before he recognized it as the name Idaan traveled under. His heart racing, he let himself be led to a smaller chamber of carved granite and worked gold. His sister sat between a small fountain and a shadowed alcove. She wore a gray robe under a colorless cloak, and her boots were soft with wear. A long scratch across the back of her hand was the dark red of scabs and old blood.

The servant made his obeisance and retreated. Otah took a pose of greeting appropriate to close family, and Idaan tilted her head like a dog hearing an unfamiliar sound.

"I had intended to meet you when you came into the city. I didn't know you were planning a festival."

"I wasn't," Otah said, sitting beside her. The fountain clucked and burbled. "Traveling quietly seems beyond me these days."

"It was all as subtle as a rockslide," Idaan agreed. "But there's some good in it. The louder you are, the less people are looking at me."

"You've found something then?" Otah asked.

"I have," Idaan said.

"What have you learned?"

A different voice answered from the darkness of the alcove at Idaan's side. A woman's voice.

"Everything," it said.

Otah rose to his feet. The woman who emerged was young: not more than forty summers and the white in her hair still barely more than an accent. She wore robes as simple as Idaan's but held herself with a mixture of angry pride and uncertainty that Otah had become familiar with. Her pupils were gray and sightless, but her eyes were the almond shape that marked her as a citizen of the Empire. This was a victim of the new poet, but she was no Galt.

"Idaan-cha knows everything," the blind woman said again, "because I told it to her."

Idaan took the woman's hand and stood. When she spoke, it was to her companion.

"This is my brother, the Emperor," Idaan said, then turned to him. "Otah-cha, this is Ashti Beg."

20

>+< When before Maati had considered death, it had been in terms of what needed to be done. Before he died, he had to master the grammars of the Dai-kvo, or find his son again, or most recently see his errors with Sterile made right. It was never the end itself that drew his attention. He had reduced his mortality to the finish line of a race. This and this and this done, and afterward, dying would be like rest at the end of a long day.

With Eiah's pronouncement, his view shifted. No list of accomplishments could forgive the prospect of his own extinction. Maati found himself looking at the backs of his hands, the cracked skin, the dark blotches of age. He was becoming aware of time in a way he never had. There was some number of days he would see, some number of nights, and then nothing. It had always been true. He was no more or less a mortal being because his blood was slowing. Everything born, dies. He had known that. He only hadn't quite understood. It changed everything.

It also changed nothing. They traveled slowly, keeping to lesser-known roads and away from the larger low towns. Often Eiah would call the day's halt with the sun still five hands above the horizon because they had found a convenient wayhouse or a farm willing to board them for the night. The prospect of letting Maati sleep in cold air was apparently too much for her to consider.

On the third day, Eiah had parted with the company, rejoining them on the fifth with a cloth sack of genuinely unpleasant herbs. Maati suffered a cup of the bitter tea twice daily. He let his pulses be measured against one another, his breath smelled, his fingertips squeezed, the color of his eyes considered and noted. It embarrassed him.

The curious thing was that, despite all his fears and Eiah's attentions, he felt fine. If his breath was short, it was no shorter than it had been for years. He tired just when he'd always tired, but now six sets of eyes shifted to him every time he grunted. He dismissed the anxiety when he saw it in the others, however closely he felt it himself.

He would have expected the two feelings to balance each other: the dismissive self-consciousness at any concern over him and the presentiment of his death. He did not understand how he could be possessed by both of them at the same time, and yet he was. It was like there were two minds within him, two Maati Vaupathais, each with his own thoughts and concerns, and no compromise between them was required.

For the most part, Maati could ignore this small failure to be at one with himself. Each morning, he rose with the others, ate whatever rubbery eggs or day-old meat the waykeeper had to offer, choked down Eiah's tea, and went on as usual. The autumn through which they passed was crisp and fragrant of new earth and rotting leaves. The snow that had plagued the school had also visited the foothills and shallow passes that divided the western plains of Pathai from the river valleys of the east, but it was rarely more than three fingers deep. In many places, the sun was still strong enough to banish the pale mourning colors to the shadows.

With rumors that Otah himself had taken up the hunt, they kept a balance between the smaller, less-traveled roads and those that were wider and better maintained. So far from the great cities, the ports and trading posts, there were no foreign faces to be seen. None of the handful of adventurous Westlands women had made their way here to try for a Khaiate husband and a better life. There was no better life to be had here. The lack of children, of babies, gave the towns a sense of tolerating a slow plague. It was only the world. It no longer troubled Maati. This was another journey in a life that seemed to be woven of distance. Apart from the overattentiveness of his traveling companions, there was no reason to reflect on his mortality; he had no cause to consider that these small chores and pleasantries of the road might be among his last.

It was only days later, at the halfway point between the school and the river Qiit, that without intending it, Eiah called the question.

They had stopped at a wayhouse at the side of a broad lake. A wide wooden deck stood out over the water, the wind pulling small waves to lap at its pilings. A flock of cranes floated and called to one another at the far shore. Maati sat on a three-legged stool, his traveling cloak still wrapping his shoulders. He looked out on the shifting water, the gray-green trees, the hazy white sky. He heard Eiah behind him, her voice coming from the main building as if it were coming from a different world. When she came out, he heard her footsteps and the leather physician's satchel bumping against her hip. She stopped just behind him.

"They're beautiful," he said, nodding at the cranes.

"I suppose," Eiah said.

"Vanjit? The others?"

"In their rooms," Eiah said, a trace of satisfaction in her voice. "Three rooms, and all of them private. Meals this evening and before we go. One length of silver and two copper."

"You could have paid them the normal price," Maati said.

"My pride won't allow it," Eiah said. She stepped forward and knelt. "There was something. If you're not tired."

"I'm an old man. I'm always tired."

Her eyes held some objection, but she didn't give it voice. Instead she un-buckled her satchel, rooted in it for a moment, and drew out a paper. Maati took it, frowning. The characters were familiar, a part of Eiah's proposed bind-ing, but the structure of them was different. Awkward.

"It isn't perfect," Eiah said. "But I thought we could consider it. I've mentioned the idea to Large Kae, and she has some ideas about how to make it consonant with the grammar."

Maati lifted his hand, palm out, and stopped the flow of words. The cranes called, their harsh voices crossing the water swifter than arrows. He sounded out each phrase, thinking through the logic as he did.

"I don't understand," he said. "This is the strongest part of the binding. Why would you change . . ."

And then he saw her intentions. Each change she had made broadened the concept of wounds. Of harm. Of damage. And there, in the corner of the page, was a play on the definitions of blood. He folded the page, slipping it into his sleeve.

"No," he said.

"I think it can—"

"No," Maati said again. "What we're doing is hard enough. Making it fit the things that Sterile has done is enough. If you try to make everything fit into it, you'll end with more than you can hold."

Eiah sighed and looked out across the water. The wind plucked a lock of hair, the black threads dancing on her cheek. He could see in her expression that she'd anticipated all he would say. And more, that she agreed. He put a hand on her shoulder. For a moment, neither spoke.

"Once we reach the river, things will move faster," Eiah said. "With the Galts' paddle boats, we should reach Utani before the worst cold comes." To their left, a fish leaped from the water and splashed back down. "Once I have you someplace with real physicians, I'm going to try the binding."

Maati drew in a deep breath and let it out slowly. A sick dread uncurled in his belly.

"You're sure?" he said.

Eiah took a pose that confirmed her resolve and also chided him. When he replied with one that expressed mild affront, she spoke.

"You sit here like something from a philosopher's daydream, refusing to let me even try to mend your heart," she said, "and then you start quaking like an old woman when I'm the one at risk."

" 'Quaking like an old woman'?" Maati said. "I think we haven't known the same old women. And of course I'm concerned for you, Eiah-kya. How could I not be? You're like a daughter to me. You always have been."

"I might not fail," she said. And a moment later, rose, kissed his hair, and walked in, leaving him alone with the world. Maati sank deeper into his cloak, determined to watch the birds until his mind calmed. Half a hand later, he went inside the building, muttering to himself.

The evening meal was a soup of ground lentils, rice, and a sweet, hot spice that made Maati's eyes water. He paid an extra length of copper for a second bowl. The commons with its low ceilings and soot-stained walls also served as a teahouse for the nearby low towns. By the time he'd finished eating, local men and women had begun to appear. They took little notice of the travelers, which suited Maati quite well.

In less interesting times, the table talk would have turned on matters of weather, of crop yields and taxes and the small jealousies and dramas that humanity drew about itself in all places and times. Instead, they spoke of the Emperor, his small caravan on its way to Pathai or else Lachi or else some unknown destination in the Westlands. He was going to broker a new contract for women, now that the Galts had been destroyed, or else retrieve the new poet and march back in triumph. He had been secretly harboring the poets all this time, or had become one himself. Nothing that approached the truth. Small Kae, listening to two of the local men debate, looked on the edge of laughter the whole evening.

As the last of the sunset faded, a pair of the older men took up drums, and the tables nearest the fire grate were pulled aside to clear space for dancers. Maati was prevented from excusing himself from the proceedings only by Vanjit's appearance at his side.

"Maati-kvo," she murmured, her hand slipping around his arm, "I spoke to Eiah-kya. I know it was wrong of me to interfere, but please, please, will you reconsider?"

The older of the two men set up a low throbbing beat on his drum. The second drummer closed his eyes and bobbed his head almost in time with the first. Maati suspected that both were drunk.

"This isn't the place to discuss it," Maati said. "Later, we can . . ."

"Please," Vanjit said. Her breath wasn't free from the scent of distilled wine. Her cheeks were flushed. "Without you, none of us matter. You know that. You're our teacher. We need you. And if Eiah . . . she pays its price, you know that I'll be there. I can do the thing. I've already managed once, and I *know* that I could do it again."

The second drum began, dry and light and not quite on its mark. No one seemed to be paying attention to the old man in the corner or the young woman attached to his arm. Maati leaned close to Vanjit, speaking low.

"What is it, Vanjit-kya?" he asked. "This is the second time you've offered to bind Wounded. Why do you want that?"

She blinked and released his arm. Her eyes were wider, her mouth thin. It was his turn to take her arm, and he did, leaning close enough to speak almost into her ear.

"I have known more poets than I can count," he said. "Only a few held the andat, and none of them took joy in it. My own first master, Heshai of Saraykeht, planned out a second binding of Seedless. It could never have worked. It was too near what he'd done before, and part of Sterile's failure was that I borrowed too much from his design."

"I don't know what you mean, Maati-kvo," Vanjit said. Three women had stepped into the dancing space and were thumping in a simple pattern, keeping time with one drum or the other.

"I mean that everyone wants a second chance," Maati said. "Clarity-of-Sight . . ."

Maati bit down, glancing to see if anyone had heard him. The music and the dance were the focus of the room.

"The little one," Maati said, more quietly, "isn't what you'd hoped. But neither would the next one be."

He might just as well have slapped her. Vanjit's face went white, and she stood so quickly the bench scraped out from under her. By the time Maati rose, she was halfway to the door leading out to the stables and courtyard, and when he reached her, they were outside in the chill. A thin fog blurred the lantern hanging above the wayhouse door.

"Vanjit!" Maati called, and she turned back, her face a mask of pain.

"How could you say that? How could you say those things to me?" she demanded. "You had as much to do with that binding as I did. You are just as much responsible for him. I offered to take Eiah's place because someone would have to, not because it's something that I want. I love him. He's my boy, and I love him. He is everything I'd hoped. *Everything!*"

"Vanjit—"

She was weeping openly now, her voice high, thin, and wailing.

"And he loves me. No matter what you say, I know he does. He's my boy, and he loves me. How could you think that I'd want a second chance? I offered this for *you!*"

He took her sleeve in his fist, and she pulled back, yelping. She tried to turn away, but he would not let her.

"Listen to me," he said sternly. "You don't need to tell me how deeply you—"

Vanjit snarled, her lips pulled back from her teeth like a pit dog's. She pulled away sharply, and Maati stumbled, falling to his knees. When he rose, he could hear her running footsteps fading into the dark, but the fog had thickened so badly that he couldn't see his own hand in front of his face.

Except that, of course, it hadn't.

He stood still, heart racing, hands trembling. The raucous sounds of the dance came from behind him and to the left. The poorly played drums became his polestar. He turned and made his slow, careful way back toward the wayhouse. The ground was rough under his feet, gravel and weeds taking him at slightly different angles with every step.

He shouldn't have tried to hold her. She was upset. He should have let her go. He cursed himself for his stubbornness and her for her lack of control. The drums had given way to a flute and a low, warbling singer. Maati's outstretched fingers found the rough planks of the wall. He leaned against it, unsure what to do next. If he went back to the main room, his sudden infirmity would call attention to him, to the others, to Vanjit. But if he didn't, what would he do? He couldn't navigate his way back to his room, couldn't reach shelter. His robes were damp with the fog, the wood under his palm slick. He could stay here, pressing against the wayhouse like he was holding it up, or he could move. If there was only some way to find Eiah . . .

He began inching away from the door. He could follow the walls around the building, and find the deck. If he waited long enough, Eiah would come looking for him, and that might well be one of the first places she'd look. He tried to recall where the deck's railing began and ended. He had been there for hours earlier, but now he found the details escaped him.

He stumbled over a log and bruised his knee, but he didn't cry out. The cold was beginning to numb him. He reached the corner and a set of stairs he didn't remember. The prospect of sitting in the cold at the edge of the unseen lake was becoming less and less sustainable. He started devising stories that would cover his blindness. He could go near the common room, cry out, and collapse. If he kept his eyes closed, he could feign unconsciousness. They would bring Eiah to him.

He stepped in something wet and soft, like mud but with a sudden, billowing smell of rotting plants. Maati lifted his foot slowly to keep the muck from pulling off his boot. It occurred to him for the first time that they had done this—precisely this—to a nation.

His boot was heavy and made a wet sound when he put weight on it, but it didn't slip. He started making his way back toward where he'd been. He thought he'd made it halfway there when the world suddenly clicked back into place. His hands pink and gray against the damp, black wood. The thin fog hardly worth noticing. He turned and found Vanjit sitting cross-legged on the stones of the courtyard. Her dark eyes were considering. He wondered how long she'd been watching.

"What you said before? It was uncalled for," she said. Her voice was steady as stone, and as unforgiving.

Maati took a pose that offered apology but also pointedly did not end the conversation. Vanjit considered him.

"I love Eiah-cha," she said, frowning. "I would never, *never* wish her ill. Suggesting that I want her to fail just so I could remain the only poet . . . it's madness. It hurts me that you would say it."

"I never did," Maati said. "I never said anything like it. If that's what you heard, then something else is happening here."

Vanjit shifted back, surprise and dismay in her expression. Her hands moved toward some formal pose, but never reached it. The shriek came from within the wayhouse. The music stopped. Vanjit stood up muttering something violent and obscene, but Maati was already moving to the door.

The large room was silent, drums and flute abandoned where they had fallen. The woman who'd screamed was sitting on a stool, her hands still pressed to her mouth, her face bloodless, and her gaze fixed on the archway that led to the private rooms. No one spoke. Clarity-of-Sight stood in the archway, its hands on the wall, its tiny hips swaying crazily as it lost and regained and lost its balance. It saw Vanjit, let out a high squeal, and waved its tiny arms before sitting down hard and suddenly. The delight never left its face.

"It is," someone said in a voice woven from awe and tears. "It's a baby."

And as if the word had broken a dam, chaos flowed through the wayhouse. Vanjit dashed forward, her hands low to scoop up the andat, and the crowd surged with her. The chorus of questions and shouts rose, filling the air. Maati started forward, then stopped. The older of the drummers appeared from amid the throng and embraced him, tears of joy in the man's eyes.

Through the press of the crowd, Maati saw Eiah standing alone. Her expression was cold. Maati pulled back from his grinning companion and struggled toward her. He heard Vanjit talking high and fast behind him, but couldn't make out the words. There were too many voices layered over it.

"Apparently we've decided not to travel quietly," Eiah said in tone of cold acid.

"Get the others," he said. "I'll prepare the cart. We can leave in the night."

"You think anyone here is going to sleep tonight?" Eiah said. "There's a baby. A full-blooded child of the cities, and Vanjit the mother. If the gods themselves walked in the door right now, they'd have to wait for a room. They'll think it's to do with me. The physician who has found a way to make women bear. They'll hound me like I've stolen their teeth."

"I'm sorry," Maati said.

"Word of this is going to spread. Father's going to hear of it, and when he does, he'll be on our heels."

"Why would he think it was you?"

"Galt went blind, and he headed west. For Pathai. For me," Eiah said.

"He can't know you're part of this," Maati said.

"Of course he can," Eiah said. "I am, and he isn't dim. I didn't think it was a problem when no one knew who or where we were."

A round of cheering broke out, and the wayhouse keeper appeared as if from nowhere, two bottles of wine in each hand. Vanjit had been ushered to a seat by the fire grate. Clarity-of-Sight was in her arms, beaming at everyone who came close. Vanjit's cheeks were flushed, but she seemed pleased. Proud. Happy.

"This was my mistake," Maati said. "My failure as much as anything. I distracted her from the thing. It has more freedom when her mind is elsewhere."

Eiah turned her head to look at him. There was nothing soft in her eyes. Maati drew himself up, frowning. Anger bloomed in his breast, but he couldn't say why or with whom.

"Why is it so important to you," Eiah asked, "that nothing she does be wrong?"

And with a sensation that was almost physical, Maati knew what he had been trying for months to ignore. A wave of vertigo shook him, but he forced himself to speak.

"Because she should never have become a poet," he said. "She's too young and too angry and more than half mad. And that beast on her lap? We gave it to her."

Eiah's startled expression lasted only a moment before something both resignation and weariness took its place. She kissed Maati's cheek. They stood together, a silence within the storm. He had said what she had already known, and she too had wished it was not truth.

Large Kae and Small Kae quietly prepared the cart and horses. While the wayhouse and every man and woman within running distance came to pay homage to child, mother, and physician, Irit and Maati packed their things. Eiah saw to it that the wine flowed freely, that—near the end—the celebratory drinks were all laced with certain herbs.

It was still four hands before dawn when they made their escape. Maati and Eiah drove the cart. Large Kae rode ahead, leading the spare horses. The others slept in the cart, exhausted bodies fitted in among the crates and sacks. The moon had already set, and the road before them was black and featureless apart from Large Kae's guiding torch. The fog had cleared, but a deep cold kept Maati's cloak wrapped tight. His eyes wanted nothing more than to close.

"We can make the river in seven days if we go through the night. Large Kae will fight against it for the horses' sake," Maati said.

"I'll fight against it for yours," Eiah said. "There was a reason I was trying to make this journey restful."

"I'm fine. I'll last to Utani and years past it, you watch." He sighed. His flesh seemed about to drip off his bones from simple exhaustion. "You watch."

"Crawl back," Eiah said. "Rest. I can do this alone."

"You'd fall asleep," Maati said.

"And use you for a pillow, Uncle. I'm fine. Go."

He looked back. There was a place for him. Irit had made it up with two thick wool blankets. He couldn't see it in the night, but he knew it was there. He wanted nothing more than to turn to it and let the whole broken world fade for a while. He couldn't. Not yet.

"Eiah-kya," he said softly. "About your binding. About Wounded . . ."

She turned to him, a shadow within a shadow. He bent close to her, his voice as low as he could make it and still be heard over the clatter of hooves on stone.

"You know the grammar well? You have it all in mind?"

"Of course," she said.

"Could you do it without it being written? It's usual to write it all out, the way Vanjit-cha did. And it helps to have that there to follow, but you could do the thing without. Couldn't you?"

"I don't know," Eiah said. "Perhaps. It isn't something I'd thought about particularly. But why . . . ?"

"We should postpone your binding," Maati said. "Until you are certain you could do it without the reference text."

Eiah was silent. Something fluttered by, the sound of wings against air.

"What are you saying?" Eiah said, her words low, clipped, and precise. Maati squeezed his hands together. The joints had started aching sometime earlier in the night. The ancient dagger scar in his belly itched the way it did when he'd grown too tired.

"If you were performing the binding, and something happened so that you couldn't see," Maati said. "If you were to go blind when you'd already started . . . you should know the words and the thoughts well enough to keep to it. Not to slip."

"Not pay its price," Eiah said. Meaning, they both knew, die. A moment later, "She'd do that?"

"I don't know," Maati said. "I don't know anything anymore. But be ready if she does."

Eiah shifted the reins, the pattern of the horses' stride altered, and the cart rocked gently. She didn't speak again, and Maati imagined the silence to be thoughtful. He shifted his weight carefully, turned, and let himself slip down to the bed of the cart. The wool blankets were where he'd remembered them. Feeling his way through the darkness reminded him of his brush with blindness. He told himself that the shudder was only the cold of the morning.

The shifting of the cart became like the rocking of a ship or a cradle. Maati's mind softened, slipped. He felt his body sinking into the planks below him, heard the creak and clatter of the wheels. His heart, low and steady, was like the throbbing drum at the wayhouse. It didn't sound at all unwell.

On the shifting edge of sleep, he imagined himself capable of moving between spaces, folding the world so that the distance between himself and Otah-kvo was only a step. He pictured Otah's awe and rage and impotence. It was a fantasy Maati had cultivated before this, and it went through its phases like a habit. Maati's presentation of the poets, the women's grammar, the andat. Otah's abasement and apologies and humble amazement at the world made right. For years, Maati had driven himself toward that moment. He had brought on the sacrifice of ten women, each of them paying the price of a binding that wasn't quite correct.

He watched now as if someone else were dreaming it. Dispassionate, cold, thoughtful. He felt nothing—not disappointment or regret or hope. It was like being a boy again and coming across some iridescent and pincered insect, fascinating and beautiful and dangerous.

More than half asleep, he didn't feel the tiny body inching its way to him until it lay almost within his arms. With the reflex of a man who has cared for a baby, instincts long unused but never forgotten, he gathered the child close.

"You have to kill her," it whispered.

21

>+< Otah stood in the ruins of the school's west garden. Half a century before, he'd been in this same spot, screaming at boys not ten summers old. Humiliating them. This was where, in a fit of childish rage, he had forced a little boy to eat clods of dirt. He'd been twelve summers old at the time, but

he recalled it with a vividness like a cut. Maati's young eyes and blistered hands, tears and apologies. The incident had begun Maati's career as a poet and ended his own.

The stone walls of the school were lower than he remembered them. The crows that perched in the stark, leafless trees, on the other hand, were as familiar as childhood enemies. As a boy, he had hated this place. With all its changes and his own, he still did.

Ashti Beg had told them of Maati's clandestine school. Of Eiah's involvement, and the others'. Two women named Kae, another—Ashti Beg's particular confidante—named Irit. And the new poet, Vanjit. Ashti Beg had escaped the school and the increasingly dangerous poet and her false baby, the andat Blindness. Or Clarity-of-Sight.

Three days after Eiah had left her in one of the low towns, she had lost her sight without warning. The poet girl Vanjit taking revenge for whatever slight she imagined. In a spirit of vengeance, Ashti Beg had offered to lead Otah to them all. Under cover of night, if he wished.

There was no need. Otah knew the way.

The armsmen had gone first, scouting from what little cover there was. No sign of life had greeted them, and they had arrived to find the school cleaned, repaired, cared for, and empty. They had come too late, and the wind and snow had erased any clue to where Maati and Eiah and the other women had gone. Including the new poet.

Idaan emerged from the building, walking toward him with a determined gait. Otah could see the ghost of her breath. He took a pose that offered greeting. It seemed too formal, but he couldn't think of one more fitting and he didn't want to speak.

"I'd guess they left before you reached Pathai," Idaan said. "They've left very little. A few jars of pickled nuts and some dry cheese. Otherwise, it all matches what she said. Someone's been here for months. The kitchen's been used. And the graves are still fresh."

"How many boys died here, do you think?" Otah asked.

"In the war, or when the Dai-kvo ran the place?" Idaan asked, and then went on without waiting for his reply. "I don't know. Fewer than have died in Galt since you and . . . the others left Saraykeht."

She had stumbled at mentioning Danat. He'd noticed more than once that it wasn't a name she liked saying.

"We have to find them," Otah said. "If we can't make her change this soon, the High Council will never forgive us."

Idaan smiled. It was an odd and catlike expression, gentle and predatory both. She glanced at him, saw his unease, and shrugged.

"I'm sorry," she said. "It's only that you keep speaking as if there was still a High Council. Or a nation called Galt, for that. If this Vanjit has done what for all the world it seems she's done, every city and town and village over there has been blinded for weeks now. It isn't winter yet, but it's cold enough. And even if they had gotten some of the harvest in before this, it would only help the people on the farms. You can't walk from town to town blind, much less steer one of these soup pots on wheels."

"They'll find ways."

"Some of them may have, but there'll be fewer tomorrow. And then the next day. The next," Idaan agreed. "It doesn't matter. However many there are, they aren't Galts anymore."

"No? Then what are they?"

"Survivors," Idaan said, and any amusement that had been in her voice was gone. "Just survivors."

They stood in silence, looking at nothing. The crows insulted one another, rose into the air, and settled again. The breeze smelled of new snow and the promise of frost.

Inside the stone walls, the armsmen had made camp. The kitchen was warm, and the smell of boiling lentils and pork fat filled the air. Ana Dasin and Ashti Beg sat side by side, talking to the air. Otah tried not to watch the two blind women, but he found he couldn't turn away. It was their faces that captured him. Their expressions, their gestures thrown into nothingness, were strangely intimate. It was as if by being cast into their personal darkness, they had lost some ability to dissemble. Ashti Beg's anger was carved into the lines around her mouth. Ana, by contrast, betrayed an unexpected serenity in every movement of her hands, every smile. Three empty bowls lay beside them, evidence of Ana's appetite. Their voices betrayed nothing, but their faces and their bodies were eloquent.

As the sun set, the cold grew. It seemed to radiate from the walls, sucking away the life and heat like a restless ghost. That night, they slept in the shelter of the school. Otah took the wide, comfortable room that had once belonged to Tahi-kvo, his first and least-loved teacher. The wool blankets were heavy and thick. The night wind sang empty, mindless songs against the shutters. In the dim flickering light from the fire grate, he let his mind wander.

It was uncomfortable to think of Eiah in this place. It wasn't only that she was angry with him, that she had chosen this path and not the one he preferred. All that was true, but it was also that this place was one part of his life and that she was another. The two didn't belong together. He tried to imagine what he would have said to her, had she and Maati and the other students in Maati's little school still been encamped there.

The truth he could not admit to anyone was that he was relieved that he hadn't found them.

The shadows at the fire grate seemed to grow solid, a figure crouching there. He knew it was an illusion. It wasn't the first time his mind had tricked itself into imagining Kiyan after her death. He smiled at the vision of his wife, but the dream of her had already faded. It was a sign, and since it was both intended for him and created by his mind, it was perfectly explicable. If killing his daughter was the price it took to save the world, then the world could die. He took little comfort in the knowledge.

In the morning, Danat woke him, grinning. A piece of paper flapped in the boy's hand like a moth as Danat threw open the shutters and let the morning light spill in. Otah blinked, yawned, and frowned. Dreams already half-remembered were fading quickly. Danat dropped onto the foot of Otah's cot.

"I've found them," Danat said.

Otah sat up, taking a pose that asked explanation. Danat held out the paper. The handwriting was unfamiliar to him, the characters wider than standard and softly drawn. He took the page and rubbed his eyes as if to clear them.

"I was sleeping in one of the side rooms," Danat said. "When I woke up this morning, I saw that. It was in a corner, not even hidden. I don't know how I missed it last night, except it was dark and I was tired."

Otah's eyes able now to focus, his mind more fully awake, he turned his attention to the letter.

> *Ashti-cha—*
>
> *We have decided to leave. Eiah says that Maati-kvo isn't well, so we're all going to Utani so that she can get help caring for him. Please, if you get this, you have to come back! Vanjit is just as bad as ever, and I'm afraid without you here to put her in her place, she'll only get worse. Small Kae has started having nightmares about her. And the baby! You should see the way it tries to get away. It slipped into my lap last night after the Great Poet had gone to sleep and curled up like a kitten.*
>
> *They've almost finished loading the cart. I'm going to sneak back in once we're almost under way so that she won't find it. You have to come back! Meet us in Utani as soon as you can.*

The letter was signed Irit Laatani. Otah folded the paper and tapped it against his lips, thinking. It was plausible. It could be a trick to send them off to Utani, but that would mean that they knew where Otah and his party were, and the errand they were on. If that was the case, there was no reason for misleading them. Vanjit and her little Blindness could stop any pursuit if she wanted it. Danat coughed expectantly.

"Utani," Otah said. "They're going north, just the way you'd planned. This is where you tell me how clever you were for heading there at the first?"

Danat laughed, shaking his head.

"You were right, Papa-kya. Coming here was the right thing. If Maati wasn't ill, they'd have been here."

"Still. It does mean they've stopped hiding. That's a risk if they've only got one poet."

Danat took a questioning pose.

"This poet," Otah said. "She's their protection and their power. As long as she has the andat in her control, they think that they're safe. In truth, though, she can only defend against things she knows. As long as there is only one poet, a well-placed man with a bow could end her before she could blind him. And then none of them are defended."

"Unless there's a second binding. Another andat," Danat said, and Otah took a confirming pose. Danat frowned. "But if there had been, then Irit would have said so, wouldn't she? If Eiah had managed to capture Wounded?"

"I'd expect her to, yes," Otah said.

"Then why would they go?"

Otah tapped the letter.

"Just what the woman said. Because Maati's ill," he said. "And because Eiah decided that caring for him was worth the risk. If he's bad enough to need other physicians' help, they may well be going slowly. Keeping him rested."

"So we go," Danat said. "We go now, and as fast as we can manage. And attack the poet before she can blind us."

"Yes," Otah said. "Burn the books, stop them from binding the andat. Go back, and try to put the world back together again."

"Only . . . only then how do we fix the people in Galt? How do we cure Ana?"

"There's a decision to make," Otah said. "Doing this quickly and well means letting Galt remain sightless."

"Then we can't kill the poet," Danat said.

Otah took a long breath.

"Think about that before you say it," he said. "This is likely the only chance we'll have to take them by surprise. The Galts in Saraykeht are safe enough. The ones in their own cities are likely dead already. The others could be sacrificed, and it would keep us alive."

"And childless, so what would the advantage be?" Danat said. "Everything you'd tried to do would be destroyed."

"Everything I wanted to do has already been destroyed," Otah said. "There isn't a solution to this. Not anymore. I'm reduced to looking for the least painful way that it can end. I don't see how we take these pieces and make a world worth living in."

Danat was silent and still, then took Otah's hand.

"I can," Danat said. "There's hope. There's still hope."

"This poet? Everything Ashti Beg says paints her as angry and petty and cruel at heart. She hates the Galts and thinks little enough of me. That's the woman we would be trying to reason with. And if she chooses, there is more than Galt to lose."

Danat took a pose that accepted the stakes like a man at a betting table. He would put the world and everything in it at risk for the chance that remained to save Ana's home. Otah hesitated, and then replied with a pose that stood witness to the decision. A feeling of pride warmed him.

Kiyan-kya, he thought, we have raised a good man. Please all the gods that we've also raised a wise one.

"I'll go tell the others," Danat said.

He rose and walked for the door, pausing only when Otah called after him. Danat, at the doorway, looked back.

"It's the right choice," Otah said. "No matter how poorly this happens, you made the right choice."

"There was no other option," Danat said.

It had been clear enough that no matter what the next step was, it wouldn't involve staying at the school. Under Idaan's direction, the armsmen were already refilling the water and coal stores for the steamcarts, packing what little equipment they had used, and preparing themselves for the road. The sky was white where it wasn't gray, the snow blurring the horizon. Ashti Beg sat alone beside the great bronze doors that had once opened only for the Dai-kvo. They were stained with verdigris and stood ajar. No one besides Otah saw the significance of it.

Midmorning saw a thinning of the clouds, a weak, pale blue forcing its way through the very top of the sky's dome. The horses were in harness, the carts showing their billows of mixed smoke and steam, and everything was at the ready except Idaan and Ana. The armsmen waited, ready to leave. Otah and Danat went back.

Otah found the pair in a large room. Ana, sitting on an ancient bench, had bent forward. Tears streaked the girl's cheeks, her hair was a wild tangle, and her hands clasped until the fingertips were red and the knuckles white. Idaan stood beside her, arms crossed and eyes as bleak as murder. Before Otah could announce himself, Idaan saw him. His sister leaned close to the Galtic girl, murmured something, listened to the soft reply, and then marched to the doorway and Otah's side.

"Is there . . . is something the matter?" Otah asked.

"Of course there is. How long have you been traveling with that girl?"

"Since Saraykeht," Otah said.

"Have you noticed yet that she isn't a man?" Idaan's voice was sharp as knives. "Tell the armsmen to stand down. Then bring me a bowl of snow."

"What's the matter?" Otah demanded. And then, "Is it her time of the month? Does she need medicine?"

Idaan looked at him as if he had asked what season came after spring: pitying, incredulous, disgusted.

"Get me some snow. Or, better, some ice. Tell your men that we'll be ready in a hand and a half, and for all the gods there ever were, keep your son away from her until we can put her back together. The last thing she needs is to feel humiliated."

Otah took a pose that promised compliance, but then hesitated. Idaan's dark eyes flashed with something that wasn't anger. When she spoke, her voice was lower but no softer.

"How have you spent a lifetime in the company of women and learned nothing?" she asked, and, shaking her head, turned back to Ana.

True to her word, a hand and a half later, Ana and Idaan emerged from the school as if nothing strange had happened. Ana's outer robe was changed to a dark wool, and she leaned on Idaan's arm as she stepped up to the bed of the steamcart. Danat moved forward, but Idaan's scowl drove him back. The two women made their slow way to the shed, where Idaan closed the door behind them.

The men steering the carts called out to one another, voices carrying like crows' calls in the empty landscape. The carts stuttered and lurched, and turned to the east, tracking back along the path to the high road between ruined Nantani and Pathai, from which they'd come. Otah rode down the path he'd walked as a boy, searching his mind for some feeling of kinship with his past, but the world as it was demanded too much of him. He searched for some memory deep within him of the first time he'd walked away from the school, of leaving everything he'd known, rejected, behind him.

His mind was knotted with questions of how to find the poet, how to persuade her to do as he asked, what Idaan had meant, what was wrong with Ana, whether the steamcarts had enough fuel, and a growing ache in his spine that came from too many days riding horses he didn't know. There was no effort to spare for the past. Whatever he didn't remember now of his original flight from the school he likely never would. The past would be lost, as it always was. Always. He didn't bother trying to hold it.

They made better time than he had expected, starting as late as they had. By the time they stopped for the night, the high road was behind them. The fastest route to Utani would be overland to the Qiit, then by boat up the river. Any hope they had of overtaking Maati and Eiah would come on the roads, where the steamcarts gave Otah an advantage. They would have to sleep in the open more than if they had kept to wider roads, and the rough terrain increased the possibility of the carts breaking or getting stuck. Even of the boiler bursting and killing anyone too near it. But Idaan's voice spoke in Otah's mind of the next day, and the next, and the next, so he pushed them and himself.

Four of the armsmen rode ahead in the lowering gloom of night to scout out the next day's path. The others prepared a simple meal of pork and rice, Ashti Beg sitting with them and trading jokes. Danat's slow circling of their camp took the name of defense but seemed more to be avoiding the still-closed shed where Idaan and Ana rested. Otah sat alone near the steamcart's kiln, reflecting that it was very much like his son to shift between noble dedication in the morning and childish pouting as night came on. He had been much the same as a young man, or imagined that he had.

The door opened, Ana's laughter spilling out into the night. Idaan led the girl forward, letting Ana keep a careful grip on her. Her dark eyes and Ana's unfocused gray ones were both light and merry. Ana's hair had been combed and braided in the style of children in the winter cities. In the dim moonlight, it made Ana seem hardly more than a girl.

Idaan steered the girl to the cart's front and helped her sit beside Otah. He coughed once to make sure the girl knew he was there, but she seemed unsurprised at the sound. Idaan placed a hand on the back of the girl's neck.

"I'll go get some food," Idaan said. "My brother here should be able to keep you out of trouble for that long."

Ana took a pose that offered thanks. She did a creditable job of it. Idaan snorted, patted the girl's neck, and lowered herself to the ground. Otah heard her footsteps crushing the snow as she walked away.

"Ana-cha," Otah said. His voice was more tentative than he liked. "I hope you're well?"

"Fine," she said. "Thank you. I'm sorry I delayed things today. It won't happen again."

"Hardly worth thinking about," Otah said, relieved that her infirmity had passed. Grief, he suspected, over what the poet had done to her, to her family, her nation.

"I misjudged you," Ana said. "I know it seems like everything we do is another round of apology, but I am sorry for it."

"It might be simpler to agree to forgive each other in advance," Otah said, and Ana laughed. It was a warmer sound than he'd expected. A tension he hadn't known he felt lessened and he smiled into the glowing coals of the kiln. "It is fair to ask in what manner you judged me poorly?"

"I thought you were cold. Hard. You have to understand, I grew up with monster stories about the Khaiem and the andat."

"I do," Otah said, sighing. "I look back, and I suspect that more than half of the problems between Galt and the Khaiem came from ignorance. Ignorance and power are a poor combination."

"Tell me . . ." Ana said, and then stopped. Her brow furrowed, and in the dim light he thought she was blushing. Otah put his hand over hers. She shook her head, and then turned her milky eyes to him. "You've forgiven me in advance if this is too much to ask. Tell me about Danat's mother."

"Kiyan?" Otah said. "Well. What do you want to know about her?"

"Anything. Just tell me," the girl said.

Otah collected himself, and then began to pluck stories. The night they'd met. The night he'd told her that he was more than a simple courier and she'd thrown him out of her wayhouse. The ways she had helped to smooth things as he learned how to become first Khai Machi and then Emperor. He didn't tell the hard stories. The conflict over Sinja's feelings for her, and Otah's poor response to them. The long fears they suffered together when Danat was young and weak in the lungs. Her death. Still, he didn't think he kept all the sorrow from his voice.

Idaan returned halfway through one story, four bowls in her hands like a teahouse servant juggling food for a full table. Otah took one without pausing, and Idaan squatted on the boards at Ana's feet and pressed another into the girl's hands. Otah went on with other little stories—Kiyan's balancing the combined populations of Machi and Cetani with Balasar Gice's crippled army in the wake of the war. Her refusal to allow servants to bathe her. The story of when the representative of Eddensea had mistaken something she'd said and thought she'd invited him to bed with her.

Danat arrived out of the darkness, drawn by their voices. Idaan gave him the last bowl, and he sat at Otah's side, then shifted, then shifted again until his back rested against Ana's shin. He added stories of his own. His mother's sharp tongue and wayhouse keeper's vocabulary, the songs she'd sung, all the scraps and moments that built up a boy's memory of his mother. It was beautiful to listen to. It wasn't something Otah himself had ever had.

In the end, Ana let Danat lead her back to her shelter, leaving Otah and his sister alone by the black and cooling kiln. The armsmen had prepared sleeping tents for them, but Idaan seemed content to sit up drinking watered wine in the cold night air, and Otah found himself pleased enough to join her.

"I don't suppose you'd care to explain to your poor idiot brother what happened today?" he said at length.

"You haven't put it together?" Idaan said. "This Vanjit creature has destroyed the only home Ana-cha had to go to. She's had to look long and hard at what her life could be in the place she's found herself, crippled in a foreign land, and it shook her."

"She's in love with Danat?"

"Of course she is," Idaan said. "It would have happened in half the time if you and her mother hadn't insisted on it. I think that's more frightening for her than the poet killing her nation."

"I don't know what you mean," he said.

"She's spent her life watching her mother linked with her father," Idaan said. "There are only so many years you can soak in the regrets of others before you start to think that all the world's that way."

"I had the impression that Farrer-cha loved his wife deeply," Otah said.

"And I had it that there's more than a husband to make a marriage," Idaan said. "It isn't her mother she fears being, it's Farrer-cha. She's afraid of having her love merely tolerated. I spent most of the day talking about Cehmai. I told her that if she really wanted to know what spending a life with Danat would be like, she should see what sort of man you were. If she wanted to know how Danat would see her, to find how you saw your wife."

Otah laughed, and he thought he saw the darkness around Idaan shift as if she had smiled.

"I'm sorry I didn't have the chance to know her," Idaan said. "She sounds like a good woman."

"She was," Otah said. "I miss her."

"I know you do," Idaan said. "And now Ana-cha knows it too."

"Does it matter?" Otah said. "All the hopes I had for building Galt and the Khaiem together are in rags around my knees. We're on a hunt for a girl who can ruin the world. What she's done to Galt, she could do to us. Or to all the world, if she wanted it. How do we plan for a marriage between Danat and Ana when it's just as likely that we'll all be starving and blind by Candles Night?"

"We're all born to die, Most High," Idaan said, the title sounding like an endearment in her voice. "Every love ends in parting or death. Every nation ends and every empire. Every baby born was going to die, given enough time. If being fated for destruction were enough to take the joy out of things, we'd slaughter children fresh from the womb. But we don't. We wrap them in warm cloth and we sing to them and feed them milk as if it might all go on forever."

"You make it sound like something you've done," Otah said.

Idaan made a sound he couldn't interpret, part grunt, part whimper.

"What is it?" he asked the darkness.

The silence lasted for the length of five long breaths together. When she spoke, her voice was low and rich with embarrassment.

"Lambs," she said.

"Lambs?"

"I used to wrap up the newborn lambs and keep them in the house. I even had Cehmai build them a crib that I could rock them in. After a few years, we had to switch to goats. I couldn't slaughter the lambs after all that, could I? By the end, I think we had sixty."

Otah didn't know whether to laugh or put his arms around the woman. The thought of the hard-hearted killer of his own father, his own brothers, cuddling a baby lamb was as absurd as it was sorrowful.

"Is it like this for everyone?" he asked softly. "Does every woman suffer this? Is the need to care for something that strong?"

"Strong? When it strikes, yes. But everyone? No," Idaan said. "Of course not. As it happened, it struck me. I assume Maati's students all feel strongly enough about it to risk their lives. But not every woman needs a child, and, thank the gods, the madness sometimes passes. It did for me."

"You wouldn't be a mother now? If it were possible, you wouldn't choose to?"

"Gods, no. I'd have been terrible at it. But I miss them," Idaan said. "I miss my little lambs. And that brings us back to Ana-cha, doesn't it?"

Otah took a pose that asked clarification.

"Who am I," Idaan asked, "to say that falling in love is ridiculous just because it's doomed?"

22

The weeks spent at the school had let Maati forget the ways in which the world broadened when he was traveling, and also the ways in which it narrowed when he was traveling with company. Living in the same walls, the same gardens, and surrounded as he had been by only a few deeply familiar faces had begun to grate on him before they left, but there had still been a way to find a moment to steal away. On the road, all of them together, the chances for private conversation were few and precious.

Since the andat had spoken, he hadn't found himself alone with Eiah, or at least not so clearly so that he would risk speaking. He didn't want either of the Kaes or Irit to know what had happened. He was afraid that they would say something where Vanjit could hear them. He was afraid that Vanjit would find out what the andat had said and take some terrible action in her fear and in her own defense.

He was afraid because he was afraid, and he was half-certain that Vanjit knew he was.

They reached the lands surrounding the river sooner than he would have wanted; if the long days and nights on the road had kept him in close quarters with the others, the days ahead sharing a boat would be worse. He had to find a way to talk with Eiah before that, and the prospect of his lessening time made him anxious.

Cold and snow hadn't reached the river valley yet. It was as if their journey were moving backward in time. The leaves here clung to the trees, some of them with the gold and red and yellow still struggling to push out the last hints of green. As they approached the water, farms and low towns clustered closer and closer. The roads and paths began to cling to irrigation channels, and other travelers—most merely local, but some from the great cities—appeared more and more often. Maati sat at the front of the cart, his robes wrapped close around him, staring ahead and trying not to put himself anywhere that the andat could catch his eye.

He was, in fact, so preoccupied with the politics and dangers within his small party that he didn't see the Galts until his horses were almost upon them.

Three men, none of them older than thirty summers, sat at the side of the road. They wore filthy robes that had once been red or orange. The tallest had a leather satchel over his shoulder. They had stepped a few feet off the path at the sound of hooves, and the tall grass made them seem like apparitions from a children's epic. Their eyes were blue, the pupils gray. None of them had shaved in recent memory. Their gaunt faces turned to the road from habit. There was no expression in them, not even hunger. Maati didn't realize he had slowed the horses until he heard Eiah call out from the cart's bed behind him. At her word, he stopped. Large Kae and Irit, taking their turns on horseback, reined in. Vanjit and Small Kae moved to the side of the cart. Maati risked a glance at Clarity-of-Sight, but it was still and silent.

"Who are you?" Eiah demanded in their language. "What are your names?"

The Galtic apparitions shifted, blinking their empty eyes in confusion. The tall one with the satchel recovered first.

"I'm Jase Hanin," he said, speaking too loudly. "These are my brothers. It isn't plague. Whatever took our eyes, miss, it wasn't plague. We aren't a danger."

Eiah muttered something that Maati couldn't make out, then shifted a crate in the back. When he turned to look, she had her physician's satchel on her hip and was preparing to drop down to the road. Vanjit, seeing this as well, grabbed Eiah's sleeve.

"Don't," Vanjit said. The word was as much command as plea.

"I'll be fine," Eiah said. Vanjit's grip tightened on the cloth, and Maati saw their eyes lock.

"Vanjit-cha," Maati said. "It's all right. Let her go."

The poet looked back at him, anger in her gaze, but she did as he'd said. Eiah slipped down to the ground and walked toward the surprised Galts.

"You're a long way from anyplace," Eiah said.

"We were out in the low towns," the tall one said. "Something happened. We've been trying to get back to Saraykeht. Our mother's there, you see. Only it seems like we're put on the wrong path or stolen from as often as we're helped."

He tried what had once been a winning smile. Maati tied the reins to the cart and lowered himself to the road as well.

"Your mother?" Eiah said.

"Yes, miss," the Galt said.

"Well," she said, her voice cool. "At least you weren't a band of those charming liars out selling the promise of women in the low towns. What's in the satchel?"

The Galt looked chagrined and desperate, but he didn't lie.

"Names of men, miss. The ones who wanted wives from Galt."

"I thought as much," Eiah said.

"Don't help them," Vanjit said. She'd climbed to the front of the cart, but hadn't taken up the reins. From the way she held her body, Maati guessed it was a matter of time before she did. He saw the andat's black eyes peering over the cart at him and looked away. Eiah might as well not have heard her.

"We were going to do the right thing with them, miss," the tall man said. "There's a man in Acton putting together women who want to come over. We had an arrangement with him. All the money's been taken, but we still have the lists. God's word, we're going to keep our end of the thing, if we can just get back to Saraykeht."

"You stole from them," Eiah said, pulling a leather waterskin from her satchel. "They stole back from you. Seems to me that leaves you even. Here, drink from this. It's not only water, so don't take more than a couple of swallows, any of you."

"Eiah-kya," Irit said. Her voice was high and anxious, but she didn't say more than the name. Large Kae's mount whickered and sidestepped, sensing something uneasing in its rider's posture. Eiah might as easily have been alone.

"These . . . put out your hand. These are lengths of silver. I've put a notch in each of them, so you'll know if someone's trying to switch them. It's enough to pay for a passage to Saraykeht. The road you're following now, it will be about another day's walk to the river. Maybe longer. Call it two."

"Thank you, miss," one of the other two said.

"I don't suppose we could ride on the back of your cart?" the tall man said, hope in his smile.

"No," Maati said. There was a limit to what Vanjit would allow, and he wasn't ready for that confrontation. "We've spent too long at this. Eiah."

Without a word, without meeting his gaze, Eiah turned back, climbed into the cart, and went back to the wax writing tablets she'd spent her morning over. Maati climbed back up into the cart and started them back down the road, Vanjit at his side.

"She shouldn't have done that," Vanjit murmured. Soft as the words were, he knew Eiah would hear them.

"There's no harm in it," Maati said. "Let it pass."

Vanjit frowned, but let the subject go. She spent the rest of the day beside him, as if guarding him from Eiah. For her part, Eiah might have been alone with her tablets. Even when the rest of them sang to pass the time, she kept to her work, steady and focused. When the conversation turned to whether they should keep riding after sunset in hopes of reaching the river, she spoke for stopping on the road. She didn't want Maati to be any more tired than was necessary. Large Kae sided with her for the horses' sake.

The women made a small camp, dividing the night into watches since they were so near the road. Vanjit sharpened their sight in the evenings but insisted on returning them to normal when dawn came. She, of course, didn't have a turn at watch. Neither did Maati. Instead, he watched the moon as it hung in the tree branches, listened to the low call of owls, and drank the noxious tea. Vanjit, Irit, and Small Kae lay in the bed of the cart, their robes wrapped tightly around them. The andat sat beside its poet, as still as a stone. Eiah and Large Kae had taken the first watch, and were sitting with their backs to the fire to keep their unnaturally sharp eyes well-adapted to the darkness.

You have to kill her, it had said, and when Maati had reared back, his fragile heart racing, the andat had only looked at him. Its childish eyes had seemed older, like something ancient wearing the mask of a baby. It had nodded to itself and then turned and crawled awkwardly away. The message had been delivered. The rest, it seemed to imply, was Maati's.

He looked at the bowl of dark tea in his hands. The warmth of it was almost gone. Small bits of leaf and root shifted in the depths. An idea occurred to him. Not, perhaps, a brilliant one, but they would reach the river and hire a boat in the morning. It was a risk worth taking.

"Eiah-kya," he said softly. "Something's odd with this tea. Could you . . . ?"

Eiah looked over at him. She looked old in the dim light of moon and fire. She came to the tree where he sat. Large Kae's gaze followed her. The sleepers in the cart didn't stir, but the andat's eyes were on him. Maati held out the bowl, and Eiah sipped from it.

"We need to speak," Maati said under his breath. "The others can't know."

"It seems fine. Give me your wrists," Eiah said in a conversational tone. Then, softly, "What's happened?"

"It's the andat. Blindness. It spoke to me. It told me to kill Vanjit-cha. This is all its doing."

Eiah switched to compare pulses in both wrists, her eyes closed as if she were concentrating.

"How do you mean?" she whispered.

"The babe was always clinging to Ashti Beg. It made Ashti-cha feel that it cared for her. Vanjit grew jealous. The conflict between them was the andat's doing. Now that it thinks we're frightened of it, it's trying to use me as well. It's Stone-Made-Soft encouraging Cehmai-cha into distracting conflicts. It's Seedless again."

Eiah put down his wrists, pressing her fingertips against his palms with the air of a buyer at a market.

"Does it matter?" Eiah murmured. "Say that the andat has been manipulating us all. What does that change?"

Eiah put down his hands. Her smile was thin and humorless. Something scurried in the bushes, small and fast. A mouse, perhaps.

"Is all well?" Large Kae called from the fire. In the cart, someone moaned and stirred.

"Fine," Maati said. "We're fine. Only adjusting something." Then, quietly, "I doubt it changes anything. Vanjit's more likely to side with Clarity-of-Sight than with us. If it is scheming against her—and, really, I can't see why it wouldn't be—it's better placed to get what it wants. It *is* her. It knows what she needs and what she fears."

"You think *she* wants to die?" Eiah asked.

"I think she wants to stop hurting. Binding the andat was supposed to stop the pain. Having a babe was supposed to. Revenge on the Galts. Now here she is with everything she wanted, and she still hurts."

Maati shrugged. Eiah took a pose of agreement and of sorrow.

"If she weren't a poet, I'd pity her," Eiah said. "But she is, and so she frightens me."

"Maati-kya?" Vanjit's voice came from the darkness over Eiah's shoulder. It was high and anxious. "What's the matter with Maati-kvo?"

"Nothing," Eiah said, turning back. Vanjit was sitting up, her hair wild, her eyes wide. The andat was clutched to her breast. Eiah took a reassuring pose. "Everything's fine."

Poet and andat looked at Maati with expressions of distrust so alike they were eerie.

THE RIVER QIIT HAD ITS SOURCE FAR NORTH OF UTANI. RAINS FROM THE MOUNTAIN ranges that divided the cities of the Khaiem from the Westlands flowed east into the wide flats, gathered together, and carved their way south. Utani,

the ruins of Udun, and then far to the south, the wide, silted delta just east of
Saraykeht.

At its widest, the river was nearly half a mile across, but that was farther
south. Here, at the low town squatting on the riverfront, the water was less
than half that, its surface smooth and shining as silver. Eight thin streets
crossed one another at unpredictable angles. Dogs and chickens negotiated
their peace in bark and squawk, tooth and beak as Maati drove past. Two wayhouses offered rest. Another teahouse was painted in characters that made it
clear there were no beds for hire there, and grudgingly offered fresh noodles
and old wine. The air smelled rich with decay and new growth, the cold water
and the dust of the road. There should have been children in the streets, calling, begging, playing games both innocent and cruel.

Maati drew the cart to a halt in the yard of the wayhouse nearest the riverfront itself. Large Kae dismounted and went in to negotiate for a room. After
the incident with the andat, the agreement was that someone would always
be in a private room with the shutters closed and the door bolted, watching the
andat. If all went as he intended it, they would be on the river well before
nightfall, but still . . .

Vanjit's scowl had deepened through the day. Twice more they had passed
men and women with pale skin and blind eyes. Two were begging at the side of
the road, another was being led on the end of a rope by an old woman. Eiah had
not insisted on stopping to offer them aid. Happily, there were no Galtic faces
at the wayhouse. Vanjit paused in the main room, her hand on Maati's shoulder.
The andat was in her other arm, concealed by a blanket and as still as death.

"Maati-kvo," she said. "I'm worried. Eiah has been so strange since we left
the school, don't you think? All the hours she's spent writing on those tablets.
I don't think it's good for her."

"I'm sure she's fine," Maati said with what he hoped was a reassuring smile.

"And giving silver to those Galts," Vanjit said, her voice creeping higher. "I
don't know what she means by that. Do you?"

Large Kae came in from a dark corridor and motioned them to follow. Maati
almost had to pull Vanjit to get her attention. She glared at Large Kae's back as
they walked.

"It seems to me," Vanjit continued, "that Eiah is forgetting who are her allies and who are her enemies. I know you love her, Maati-kvo, but you can't let
that blind you. You can't ignore the truth."

"I won't, Vanjit-kya," Maati said. The room was on the first floor. Fresh
rushes on the floor. A small cot of stretched canvas. Oak shutters closed against
the daylight. "You leave this to me. I'll see to it."

Large Kae left, murmuring something about seeing to the animals. When
the door closed behind her, Vanjit let the blanket fall and set the andat on the
cot. It cooed and burbled, waving its hands and grinning toothlessly. It was a
parody of infantile delight, and seeing Vanjit's smile—pleasure and fear and
anger all in the smallest stretching of her lips—made Maati's flesh crawl.

"You have to do something," she said. "Eiah-kya can't be trusted with the andat. You wouldn't . . ."

The baby shrieked and flopped to its side, trying to lower itself to the floor. Vanjit moved forward and lifted it back up before she went on.

"You wouldn't let someone you can't trust bind the andat. You wouldn't do that."

"Certainly, I'd try not to," Maati said.

"That's a strange answer."

"I'm not a god. I use the judgment I have. It isn't as if I can see into someone's heart."

"But if you think Eiah can't be trusted," Vanjit said, anger growing in her voice, "you *will* stop her. You have to."

Who am I speaking to? he wondered. The girl? The andat? Does Vanjit know what she's saying?

"Yes," Maati said slowly. "If she isn't fit to be a poet to wield the andat, it would be my duty to see that she does not. I will stop her. But I have to be sure. I can't do this thing until I'm sure there's nothing I can do that will mend her."

"Mend her?" Vanjit said and took a pose that scorned the thought.

"I won't kill someone unless there is no other way."

Vanjit stepped back, her face going pale. The andat's gaze shifted from one to the other and back, its eyes shining with unfeigned delight.

"I never said to kill her," Vanjit said, her voice soft.

"Didn't you?" Maati said as if making it an accusation. "You're sure of that?"

He turned and left the room, his hands trembling, his heart racing.

He'd been an idiot. He'd slipped. Perhaps making him say more than he'd intended had been the point; perhaps the andat had guessed that it could make him go too far. He paused in the main room, his head feeling light. He sat at one of the tables and lowered his head to his knees.

His heart was still pounding, and his face felt hot and flushed. The voices of the keeper and Irit seemed to echo, as if he were hearing them from the far end of a tunnel. He gritted his teeth, willing his body to calm itself, to obey him.

Slowly, his pulse calmed. The heat in his face lessened. He didn't know how long he'd been sitting at the little table by the back wall. It seemed like only moments and it also seemed like half the day. Both were plausible. He tried to stand, but he was weak and shaking. Like a man who'd just run a race.

He motioned to the keeper and asked for strong tea. The man brought it quickly enough. A cast-iron pot in the shape of a frog, the spigot a hollow tongue between its lips. Maati poured the rich, green tea into a carved wooden bowl and sat for a moment, breathing in the scent of it before trying to lift it to his lips.

By the time Irit arrived, he felt nearly himself again. Exhausted and weak, but himself. The woman sat across from him, her fingers knotted about one another. Her smile was too wide.

"Maati-kvo," she said and belatedly took a pose of greeting. "I've just come from the riverfront. Eiah has hired a boat. It looks like a good one. Wide enough that it isn't supposed to rock so much. Or get stuck on sandbars. They talked a bit about sandbars. In any case—"

"What's the matter?"

Irit looked out toward the main room as if expecting to see someone there. She spoke without looking at him.

"I'm not ever going to make a binding, Maati-kvo. I may have helped, I may not. But we both know I'm not going to do the thing."

"You want to leave," Maati said.

She did look at him now, her mouth small, her eyes large. She was like a picture of herself drawn by someone who thought poorly of her.

"Take your things," Maati said. "Do it before we get on the river."

She took a pose that accepted his orders, but the fear remained in the way she held her body. Maati nodded to himself.

"I'll tell Vanjit that I've sent you on an errand for me. That Eiah needed some particular root that only grows in the south. You're to meet us with it in Utani. She won't know the truth."

"Thank you," Irit said, relief in her expression at last. "I'm sorry."

"Hurry," Maati said. "There isn't much time."

Irit scuttled out, her hands fluttering as if they possessed a life of their own. Maati sat quietly in the growing darkness, sipped his tea, and tried to convince himself that his strength was coming back. He'd let himself get frightened, that was all. It wasn't as if he'd fainted. He was fine. By the time Eiah and Small Kae came to collect Vanjit and Clarity-of-Sight, he mostly believed it.

Eiah accepted the news of Irit's departure without comment. The two Kaes glanced at each other and kept loading their few remaining crates onto the boat. Vanjit said nothing, only nodded and took Clarity-of-Sight to the bow of the little craft to stare out at the water.

The boat was as long as six men laid end to end, and as wide across as five. It sat low in the water, and the back quarter was filled with coal and kiln, boiler and wide-slatted wheel ready to take to the river. The boatman who watched the fires and the rudder was older than Maati, his skin thin and wrinkled. The second who took duty whenever the old man rested might have been his son. Neither man spoke to the passengers, and the sight of the baby struggling in Vanjit's arms seemed to elicit no reaction.

Once they were all on and their belongings tied down, Eiah took a pose that indicated their readiness. The second called out, his voice almost a song. The riverfront clerk called back. Ropes were untied, the evil chuffing from the wheel grew louder, and the deep, violent slap of wood against water jerked them away from the bank and into the river. It seemed as if a breeze had come up, though it was likely only the speed of the boat. Eiah sat beside Maati, taking his wrists.

"We told them the child was the get of one of the utkhaiem on a Westlands girl. Vanjit is the nurse."

Maati nodded. It was as good a lie as any. At the bow, Vanjit looked back at the sound of her name. Her eyes were clear, but something in the set of her face made him think she'd been crying. Eiah frowned, pinching his fingertips until they went white, then waiting for the blood to pour back into them.

"She asked about your tablets," he said. "You have been busy with them. The binding?"

"I'm trying to cut deep enough that I can read it with my fingers," Eiah said quietly. "It's a better exercise than I'd expected. I think I've seen some ways to improve the grammar itself. It will mean another draft, but . . . How are you feeling?"

"What? Ah, fine. I feel fine."

"Tired?"

"Of course I'm tired. I'm old and I've been on the road too long and . . ."

And I have loosed a mad poet on the world, he thought. All the cruelties and tricks of the Dai-kvo, all the pain and loss that I suffered to be a poet was justified. If it kept people like Vanjit from the power of the andat, it was all justified. And I have ignored it.

As if reading the words in his eyes, Eiah glanced over her shoulder at Vanjit. The sun was shining off the water, surrounding the dark, huddled girl with a brilliant halo of gold and white. When Maati looked away, the image had scarred his eyes. It lay over everything else he saw, black where it had been light, and a pale shape the color of mourning robes where Vanjit had been.

"I'm making your tea," Eiah said, her voice grim. "Stay here and rest."

"Eiah-kya? We . . . we have to kill her," Maati said.

Eiah turned to him, her expression empty. He gestured to Vanjit's back. His hand trembled.

"Before your binding," he said, "we should be sure that it's safe for you. Or, that is, as safe as we can make it. You . . . you understand."

Eiah sighed. When she spoke again, her voice was distant and reflective.

"I knew a physician in Lachi. She told me about being in a low town when one of the men caught blood fever. He was a good person. Well-liked. This was a long time ago, so he had children. He'd gone out hunting and come back ill. She had them smother him and burn the body. His children stayed in their house and screamed the whole time they did it. She didn't sleep well for years afterward."

Her eyes were focused on nothing, her jaw forward as if she was facing someone down. Man or god or fate.

"You're saying it's not her fault," Maati said softly, careful not to speak Vanjit's name. "She was a little girl who had her family slaughtered before her. She was a lost woman who wanted a child and could never have one. What's wrong with her mind was done to her."

Eiah took a pose that disagreed.

"I'm saying no matter how little my physician friend slept, she saved those children's lives," Eiah said. "There are some herbs. When we stop for the night, I can gather them. I'll see it's done."

"No. No, I'll do the thing. If it's anyone, it should—"

"It will have to be quick," Eiah said. "She mustn't know it's coming. You can't do that."

Maati took a pose that challenged her, and Eiah folded his hands gently closed.

"Because you still want to save her," she said. Something about weariness and determination made her look like her father.

Otah, who had killed a poet once too.

23

>+< Otah rose in the mornings with stiff, aching joints and a pain in his side that would not fade. The steamcarts allowed each of them the chance to sleep for a hand or two in the late mornings or just after the midday meal. Without the rest, Otah knew he wouldn't have been able to keep pace with the others.

The courier found them on the road. His outer robe was the colors of House Siyanti and mud-spattered to the waist. His mount cantered alongside the carts now, cooling down from the morning's travel as its rider waited for replies. The man's satchel held a dozen letters at least, but only one had occasioned his speed. It was written on paper the color of cream, sewn with black thread, and the imprint in the wax belonged to Balasar Gice. Otah sat in his saddle, afraid to open it and afraid not to.

The thread ripped easily and the pages unfolded. Otah skimmed the letter from beginning to end, then began again, reading more slowly, letting the full import of the words wash over him. He folded the letter and slipped it into his sleeve, his heart heavy.

Danat drew closer, his hands in a pose that both called for inclusion and offered sympathy. The boy might not know what had happened, but he'd drawn the fact that it wasn't good.

"Chaburi-Tan," Otah said, beginning with the least of the day's losses. "It's gone. Sacked. Burned. We don't know whether the mercenaries turned sides or simply wouldn't protect it, but it comes to the same thing. The pirates attacked the city, took what they could, and set the rest alight."

"And the fleet?"

Otah looked at the roadside. Sun had melted the snow as far as its light could reach, but the shadows were still pale. Otah had known Sinja Ajutani for more years than not. The dry humor, the casual disrespect of all things pompous or self-certain, the knife-sharp and unsentimental analysis of any issue. When Kiyan died, they had been the only two men in the world who truly understood what had been lost.

Now, only Otah knew.

"What ships remain have been set to guard the seafront at Saraykeht," he said when he could speak again. "The thought is that winter will protect Yalakeht and Amnat-Tan. When the thaw comes in spring, we may have to revisit the plan."

"Are you all right, Papa-kya?"

"I'll be fine," Otah said, then he raised his hand and called the courier close. "Tell them I read it. Tell them I understood."

The courier made his obeisance, turned his mount, and rode away. Otah let himself sit with his grief. The other letters for him could wait. They had come from his Master of Tides, and from others he'd named to watch the Empire crumble in his absence. Two had been for Ana Dasin, and he assumed they were from her parents. The letters had made their way up from Saraykeht and then along the low roads, tracking Otah and his party for days. And each day had marked the ending of lives, in Galt especially, but everywhere.

He had known that Sinja might die. He'd sent the fleet out knowing it might happen, and Sinja had gone without any illusions of safety. If it hadn't been this and now, it would have been something else at some other time. Every man and woman died, in time.

And in truth, death wasn't the curse he'd set out to break. All his work and sacrifice had been only so that they could balance the constant withering of age with some measure of renewal. He thought of his own children: Eiah, Danat, and even long-dead Nayiit. They had each of them been wagers he'd placed against a cruel world. A child comes into the world, and its father holds it close and thinks, If all goes as it should, I will die first. This one, I can love and never mourn for. That was all he wanted to leave for Danat and Eiah. The chance of knowing a love that they would never be called to bury. It was the world as it was intended to be.

He didn't notice Idaan riding close to him until she spoke. Her voice was gruff, but he imagined he could hear some offer of comfort in it.

"It's past time to shift. Crawl up on that cart and rest awhile. You've been riding that thing for five hands together."

"Have I?" Otah said. "I didn't notice."

"I know. It's why I came," she said. After a moment's pause, she added, "Danat told us what happened."

Otah took a pose that acknowledged having heard her, but nothing more than that. There wasn't anything more that could be meaningfully said. Idaan respected it and let him turn his horse aside and shift to the steamcart where Ana Dasin and Ashti Beg sat, their sightless eyes fixed on nothing. Otah sat on the wide boards not far from them, but not so near that their conversation would include him. Ana laughed at something Ashti Beg had said. The older woman looked vaguely pleased. Otah lay back, his closed eyes flooded with the red of sun and blood. He willed himself to sleep, certain that it would elude him.

He woke when the cart jerked to a halt. He sat up, half-thoughts of snapped axles and broken wheels forming and falling apart like mist in a high wind. When he was awake enough to make sense of the world, he saw that the sun had sunk almost to the treetops, and the cart was sitting in the yard of a way-house. The memory of the morning's foul message flooded back into him, but not so deeply as before. It would rise and fall, he knew. He would be jarred by the loss of his friend again and again and again, but less and less and less. It said something he didn't want to know that mourning had become so familiar. He plucked his traveling robes into their proper drape and lowered himself to the ground.

The one thing he truly didn't regret about the journey was that his servants were all in Utani or Saraykeht. Walking into the low, warm main room of the wayhouse without being surrounded by men and women wanting to change his robes or powder his feet was a small pleasure. He tried to savor it.

"Half a day east of here," a young man in a leather apron was saying, but he was pointing north. "Must have been five or six days ago. Raised ten kinds of trouble, then left in the middle of the night. So far as I can see, no one's talked about anything else since."

"Did you see them?" Danat asked. His voice had an edge, but Otah couldn't see his face to know if it was excitement or anger.

"Not myself, no," the young man said. "But it's the ones you asked after. An old man with a physician, and nothing but women traveling with him. There was even some talk he was trying to start a comfort house or something of that kind, but that was before the baby."

"Baby?" The voice was Ana's.

"Yes. Little one, not more than eight months old from the size. So I'm told. I didn't see him either, but they all saw him over at Chayiit's place. Walked right out in the middle of the main room."

Otah slipped down at a bench by the fire grate. The fire was small but warm. He hadn't realized how cold he'd gotten.

"Those are the people," Danat said.

"Five, six days then," the young man said with a pleased nod. He glanced over at Otah, their eyes meeting briefly. The other man paled as Otah took a pose of casual greeting and then turned his attention back to the flames. The conversation behind him grew softer and ended. Danat came to sit at his side. Through the open door, the yard fell into evening as the armsmen finished unloading and leading away their horses.

"We've gotten closer," Danat said. "If they keep traveling as slowly as they have up to now, we'll overtake them well before Utani."

Otah grunted. There was a deep thump from overhead and voices lifted in annoyance. Danat's fingers laced his knee.

"I told Balasar that I would beg," Otah said. "I told him that I would bend myself before this new poet and beg if it meant restoring him and Galt."

"And now?"

"I don't believe I can. And more than that, having heard Ashti Beg talk about this Vanjit, it's hard work thinking it would help."

"Maati, perhaps. He holds some sway with her."

"But what can I say that would move him?" Otah asked, his voice thick. "We were friends once, and then enemies, and friends again, but I'm not sure we know each other now. The more I look at it, the more I'm tempted to set some sort of trap, capture the new poet, and give her over to blind torturers until she makes the world what it should be."

"And what about Eiah?" Danat asked. "If she manages her binding—"

"What if she does?" Otah said. "She's been against me from the start. She's gone with Maati, and between them they've sunk the fleet, burned Chaburi-Tan, blinded Galt, and killed Sinja. What would you have me say to her?"

"You'll have to say something," Danat said, his voice harder than Otah had expected. "And we'll be upon them soon enough. It's a thing you should consider."

Otah looked over. Danat's head was bowed, his mouth tight.

"You'd like to suggest something?" Otah asked, his voice low and careful. The anger in his breast shifted like a dog in sleep. Danat either didn't hear the warning or chose to ignore it.

"We're trading revenge," Danat said. "The Galts came from anger at our arrogance and fear of the andat. Maati and Vanjit have struck back now for the deaths during their invasion. This can't go on."

"It isn't in my power to stop it," Otah said.

"It isn't in your power to stop them," Danat said, taking a pose of correction. "Only promise me this. If you have the chance, you'll forgive them."

"Forgive them?" Otah said, rising to his feet. "You want them forgiven for this? You think it can all be put aside? It can't. If you ask Ana-cha, I will wager anything you like that she can't look on the deaths in Galt with calm in her heart. Would you have me forgive them for what they've done to her as well? Gods, Danat. If what they've done isn't going too far, nothing is!"

"He isn't worried for them," Idaan said from the shadows. Otah turned. She was sitting alone at the back of the room, a lit pipe in her hand and pale smoke rising from her lips as she spoke. "He's saying there are crimes that can't be made right. Trying to make justice out of this will only make it last longer."

"So we should let it go?" Otah demanded. "We should meekly accept what they've done?"

"It was what you told Eiah to do," Danat said. "She wanted to find a way to heal the damage from Sterile; you told her to let it go and accept what had happened. Didn't you?"

Otah's clenched fists loosened. His mind clouded with rage and chagrin. Idaan's low chuckle filled the room like a growl.

"Which of us is innocent now, eh?" she said, waving her pipe. "It's easy to counsel forgiveness when you aren't the one swallowing poison. It's harder to forgive them for having won."

"What would you have me do, then?" Otah snapped.

"In your place, I'd kill them all before they could do more damage," Idaan said. "Maati, Vanjit, Eiah. All of them. Even Ashti Beg."

"That isn't an option," Otah said. "I won't kill Eiah."

"So you won't end them and you won't forgive them," Idaan said. "You want the world saved, but you don't know what that means any longer. There isn't much time to clear your mind, brother. And you can't put your thoughts in line when you're half-sunk in rage."

Danat took a pose of agreement.

"It's what I was trying to say," he said.

"Lift yourself above this," Idaan said. "See it as if you were someone else. Someone less hurt by it."

Otah lifted his hands, palms out, refusing it all. His jaw ached, but the heat in his chest and throat, the blood in his ears, washed him out of the room. He heard Danat cry out behind him, and Idaan's softer voice. He stalked out to the road. No one followed. His mind was a cacophony of voices, all of them his own.

Alone on the dimming road, he excoriated Maati and Eiah, Danat and Idaan, Balasar and Sinja and Issandra Dasin. He muttered all the venom that rose to his lips, and, in time, he sat at the base of an ancient tree, throwing stones at nothing. The rage faded and left him as empty as an old skin. The sun was gone and the sky darkening blue to indigo and indigo to starlit black.

Alone as he had not been in years, he wept. At first it was only the loss of Sinja, but then of the fleet and Chaburi-Tan. Eiah and his warring senses of guilt and betrayal. Galt, blind and dying. It ended where he had known it would. All rivers led to the sea, and all his sorrows to the death of Kiyan.

"Oh, love," he said to the empty air. "Oh, my love. Can this never go well?"

Nothing answered back.

The tears faded. The sorrow and rage, spent, left his heart and mind clearer. The tree at his back scratched, its bark as rough as broken stone. It offered no comfort, but he let himself rest against it. He noticed the scent of fresh earth for the first time, and the hushing of a breeze that stirred the treetops without descending to the path they covered. A falling star lit the sky and was gone.

He must, Otah thought, have looked like he was on the edge of murder the whole day for his son and his sister to face him down that way. He must have seemed like a man gone mad. It was near enough to the truth.

The night air was cold and his robes insufficient. He went back to the way-house more for warmth than the desire to continue any conversation. There was an odd silence in his mind now that felt fragile and comforting. He knew as he stepped into the yard that he wouldn't be able to maintain it.

Voices raised in anger filled the yard. Danat and the captain of the armsmen stood so close to each other their chests nearly touched, each of them shouting at the other. Idaan stood at Danat's right, her arms crossed, her expression deceptively calm. The captain had his armsmen arrayed behind him, lit torches in their hands. Otah made out words like *protection* and *answerable* from the captain and *disrespect* and *mutiny* from Danat. Otah rubbed his hands together to fight off the numbness and made his way toward the confrontation. The captain saw him first and stopped talking, his face flushed red by blood and torchlight. Danat took a moment longer, then glanced over his shoulder.

"I suppose this is to do with me," Otah said.

"We only wanted to see that you were safe, Most High," the captain said. The words were strangled. Otah hesitated, then took a pose of apology.

"I needed solitude," he said. "I should have told you before I left. But if I'd been clear-minded, I likely wouldn't have needed to leave. Please accept my apology."

There was little enough the man could do. Moments later, the armsmen were scattering back to the wayhouse or the stables. The smell of doused torches filled the air like a forest on fire. Danat and Idaan stood side by side.

"Should I apologize to you as well?" Otah asked with a half-smile.

"Isn't called for," Idaan said. "I was only keeping your boy near to hand in case you reconsidered my death order."

"Next time, maybe," Otah said, and Idaan grinned. "Is there anything warm to drink in this place?"

The young keeper brought them the best food the wayhouse had to offer—river fish baked with red pepper and lemon, sweet rice, almond milk with mint, hot plum wine, and cold water. They arrayed themselves through the main room, all other guests being turned away by the paired guards at every door. Ana and Ashti Beg were in a deep conversation about the strategies they'd developed in their new sightlessness. Danat sat nearer the fire, watching them with a naked longing in his expression that would have made Ana blush, Otah thought, had she been able to see it. Otah and Idaan sat together at a low table, passing the chipped lacquer bowls back and forth. The armsmen who weren't on duty had taken a back room, and their voices came in occasional outbursts of hilarity and song.

It could have been the image of peace, of something approaching a family passing a road-wearied night in warmth and companionship. And perhaps it was. But it was other things as well.

"You look better," Idaan said, freshening the wine in his bowl. Fragrant steam rose from it, astringent and rich with the scent of the fruit.

"I am for now," Otah said. "I'll be worse again later."

"Have you made up your mind, then?" she asked. He sighed. Ashti Beg illustrated some point with a wide, vague gesture. Danat placed a new length of pine on the fire.

"There isn't an answer," Otah said. "They have all the power. All I can do is ask them to reconsider. So I suppose I'll do that and see what happens next. I know that you think I should go in and kill them all—"

"I didn't say that," Idaan said. "I said it was what I would do. My judgment on those matters is . . . occasionally suspect."

Otah sipped his wine, then put the bowl down carefully.

"I think that's the nearest you've ever come to apologizing," he said.

"To you, perhaps," Idaan said. "I spent years talking to the dead about it. They didn't have much to say back."

"Do you miss them?"

"Yes," Idaan said without hesitation. "I do."

They lapsed into silence again. Danat and Ashti Beg were in the middle of a lively debate over the ethics of showfighting, Ana listening to them both with a frown. Her hand pressed her belly as if the fish was troubling her.

"If Maati were here tonight," Otah said, "and demanded that he be named emperor, I think I'd give it to him."

"He'd hand it back in a week," Idaan said with a smile.

"Who's to say I'd take it?"

They left in the morning, the horses rested or changed for fresh, the carts restocked with wood and coal and water. Ana looked worse, but kept a brave face. Idaan stayed with her like a personal guard, to Danat's visible annoyance. A cold wind haunted them, striking leaves from the trees.

News of the Emperor's party came close to overwhelming stories of the mysterious baby at the wayhouse. No couriers came to trouble Otah with word of fire or death. Twice, Otah dreamed that Sinja was riding at his side, robes soaked with seawater and black as a bat's wing, and he woke each time with an obscure feeling of peace. And with every stop, they found the poets had passed before them more and more recently.

Three days ago. Then two.

When they reached the river Qiit, tea-dark with newly fallen leaves, just the day before.

24

>+< The cold caught up with them in the middle of the day, a wind from the west that rattled the trees and sent tiny whitecaps across the river's back. They had covered a great stretch of river in their day's travel, but night meant landing. The boatman was adamant. The river, he said, was a living thing; it changed from one journey to the next. Sandbars shifted, rocks lurked where none had been before. The boat was shallow enough to pass over many dangers, but a log invisible in the darkness could break a hole in the deck. Better to run in the daylight than swim in the dark. The way the boatman said it left no room for disagreement.

They camped at the riverside, and awakened with tents and robes soaked heavy by dew. Morning light saw them on the water again, the boiler at the stern muttering angrily to itself, the paddle wheel punishing the water.

Maati sat away from the noise, huddled in two wool robes, and watched the trees march from the north to the south like an army bent on sacking Saraykeht. Large Kae and Small Kae sat in the stern, making conversation with the boatman and his second when the men would deign to speak. Vanjit and Eiah turned around each other, one in the bow, the other in the center of the craft, both maintaining a space between them, the andat watching with rage and hunger in its black eyes. It was like watching an alley-mouth knife fight drawn out over hours and days.

It was hard now to remember the days before they had been splintered. The years he had spent in hiding had seemed like a punishment at the time. Living in warehouses, giving the lectures he half-recalled from his own youth and half-invented anew, trying to understand the ways in which a woman's mind was not a man's and how that power could be channeled into grammar. He had resented it. He recalled crawling onto a cot, exhausted from the day's work. He could still picture the expressions of hunger and determination on their faces. He had not seen it then, but it had all of it been driven by hope. Even the sorrow and mourning that came after a binding failed and they lost someone to the andat's grim price had held a sense of community.

Now they had won, and the world seemed all cold wind and dark water. Even the two Kaes seemed to have set themselves apart from Vanjit, from Eiah, from him. The nights of conversation and food and laughter were gone like a pleasant dream. They had created a women's grammar and the price was higher than he could have imagined.

Murder. He was planning to murder one of his own.

As he had expected, the boat was too small for any more private conversations. He had managed no more than a few moments with Eiah when none of the others were paying them attention. Something in Vanjit's wine, perhaps, to slow her mind and deepen her sleep. She mustn't know that the blow was coming.

He could see that it weighed on Eiah as much as it did upon him. She sat carving soft wood with a knife wherever Vanjit was not, her mouth in a vicious scowl. The wax tablets that had been her whole work before he'd come to her lay stacked in a crate. The latest version of Wounded, waiting for his analysis and approval. He imagined the two of them would sit nearer each other if it weren't for the fear that Vanjit would suspect them of plotting. And he would not fear that except that it was truth.

For their own part, Vanjit and Clarity-of-Sight held to themselves. Poet and andat in apparent harmony, watching the night sky or penetrating the secrets of wood and water that only she could see. Vanjit hadn't offered to share the wonders the andat revealed since before they had left the school, and Maati couldn't bring himself to ask the favor. Not knowing what he knew. Not intending what he intended.

When evening came, the boatman sang out, his second joining the high whooping call. There was no reason for it that Maati could see, only the habit of years. The boat angled its way to a low, muddy bank. When the water was still enough, the second dropped over the side and slogged to the line of trees, a rope thick as his arm trailing behind him. Once the rope had been made fast to the trees, he called out again, and the boatman shifted the mechanism of the boiler from paddle wheel to winch, and the great rope went taut. It creaked with the straining, and river water flowed from the strands as if giant hands were wringing it. By the time the boatman stopped, the craft was almost jumping distance from the shore and felt as solid as a building. It made Maati uncomfortable, afraid that they had grounded it so well that they wouldn't be able to free it in the morning. The boatman and his second showed no unease.

A wide plank made a bridge between boat and shore. The boatman wrestled it into place with a stream of perfunctory vulgarity. The second, his robes soaked and muddied, trotted back onto the deck.

"We're doing well, eh?" Maati said to the boatman. "The distance we went today must have been four days' ride."

"We'll do well enough," the boatman agreed. "Have you in Utani before the last leaf drops, that's certain."

Large Kae went across to the shore, two tents on her wide back. Eiah was just behind her with a crate of food to make the evening meal. The twilight sky was gray streaked with gold, and the calls of birds gave some hint to where the boatman's songs had found their start. On another night, it would have been beautiful.

"How many days do you think that would be?" Maati asked, trying to keep his tone light and friendly. From the boatman's perfunctory smile, it wasn't an unfamiliar question.

"Six days," the boatman said. "Seven. If it's been raining to the north and the river starts running faster, it could go past that, but this time of year, that's rare."

Vanjit shifted past them, brushing against Maati as she stepped onto the plank. The andat was curled against her, its head resting on her shoulder like a tired child might.

"Thank you," Maati said.

They made camp a dozen yards inland, where the ground was dry. It was habit now. Routine. Eiah dug the fire pit, Small Kae gathered wood. Large Kae put the sleeping tents in place. Irit would have started cooking, but Maati knew well enough how to take her part. A few bowlfuls of river water, crushed lentils that had been soaking since morning, slivers of salted pork, an onion they'd hauled almost from the school. It made for a better soup than Maati had first expected, though the gods all knew he was tired of it now. It would keep them alive until morning.

Just as Maati filled a bowl for the boatman, Vanjit stepped out of the shadows, the andat on one hip, a satchel on the other. Everyone was aware that she hadn't helped to make camp. No one complained. In the firelight, she looked younger even than she was. Her eyes flashed, and she smiled.

Vanjit sat at Maati's side, accepting the next full bowl. The andat rested at her feet, shifting its weight as if to crawl away but then shifting back. The boatman and his second went back to their boat, bowls steaming in their hands. It was, Maati supposed, all well for passengers to sleep on the shore, but someone needed to stay with the boat. Better for them as well. It would have been awkward, explaining why the baby's breath didn't fog.

When they had gone, Eiah rose to her feet. The darkness under her eyes was dispelled by her smile. The others looked up at her.

"I would like to announce a small celebration," she said. "I've been reworking the binding for Wounded, and as of today, the latest version is complete."

Small Kae smiled and applauded. Large Kae grinned. Eiah made a show of pulling a wineskin from her bags. They all applauded now. Even Vanjit. But Eiah's gaze faltered when her eyes met Maati's, and his belly soured.

Something in her wine to deepen her sleep. She mustn't see the blow coming.

"Yes," Maati said, trying to hide his fear. "Yes, I think celebration is in order."

"You've seen the new draft?" Vanjit asked as Eiah poured the wine into bowls. "Is it ready?"

"I haven't been through it all as yet," he said. "There are some changes that make me optimistic. By Udun, I'll have a better-informed opinion."

The two Kaes were toasting each other, the fire. Eiah came to Maati and Vanjit. She pressed bowls into their hands, and went back to pour one for herself. Maati drank quickly, grateful for something to do that would occupy his hands and his mind. If only for a moment.

Vanjit swirled her wine bowl, looking down at it with what might have been serenity.

"Maati-kvo," Vanjit said. "Do you remember when I first came to you? Gods, it seems like it was a different life, doesn't it? You were outside Shosheyn-Tan."

"Lachi," Eiah said from across the fire.

"Of course," Vanjit said. "I remember now. I met Umnit at a bathhouse, and we'd started talking. She brought me to Eiah-cha, and Eiah brought me to you. It was that abandoned house, the one with all the mice."

"I remember," Maati said. The two Kaes exchanged a glance that Maati didn't understand. Vanjit laughed, throwing back her head.

"I can't think what you saw in me back then," she said. "I must have looked like something the dogs wouldn't eat."

"They were lean times for all of us," Maati said, forcing a jovial tone.

"Not for you," she said. "Not with Eiah to look after you. No, don't you pretend that she hasn't supported us all from the start. Without her, we would never have come this far."

Eiah took a pose that accepted the compliment and raised her wine bowl, but Vanjit still didn't drink from her own. Maati willed her to drink the poison, to end this.

"I think of who I was then," Vanjit said, her voice soft and contemplative. She sounded like a child. Or worse, like a grown woman trying to sound childish. "Lost. Empty. And then the gods touched my shoulder and turned me toward you. All of you, really. You've been the only family I've ever had. I mean, since the Galts came."

At her feet, Clarity-of-Sight wailed as if heartbroken. Vanjit turned to it, her brow furrowed in concentration. The andat squirmed, shuddered, and became still. The tension in Maati's shoulders was spreading to his throat. He could see Eiah's hands clutching her bowl.

"The only family I've had," Vanjit said, as if finding her place in a practiced speech. And then softly, "Did you think I wouldn't know?"

Large Kae put down her bowl, her gaze shifting from Eiah to Vanjit and back. Maati shifted to the side, his throat almost too tight for words.

"Know what?" he asked. The words came out stilted and rough. Even he wasn't convinced by them. Vanjit stared at him, disappointment in her expression. No one moved, but Maati felt something shifting in his eyes. The andat's attention was on him, the tiny face growing more and more detailed with each heartbeat.

Vanjit held out the poisoned wine bowl. The color was wrong. No human would ever have seen the difference, but with the andat driving his vision and hers, there was no mistaking it. The deep red had a greenish taint that no other bowl suffered.

"What . . . what's that?" Maati squeaked.

"I don't know," Vanjit said in a voice that meant she did. "Perhaps you should drink it for me, and we could see. But no. You're too valuable. Eiah, perhaps?"

"I'm sorry. Did I not clean the bowl well enough?" Eiah asked.

Vanjit threw her bowl into the fire, flames hissing and smoke rushing up in a cloud. There was rage in her expression.

"Vanjit," Eiah said. "I don't think . . ."

Vanjit ignored them, untying her satchel with a fast scrabbling motion. When she lifted it, blocks of wax spilled out, gray and white, like rotten ice. Maati saw bits of Eiah's writing cut into them.

"You were going to kill me," Vanjit said.

Eiah took a pose that denied the charge. The firelight flickered over Vanjit's face, and for a moment, Maati thought the poet might believe the lie. He cleared his throat.

"We wouldn't do that," he said.

Vanjit turned to him, her expression empty and mad. At his feet, the andat made a sound that might have been a warning or a laugh.

"Do you think he only speaks to you?" Vanjit spat.

Maati sputtered, falling back a step when Vanjit lunged forward. She only scooped up the andat, turned, and ran into the darkness.

Maati scrambled after her, calling her name with a deepening sense of despair. The trees were shadows within the night's larger darkness. His voice seemed too weak to carry more than a few paces before him. It couldn't have been more than half a hand—less than that, certainly—when he stopped to catch his breath. Leaning against an ancient ash, he realized that Vanjit was gone and he was lost, only the soft rushing of the river away to his left still there to guide him. He picked his way back, trying to follow the route he had taken and failing. A carpet of dry leaves made his steps loud. Something shifted in the branches overhead. The cold numbed his fingers and toes. The half-moon glimmering among the branches assured him that he had not been blinded. It was the only comfort he had.

In the end, he made his way east until he found the river, and then south to the wide mud where the boat still rested. It was simple enough to find the little camp after that. He tried to nurture some hope that he would step into the circle of firelight to find Vanjit returned and, through some unimagined turn of events, peace restored. The laughter and soft company of the first days of the school returned; time unwound, and his life ready to be lived again without the errors. He wanted it to be true so badly that when he stumbled into the clearing and found Eiah and the two Kaes seated by the fire, he almost thought they were well.

Eiah turned gray, fogged eyes toward him.

"Who's there?" she demanded at the sound of his approaching steps.

"It's me," Maati said, wheezing. "I'm fine. But Vanjit's gone."

Large Kae began to weep. Small Kae put an arm over the woman's shaking shoulders and murmured something, her eyes closed and tear-streaked. Maati sat at the fire. His bowl of soup had overturned.

"She's done for the three of us," Eiah said. "None of us can see at all."

"I'm sorry," Maati said. It was profoundly inadequate.

"Can you help me?" Eiah said, gesturing toward something Maati couldn't fathom. Then he saw the pile of wax fragments. "I think I have them all, but it's hard to be sure."

"Leave them," Maati said. "Let them go."

"I can't," Eiah said. "I have to try the thing. I can do it now. Tonight."

Maati looked at her. The fire popped, and she shifted her head toward the sound. Her jaw was set, her gray eyes angry. The cold wind made her robes flutter at her ankles like a flag.

"No," he said. "You can't."

"I have been studying this for weeks," Eiah said, her voice sharpening. "Only help me put these back together, and I can . . ."

"You can die," Maati said. "I know you've changed the binding. You *won't* do this. Not until we can study it. Too much rides on Wounded to rush into the binding in a panic. We'll wait. Vanjit may come back."

"Maati-kvo—" Eiah began.

"She is alone in the forest with nothing to sustain her. She's cold and frightened and betrayed," Maati said. "Put yourself in her place. She's discovered that the only friends she had in the world were planning to kill her. The andat must certainly be pushing for its freedom with all its power. She didn't even have the soup before she went. She's cold and hungry and confused, and we are the only place she can go for help or comfort."

"All respect, Maati-kvo," Small Kae said, "but that first part was along the lines that you were going to *kill* her. She won't come back."

"We don't know that," Maati said. "We can't yet be sure."

But morning came without Vanjit. The sky became a lighter black, and then gray. Morning birds broke into their chorus of chatters and shrieks; finches and day larks and other species Maati couldn't name. The trees deepened, rank after ragged rank becoming first gray and then brown and then real. Poet and andat were gone into the wild, and as the dawn crept up rosy and wild in the east, it became clear they were not going to return.

Maati built a small fire from last night's embers and brewed tea for the four of them still remaining. Large Kae wouldn't stop crying despite Small Kae's constant attentions. Eiah sat wrapped in her robes from the previous night. She looked drawn. Maati pressed a bowl of warm tea into her hand. Neither spoke.

At the end, Maati took the belts from their spare robes and used them to make a line. He led Eiah, Eiah led Small Kae, and Small Kae led Large Kae. It was the obscene parody of a game he'd played as a child, and he walked the path back to the boat, calling out the obstacles he passed—log, step down, be careful of the mud. They left the sleeping tents and cooking things behind.

To Maati's surprise, the boat was already floating. The boatman and his second were moving over the craft with the ease and silence of long practice. When he called out, the boatman stopped and stared. The man's mouth gaped in surprise; the first strong reaction Maati had seen from him.

"No," the boatman said. "This wasn't the agreement. Where's the other one? The one with the babe?"

"I don't know," Maati called out. "She left in the night."

The second, guessing the boatman's mind, started to pull in the plank that bridged boat and sticky, dark mud. Maati yelped, dropped Eiah's lead, and lumbered out into the icy flow, grabbing at the retreating wood.

"We didn't contract for this," the boatman said. "Missing girls, blinded ones? No, there wasn't anything about this."

"We'll die if you leave us," Eiah said.

"That one can see after you," the boatman called, gesturing pointlessly at Maati, hip deep in river mud. It would have been comic if it had been less terrible.

"He's old and he's dying," Eiah said, and lifted her physician's satchel as if to prove the gravity of her opinion. "If he has an attack, you'll be leaving all the women out here to die."

The boatman scowled, looking from Maati to Eiah and back. He spat into the river.

"To the first low town," he said. "I'll take you that far, and no farther."

"That's all we can ask," Eiah said.

Maati thought he heard Small Kae mutter, *I could ask more than that*, but he was too busy pulling the plank into position to respond. It was a tricky business, guiding all three women into the boat, but Maati and the second managed it, soaking only Small Kae's hem. Maati, when at last he pulled himself onto the boat, was cold water and black mud from waist to boots. He made his miserable way to the stern, sitting as near the kiln as the boatman would allow. Eiah called out for him, following the sound of his voice until she sat at his side. The boatman and his second wouldn't speak to either of them or meet Maati's eyes. The second walked to the bow, manipulated something Maati couldn't make out, and called out. The boatman replied, and the boat shifted, its wheel clattering and pounding. They lurched out into the stream.

They were leaving Vanjit behind. The only poet in the world, her andat on her hip, alone in the forest with autumn upon them. What would she do? How would she live, and if she despaired, what vengeance would she exact upon the world? Maati looked at the dancing flames within the kiln.

"South would be faster," Maati said. The boatman glanced at him, shrugged, and sang out something Maati couldn't make out. The second called back, and the boatman turned the rudder. The sound of the paddle wheel deepened, and the boat lurched.

"Uncle?" Eiah asked.

"It's all fallen apart," Maati said. "We can't manage this from here. Tracking her through half the wilds south of Utani? We need men. We need help."

"Help," Eiah said, as if he'd suggested pulling down the stars. Maati tried to speak, but something equally sorrow and rage closed his throat. He muttered an obscenity and then forced the words free.

"We need Otah-kvo," Maati said.

25

"Will you go back?" Ana asked. "When this is over, I mean."

"It depends on what you mean by *over*," Idaan said. "You mean once my brother talks the poets into bringing back all the dead in Galt and Chaburi-Tan, rebuilding the city, killing the pirates, and then releasing the andat and drowning all their books? Because if that's what *over* looks like, you're waiting for yesterday."

Otah shifted, pretending he was still asleep. The sun of late morning warmed his face and robes, the low chuckle of the river against the sides of the boat and the low, steady surge of the paddle wheel became a kind of music. It had been easy enough to drowse, but his body ached and pinched and complained despite three layers of tapestry between his back and the deck. If he rose, there would be conversations and planning and decisions. As long as he could maintain the fiction of unconsciousness, he could allow himself to drift. It passed poorly for comfort, but it passed.

"You can't think we'll be chasing these people for the rest of our lives, though," Ana said.

"I'm hoping we live longer than that, yes," Idaan said. "So. If this ends in a way that lets me return to him, then I will. I enjoy Cehmai's company."

"And he'll take you back in, even after you've been gone this long?"

Otah could hear the smile in Idaan's voice when she replied.

"He's overlooked worse from me. Why do you ask?"

"I don't know," Ana said. And then a moment later, "Because I'm trying to imagine it. What the world will be. I've never traveled outside Galt before, except one negotiation in Eymond. I keep thinking of going back to it. Acton. Kirinton. But it's not there anymore."

"Not the way it was," Idaan agreed. "We can't be sure how bad it is, but I'll swear it isn't good."

The silence was only a lack of voices. The river, the birds, the wind all went on with their long, inhuman conversation. It wasn't truly silence, it only felt that way.

"I think about what I would do without all of you," Ana said. "And then I imagine . . . What would you do if a city caught fire and no one could see it? How would you put it out?"

"You wouldn't," Idaan said. Her voice was cool and matter-of-fact.

"I think about that," Ana said. "I think about it more now. The future, the things that can go wrong. Dangers. I wonder if that always happens when—"

Idaan had made a clicking sound, tongue against teeth.

"You're not fooling anyone, brother," Idaan said. "We all know you're awake."

Otah rolled onto his back, his eyes still closed, and took a pose of abject denial. Idaan chuckled. He opened his eyes to the great pale blue dome of the sky, the sun burning white overhead and searing his eyes. He sat up slowly, his back as bruised as if someone had beaten him.

Ashti Beg lay a few yards off, her arm curved under her to cradle her sleeping head. Two armsmen sat at either side of their boat with pairs at the stern and the bow, keeping watch on the changeless river. Danat had joined the watchers at the bow and seemed to be having a conversation with them. It was good to see it. Otah had been concerned after his disappearance at the wayhouse that Danat and the captain of the guard might have found themselves on bad terms. Danat seemed to be making it his work to see that didn't happen.

The boat itself was smaller than Otah would have chosen, but the kilns at the back were solid, the wheel new, and the alternatives had been few. When there are only three boats on the riverfront, even being emperor won't create a fourth. Ana and Idaan were sitting side by side on a shin-high bench, their hands clasped.

It was something Otah had noticed before, the tendency of Ana and Ashti Beg to touch people. As if the loss of their eyes had left them hungry for something, and this lacing of fingers was the nearest they could come.

"You both look lovely," Otah said.

"Your hair looks like mice have been building a nest in it," Idaan said.

Otah confirmed her assessment with his fingertips. The fact of the matter was that none of them was presentable. Too many weeks on the road bathing with rags and tepid water had left them looking disreputable. Somewhere just east of Pathai, they had been joined by a colony of lice that still took up their evenings. Otah imagined walking into the palaces at Utani as he now was and smiled.

He walked to the edge of the boat where a bucket and rope stood ready for moments like this. With the armsmen looking on, he lowered the line himself and hauled up the water. When he knelt and poured it over his head, it was as if he could feel ice forming in his mind. He whooped and shuddered, pulling his hair back. Idaan, behind him, was laughing. He made his way back to them, Ana holding out a length of cloth for him to take and dry himself.

And that was the nature of the journey. Tragedy lay behind them, and desperate uncertainty ahead. He was gnawed by his fears and his guilt and his sorrow, but his sister was there, laughing with him. His son. The river was cold and uncomfortable and beautiful. Every day meant more dead, and yet there was no way for them to move faster than the boat would carry them. Otah knew that as a younger man, he would have been sitting at the bow, frowning at the water as if by will alone he could make things into something they weren't. As an old one, he was able to put it all aside for as much as a hand at a time, holding his energy for the moment when it might effect a change and resting until then. Perhaps it was what the philosophers meant by wisdom.

Somewhere ahead, Maati and Eiah and the new poet were making their own way to Utani and, he thought, the proclamation of their victory. Perhaps Eiah would bind her andat as well, and return to the women of the Khaiate cities their wombs. There would be children again, a new generation to take the place of the old. All that would be sacrificed was Galt, and the world would be put back as it was. An empire now, instead of a scattering of cities, but with the andat, slaves of spirit and will, putting them above the rest of the world.

Until a new Balasar Gice found a way to bring it all down, and the cycle of suffering and desperation began anew.

"You've gone solemn," Idaan said.

"Steeling myself for failure," Otah said. "We'll be on them soon, I think. And . . ."

"You've been thinking about forgiveness," Idaan said. Otah looked at Ana, listening, rapt. Idaan shook her head. "The girl's strong enough to know the truth. There's no virtue in softening it."

"Please," Ana said.

Otah took a deep breath and let it slide out between his teeth. River water traced a cold path down his back. On the east bank, half a hundred crows took to the air, startled by something on the ground or just one another.

"If we lose Galt," Otah said, stopped, and began again, more slowly. "If we lose Galt, I don't believe I can forgive them. I know what you said, and Danat. I should. I should do whatever it takes to stop all this, even if it means agreeing that I've lost, but it's beyond me. I'm too old to forgive anymore, and . . ."

"And," Idaan said, making it sound like agreement.

"I don't understand," Ana said.

"That's because you haven't killed anyone," Idaan said. Otah looked up at her. Idaan's eyes were dark but not unsympathetic. When she went on, the words were addressed to Ana, but her gaze was fixed on his. "There are some things about my brother that few people know. His best friend, Maati, was one who knew his secrets. And because of Maati, Cehmai. And so I am also one of the few to know what happened all those years ago in Saraykeht."

To his surprise, Otah found himself weeping silently. Ana leaned forward, her brow fierce.

"What happened?" she asked.

"I killed a good man. An honorable, unwell man with a wounded soul," Otah said softly. "I strangled him to death in a little room off a mud-paved alley in the soft quarter."

"Why?" Ana asked.

The answers to that seemed so intricate, so complex, he couldn't find words. Idaan could.

"To save Galt," she said. "If the man had lived, all of Galt would have at least suffered horribly, and likely been wiped from the map. Otah had the choice of condemning his city or letting thousands upon thousands upon thousands of your countrymen die. He chose to betray Saraykeht. He's carried it ever since. He's ordered men killed in war. He's sentenced them to death. But he's only ever ended one life himself. Seen something that had been a man become only a body. If you haven't done it, it's a hard thing to understand."

"That's truth," Otah said.

"And along with all the other insults and injuries and pain that he's caused. Along with the deaths," Idaan said, sorrow and amusement mixed in her voice, "Maati Vaupathai has taken away the thing that made Otah's slaughter bearable. He took away the reason for it. Galt is dying anyway."

"I also did it for Maati," Otah said. "If I hadn't, he'd be fighting against Seedless today."

"And I wouldn't have been born," Ana said. She put out a wavering hand to him, and Otah took it. Her grasp was stronger than he'd expected. There were tears in her milky eyes. "I won't forgive him either."

Idaan sighed.

"Well," his sister said, "at least we'll be damned for what we are."

The second sang something from the bow, a high trill that ended in words Otah couldn't make sense of. The paddle wheel, in the stern, shifted and creaked, the deck beneath him lurching. Otah stood, unsteadily.

"Sandbar," Danat called to him. "It's all right. We're fine."

"Ah, well then. You see?" Idaan said with a chuckle. "We're fine."

They stayed on the river as long into the twilight as they could. Otah could see the unease in the boatman's expression and hear it in his voice. Otah's assumption was that the boats would travel at nearly the same speed. The gap between his party and Maati's would only keep narrowing if he pushed farther past the point of safety than they were willing to do. He thought his chances good. Maati, after all, had all the power, and time was his ally. There was no reason that he should rush.

They put in at a riverfront town half a hand after sundown. A small, rotting pier. A pack of half-feral dogs baying at the boatman's second as he made the boat fast and stretched a wide, arching bridge between the deck and the land. A handful of lights in the darkness that showed where lanterns burned like fireflies in the night.

While the armsmen unloaded their crates and skipped stones at the dogs' feet, Otah led Ashti Beg across to solid land, Idaan and Ana close behind. In the night, the moon and stars obscured by almost-bare branches, Otah felt hardly more sure of himself than did Ashti Beg. But then a local boy appeared with a lantern dancing at the end of a pole to lead them to the wayhouse. They walked slowly despite the cold, as if sitting on the deck all day had been the most wearying work imaginable. Otah found himself walking to one side of the group, hanging back with Danat at his side. It wasn't until his son spoke that Otah noticed that he'd been herded there like an errant sheep.

"I'm sorry, Papa-kya," Danat said, softly. "I need to speak with you."

Otah took a pose that granted his permission.

"You spoke with Ana earlier," Danat said. "I saw she took your hand. It looked . . . it looked like she was crying."

"Yes," Otah said.

"Was it about me?" Danat asked. "Was it something I've done wrong?"

Otah's expression alone must have been enough to answer the question. Danat looked around, shame in his face.

"She's avoiding me," Danat said.

"She's blind, and we've been sunrise to sunset on a boat smaller than my bedchamber," Otah said. "How could she possibly avoid you?"

"It wasn't today. It's been . . . it's been weeks. I thought at first it was only that Idaan and Ashti Beg joined us. There were women here, and Ana-cha felt more comfortable in their company. But it's more than that, and . . ."

Danat ran a hand through his hair. In the dim light of the lantern, Otah could see the single crease in his brow, like a paint mark.

"I don't know what to say. She's done nothing in my presence to make me suspect she's anything but fond of you. If anything, she seems stronger for having come with us."

Danat raised his hands toward some formal pose, but skidded in the mud. When he regained his balance, whatever he'd intended to express was forgotten. Otah put a hand on the boy's shoulder.

The wayhouse was a series of low buildings built of fired brick. The stable squatted across a thin, stone-paved road, a single light burning at its side where, Otah assumed, a guard slept. The wayhouse keeper stood outside, her hands on her hips and a dusting of flour streaking her robe. The captain of the guard stood before her, his arms crossed, while the keeper turned her head from side to side like a cat uncertain which window to flee through. When she saw Otah walking toward them, her face went pale and she took a pose of welcome and obeisance that bent her almost double.

"There's a problem?" Otah asked.

"There aren't rooms," the captain said. "All filled up, she says."

"Ah," Otah said, but before he could say more the captain turned on him. Even in the dim light, he could see a banked rage in the man's eyes. The captain took a pose that requested an audience more formal than the occasion called for. Otah replied with one, equally formal, that granted it.

"All respect, Most High, I have done my best all this campaign to respect your wishes. You want to dunk your head in river water, I haven't objected. You run off into the wilderness for half an evening with no guard or escort, and I've accepted that. But if you are about to suggest that we put the Emperor of the Khaiem in a sleeping tent in a wayhouse courtyard because someone else *got here first*, I'm resigning my commission."

"Actually, I was going to suggest that we offer the present guests our tents and compensation for their rooms," Otah said. "It seemed polite."

"Ah. Yes, Most High," the captain said. It was hard to tell in the night whether the man was blushing.

"There's room in the stables," the keeper said. She had an eastern accent.

"Yalakeht?" Otah asked, and the woman blinked.

"I grew up there," she said, a note of awe in her voice. As if recognizing an accent were a sign of supernatural power.

"It's a good city," Otah said. "Would there be room enough for your present guests if we put my guardsmen in the stables as well?"

"We'll *find* space, Most High," the keeper said.

"Then I'll go negotiate rooms for us," Otah said, and to the captain, "It might be more impressive if I went in with a guard. They'll be less likely to mistake me for a fraud."

"I . . . yes, Most High," the captain said.

The air in the wayhouse was thickened by a chimney with a poor draw. Smoke haze gave the place a feeling of dread and poverty. The tables were dark wood, the floors packed earth. A dozen men and women sat in groups, a few in a smaller room to the side. All eyes were on the guard as they strode in and took formal stances. Otah stepped in.

The movement that stopped him was so slight it might almost not have existed, and familiar enough to disorient him. A woman by the fire grate with her back to him shifted her shoulders. In anyone else, it would have been beneath notice. Otah stood, stunned, his heart thudding like it was trying to break free of his ribs. Idaan appeared at his side, her hand on his arm. He motioned her back.

"Eiah?" he said.

The woman by the fire turned to him. Her face was thin and drawn, older than time alone could explain. Her eyes were the same milky gray as Ana's.

"Father," she said.

26

>+< The years had changed Otah Machi. The last time Maati had seen him, his hair had been black or near enough to pass. His shoulders had been broader, his eyebrows smooth. The man who stood before the smoking fire grate now was thinner, his skin loose against his face. His robes, though travel-stained, were of the finest cloth. They draped him like an altar; they made him more than a man. Or perhaps Otah Machi had always been something more than the usual and his robes only reminded them.

Danat, at his father's side, was unrecognizable. The ill, coughing boy confined to his bed had grown into a hale young man with intelligent eyes and his father's distant, considering demeanor. The others Maati had either seen recently enough that they held no disturbing sense of change or were strangers to him.

They had all come. Large Kae and Small Kae and Eiah, but to his discomfort also Idaan Machi, sitting on a bench with a bowl of wine in her hand and her face as expressionless as the dead. A Galtic girl sat apart, her head held high, sightless and proud to cover the disgust and horror she must feel at all Maati had done. Ashti Beg sat at her side, another victim of Vanjit's malice. After all that had happened, after all his many failures of judgment, seeing her among his arrayed enemies was still wrenching.

Otah's armsmen cleared the wayhouse. The conversation that should have taken place in the finest of meeting rooms in the high palaces instead found its place in a third-rate wayhouse, free of ceremony or ritual or even well-brewed tea. Maati felt himself trembling. He had the powerful physical memory of being a boy at the school, holding himself still and waiting for Tahi-kvo's lacquer rod to split his skin.

"Maati Vaupathai," the Emperor said.

"Most High," Maati replied, crossing his arms.

"I suppose I should start by asking why I shouldn't have you killed where you stand."

Eiah, beside him, twitched as if wasp-stung. Maati stared at his old friend, his old enemy, and all the conciliatory words that he had imagined in the last day vanished like a snuffed candle. There was rage in Otah's stance, and Maati found himself more than matching it.

"How dare you?" Maati said, his voice little more than a hiss. "How *dare* you? I thought, coming here, I would at least be treated with respect. I thought at the very least, that. And instead you stand me up like a common thief in a low-town courtroom and have me defend my life? Justify my right to breathe to the man who killed my son?"

"Nayiit has nothing to do with this," Otah said. "Sinja Ajutani, to contrast, died because of you. Every Galt who has starved since you exacted this sick, petty revenge is dead because of you. Every—"

"Nayiit has *everything* to do with this. Your sick love of all things Galtic has everything to do with it. Your disloyalty to the women you claim to rule. Your perfect calm in making me an outcast living in gutters for something you were just as guilty of. You are a hypocrite and a liar in everything you've done. I owe you nothing, Otah-kvo. *Nothing!*"

Otah was shouting something, but Maati's ears were rushing with blood and raw anger. He saw the armsmen shift forward, blades at the ready, but Maati was far past caring. Every injustice, every slight, every cupful of pent-up outrage spilled out, all made worse by the fact that Otah—self-righteous, entitled, and arrogant—was so busy shouting back that he wasn't hearing a word of what Maati was saying.

When he noticed through his rage that a third voice had entered the fray, he couldn't say how long it had been going.

"I said *stop!*" the Galt shouted again. "Stop it! Both of you!"

Maati turned to the girl, a sneer on his lip, but he was having a hard time catching his breath. Otah also was now silent, his imperial face flushed bright red. Maati felt the urge to offer up an obscene gesture, but he restrained himself. The girl stood in the space between the two, her hands outstretched. Danat stepped to her side. If anything, her anger appeared as high as either of her elders', but she was able to speak coherently.

"Gods," she said. "Is this really what we've been doing? Someone please tell me that the world is on its knees over something more than two old men chewing over quarrels from their boyhood."

"This is much, much more than that," Otah said. His voice, though severe, had lost some of its certainty.

"I wouldn't know from listening to that display," Idaan said. "Ana-cha has more sense than you on this, brother. Listen to her."

Otah had calmed down enough to look merely peeved. Maati held his fist to his chest, but his heart was slowing to its usual pace. Nothing had happened.

He was fine. Otah, across from him, took a pose appropriate to the beginning of a short break in a negotiation. His jaw was tight and his stance only civil. Maati replied with one that accepted the proposal. He wanted to sit at Eiah's side, to talk with her about what to do next and how to go about it. It would have been a provocation, though, so instead, Maati retreated to the door leading out into the cold, black courtyard and the clean night air.

It had been a mistake. Otah was too proud and self-centered to help them. He was too wrapped up in anger that the world hadn't followed his one and only holy and anointed plan. They should have gone on to Utani, found someone in the utkhaiem who would support them. Or they should have gone after Vanjit themselves.

They should have done anything but this.

Voices came from behind him. Danat's, Otah's, Eiah's. They sounded tense, but they weren't shouting. Maati pressed his hands into their opposite sleeves and watched his breath steam like a soup kettle. He wondered where Vanjit was and how she was keeping warm. It seemed the woman had become two different people in his mind—one, the girl who had come to him in despair and been given hope again, the other a half-mad poet he'd loosed on the world. The impulses to kill her and to see to her care shouldn't have been able to exist in him at the same time, and yet there they were. He prayed she was dead, and he hoped she was well.

Between that and seeing Otah again, his head was buzzing like a hive.

"We've reached a conclusion," Idaan said from behind him. He turned. She was standing in the doorway, blocking the light. His belly itched where her assassin had stabbed him all those years before.

"Should I be grateful?" Maati asked. Idaan ignored the jab.

"If you and Otah can't play gently, and it's clear as the moon that you can't, we're going to go through channels. Eiah's talking with Danat. They sent me to speak with you."

"Ah, because we're such excellent friends?"

"Say it's because our relationship is simpler," Idaan said. Her voice took on the texture of cast iron. "Tell me what happened."

Maati leaned against the rough wall and shook his head. He'd become too excited, and now that he was calming, it was coming out in an urge to weep. He would not under any circumstances allow that in front of Idaan. Idaan, who'd tried to have Otah killed and had now become his traveling companion. What more did anyone need to know to understand how far Otah had fallen?

"Maati," Idaan said, her voice still hard. "Now."

He began with leaving the school, Eiah's opinion of his health, Vanjit's escalating unreliability. The story took on a rhythm as he told it, the words putting themselves in order as if he had practiced it all before. Idaan didn't speak, but her listening was intense, drawing detail from him almost against his will.

It was as if he were telling himself what had happened, offering a kind of confession to the empty night, Idaan Machi—of all people in the world, Idaan Machi—as his intercessor.

He reached the end—Vanjit's discovery of the poison, her escape, his decision to find help. Somewhere in the course of things, he'd let himself slip to the ground, sitting with his legs stuck out before him and the stone paving leaching the warmth from his body. Idaan squatted beside him. He imagined that the manner of her listening had softened, as if silences could differ like speech.

"I see," she said. "Well. Who'd have thought this would become worse?"

"You led him to us," Maati said.

"I did my best," Idaan agreed. "It's been years since I put my hand to this kind of work. I'm out of practice, but I did what I could."

"All to regain his imperial favor," Maati said. "I would never have guessed that you'd become his toady."

"Actually, I started it to protect Cehmai," Idaan said as if he had offered her no insult. "With you stirring up the mud, I was afraid for him. I wanted Otah to know that he wasn't part of it. And then, once I was at the court . . . well, I had amends to make to Danat."

"The boy?"

"No. The one he's named for," Idaan said. She heaved a great sigh. "But back to the matter at hand, eh? I understand how hard and confusing it is to love someone you hate. I really do. And if you call me his toady again, I swear by all the gods there ever were, I'll disjoint your fingers. Understood?"

"I didn't mean for it to happen like this," Maati said. "I wanted to heal the world, not . . . not this."

"Plans go awry," Idaan said. "It's their nature. I'm going back in. Join us when you're ready. I'll get something warm for you to drink."

Maati sat alone, growing colder. Behind him, the wayhouse ticked as the day's heat radiated away. An owl gave its low coo to the world, and the darkness around him seemed to lessen. He could make out the paving stones, the outline of the stable, the high branches rising toward the stars like thin fingers. Maati rested his head against the wall and let his eyes close.

The trembling had stopped. The anger was less immediate, chagrin slowly taking its place. He heard Eiah's calm voice, as solid as stone, from within. He should be with her. He should be at her side. She shouldn't have to face them by herself. He rose, grunting, and lumbered inside, his knees aching.

Otah was sitting in a low wooden chair, his fingers pressed to his lips in thought. He glanced up as Maati stepped into the room but made no other acknowledgment. Eiah, speaking, gestured to the space between Otah and Danat. Her voice had neither rancor nor apology, and Maati was reminded again why he admired her.

"Yes," she said, "the andat outplayed us. From the beginning with Ashti Beg to the end with me, we wanted to think of it as a baby. We all knew it wasn't. We all understand perfectly well that it was some part of Vanjit's mind made flesh, but . . ."

She raised her hands, palms out. Not a formal pose, but the gesture was eloquent enough.

"So what does it want?" Danat said. "If it truly wants Vanjit killed, why didn't it help you? That would have done all it wanted to do."

"It may want more than freedom," Idaan said, speaking over her shoulder as she pressed a warm bowl into Maati's hand. "There's precedent. Seedless wanted his freedom, but he also wanted his poet to suffer. Clarity-of-Sight may want something for Vanjit besides death."

"Such as?" Large Kae asked.

"Punishment," Eiah suggested. "Or isolation. Or . . ."

"Or a sense of family," Ashti Beg said, her voice oddly contemplative. "If we think of the babe as having more than one agenda, this could be its way of making a world that was only mother and child. Alienating all the rest of us."

"But it also wants its freedom," Maati said. Small Kae shifted on her bench at the sound of his voice, making room for him. He moved forward and sat. "Whatever else it wants, it must want that."

A puff of smoke escaped from the fire grate. Maati sipped the drink Idaan had given him—rum with honey and apple. It warmed his throat and made his chest glow.

"Is this really what we should care about?" the Galtic girl—Ana—asked. "I don't mean that as an attack, but it seems that we've established that the girl's less than sane. Is there something we gain by trying to guess at the shape of her madness?"

"We might have a better idea of where she's gone," Small Kae offered. "What she might do next?"

"Ana's right," Danat said. "We could roll dice about it, but there are some things we know for certain. She set out half a day's boat ride north of here a night ago. If she goes upriver, she'll need to hire a boat. If she goes down, she could hire one or build a raft and rely on the current. Or she can go east over land. What about the low towns? Could she have found shelter in a low town?"

The group was silent, then Danat said, "I'll get the keeper. She may know something of the local geography."

It was, Maati thought, a strangely familiar feeling. A handful of people sitting together, thinking aloud about an insoluble problem. The weeks at the school, sitting in the classrooms with chalk marks on the walls. All of them offering suggestion, interpretation, questions opened for anyone to answer if they could. He took an unexpected comfort from it.

The only one who didn't speak was Otah.

The conversation went on long into the night. The longer they took to find Vanjit, the greater her chance of escape. The greater her chance of dying alone in the wild. The Galtic girl and Small Kae had a long discussion of whether they were going to rescue Vanjit or if the aim was to kill her; Small Kae advocated a fast death, Ana wanted the chance to ask Vanjit to undo the damage to

Galt. Danat counted the days to Utani, the days back, guessed at the size of the search party that could be raised.

"There is another option," Eiah said, her pearl-gray eyes focused on nothing. "I had a binding prepared. Wounded. If I can manage it, we would have another way to heal the damage done to Galt."

Ana turned toward Eiah's voice, raw hope on her face. Maati almost felt sorry to dash it.

"No," he said. "It can't be done. Even if you knew it well enough to perform it blind, we hadn't looked over the most recent version. And Vanjit ruined the notes."

"But if Galt could be given its eyes again . . ." Danat said.

"Vanjit could take them away again," Maati said. "Clarity-of-Sight and Wounded could go back and forth until eventually Eiah tried to heal someone just as Vanjit tried to blind them, and then the gods alone know what would happen. And that matters less than the fact that Eiah would die if she tried the thing."

"You don't know that," Idaan said.

"I'm not willing to take the risk," Maati said.

Otah listened, his brow furrowed, his gaze shifting now and again to the fire. It wasn't until morning that Maati and the others learned what the Emperor was thinking.

The morning light transformed the wayhouse. With the shutters all opened, the benches and tables and soot-stained walls seemed less oppressive. The fire still smoked, but the breeze moving through the rooms kept the air fresh and clear, if cold. The wayhouse keeper had prepared duck eggs and peppered pork for their morning meal, and tea brewed until it was rich with taste and not yet bitter.

They were not all there. Ashti Beg and the two Kaes had stayed up after many of the others had faded into their restless sleep. Maati had slipped into dream with the sound of their voices in his ears, and none of them had yet risen. Danat and Otah were sitting at the same table, looking like a painter's metaphor of youth and age. Eiah and Idaan shared his own table, and he did not know where the Galtic girl had gone.

"She didn't blind Maati. Why?" Otah asked, gesturing at Maati as if he were an exhibit at an audience rather than a person. "Why spare him and not the others?"

"Well, for Eiah it's clear enough," Danat said around a mouthful of pork. "She didn't want another poet binding the andat. As long as Vanjit's the only one, she's . . . well, the only one."

"And the two Kaes," Eiah said, "so that they couldn't follow her."

"Yes," Idaan said, "but that's not the question. *Why not Maati?*"

"Because . . ." Maati began, and then fell short. Because she cared for him more? Because she didn't fear him? Nothing he could think of rang true.

"I think she wants to be found," Otah said. "I think she wants to be found, in specific, by Maati."

Idaan grunted appreciatively. Eiah frowned and then nodded slowly.

"Why would she want that?" Maati asked.

"Because your attention is the mark of status," Eiah answered. "You are the teacher. The Dai-kvo. Which of us you choose to give your time to determines who is in favor and who isn't. And she wants to show herself that she can take you from me."

"That's idiotic," Maati said.

"No," Idaan said, her voice oddly soft. "It's only childish."

"It fits together if you've raised a daughter," Otah agreed. "It's just what Eiah would have done when at twelve summers. But if I'm right, it changes things. I didn't want to say it in front of Ana-cha, but if your poet's truly gone to ground, I can't believe we'd find her before spring. She can find new allies if she needs them, or use the andat to threaten people and get what she wants from them. At best, we might have her by Candles Night."

"But if she's waiting to *be* found," Danat said.

"Then it's a matter of guessing where she'd wait," Otah said. "Where she'd expect Maati to go looking for her."

"I don't know the answer to that," Maati said. "The school, maybe. She might make her way back there."

"Or at the camp where we lost her," Eiah suggested.

Silence fell over the room for a moment. A decision had just been made, and Maati could tell that each of them knew it. Utani would wait. They were hunting Vanjit.

"The camp's nearest," Danat said.

"You can send one of the armsmen north with a letter," Eiah said. "Even if we fail, it doesn't mean a larger search can't be organized while we try."

"I'll round up the others," Idaan said, rising from the table. "No point wasting daylight. Danat-cha, if you could tell our well-armed escorts that we're leaving?"

Danat swilled down the last of his tea, took a pose that accepted his aunt's instructions, and rose. In moments, only Otah, Eiah, and Maati himself were left in the room. Otah took a bite of egg and stared out into nothing.

"Otah-kvo," Maati said.

The Emperor looked over, his eyebrow raised in something equally query and challenge. Maati felt his chest tighten as if it were bound by wire. He sat silent for the rest of the meal.

To Maati's dismay, Ashti Beg, Large Kae, and Small Kae all preferred to stay behind. There was a logic to it, and the keeper was more than happy to take Otah's silver in return for a promise to look after them. Still, Maati found himself wishing that they had come.

The Emperor's boat was, if anything, smaller than the one Maati had hired.

One of the armsmen had been sent north with letters that Otah had hastily drafted, another to the south. Half of the rest were set to finding a second boat and following with the supplies, and yet the little craft felt crowded as they nosed out into the river.

Otah stood at the bow, Danat at his side. Idaan had appointed herself shepherd of Eiah and Ana, the blinded women. Maati sat alone near the stern. The sky was pale with haze, the river air rich with the scent of decaying leaves and autumn. The kiln roared to itself, and the wheel slapped the water. Far above, two vees of geese headed south, their brash unlovely voices made beautiful by distance.

His rage was gone, and he missed it. All his fantasies of Otah Machi apologizing, of Otah Machi debased before him, melted like sugar in water when faced with the man himself. Maati felt small and alone, and perhaps that was merely accurate. He had lost everything now except perhaps Eiah. Irit was gone, and the wisest of them all for fleeing. He couldn't imagine Large Kae and Small Kae would return to him. Ashti Beg had left once already. And then Vanjit. All of his little family was gone now.

His family. Ashti Beg's voice returned to him. Vanjit and Clarity-of-Sight and the need for family.

"Oh," he said, almost before he knew what he meant. And then, "*Oh.*"

Maati made his unsteady way to the bow, touching crates with his fingertips to keep from stumbling. Otah and Danat turned at the sound of his approach, but said nothing. Maati reached them short of breath and oddly elated. His smile seemed to surprise them.

"I know where she's gone," he said.

27

>+< Udun had been a river city. A city of birds.

Otah remembered the first time he'd come to it, a letter of introduction from a man he had known briefly years before limp in his sleeve. After years of life in the eastern islands, it was like walking into a dream. Canals laced the city, great stone quays as busy as the streets. Great humped bridges with stairs cut in each side rose up to let even the tallest boats pass. On the shores, tree branches bent under the brightly colored burden of wings and beaks and a thousand kinds of song. The street carts sold food and drink as they did everywhere, but with each paper basket of lemon fish, every bowl of rice and sausage, there would be a twist of colored cloth.

Open the cloth, and seeds would spill out, and then within a heartbeat would come the birds. Fortunes were told by which birds reached you. Finches for love, sparrows for pain, and so on, and so on. Wealth, birth, death, love, sex,

and mystery all spelled out in feathers and hunger for those wise enough to see
or credulous enough to believe.

The palaces of the Khai Udun had spanned the wide river itself, barges
disappearing into the seemingly endless black tunnel and then emerging again
into the light. Beggars sang from rafts, their boxes floating at the side. The
firekeepers' kilns had all been enameled the green of the river water and a
deep red Otah had never seen elsewhere. And at a wayhouse with a little garden, there had been a keeper with a fox-sharp face and threads of white in her
black hair.

He had entered the gentleman's trade there, become a courier and traveled
through the world, bringing his messages back to House Siyanti and sleeping
at Kiyan's wayhouse. He knew all the cities and many of the low towns as they
had been back then, but Udun had been something precious.

And then the Galts had come. There were tales afterward that the river
downstream from the ruins stank of corpses for a year. Thousands of men and
women and children had died in the bloodiest slaughter of the war. Rich and
poor, utkhaiem and laborer, none had been spared. What survivors there were
had abandoned their city's grave, leaving it to the birds. Udun had died, and
with it—among unnumbered others—the poet Vanjit's parents and siblings
and some part of her soul.

And so, Maati argued, it was where she would return now.

"It's plausible," Eiah said. "Vanjit's always thought of herself as a victim.
This would help her to play the role."

"How far would it be from here?" Danat asked.

Otah, his mind already more than half in the past, calculated. They were
six days south of Utani on this steamcart for water. Udun had been a week's
ride or ten days walking south from Utani. . . .

"She could reach it in three days," Otah said, "if she knew where she was
headed. There are more than enough streams and creeks feeding the river
here. Water wouldn't be a problem."

"If we go there now, we might reach it before she does," Idaan said, looking
out over the river.

"The camp's still the better wager," Danat said. "It's where she parted ways
with them. They left their sleeping tents, so there's shelter of a sort. And it
doesn't require walking anywhere."

Maati started to object, but Otah raised his hand.

"It's along the way," Otah said. "We'll stop there and look. If she's been to the
camp, we should be able to tell. If not, we won't have lost more than half a day."

Maati straightened as if the decision were a personal insult, turned and
walked back to the stern of the boat. Time had not been gentle to the man.
Hard fat had thickened his chest and belly. His skin was gray where it wasn't
flushed. Maati's long, age-paled hair had an unhealthy yellow, and his movements were labored as if he woke every morning tired. And his mind . . .

Otah turned back to the water, the trees, the soft wind. The white haze of

sky was darkening as the day wore on, the scent of rain on the air. The others—
Idaan, Danat, Eiah, Ana—moved away quietly, as if afraid their conversation
might move him to violence. Otah breathed in and out, slow and deep, until
both his disgust and his pity had faded.

Maati had lost the right to feel anger when his pupil had killed Galt, and
any sentimental connection between Otah and his once-friend had drowned
outside Chaburi-Tan. If Maati thought that stopping at the camp was a poor
decision, he could make his case or he could choke on it. It was the same to
Otah.

In the event, they lost more than half a day. Maati identified the wrong
stretches of river twice, and Eiah had no eyes to correct him. When at last they
found the abandoned campsite, a soft, misting rain had started to fall and the
daylight was beginning to fail them. Maati led the way into the small clearing,
walking slowly. Otah and two of the armsmen were close behind. Eiah had
insisted that she come as well, and Idaan was helping her, albeit more slowly.

"Well," Otah said, standing in the middle of the ruins. "I think we can
fairly say that she's been here."

The camp was destroyed. The thick canvas sleeping tents lay in shreds and
knots. Stones and ashes from the fire pit had been strewn about, and two
leather bags lay empty in the mud. One of the armsmen crouched on his heels
and pointed to a slick of black mud. A footprint no longer than Otah's thumb.
Idaan's steps squelched as she paced near the ruined fire pit. Maati sat on a
patch of crushed grass, his hem dragging in the mud, his face a mask of desola-
tion.

"Back to the boat, I think," Otah said. "I can't see staying on here."

"We may still beat her to Udun," Idaan said, prying the gray wax shards
that had been Eiah's binding from the muck. "She spent a fair amount of time
doing this. Tents like those are hard to cut through."

One of the armsmen muttered something about the only thing worse than a
mad poet being a mad poet with a knife, but Otah was already on his way back
to the river.

The boatman and his second had fitted poles into thick iron rings all along
the boat's edge and raised a tarp that kept the deck near to dry. As darkness
fell and the rain grew heavier, the drops overhead sounded like fingertips tapping on wood. The kiln had more than enough coal. The wide-swung doors lit
the boat red and orange, and the scent of pigeons roasting on spits made the
night seem warmer than it was.

Maati had returned last, and spent the evening at the edge of the light.
Otah saw Eiah approach him once, a few murmured phrases exchanged, and
she turned back to the sound of the group eating and talking in the stern. If
Idaan hadn't risen to lead her back, he would have. The boatman's second
handed her a tin bowl, bird's flesh gray and steaming and glistening with fat.
Otah shifted to sit at her side.

"Father," Eiah said.

"You knew it was me?"

"I'm blind, not dim," Eiah said tartly. She plucked a sliver of meat from her bowl and popped it into her mouth. She looked tired, worn thin. He could still see the girl she had been, hiding beneath the time and age. He felt the urge to stroke her hair the way he had when she was an infant, to be her father again.

"This is, I assume, when you point out how much better your plan was than my own," she said.

"I didn't intend to, no," Otah said.

Eiah turned to him, shifting her weight as if she had some angry retort that had stuck in her throat for want of opposition. When he spoke, he was quiet enough to keep the conversation as near to between only the two of them as the close quarters would allow.

"We each did our best," Otah said. "We did what we could."

He put his arm around her. She bit down on her lip and fought the sobs that shook her body like tiny earthquakes. Her fingers found his own, and squeezed as hard as a patient under a physician's blade. He made no complaint.

"How many people have I killed, Papa-kya? How many people have I killed with this?"

"Hush," Otah said. "It doesn't matter. Nothing we've done matters. Only what we do next."

"The price is too high," Eiah said. "I'm sorry. Will you tell them that I'm sorry?"

"If you'd like."

Otah rocked her gently, and she allowed him to do it. The others all knew what they were saying, if not in specific, then at least the sketch of it. Otah saw Danat's concern, and Idaan's cool evaluating glance. He saw the armsmen turn their backs to him out of respect, and at the bow, Maati turned his back for another reason. Otah felt a flicker of his rage come back, a tongue of flame rising from old coals. Maati had done this. None of it would have happened if Maati hadn't been so bent by his own guilt or so deluded by his optimism that he ignored the dangers.

Or if Otah had found him and stopped him when that first letter had come. Or if Eiah hadn't made common cause with Maati's clandestine school. Or if Vanjit hadn't been mad, or Balasar ambitious, or the world and everything in it made from the first. Otah closed his eyes, letting the darkness create a space large enough for the woman in his arms and his own complicated heart.

Eiah murmured something he couldn't make out. He made a small interrogative sound in the back of his throat, and she coughed before repeating herself.

"There was no one at the school I could talk with," she said. "I got so tired of being strong all the time."

"I know," he said. "Oh, love. That, I know."

Otah slept deeply that night, lulled by exhaustion and the soft sounds of familiar voices and of the river. He slept as if he had been ill and the fever had only just broken. As if he was weak, and gaining strength. The dreams that possessed him faded with his first awareness of light and motion, less substantial than cobwebs, less lasting than mist.

The air itself seemed cleaner. The early-morning haze burned off in sunlight the color of water. They ate boiled wheat and honey, dried apples, and black tea. The boatman's second made his call, the boatman responded, and they nosed out again into the flow. Maati, sulking, kept as nearly clear of Otah as he could but kept casting glances at Eiah. Jealous, Otah assumed, of the conversation between father and daughter and unsure of her allegiance. Eiah for her part seemed to be making a point of speaking with her brother and her aunt and Ana Dasin, sitting with them, eating with them, making conversation with the jaw-clenched determination of a horse laboring uphill.

The character of the river itself changed as they went farther north. Where the south was wide and slow and gentle, the stretch just south of Udun was narrower—sometimes no more than a hundred yards across—and faster. The boatman kept his kiln roaring, the boiler bumping and complaining. The paddle wheel spat up river water, slicking the deck nearest the stern. Otah would have been concerned if the boatman and his second hadn't appeared so pleased with themselves. Still, whenever the boiler chimed after some particularly loud knock, Otah eyed it with suspicion. He had seen boilers burst their seams.

The miles passed slowly, though still faster than the poet girl could have walked. Every now and then, a flicker of movement on the shore would catch Otah's attention. Bird or deer or trick of the light. He found himself wondering what they would do if she appeared, andat in her arms, and struck them all blind. His fears always took the form of getting Danat and Eiah and Ana to safety, though he knew that his own danger would be as great as theirs and their competence likely greater.

The spitting waterwheel slowly drove them toward the bow. Near midday, the captain of the guard brought them tin bowls of raisins and bread and cheese. They all sat in a clump, and even Maati haunted the edges of the conversation. Ana and Eiah sat hand in hand on a long, low bench; Danat, cross-legged on the deck. Otah and Idaan kept to leather and canvas stools that creaked when sat upon and resisted any attempt to rise. The cheese was rich and fragrant, the bread only mildly stale, and the topic a council of war.

"If we do find her," Idaan said, answering Otah's voiced concerns, "I'm not sure what we do with her. Can she be made to see reason?"

"A month ago, I'd have said it was possible," Eiah said. "Not simple, but possible. I'm half-sorry we didn't kill her in her sleep when we were still at the school."

"Only half?" Danat asked.

"There's Galt," Eiah said. "As it stands now, she's the only one who can put it back. It's harder for her to do that dead."

Danat looked chagrined, and, as if sensing it, Idaan put a hand on his shoulder. Eiah squeezed Ana's hand, then gently bent it at the wrist, as if testing something.

"She's alone. She's hurt and she's sad. I'm not saying that's all certain to work in our favor," Maati said, "but it's something." Otah thought he sounded petulant, but none of the others appeared to hear it that way.

Eiah's voice cut the conversation like a blade. Even before he took the sense of the words, Otah was halfway to his feet.

"How long?" Eiah asked.

Her hands were around Ana's wrists, her fingers curled as if measuring the girl's pulses. Eiah's face was pale.

"Ah," Idaan said. "Well. Sitting those two together was a mistake."

"Tell me," Eiah said. "How far along?"

"A third, perhaps," Ana said softly.

"We hadn't mentioned it to the men," Idaan said. "I understand the first ones don't always take."

It took him less than a breath to understand.

"Ah," Otah said, a hundred tiny signs falling into place. Ana's weeping at the school, her avoidance of Danat, the way she'd kept to herself in the mornings and eaten with Idaan.

"What?" Danat asked, baffled.

"I'm pregnant," Ana said, her voice calm and matter-of-fact, her cheeks as bright as apples with her blush. The whole boat seemed to breathe in at once.

"And how long has *this* been going on?" Otah demanded, shifting his gaze to the dumbstruck Danat at his feet. His son blinked up, uncomprehending. It was as if Otah had asked in an unknown language.

"You're joking," Idaan said. "You have a boy who's just ended his twentieth summer and a girl not two years younger, an escort of professional armsmen as chaperone, and a steamcart with private quarters built on its back. What did you expect would happen?"

"But," Otah began, then found he wasn't sure what he intended to say. *She's blinded*, or *They aren't wed*, or *Farrer Dasin will say it's my fault for not keeping better watch over them*. Each impulse seemed more ridiculous than the last.

"I'm going to be a father," Danat said as if testing out the words. He turned to look up at Otah and started to grin. "*You're* going to be a grandfather."

Eiah was weeping openly, her arms around Ana. A clamor of voices and a whoop from the stern said that whatever hope there might have been that the thing would be kept quiet once they returned to court was gone. Otah sat back, his stool creaking under his weight. Idaan took a pose of query that carried nuances of both pity at his idiocy and congratulations. Otah started laughing and found it hard to stop.

It had been so long since he'd felt joy, he'd almost forgotten what it was like.

The rest of the day was spent in half-drunken conversation. Otah was made to retell the details of Danat's birth, and of Eiah's. Danat grew slowly more pleased with himself and the world as the initial shock wore thin. Ana Dasin smiled, her grayed eyes taking in nothing and giving out a pleasure and satisfaction that seemed more intimate in that she couldn't see its reflection in the faces around her.

Stories came pouring out as if they had only been waiting for the chance to be told. Idaan's spectacularly failed attempts to care for a younger half-sister when she'd been little more than fourteen summers old. Otah's work in the eastern islands as an assistant midwife, and the awkward incident of the baby born to an island mother and island father and with a complexion that sang to the stars of Obar State. Eiah spilled out every piece of secondhand wisdom she'd ever heard about keeping a new babe safe in the womb until it was ready to be born. At one point the armsmen broke into giddy song and, against Danat's protests, lifted him onto their shoulders, the deck shifting slightly under them. The sun itself seemed to shine for them, the river to laugh.

Maati alone seemed not to recover entirely from the first surprise. He smiled and chuckled and nodded when it fit the moment, but his eyes were reading letters in the air. He looked neither pleased nor displeased, but lost. Otah saw his lips moving as Maati spoke to himself, as if trying to explain something to his body that only his mind knew. When the poet hefted himself up and came to take Ana's hand, it was with a formality that might have been mixed feelings on his part or only a fear that his kind thoughts would be unwelcome. Ana accepted the formal, somewhat stilted blessing, and afterward Eiah took Maati's hand, pulling him down to sit at her side.

Even braided together, Otah's anger and distrust and sorrow couldn't overcome the moment. The blood and horror of the world lifted, and a future worth having peeked through the crack.

It was only much later, when the sun fell carelessly into the treetops of the western bank and shadows darkened the water, that the celebration faltered. The boat passed a brickwork tower standing on the riverbank, ivy almost obscuring the scars where fire had burned through timber and stripped the shutters from the empty windows. Otah watched the structure with the eerie feeling that it was watching back. The river bent, and a great stone bridge came into sight, gaps in its rail like missing teeth. Birds as bright as fire sang and fluttered, even in the autumn cold. Their songs filled the air, the familiar trills greeting Otah like the wail of a ghost.

The ruins of the river city. The corpse of a city of birds.

They had come to dead Udun.

28

Maati tramped through the overgrown streets, Idaan walking silently at his side. The hunter's bow slung over her shoulder was meant more as protection from feral dogs than to assassinate Vanjit, though Maati knew Idaan could use it for either. To their left, an unused canal stank of stale water and rotting vine. To the right, walls stood or leaned, roofs sagged or had fallen in. Every twenty steps seemed to offer up a new display of how war and time could erase the best that humanity achieved. And above the ruins, rising like a mountain over the city, the ruined palaces of the Khai Udun were grayed by the moisture in the air. The towers and terraces of enameled brick as soft as visions.

He had lost Eiah too.

Squatting on the boat as they made their way upriver, he had watched her turn to Otah, watched her become his daughter again where before she had chosen the role of outcast. She had lost faith in Maati's dream, and he understood why. She had delighted in the Galtic girl's condition as if it weren't the very thing that they had feared and fought against.

Maati had wanted the past. He had wanted to make the world whole as it had been when he was a boy, none of his opportunities squandered. And she had wanted that too. They all had. But with every change that couldn't be undone, the past receded. With every new tragedy Maati brought upon the world, with each friend that he lost, with failure upon failure upon failure, the dim light faded. With Eiah returned to her father's cause, there was nothing left to lose. His despair felt almost like peace.

"Left or right?" Idaan asked.

Maati blinked. The road before them split, and he hadn't even noticed it. He wasn't much of a scout.

"Left," he said with a shrug.

"You think the canal bridge will hold?"

"Right, then," Maati said, and turned down the road before the woman could raise some fresh objection.

It was only a decade and a half since the war. It seemed like days ago that Maati had been the librarian of Machi. And yet the white-barked tree that split the road before them, street cobbles shattered and lifted by its roots, hadn't existed then. The canals he walked past had run clean. There had been no moss on the walls. Udun had been alive, then. The forest and the river were eating the city's remains, and it seemed to have happened in the space between one breath and the next. Or perhaps the library, the envoys from the Dai-kvo, the long conversations with Cehmai-kvo and Stone-Made-Soft had been part of some other lifetime.

The sound was low and violent—something thrashing against wood or stone. Maati looked around him. The square they'd come to was paved in wide, flat stones, tall grass a yellow gray at the joints. A ruined fountain with black muck where clear water had been squatted in the center. Idaan's bow was in her hands, an arrow between her fingers.

"What was that?" Maati asked.

Idaan's dark eyes swept over the ruins, and Maati tried to follow her gaze. They might have been houses or businesses or something of both. The sound came again. From his left and ahead. Idaan moved forward cat-quiet, her bow at the ready. Maati stayed behind her, but close. He remembered that he had a blade at his belt and drew it.

The buck was in a small garden with an iron fence overgrown now with flowering ivy. Its side was cut, the fur black with dried blood and flies. The noble rack of horns was broken on one side, ending in a cruel, jagged stump. As Idaan stepped near, it moved again, lashing out at the fence with its feet, and then hung its head. It was an image of exhaustion and despair.

And its eyes were gray and sightless.

"Poor bastard," Idaan said. The buck raised its head, snorting. Maati gripped the handle of his blade, readying himself for something, though he wasn't certain what. Idaan raised her bow with something akin to disgust on her face. The first arrow sunk deep into the neck of the once-proud animal. The buck bellowed and tried to run, fouling itself in the fence, the vines. It slipped to its knees as Idaan sank another arrow into its side. And then a third.

It coughed and went still.

"Well, I think we can say how your little poet girl was planning to get food," Idaan said, her voice acid. "Cripple whatever game she came across and then let it beat itself to death. She's quite the hunter."

She slung the bow back over her shoulder, walking carefully into the trampled garden. Flies rose from the beast in a buzzing cloud. Idaan ignored them, putting her hand on the dead buck's flank.

"It's a waste," she said. "If I had rope and the right knife we could at least dress him and eat something fresh tonight. I hate leaving him for the rats and the foxes."

"Why did you kill him then?"

"Mercy. You were right, though. Vanjit's in the city somewhere. That was a good call."

"I'm half-sorry I said anything," Maati said. "You'd kill her just as quickly, wouldn't you?"

"You think you can romance her into taking back her curse. I'm no one to keep you from trying."

"And then?"

"And then we follow the same plan each of us had. It's the one thing we agree upon. She's too dangerous. She has to die."

"I know what I intended. I know what Eiah and I were planning. But that was the andat's scheme. I think there may be another way."

Idaan looked up, then stood. The bow was still in her hand.

"Can you give her her parents back?" she asked. "Can you give her the brothers and sisters she lost? Udun. Can you rebuild it?"

Maati took a pose that dismissed her questions, but Idaan stepped close to him. He could feel her breath against his face. Her eyes were cold and dark.

"Do you think that Galt died blind because of something you can remedy?" she demanded. "What's happened, happened. You can't will her to be the woman you hoped she was. Telling yourself that you can is worse than stupidity."

"If she puts it to rights," Maati said, "she shouldn't have to die."

Idaan narrowed her eyes, tilted her head.

"I'll offer you this," she said. "If you can talk the girl into giving Galt back its eyes—and Eiah and Ashti Beg. Everyone. If you can do that and also have her release her andat, I won't be the one who kills her."

"Would Otah let her live?" Maati asked.

"Ask him and he might," Idaan said. "Experience suggests he and I have somewhat different ideas of mercy."

At midday, they returned to their camp. The boat was tied up at an old quay slick with mold. The scent of the river was rich and not entirely pleasant. Two of the other scouting parties had returned before them; Danat and one of the armsmen were still in the city but expected back shortly. Otah, in a robe of woven silk under a thicker woolen outer robe, sat at a field table on the quayside, sketching maps of the city from memory. Idaan made her report, Maati silent at her side. He tried to imagine asking Otah for clemency on Vanjit's behalf. If Maati could persuade her to restore sight to everyone she'd injured and release the andat, would Otah honor Idaan's contract? Or, phrased differently, if Maati couldn't save the world, could he at least do something to redeem this one girl?

He didn't ask it, and Idaan didn't raise the issue.

After Danat and the armsmen returned, they all ate a simple meal of bread and dried apples. Danat, Otah, and the captain of the guard consulted with one another over Otah's sketched maps, planning the afternoon's search. Idaan tended to Ana; their laughter seemed incongruous in the grim air of their camp. Eiah sat by herself at the water's edge, her face turned up toward the sun. Maati went to her side.

"Did you drink your tea this morning?" she asked.

"Yes," he lied petulantly.

"You need to," she said. Maati shrugged and tossed the last round of dried apple into the water. It floated for a moment, the pale flesh looking nearly white on the dark water. A turtle rose from beneath and bit at it. Eiah held out her hand, palm up, fingers beckoning. Maati was vaguely ashamed of the relief he felt taking her hand in his own.

"You were right," Maati confessed. "I still want to save Vanjit. I know better. I do, but the impulse keeps coming back."

"I know it does," Eiah said. "You have a way of seeing things the way you'd prefer them to be rather than the way they are. It's your only vice."

"Only?"

"Well, that and lying to your physician," Eiah said, lightly.

"I drink too much sometimes."

"When was the last time?"

Maati shrugged, a smile tugging at his mouth.

"I used to drink too much when I was younger," he said. "I still would, but I've been busy."

"You see?" Eiah said. "You had more vices when you were young. You've grown old and wise."

"I don't think so. I don't think you can mention me and wisdom in the same breath."

"You aren't dead. There's time yet." She paused, then asked, "Will they find her?"

"If Otah-kvo's right, and she wants us to," Maati said. "If she doesn't want to be found, we might as well go home."

Eiah nodded. Her grip tightened for a moment, and she released his hand. Her brow was furrowed with thought, but it was nothing she chose to share. *Don't leave me,* he wanted to say. *Don't go back to Otah and leave me by myself. Or worse, with only Vanjit.* In the end, he kept his silence.

His second foray into the city came in the middle of the afternoon. This time they had set paths to follow, rough-drawn maps marked with each pair's route, and Maati was going out with Danat. They would come back three hands before sunset unless some significant discovery was made. Maati accepted Otah's instructions without complaint, though the resentment was still there.

The air was warmer now, and with the younger man's pace, Maati found himself sweating. They moved down smaller streets this time, narrow avenues that nature had not quite choked. The birds seemed to follow them, though more likely it was only that there were birds everywhere. There was no sign of Vanjit or Clarity-of-Sight, only raccoons and foxes, mice and hunting cats, feral dogs on the banks and otters in the canals. They were hardly a third of the way through the long, complex loop set out for them when Maati called a halt. He sat on a stonework bench, resting his head in his hands and waiting for his breath to slow. Danat paced, frowning seriously at the brush.

It struck Maati that the boy was the same age Otah had been in Saraykeht. Not as broad across the shoulders, but Otah had been Itani Noygu and a seafront laborer then. Maati himself had been born four years after the Emperor, hardly sixteen when he'd gone to study under Heshai and Seedless. Younger than Ana Dasin was now. It was hard to imagine ever having been that young.

"I meant to offer my congratulations to you," Maati said. "Ana-cha seems a good woman."

Danat paused. The reflection of his father's rage warmed the boy's face, but not more than that.

"I didn't think an alliance with Galt would please you."

"I didn't either," Maati said, "but I have enough experience with losing to your father that I'm learning to be generous about it."

Danat almost started. Maati wondered what nerve he had touched, but before he could ask, a flock of birds a more violent blue than anything Maati had seen burst from a treetop down the avenue. They wheeled around one another, black beaks and wet eyes and tiny tongues pink as a fingertip. Maati closed his eyes, disturbed, and when he opened them, Danat was kneeling before him. The boy's face was a webwork of tiny lines like the cracked mud in a desert riverbed. Fine, dark whiskers rose from Danat's pores. His eyelashes crashed together when he blinked, interweaving or pressing one another apart like trees in a mudslide. Maati closed his eyes again, pressing his palms to them. He could see the tiny vessels in each eyelid, layer upon layer almost out to the skin.

"Maati-cha?"

"She's seen us," Maati said. "She knows I'm here."

In spite of the knowledge, it took Maati half a hand to find her. He swept the horizon and from east to west and back again. He could see half-a-hundred rooftops. He found her at last near the top of the palaces of the Khai Udun on a balcony of bricks enameled the color of gold. At this distance, she was smaller than a grain of sand, and he saw her perfectly. Her hair was loose, her robe ripped at the sleeve. The andat was on her hip, its black, hungry eyes on his own. Vanjit nodded and put the andat down. Then, with a slow, deliberate motion, she took a pose of greeting. Maati returned it.

"Where? Where is she?" Danat asked. Maati ignored him.

Vanjit shifted her hands and her body into a pose that was both a rebuke and an accusation. Maati hesitated. He had imagined a thousand scenarios for this meeting, but they had all involved the words he would speak, and what she would say in return. His first impulse now was toward apology, but something in the back of his mind resisted. Her face was a mask of self-righteous anger, and, to his surprise, he recognized the expression as one he himself had worn in a thousand fantasies. In his dreams, he had been facing Otah, and Otah had been the one to beg forgiveness.

Like a voice speaking in his ear, he knew why his hands would not take an apologetic pose. *She is here to see you abased. Do it now, and you have nothing left to offer her.* Maati pulled his shoulders back, lifted his chin, and took a pose that requested an audience. Its nuances didn't claim his superiority as a teacher to a student but neither did they cede it. Vanjit's eyes narrowed. Maati waited, his breath short and anxiety plucking at him.

Vanjit took a pose appropriate to a superior granting a servant or slave an indulgence. Maati didn't correct her, but neither did he respond. Vanjit looked down as if the andat had cried out or perhaps spoken, then shifted her hands and her body to a pose of formal invitation appropriate for an evening's meal. Only then did Maati accept, shifting afterward to a pose of query. Vanjit indicated the balcony on which she stood, and then made a gesture that implied either intimacy or solitude.

Meet me here. In my territory and on my terms. Come alone.

Maati moved to an accepting pose, smiling to himself as much as to the girl in the palaces. With a physical sensation like that of a gnat flying into his eye, Maati's vision blurred back to merely human acuity. He turned his attention back to Danat.

The boy looked half-frantic. He held his blade as if prepared for an attack, his gaze darting from tree to wall as if he could see the things that Maati had seen. The moons that passed around the wandering stars, the infinitesimal animals that made their home in a drop of rain, or the girl on her high balcony halfway across the city. Maati had no doubt she was still watching them.

"Come along, then," he said. "We're done here."

"You saw her," Danat said.

"I did."

"Where is she? What did she want?"

"She's at the palaces, and there's no point in rushing over there like a man on fire. She can see everything, and she knows to watch. We could no more take her by surprise than fly."

Maati took a deep breath and turned back along the path they'd just come. There was no reason to follow Otah's route now, and Maati wanted to sit down for a while, perhaps drink a bowl of wine, perhaps speak to Eiah for a time. He wanted to understand better why the dread in his breast was mixed with elation, the fear with pleasure.

"What does she want?" Danat asked, trotting to catch up to Maati.

"I suppose that depends upon how you look at things," Maati said. "In the greater scheme, she wants what any of us do. Love, a family, respect. In the smaller, I believe she wants to see me beg before I die. The odd thing is that even if she had that, it wouldn't bring her any lasting peace."

"I don't understand."

Maati stopped. It occurred to him that if he had taken the wrong pose, made the wrong decision just now, he and the boy would be trying to find their way back to camp by smell. He put a hand on Danat's shoulder.

"I've asked Vanjit to meet with me tonight. She's agreed, but it can only be the two of us," Maati said. "I believe that once it's done I'll be able to tell you whether the world is still doomed."

29

>+<   "No," Otah said. "Absolutely not."

"All respect," Maati said. "You may be the Emperor, but this isn't your call to make. I don't particularly need your permission, and Vanjit's got no use for it at all."

"I can have you kept here."

"You won't," Maati said. The poet was sure of himself, Otah thought, because he was right.

When Danat and Maati had returned early, he had known that something had happened. The quay they had adopted as the center of the search had been quiet since the end of the afternoon meal. Ana and Eiah sat in the shadow of a low stone wall, sleeping or talking when Eiah wasn't going through the shards of her ruined binding, arranging the shattered wax in an approximation of the broken tablets. The boatman and his second had taken apart the complex mechanism connecting boiler to wheel and were cleaning each piece, the brass and bronze, iron and steel laid out on gray tarps and shining like jewelry. The voices of the remaining armsmen joined with the low, constant lapping of the river and the songs of the birds. At another time, it might have been soothing. Otah, sitting at his field table, fought the urge to pace or shout or throw stones into the water. Sitting, racking his brain for details of a place he'd lived three decades ago, and pushing down his own fears both exhausted him and made him tense. He felt like a Galtic boiler with too hot a fire and no release; he could feel the solder melting at his seams.

If they had followed his plan, Danat and Maati would have returned to the quay from a path that ran south along the river. They came from the west, down the broad stone steps. Danat held a naked blade forgotten in his hand, his expression set and unnerved. Maati, walking more slowly, seemed on the verge of collapse, but also pleased. Otah put down his pen.

"You've found her?"

"She's found us," Maati said. "I think she's been watching us since we stepped off the boat."

The armsmen clustered around them. Eiah and Ana rose to their feet, touching each other for support. Maati lumbered into the center of the quay as if it were a stage and he was declaiming a part. He told them of the encounter, of Vanjit's appearance, of the andat at her side. He took the poses he'd adopted and mimicked Vanjit's. In the end, he explained that Vanjit would see him—would see *only* him—and that it was to happen that evening.

"She doesn't know you," Maati continued, "and what little she does know, she doesn't have a use for. To her, you're the man who turned against his own people. And I am the teacher who gave her the power of a small god."

"And then plotted to kill her," Otah said, but he knew this battle was lost. Maati was right: neither of them had the power here. The poet and her andat were their masters whether he liked it or not. She could dictate any terms she wished, and Maati was important to her in a way that Otah himself was not.

It was a meeting with the potential to end the world or save it. He would have given it to a stranger before he trusted it to Maati.

"What are you going to tell her?" Ana asked. Her voice sounded hungry. Weeks—months now—Ana had been living in shadows, and here was the chance to make herself whole.

"I'll apologize," Maati said. "I'll explain that the andat manipulated us, playing on our fears. Then, if Vanjit will allow it, I'll have Eiah brought so that she can offer her apologies as well."

Eiah, standing where Otah could see her face, lifted her chin as if something had caught her attention. Something ghosted across her face—alarm or incredulity—and then was gone. She became a statue of herself, a mask. She had no more faith in Maati than he did. And, to judge from her silence, no better idea of what to do either.

"She has killed thousands of innocent people," Otah said. "She's crippled women she had numbered among her friends. Are you sure that apologizing is entirely appropriate?"

"What would you have me do?" Maati asked, his hands taking a pose that was both query and challenge. "Should I go to her swinging accusations? Should I tell her she's not safe and never will be?"

The voice that answered was Idaan's.

"There's nothing you can say to her. She's gone mad, and you talk about her as if she weren't. Whatever words you use, she's going to hear what she wants. You might just as well send her a puppet and let her speak both parts."

"You don't know her," Maati said, his face flushing. "You've never met her."

"I've *been* her," Idaan said dismissively as she walked down the steps to the now-crowded quay. "Give her what she wants if you'd like. It's never made her well before, and it won't make her well now."

"What would you advise?" Otah asked.

"She'll be distracted," Idaan said. "Go in with a bowman. Put an arrow in the back of her head just where the spine touches it."

"*No,*" Maati shouted.

"No," Eiah said. "Even if killing her is the right thing, think of the risk. If she suspects, she can always lash out, and we haven't got any protection against her."

"There doesn't need to be anyone there for her to be suspicious," Idaan said. "If she's frightened by shadows, the end is just as bloody."

"So we're giving up on Galt," Ana said. Her voice was flat. "I listen to all of you, and the one thing I never hear mentioned is all the people who've died because they happened to be like me."

Maati stepped forward, taking the girl's hand. Otah, watching her, didn't believe she needed comfort. It wasn't pain or sorrow in her expression. It was resolve.

"They don't think they can move her to mercy," Maati said. "I will do everything I can, Ana-cha. I'll swear to anything you like that I will—"

"Take me with you," Ana said. "I'm no threat to her, and I can speak for Galt. I'm the only one here who can do that."

Her orders were met by silence until Idaan made a sound that was equally laughter and cough.

"She told me to come alone," Maati said. "If she sees me leading a blind Galt to her—"

"Vanjit has the right to see her mistakes," Otah said. "She's done this. She should look at it. We all should look at what we've done to come here."

Maati looked at him as if seeing him for the first time. There was a deep confusion in the old poet's face. Otah took a pose that asked a favor between equals. As a friend to a friend.

"Take Ana," Otah said.

Maati's jaw worked as if he were chewing possible replies.

"No," he said.

Otah took a pose that was at once a query and an opportunity for Maati to recant. Maati shook his head.

"I have trusted you, Otah-kvo. Since we were boys, I have had to come to you with everything, and when you weren't there, I tried to imagine what you might have done. And this time, you are wrong. I know it."

"Maati—"

"Trust me," Maati hissed. "For once in your life *trust me*. Ana-cha must not go."

Otah's mouth opened, but no words came forth. Maati stood before him, his breath fast as a boy's who had just run a race or jumped from a high cliff into the sea. Maati had defied Otah. He had betrayed him. He had never in their long history refused him.

For a moment, Otah felt as if they were boys again. He saw in Maati the balled fists and jutting chin of a small child standing against an older one, the bone-deep fear mixed with a sudden, surprising pride in his own unexpected courage. And in Otah's own breast, an answering sorrow and even shame.

He took a pose that acknowledged Maati's decision. The poet hesitated, nodded, and walked to the riverside. Idaan leaned close to Ana, whispering all that had happened which the girl could not see.

Kiyan-kya—

Sunset isn't on us yet, but it will be soon. Maati is sulking, I think. Everyone's frightened, but none of us has the courage to say it. I take that back. Idaan isn't afraid. Just after Maati refused to take Ana Dasin with him to this thrice-damned meeting, Idaan came to me and said that she was fairly certain that if Vanjit kills us all, she'll die of starvation herself within the year. Vanjit's hunting ability hasn't impressed her, and Idaan has a way of finding comfort in strange places.

Nothing has ever come out the way I expected, love. It seemed so simple. We had men who could sire a child, they had women who could bear. And instead, I am sending the least reliable man I know to save everything and everyone by talking a madwoman into sanity. If I could find any way not to do this, I'd take it. I appealed to what Maati and I once were to each other when I tried to convince him to accept Ana's company. It was more than half a lie. In truth I can't say I know this man. The boy I knew in Saraykeht and the man we knew in Machi has become a stew of bitterness and blind optimism. He wants the past back, and no sacrifice is too high. I wonder if he never saw the weakness and injustice and rot at the heart of the old ways, or if he's only forgotten them.

If I had it all to do again, I'd have done it differently. I'd have married you sooner. I'd never have gone north, and Idaan and Adrah could have taken Machi and had all this on their heads instead of my own. Only then we'd have been in Udun, you and I, and I would have had your company for an even shorter time. There is no winning this game. I suppose it's best that we can only play it through once.

You wouldn't like what's become of Udun. I don't like it. I remember Sinja saying that he kept your wayhouse safe during the sack, but I haven't had the heart to go and look. The river still has its beauty. The birds still have their song. They'll still be here when the rest of us are gone. I miss Sinja.

There's something I'm trying to tell you, love. It's taking me more time than I'd expected to work up the courage. We all know it. Even Maati, even Ana, even Eiah. None of us can speak the words; not even me. You're the only one I can say this to, because, I suppose, you've already died and so you're safe from it.

Love. Oh, love. This meeting is all we can do, and it isn't going to work.

Maati left in twilight. The stars shone in the east, the darkness rising up like a black dawn as the western sky fell from blue to gold, from gold to gray. Birdsong changed from the trills and complaints of the day to the low cooing and complexities of the night. The river seemed to exhale, and its breath was green and rotting and cold. Maati had a small pack at his side. In the light of the failing day and the flickering orange of the torches, he looked older than Otah felt, and Otah felt ancient.

He tried to see something familiar in Maati's eyes. He tried to see the boy he'd gone drinking with in dark, lush Saraykeht, but that child was gone. Both of those children.

"I will do my best, Otah-kvo," Maati said.

Otah bit back his first reply, and then his second.

"Tomorrow's going to be a very different day, Maati-cha," Otah said. Maati nodded. After so much and so long, there should have been more. Sinja appeared for a moment in the back of Otah's mind. There had been no last good-bye for him. If this was to be the ending between the two of them, Otah thought he should say something. He should make this parting unlike the others that had come before. "I'm sorry it's come to this."

Maati took a pose that agreed but kept the meaning as imprecise as Otah had. One of the armsmen called out, pointing at the looming threat of the Khai Udun's palaces. In a wide window precisely above the river, a light had appeared, glittering like gold. Like a fallen star.

Ana and Danat were in a corner of the quay, their arms wrapped around each other. Idaan stood among the armsmen, her expression grim. Eiah sat alone by the water, listening. Otah saw Maati's gaze linger on her with something like sorrow.

With a lantern in his unsteady hand, Maati walked off along the ruined streets that ran beside the river. Otah guessed it would take him half a hand to reach the palaces.

"All right," Idaan said. "He's gone."

Otah turned to look at her, some pale attempt at wit on his lips, and saw that the comment hadn't been meant for him. Idaan crouched beside Eiah. His daughter's face was turned toward nothing, but her hands were digging through the physician's satchel. Danat glanced at Otah, confusion in his eyes. Eiah started drawing flat stones from her bag and laying them gently on the flagstones before her.

No, he was wrong. Not stones, but triangles of broken wax. The contents of old, broken tablets with symbols and words inscribed on them in Eiah's hand.

"You could try being of help," Idaan said and gestured toward the shards at his daughter's knees. "There's a piece that goes right here I haven't been able to find."

"You did enough," Eiah said, her hands shifting quickly, fitting the breaks together. Already the wax was taking the shape of five separate squares, the characters coming together. "Just going to the campsite and bringing back the bits you did was more than I could have asked."

"What is this?" Otah asked, though he already knew.

"My work," Eiah said. "My binding. I hoped I'd have time. Before we actually came across Vanjit-cha, there was the chance she was spying on us. She'd always planned to kill me by distracting me during the binding. But now, and for I think at least the next hand and a half, her attention is going to be on Maati-kvo. So . . ."

Idaan shook her head, clearing some thought away, and gestured to the captain of the guard.

"We'll need light," she said. "Eiah may be able to work puzzles in the dark, but I'm better if I can see what I'm doing."

"I thought you couldn't do this," Otah said, kneeling.

"Well, I haven't managed it yet," Eiah said with a wry smile. "On the other hand, I've studied to be a physician. Holding things in memory isn't so difficult, once you've had the practice. And there's enough here, I think, to guide me through it, no matter what Maati-kvo believes."

Idaan made a low grunt of pleasure, reached across Eiah and shifted a stray chunk of wax into place. Eiah's fingers caressed the new join, and she nodded to herself. Armsmen brought the wild, flickering light close, the waxwork lettering seeming to breathe in the shadows.

"Maati's warnings," Otah said. "You can't know what will happen if you pit your andat against hers."

"I won't have to," Eiah said. "I've thought this through, Papa-kya. I know what I'm doing. There was another section. It was almost square with one corner missing. Can anyone see that?"

"Check the satchel," Idaan said as Otah plucked the piece from the hem of Eiah's robe. He pressed it into her hand. Her fingertips traced its surface before she placed it at the bottom of the second almost-formed tablet. Her smile was gentler than he'd seen from her since he'd walked into the wayhouse. He touched her cheek.

"Maati doesn't know you're doing this, then?" Otah asked.

"We didn't think we'd ask him," Idaan said. "No disrespect to Eiah-cha, but that man's about half again as cracked as his poet."

"No, he isn't mad," Eiah said, her hands never slowing their dance across the face of the broken tablets. "He's just not equal to the task he set himself. He always meant well."

"And I'm sure the two dozen remaining Galts will feel better because of it," Idaan said acidly. And then, in a gentler voice, "It doesn't matter what story you tell yourself, you know. We've done what we've done."

"I wish you would stop that," Eiah said.

Idaan's surprise was clear on her face, and apparently in her silence as well. Eiah shook her head and went on, her tone damning and conversational.

"Every third thing you say is an oblique reference to killing my grandfather. We all know you did the thing, and we all know you regret it. None of this is anything to do with that. Papa-kya and Maati love each other and they hate each other, and it doesn't pertain either. Maati's overwhelmed by the consequences of misjudging Vanjit, and he might not be if he weren't hauling Nayiit and Sterile and Seedless along behind him."

Idaan looked like she'd been slapped. The armsmen were crowded so close, Otah could hear the low flutter of the torches burning, but the men pretended not to have heard.

"The past doesn't matter," Eiah said. "A hundred years ago or last night, it's all just as gone. I have a binding to work, and I'd like to make the attempt before Vanjit blinds Maati and walks him off something tall. I think we have something like half a hand."

They worked together in silence, three pairs of hands putting the wax into place quickly. There were still sections missing, and some parts of the tablets were shattered so thoroughly that Eiah's markings were all but lost. His daughter passed her fingertips slowly over each of the surfaces, her brow furrowed, her lips moving as if reciting something under her breath. Whether it was the binding or a prayer, Otah couldn't guess.

Idaan leaned close to Otah, her breath a warm and whispering breeze against his ear.

"She takes the tact from her mother's side, I assume?"

His tension and fear gave the words a hilarity they didn't deserve, and he fought to contain his laughter. The quay was dark around them; the torches kept his eyes from adapting to the darkness. It was as if the world had narrowed to a few feet of lichen-slicked flagstone, a single unshuttered window in the distance, and countless, endless, unnumbered stars.

"All right," Eiah said. "I can't be disturbed while I do this. If we could have the armsmen set up a guard formation? It would be in keeping with my luck to have a stray boar stumble into us at the wrong moment."

The captain didn't wait for Otah's approval. The men shifted, Idaan and Danat with them. Only Otah stayed. As if she saw him there, Eiah took a querying pose.

"You may die from this," he said.

"I'm aware of it," she said. "It doesn't matter. I have to try. And I think you have to let me."

"I do," Otah agreed. Smiling, she looked young.

"I love you too, Papa-kya."

"May I sit with you?" he asked. "I don't want to distract you, but it would be a favor."

He brushed the back of her hand with his fingertips. She took him by the sleeve of his robe and pulled him down to sit beside her. The fingers of her left hand laced with his right. For a moment, the only sounds were the gentle lapping of the river against the stone, the diminished hush of torch fire, the cooing of owls. Eiah leaned forward, her fingertips on the first tablet. Otah let go, and both of her hands caressed the wax. She began to chant.

The words were only words. He recognized a few of them, some phrases. Her voice went out on the cool night air as she moved slowly across each of the shattered tablets. When she reached the end, she went back to the beginning.

Though there were no walls or cliffs to sound against, her voice began first to resonate and then to echo.

30

Maati traveled through the darkness alone. The sense of unreality was profound. He had refused Otah Machi, Emperor of the Khaiem. He had refused Otah-kvo. For years, perhaps a lifetime, he had admired Otah or else despised him. Maati had broken the world twice, once in Otah's service, and now, through Vanjit, in opposition to him. But this once, Otah had been wrong, and he had been right, and Otah had acknowledged it.

How strange that such a small moment should bring him such a profound sense of peace. His body itself felt lighter, his shoulders more nearly square. To his immense surprise, he realized he had shed a burden he'd been carrying unaware for most of his life.

Maati traveled through the darkness of Udun alone, because he had chosen to.

The brown vines and bare branches stirred in a soft breeze. The flutter of wings came from all around him, from nowhere. The air was cold enough to make his breath steam, and the voice of the river was a constant hush. With each step, some new detail of his path would come clear: an axe consumed by rust, a door still hanging from rotten leather hinges, the green-glowing eyes of some small predator. Cracks appeared in the paving stones, running out before him as if his passage were corrupting the city rather than revealing the decay already there.

He and Vanjit carried a history together. They had known each other, had helped each other. She would see that it was the andat's intervention that had turned him against her. The palaces of the Khai Udun grew taller and taller without ever seeming to come close until, it seemed between one breath and the next, he stepped into a grand courtyard. Moss and lichen had almost obscured the swirling design of white and red and gold stones. Maati paused, his lantern held over his head.

Once, it would have been a breathtaking testament to power and ingenuity and overwhelming confidence. Columns rose into the black air. Statues of women and men and beasts towered over the entranceway, the bronze lost under green and gray. He walked alone into a welcoming chamber too vast for his lantern to penetrate. There was no ceiling, no walls. The river was silent here. Far above, wings fluttered in still air.

Maati took a deep breath—dust and rot and, after a decade and a half of utter ruin, still the faint scent of smoke. It smelled like the corpse of history.

He walked forward over parquet of ebony and oak, the pattern ruined and pieces pried up by water and time. He expected his footsteps to echo, but no sound he made returned to him.

A light glimmered high up and to his left. Maati stopped. He lowered his lantern and raised it again. The glimmer didn't shift. Not a reflection, then. Maati angled toward it.

A great stone stairway swept up in the gloom, a single candle burning at its top. Maati made his way slowly enough to keep from tiring. The hall that opened before him was not as numbingly huge as the first chamber; Maati could make out the ceiling, and that the walls existed. And far down it, another light.

The carpets underfoot had rotted to scraps years before. The shattered glass and fallen crystal might have been the damage of the elements or of the city's fall. The next flight of stairs—equally grand and equally arduous—could only have been a testament to that first violence, long ago. A human skull rested at the center of every step, shadows moving in the sockets as Maati passed them. He hoped the Galts had left the grim markers, but he didn't believe it.

Here, Vanjit was saying, *each of these is a life the soldiers of Galt ended*. They were her justification. Her honor guard.

He should have guessed where the candles were leading him. The grand double doors of the Khai's audience chamber stood closed, but light leaked through at the seams. After so long in the dark, he half-expected them to open onto a fire.

In its day, the chamber must have inspired awe. In its way, it still did. The arches, the angles of the walls, the thin ironwork as delicate as lace that held a hundred burning candles—everything was designed to draw the eyes to the dais, the black lacquer chair, and then out a wide, unshuttered window that reached from ceiling to floor. The Khai would have sat there, his city arrayed out behind him like a cloak. Now the cloak was only darkness, and in the black chair, Clarity-of-Sight cooed.

"I didn't think you'd come," Vanjit said from the shadows behind him. Maati startled and turned.

Exhaustion and hunger had thinned the girl. Her dark hair was pulled back, but what few locks had escaped the bond hung limp and lank, framing her pale face.

"Why wouldn't I?"

"Fear of justice," Vanjit said.

She stepped out into the candlelight. Her robes were silken rags, scavenged from some noble wardrobe, fourteen years a ruin. Her head was bowed beneath an invisible weight and she moved like an old woman bent with the pain for years. She had become Udun. The war, the damage, the ruin. It *was* her. The baby—the inhuman thing shaped like a baby—shrieked with joy and clapped its tiny hands. Vanjit shuddered.

"Vanjit-cha," Maati said, "we can talk this through. We can . . . we can still end this well."

"You tried to murder me," Vanjit said. "You and your pet poisoner. If you'd had your way, I would be dead now. How, Maati-kvo, do you propose to talk that through?"

"I . . ." he said. "There must . . . there must be a way."

"What was I supposed to be that I wasn't?" Vanjit asked as she walked toward the black chair with its tiny beast. "You knew what the Galts had done to me. Did you want me to get this power, and then forget? Forgive? Was this supposed to be the compensation for their deaths?"

"No," Maati said. "No, of course not."

"No," she said. "Because you didn't care when I blinded them, did you? That was my decision. My burden, if I chose to take it up. Innocent women.

Children. I could destroy them, and you could treat it as justice, but I went too far. I blinded you. For half a hand, I turned it against you, and for *that,* I deserved to die."

"The andat, Vanjit-kya," Maati said, his voice breaking. "They have always schemed against their poets. They have manipulated the people around them in terrible ways. Eiah and I . . ."

"You hear that?" Vanjit said, scooping up Clarity-of-Sight. The andat's black eyes met hers. "This is your doing."

The andat cooed and waved its arms. Vanjit smiled as if at some unspoken jest, shared only between those two.

"I thought I would make the world right again," Vanjit said. "I thought I could make a baby. Make a family."

"You thought you could save the world," Maati said.

"I thought *you* could," she said in a voice like cold vinegar. "Look at me."

"I don't understand," he said.

"Look."

Her face sharpened. He saw the smudge of dust along her cheek, the stippled pores along her cheek, the individual hairs smaller than the thinnest threads. Her eyes were labyrinths of blood mapped on the whites, and the pupils glowed like a wolf's where the candlelight reflected from their depths. Her skin was a mosaic, tiny scales that broke and scattered with every movement. Insects too small to see scuttled through the roots of her hair, her eyelashes.

Maati's stomach turned, a deep nausea taking him. He closed his eyes, pressing his palms into the lids.

"Please," he said, and Vanjit wrenched his hands away from his face.

"Look at me!" she shouted. "Look!"

Reluctantly, slowly, Maati opened his eyes. There was too much. Vanjit was no longer a woman but a landscape as wide as the world, moving, breaking, shifting. Looking at her was being tossed on an infinite sea.

"Can you see my pain, Maati-kvo? Can you see it?"

No, he tried to say, but his throat closed against his illness. Vanjit pushed him away, and he spun, a thousand details assaulting him in the space of a heartbeat. He fell to the stone floor and retched.

"I didn't think you would," she said.

"Please," Maati said.

"You've taken it from me," Vanjit said. "You and Eiah. All the others. I was ready to do anything for you. I risked death. I did. And you don't even know me."

Her laugh was short and brutal.

"My eyes," he said.

"Fine," Vanjit said, and Maati's vision went away. He was once again in the fog of blindness. "Is that better?"

Maati reached toward the sound of her voice, then stumbled. Vanjit kicked him once in the ribs. The surprise was worse than the pain.

"There is nothing you have to teach me anymore, old man," she said. "I've learned everything you know. I understand."

"No," Maati said. "There's more. I can tell you more. I know what it is to lose someone you love. I know what it is to feel betrayed by the ones you thought closest to you."

"Then you know the world isn't worth saving," Vanjit said.

The words hung in the air. Maati tried to rise, but he was short of breath, wheezing like he'd run a race. His racing heart filled his ears with the sound of rushing blood.

"It is," he said. "It's worth . . ."

"Ah. There's Eymond. Everyone in Eymond, blind as a stone. And Eddensea. There. Gone. Bakta. But why stop there, Maati-kya? Here, the birds. All the birds in the world. There. The fish. The beasts." She laughed. "All the flies are blind. I've just done that. All the flies and the spiders. I say we give the world to the trees and the worms. One great nation of the eyeless."

"Vanjit," Maati said. His back hurt like someone had stabbed him and left the blade in. He fought to find the words. "You mustn't do this. I didn't teach you this."

"I did what you told me," she said, her voice rising. The andat's cry rose with her, an infantile rage and anguish and exultation at the world's destruction. "I did what you wanted. More, Maati-kvo, I did what you couldn't do yourself, and you hated me for it. You wanted me dead? Fine, then. I'll die. And the world can come with me."

"No!" Maati cried.

"I'm not a monster," Vanjit said. Like a candle being snuffed, the andat's wail ceased. Vanjit collapsed beside him, as limp as a puppet with cut strings.

There were voices. Otah, Danat, Eiah, Idaan, Ana. And others. He lay back, letting his eyes close. He didn't know what had happened. For the moment, he didn't care. His body was a single, sudden wash of pain. And then, his chest only ached. Maati opened his eyes. An unfamiliar face was looking down at him.

The man had skin as pale as snow and flowing ink-black hair. His eyes were deep brown, as soft as fur and as warm as tea. His robe was blue silk embroidered with thread of gold. The pale man smiled and took a pose of greeting. Maati responded reflexively. Vanjit lay on the floor, her arm bent awkwardly behind her, her eyes open and empty.

"Killed her," Maati said. "You. Killed her."

"Well. More precisely, we wounded her profoundly and then she died," the pale man said. "But I'll grant you it's a fine point. The effect is much the same."

"Maati!"

He lifted his head. Eiah was rushing toward him, her robes pressed back like a banner by her speed. Otah and Idaan followed her more slowly. Ana and Danat were locked in a powerful embrace. Maati lifted his hand in greeting. When she drew near, Eiah hesitated, her gaze on the fallen girl. The pale man—Wounded—took a pose that offered congratulations, and there was irony in the cant of his wrists. Eiah knelt, touching the corpse with a calm, professional air.

"Oh, yes," the andat said, folding its hands. "Quite dead."

"Good," Eiah said.

"*He* isn't standing," Idaan said, nodding toward Maati.

Eiah's attention shifted to him and her face paled.

"Just need. To catch my breath."

"His heart's stopping," Eiah said. "I knew this would happen. I told you to drink that tea."

Maati waved his hand, shooing her concerns away. Danat and Ana had come. He hadn't noticed it. They were simply there. Ana's eyes were brown and they were beautiful.

"Can't we . . . can't we do something?" Danat asked.

"No," said the andat in the same breath that Eiah said, "Yes. I need my satchel. Where is it?"

Danat rushed back to the great doors, returning half a moment later with the physician's satchel in his hands. Eiah grabbed it, plucked out a cloth bag, and started shuffling through sheaves of dried herbs that to Maati looked identical.

"There's another bag. A yellow one," Eiah said. "Where is it?"

"I don't think we brought it," Danat said.

"Then it's back at the quay. Get it now."

Danat turned and sprinted. Gently, Eiah took Maati's hand. He thought at first she meant to comfort him, but her fingers pressed into his wrist, and then she reached for his other hand. He surrendered himself to her care. He didn't have a great deal of choice. Idaan squatted at his side, Otah sitting on the dais. The andat rose, stepping back by Ana's side as if out of respect.

"How bad?" Idaan asked.

"He hasn't died. That's what I can offer for now," Eiah said. "Maati-kya, open your mouth. I don't have time to brew this, but it will help until I can get the rest of my supplies. It's going to be sweet first and then bitter."

"You've done it," Maati said around the pinch of leaves she put on his tongue.

Eiah looked at him, her expression startled. He smiled at her.

"You bound it. You've cured the blindness."

Eiah looked up at her creation, her slave. It nodded.

"Well, no," she said. "I mean, yes, I bound him. And I did undo Vanjit's damage to Ana and myself. And then you, when I saw that she'd done it."

"Galt?" Ana asked.

"I hadn't . . . I hadn't even thought of it. Gods. Is there anything different to be done? I mean, a whole nation at once?"

"You have to do everything," Maati said. "Birds. Beasts. Fish. Everyone, everywhere. You have to hurry. It's only a thought." The herbs were making his mouth tingle and burn, but the pain in his breast seemed to ebb. "It's no different."

Eiah turned to the andat. The kind, pale face hardened. No matter how it seemed, the thing wasn't a man and it wasn't gentle. But it was bound to her will, and a moment later Eiah caught her breath.

"It's done," she said, wonder in her voice. "They've been put back. The ones who are left."

Ana stepped forward and knelt, wordlessly enfolding Eiah in her arms. From where he lay, he could see Eiah's eyes close, watch her lean into the embrace. The two women seemed to pause in time, a moment that lasted less than two long breaths together but carried the weight of years within it. Eiah raised her head sharply and the andat twitched. Idaan leaped up, yelping. All eyes turned to her as she pressed a flat palm to her belly.

"That," she said, "felt very odd. You should warn someone when you're planning something like that."

"Sterile?" Otah asked. His voice was low. There was no joy in it.

"Repaired," Eiah said. "We can bear again. Galts can father children and we can bear them."

"I don't suppose you could leave me as I was?" Idaan asked.

"So we've begun again," Otah said. "It is all as it was. We've only changed a few names. Well—"

Wounded cut him off with a low bark of a laugh. Its eyes were fixed upon Eiah. Otah looked from one to the other, his hands taking a querying pose. Woman and slave both ignored him.

"Everyone?" the andat asked.

"Everyone, everywhere," Eiah said. "It's only a thought, isn't it? That's all it needs to be."

"What are you doing?" Ana asked. It seemed like a real curiosity.

"I'm curing everyone," Eiah said. "If there's a child in Bakta who split her head on a stone this morning, I want it fixed. A man in Eymond whose hip was broken when he was a boy and healed poorly, I want him walking without pain in the morning. Everyone. Everywhere. Now."

"Eiah Machi," the andat said, its voice low and amused, "the little girl who saved the world. Is that how you see it? Or is this how you apologize for slaughtering a whole people?"

Eiah didn't speak, and the andat went still again. Anger flashed in its eyes and Maati's hand went out, touching Eiah's. She patted him away absently, as if he were no more than a well-intentioned dog. The andat hissed under its breath and turned away. Maati noticed for the first time that its teeth were pointed. Eiah relaxed. Maati sat up; his breath had almost returned. The andat shifted to look at him. The whites of his eyes had gone as black as a shark's; he had never seen an andat shift its appearance before, and it filled him with sudden dread. Eiah made a scolding sound, and the andat took an apologetic pose.

Maati tried to imagine what it would be like, a thought that changeable, that flexible, that filled with violence and rage. *How did we ever think we could do good with these as our tools?* For as long as she held the andat, Eiah was condemned to the struggle. And Maati was responsible for that sacrifice too.

Eiah, it seemed, had other intentions.

"That should do," she said. "You can go."

The andat vanished, its robe collapsing to the floor in a pool of blue and gold. The scent of overheated stone came and went, a breath of hell on the night air. The others were silent. Maati came to himself first.

"What have you *done*?" he whispered.

"I'm a physician," Eiah said, her tone dismissive. "Holding that abomination the rest of my life would have gotten in the way of my work, and who told you that you were allowed to sit up? On your back or I'll call in armsmen to hold you down. No, don't say anything. I don't care if you're feeling a thousand times better. Down. Now."

He lay back, staring up at the ceiling. His mind felt blasted and blank. The enameled brick was blurred in the torchlight, or perhaps it was only that his eyes were only what they had been. The cold air that breathed in through the window too gently to even be a breeze felt better than he would have expected, the stone floor beneath him more comfortable. The voices around him were quiet with respect for his poor health or else with awe. The world had never seen a night like this one. It likely never would again.

She had freed it. Gods, all that they'd done, all that they'd suffered, and she'd just *freed* the thing.

When Danat returned, Eiah forced half a handful of herbs more bitter than the last into his mouth and told him to leave them under his tongue until she told him otherwise. Idaan and one of the armsmen hauled Vanjit's body away. They would burn it, Maati thought, in the morning. Vanjit had been a broken, sad, dangerous woman, but she deserved better than to have her corpse left out. He remembered Idaan saying something similar of the slaughtered buck.

He didn't notice falling asleep, but Eiah gently shook him awake and helped him to sit. While she compared his pulses and pressed his fingertips, he spat out the black leaves. His mouth was numb.

"We're going to take you back down in a litter," she said, and before he could object, she lifted her hand to his lips. He took a pose that acquiesced. Eiah rose to her feet and walked back toward the great bronze doors.

The footsteps behind him were as familiar as an old song.

"Otah-kvo," Maati said.

The Emperor sat on the dais, his hands between his knees. He looked pale and exhausted.

"Nothing ever goes the way I plan," Otah said, his tone peevish. "Not ever."

"You're tired," Maati said.

"I am. Gods, that I am."

The captain of the armsmen pulled open the doors. Four men followed, a low weaving of branches and rope between them. Eiah walked at their side. One of the men at the rear called out, and the whole parade stopped while the captain, cursing, retied a series of knots. Maati watched them as if they were dancers and gymnasts performing before a banquet.

"I'm sorry," Maati said. "This wasn't what I intended."

"Isn't it? I thought the hope was to undo the damage we did with Sterile, no matter what the price."

Maati started to object, then stopped himself. Outside the great window, a star fell. The smear of light vanished as quickly as it had come.

"I didn't know how far it would go."

"Would it have mattered? If you had known everything it would take, would you have been able to abandon the project?" Otah asked. He didn't sound angry or accusing. Only like a man who didn't know the answer to a question. Maati found he didn't either.

"If I asked your forgiveness . . ."

Otah was silent, then sighed deeply, his head hanging low.

"Maati-kya, we've been a hundred different people to each other, and tonight I'm too old and too tired. Everything in the world has changed at least twice since I woke up this morning. I think about forgiving you, and I don't know what the word means."

"I understand."

"Do you? Well, then you've outpaced me."

The litter came forward. Eiah helped him onto the makeshift seat, rope and wood creaking under his weight, but solid. The gait of the armsmen swayed him like a branch in the breeze. The Emperor, they left behind to follow in the darkness.

31

>+< The formal joining of Ana Dasin and Danat Machi took place on Candles Night in the high temple of Utani. The assembled nobility of Galt along with the utkhaiem from the highest of families to the lowest firekeeper filled every cushion on the floor, every level of balcony. The air itself was hot as a barn, and the smell of perfume and incense and bodies was overwhelming. Otah sat on his chair, looking out over the vast sea of faces. Many of the Galts wore mourning veils, and, to his surprise, the fashion had not been lost on the utkhaiem. He worried that the mourning was not entirely for fallen Galt, but also a subterranean protest of the marriage itself. It was only a small concern, though. He had thousands more like it.

The Galtic ceremony—a thing of dirgelike song and carefully measured wine spilled over rice, all to a symbolic end that escaped him—was over. The traditional joining of his own culture was already under way. Otah shifted, trying to be unobtrusive in his discomfort despite every eye in Utani being fixed on the dais.

Farrer Dasin wore a robe of black and a red ocher that suited his complexion better than Otah would have expected. Issandra sat at his side in a Galtic gown of yellow lace over a profoundly celebratory red. Danat knelt before them both.

"Farrer Dasin of House Dasin, I place myself before you as a man before my elder," Danat said. "I place myself before you and ask your permission. I would take Ana, your blood issue, to be my wife. If it does not please you, please only say so, and accept my apology."

The whisperers carried his words out through the hall like wind over wheat. Ana Dasin herself knelt on a cushion off to her parents' right and Danat had been sitting to Otah's left. The girl's gown had been an issue of long and impassioned debate, for the swell of her belly was unmistakable. With only a few minor modifications, the tailors could have done much to hide it. Instead, she had chosen Galtic dress with its tight fittings and waist-slung ribbons, which would make it clear to the farthest spectator in the temple that summer would come well after the child. Etiquette masters from both courts had gone at the issue like pit dogs for the better part of a week. Otah thought she looked beautiful with her garland of ribbons. Her father apparently thought so as well. Instead of the traditional reply, *I am not displeased*, Farrer looked Danat square in the eyes, then turned to Ana.

"Bit late for asking, isn't it?" Farrer said.

Otah laughed, giving his implicit permission for all the court to laugh with him. Danat grinned as well and took a pose of gratitude somewhat more profound than strictly required. Danat rose, came to Otah, and knelt again.

"Most High?" he said, his mouth quirked in an odd smile. Otah pretended to consider the question. The court laughed again, and he rose to his feet. It felt good to stand up, though before it was all finished, he'd be longing to sit down again.

"Let it be known that I have authorized this match. Let the blood of the House Dasin enter for the first time into the imperial lineage. And let all who honor the Khaiem respect this transfer and join in our celebration. The ceremony shall be held at once."

The whisperers carried it all, and moments later a priest came out, intoning old words whose meanings were more than half forgotten. The man was older than Otah, and his expression was as serene and joyous as that of a man too drunk to stagger. Otah took a welcoming pose, accepted one in return, and stepped back to let the ceremony proper begin.

Danat accepted a long, looped cord and hung it over his arm. The priest intoned the ritual questions, and Danat made his answers. Otah's back began to spasm, but he kept still. The end of the cord, cut and knotted, passed from Danat to the priest and then to Ana's hand. The roar that rose up drowned out the whisperers, the priest, the world. The courts of two nations stood cheering, all decorum forgotten. Ana and Danat stood together with a length of woven cotton between them, grinning and waving. Otah imagined their child stirring in its dark sleep, aware of the sound if not its meaning.

Balasar Gice, wearing the robe of a high councilman, was at the front of the crowd, clapping his small hands together with tears running down his cheeks. Otah felt a momentary pang of sorrow. Sinja hadn't seen it. Kiyan hadn't. He took a deep breath and reminded himself that the moment wasn't his. The celebration was not of his life or his love or the binding of his house to a wayhouse keeper from Udun. It was Danat's and Ana's, and they at least were transcendent.

The rest of the ceremony took twice as long as it should have, and by the time the procession was ready to carry them out and through the streets of Utani, the sunset was no more than a memory.

Otah allowed himself to be ushered to a high balcony that looked down upon the city. The air was bitterly cold, but a cast-iron brazier was hauled out, coals already bright red so that Otah could feel the searing heat to his left while his right side froze. He huddled in a thick wool blanket, following the wedding procession with his eyes. Each street they turned down lit itself, banners and streamers of cloth arcing through the air.

Here is where it begins, he thought. And then, Thank all the gods it isn't me down there.

A servant girl stepped onto the balcony and took a pose that announced a guest. Otah wasn't about to stick his hands out of the blanket.

"Who?"

"Farrer Dasin-cha," the girl said.

"Bring him here," Otah said. "And some wine. Hot wine."

The girl took a pose that accepted the charge and turned to go.

"Wait," Otah said. "What's your name?"

"Toyani Vauatan, Most High," she said.

"How old are you?"

"Twenty summers."

Otah nodded. In truth, she looked almost too young to be out of the nursery. And yet at her age, he had been on a ship halfway to the eastern islands, two different lives already behind him. He pointed out at the city.

"It's a different world now, Toyani-cha. Nothing's going to stay as it was."

The girl smiled and took a pose that offered congratulations. Of course she didn't understand. It was unfair to expect her to. Otah smiled and turned back to the city, the celebration. He didn't see when she left. The wedding procession had just turned down the long, wide road that led to the riverfront when Farrer stepped out, the girl Toyani behind them bearing two bowls of wine that plumed with steam and a chair for the newcomer without seeming awkward or out of place. It was, Otah supposed, an art.

"We've done it," Farrer said when the girl had gone.

"We have," Otah agreed. "Not that I've stopped waiting for the next catastrophe."

"I think the last one will do."

Otah sipped his wine. The spirit hadn't quite been cooked out of it, and the spices tasted rich and strange. He had been dreading this conversation, but now that it had come, it wasn't as awful as he'd feared.

"The report's come," Otah said.

"The first one, yes. Everyone on the High Council had a copy this morning. Just in time for the festivities. I thought it was rude at the time, but I suppose it gives us all more reason to get sloppy drunk and weep into our cups."

Otah took a pose of query simple enough for the Galt to follow.

"Every city is in ruins except for Kirinton. They did something clever there with street callers and string. I don't fully understand it. The outlying areas suffered, though not quite as badly. The first guesses are that it will take two generations just to put us back where we were."

"Assuming nothing else happens," Otah said. Below, a fanfare was blaring.

"You mean Eymond," Farrer said. "They're a problem, it's true."

"Eymond. Eddensea, the Westlands. Anyone, really."

"If we had the andat . . ."

"We don't," Otah said.

"No, I suppose not," Farrer said, sourly. "But to the point, how many of us are aware of that fact?"

In the dim light of the brazier's coals, Farrer's face was the same dusky red as the moon in eclipse. The Galt smiled, pleased that he had taken Otah by surprise.

"You and I know. The High Council. That half-bastard council you put together when you headed out into the wilderness. Ana. Danat. A few armsmen. All in all, I'd guess not more than three dozen people actually know what happened. And none of them is at present working for Eymond."

"You're saying we should pretend to have an andat?"

"Not precisely," Farrer said. "As many people as already know, the story will come out eventually. But there might be a way to present it that still gave other nations pause. Send out letters of embassage that say the andat, though recovered, have been set aside and deny the rumors that certain deaths and odd occurrences are at all related to a new poet under the direction of the Empire."

"What deaths?"

"Don't be too specific about that," Farrer said. "I expect they'll supply the details."

"Let them think . . . that we have the andat and are hiding the fact?" Otah laughed.

"It won't last forever, but the longer we can stall them, the better prepared we'll be when they come."

"And they do always come," Otah said. "Clever thought. It costs us nothing. It could gain us a great deal. Issandra?"

Farrer leaned back in his chair, setting his heels on the parapet and looking up at the stars, the full, heavy moon. For the space of a heartbeat, he looked forlorn. He drank his wine and looked over at Otah.

"My wife is an amazing woman," he said. "I'm fortunate to have her. And if Ana's half like her, she'll be running both our nations whether your son likes it or not."

It was the opening to a hundred other issues. Galt and the cities of the Khaiem were in a state of profound disarray. Ana Dasin might be the new Empress, but that meant little enough in practical terms. In Galt the High Council and the full council were each in flux, their elections and appointments in question now that their cities were little more than abandoned. Otah would be hated for that destruction or else beloved for the mending of it.

"It is the point, isn't it? If we are two nations, we're doomed," Farrer said, reading his concerns. "We have too many enemies and not enough strengths between us."

"If we're one . . . how do we do that? Will the High Council be ruled by my edict? Am I supposed to cede my power to them?"

"Compromise, Most High," Farrer said. "It will be a long process of compromise and argument, idiotic yammering debate and high melodrama. But in its defense, it won't be war."

"It won't be war," Otah repeated. Only when the words had come out into the night air, hanging as if physical, did he realize he had meant it as an agreement. One nation. His empire had just doubled in size, tripled in complexity and need, and his own power had been cut at least by half. Farrer seemed surprised when he laughed.

"Tomorrow," Otah said. "Call the High Council tomorrow. I'll bring my council. We'll start with the report and try to build something like a plan from there. And tell Issandra that I'll have the letters of embassage sent. Best get that done before there's a debate about it, ne?"

They sat for a time without speaking, two men whose children had just joined their families. Two enemies planning a house in common. Two great powers whose golden ages had ended. They could play at it, but each knew that it was only in their children, in their grandchildren, that the game of friendship could become truth.

Farrer finished his wine, leaving the bowl by his chair. As he walked out, he put a hand on Otah's shoulder.

"Your son seems a fine man," he said.

"Your daughter is a treasure."

"She is," Farrer Dasin said, his voice serious. And then Otah was alone again, the night numbing his feet and biting his ears and nose. He pulled the blanket around himself more tightly and left the balcony and the city and the celebrations behind him.

The palaces were as quiet and busy as the backstage at a performance. Servants ran or walked or conducted low, angry conversations that died at Otah's approach. He let the night make its own path. He knew the bridal procession had returned to the palaces by the number of robes with bits of tinsel and bright paper clinging to the hems. And also by the flushed faces and spontaneous laughter. There would have been celebration on into the night, even if they hadn't scheduled the wedding on Candles Night. As it was, Utani as a whole, from the highest nobility to the lowest beggar, would sleep late and speak softly when they woke. Otah doubted there would be any wine left by spring.

But there would be babies. He could already name a dozen women casually who would be giving birth when the summer came. And everywhere, in all the cities, the conditions were the same. They would miss a generation, but only one. The Empire would stumble, but it need not fall.

Even more than the joining of the Empire and Galt, the night was the first formal celebration of a world made new. Otah wished he felt more part of it. Perhaps he understood too well what price had brought them here.

He found Eiah where he knew he would. The physicians' house with its wide, slate tables and the scent of vinegar and burning herbs. Cloth lanterns bobbed in the breeze outside the open doors. A litter of stretched canvas and light wood lay on the steps, blood staining the cloth. Within, half a dozen men and two women sat on low wooden benches or lay on the floor. One of the men tried to take a pose of obeisance, winced in pain, and sat back down. Otah made his way to the rear. Three men in leather aprons were working the tables, servants and assistants swarming around them. Eiah, in her own apron, was at the back table. A Galtic man lay before her, groaning. Blood drenched his side. Eiah glanced up, saw him, and took a pose of welcome with red hands.

"What's happened?" Otah asked.

"He fell out of a window and onto a stick," Eiah said. "I'm fairly sure we've gotten all the splinters out of him."

"He'll live, then?"

"If he doesn't go septic," Eiah said. "He's a man with a hole in his side. You can't ask better odds than that."

The wounded man stuttered out his gratitude in his own language while Eiah, letting him hold one of her hands, gestured with the other for an assistant.

"Bind the wound, give him three measures of poppy milk, and put him somewhere safe until morning. I'll want to see his wound again before we send him back to his people."

The assistant took a pose that accepted instruction, and Eiah walked to the wide stone basins on the back wall to wash the blood from her hands. A woman screamed and retched, but he couldn't see where she was. Eiah was unfazed.

"We'll have forty more like him by morning," she said. "Too drunk and happy to think of the risks. There was a woman here earlier who wrenched her knee climbing a rope they'd strung over the street. Almost fell on Danat's head, to hear her say it. She may walk with a cane the rest of her life, but she's all smiles tonight."

"Well, she won't be dancing," Otah said.

"If she can hop, she will."

"Is there a place we can speak?" Otah asked.

Eiah dried her hands on a length of cloth, leaving it dark with water and pink with blood. Her expression was closed, but she led the way through a wide door and down a hall. Someone was moaning nearby. She turned off into a small garden, the bushes as bare as sticks, a wide-branched tree empty. If there had been snow, it would have been lovely.

"I'm calling a meeting with the Galtic High Council tomorrow," he said. "And my own as well. It's the beginning of unification. I wanted you to hear it from me."

"That seems wise," Eiah said.

"The poets. The andat. They can't be kept out of that conversation."

"I know," she said. "I've been thinking about it."

"I don't suppose there are any conclusions you'd want to share," he asked, trying to keep his tone light. Eiah pulled at her fingers, one hand and then the other.

"We can't be sure there won't be others," she said. "The hardest thing about binding them is the understanding that they can be bound. They burned all the books, they killed every poet they could find, and we remade the grammar. We bound two andat. Other people are going to try to do what we did. Work from the basic structures and find a way."

"You think they'll do it?"

"History doesn't move backward," she said. "There's power in them. And there are people who want power badly enough to kill and die. Eventually, someone will find a way."

"Without Maati? Without Cehmai?"

"Or Irit, or Ashti Beg, or the two Kaes?" Eiah said. "Without me? It will be harder. It will take longer. The cost in lives and failed bindings may be huge."

"You're talking about generations from now," Otah said.

"Yes," Eiah said. "Likely, I am."

Otah nodded. It wasn't what he'd hoped to hear, but it would do. He took a pose that thanked Eiah. She bowed her head.

"Are you well?" he asked. "It isn't an easy thing, killing."

"Vanjit wasn't the first person I've killed, Father. Knowing when to help someone leave is part of what I do," Eiah said. She looked up, staring at the moon through the bare branches that couldn't shelter them, even from light. "I'm more troubled by what I could have done and didn't."

Otah took a pose that asked her to elaborate. Eiah shook her head, and then a moment later spoke softly, as if the words themselves were delicate.

"I could have held all our enemies at bay just by the threat of Wounded," she said. "What army would take the field, knowing I could blow out their lives like so many candles? Who would conspire against us knowing that if their agents were discovered, I could slaughter their kings and princes without hope of defense?"

"It would have been convenient," Otah agreed carefully.

"I could have slaughtered the men who killed Sinja-kya," Eiah said. "I could have ended every man who had ever taken a woman against her will or hurt a child. Between one breath and the next, I could have wiped them from the world."

Eiah turned her gaze to him. In the cool moonlight, her eyes seemed lost in shadow.

"I look at those things—all the things I might have done—and I wonder whether I would have. And if I had, would they have been wrong?"

"And what do you believe?"

"I believe I saved myself when I set that perversion free," she said. "I only hope the price the rest of the world pays isn't too high."

Otah stepped forward and took her in his arms. Eiah held back for a moment, and then relaxed into the embrace. She smelled of herbs and vinegar and blood. And mint. Her hair smelled of mint, just as her mother's had done.

"You should go see him," she said. He knew who she meant.

"Is he well?"

"For now," she said. "He's weathered the attacks so far. But his blood's still slowing. I expect he'll be fine until he isn't, and then he'll die."

"How long?"

"Not another year," she said.

Otah closed his eyes.

"He misses you," she said. "You know he does."

He stepped back and kissed her forehead. In the distance, someone screamed. Eiah glanced over his shoulder with disgust.

"That will be Yaniit," she said. "I'd best go tend to him. Tall as a tree, wide as a bear, and wails if you pinch him."

"Take care," Otah said.

His daughter walked away with the steady stride of a woman about her own business, leaving the bare garden for him. He looked up at the moon, but it had lost its poetry and charm. His sigh was opaque in the cold.

Maati's cell was the most beautifully appointed prison in the cities, possibly in the world. The armsmen led Otah into a chamber with vaulted ceilings and carved cedar along the walls. Maati sat up, waving the servant at his side to silence. The servant closed the book she'd been reading but kept the place with her thumb.

"You're learning Galtic tales now?" Otah asked.

"You burned my library," Maati said. "Back in Machi, or don't you recall that? The only histories your grandchild will read are written by *them*."

"Or by us," Otah said. "We can still write, you know."

Maati took a pose that accepted correction, but with a dismissive air that verged on insult. So this was how it was, Otah thought. He motioned to the armsmen to take the prisoner and follow him, then spun on his heel. The feeble sounds of protest behind him didn't slow his pace.

The highest towers of Utani were nothing in comparison to those in Machi; they could be scaled by stairways and corridors and didn't require a rest halfway along. Under half the height, and Otah liked them better. They were built with humanity in mind, and not the raw boasting power of the andat.

At the pinnacle, a small platform stood high above the world. The tallest place in the city. Wind whipped it, as cold as a bath of ice water. Otah motioned for Maati to be led forward. The poet's eyes were wild, his breath short. He raised his thick chin.

"What?" Maati spat. "Decided to throw me off, have you?"

"It's almost the half-candle," Otah said and went to stand at the edge. Maati hesitated and then stepped to his side. The city spread out below them, the streets marked by lanterns and torches. A fire blazed in a courtyard down near the riverfront, taller than ten men with whole trees for logs. Otah could cover it with his thumbnail.

The chime came, a deep ringing that seemed to shake the world. And then a thousand thousand bells rang out in answer to mark the deepest part of the longest night of the year.

"Here," Otah said. "Watch."

Below, light spread through the city. Every window, every balcony, every parapet glowed with newly lit candles. Within ten breaths, the center of the Empire went from any large city in darkness to something woven from light, the perfect city—the *idea* of a city—made for a moment real. Maati shifted. When his voice came, it was little more than a whisper.

"It's beautiful."

"Isn't it?"

A moment later, Maati said, "Thank you."

"Of course," Otah replied.

They stood there for a long time, neither speaking nor arguing, concerned with neither future nor past. Below them, Utani glowed and rang, marking the moment of greatest darkness and celebrating the yearly return of the light.

EPILOG

We say that the flowers return every spring, but that is a lie.

CALIN MACHI, ELDEST SON OF THE EMPEROR REGENT, KNELT BEFORE HIS FATHER, his gaze downcast. The delicate tilework of the floor was polished so brightly that he could watch Danat's face and seem to be showing respect at the same time. Granted, Danat was reversed—wide jaw above gray temples—and it made the nuances of expression difficult to read. It was enough, though, for him to judge approximately how much trouble he was in.

"I've spoken to the overseer of my father's apartments. Do you know what he told me?"

"That I'd been caught hiding in Grandfather's private garden," Calin said.

"Is that true?"

"Yes, Father. I was hiding from Aniit and Gaber. It was a part of a game."

Danat sighed, and Calin risked looking up. When his father was deeply upset, his face turned red. He was still flesh-colored. Calin looked back down, relieved.

"You know you're forbidden from your grandfather's apartments."

"Yes, but that was what made them a good place to hide."

"You're sixteen summers old and you're acting twelve of them. Aniit and Gaber look to you for how to behave. It's your duty to set an example," Danat said, his voice stern. And then he added, "Don't do it again."

Calin rose to his feet, trying to keep his rush of joy from being obvious. The great punishment had not fallen. He was not barred from the steam caravan's arrival. Life was still worth living. Danat took a pose that excused his son and motioned to his Master of Tides. Before the woman could glide over and lead his father back into the constant business of negotiating with the High Council, Calin left the audience chamber, followed only by his father's shouted admonition not to run. Aniit and Gaber were waiting outside, their eyes wide.

"It's all right," Calin said, as if his father's lenience were somehow proof of his own cleverness. Aniit took an exaggerated pose of congratulations. Gaber clapped her hands. She was young, though. Only fourteen summers old and barely marriageable.

"Come on, then," Calin said. "We can pick the best places for when the caravan comes."

The roadway had been five years in the building, a shallow canal of smooth worked iron that began at the seafront in Saraykeht and followed the river up to Utani. The caravan was the first of its kind, and the common wisdom in the streets and teahouses was evenly divided between those who thought it would arrive even earlier than expected and those who predicted they'd find splinters of blown boilers and nothing else.

Calin dismissed the skeptics. After all, his grandmother was arriving from her plantations in Chaburi-Tan, and she would never put herself on the caravan if it was going to explode.

The sweet days of early spring were short and cold. Frost still sent white fingers up the stones of the palaces in the morning and snow lingered in the deep shadows. A hundred times Calin and his friends had gone through the elaborate ritual of how they would greet the caravan, rehearsing it in their minds and conversations. The event, of course, was nothing like what they'd planned.

When word came, Calin was with his tutor, an ancient man from Acton, working complex sums. They were seated in the sunlight of the spring garden. Almond blossoms turned the tree branches white even before the first leaves had ventured out. Calin frowned at the wax tablet on his knees, trying not to count on his fingers. Hesitating, he lifted his stylus and marked his answer. His tutor made a noncommittal sound in the back of his throat and Gaber appeared at the end of the arcade, running full out.

"It's here!" she screamed. "It's here!"

Before any adult could object, Calin joined her flight. Tablet, stylus, and sums were forgotten in an instant. They ran past the pavilions that marked palaces from merchants' compounds, the squares and open markets that showed where the great compound gave way to the haunts of common labor. The streets were thick with humanity, and Calin threaded his way through the press of bodies aided by his youth, the quality of his robes, and the boyish instinct that saw all obstacles as ephemeral.

He reached the Emperor's platform just before the caravan arrived. Wide plumes of smoke and steam stained the southern sky, and the air smelled of coal. Danat and Ana were already there, seated in chairs of carved stone with silk cushions. Otah Machi—the Emperor himself—sat on a raised dais, his hands resting like fragile claws on the arms of a black lacquer chair. Calin's grandfather looked over as he arrived and smiled. Danat's expression was distracted in a way that reminded Calin of doing sums. His mother was craning her neck and trying not to seem that she was.

It hardly mattered. The crowd that pressed and seethed around the yard at the caravan road's end had eyes only for the great carts speeding toward them, faster than horses at full gallop. Calin sat at his mother's feet, his intended perch nearest his friends forgotten. The first of the carts came near enough to make out the raised dais, twin of his grandfather's, and the stiff-backed white-haired woman sitting atop it. Calin's mother left all decorum, and stood, waving and calling to her mother.

Calin felt his father's hand on his shoulder and turned.

"Watch this," Danat said. "Pay attention. That caravan reached us in half the time even a boat could have. What you're seeing right now is going to change everything."

Calin nodded solemnly as if he understood.

It is true that the world is renewed. It is also true that that renewal comes at a price.

CEHMAI TYAN SAT ACROSS THE MEETING TABLE FROM THE HIGH COUNCIL'S special envoy. The man was nondescript, his clothing of Galtic cut and unremarkable quality. Cehmai didn't like the envoy, but he respected him. He'd known too many dangerous men in his life not to.

The envoy read the letters—ciphered and sent between a fictional merchant in Obar State and Cehmai himself here in Utani. They outlined the latest advance in the poetmaster's rebuilding of the lost libraries of Machi, which also had not happened. Cehmai sipped tea from an iron bowl and looked out the window. He couldn't see the steam caravan from here, but he had a good view of the river. It was at the point he liked it most, the water freed by the thaw, the banks not yet overgrown by green. No matter how many years passed, he still felt a personal affinity with earth and stone.

The envoy finished reading, his mouth in a smile that would have seemed pleasant and perhaps a bit simple on someone else.

"Is any of this true?" the envoy asked.

"Danat-cha did send a dozen men into the foothills north of Machi," Cehmai said, "and Maati-kvo and I did spend a winter there. Past that, nothing. But it should keep Eddensea's attention on sneaking through to search for it themselves. And we're in the process of forging books that we can then 'recover' in a year or so."

The envoy tucked the letters into a leather pouch at his belt. He didn't look up as he spoke.

"That brings a question," the man said. "I know we've talked about this before, but I'm not sure you've fully grasped the advantages that could come from leaning a little nearer the truth. Nothing that would be effective. We all understand that. But our enemies all have scholars working at these problems. If they were able to come close enough that the bindings cost them, if they paid the andat's price—"

Cehmai took a pose of query. "Wouldn't that be doing your work for you?" he asked.

"My job is to see they don't succeed," the envoy said. "A few mysterious, grotesque deaths would help me find the people involved."

"It would give away too much," Cehmai said. "Bringing them near enough to be hurt by the effort would also bring them near to succeeding."

The envoy looked at him silently. His placid eyes conveyed only a mild distrust.

"If you have a threat to make, feel free," Cehmai said. "It won't do you any good."

"Of course there's no threat, Cehmai-cha," the envoy said. "We're all on the same side here."

"Yes," the poetmaster said, rising from his chair with a pose that called the meeting to its close. "Try to keep it in mind."

His apartments were across the palaces. He made his way along the pathways of white and black sand, past the singing slaves and the fountain in the shape of the Galtic Tree that marked the wing devoted to the High Council. The men and women he passed nodded to him with deference, but few took any formal pose. A decade of joint rule had led to a thousand small changes in etiquette. Cehmai supposed it was small-minded of him to regret them.

Idaan was sitting on the porch of their entranceway, tugging at a length of string while a gray tomcat worried the other end. He paused, watching her. Unlike her brother, she'd grown thicker with time, more solid, more real. He must have made some small sound, because she looked up and smiled at him.

"How was the assassin's conference?" she asked.

The tomcat forgot his string and trotted up to Cehmai, already purring audibly. He stopped to scratch its fight-ragged ears.

"I wish you wouldn't call it that," he said.

"Well, I wish my hair were still dark. It is what it is, love. Politics in action."

"Cynic," he said as he reached the porch.

"Idealist," she replied, pulling him down to kiss him.

Far to the east, an early storm fell from clouds dark as bruises, a veil of gray. Cehmai watched it, his arm around his lover's shoulder. She leaned her head against him.

"How was the Emperor this morning?" he asked.

"Fine. Excited to see Issandra-cha again as much as anything about the caravan. I think he's more than half infatuated with her."

"Oh please," Cehmai said. "This will be his seventy-ninth summer? His eightieth?"

"And you won't still want me when you've reached the age?"

"Well. Fair point."

"His hands bother him most," Idaan said. "It's a pity about his hands."

Lightning flashed on the horizon, less that a firefly. Idaan twined her fingers with his and sighed.

"Have I mentioned recently how much I appreciate you coming to find me? Back when you were an outlaw and I was still a judge, I mean," she asked.

"I never tire of hearing it," Cehmai said.

The tomcat leaped on his lap, dug its claws into his robe twice, kneading him like bread dough, and curled up.

For even if the flower grows from an ancient vine, the flowers of spring are themselves new to the world, untried and untested.

———

Eiah motioned for Otah to sit. She was gentle as always with his crippled hands. He sat back down slowly. The servants had brought his couches out to a wide garden, but with the coming sunset he'd have to be moved again. Eiah tried to impress on her father's servants that what he needed and what he wanted weren't always the same. She'd given up convincing Otah years earlier.

"How are you feeling?" she asked, sitting beside him. "You look tired."

"It was a long day," Otah said. "I slept well enough, but I can never stay in bed past dawn. When I was young, I could sleep until midday. Now that I have the time and no one would object, I'm up with the birds. Does that seem right to you?"

"The world was never fair."

"Truth. All the gods know that's the truth."

She took his wrists as if it were nothing more than the contact of father and daughter. Otah looked at her impatiently, but he suffered it. She closed her eyes for a moment, feeling the subtle differences of his pulses.

"I heard you woke confused again," she said. "You were calling for someone called Muhatia-cha?"

"I had a dream. That's all," Otah said. "Muhatia was my overseer back when I was young. I dreamed that I was late for my shift. I needed to get to the seafront before he docked my pay. That was all. I'm not losing my mind, love. My health, maybe, but not my mind. Not yet."

"I didn't think you were. Turn here. Let me look at your eyes. Have the headaches come back?"

"No," Otah said, and she knew by his voice he was lying. It was time to stop asking details. There was only so much physician's attention her father would permit. She sat back on the couch, and he let out a small, satisfied breath.

"You saw Issandra Dasin?" she asked.

"Yes, yes. She spent the better part of the afternoon here," Otah said. "The things they've done with Chaburi-Tan are amazing. I was thinking I might go myself. Just to see them."

"It would be fascinating," Eiah agreed. "I hear Farrer-cha's doing well?"

"He's made more out of that city than I could have. But then I was never particularly brilliant with administration. I had other skills, I suppose," Otah said. "Enough about that. Tell me about your family. How is Parit-cha? And the girls?"

Eiah let herself be distracted. Parit was well, but he'd been kept away from their apartments three nights running by a boy who worked for House Laarin who'd broken his leg falling off a wall. It had been a bad break, and the fever hadn't gone down quickly enough to suit anyone. It seemed as if the boy would live, and they were both happy to call that a success. Of Otah's grand-daughters, Mischa was throwing all her free time into learning to dance every new form that came in from Galt, and wearing the dance master's feet raw in the effort. Gaber had talked about nothing besides the steam caravan for weeks, but Eiah suspected it was more Calin's enthusiasm than her own. Gaber assumed that Calin rose with the sun and set with the moon.

Eiah didn't realize how long she'd been telling the small stories of her family until the overseer came out with an apologetic pose and announced that the Emperor's meal was waiting. Otah made a show of rubbing his belly, but when Eiah joined him, he ate very little. The meal was fresh chicken cooked in last year's apricots, and it was delicious. She watched her father pluck at the pale flesh.

He looked older than his years. His skin had grown as thin as paper; his eyes were always wet. After his hands had fallen to their weakness, the headaches had begun. Eiah had tried him on half a dozen different programs of herbs and baths. She wasn't convinced he'd followed any of them very closely.

"Stop," Otah said. Eiah took a pose that asked clarification. He frowned at her, his eyebrows rising as he spoke. "You're looking at me as if I were a particularly interesting bloodworm. I'm fine, Eiah-kya. I sleep well, I wake full of energy, my bowels never trouble me, and my joints don't ache. Everything that could be right about me is right. Now I'd like to spend an evening with my daughter and not my physician, eh?"

"I'm sorry, Papa-kya," she said. "It's only that I worry."

"I know," he said, "and I forgive you. But don't let tomorrow steal what's good about tonight. The future takes care of its own. You can write that down if you like. The Emperor said it."

The flower that wilted last year is gone. Petals once fallen are fallen forever.

IDAAN ROSE BEFORE THE DAWN AS SHE ALWAYS DID, PARTING THE NETTING silently and stealthily walking out to her dressing chamber so as not to disturb Cehmai. She was not so important a woman that the servants wouldn't leave her be or that armsmen were needed to hold the utkhaiem and councilmen at bay. She was not her brother. She picked a simple robe of dusty red and rich blue and fastened all the ties herself. Then sandals and a few minutes before a mirror with a brush and a length of stout ribbon to bring her hair into something like order.

No one had assigned her the daily task of carrying breakfast to the Emperor. It was one she'd simply taken on. After two weeks of arriving at the kitchens to collect the tray with its plates and bowl and teapot, the servant who had been the official bearer simply stopped coming. She'd usurped the work.

That morning, they'd prepared honey bread and raisins, hot rice in almond milk, and a slab of roast pork with a pepper glaze. Idaan knew from experience that she would end with the pork and the honey bread. The rice, he might eat.

The path to the Emperor's apartments was well-designed. The balance between keeping the noises and interruptions away—not to mention the constant possibility of fire—and getting the food to him still warm meant a long, straight journey almost free from the meanderings to which the palaces were prone. Archways of stone marked the galleries. Tapestries of lush red and gold hung on the walls. The splendor had long since ceased to take her breath away. She had lived in palaces and mud huts and everything in between. The only thing that astounded her with any regularity was that so late in her life, she had found her family.

Cehmai alone had been miraculous. The last decade serving in court had been something greater than that. She had become an aunt to Danat and Eiah and Ana, a sister to Otah Machi. Even now, her days had the feel of relaxing in a warm bath. It wasn't something she'd expected. For that, it wasn't something she'd thought possible. The nightmares almost never came now; never more than once or twice in a month. She was ready to grow old here, in these halls and passageways, with these people. If anyone had the poor judgment to threaten her people, Idaan knew she would kill the idiot. She hoped the occasion wouldn't arise.

She knew something was wrong as soon as she passed through the arch that led to Otah's private garden. Four servants stood in a clot at the side door, their faces pale, their hands in constant motion. With a feeling of dread, she put the lacquer tray on a bench and came forward. The oldest of the servants was weeping, his face blotchy and his eyes swollen. Idaan looked at the man, her expression empty. Whatever strength remained in him left, and he folded to the ground sobbing.

"Have you sent for his children?" Idaan asked.

"I . . . we only just . . ."

Idaan raised her eyebrows, and the remaining servants scattered. She stepped over the weeping man and made her way into the private rooms. All together, they were smaller than Idaan's old farmhouse. It didn't take long to find him.

Otah sat in a chair as if he were only sleeping. The window before him was open, the shutters swaying slow and languorous in the breeze. The motion reminded her of seaweed. His robe was yellow shot with black. His eyes were barely open and as empty as marbles. Idaan made herself touch his skin. It was cold. He was gone.

She found a stool, pulled it to his side, and sat with him one last time. His hand was stiff, but she wrapped her fingers around his. For a long while, she said nothing. Then, softly so that just the two of them could hear, she spoke.

"You did good work, brother. I can't think anyone would have done better."

She remained there breathing the scent of his rooms for the last time until Danat and Eiah arrived, a small army of servants and utkhaiem and councilmen at their backs. Idaan told Eiah what she needed to know in a few short sentences, then left. The breakfast was gone, cleared away. She went to find Cehmai and tell him the news.

*Flowers do not return in the spring, rather they are replaced. It is in this difference
between returned and replaced that the price of renewal is paid.*

"No," Ana said. The ambassador of Eymond lifted a finger, as if begging
leave to interrupt the Empress. He made a small noise at the back of his
throat. Ana shook her head. "I said no. I meant no, Lord Ambassador. And if
you raise your finger to me again like I was a schoolgirl talking out of turn, I
will have it cut off and set in a necklace for you."

The meeting room was as silent as a grave. Even the candle flames stood
still. The dark-stained wood of the floor and beautifully painted abstract fres-
coes of the walls seemed out of place, too rich and peaceful for the moment. A
back room at a teahouse was the better venue for this kind of negotiation. Ana
enjoyed the contrast.

She knew when she first heard of Otah Machi's death that she was going to
have to be responsible for holding the Empire together until Danat regained
his balance. She hadn't yet lost a parent. Her husband and lover now had neither of his. The lost expression in his eyes and the bewildered tone in his
voice made her heart ache. And so when their partners and rivals in trade took
the opportunity to renegotiate treaties in hopes of winning some concession in
the fog of grief, Ana found herself taking it personally.

"Lady Empress," the ambassador said, "I don't mean disrespect, but you
must see that—"

Ana raised her finger, the mirror of the man's gesture. He went silent.

"A necklace," she said. "Ask around if you'd like. You'll find I have no sense
of proportion. None."

Very quietly, the ambassador took the scroll up from the table between
them and put it back in its satchel. Ana nodded and gestured to the door. The
man's spine could have been made of a single, unarticulated iron bar as he left.
Ana felt no sympathy for him.

The Master of Tides came in a moment later, her face amused and alarmed.
Ana took what she thought was the proper pose to express continuity. The
Khaiate system of poses was something that was best born into and learned
from infancy. She did her best, and no one had the audacity to correct her, so
Ana figured she was close enough.

"I believe that is all for the day, Most High," the Master of Tides said.

"Excellent. We got through those quickly, didn't we?"

"Very quickly," the woman agreed.

"Feel free to offer any other audiences the choice of meeting with me or
waiting for my husband until after the mourning rites."

"I will be sure to sketch out the options," the woman said in voice that assured Ana that she would make room in her schedule to help Danat with his
father's arrangements.

Ana found her mother in the guests' apartments. Her return trip had been postponed, the steam caravan itself waiting for her. The blue silk curtains billowed in the soft breeze; the scent of lemon candles lit to keep the insects away filled the air. Issandra sat before the fire grate, her hands folded on her lap. She didn't rise.

Ana would never have said it, but her mother looked old. The sun of Chaburi-Tan had darkened her skin, making her hair seem brilliantly white.

"Mother."

"Empress," Issandra Dasin said. Her voice was warm. "I'm afraid our timing left something to be desired."

"No," Ana said. "It wouldn't have mattered. Tell father that I appreciate the invitation, but I can't leave my family here."

"He won't hear it from me," Issandra said. "He's a good man, but time hasn't made him less stubborn. He wants his little girl back."

Ana sighed. Her mother nodded.

"I know his little girl is gone," Issandra said. "I'll try to make him understand that you're happy here. It may come to his visiting you himself."

"How are things at home?" Ana asked. She knew it was a telling question. She started to take a pose that unasked it but lost her way. It wasn't part of their conversation anyway.

"The word from Galt is good. The trade routes are busier than Farrer's seafront can accommodate. He's filling his coffers with silver and gems at a rate I've never seen," Issandra said. "It consoles him."

"I am happy here," Ana said.

"I know you are, love," her mother said. "This is where your children live."

They talked about small things for another hour, and then Ana took her leave. There would be time enough later.

The Emperor's pyre was set to be lit in two days. Utani was wrapped in mourning cloth. The palaces were swaddled in rags, the trees hung heavy with gray and white cloth. Dry mourning drums filled the air where there had once been music. The music would come again. She knew that. This was only something that had to be endured.

She found Danat in his father's apartments, tears streaking his face. Around him were spread sheets of paper as untidy as a bird's nest. All of them were written upon in Otah Machi's hand. There had to be a thousand pages. Danat looked up at her. For the length of a heartbeat, she could see what her husband had looked like as a child.

"What is it?" Ana asked.

"It was a crate," Danat said. "Father left orders that it be put on his pyre. They're letters. All of them are to my mother."

"From when they were courting?" Ana asked, sitting on the floor, her legs crossed.

"After she died," Danat said. Ana plucked a page from the pile. The paper was brittle, the ink pale. Otah Machi's words were perfectly legible.

Kiyan-kya—

You have been dead for a year tonight. I miss you. I want to have something more poetic to say, something that will do you some honor or change how it feels to be without you. Something. I had a thousand things I thought I would write, but those were when it was only me. Now, here, with you, all I can say is that I miss you.

The children are starting to come back from the loss. I don't know if I ever will. I have no experience with this. I had no mother or father. As a child, I had no family. I don't have any experience losing a family.

The closest thing I have to solace is knowing that, if I had gone first, you would have suffered all this darkness yourself. That I have to bear it is the price of sparing you. It doesn't make the burden lighter, it doesn't make the pain less, it doesn't take away any of the longing I have to see you again or hear your voice. But it does give the pain meaning. I suppose that's all I can ask: that the pain have meaning.

I love you. I miss you. I will write again soon.

Ana folded the letter. Thousands of pages of letters to the Empress who had died. The last Empress before her.

"I don't know what to do," Danat said.

"I love you. You know I love you more than anything except the children?"

"Of course."

"If you burn these, I will leave you. Honestly, love. You've lost enough of him. You have to keep these."

Danat took a deep shuddering breath and closed his eyes. His hands pressed flat on his thighs. Another tear slipped down his cheek, and Ana leaned forward to smooth it away with her sleeve.

"I want to," Danat said. "I want to keep them. I want to keep *him.* But it was what he asked."

"He's dead, love," Ana said. "He's dead and gone. Truly. He doesn't care anymore."

When Danat had finished crying, his body heavy against her own, the sun had set. The apartments were a collection of shadows. Somewhere in the course of things, they had made their way to Otah Machi's bed—a soft mattress that smelled of roses and had, so far as Ana could tell, never been slept in. She stroked Danat's hair and listened to the chorus of crickets in the gardens. Her husband's breath became deeper, more regular. Ana waited until he was deeply asleep, then slipped out from under him, lit a candle, and by its soft light gathered the letters and began to put them in order.

And as it is for spring flowers, so it is for us.

THE WORLD ITSELF SEEMED TO HAVE CONSPIRED TO MAKE THE DAY SOMBER. Gray clouds hung low over the city, a cold constant mist of rain darkening the mourning cloths, the stones, the newly unfurled leaves of the trees. The pyre stood in the center of the grand court, stinking of coal oil and pine resin. The torches that lined the pyre spat and hissed in the rain.

The assembly was huge. There weren't enough whisperers to take any words he said to the back edges of the crowd. If there was a back. As far as he could see from his place at the raised black dais, there were only faces, an infinity of faces, going back to the edge of the horizon. Their murmuring voices were a constant roll of distant thunder.

The Emperor was dead, and whether they mourned or celebrated, no one would remain unmoved.

At his side, Ana held his hand. Calin, in a pale mourning robe and a bright red sash, looked dumbstruck. His eyes moved restlessly over everything. Danat wondered what the boy found so overwhelming: the sheer animal mass of the crowd, the realization that Danat himself was no longer emperor regent but actually emperor, as Calin himself would be one day, or the fact that Otah was gone. All three, most likely.

Danat rose and stepped to the front of the dais. The crowd grew louder and then eerily silent. Danat drew a sheaf of papers from his sleeve. His farewell to his father.

"We say that the flowers return every spring," Danat said, "but that is a lie. It is true that the world is renewed. It is also true that that renewal comes at a price, for even if the flower grows from an ancient vine, the flowers of spring are themselves new to the world, untried and untested.

"The flower that wilted last year is gone. Petals once fallen are fallen forever. Flowers do not return in the spring, rather they are replaced. It is in this difference between *returned* and *replaced* that the price of renewal is paid.

"And as it is for spring flowers, so it is for us."

Danat paused, the voices of the whisperers carrying his words out as far as they would travel. As he waited, he caught sight of Idaan and Cehmai standing before the pyre. The old poet looked somber. Idaan's long face carried an expression that might have been amusement or anger or the distance of being lost in her own thoughts. She was unreadable, as she always was. He saw, not for the first time, how much she and Otah resembled each other.

The rain tapped on the page before him as if to recall his attention. The ink was beginning to blur. Danat began again.

"My father founded an empire, something no man living can equal. My father also took a wife, raised children, struggled with all that it meant to have us, and there are any number of men and women in the cities or in Galt, Eymond, Bakta, Eddensea, or the world as a whole who have taken that road as well.

"My father was born, lived his days, and died. In that he is like all of us. All of us, every one, without exception. And so it is for that, perhaps, that he most deserves to be honored."

The ink bled, Danat's words fading and blurring. He looked up at the low sky and thought of his father's letters. Page after page after page of saying what could never be said. He didn't know any longer what he'd hoped to achieve with his own speech. He folded the pages and put them back in his sleeve.

"I loved my father," Danat said. "I miss him."

He proceeded slowly down the wide stairs to the base of the pyre. A servant whose face he didn't know presented Danat with a lit torch. He took it, and walked slowly around the base of the pyre, cool raindrops dampening his face, his hair. He smelled of soft rain. Danat touched flame to tinder as he went, the coal oil flaring and stinking.

The fire roared. Smoke rose through the falling rain, carrying the body of Otah Machi with it. And pale petals of almond blossoms floated over the crowd and the pyre, the palaces and the city, like the announcement that spring had come at last.

ABOUT THE AUTHOR

Daniel Abraham is the author of The Long Price Quartet: *A Shadow in Summer, A Betrayal in Winter, An Autumn War,* and *The Price of Spring*. His most recent novel is *The Dragon's Path*. His short fiction has been published in the anthologies *Vanishing Acts, Bones of the World, The Dark,* and *Logorrhea,* and included in Gardner Dozois's *Year's Best Science Fiction* and *The Year's Best Fantasy and Horror,* edited by Ellen Datlow, Kelly Link, and Gavin J. Grant, as well. His story "Flat Diane" won the International Horror Guild Award for best short story. His novelette "The Cambist and Lord Iron" was runner-up for the Hugo Award. He is also the coauthor of *Hunter's Run* with Gardner Dozois and George R. R. Martin. He lives in New Mexico with his family.